LAMENT:
A SOVIET WOMAN AND HER TRUE STORY

LAMENT

A Soviet Woman and Her True Story

A Novel By
Liz Mackie

• NOSTALGISTUDIO : NEW YORK •

2018 / 2020

Second Edition
Published by Nostalgistudio
© Copyright 2020 by Elizabeth Mackie
ISBN 978-1-7323931-3-4
Cover images: Altered photographs, Bira River and Factory, Birobidzhan
The First Edition was published and copyrighted in 2018.

This book is dedicated to my sister Claudia.

CONTENTS

PART ONE

ODESSA | BIROBIDZHAN | ODESSA

(1)

Two sisters grew up in a small Ukrainian town on the outskirts of Odessa. They lived with their mother and father in a small house on a narrow, muddy street. They often said how glad they were to be their parents' only children. Many families in their town were much larger and those children had far fewer toys or nice things in their homes; sometimes those families had even too little food for everyone to eat more than one meal a day. The two sisters never went hungry, although they were poor. They knew they were poor because their mother said so, they heard her complain about it a great deal as she sat day and night in the front room, sewing dresses. She suffered from grief, disappointment and eye-strain headaches and was not an affectionate mother but rather a proud one. She insisted that her two daughters be cleaner, more polite, better-dressed and better-educated than all the other girls in their neighborhood; and for the most part they were. From their mother they'd learned to be thankful to be only two.

Their father in his bachelor days had peddled dress trimmings bought wholesale— ribbons, beaded fringes, bands of embroidery and lace—town-to-town to home seamstresses; this was how he'd met his wife-to-be. The trimmings dwindled to a sideline once he began peddling the dresses she made. His clientele which he described as "specialized" encompassed some dozen penny pinching old women who clung to the elaborately-trimmed flounces and wraps of their youth. Upon delivery every stitch they'd examine through various magnifying lenses and some deduction for every crookedness perceived would be marked against the bill. Reporting home with the final payment the poor man would cringe as his wife shook fistfuls of worn small bill currency and summarized: she'd ruined her hands and her eyesight, squandered her talents on sewing these freakish old-fashioned dresses he insisted on selling, now she was good for nothing else, to produce a wardrobe for a normal human woman she couldn't, only for hideous ungrateful miserly crones. Which was her punishment, of course, for erring, misled by who knows what and choosing—him, to marry. Her husband. Their father. She'd retreat into a darkened curtained corner and he might spend a night or even two sleeping on top of the work table. Their mother couldn't help her emotions, he'd explain to the two girls. She was grieving her parents, who'd been killed in a pogrom during the Civil War, both in one night; she still blamed herself for not being there to protect them even though she'd certainly have failed to. As for his own parents, dead too, in separate pogroms, as a man he grieved them less, he said.

His daughters appreciated their father as a basically cheerful presence in and around the home but always agreed with their mother, that he was a foolish failure of a man who couldn't really do anything.

The older daughter's name was Liza. Tall, with the mother's long tapered hands, thin face, and ferocious gray eyes, she possessed an excellent set of teeth but her skin was blemish-prone. Unmusical and bad at games, Liza was a great reader of Party-sanctioned material, an ardent and opinionated socialist who idolized the Revolution and its heroes. At fourteen, claiming political cause, Liza ate a bread roll on Yom Kippur and forbade her family any further signs or practice of the Jewish faith. Or tongue: if one of them let a Hebrew word slip back into their household Yiddish, she'd hit the roof. Already less religious than many in their neighborhood, the family acquiesced without protest. Liza's will was strong, she could even be a bully. But when it came to learning to speak Ukrainian in accord with Comrade Stalin's policy for the national cultures, they left Liza on her own. Ukrainian was very hard—in truth, even she never spoke it easily or well. The rest of them stuck with the Yiddish-Russian mix they knew.

Little Musya was almost six years younger and never reached much past her sister's shoulder height-wise. Quicker, lighter, merrier, she laughed more showing smaller teeth, ran more, played more; she loved games, crowds, promenades, most public amusements. She hated fighting. Her earliest dream in life was to become a major motion picture star. Pinned to the wall above her mother's work table was a postcard photograph of the most beautiful woman in history, a great actress of silent film tragically dead at a young age of the 1919 influenza: Vera Kholodnaya, whose funeral cortege Musya's mother had glimpsed from the very front of a curb, one among thousands of mourners thronging Odessa's streets on that mournful occasion. Musya wanted to be exactly like this woman—except she would live. She'd live and thrive and be even more famous, more beautiful; she might even go to America like Anna Sten and make movies in Hollywood. Into the looking glass that hung in the tiny room she shared with her sister, Musya spent long afternoons staring. Big dark brown eyes like her father's, a round face, full lips—not narrow like Liza's—clear skin unlike Liza's, a thick head of reddish-brown hair with an interesting wave: she considered her hair to be probably her best feature. As a great actress she was sure to have many suitors, men who would crave her, men who would threaten themselves for her. Some—most!—she'd reject. One knelt trembling at her feet, he clutched a razor, he could only sob. Down she reached with one small sturdy hand, a gesture to console, a gentle smile playing across her lips because she must refuse him. The scene swam, wavered, her eyes had filled with tears.

Why did she refuse? Was there another? No, there was no one. No one yet.

At thirteen she amazed everybody by publishing a prize-winning poem in one of Odessa's Yiddish-language journals. Musya had never really distinguished herself in the intellectual sphere, she'd never struggled in school but neither had she made notable efforts or successes. And here she was, an author. Modestly, she acknowledged what had happened: the girls in her class had created a collection of poems to circulate among family and friends; her poem had impressed an instructor who'd submitted it for competition. Best of all the poem would soon appear alongside its Russian translation among other Voices of Soviet Youth, hard-bound in a book from Moscow, an honor to be accompanied by state store coupons for rationed goods.

Musya had titled her poem Who Will Love Me? A young woman ponders her future; she tries to match her flaws and her advantages to the requirements of several nameless, handsome and intrepid men. A soldier, a writer, a worker, an engineer, a famous actor (naturally), a doctor in the provinces—each will find some traits of hers irresistible and others less so; the wrong fit in every case. She resigns herself to being alone. What Musya never told anyone was that her poem came almost word-for-word from dramatic speeches she'd delivered at her mirror, practicing farewells to devastated lovers. She had no intention of ending up alone, absolutely none. And in the end the Moscow edition contained a new concluding line to the effect that she would be loved always, in the best way, by the Revolution's wise and compassionate leaders. The state store coupons arrived at the same time, as promised. Musya promptly traded them at a market near her street for an old gramophone and two recordings of fast jazz foxtrots.

A year or two later, it was Liza's turn to astonish the household with a sudden demand that they start keeping shabes. Where, she asked to know, were the family's tablecloth, candlesticks, cups, prayer books—were they hidden in the floor? Shocked, her mother and father protested. They owned nothing of the kind. Whatever they'd customarily used, some of it silver, had been burned up with their parents in their cottages by Ukrainian Jew-haters in 1918. It was sad, but there were no heirlooms. And there'd be no shabes celebrated in this home, not after so many years. Who even remembered the words? Or the recipes to which dishes to serve? They were a modern family, Soviets down to the tips of their tongues as she herself had insisted they be.

Infuriated by everything in this conversation Liza stormed out again, gone they had no idea where, leaving them mystified. Her behavior and habits had changed of late, true. At twenty, she worked as a junior inspector at an electrical supply warehouse, a good position. The Komsomol and study groups had always claimed her spare time. Zealous since girlhood in soliciting volunteers for every Party initiative of the day, she was tolerated and avoided by their neighbors in equal measure. Just that week, Musya had been unsurprised to spot Liza receiving a firm rebuff at a nearby doorstep; this was as usual. The difference was in her sister's manner, slightly stooped and strangely humble. And the plain dark shawl—that was a change. So was the way she'd taken to covering her hair. She'd never sat on the edge of their bed rocking forward and back as her lips moved almost silently in every appearance of prayer before, either. The tiny book she kept studying was beaten-up but new. It had been months since they'd heard her try to speak one word of Ukrainian. And now this—shabes. Why did she want such a thing? What was she up to now? And why was she so angry? The signs were ominous.

Now Liza absented herself on Friday evenings without explanation. Her family didn't seek one. While curious, all three, to see what happened next in this drama unfolding so close to their lives, at the same time they hoped to avoid nearer involvement. Unlike Liza, they didn't enjoy meetings and politics frightened them, they never joined anything. As the father said, this way they avoided many crooks and murderers. So when the denouement came—when the denouement entered, shook hands, sat down erect in a chair—their initial relief was intense. Because clearly this had nothing to do with any decision taken by committee.

It was only a man.

His name was Kotz. He was reading to become a law student. Boris was his first name but Liza only ever called him Kotz. They'd met in a bookstore. Then they'd courted at a weekly shabes meal nearby, an underground affair of strange nostalgists—older students, mostly, it sounded like. Kotz was several years older than Liza and a few inches shorter. Above an unimpressive beard his colorless hair was thinning; his handshake was sponge-like; he had a metallic voice and a nervous cough. Without explicit shabbiness, his appearance advertised an utter absence of prosperity. His suit was probably his own but was badly made and no longer fit limbs nor trunk, especially the arms of the jacket looked stuffed with bread dough. Facially not one of the Kotz features was prepossessing, the lips, in Musya's view, least of all, being long, moist and notably purplish. She felt really disturbed. Granted, no one would have expected her humorless, thin-faced sister to attract and capture a male of the heroic type—but surely even Liza could do better than this!

Her mother and father might have been thinking exactly the same. An uncomfortable silence prolonged itself in the cramped front room. The work table, shoved to one side for the hour, seemed poised in threat to reclaim its territory. The stranger called himself a student-worker correspondent, he'd published letters in the Russian and Yiddish press, both: he wrote beautiful letters, Liza said. Kotz gave a complacent nod and through wire-rimmed spectacles directed a watery, unemotional gaze at his surroundings. The family's quarters, he observed, were large: had the house many other tenants? Of course many, three or four households on each floor plus the man in the basement (a drunkard, they didn't add), him; to count all the others was not even possible. Sinking back into their own indignation as into a featherbed, Musya, mother and father fell silent again. Liza didn't say anything. Pale, blemish-striped, she sat rigid with up-tilted chin, gripped by a high-pitched tremor, she kept glancing between her family and the man at her side, her eyes triumphant, as if Kotz represented proof of some claim she'd made that everyone had doubted. The couple displayed no recognizable signs of mutual affection.

Yet a couple they were. With a last, quick cough, Kotz made it official. He said he wished to marry Liza the first rose of their family but that he considered even more important than his wish to be her husband was his desire to make Jewish history with her. Marriage he regarded as a means to advance the Jewish race and populate its future; he and Liza would be pioneers and their children the premier citizens of a new homeland for Jewish culture, national in form, socialist in content—in fact a future socialist republic of Soviet Jewry. Which, he explained, was a place already as real as the room they were sitting in—even as they sat talking, with every second that passed it grew realer; for the realization of another plan sprang up every minute there, with new buildings, new streets, new factories, new telegraph lines; while Jewish plows claimed huge tracts of wilderness for high-yielding agriculture. Where? In the Far East, near the southern border with Japanese Manchuria, a place called Birobidzhan.

"No," said the mother.

Liza shouted, "Mommy—yes!"

At once the room became noisy and hot with all the passion the strange scene had lacked. Their gray eyes flashing, mother and daughter raged at each other: "This, this!" cried the mother was what she'd heard whispered, she hadn't believed it at first, her crazy daughter knocking on people's doors again—where she used to order all the old women to disinfect their doorsteps, now she was selling this scheme to move to the end of the world? Wholly discredited, by the way—people had been coming back from Birobidzhan for years saying how awful it was there. The neighbors were dumbfounded, they were complaining. How could Liza's family show their faces again on the street? They couldn't, she'd shamed them too badly. The only shame, Liza rejoined, was unbelief. Which meant—the mother demanded to be told—what? Of what was she accusing them?

"Hah!" said Liza.

"Hah?" the mother said, and flung more recriminations. From the random words and wheezy noises he was producing it was evident that Kotz felt duty-bound to impose calm but lacked the capacity. Musya looked across at her father's bewilderment. She reached over to give his coat sleeve a tug and he roused himself as if from stupor.

"Liza," he said, "you want to leave us? Why?"

She burst into tears. With extraordinary hesitation and awkwardness, Kotz took her hand and patted it, displaying short thumbs. He answered in Liza's stead, "Tovarisch, sir, you know, soon it will be very bad for the Jews here."

"But it's always bad for the Jews everywhere," the older man answered reasonably. "Why go to China for it?"

Collecting herself a little, Liza managed to sob that she didn't care, she didn't, whether her family approved, their approval meant even less than their permission, it meant nothing. When at last she'd found a man she truly respected, a man of faith and not a man of surfaces. "He doesn't care that I'm not pretty like Musya!" she declared.

They all looked at Kotz; through her tears Liza looked at him hardest. He let a few seconds pass before it occurred to him to speak. Then he blinked several times, his froggy lips twisting. At last he murmured: "But dearest, to me you are much prettier than your sister!" And Liza leaned against him gratefully.

Musya shrugged to herself. Boris Kotz had produced a gallant phrase. She didn't believe him.

Everything happened as Liza wanted, of course, so that she wouldn't make life impossible. Mother and daughter reconciled over the wedding arrangements, their tastes coinciding. The in-laws were polite, normal people, less inclined than their son to ideology and not religious in the least; the rotund Papa Kotz kept the accounts in a wine warehouse and his pretty wife liked birds, she kept doves and finches. The warehouse was controlled by her brother-in-law, who not only loaned them the upper floor for the wedding feast and hired musicians but also made a risqué toast and a generous cash gift to the new couple. That they would need it nobody doubted. Flushed with celebration, his lenses steamed, Liza's new husband cried out that he'd toiled long enough among books—today he was trading his pen for the handles of a plow. He wanted to farm, he wanted to raise wheat and grapes and pumpkins big as planets for the glory of the Soviet Zion. The speeches dragged on; then came more drinking, more singing, more dancing. While she had a good time, Musya vowed that her own wedding would be a far more sophisticated affair, one with a jazz band and a husband who didn't pass out at the table, one with less motherly weeping.

Their train left the next day in May 1934.

(2)

With Liza gone the place felt bigger and very much more peaceful. The angry ever-shifting world of politics and policies, sloganeering, five-year plans and Party leaders, all receded. This was a relief.

Musya didn't mind being the only child at home, in fact it suited her. She adjusted happily to having more space—all the space—in the tiny room she'd shared with her sister. The whole bed, the whole little armoire, every shelf and all the drawers were hers. She expanded accordingly, happy to find that she could be almost as untidy as she liked and not be scolded. What's more, bitter complaints no longer greeted her choice to play gramophone records on Saturdays. Her delicate experimental hairstyles ceased to raise a single condescending sneer and she could spend hours at a time posing and speechifying before the looking glass—hers now, too—without interruption. All this she felt could only benefit her career: for film stardom still drew Musya.

She was popular and had a circle of noisy, lively girlfriends whom her mother called The Geese. The friends shared a passion for cinema and labored nightly over thick scrapbooks devoted to favorite performers whose lives and loves and looks were their incessant study. As for the classroom, her last few years at school left Musya uninspired. She no longer wrote poems, although she kept a brooding photo-portrait of the tragic Mayakovsky pinned to her bookshelf. She did well at tests and might have qualified for university but didn't want to try, the regimentations of student life held no appeal for her. What she wanted was to surround herself with freedom and empty space, she wanted to ease the way for fame to find her.

Fame—and love. Somewhere out in the world, the man who would love her drew breath. He was parting his hair, straightening his necktie, smoothing the edges of his moustache with a polished thumbnail. In acts of clairvoyance she pictured her own image appearing, sudden as a comet, in his mind; she looked into his green eyes and watched how the pupils expanded and shrank, as if gulping the thought of her.

One night she and The Geese went to a party with dancing and there he stood, the man of her imagination, waiting in line by the punch bowl. In life he looked older but better, more tangible. Someone told her he had a good job in Odessa at the film studio. So it was meant to be. Next they were introduced; he reacted with boredom and Musya couldn't think of anything to say; his name had sounded like Rudy but she couldn't be sure; perfumed overpoweringly with attar of roses, his hair oil made her sneeze three times in quick succession; he wished her good health after the first two and walked away during the third. Their encounter had lasted sixty seconds, even less. It didn't matter—time was a trifle, three sneezes were probably lucky. Fate was at work. She awaited their next meeting. Months passed, most of her seventeenth year which she filled with daydreams of long conversations and kisses passed, she loved this man who might be named Rudy. But she never saw him again.

Almost without noticing she finished with school. At the age where Liza had clamored for permission to enter the professional workforce, the younger daughter asked nothing of the kind. Instead she announced her choice to join the family trade. On the sales side, that is, not production: she was a decent seamstress but sewing tired her. Lately the father's elderly clientele had grown almost numerous; for Musya to take a hand in fittings and deliveries made sense. She'd be helping. And since the city streetcar had extended a line right to the edge of their town, she could make half a dozen house calls in Odessa and be home for dinner—all on her discounted student fare, still unexpired. Motion, interest, variety, fresh air—how far preferable to a dull dingy warehouse position was this job she proposed to do? And for the meanest of salaries, just a little pocket money she asked, plus a small commission.

Her parents hesitated. The father had a nominal employment at the Privoz market and knew how to get his daughter added to the rolls there; but his dress sideline was illegal and how much help he needed was uncertain. The mother who possessed a long-standing health exemption knew she could have used the extra needlework; but getting Musya to sit quietly at the work table for any length of time had never been possible. At the same time the parents knew her lively spirits would suffer cruelly from the routines of a Soviet workplace. So they agreed to her half-whimsical scheme—not without reluctance, and not without warnings. If she wanted to do nothing but ride around on streetcars and put up with Odessa's worst old women all day long by herself, Musya's mother insisted she learn and memorize a few hard truths suitable for adulthood.

Truths about men, especially.

Men were prisoners of violence, the mother explained. Screaming from birth, fighting by instinct, they passed their lives in violence until they died of a build-up of wounds. Nothing Musya did, nothing she could ever do would change the nature of one single man. However placid he seemed, however many consecutive years he might appear to be passing in peace, all this was vapor, illusion. Violence would find him. Suddenly, the lunging attack, the bloody scream; murderous mindless horrors were never more than a heartbeat away wherever men were. Their prison came with them, bringing no hope of escape. And while women must naturally pity this sad fate of men, they shared the dangers and suffered its consequences. More than their fair share, women suffered. Women grew wary and went in fear of what might befall their daughters, especially in cities and most especially in Odessa, a city so full of students, sailors, draymen, drunkards, artists, thieves, pimps, foreign tourists, financiers. Only if their daughters swore to exercise the utmost care at every moment, only if they vowed to make a daily pledge of silence modesty and chastity, could mothers continue to breathe evenly and sleep a little at night.

Musya looked over at the father and thought he seemed embarrassed by this speech. She didn't associate him with any sort of violence—neither did she most grown men she knew. Granted, the majority of her screen idols led with their fists or their bayonets; but that was cinema. Mommy had clearly spent too much time at her work table, she'd fallen out of touch with real life and into some dark sort of dream world. Nevertheless, Musya made a solemn promise to shun strange men in every form.

Now began a wonderful time for the younger sister. Relieved beyond words not to be stuck like some of her friends behind a hot lunch counter or on an assembly line, she greeted each new day with the sensation of spreading her wings into luxurious flight. Freedom was the sound of the streetcar tracks, humming to herald the trolley's approach, rattling beneath the grooved wheels, shrieking when the hand brakes tickled too hard. Her arms laden with bagged dresses, Musya held the joy of these morning rides tight and devoured the fast-moving views. The right side, the left side, the front window, the rear platform, she tried every vantage point; they were all good. Odessa was gorgeous. Sunshine spangled down through blossoming tree branches onto pavements and cobblestones. Women draped mattresses over balconies and lingered there to converse across housefronts. Sailors in white walked arm in arm laughing or leaned at the windows of newspaper kiosks counting out cigarette change. Great sculpture-decked buildings of stone reared up like icebergs at street corners, where whole avenues ran ribbon-lined with bright awning canvas shading the windows of elegant shops. An enormous floating opera house drifted in and out of view. The next vista opened briefly onto an ancient world; Musya spied golden temples stacked on a lush green hillside. Then it was gone and in its place came glimpses of white sails, towering ship masts, hoisting cranes, steam funnels painted with stripes—the great fleets at anchor and docked in the emerald harbor.

Another year had passed. Musya knelt comfortably on the thick pile of an old Turkish rug, her mouth full of pins, adjusting a hem on an ankle-length skirt for a client. Along with a taste for the previous century's fashions and a controlling share of the flat above her late husband's former drapery concern, the widow Tsigal maintained an important collection of memories whose major highlights dated to the reign of Alexander II. Four prolonged sightings of the tragic Liberator and his Empress on holiday had stocked the widow's shelves with anecdotes for life. Maria Alexandrovna she recalled as a great beauty:

"And around her a light, it shone, this I saw myself, a light not from nature. She was a saint."

The widow bought many dresses, far more than she needed, really, more than an old woman could wear; Musya's mother suspected her of running a re-sale line among her former drapery customers and had tasked Musya with seeking signs or proof but Musya hadn't found any. The widow Tsigal liked Musya and had given her some silk handkerchiefs and several boxes of imported chocolate as gifts. Milord, the Tsar's setter, she'd seen too, for he and Alexander were never parted:

"The dog also was a saint," the widow said.

Musya nodded vaguely, happily. She'd heard all this before and wasn't really paying attention; no answer was required with her mouth full of pins. She looked up. Lemony light skimmed from the waves in the distant harbor had spilled all the way down Vorovskogo Street to dance in laughing ranks on the low ceiling, drawn there by her secret happiness.

His name was Leon Flohr. He had soft brown curls and a small soft brown moustache that Musya's lips adored—to be brushed and tantalized by this moustache her mouth yearned like a castaway for home and shelter. Leon Flohr's lips were shapely and usually curved in a smile. His brown eyes were merry and mocking. He dressed in the latest styles, mastered dance steps in minutes, and had the biography of every top film star and director by heart. Musya smiled. They were soul mates.

All at once the widow Tsigal said something very shocking to Musya. "Don't get a baby," she said. A pin dropped from between Musya's lips onto the carpet and vanished among the hand-knotted fibers. She combed with her fingertips in search. "Oof," the old woman grunted above her head. "Already? You're sure?"

Musya denied it, truthfully, she wasn't pregnant; but her alarm was extreme. How obvious was it that she had a man and his love? To what other eyes had she become transparent? Did her mother know? A little cry escaped her as she located the sharp end of the pin with an index finger.

She'd met Leon Flohr in City Park where she'd been walking with The Geese, a slightly melancholy old school friends' reunion that she hadn't been enjoying. Other people's news made her own life feel insubstantial. The park was too crowded as usual, the pebbled paths overrun by noisy children. Finding nowhere for their whole group to sit down, the friends had hardly room to walk. An orchestra flung discordant patriotic songs into the dusty twilight from a bandstand perch. Musya had been wondering how long before she could leave when a strange man suited in cream-colored gabardine swooped into their midst and started talking: one young man to five young women. Despite his fine suit, her initial impression of Leon Flohr was that he planned to ask one of them or perhaps all five of them to loan him some money. It was strange. Handsome, slim, not very tall, he talked fast in a fluent jumble of Russian and Yiddish. The Geese stood blinking beneath his confident dual barrage of self-promotion and relentless flattery. To one of them he sang a phrase from a popular dance tune, he had a pleasing tenor voice. In the midst of a silly boastful tale about racing a motorbike illegally up and down the Richelieu steps he kept catching Musya's eye with his own. Behind him a fountain was playing, he stood in his pale well-tailored suit before a curtain of silvery water. She wished, Musya realized, he'd really ask her for a loan after all because that would give her a reason to see him again; maybe they could even craft an arrangement pledging him to pay her back gradually across multiple meetings. With this thought, she'd smiled her first of many smiles at Leon Flohr. He appealed to her.

The loan request never transpired. Leon always had plenty of cash, from a hundred different sources all around Odessa it came to him, handed over in the pursuit or conclusion of various deals. What did he do? Nothing specific. He introduced sellers to buyers, he helped men move contraband, he brokered small unregistered property transfers and publicized some private gambling rooms discretely. Even more than Musya's his workday crisscrossed the city; he took most of his meetings at cafés and hotels. Where did he live? Officially, with his family in the Moldavanka. He still visited and paid his mother's rent sometimes but had no fixed address, only here and there a room, a club, a corner of a flat, even a limestone cubbyhole he'd reach through someone's cellar floor. Leon worked night and day: sleep bored him. He disliked sitting motionless except in a cinema and he hated to read more than a paragraph. Even so, by noon each day he knew the entire contents of all newspapers solely from conversations he'd had or overheard. He got a lot of shoe shines. His life's ambition was to own a steam yacht and a stable of racehorses; admiring extravagance, he never saved a kopek. He took Musya to beautiful restaurants, he drove her all around town and even out to the countryside in a car he owned for a month or two. That summer he'd taught her to swim in the Black Sea, they'd gotten sunburnt and tanned together, lying side by side on the crowded strip of yellow beach, watching processions of clouds like giant gleaming brass-fronted warships breast the azure heavens at full sail. She'd gone to bed with him, maybe a dozen times in four different rooms. Musya enjoyed this although the mad passionate obsesssion she'd been led by cinema and fiction to expect had so far failed to seize her. Most of all she liked to lie quietly beside Leon Flohr while he talked—sex made him talkative—and stroke his naked chest: she liked the way the hair grew in sparse uneven patches down his sternum, on his stomach, across his upper arms. His pale gently muscled flesh emitted light, he was like the Tsar's setter dog to her that way, Musya supposed; except she knew he was no saint. He'd said they could marry if she became pregnant but somehow or other she hadn't.

"Pray to be childless." The widow Tsigal gripped Musya by the shoulder now as she guided herself off the footstool onto the floor. Musya stood up to help her out of the new dress in progress; she was small but felt herself towering over the old woman. Who told her that the next big war had begun—another from Germany—and a Jew-hater was leading it. Terrible times were at hand, soon, times worse than the worst of the bad times before, such times were coming. "That you bring no child into these years—this is my prayer for you."

That day she sent Musya off with more chocolate than usual. Was it a premonition? Feeling uneasy, unlike herself, Musya boarded the streetcar towards home. She wished she could stay in Odessa and dine out with Leon but he was selling some live pheasants, or buying them—Musya wasn't sure only she knew he wasn't free. The streetcar grew uncrowded as it rattled further into the outskirts. Musya looked around at the passengers who remained. They all looked familiar; she must have seen every one of their faces dozens of times. And yet they were strangers. Of their feelings, their hearts, she knew nothing—of what they might be capable, she was suddenly afraid. Their eyes looked like stones to her and the rolling streets seemed full of shadows unrelated to the lateness of the day or the nearness of autumn. At the end of the line, her stop, Musya leapt off the platform before anyone else and hurried homeward.

The mother held a telegram. The father, home first today, was holding the envelope. That these printed, folded, flimsy yellow paper scraps signified disaster, Musya had no doubt; the details, she wished she could be spared from knowing. She didn't want to know. Her knees knocked together like jellies in bowls at the sight of her parents' solemn, unspeaking faces. What could it be?

Leon Flohr!

It flashed into her mind that Leon had been badly injured, maybe some freak poultry accident had occurred and she was summoned her to his bedside, he was probably hospitalized, possibly he was dying; Leon, from his deathbed, had dictated a message of love that he'd sped to her, here, at home. Where her parents had no idea of his existence. Musya took a big lungful of breath and prepared herself for a terrible scene with tears— her own tears, at least.

Then the mother spoke. With difficulty, through clenched teeth:

"Your sister," she said.

Musya blinked, she flinched at this absurdity. Her sister? It made no sense. Liza her married sister had returned home to attack Leon Flohr and put him in the hospital? How could this be? And why? Her mouth opened and closed several times, she couldn't speak; like a fish she stood gaping, the father said. He told her to sit down with them at the work table. Then he tugged the telegram from between his wife's fingers and passed it across. She read:

SEND MUSYA TO ME URGENT & SUPREME IMPORTANCE. MUST COME AT ONCE. PRAY FOR US.

That was all. Front, back, she looked: no more message. Two, three times more she read the message that was there. It said no more to her. Pity gripped her heart for Liza who had clearly lost her mind. Panting, at the same time, with relief that Leon wasn't involved, she wrestled back a shout of laughter. When the mother told her to start preparing for a journey, Musya did laugh. She couldn't grasp what she was hearing—a mother who never made jokes produced this gem so unexpectedly. Astonishment kept her open-mouthed with goggling eyes until the father said to stop and not to worry. A brief visit, a month, nothing more, with the travel she'd be gone all of two months at the most. After all, she owed a visit, long overdue. She'd never met her nephews, Liza's boys. Finally that would happen. This trip would be good.

"Yes, good," said the mother in an absent voice. "One bag only you'll need."

Musya said she didn't think so. In her view the probability ran far higher that this trip would be bad, very bad, terrible. To deny it and pretend otherwise was almost as ludicrous as the idea that a single bag could accommodate any two-month travel wardrobe. How could her mother be serious? She couldn't, she wasn't—she was simply infected by Liza's incredible craziness; here it was again, worse than ever, strong and direct from the Far East, insanity folded in yellow paper and flung at them like a poisoned dart across the length of the continent. Remembering a newsreel she'd seen not long before, Musya added an objection: the Far East was a war zone.

The father waved a hand. "We won that war."

Of course this had been in the newsreel, too. Feeling trapped, she slammed the telegram down onto the work table and started shouting. First her lunatic sister had tried to turn them into socialists—then into Ukrainians—then into Jews. What next? When would the tyranny end?

"We are Jews." The father spoke calmly. He covered both the mother's hands that she'd been wringing with one of his own, to still them. "Yevrei—look. Even the government says so." He always kept Musya's internal passport with his own because she was careless. Now he pushed the folder across the table at her. There it was in black and white, her nationality. ЄВРЕИ: Hebrew. "Don't lose that, now. You'll need it to travel."

Musya kept up a struggle, she argued and wept, she fought like a lynx but it was no use, she could tell the mother wasn't really paying attention. Which became obvious when she slipped her hands from her husband's to take a pencil from her apron pocket and jotted ".1" on the back of the telegram envelope.

It was the start of a packing list for Musya's trip to the Soviet Zion.

(3)

The train journey lasted thirteen days, including the two it took to reach Moscow. That was north; then Musya's way led east, almost to the last stop on the Trans-Siberian line, almost to Vladivostok on the Pacific Ocean coast.

About one quarter way around the planet.

In 1934, when Liza and Kotz embarked as honeymooning pioneers on the Russiya Number Two to Birobidzhan, the movement of Jews to the Soviet Far East was still a respectable project. The settlers came from all over the world, even America, to public fanfare; they starred in newsreels and inspired musical films; literary celebrities visited and returned home to write novels about them. The new couple's train fare had been nothing at all—and they'd been given cash travel grants. All this Musya remembered.

Five years later the project looked close to defunct, all unattended desks and fading poster slogans on the walls of the connecting stations. Why this state of things should be, Musya had no idea; what's more, she didn't care. All she knew was that instead of being cheap, her fare to what was now called the Jewish Autonomous Region was rather expensive. Adding its cost to the countless gifts, toys, bolts of cloth, sewing tools and sweets and other foodstuffs that her parents had gathered and wrapped into parcels—six in number, all large, an outrageous burden—the family's savings were practically drained; for her return fare they'd have to rely on the kindness of Kotz as son- and brother-in-law. Musya had nothing to contribute, she'd lived like a bird on the wing, living on air, spending everything she earned. Now she was travelling with just enough cash money to sustain herself for two weeks on tea, hard-boiled eggs, biscuits, meat pies, the occasional blintz or a chicken leg; she shopped through the train window at stops where food vendors thronged the station platforms. She budgeted carefully, never let go of her purse, and still arrived penniless.

For the first week of her journey she expected Leon Flohr to appear at any moment. She hadn't been able to send him a message, not knowing where in Odessa to send it; but Leon knew where she lived, she'd told him. After a day, maybe two, when he missed her, he'd speed there. She pictured the scene in the front room, Leon in a pale suit, gleaming, fists clenched, tall with outrage. Muschka (he tells her parents who crouch in gloom, shame-faced) is his now: they don't deserve her. Then he rushes off in pursuit. Every stop and delay on the Moscow-bound train Musya thought her lover must have engineered for the purpose of boarding—her heart pounded—and searching the cars for her. She clutched the bakelite handle of her travel bag. The authorities must be on Leon's side, for once; quite likely her parents' treatment of her was criminal, sending her like this to Birobidzhan, their presumption trampling her basic rights. Under the soaring vaults of the Kievsky station she looked all around for him, she thought he might have overtaken her and would appear to welcome her to Moscow with flowers; he'd have a car waiting or even a carriage drawn by midnight black steeds, and their hotel room would end in a balcony with panoramic river views.

Her train departed Moscow late at night. Soldiers were everywhere, in the streets, the squares, the stations. She lingered on the Yaroslavsky platform until the last possible moment, straining her eyes to pierce steam clouds thickened by coal smoke for a glimpse of Leon Flohr among the drab uniforms, but he didn't appear. The next morning she awoke in motion. Greenish-brown at the bottom, bluish-gray at the top, bisected by a horizon line perfectly level, the view was monotonous to say the least. Musya decided to be realistic. Leon would never come looking for her after only a day or two: it might take him almost a week to go pound on the door of her home and demand information. Would he strike her father in the face and knock him to the floor? Her poor father! Musya hoped not. In distant parallel another motorcar appeared and rode alongside the Trans-Siberian line, toy-like, tethered to her soaring heart. Then gone. Next time Leon would be driving, she'd recognize the love that fueled his breakneck pace.

The hours after sundown when she lost her view were awful.

The triple shelves of her platskartny carriage were full of women travelling alone or with young children. The sounds and smells of infant care were fairly relentless. The W/Cs at either end were occupied around the clock and a steady crowd ringed the huge carriage samovar, whose hot water always seemed to run out just before Musya got there. By the samovar the carriage provodnitsa—as the conductresses were called—had their den. The bench Musya shared with her heaped belongings doubled as a sleeping bunk with an inadequate curtain for privacy. She couldn't keep the curtain drawn by day because it wasn't allowed, the provodnitsa scolded her for trying. They scolded her for oversleeping, too. She was vaguely aware of a feminine conviviality that ebbed and flowed around the carriage as other women boarded, met, exclaimed, boasted, shared amusing stories, reached their destinations, parted friends. Musya heard herself described as the little zhid who was going to Birobidzhan. She made no friends nor did she try to. Hourly she imagined her fellow passengers' consternation and envy when the whole train screeched to a grinding halt at the very midpoint of desolation and Leon Flohr with his curls windblown and fresh leapt aboard, dashing the provodnitsa's senile protests to atoms with an easy laugh. Then yet another dusk surprised and drove the daylight to extinction. Jammed in among the six enormous parcels, Musya studied her own round pale face reflected in the window glass, forlorn.

One day they passed nothing but tree stumps in every direction for six full hours. Musya began to picture Leon arriving with an accomplice or two—for he could never reach her now without the aid of a dedicated team, not realistically. The distances involved were too enormous. This, she heard the other passengers agreeing, was the part that always felt long. Maybe Leon's handsome accomplice would be sympathetic to Musya, he might become a friend to her, even something like a brother. She heard a passenger's voice rise from the doldrums:

"What kind of maniacs can believe they rule this far away?"

Musya had to laugh although she didn't see the good of criticizing. A few others laughed and other women hushed them. The carriage fell into an uneasy silence, hypnotically rocked to a steel rail lullaby. When Musya opened her eyes again, a low bright green forest was almost crowding her view; this was the taiga. Its great cool breath enclosed her like tunnel walls. Up and down the carriage mothers were unpacking shawls and little mufflers and supplemental swaddling clothes while the porters fed the iron boiler stove until it roared. Distantly from another carriage they heard voices and handclaps, rhythmic and musical—men in song, the wheezy reeds and bass stops of a bayan accompanying.

The taiga revealed itself. Trees gave way to marshes that led into forests that ended in swamps; the cycle repeated; ground level was a cloak of bright green, every shade, some aglow. The monotony was total, just as it had been on the steppe: indeed it felt a little like the grasses of the steppe had turned gigantic around the train that burrowed busily past stems thick as tree trunks and flooded hoof prints big as ponds. Otherwise a chill damp was pervasive and thick fogs were chronic at any hour of day or night. It was a region of heavy industry and mass labor, Musya gathered, into which many of her fellow passengers would be disembarking on the way to work settlements, assigned there. A few other women she thought very romantic, the ones headed for the environs of prison camps to be near their husbands. Admiring their saintly glamour she wished for a way to befriend them but spent more time picturing herself in their place, with her beloved condemned to hard labor in Siberian chains; she'd be self-sacrificial as a Dekabristi princess, another Trubetskaya choosing exile by his side. Maybe Leon would be guilty as charged of a genuine crime and he'd beg her from his knees to forgive him. She'd touch his poor unbarbered face. She'd leave herself in tears.

The train went along day and night. With the carriage emptying of wives and children, more men boarded. Bound for eastern ports and sea voyages, freight seamen, a pair of them, had found their way onto the bunk facing her own. Musya turned from the dull fogbound view to converse, she could see no harm in this although the provodnitsa's disapproval was obvious. Neither sailor was at all good looking but they'd both spent time ashore in Odessa. She found a lot to talk about with them in easy Russian. Soon the conversation turned to the present journey's apparent endlessness and one of the sailors told of an amazing invention that the Americans were keeping top secret, one which enabled them to travel vast distances without the use of fuel or even motion. It was a suit, he explained, whose wearer could simply levitate, hang in mid-air, and let Earth's rotation do the rest:

"Over Europe one continent, over Atlantic first Ocean, over North America second continent, over Pacific second Ocean—in less than one day only, from Moscow longitude to Vladivostok longitude. Then, what, a few hours south? Think how fast compared to now!"

Musya nodded eagerly. Although a little frightening the floating suit sounded terrific. No doubt about it, she agreed, these American United States with their capitalism, sometimes it really seemed to help them get ahead.

An angry shout and a few loud footfalls heralded the appearance of a tall man in a handsome tunic uniform with red stars on the sleeves and hat brim: he was security police, NKVD. And not disposed, he said, to listen to degenerates spread misinformation about advances in effortless travel. "Suit—what suit?" He barked a disparaging laugh. "Do you not know it does a man no damn good to levitate—not unless he escapes the planet's gravitational pull!"

"Yes," one of the sailors said instantly. "This does."

The newcomer sneered. "An anti-gravity suit? You say the Americans have invented an anti-gravity suit?"

They said yes and he started shouting, threatening the seamen with kicks and arrest; he chased them off. Then he took their place on the bench opposite Musya's, gave her a long hot-eyed look, and begged her pardon; but he was a patriot. America-worship was a poison corroding the veins of the Soviet people. He said to put her worries over the matter away. Latitudinal or otherwise, American physics would get its people exactly nowhere. Humanity's first functioning anti-gravity products were bound to originate in the Soviet Union whose socialist science, he explained, was vastly superior to all science elsewhere because it had never been polluted by foreign influences. Musya didn't know what this was supposed to mean but she agreed with him. She found him terrifically good-looking once she got used to the sight of him and his large pores. He was a black-haired man, very close-shaven. How was she enjoying her journey—how did she find the views, he wondered, of this great land they crossed? It was very big, she hazarded. He agreed in full:

"Immense!"

His name, she learned, was NKVD Trooper Alexey and the salient facts about him were two in number: he loved his country, and he loved pretty girls. Thus he was the happiest of men. To his way of thinking, in the productive force of pretty Soviet girls the unstoppable advance of historical materialism achieved its latest triumph—for were they not all singularly forward-thinking and accomplished? She admitted that she might be.

"I am a poet," she said.

He removed his cap with exaggerated pathos. *"Farewell, leafy groves! You faithful ones, you*—ah, Pushkin." They discussed books for a while and then, more knowledgably, films. The officer loved epics, battle scenes. She ventured to ask whether their train was nearing a war zone even now. This amused, even charmed him. She felt her hand patted: "Ah, my dear. All over, finished. Our Red Army knocked the clockwork out of those Japanese and sent them back to the toy factory. Those maniacs will not be heard from again for three hundred years, mark my words."

She and Alexey talked for almost two hours, a full-out flirtation on both their parts, Musya felt. When one of his colleagues came rattling through on a carriage inspection he sprang up hastily and left her in an instant, tempering the exit's rudeness with a wink that seemed to vow his swift return. Certainly she expected him to return.

Smiling at the window, Musya thought of her silly old poem, the prize-winner. Who would love her? Would it be the black-haired trooper—would he love her? Was she now and had she always been fated to be loved by him? This particular man—his career advanced by leaps as she pictured the effects of her influence—was she about or destined to become the wife of an NKVD commandant? If so, her eyes popped wider. She pictured some opulence, an elegant party, with fingertips to painted lips lifting toast triangles heaped with black caviar, careful of her champagne satin gloves. Would she love only Alexey now? Or would she take a lover? Musya pictured the entrance of Leon Flohr—she threw herself into his arms! And then in the next scenario, she didn't. She pictured him in tears, she pictured herself torn, suspicious. Why had he not come for her sooner? Then Leon Flohr didn't come for her, they met by chance, they met in passing at a nightclub—nothing happened, not right away. At last Leon fell to his knees and begged her for another chance but she said no, she chose fidelity to her husband, Alexey, whom she called Alyosha.

She expected the trooper's return at every moment for the next three days; then hourly; then less. But she never saw him again. The journey dragged its way along enormous rivers into a stretch of warmer climate, marshier, steaming where sun-struck. Evening brought the welcome signals of a station's approach. But it was barely a depot, where a handful of snack vendors passed alongside on the bare ground. Chips of light marked the windows of a small settlement carved out of the taiga. Yet surely the place ought to have been ablaze with light, given the volume of audible current flooding the area—the power plant had to be immense to make so loud a humming sound, so steady.

"*Gnus!*"

The carriage floorboards clattered as the passengers and provodnitsa rushed into violent action together on every side. "*Gnus! Gnus!*" Some lit lamps and citronella coils, others rushed from window to window slamming what they could. Sooty smoke stung Musya's eyes and throat. She slapped at her arm and saw insect wings smashed up in blood—her own, she realized. Gnus: they bit. That had been the sound of them—that many. And people lived here! Musya exclaimed, she thought it was really horrible to establish inhabitants in a place where they'd be driven mad and devoured.

"Where you are going is worse," they told her.

She didn't believe them; although a memory stirred of the mother reading aloud from a letter Liza had sent, an early one, in which she'd complained about the Biting Insect Population, she'd called it. Had this complaint been a recurring one in Liza's letters home? Perhaps it had been, Musya thought now. In truth she hadn't always listened with full attention when the mother read them aloud at the work table; and she hadn't read more than a handful on her own because she hated her older sister's handwriting, the sight of it always depressed and strained her nerves.

She'd absorbed enough, even so, to have gathered that Birobidzhan was a kind of paradise-in-the-making for people exactly like her sister: industrious, high-minded, tiresome. But Musya wondered; for some at least among the settlers might feel much the same as she. A picture rose to mind of her own arrival there, its first catalyzing effects upon the region and an isolated, disaffected minority begun to coalesce into a clique, even a circle with herself dead-center, its leading light and star. A handsome boy she pictured, too, coming from the pumpkin fields outside town one day to market and meeting her eye in the sunshine; she based his image on a boy she'd glimpsed some-where among the steppes who'd stopped loading hay into a cart to watch the train pass by, she could see him leaning on his pitchfork, easeful and attentive. And so handsome: a farmer. Bored, just as she was bored, by all this modernity, all this civilization surrounding them with its niceties and chatter, its politics and news, its cafés and motorcars, its pale suits—this intelligent, sensitive young Jewish pioneer, his skin smooth and honestly sun-browned, his large hands roughened by productive labor, his plush mouth sweet from the apple that she'd toss him when they met, that first day, soon—would he love her? Their love at first sight sealed, of course so.

Maybe a couple of months on the land would do her good, Musya decided.

What else did she know about the Soviet Zion from five years' worth of Liza's telling? That its climate saw extremes of heat and cold unknown in Odessa raised no concern as she'd be gone before the winter came; it was now early October 1939. That famous writers came and visited and sometimes shook hands with Liza before they left, she remembered with traces of her original envy. She knew that the American settlers had all come and gone; that the local government was always changing; and that a sizeable population of Korean families lived there and grew rice, which she thought must be picturesque if not quite worth seeing. That downtown Birobidzhan boasted its own modern Yiddish Theater was the fact whose recollection kindled Musya's imagination into the liveliest activity now. She'd been able to pack one nice fashionable dress she felt sure would outclass any other in so provincial an audience. Maybe at some point in her visit the company would even be casting for extras or an ingénue; or else the production's leading lady could fall ill, quit the stage, or elope with an aviator, leaving the handsome playwright-turned-director brokenhearted and in extremis, mere hours from ruin. Musya his future savior smiled to herself: she was on the way.

Through a late morning the train drew near to Birobidzhan, capital city of the Jewish Autonomous Region and in the approach little different from its brother and sisters cities that lined—widely spaced—the Trans-Siberian's eastern frontier route. Blasted and barren and waterlogged, scarred by earth machines, virtually treeless, dotted with ramshackle mining works where she'd pictured melon fields and wheat, hay wagons creaking on chalk roads and lambs leaping in green grass paddocks; but she didn't see a single farm, not one, before the brake whistle's long shrill cry signaled the station's approach. The sound plunged Musya into a painful dilemma.

For, arriving penniless, she had still to thank the provodnitsa with a little something. Though hard on her at times the conductress and her colleagues had been vigilant in Musya's service for over ten days now, of this they were using these final minutes to remind her; and she admitted it readily. It was true. She owed the provodnitsa. Who knew, somehow, she didn't know how they knew, exactly how much cash she had left upon her person—none, zero—and they joined her in hoping that any relatives waiting to greet her on the Birobidzhan station platform had come equipped with moderate to heavy sums in bill or coin. Otherwise, if not, they could discuss the bolts of cloth and dry goods and other contents of her parcels; which the provodnitsa knew backwards and forwards as well, they knew better than Musya did, actually. She hoped it wouldn't come to that but was preparing herself to part with an ample moiety. In the meantime she regretted having to fix every bit of her attention on this debate in the carriage interior whilst her first views of the city presumably rolled past unseen; in sum, she arrived penniless, fretful and vexed.

(4)

Boris Kotz had already hired a handcart for the baggage before her arrival. What that transaction had left in his pocket could have bought a few sticks of candy, but not very good ones. He said, "But surely they know that tipping is not permitted in the Soviet Union." Musya didn't answer. The handcart creaked, jiggled, its boards loose; fortunately the parcels were much more compact now, minus the provodnitsa's share. It surprised her that she'd recognized her brother-in-law so immediately in the crowds and chaos of the platform. A few dozen passengers had disembarked with her but many more were boarding, whole family groups leaving, heading east to where the Soviet Union ended in harbors full of ships. Taking her first strangely uncertain steps on the immobile ground, Musya had caught hold of the handcart and dislodged a board that fell and broke apart, the wood was rotten. No one had offered to help them patch the gap or resettle the baggage, least of all the station porters who'd already seen what they could expect from Boris Kotz by way of baksheesh. He told her to climb on top if she preferred being pushed to walking but she declined, she walked, using her arm and shoulder to brace the broken side; she walked with firmer steps and growing certainty that the man between its handles had overpaid five times too much to hire this sorry cart—five being a minimum. Now he was worried that its owner might ask extra for damages. Any shyster ever born could see he was a dupe. Where, she wondered, was Liza? Her sister was waiting at home, he said.

Then again, maybe the way his froggy face had leapt out from her memory in a crush and throng wasn't such a surprise. His homeliness was really striking. The years had not improved Boris Kotz, he'd changed barely at all. Still unhealthily plump and light-deprived-looking, he labored already to push the handcart through the station's rather modest confines—how he'd expected to make it all the way to the exit with her riding on top she couldn't imagine. He'd greeted her with the same soft squelching handshake; Musya even recognized the suit jacket from their very first meeting. The plain cotton tunic shirt beneath was newer and not well-maintained, his boots were fairly clean but shoddy. How would they be riding to the farm, she wondered?

"Oh, no," he said. "We live here in the city now."

Exciting news, to Musya: her reaction to it she'd remember always—*The City!*—the exciting picture set alight in her mind with such clarity: the spacious flat surrounded by accomplished neighbors, shops, shaded park benches, cafés. Maybe Boris and Liza were intelligentsia now, with interesting friends; they might have gotten to know one or two full-bearded poets who'd recognize something akin in Liza's frankly prettier little sister. The life of the mind: here, now, having reached a point inconceivably far from all she knew of civilization, Musya saw its appeal. She would write again, she vowed this, she would make contributions equally treasured among the avant-garde and in the worker's home. A sense of mission thrilled her as they stepped outdoors into the city bustling at the shadowless peak of noon.

But Musya's first impression of Birobidzhan was that she did not consider this to be a city. It looked to her instead like some actual city's most unfinished edge or outskirts had been torn off and dropped into a muddy wilderness several thousand miles away. Beyond the railway station there was hardly one block of stone to be seen; outside the road from the station there wasn't any pavement. The buildings, a collection of hulking boxes hammered together from logs, planks, shingles so rough-hewn as to look raw, had iron chimney vents crowning their steep roof peaks and hardly any windows; some advertised their tenancy by shops and offices with signboard-covered facades; few were painted. Fresh-cut wood perfumed the heavy atmosphere in welcome counterpoint to a more aggressive reek of petrol mixed with sewage.

"It's not so far to walk from here," said her host.

They were just outside the station entrance, paused there. A little stunned, Musya felt the pull of the tracks at her rear quarter. She hadn't fully left the state of transit and now an urgent instinct tugged her towards retreat and flight; maybe she ought to board the next train headed in either direction and go. Her next step would be decisive—or would have been, only she didn't have a ticket or anything to put towards a fare.

Her first steps into Birobidzhan felt more like sleepwalking. Out of a dim quiet, battered trucks and the infrequent motorcar began to rattle past. The felled tree trunks supporting the roadbed had broken through the paved surface in places. The road was almost two years old now, she heard Boris tell her. Along its verges, parallel rows of fragile-looking saplings stood dwarfed by towering electrical poles; there was not a spot of shade here. Open ground lay exposed in a squalid jumble of woodpiles, ditches, fences (ditches outnumbered fences), privies and outbuildings, overgrown kitchen gardens, animal pens, wash lines, rubbish heaped in piles, rubbish thrown in pits, rubbish left uncollected—the whole place was covered with rubbish and looked and smelled filthy. Enormously deep-looking mud puddles the size of public rooms lay here and there, plank walkways skirting and crossing their litter-scummed surfaces. The month just past, Boris Kotz supplied, like the month before had been a rainy one.

"Here, Musya, if you can believe," he seemed to boast, "ten years ago was only a small village."

"What happened to your farm?" she asked.

He said, "Oh, that. Farming didn't work out for us." Of course all the farms in the region were collectivized in accordance with Soviet policy. Jews were in charge at some dozen kolkhozes scattered within a day trip or so. There were also some Jewish settlements organized around light industry; they even ran a health resort village; but Boris and Liza had wanted to farm. They'd arrived on the land as newlyweds in time to help fertilize a rye crop that never sprouted at one kolkhoz. Later at a horrible place called Red October they'd tended melon beds that a freak ground frost transformed into slime.

Their unprivate nights they'd passed in communal tents or bunkhouses. Boris had no regrets at all about their move to the regional capital, where he worked in an office at a wooden chair factory. "But your sister didn't write to tell you about all this?"

"I don't remember," Musya told him. She wondered what he did there at his chair factory: not much, she guessed. Something else that remained unchanged about Boris Kotz was his air of being as Musya's father said of him, not such a hardworking fellow. Yet he did appear careworn. His breath came in puffs as they attained a sort of inter-section marked by a hodgepodge of overlapping ruts and boards across which the cartwheels labored. Musya moved around to pull, there was a rope handle in front. She tugged with all her might; and in a vivid little show, a few snippets of her tree-lined boulevard café society fantasies returned to taunt her. The cart groaned and then jolted forward. She stumbled but kept her footing, looked around. The closest thing here to a café wasn't even a restaurant, it was an alleyway tavern with canvas walls and a very grisly appearance, gray and purple drunkards sprawled out front like human shrubbery. And what passed for restaurants were only cheerless eating houses all exhaling the same sour dumpling dough steams. This month-long visit would feel very much longer, she feared.

For sure, the people of Birobidzhan looked to promise little by way of diverting mental stimulation or romance. In every respect that mattered to Musya, their way of life obviously lacked. All she could see were men and woman toughened by the elements, scarred by the austerities of daily existence, condemned to a choice between out-of-date fashions and no fashions at all; the hats and dresses were horrible and some were quite tawdry. Men far outnumbered women, but the handsome young Jewish farmer she'd pictured meeting when he came to market was, much like the marketplace, nowhere in sight. So far as Musya could see, while the capital of the Jewish Autonomous Region was probably some things (for instance small, unsightly, unsanitary) one thing it did not appear to be was especially full of Jews. She recognized Russians or Ukrainians, blondish, round-faced, strapping, and a lot a Asian-featured faces she guessed belonged to Korean people. And there were Jews, unmistakable though mostly clean-shaven and dressed in what passed for the popular mode here, Jews as usual: outnumbered, poor, and subjected to authority. They weren't in charge here.

Musya felt a little disappointed but far from surprised. Of course her sister's hopes had been unrealistic, of course Boris Kotz had picked a losing course to follow. They were a ridiculous couple who'd chosen a life in their own utopia only for the husband not to buy a new suit jacket in five years. Frowning, she thought about the yards of brown worsted she'd relinquished to the her keepers on the train: had Boris only brought enough cash today he might have had one—plus trousers, possibly. His faults were manifold.

At last he pointed at one small window cut in the side of a long shambling structure, where the young Kotz family was established on an upper floor in two rooms of its own, this Boris noted with pride. No kitchen, it was a rooming house. Puddles and sewage pools encircled its foundations, a ditch fronted it. Musya crossed and re-crossed the sagging planks laid from roadway to entrance, helping Boris carry her parcels inside. Still Liza didn't appear. A strange delay, her sister felt, considering the urgency of her summons. Boris said that Liza couldn't leave the boys upstairs but still it was strange, this absence of welcome. Musya might have been anyone, a distant acquaintance. She agreed sullenly to postpone her proper greeting even longer while Boris returned the handcart to the man he'd hired it from without delay.

Her brother-in-law's thralldom to this handcart business added to Musya's vexation. He'd led her to a small room that served the house as common parlor and mail drop and left her there to wait. It was a cheerless room with a layer of tobacco ash coating every surface and she was alone in it. Framed on the walls behind nicotine-yellowed glass were the standard portraits of Soviet leaders and two identical lists of house rules printed in Russian and Yiddish. No animals including livestock were permitted on the premises. Visitors and guests were required to register but Musya saw no sign of any book. Windowsill and floor below it were littered with dead flies. Mud, weeds, corners of walls, a paddock of some kind: to Musya's eyes the view through the murky panes appeared to be of nothing, blank emptiness. She dropped onto the hard lumpy seat of a chair by the cold stove. Her feet hurt, her whole body ached, she was thirsty. She loosened the collar of her dress and drew a deep dispirited breath.

A whole month here!

From a table nearby she took up a newspaper printed in Yiddish, only to find it filled with stultifying accounts of the Jewish Autonomous Region's industrial and agricultural output measured against the goals of the latest Five-Year Plan. Blotchy photographs, impossible to decipher without the aid of their captions, immortalized a tractor, a logging crew, some factory gates. The local branch of the League of the Militant Godless, she read, was preparing another extraordinary lecture series. Her search for local theater news or listings turned up none; the arts section featured only a few poems she thought very inferior. Then came four pages in praise of the man whose bristling portrait faced her from the parlor wall. The Lenin of Today, she reflected, for all his faults as a subject of prose, would have hired a sturdy well-oiled handcart and returned it at his leisure.

She rose at the sound of footsteps descending the wooden stairs beyond the wall and looked to the parlor doorway where, instead of Liza, a strange short woman appeared and exclaimed at the sight of her:

"You! The sister? Little sister from Odessa?" She had a thick accent to her Russian and a charge-taking look on a wrinkled red-brown shiny face. Her dress was Liza's, about eight years old, Musya recognized it perfectly, folded over at the waist and belted to raise the hem from the floor as a child in her mother's dress would wear it. Decrepit lapti toes peeked out. Before Musya could produce a syllable the woman waved her arms and hissed, "Him! Him!" A mystifying whispered shout: now the woman rolled her eyes and spittle flew. "Where is he? The idiot!"

"Ah," said Musya. "He's gone with the handcart." Before she could say anything else her companion boiled over with furious carefully quieted noise. She sputtered, seemed to curse, waved her fists, stamped a bast boot sole, snapped her red bony jaws, cried, "The end! The end!" She was livid.

"Excuse me," Musya tried to ask. "Who are you?"

But here the front door of the rooming house scraped open to admit a stooped and muddy-booted figure: Boris Kotz had returned. The old woman lunged at him and then shushed the hoarse cry he gave as her hard yellow nails found flesh through the upper sleeve of his jacket. These were definitely curses she was spewing now, whispered, croaked, suddenly tearful as she yanked at and shoved him. Boris struggled in her grip and Musya wondered which would give first, seams or fabric. "I had to return the cart, Magga! I didn't want to pay the late charge."

Her throat straining to whisper, Musya cried, "Who is this woman?"

"She's only the dvornik." The house porter, then. Boris was wild-eyed. He was also, Musya decided once and for all, an extremely stupid person. Only the dvornik? He didn't know anything. "Let me go, Magga!" Another helpless heave of his arm left a sizeable rip before the dvornik released him in disgust; the shoulder seam was torn as well. The old woman turned her wet red face to Musya.

"I run things around here," she said.

"Of course," said Musya, vowing that this woman would have none of her dresses— not one.

"Your sister waits for you."

"Yes. Good."

But nobody moved. They stood quiet. Then Musya started at a sound behind, a loud, buzzing, tap-tap-tapping where a fat fly beat itself against the windowpanes; twice more it struck the glass before it dropped to the sill, heaved around on its wings and fell down dead to lie among its fellows on the floor. The whole thing was very odd because the window was open. She turned again and met the dvornik's dark, glittering eyes. Tears made them glitter.

"You put too much poison again, Magga, I told you. It isn't safe," Boris scolded.

"Who asked you?" the old woman shot back. "No body."

On this last somewhat ambiguous note they divided the luggage, left the parlor and started upstairs, the dvornik in the lead. Musya managed the heaviest parcel, the one with the old wooden toys she and Liza had shared, the small blankets, some good secondhand boys' shoes and trousers—back there on the train she'd refused the provodnitsa any share of what came marked for the nephews. She'd looked forward to presenting gifts in her role as benefactress and aunt; she'd seen herself bending to help tie a shoelace, tossing a ball on a lawn, teaching the rules of a board game; she'd thought she might even go so far as to tell a bedtime story and share a kiss or two goodnight, although she wasn't especially fond of children.

"Sender and Anshel—and Anshel is the younger, yes?" She had to ask.

Boris was plodding heavily up the stairs behind her. "Anton," he said. "Anton is the baby."

"Anton." A Russian name. Musya frowned. Whatever they were called, these two were unusually silent and invisible for boys—the rowdier sex, she'd thought. And her sister Liza for all her reading had always been active, overflowing with projects and sometimes manic energy; maybe Liza's sons took after their father, two squat little bodies already bookish, sedentary, unenthused. Or maybe they were sick—or dead—or dying. It would explain a great deal; but this she couldn't ask. Only the staircase seemed too short when she'd rather have climbed much longer.

Near the end of a dim foul-smelling hall they came to a plain door and followed the dvornik inside. "Here we are!" Boris called strangely.

The first room was dimmer than the hall, airless, wildly overstuffed with unmatching furniture and blanketed with boxes, books and papers, plates and glassware including parts of what looked like a chemistry kit. Near the wall sink were two samovars, one in use, and a large incongruously pristine white boiler on a stand, its bottom vents glowing blue. Deposited all in a heap only seconds ago at the host's vague direction, the six parcels from Odessa were already imbued with the room's uncared-for atmosphere, Musya thought. She made a move across the hexagon pattern of a gritty threadbare kilim towards the working samovar, where the hissing dvornik helped her to some tea, badly overbrewed but welcome. From an adjoining space divided from this one by a curtain on rings came a collection of quiet sounds, rhythmic like birdcalls, in which she recognized children's sobs. And an overwhelming wish for Leon Flohr assailed her spirit and seemed to cast a spotlight's glare on her hollowness, her incapacity, her youth. Where was her lover? Two weeks: he'd had two weeks to come after her. What if he'd decided that she wasn't worth his time or effort to pursue? In which case could she—looking at this room, this situation, looking at her mess of a family—could she really blame him?

The curtain twitched, one edge pulled aside. In the gap a face less wrinkled, pinker than red but otherwise a copy of the house porter's down to the tearstains confronted them with an urgent and questioning look. "Kitty, my daughter," Musya heard, while in the small of her back she felt the mother's hard little hand prodding her forward. Across the room, Boris fussed with some tools in a case, his mouth slack. At the vicious noise the dvornik sent his way through her teeth he looked up and started obediently towards the curtain. On the other side two sleeping alcoves and a commode closet lined a short passageway that ended in a door. This opened onto the room with the window.

"Oh, Liza! Oh!" Musya exclaimed. "How wonderful to see you—your skin looks wonderful!" It was a small white room stripped of furniture but for the bed, a chair or two, a narrow table heaped with white linen towels. Her sister lay in the bed. On the table and the windowsill were basins filled with bloody towels and blood. Two little red-haired boys sat near the bed, undefended from their view, both in one chair, one on the other's lap. "And you must be Simkhe and Semyon and, no, wait, that isn't right, I know, I know." She didn't know. She raised a hand to her hair. "I'm your aunt, your Mumeh Musya, I've brought you beautiful toys from Odessa and—I'll buy you some sweets. We'll go out later for sweets." They looked to her like puppet children made from dyed lamb's fleece and porcelain and glass, huge glass eyes that seemed to click each time they blinked releasing fresh tears to fall, as if there were a hidden mechanism for it. "I brought things for you, too, Liza, sewing things from Mama, you'll like them. And some cloth— oh, and the best buttons!" The room was cool, the window wide open; white curls of camphor-laced aromatics were rising from an incense burner on a stand; still the smell was close and rotten. Was she already infected, standing here—already doomed? "I was so glad to hear you'd moved to the city. There's always so much more to do in a city. Culturally, I mean. You have your theater for instance, that must—"

A horrible noise came from the bed. Then a voice croaked:

"Musya. Stop talking."

"I'm sorry, Liza, let me—let me embrace you." She tried moving forward but her legs and feet refused to take her even one step, though she tried to force them. "Please. My sister."

A spidery hand rose from the blood-spattered counterpane, made a rebuffing gesture and dropped back. "Don't be a fool," Liza told her. "Try not to be."

"Yes," said Musya. "All right."

This was Consumption. Her sister was skeletal. A stack of pillows kept her vanishing torso half-upright and her head supported; the neck was nothing but a pulse and a handful of reeds collected in a parchment sheath. Contours pressed unevenly from chalk, through skin stretched sheer as gauze all Liza's bones showed clearly, even a zigzagging seam in her skull ran legible from eyebrow to sweat-beaded hairline. She wore a lovely patterned kerchief tied around her hair and a linen nightdress from her bridal kit, the one with the blue embroidery at cuffs, yoke and collar, the front stained brown in overlapping blots by successive eruptions of hemorrhage. It was true, though: her skin had never looked better. Every blemish had fled.

"Listen to me," Liza commanded. Swollen and red with bloodshot and fever her gray eyes were vast, luminous, twin angry planets with molten metal cores. "I haven't got much time." Musya answered automatically:

"Oh, no, I'm sure that's not true. You'll be—you just need to get some rest."

Something like a laugh shook Liza's frame and then one or two cupfuls of brilliantly red blood spouted from her lower jaw, down her chin and across the front of the ruined nightdress. Keening cries broke from the chair where the little boys huddled and hoarser exclamations from the dvornik and her quick-footed daughter who rushed forward with towels, hiding the sick woman briefly from her sister's view. *Poor Liza!* her sister thought. After all the energy she'd put into berating the neighbors over their deficient household hygiene—as a child hadn't Liza even earned a ribbon and commendation in some long-ago anti-tuberculosis campaign? For Heroic Efforts to Eradicate the Worker's Enemy: a red ribbon, yes, Musya was sure of it. And now this, like a cruel joke, terrible.

Yet people recovered from tuberculosis all the time. They came by the thousands to the warm dry shores of the Black Sea and the famous sanatoriums around Odessa, seeking to regain their health; not in vain, not always. Camps for consumptive children ringed the city, she'd seen them on outings in parks, lined up two by two in their little white outfits, plump, cherubic, flourishing on milk diets. It was a disease that came and went. Many years might be left to Liza, even a long life ahead. Loading her voice with cheerfulness and firm resolve, Musya said, "You need to come back to Odessa, that's all. You'll get better there."

"Never." This was Liza. As the other women bore away their bloody towels and basins Musya faced her whole again and had to agree: a recovery looked worse than doubtful. "I'll never see Odessa again. I'll never see Mommy and Daddy again."

"You could have seen Mommy again! You could have sent for her! Why not Mommy—why me?" Musya heard her own voice rise and shake and ring against the walls, shockingly. She couldn't help it. "This isn't fair!"

In bitter amusement Liza let her stained lips part and lift across long front teeth hideous with blood. "Fair," she echoed.

They always fought. "Yes—fair! Did you give any thought to me? I have my own life, you know." She'd gone too far to back down now. "I'm not a nurse. I can't help you. Did you want to bring me here to make me sick like you? To kill me? Is that how jealous you are?" Musya gave a desperate look around the room, saw Boris Kotz slumped like a water stain against the wall, saw the grief-stricken faces of the little puppet boys turned her way, open-mouthed with shock and horror; because she was monstrous. "I'm sorry!" she cried.

Liza raised one hand to silence her and let it drop, at which a whispering rustle of bones reached Musya's ears; she wanted to cover her ears with both hands but she seemed to be paralyzed. Her sister, with a tremendous heaving effort of throat and chest, swallowed and began to speak, gasping between every few words:

"You're a frivolous person, Musya. You always were. *Your own life*, you call it. All you've ever done is dream of film stardom and fantasy men—that's your life. What's to become of you? Don't you wonder? Doesn't it worry you?"

Musya said, "Not really."

As if she hadn't spoken, Liza droned on. "I've worried about you and your lack of direction for years. So has Mommy. You've never been serious. You're full of yourself. You'll fall prey to the first fancy man who comes along and smiles at you."

"No. That's not true. I won't."

"Let me give you a chance to do something with your life, something meaningful and important—let me die knowing that your life won't be completely frivolous and empty and wasted on trifles. Don't you see? I want to help you, for your own good—*oh!* I can't— give me some water!"

She called for water and the dvornik hurried forward with a glass as Musya stood there shaking her head: she didn't see. Where was Leon Flohr? Where was his soft brown moustache? Where was Leon? He should have been standing there beside her, defending her, visibly present and forceful and not only a figure of memory, not only wished for like riches or fame.

But he'd failed her.

"Listen to me, Musya, I've haven't much time. Look at my sons—my babies." Musya glanced that way. They had their mother's gray eyes and probably her fatal infection, given the close quarters here. It was sad but tuberculosis was a killer of multitudes. "You, Musya—you be their mother now."

"I—what?"

"Take my boys and be their mother."

"Take them back to Odessa? All right." *Gladly*, she almost added. For an idea of Liza's this one made surprising quantities of sense. The boys could live with their grandparents where Musya could certainly visit them; a children's sanatorium would admit them if necessary; meanwhile she'd have moved from the outskirts to someplace nearer central Odessa; she'd visit often, every week, and be in some ways like a mother to them. Why not? Her sister's gaunt, sweat-sheened face was moving back and forth against the pillows, though. Musya had it wrong, all wrong:

"No. Listen. Pay attention." The huge fevered eyes burned a way into her own with their red intensity. "A mother to my boys—and a wife to their father." Musya put a hand to her head and stared, dizzied. She couldn't speak. She thought she might fall down. She listened to what her insane sister was saying. "This is our home, Musya, our home and our homeland as Soviet Jews—this land is our rightful share in the victory of socialism. My sons will grow strong here in the Jewish Autonomous Region, they'll become men, they'll be leaders, great leaders—yes, both of you." The boys seemed to have exhausted their store of sobs, they returned their mother's look and trembled.

"Liza, it's awful here!" Again Musya couldn't contain herself. "It's dirty and awful, it smells bad, it's not at all finished, it's not even Jewish here—Odessa is a thousand times more Jewish!"

"Odessa is decadent. Dying. For Birobidzhan I have hope. I have always had hope."

Musya recognized the elevated look on her sister's face, she remembered it very well. She sighed, knowing reason was powerless.

Softly clearing his throat, her brother-in-law materialized at Musya's shoulder. She'd forgotten he was in the room. The look he gave her was embarrassed, she thought. It was hard to tell: the eyes were quite unreadable through the smudges on his eyeglass lenses. Weeping had swollen his features and heightened their amphibious cast. He addressed the bed. "My dear." His voice cracked and he cleared his throat again. "My dear."

Liza had drifted. It took her almost a minute and who knew how much strength to direct her gaze at her husband. When she finally had him in her sights, she frowned. "I'm leaving you too soon, Kotz," she told him.

He agreed. "Yes." His shoulders started heaving. Musya raised the comfort of a hand to his back and left a few pats on the unpleasantly damp suitcloth. From the bed she heard:

"Musya, please. Take my place."

"What? No—what place?"

"As my babies' mother. As my husband's wife—please. I beg of you."

"But—but I don't even like Boris!"

"Look at him," Liza answered. "He needs someone."

"He can find someone—he found you!" she cried reasonably. "There are other women. There—" There were even other women in the room. But the old dvornik drew back from her wild entreating glance with a scandalized grunt, while the daughter went so far as to raise both forearms in a prohibitory gesture and shake her hands as if Musya had offered her something that was on fire. Feeling she could sympathize, Musya went for an authoritative tone. "There are plenty of other women in the Soviet Union for your husband to marry."

Naturally Liza ignored both tone and sentiment. "This is the best thing for you, too, Musyu. It will give you a purpose in life."

"I have a purpose already in life without you, Liza!"

"You don't," came the inexorable reply. "None. But you have a duty, you have a sister's duty to do as I ask—as I beg you—and take my place in this family and this home."

This home! The dust-glazed riot of end tables and crockery in the next room seemed to crash down through her thoughts and bury her in rubble. She stared, panting. "So this is why you didn't send for Mommy, this is why you sent for me instead, all this way, two weeks, for this crazy—you're crazy!" She felt Boris touch her arm and she batted him away, she couldn't stand for him to touch her. "I don't want your ugly husband you—you crazy woman!"

Liza closed her eyes. The lids were huge, wet, greenish-purple. "Musya, can't you see this is my dying wish?"

"So? So?" The dvornik's tongue clucked disapproval but Musya was very far past caring how nice an impression she made here. "You're so greedy, Liza! Dying has nothing to do with it."

"Don't die, Mamenyu, don't die."

With a start, Musya looked at the chair where her nephews huddled, watching, hearing everything. The younger one had a musical voice, really lovely. Tears soaked the collars and fronts of their little gray blouses. She wished she could cut her own head off and be done.

The dying woman's lips twitched—possibly with effort and maybe it was really painful to force eyelids ajar across orbs so swollen and feverish. Liza spared no look for Musya. Instead her gaze fell upon her children and rested as it might have on a famous view attained at the high point of some one-time holiday: she absorbed every detail of them.

"Don't die, Mama," the elder boy pleaded.

Liza said to tell their aunt. "Tell her, tell your Mumeh Musya to promise."

"Oh, Mamenyu!"

"To take—my place. Tell her—to promise."

He bargained. "Then don't die!" Some assent he read then in his mother's face made him wheel on Musya and shout at her. "Promise! Promise!" His little brother screamed, kept screaming, his voice throwing spears.

"I can't—I can't!" She tried to tell them but their terrible racket only grew louder.

And Boris Kotz didn't do anything. He didn't say one word.

"Promise! Promise!"

Liza's eyes had fallen shut again, she lay there and listened to the howling cries, a strange smile playing across her wasted features. Blue-gray beneath the bloodstains her narrow lips looked poisoned. Suddenly Musya remembered the dead flies on the parlor floor. Maybe this wasn't disease at all! Maybe there'd been a careless mistake and her sister was nothing more than a pesticide accident victim, suffering from nothing that a good dose of castor oil wouldn't set to rights. What they needed here was a doctor—where was the doctor? And quiet. They needed quiet, they needed this noise to stop:

"Yes, I promise! All right! I promise."

"Mama!" He plunged at the bed with a cry, squeezing his little brother into near silence. "Mamenyu, she promised!"

Musya grabbed Boris by the arm and shook him; instantly she felt the jacket sleeve come loose beneath her hands. "Where is the doctor? Don't you have a doctor here?"

"He—he comes, yes." Looking at his children and his dying wife with helpless bewilderment, Boris seemed to welcome this new topic. "A very able man," he murmured. "Really an excellent doctor—he trained abroad, in Warsaw. No—Krakow. I'm sorry, it was—it was Krakow."

The older boy shot his father a look and then reached for Liza's shoulder, he squeezed it and even shook her a little. "Mamenyu—look at me. Mama!" An excruciating moment passed before the eyelids which all at once looked swampier and more sunken finally moved, almost a flutter. Then both eyes flew open and Liza stared in blind agony at the ceiling, her swollen blood-filled eyes were starting from her head. They watched her jaws part, her throat jerk backwards and her spine become an arch, raising the bedcovers. Her tongue protruded. Now came the worst noise imaginable.

Without stopping to think Musya dashed forward and yanked the two little boys away from the bed, pulled them to herself and held them tightly, she held their faces to her skirt and tried to retreat from the scene but Boris was behind her, immobile and groaning steadily. She didn't recognize the language of the rapid singsong chant the dvornik had commenced as she and her daughter busied themselves around the pillows, giving what comfort they could; the daughter also chanted. A gust of cold air rattled the window frame.

Soon she felt a soft damp object descend upon her shoulder and rest there; she recognized the hand. The sons of Boris Kotz burrowed closer and tightened their fists on her clothes. Here was her sister's family.

She was alone with them.

(5)

The Jewish cemetery lay on the southwest side of Birobidzhan, occupying a stretch of ground within distant earshot of the passing trains. After the funeral, Musya walked there every day, never setting off without the thought that her way led in the direction of Odessa—of home.

Each morning when Boris Kotz was safely gone to his office she went to their single window and looked out at the weather. Save for this purpose she almost never entered this room, only for weather spotting or for when the clutter in the front room had become too much and she'd lug some in here for Boris to contend with; he, the clutter's source, occupied his wife's death chamber and deathbed in bachelor solitude. His sons would slip into the room when it was empty, they spent hours at a time there. At night they shared the sleeping alcoves in the passage. Their aunt on the chaise lounge in the front room went to sleep and woke again in a never-ceasing state of craving for fresh air. She used her morning visit to the window to determine how many layers of wraps and waterproofing the day would require. By the end of November nothing worked terribly well but it took the very worst weather to prevent Musya's daily visit to her sister's grave.

Freezing rain could come in leaden mists or wind-swirled sheets and freezing mud run down the unpaved roads in torrents. An hour of sun might beam warmthless sparks through icicles and frost-furred wires. Snow could pile in drifts, then melt, then freeze again to lie in treacherous slicks beneath fresh snowfalls. Or the weather could simply be what it was for the most part: ever colder. The hours of daylight dwindled day by day, the cold grew hard as iron and still Musya ventured. Her nephews always went along, they'd both insisted from the first. Not having brought any winter clothes of her own from Odessa she improvised cloaks, hoods, fur linings, galoshes, long mittens, face scarves and leggings for herself from what she found at hand among Liza's old things. And how she regretted now the bolts of good cloth she'd lost—surrendered—to the provodnitsa! Her memory spun them to fantastic lengths of miraculous insulating power as she sat and cut and sewed what remained into roomy boy-sized snowsuits of padded broadcloth. She'd carved out a workspace with table amid the front room's clutter. Which had actually yielded a sewing machine that worked once she cleaned and oiled the foot pedal: the thing was ancient, Boris couldn't remember how he'd acquired it. Her sister hadn't sewn much, he said. Surprisingly, Liza had amassed a large collection of lovely patterned headscarves, real silk. "Oh yes," Boris sighed. "She loved a little finery." Otherwise Musya found the family's stock of clothes and linens (much of it bought second-hand) in poor shape. She repaired most everything and used the rest for stuffing and patches. With the dvornik's daughter Kitty lending occasional help, four year-old

Sender Kotz shared the labor. He loved to baste—Musya's least favorite aspect of tailoring, next to taking measurements—but he was still a little young for adding figures, he made a few mistakes. The snowsuits turned out fine, however, they were even rather handsome.

And to be sure, the snow fell just in time. Two year-old Anton who still needed occasional carrying was impossibly cumbersome in winter wear. Behind a pile of junk in the front room they'd found an old wooden sled that Boris had dragged in ages ago and forgotten. With the dvornik looking on, they'd waxed it. Now Musya and Sender could take turns pulling Anton like a prince through the frozen town.

"What do I write?" An hour from the funeral, she'd hit desperation. "What on earth can I write? What words are there for this?" Dim and yellow, the letter paper lay before her on the table, the letter barely started; numb, her fingers curled around a useless pen that left a trail of pinprick blotting from its clogged nib. *Dearest Mama and Papa, I must* was followed by nothing, a blank. "How can I tell them—what's happened? It can't be done!" And Boris had pulled the paper to him and taken the pen from her hand, saying that this was not a problem; he knew what to say and it was his place to write it anyhow. "Your place as what?" she'd asked. "What place?"

But he'd made no answer. Already composition held him rapt.

Boris Kotz enjoyed writing letters, especially formal ones. In Russian or Yiddish, he took pleasure in matching his large store of stock phrases to proper sentiments each in their given place. To the experts on all manner of subjects whose printed works he brought home by the bushel and read only bits of, he'd nonetheless make a point of sending a page or three of fulsome praise leavened with factual corrections. The occasional reply he'd commit almost to memory and carry about with him for days before adding it to the heaps of paper marked for later cataloging that took up tabletops, drawers and cupboards in every corner of the flat. Especially voluminous was a correspondence generated by his long pursuit of a position Boris deemed better suited to his abilities than a petty clerkship in a chair factory. His goal was specific: he sought classification as a Regional Soil Specialist and a large salary upgrade. To date officialdom had not responded encouragingly and indeed he lacked any qualifications—he'd prepared to study law, not the sciences, and had earned no advanced degree.

But one fatal autumn day in 1934, his first year on the kolkhozes, he'd fallen into conversation with a mobile soil study team at work in the locale. Which featured at least three extinct volcanoes; there were floodplains, too. The farming should have been much better. The team had also told him that all the real and only necessary training for what they did happened in the field, on the job. Had it been their big shiny truck? Their shovels and instruments, their boot leather or the felt of their hats? Their teeth? Their merriness? Musya would never know for sure what it was about those soil specialists that Boris had found so beguiling, nor why he'd coveted their life ever since. The fact remained that their indelible glowing image was the reason for all the pieces of chemistry sets in the flat, the cupboard shelves crammed with specimen jars and bottled acids, the scattered tools, the bags of rocks, the layers of dust and grittiness on every surface down to the last inch of bedclothes.

That bleak day, an hour from the funeral, Musya had nodded at her pushy brother-in-law: yes, to address both her parents at once was fine if he preferred. He was already writing. One thing he could do was talk and write at the same time: "I'll explain to your parents that my position here will improve very shortly—but in the meantime you will enjoy every comfort here, just as your sister did." She watched ink-sprayed phrases pile up above the fluent progress of his thick white fist. *Deepest sorrow—irreplaceable loss—a greater will than ours—kindly consented—the future.* "Your sister had no complaints about her life here—did she? Did she ever write that she was dissatisfied? Unhappy?" He glanced up, really wanting to know.

"She died, Boris."

"Yes." He blinked behind his dusty spectacles and went back to writing. "Yes of course, but, I only meant, in her letters, she might have, somewhere—" An irritated breath escaped him as he missed a word: he drew a line and kept going. "In any case, she couldn't say everything—some things, that is. You can never know what the authorities here—elsewhere—they—it's important to know how to phrase things correctly."

Annoyed by his pompous tone she said, "I didn't read everything. It wasn't interesting." His hand kept on evenly, making scratching sounds, precise. She read: *a second mother—companion—wife.* The boys were tucked up together on one of the half-sofas, she thought they'd cried themselves to sleep. Or else they were stupefied. The room was suffocating, every particle of air used and used again, every breath tarnished by sorrow and freighted with death. The working samovar gave a hiss like a last gasp of oxygen. "I didn't consent, Boris," she told him suddenly. "I didn't—to be your wife. I didn't consent."

He gave her another look, mild, almost quizzical. "You did, Musya. You promised."

"Yes, I promised," she began. But what came next? It was as if she'd lost a game she hadn't realized that she was even playing, one with fatal rules laid down by distant and unknowable powers. What could she have done differently? Had she overlooked the proper move or step? Had she ever stood a chance? She looked at Boris Kotz, possibly the least desirable man in the Soviet Union—she'd been across the whole length of it, seen it end to end. Here he was. "But you don't want me," she objected.

With a slight frown and an unreadable shrug of his rusty black-clad shoulder, his funeral suit, he'd said, "It doesn't matter what I want." Then he'd returned his attention to the darkening page.

The next month they were married. Her parents' consent, short and grief-stricken, had arrived in the interim, extinguishing Musya's last hope. She couldn't run away because she had no money. One week she'd passed in bed with fever when, longing to die, she'd only lost a little weight. She would have looked delightful in a bridal gown but she didn't have one—nor a wedding ceremony, nor gifts, nor guests, nor a bridal feast. She wore the dress she'd brought for play-going. They signed their two names in a register at the local ZAGS office in front of slow, rude clerks and a dirty floor. Musya didn't care, she had no wish to celebrate; but it surprised her to learn at the time that in the capital of the Jewish Autonomous Region there was not a single working rabbi and no synagogue.

Boris tried to explain. Religious freedom was here, yes, it was bedrock; but religious expression was frowned on, he said. Because this wasn't a shtetl, it was an advanced model society. "Here we must distinguish between fact and fiction. As follows: fact. We are Jews. Not Russians—Jews. But what else is our difference? What else separates us, divides us from them? Only our fictions—our religious tales, our rituals, our superstitions, yes, even our language. What we need to live, what we require, are facts. Bread is a fact. Roads, shelter, work—facts. To know who we are, Jews—this fact—and to recognize our place in the struggle we share with the rest of mankind—that one. The rest doesn't matter. Facts are the only true necessities."

To Musya his words had the sound of something he must have read in a pamphlet, one espousing some extremist view; she recognized the tone from her late sister's radical schooldays. Musya never took extremism seriously. It always seemed to pass. She'd never bothered, for instance, to get her hair cut into an asymmetrical bob—and look how her poor friends who had done always envied her the rich long tresses she'd kept inviolate. Still:

"You've changed, Boris," she observed. "You wanted everything Jewish, before."

"Being a pioneer changes one, Musya. It does. My dear," he added, clearing his throat. Again his weak eyes brushed her foil-trimmed neckline. In lieu of a bridal feast they were enjoying the wild extravagance of a restaurant meal at a table for four; the boys were along. Anton at this time would eat only canned green peas mashed with a fork and lightly salted. The restaurant seemed mainly popular with Jewish families and was the most cheerful place Musya had seen in Birobidzhan. A machine in the corner played a few Leonid Utesov songs, which made her feel homesick. Even for peas the prices were steep. There was wine on the menu but without his uncle on hand to foot the bill as at his previous wedding, Boris stayed quite sober on a single glass.

That night back at the flat he sent her an expectant look. She returned him a look practically blazing with shock and moral outrage and he didn't ask again, by any means, for months.

While the young city would always strike her Odessa-shaped tastes as primitive and bare, it didn't lack every amenity. The streets were a little more paved and some structures slightly less impermanent than Musya had first imagined. Not far from the pleasant restaurant was a modest-sized cinema with a big program board out front she checked constantly for new arrivals. She'd already seen every picture that played there, months if not years before, but even the proximity of celluloid and screen soothed her awful homesickness. A few times she went to the evening show with Kitty, the dvornik's young daughter, braving the rough crowd, the hard seats, the unheated hall, the noisy projector, the popping soundtrack on the invariably bad print—things she'd find too distracting to bear right up until the moment that came without fail, when she'd sink and lose herself inside the story's silvery, music-laden flow. She'd vanish with relief. Sadly, Boris wouldn't give her money to do this very often, calling it extravagance and backsliding on her part; and in his loyalty to dead Liza's wishes he wouldn't consider permitting her to take the boys to the cinema, not even for a matinee; which was depressing. With great ineptitude and fuss he finally ran a wire from outside in the hallway to a battered tabletop tarelka, in working order, surprisingly. Soviet radio was entertainment enough for anyone with brains, Boris asserted, further recommending Musya listen to the Broadcast for Housewives sometimes.

She didn't.

Their poverty frustrated her. Their life, it's true, wasn't exactly one of hardship. Their meals from the rooming house kitchen were clean, meaty, bland, plentiful. Drinking water had to be boiled but this was customary. The closet commode in their flat spared them many of the outhouse trips that were a common feature of life elsewhere, even in Odessa. Still, to Musya, the situation felt squalid, mean. Why were they so poor? Did Boris merely trade and scavenge? Or did he actually buy the worn-out books, papers, parlor furnishings and all the other junk that lay in heaps around the flat, around their ears, almost reaching the ceiling in places? He rarely came home empty-handed and yet claimed to spend nothing; sometimes he even claimed to have spent "less than nothing" on some unusually damaged or meaningless object. He idolized his own discernment and planned to realize extraordinary profits from his hoard. Upon the appeal of the Far East's exoticism to Western-bred tastes he especially counted, with four crates of painted dishware from nearby Manchukuo to prove it. His scientific fancies had filled large amount of what room space remained with soil collections and chemistry set apparatus.

There was also a pungent sack inside which Musya and the boys found a rolled-up Siberian tiger skin, its brilliance damaged only in spots by insects and time. Boris said it was quite valuable even with a missing head. How was it, Musya wondered, that a man could be in possession of such a valuable tiger skin yet find himself unable to provide his domestic companion with a regular sum for personal and home expenses? How? Why was this happening?

Boris replied with the suggestion that she register for work papers if she wanted pocket money. To which Musya objected with heat and tears. She hadn't come to Birobidzhan to work, she hadn't come there to be his unwilling bride—she'd come as a visitor, and a visitor she would most adamantly remain.

"That is your choice, then." With these words, Boris walked out as if he'd won the argument. Sometimes she really hated him. Her temper flared:

"You're afraid to give me money because if I have it, I'll leave!"

The older nephew shot up from his seat, roused to alarm: "Don't leave! Musya—Mumeh—no!"

She whispered, "Of course I won't—don't worry."

"No," Boris spoke from the next room. "I'm afraid you'll spend it all on candy and cinema tickets and worthless magazines."

But he was moved to approach her not long afterwards with some columns from the local news: apparently, the State Yiddish Theater was mounting a musical show about the lives of Jewish farmers in Birobidzhan. "I don't want to see that," said Musya in a bad mood, sore with cramps. Boris didn't really want to see it either, he said, adding:

"Your sister loved the theater."

She was surprised, even shaken. "Liza loved theater?"

"Here she did, yes. When it was, before. When—it was different. The people were, that is." He trailed off. She tried but couldn't get him to continue; what had happened, he wouldn't explain. Indeed he looked at her in a way that made her uneasy. She inched back before he spoke.

"What do you do?" he asked, surprising her. "With Liza? When you—at her grave— you go every day. In this cold, this weather, what do you do there?"

"I—think. I go there to think." She found herself trembling. They'd never discussed this before, not once.

"Do you—talk? You talk to her?"

"I suppose. Not always."

He looked down at the floor and cleared his throat; she'd known he would. "And she—Liza talks to you?"

"She doesn't Boris, no." She felt his disappointment reach her like a shockwave. "I don't hear her. I can't hear her. I'm sorry," she added.

"It's—no. Don't be." He looked up with a flash of eyeglass lens, she saw his long lips twist into a faint smile. "Please tell her hello, Musya. *From Kotz*, say."

"Yes, of course." She watched him go off to bed. In the night Anton climbed onto Musya's chaise lounge and curled up beside her as usual; Sender joined them near dawn as a rule. Four months from the funeral they still wept at night but sleep would overtake them sooner.

Not long after this she went back to the town hall and filed some papers. She got a propiska for Birobidzhan stamped in her internal passport; now she could have worked but still she avoided it.

One day Musya received a visit from the dvornik, who knocked and entered immediately in a state more hunched, secretive and whispery even than usual, her voice seemed to be issuing from a hole in a steam vent. Musya came closer but still had to ask, "What, Magga? What are you saying?"

Magga looked her in the eye. "Married life. He touches you?"

"Of course not!" She blushed, offended. "Why would I let him?"

The old woman nodded some kind of approval and looked her up and down now. "You. Virgin?"

"No!" Musya's voice emerged with cracks. She took a breath and added, calmer, "No. I have a man, a very—a fine man, in Odessa. I only left him—this was only to be a short visit, he doesn't know I'm—where I am. This is all a mistake." Saltwater began to sting her eyes, she had to squeeze them shut.

A grunt came. "Everything is a mistake," Musya heard. "Just know, I run a clean house here. No whoring." Her eyes snapped open as she made to object but a quick gesture stopped her. "I told him first. He knows I mean it."

"I am not like that," Musya said. The survey of her person this reply invited, ended in a more lenient verdict.

"You are soft. Nice. Not like your sister. She was hard woman, like stone woman. Made for trouble. A great kind of woman." The dvornik sighed, not all that sadly, a philosophical sigh, and sucked a tooth. "It's too bad for you here. Listen, you need anything, ask me, ask Kitty. Never try this alone, this married life."

Indeed the circumstances of her arrival in Birobidzhan might have been bound to precipitate an unusual and permanent closeness between Musya and the dvornik and her daughter. Magga ran the rooming house for the drunkard who'd built and run the place first. She kept him alive in an upper-floor room on some clear sharp samogon spirit she distilled herself; he raved without it. Kitty's father was a black-haired railroad man from Belarus, a hard worker and a fast worker: he was gone. Magga's people had always been there in the Far East, taking gigantic pike from its icy lakes and rivers, tending traps deep in its boundless forests, trading dried meat and furs for ammunition: a good life. By the bursting growth of the city around them the dvornik remained resolutely unimpressed; the place had been better ten years ago as a village, she thought. Her daughter was another story. Kitty longed to throw herself onto the bosom of some great metropolis and be surrounded day and night by chromium, motor-cars, electric chandeliers, cigarette smokers, patterned hosiery, hushed salon floors dotted with chic workers manufacturing permanent waves; she almost pestered Musya for descriptions of Odessa life and imbibed every detail. For Kitty, Birobidzhan couldn't become a real big city fast enough. She was fifteen. Mother and daughter lived in a room off the kitchen where they kept an altar in a cupboard, fascinating to Sender Kotz for the way the goyish icons hung there among the Holy Buddha picture postcards glowed. Another faith, very old and native to Siberia, Magga and Kitty kept in reserve for emergencies—Musya remembered their chant over Liza's deathbed. Against Russian Jews they held no prejudices at all, none; but that Polish Jews had actual tails they were convinced beyond anything. They'd seen photographs.

Spending time with the ones who'd tended Liza in her final illness and who'd known her for years before that, supplied many missing details to Musya's picture of her sister's life in Birobidzhan. Kitty would chatter, still a bit under a spell, maybe. To hear her tell it, everyone knew Liza Kotz—or knew of her—and she'd known them, too, most of the people and every last leader. Right up until it was abolished she'd practically led Birobidzhan's Citizens' Advisory Brigade for Public Administration. The woman had been a dynamo, helping power every sort of enterprise in town: the Yiddish newspapers, the schools, the theater, the tree plantings, the minyans that were forming, the public hygiene committee ("Ah, not again!" cried Muysa). To newcomers who'd needed it she'd offered Yiddish lessons, free.

"But her Yiddish was not so great," Musya said.

"Yes it was," said Kitty, who didn't speak it.

Musya shrugged. "And what about Boris, where was he in all of this?"

She couldn't get an answer. Kitty's plain pink face, like a purse with a catch, snapped closed. "I have work to do," she said, and left the flat.

As for getting information out of Boris, he had a trick of crumpling up his personality into one of those pompoms the magicians came to buy for vanishing balls from her father's friend in the Privoz market. There'd be nothing left for her to question, only a pellet of man-fluff with a pair of pale eyes wide with vacancy suggesting fright. It was clear that he regretted his reminiscence about the State Yiddish Theater, he was always on his guard now.

"She was a wonderful mother, a wonderful wife. I worshipped her, we all did."

"But what about you, Boris?" she pressed. "Didn't you ever help with her committees? You must have had some of the same friends—what about the people at her funeral?" There'd been half a dozen there, men and women both, who'd offered condolences but hadn't introduced themselves; she hadn't seen any of them since. "Where are your friends?"

"Most people work, you know." Boris rattled glassware. She'd begged him to tidy up around the sink. "Of course she had friends, but I was always very busy with my work and she was sick, you know, for a very long time." His chin was trembling and his entire manner suggested that her carelessness had cracked him and made all his grief flood back at once. "Your sister and I were friends to each other first. Always," he said.

And so she resigned herself to living with ciphers.

The boys had never spent much time outdoors nor even outside the home. There was a day nursery not far away they'd both attended briefly. As for infant school, since the authorities had shut down all the cheders during the previous year, the eldest hadn't gone. Liza his mother hadn't wished him to attend the Russian school, Boris explained, so she'd taught him herself. On the shelves were Yiddish schoolbooks she'd used, along with many children's storybooks, about half in Russian. Liza's own collection was less mixed, more Yiddish. She and Musya had always had different tastes in authors. Musya didn't care for Dovid Bergelson, for instance. The glamorous booster of Birobidzhan took up half a shelf here, every volume crawling with her sister's spiky marginalia—True! Beautiful!—impossible to ignore.

But why had the authorities closed the Yiddish schools? Boris had no idea; those were their orders, he said, which was all anyone could know. As usual when she asked him anything about the Current Local Situation, as he called it, he avoided meeting Musya's eyes and changed the subject fast. In the office where he worked nothing but Russian was spoken, a practice he made a point of carrying into the home through stilted conversations with his sons that he meant to double as valuable instruction; everything they said in Yiddish he insisted they translate and repeat in Russian "for their own good." Often he gave Musya the same treatment, which she resented for the simple reason that she spoke excellent Russian. He disagreed. Meanwhile his sons complained that he'd used to speak Yiddish all the time, before. They missed their father in Yiddish and their dead mother completely. At night in bed they wept. But their health was good and their spirits seemed to be improving daily with the exercise and fresher air. Two sturdy redheads, as children went, Musya supposed, they were the better sort of company: sweet-natured and kind, intelligent enough yet neither too talkative nor intrusively curious. Their father had ordered them to call her Mama but she'd asked them not to and they never did; for this she liked them most of all.

"Should we read Jungle Book tonight, or Treasure Island?" she asked Sender Kotz.

He said, "Mama always picked the story. She always told us what to do. She told Papa everything to do."

This Musya could have guessed. Just beyond the newspaper office she stopped and waited for an empty lumber truck to churn past with a tremendous din of chains through the slurry of mud, snow, ice, trash, wood chips and cinders that carpeted the road. A quick check over her shoulder confirmed that Anton was in ecstasy: he loved a loud noise. Wrapped in the tiger skin, he was playing Emperor over them today and had both Musya and Sender pulling the sled, an obedient pair in tandem. White steam poured from his throat as he roared commands at them. "Go! Iditeh!"

Their way led across the railroad tracks. Some days they timed their walk to bring them to a halt at the crossing while a train passed, arriving or departing, groaning, slow, the long line of windows filled with bustle punctuated by figures and faces still or slumbering, unconcerned, unconnected to this place. But not today: the gates were open and they crossed. On the other side a short incline made a snow hill and Sender (it was his turn, she'd gone yesterday) climbed onto the sled behind Anton, wrapped his arms around the tiger skin, waited for her push and rode, squealing almost as happily as his little brother. As she picked her own way down the slope on a snowy footpath worn to slickness yet again, Musya vowed again to complain to the authorities who never put down enough cinders. But she wouldn't complain, she knew she wouldn't. At the foot of the hill she resumed her place at the sled rope—pulled—marched.

This side of the tracks made for easier towing, with fewer street corners and streets to cross. Buildings rose up here and there, factories, warehouses, long grim dormitories for workers. Truck roads snaked among storage lots and supply yards. Beyond the busiest district, empty expanses of snow blanketing what might have been fields or waste ground lay interspersed with clumps of willow and vine-woven copses where blackbirds fluttered. Today the low sky was a uniform heavy cream hue except where a small primrose sun appeared to be dissolving. They had another hour of daylight left to spend.

"Mama wanted some people to take her away." To Musya's surprise, her nephew had resumed their conversation and was revealing something of interest. But asked where, he said, "I don't know. With the others."

"What others?" Sender didn't know. "You mean when she was sick, to go away to a place to get well?" Maybe he meant a sanatorium.

But that wasn't it. "No. Before." They pulled as he searched the past and she wondered what his memory looked like. A toy memory, miniaturized, simplified but solid and whole? Or was it mostly formless and dim, with a door at one end still open to the dark land before birth? "She said because it was right. She said she didn't want to go but she wanted the people to take her away where they took the others."

Musya frowned. For all its obscurities, the tale's most puzzling aspect was that Liza should have wanted something she hadn't managed to get. "That must have been confusing," she said.

"Yes." They plodded on a few more paces, slowed by thought. He said, "You don't tell us what to do."

"I—but you know what to do."

"Pull! Fast! Bystra!" cried Anton. They put on speed.

She was well aware of being no kind of mother. Aside from a few uninspiring school visits to the local crèche, her experience with small children had been limited to those she'd met in the homes of her friends—and the complaints she'd heard about them. They also died quite easily, she knew this. Finding two in her care had put her in a state of terror from which she never expected to emerge until either she or they were tucked in their graves. Boris, although he must have taken charge of his sons during Liza's final illness, wasn't any help, he left everything to Musya from her first night among them. In the end, obeying the dictates of some ancient half-forgotten hour of hygiene instruction, she concentrated on keeping the boys very clean. Their skin, hair, teeth, fingernails, clothes and bedding she scrubbed with equal dispassionate thoroughness and extreme frequency. Otherwise, she fed them according to their appetites, read to them from whatever they brought her to read, warmed them with her body in sleep when they slipped beneath her covers, kept them near her by day. They really did seem to know far better than she did what they required.

Soon came the cemetery, confined by a low wooden rail fence to a treeless square of ground within an untilled field beside the road—or really the parallel ruts that passed for a road—across which the field continued on a rise. Trucks passed by now and then but it was a desolate, neglected spot. The road went on to disappear inside a wall of pine trees that extended right to left as far as she could see. Here where the city's traces were faintest, wide-winged hunting birds circled the heights of the pale sky on endless patrol, and animal tracks perforated the snows all around like sunken chains. On different occasions they'd spotted live hare, a fox, and something beautiful, two sables at play that leapt and chased one another in wild figure-eights through sparkling ice sprays in a rare hour of sunshine.

Around the cemetery only the topmost fence rail could be seen above the accumulated months of snowfall. Two posts and a simple wooden crossbeam marked the gateless entrance, where the drifts had piled so high that Musya's head brushed the lintel when she passed underneath. No sign or symbol had been hung to indicate the nature of the place which of course was relatively obvious, given the clumps of tall grave markers, tipped and tilted by ground frosts, overlapping like crooked teeth, that protruded from the snowy ground within. Far less frequented in every season than the bigger cemetery on the other side of town, this was the one—the Jewish one—Liza had specified among her final wishes; her wishes that were orders. Musya had worn a path by now to the smooth white painted board, the newest there, inscribed in Yiddish like all the others there. Interspersed among the wood were a few slabs and even obelisks of stone, mostly a green stone quarried and carved in another part of the Jewish Autonomous Region, Boris had told her. Once or twice he'd murmured an intention to replace Liza's wooden marker with an excellent stone "when it had been a year" but Musya was doubtful. There were so many more of wood than stone that only by changing he risked being conspicuous, which he dreaded. And Liza had left no orders as to marble or malachite, either she'd overlooked this detail or she hadn't cared. She'd only asked for an inscription, the simplest possible:

WIFE AND MOTHER.

After enough hours spent with Musya beside their mother's grave, the boys had drifted from her side into other rows, other precincts. Gradually they'd explored every corner—the place was compact, all its boundaries visible from every point within. Lately they were more inclined to stay outside and sled down the hill across the road, follow paw tracks, throw snowballs and shout. Musya wouldn't have scolded them for playing among the graves, there were never any other visitors, they were all alone here; but they seemed to have outgrown the cemetery. While inside its fence they were motherless children, mourning, subdued, outside it they were big boys, free and energized by nature.

And she? In the living world a wife of sorts and a mother of no kind, among the dead Musya reclaimed herself. The comfort she derived from doing so might have been what kept her coming back each day. Once more she was a guest and stranger here, a younger sister visiting, divided from her lover in Odessa and her life in a happier, warmer, altogether more advanced society. As she watched, the stark black Yiddish letters of her sister's name would seem to detach themselves, shimmer, almost to dance in mid-air while the bare white plank below them turned into a kind of looking glass. When she stared long enough, Musya could see herself, her youth in bloom, her traveling frock wrinkled: she was just off the train. It was that day again—it was always that day—and she was in Liza's bedroom—she'd never left that spot, she'd never moved an inch. Her loss had been so great, her poor innocence so completely wronged and violated, time for her had stopped and frozen. Events might appear to intervene, she might get a fever, mend a pile of ragged clothes, read her nephews the story of Mowgli, marry her brother-in-law, gossip with the dvornik's daughter about Lyubov Orlova—but none of this was real, nothing was happening. At Liza's grave alone, Musya's clock hands read the proper hour while chimes perpetual tolled her sentence:

Exile. Eternal exile.

Some days the arctic winds had howled down and laid about her with heavy whips. Ice had clung to her eyelashes like metal filings. She'd been blasted, buried up to her knees as she'd stood there in blizzards. Yet she'd suffered not at all, she'd barely felt the cold and might have lingered by the grave through the worst—beyond the worst—forever—had it not been for the boys, her concern for them had always nagged her away from her secret looking glass into retreat, an awful trudge back to town. Even today as they played happily among the mild drifts she was conscious of keeping them within earshot. Sender and Anton: she hadn't even known both their names, she'd never thought about them much at all, they'd been nothing but abstractions. Now they shared her bed. She'd lost her own life.

The dead ruled the living, she'd realized. Confronted daily with the moment of her own ruin, in her reveries at the grave she'd occasionally seen beyond the grave and through the looking glass; her gaze penetrating snow and earth, she'd reached the solid sheet of ice, transparent in places, beneath which the dead passed their eternity in luxurious splendor. The dead sat erect in high thrones. They wore gemstones in their crowns and embroidered robes with long ermine-trimmed trains. Their palace walls were inlaid with enameled mosaics and amber. From Musya's side of the ice their world was silent, their ceremonies mute. She'd watched them process between dual ranks of spear-bearers ten thousand strong and feast on skewered larks at banquet tables groaning beneath vessels of silver and gold; she'd seen the dead drape themselves in chain mail, wheel gigantic armored horses into battle array and charge, raising pennants and lowering lances. And there, in a tent above the carnage, she could always find Liza, dressed in a tunic woven from steel, dark hair tumbling loose beneath a bronze helmet fringed with chains and tipped with a spike; her gray kohl-darkened eyes would be gleaming, her mouth painted to be sharp red and cruel would be twisted in a savage smile. With a hand sporting dozens of rings, her wedding band not among them, she'd be raising a goblet, its crystal bowl filled to the brim. And as the bearded hero she saluted—her lover—bare-chested, wrapped in robes of wolves' fur, raised high a goblet in turn, his huge domed brow would flash in the torchlight: naturally, it was Ulyanov himself, V.I. Lenin, his keen feline eyes blacked with emphatic stripes in the Egyptian style. Musya would see Liza's long teeth bared to the gums in silent hilarity, laughing for triumph, before she drank the red wine.

At last, her sister was happy.

So it was true, what she'd told Boris that night after the theater: she and Liza, Empress of Death, didn't speak. Even had the thickness of the ice pane not prevented it, a social gulf divided them. Inequality, for sure, was far from banished in the next and better world but rather enshrined there. Musya stood, yes, she stood and neither knelt nor bowed; but she was her sister's subject. How to get free, how to liberate herself in the complete absence of means, money, aid—she'd lost all hope of Leon Flohr's appearing— how to throw off the bonds of her exile and resume the normal life her journey to Birobidzhan had interrupted? These were questions that impossibility made petty. Freedom wishes were like dance tunes for gramophone in a land without gramophones, dances, or shoes; eccentric relics, even annoying, clutter of a kind. Best to stand and face the facts instead: Boris was right about that at least. Facts were all a person really needed. Fact: her tyrant sister had trapped and crushed her.

Its top cleared of snow, a wooden column shorter than the rest made a seat when she wanted one. She sank back onto it today and closed her eyes. Punctuated by the sled runners' swish, her nephews' play cries echoed, they sounded almost like a crowd. A long whispering rumble of train wheels reached her somewhat pleasantly. It occurred to her that Magga had promised roasted chicken with potatoes for supper. Musya felt hungry, which was unexpected. When had she ever thought of food at Liza's grave? She was trying to remember when a sound made her turn—someone was at the entrance, a woman. She had to duck her kerchiefed head to pass beneath the lintel, which she gripped with one hand at the same time as if she were climbing down into a cave. Down the drift she came, into the cemetery, expensively dressed for Birobidzhan; and Musya recognized her as one of the women who'd been at Liza's funeral.

She introduced herself in a deep and melodious voice, with an accent Musya couldn't identify. "Call me Fanny, please. I was your sister's good friend. Best."

"Oh!" Musya realized. "You must have given her the silk scarves."

"Of course," Fanny nodded.

They'd have made a striking pair, high on contrast, Musya reflected. Older and quite a bit taller, plump and round-limbed, golden brown where her friend had been pale, with a plush pomegranate-colored mouth, thick black unruly curls (possibly tinted) and heavy brows shading purple-brown eyes, the stranger radiated good health and—at the moment—curiosity. With a look around, she exclaimed over the depth of the snow. A certain obelisk that had topped their heads at the funeral reached only to her waist today.

The two of them stood in silence and looked at the grave together. Musya this time saw nothing but black painted words on a board. Her sister's friend sighed and struggled with emotion. "The best woman in Jewish Autonomous Region—dead," she pronounced at last. "Ah well."

Musya asked, "But was she? The best—was she really?"

"Without question." A last heavy glance, then Fanny turned to face her. "So. It all happened as she planned. You, now, the wife." Musya nodded weakly. The older woman continued: "And the husband—he doesn't try to bother you, I hope not, in the home. You understand me?"

Musya did, very well. "Oh, no, he doesn't but—you say she, my sister, she planned—this?"

"Of course she planned—for her babies to have a real mama, she planned. Because she knew, everything, it was coming—you know she knew."

Now it was Musya's turn to sigh. "I suppose so."

"You suppose right," Fanny told her. The younger sister had nothing to add. The information was by no means surprising. She followed Fanny from the cemetery; they helped one another up and down the steep drift. Fanny apologized for having to creep. "My womb is a little fallen," she said.

They exited into cacophony. Brilliant in tiger stripes at the summit, Anton stood howling his loudest for another ride down the sled hill which was thronged. "Where did all these children come from?" Musya marveled, crossing the road towards the scene.

"Mine, yours, others. With no Jewish school they sit home," Fanny said. "Fresher air is better."

And here was the plan which was in about two minutes decided, that Musya would lead a more or less large group of children out here to the fields every day. Since she was going anyhow, why not? While their mothers were working or resting or busy or unwell in the home—all who'd been fit to vote had agreed, it would be a tremendous help to them. So wouldn't she? A brief objection that she wasn't qualified, that she possessed zero knowledge of children and shouldn't be entrusted with their care, that her sister had miscalculated, badly, in her late last disposal, went nowhere. Around her sister's friend a force Musya recognized—here was what they'd had in common, she could see it now—hung like an atmosphere, one that extinguished contradiction. Indeed:

"So, that's settled," Fanny said. "Good. Now tell me. Happy husband, Kotz. Did he get his position with his, what do you say, his dirt?"

"Soil," Musya realized in time. "Soil specialist. No, he's still at the chair factory. At least—he hasn't told me." She paused to think. Morose, pettish, burping dyspeptically: no, the man she'd breakfasted with a few hours since had not seen his life's ambitions fulfilled. She shook her head, certain. "His application hasn't been accepted," she said.

"They didn't give it to him?"

"Not yet."

"Interesting." Fanny glowered. "Interesting. Hey—you!" She surged forward into a fresh brawl at the foot of the snow hill; within moments two red-faced combatants dangled from either fist. She shook them and commanded niceness, then tossed them both into a soft snowbank and returned to Musya's side, slapping ice from her mittens. Seconds later Anton was there, both fists tugging at Fanny's coat skirts in a clamorous demand to be thrown into the same snowbank which Fanny ignored. Admiring the tiger skin instead, she touched it gently, smiling. "My papa had one like this," she said.

Anton reeled back, amazed. "Your papa tiger?"

Fanny regarded him. "Yes. Of course."

"Ah!" Anton's world, plain to see, burned with delights, always. He waved his arms and hollered: "Throw! Brosit!" Musya picked him up and threw him easily into the snowbank; he weighed a good deal and her own strength surprised her. It was all that sled-pulling, she supposed, as he scrambled back and she tossed him three or four times more. The effort left her exhilarated.

"You see?" The tiger's daughter approved. "Children are simple. Don't worry, be rough, they like you." Fanny's philosophy saw her dispense kisses caresses and smother-ing embraces as liberally as she did smacks, pinches, hair tugs and smart walking spanks. To her children she was a goddess, incapable of fault; they misbehaved terribly at all times, loving her discipline as much as her forgiveness. "Terrors," she called them proudly, and the image of their father, she said. Infatuation moved her handsome features when Fanny spoke of him, her husband, in her voluble way.

They'd met in Baku, city of the heavenly synagogues, at the Bolshevik-built Cultural Palace of Emancipated Turkish Womanhood. A local girl, Fanny had been taking classes there to qualify for work in scientific research. Sergey had been her instructor in organic chemistry, a Russian volunteer, idealistic, Komsomol-trained, on a year's assignment in Azerbaijan. The pair fell hard for each other but faced obstacles. "Romance!" Fanny explained. Her people were Mountain Jews who spoke an old form of Persian and frowned on mixed marriages. But Fanny was everyone's special darling and before her love match they'd relented. Her family had means: one grandfather was a sorcerer who made elixirs from mummy parts, a very lucrative concern. The scale of the wedding feast had been staggering, the photographs didn't do it any justice, Fanny said. As for the union it marked, blissfully happy and abundantly blessed best described it. Soon the young family found itself in the Jewish Autonomous Region, the husband's first important post. There were the makings of chemicals in the ground all over the Far East and Sergey was needed to help find them. He'd done his best. But now he was away, to another part of Siberia. "My heart longs," Fanny said simply.

"I understand," Musya said, picturing pale-suited Leon in the mossy green park where curtains of fountain spray sparkled, sparkled forever: he'd loved her. "When will your husband return?"

The older woman smiled and called the subject complicated; sometime later she'd explain that he was in a labor camp where he'd been sent upon his conviction for sabotage. He hadn't found enough chemicals to meet enough major quotas. "Your sister, she was good friend to my Sergey too," she told Musya now, as her story continued. Arriving in Birobidzhan with her Russian still rather shaky, hopeful that Yiddish might be easier to learn, Fanny had cast around for a tutor. This had brought Liza Kotz to her door. "But I'm better friend than Yiddish student," she admitted. Fanny worked behind the belt and glove counter at the Universal Stores downtown; if Musya had ever been inside the place they might have spoken sooner. Fanny frowned. "Don't let him keep you penniless—do not ever!"

She walked Musya home that first day and invited herself upstairs, "For the good memories," she said. In the familiar rooms she sighed and wept a little. Magga came in and the two women embraced with a fond, conspiratorial air. While Musya readied tea, Magga leafed through the latest heap of correspondence that Boris had left on the worktable although this was Musya's space, as she reminded him almost daily. Nothing was sealed yet, he had more enclosures to add.

"All going west," the dvornik snarled. "So he wants to run."

"Of course he wants to run," Fanny said. Perched on a half-sofa; she'd dumped some of the decrepit stuff piled there onto the floor, an old habit apparently. "He should run." She and Magga exchanged a look of dark accord.

"But why?" Musya asked them. "What did he do?"

Magga crossed to the samovar and hid herself in steam clouds, leaving Fanny to pronounce: "Nothing. And too much. Maybe." Musya couldn't get either one to say another word.

Later that night, she and the boys were telling Boris about their adventure when he went pale and recoiled. "Her?" he said. "Her?" He masked his discomfort fairly quickly. "Ah, yes, I remember who you mean." He nodded and managed half a pleased look, but he was still wringing his hands. He continued, "Only I fear I must warn you, my dear, against forming too many attachments, considering our plans."

"Your plans, Boris," she replied.

He didn't disagree. They'd fought it out before. Because he was the husband and head of household, their days in the Far East might be few.

For with this particular war going on, real opportunity lay much further westward, or would, Boris said, once Germany conquered its continent. Already half of Poland was back where it belonged, in Soviet hands. Why not the rest, Poland entire, a gift between allies? It could happen any day now. At which point, in order to modernize agricultural production across those ancient battlefields, experts trained in the science of soil would be required, urgently, in vast numbers. Boris listened to the radio reports at night, when the tarelka got any reception, with impatient hope. Depending on the success of his latest applications to Moscow he might be collecting a specialist's pay within the year and raising his sons, ideally, in a great seat of learning, Poland's great Jewish city of Lublin, which he'd be helping to modernize—this best of both worlds was the goal always before him these days. He scribbled busily, consulting armloads of maps and rainfall tables from a battered out-of-date almanac.

The new childcare arrangement was an even bigger hit than Fanny had predicted. Within a week their numbers had doubled: a child mob equipped with additional sleds, a few pairs of skis and two sets of snowshoes, a telescope and binoculars, a tin trumpet and dogs, sometimes as many as ten, family pets or strays that tagged along. The dogs helped keep the herd intact while going to and from the fields and Musya never lost a single child. She even made a little pocket money from the manufacture and sale of snowsuits for several of her charges—very little, after materials costs and pay for Kitty plus some for Sender, whose skills with a needle had grown impressively.

The children were all types. Some she liked better than others. Her favorite was Fanny's six year-old daughter Zara, who liked Sender Kotz—a regard he reciprocated, their bond had been immediate. Some days they'd spend all their time at the fields together, tracking a lynx they were certain they'd detected from a single snow-print. But other days Sender preferred the company of a strange boy named Mendel whose sister was a rotten doll thief, according to Zara, whose family and Mendel's lived in the same block of flats. Sender seemed enthralled by the pair, who made much of him. Disgusted and bereft, pretty Zara would come sit among the graves beside Musya and complain in a forceful and diverting manner. Musya didn't mind the distraction. As a child she'd stolen every one of Liza's dolls at least once, she remembered, although she didn't admit this to Zara.

The grove of boards and stones had risen higher as the wet drifts sank beneath their own weight, creaking. Among what passed for the paths between them almost all the other little girls could be found today, while boy's voices rioted outside—their ice games were rough. Sender with Mendel and the rotten sister were also within, conferring in a corner. Zara gave another glare that way.

"And their stupid girl, Sonya's friend." Sonya was the cross-eyed Cossack girl who scrubbed and did chores at Fanny's in exchange for a cubbyhole bed. Sonya was another one Zara didn't like. "She steals too, even worse than Sonya."

Musya let out a puff of breath and watched it dissipate. "You have so many thieves where you live—how terrible."

With a morose kick the little girl agreed. "They should be in prison for it. Like Mendel's papa."

"Mendel's father is also in prison?" She was startled. Sender talked day and night about Mendel and Mendel's magazine collection but he'd never mentioned this. "Why? What did he steal?"

The little girl kicked. "Nothing. He made shows at the theater."

Musya frowned. "What kind of shows?"

"I don't know!" Zara laughed. "I was too little to go there." She slid off their grave-stone, packed some snow between her mittens and threw it, not far. "All the papas where we live are in prison, and lots of the mamas. All the people from Yiddish theater, and the newspapers, and the schools, from this whole town it's almost everyone in prison who used to be important here. Except not your sister because she died." A respectful pause followed; then a caution: "Be careful you don't go to prison!" Musya said she didn't plan to go to any prison, which was the truth.

Her new role introduced her into a little social circle, a nice change. One day when the weather was almost warm, almost not freezing, she went hat shopping with one of Fanny's neighbors. All the hats were awful but it was nice to go shopping. Another refugee from conditions on the Jewish collective farms, her new acquaintance had barely avoided tuberculosis herself, she'd said. Conversation lagged until Musya spotted a cart drawn by black oxen, not a rare sight, coming towards them up the road; the driver and the woman beside him on the front board seat reminded her:

"And there are Korean kolkhozes, yes?" she asked brightly. "I've heard they grow rice there."

Her companion blushed and stammered. "Those aren't—that couple is probably Chinese. We have more Chinese here now. All the Koreans are gone," she finally said. Her face wore a look of alarm. Musya found this easily startled sort of person hard to take.

"That's impossible," she said sharply.

"No. No, it isn't. They took them away."

"Who did? Who took them? When?"

"The government. Last year. They took them away in trucks. And—trains."

"Trucks? Trains? To where?"

"To—I don't know. Back to Korea, I suppose." That was all she'd say.

So that night, after the boys were asleep, Musya asked, "Boris, is it true the government took all the Koreans away from their rice farms last year?"

"What Koreans?" he said. She was getting better at forcing him to communicate and managed to pry from him, eventually: "Musya, you must know that resources aren't infinite. Where there are rice fields in the Soviet Union, they must be for the Soviet people to farm and to harvest. What—do you want a Korean woman sharing your dresses, your shoes?"

"I wouldn't mind," she insisted, as he snatched up a stack of papers and retreated with them towards his bedroom. At the door he turned and said, "By the way, I don't care for your friendship with those women. Their husbands are convicts, you know."

She said, "That doesn't mean anything."

His face twisted. "Of course it does."

"But they only," she tried to argue. "They worked in the theater. They're not criminals."

"They committed political crimes."

"But what did they do?"

"How should I know?" Boris said. He went into the bedroom. This time Musya followed him. He gave her a startled look from where he sat at a writing desk, one of several small desks squeezed into the space between the deathbed and the battery of armoires that lined the walls. Musya stood against the door, blocking his escape. She hadn't been in this room after dark since her first night in Birobidzhan; this had been her policy, unshakable. But now she'd launched an invasion. She wanted facts.

"I want facts, Boris," she said. "I want information. I want honesty."

"But when have I ever refused you these things?" He removed his eyeglasses and rubbed his face with an ink-stained hand. He was stalling, she understood this. "Don't you realize the current local situation is very complex?"

"Why is everyone who ran the Yiddish theater in prison?"

"They're not—are they?"

"Boris Kotz!"

He gave a kind of whimper and raised some fingertips to his forehead. "My dear, I've told you. It's not really prison, not like you understand it. You see, they're in political prison."

"And you don't know why." A sextet of stacked chairs, a barrel missing staves and a desk with the drawers out divided them. Musya tried to burn the man with her gaze; she lacked all Liza's gifts in this regard but a slight sibling resemblance appeared to reach and touch him in a place still tender. He sighed and made fists, then bent his head, balding and downy. She took a half-step into the room. "Boris. What happened here?"

He stood up and sat down again; he couldn't pace, there was nowhere to move. Frustration pinched his voice so hard the words released came high and querulous. "How could you not have known?" he began. "How could you have been so unaware—is it from all your cinema? Do you live entirely in a dream world as Liza said you did—is this the truth?" She waited, controlling her temper, glaring, before she spoke:

"If you allowed me the cinema more often I might have seen whatever you're talking about in the newsreels."

"Oh—this wouldn't have been in any newsreel!" He picked up a pen from the writing desk and tapped with it upon the cracked veneer as if he were telegraphing for help, reinforcements, relief. Nothing happened. He lay down the pen. "I have wished to spare you certain facts," he tried.

"Don't. I don't want you to."

"Very well. Then. You must know." His gaze swept the room and settled on a group of table lamps, all missing shades and sprouting wires. "You must understand, as I've tried to explain to you before, that the Jewish Autonomous Region represents a great social experiment—a laboratory if you will—not only for the Jewish people of the Soviet Union—not only this at all—but more especially for socialism. You understand?"

"Keep talking."

He sighed. "Think—think of a pendulum, Musya, on a great clock, an enormous pendulum moving back, forth, back and forth." His left hand was tracing an arc, almost languidly. Musya sniffed. His ghost telegraphy having failed, was Boris trying to hypnotize her now? She shook her head but looked away. He kept on: "What does the pendulum do, Musya? It powers the clock, it makes the clock run. And what is the clock?"

She didn't want to but she guessed. "Socialism?"

"Exactly!" She hated feeling gratified but still she did, even when he continued: "Very good. Now. So. We have our pendulum—"

"But what about the State Yiddish Theater?" she cried. "What happened? What happened to the schools, the newspapers, the leaders here?"

He said, "This is what I'm trying to explain to you, that it was a question of extremes in balance. Action and reaction. Thesis and antithesis. You take Birobidzhan, here is your example. You start with—what? Wilderness, Cossacks, Koreans, some people who worship, I don't know, a few bones tied together. And what do you want? A Jewish homeland in the Soviet Union, built by Jewish hands, planted and developed by the labor of free, healthy, forward-thinking Jewish socialists. My dream, your dear sister's dream, this was what we wanted. And others who shared this dream, so many others, they came here, even from America they came, whole families. We all had this dream, you see." His look seemed to appeal to her for understanding and Musya nodded gravely although no conclusion had ever been more obvious to her. Yes—dreamers! And they criticized her life!

"So yes, a dream," she said.

"And to make of that dream a reality, this was our goal." He paused again for her to speak but she wouldn't give him the satisfaction. She waited. Reluctantly, he continued. "So. We began—many of the Jews here, that is—began with being very strong in Yiddish. In everything, street signs and shops, newspapers, schools, the theater, yes, all was for Jews in the language of Jews—a Yiddish life. Which—went on." He glanced at the window, its sealed panes dusty and night-blackened. "Went on until it became—it became clear that extremes had been reached. Really, no one, my dear, no one respect-ed your sister more than I did but there were extremes here. Even some people were wanting to open a synagogue, hold prayers, revive who knows how many superstitions. I'm saying there was excess." He swiped an unsteady hand across anemic-looking lips and came to rest in a hunched posture at which she frowned.

"You're saying that the capital of the Jewish Autonomous Region became too Jewish?"

"I'm saying—yes. Yes. In a way." He made the pendulum again. "From not Jewish at all, it became, yes, too Jewish. From one, you see, to the other—thesis to antithesis—always moving towards the unity of opposites, the joining of opposing forces in the progressive balance and synthesis that is socialism. For the true goal we all share is progress, always progress towards true socialism, always to keep the clock hands moving."

She shook her head impatiently. "But time happens without clocks, Boris! It passes anyhow. Clocks are only for people so they can catch trains and go to their work on time and—" All that occurred to her otherwise were cinema schedules which she felt loath to mention. "Would it hurt socialism to have a synagogue in Birobidzhan?"

"Of course," he said. "That is, it might. Religion is reactionary."

"And who decides this?"

He shrugged. "Cadres in the oblast. The regional soviet. And the central government, of course. The planners in Moscow. The leaders, possibly, if they concern themselves with such things."

"And so in Moscow the planners decide to send the leaders here to prison?"

"Political prison. My dear, you know, this is my point. In political prison they do work, they cut trees and build—they're kept active. This isn't punishment alone, it's simply that a judgment has been made that what they did previously wasn't productive for the Soviet Union. Productive enough, that is."

"Oh, Boris—imagine if you had to cut trees—how productive would that be for anyone?"

He was hurt. "I'm fully capable of cutting down a tree, Musya. If I had to."

"Yes?" She looked around. "Boris, I think you would only bring more wood to the forest, more and more. No one could cut it down fast enough." He didn't answer. She met his sullen look and asked him directly: "Why didn't Liza go to prison, then? If she was such a leader here—and what about you?"

He'd turned pale, almost gray. "Her health," he nearly shouted. "Was—she was spared by reason of her health. And I—my studies, my correspondence required all my time, I've had no leisure to involve myself in those circles. There was never any question—never. Not to this day. Never. Now, if you'll please." He waved a handful of papers at her to signal their urgency. She left him alone but returned moments later with news, the boys had been listening to the tarelka and told her.

"We won the war, Boris," she said.

With a sharp cry he rushed into the front room to lean close by the platter, open-mouthed. His face looked soft and very young again—for a minute, before he relapsed into irritated gloom.

"Ridiculous. This is only the frontier war with Finland."

"But we won, Papa." Sender spoke in careful Russian. "It is good, yes?"

"It could be better."

"Boris!" she objected. A chocolate bar brought out of hiding from her special stores acted as a mild antidote but he'd spoiled any victorious mood past saving.

The next day she led the final charge through snow flurries as Finland—invaded, laid waste, demoralized by desertion, nearly obliterated by snowballs—rose in desperate counterattack and this time conquered; perhaps, as Zara said, unfairly. Musya was bigger than the biggest child on either side. But not by much. Towed by her prisoners, trailed by cheers and a dozen dogs barking, she wore the tiger skin and entered Leningrad (the cemetery, for the day) in triumph. "Peace!" she declared, and a thousand years of justice under Finnish rule to follow. It was a stirring moment.

Then her subjects dispersed and Musya found herself alone before her sister's grave once more. Some clumped snowflakes struck the black letters and slid earthward:

פרוי און מוטער

Wife, mother—and leader. Tutor. Friend. Influence—a dangerous influence, all too clearly, this sister of hers with the blood-filled mouth and the faith in dubious, even doomed, endeavors. As if there could have been in this place such a place as she'd wanted—civilized, meaning well-run, cultured, hygienic, Yiddish-speaking but trumpeting modern propriety. Not like Odessa! Musya smiled. For Liza, Odessa had never been civilized enough. She must have thought she'd found more promising material to work her will on here on this savage blank frontier. Maybe she'd been right— her plans had prospered, for a while—but she hadn't been alone here. The territory was contested, her opponents were stronger. If she hadn't died in bed she might have died a prisoner, laboring in a camp, collapsed in the mud at the foot of a tree trunk sawn not halfway through.

On the other hand, if she hadn't gotten sick she might have fought, survived heroic struggles and prevailed; and Birobidzhan would have been a better place because of it, no question. Liza Kotz had been the kind of woman city streets get named for, the kind who models her profile for postage stamps and patriotic banners. Whereas she, Musya (Kotz, as she remembered with the customary start and then a sigh) sturdy little Musya Kotz could play at being Queen of Finland and all the Russias but in life she was no hero. In death she'd never be a martyr—at least she hoped not. The film stardom on which she'd set her youthful heart: would any studio head ever discover her sitting here, somewhat north of Manchuria, draped in shawls, belted into a secondhand coat, perched on a crooked gravestone? That wasn't going to happen. As for lovers, who was there to love or love her in return? Her love life was past, brief and inconclusive, done. She'd dry up like a pea. Then she'd be fit for the small future left inscribed for her across a few inches of bare board, to which she raised gloved fingertips:

Mother. Wife.

She traced the wet black letters and noticed with surprise that the wetness was from rain. At that moment she heard a booming sound like a thunderclap, close enough she seemed to feel it underfoot. She gasped.

The war!

"Girls!" A few were in the corner. She clapped her hands. "Girls!" Hurrying them before her from the cemetery Musya didn't even need to duck her head, with the drifts beneath the lintel so far receded. Play was going on at top volume on the icy rain-slicked sled runs; Anton's sudden crying fit turned out to be for the tiger skin which she restored hastily to his shoulders. "Listen, everyone!" The rumbling continued. Now that they noticed it, the children were variously curious and bothered. They thought it had to be giants, monsters, not bombs. A few started crying. With relief as well as dread—its arrival seemed like a sign of emergency—Musya spotted a rare truck coming down the road from the direction of the pine woods, sides rattling, gears whining. She managed to wave it to a halt but failed to make herself understood above the noise of the engine the driver left idling. Were they under attack? What was that noise? She gestured with her arms at the ground and the landscape, then pointed to her ears, reduced to cries of "Boom! Boom!" It was hopeless: the children were all shouting, the engine screamed, nothing thunder-like was audible anymore. There were three men crowded into the driving cab and several more in the wooden truck bed, all looking mystified and amused by the scene but not enough to linger. With an apologetic shrug the driver jerked the truck into motion again. The moment it was gone the rumbling returned. A giant's kettledrum, she thought it really might be.

At last it was Mendel of the magazine collection who resolved the crisis, pausing in his show of hysterical panic long enough to suggest that the noise was coming from the direction of the river. Musya looked around.

"There's a river?"

They found it not too far away, beyond the pine forest which was deceptively dark, not deep. The road emerged upon a bluff that overlooked an immense river bordered by low brown banks, its surface covered by a winter's ice, white with swirls of gray. Roaring agitation shook the air but nothing solid moved—not yet, not here. Not a battle on the ice but the ice itself, Musya realized, was raging towards extinction. Carried down the river's length from parts unseen, the cataclysms of its crack-up were being broadcast at Birobidzhan as if from an enormous tarelka. She told the children not to worry: this was only springtime, she explained.

Boris disagreed. Spring was not yet, he insisted over dinner that same night: it was winter still. She might have argued with him but didn't want to risk discouraging his latest, very sudden project. He'd started clearing out the clutter from his room. With hammer and chisel he'd knocked some desks and chairs apart and he'd been tossing them in pieces out the window for the firewood scavengers. Two of the armoires were next, he claimed. He'd also presented her with a bouquet of tulips on Women's Day. "Of course, scientifically, I'm sure you're absolutely right, Boris. It only felt like spring-time," Musya said.

To her new surprise he blushed, cleared his throat, wiped his mouth on a table napkin, stood up from the table with an awkward bow and left the room. They heard some hammering. Then he returned and bowed to her again. "Please accept my apologies. It is true that when—I believe the feeling—to feel that it is spring makes it spring indeed. In fact. I mean to say, you were right."

"Yes," she said. "Thank you."

"And this river you've—discovered. This is the Bira River."

"Thank you, Boris."

Rain persisted. Bypassing the cemetery fields, Musya and the children made the bluff above the Bira into the destination of their daily walks and played among the sheltering pines instead, often startled but barely afraid as the ice howled and the soft ground beneath them shuddered. Then one night, lying awake beside the work table, Musya heard a massive distant detonation that left her heart pounding. The echoes went on and on, uncannily prolonged. The next day they found the river clogged from shore to shore with what appeared to be gigantic milk curds sluggishly escaped from an upstream dairy—broken ice that flowed past with the gurgling sound of next door's conversation, lively and indecipherable. Hundreds of seagulls had arrived at the same time, they wheeled overhead with their bright beaks parted around homesick-making cries; for here and there a black streak in the foam marked a patch of open water that the seagulls, dipping, hovering, nursed and tended.

Back at the flat, more clutter evaporated. The second, broken samovar was gone. A quantity of rolled-up charts from 1925 was sold for scrap paper, Boris had a handful of rubles to show for that transaction. Whole shelves of crockery and glassware he'd turned over to Magga and Kitty for general household use but the export dishes remained in their crates, his plans to sell those held firm. Also preserved were his soil specimens and test tubes and such, which Boris never seemed to go near. In his room, he'd put up some shelves inside the extra armoires and there his books and papers were consolidated, if not exactly ordered. He'd dusted almost everything. He was immensely proud of all the progress he'd made. Even the windowpanes he'd polished. Musya had to agree, the room looked better than she'd ever seen it look. He'd put a fresh quilt on the bed, blue and white, he'd bought it new that day. She stood and studied the pattern, a very dull one. She waited.

"I always thought, my dear." He paused; she caught a glimpse of pink inner flesh as he wiped his mouth with the back of his hand. "I always thought you were prettier than your sister."

Musya gave Boris Kotz a long look that ended in a small sigh.

She didn't believe him this time, either.

(6)

A year later, in June, the family set out for a long-postponed visit to Odessa. Sender and Anton Kotz would finally meet their grandparents and the uncles, aunts, and cousins Boris almost never mentioned; he disliked his siblings. Neither did he like Odessa, really, but it was nearer to Lublin, which remained his aspiration. Beyond openings in soil he'd been pursuing all sorts of administrative posts there and elsewhere in Western Ukraine, formerly Poland. No one had answered his letters for months now. He blamed the muddle-headedness of Soviet bureaucracy; ideally, he hoped to find work under new management. He'd bought some German phrasebooks and a grammar that he planned to study on the two-week train journey. Elsewhere among the baggage were some of the Far Eastern curiosities he'd always planned to sell, including the tiger skin. The crates of Manchukuo dishware he'd left behind with instructions for Magga to send them to Odessa in mid-July, unless he wrote otherwise; for now he'd packed some samples in a hatbox. He was on vacation leave from his place at the wooden chair factory to which he hoped not to return, although he'd secured their flat through September. One-way fares in a four-berth compartment had used up nearly all his other funds but in the worst case, Boris said, he could always borrow enough from his uncle the wine merchant to get them back east in a lower-grade carriage. That the worst was very far from his thoughts was apparent. When the train with great huffing breaths and a series of jolts pulled away from Birobidzhan station Boris cheered as lustily as his sons and waved as frenetically at Fanny's children and the other farewell partygoers who ran alongside to the end of the platform; he was beaming with optimism and high spirits.

Musya was not. Although relieved beyond words to be escaping the Far East before the full onset of its biting insect season, the plain fact remained that she was pregnant and she didn't feel well. She thought longingly of the sex-segregated car she'd travelled out in: two weeks cooped up with this man and his German grammar and his optimism appeared in prospect as a brutal ordeal. Not that she disliked him—because she didn't, not completely. This, too, was apparent, and would be very much more so by summer's end, apparent that she liked Boris even well enough to accept the makings of a child from him. Musya wasn't proud of this behavior, she felt it as a weakness in herself that she allowed, sometimes, her loneliness and his to meet that way in private; like a kind of drunkenness, somehow. Rarely but undeniably, it happened. Though much paler, without his spectacles Boris Kotz bore an occasional resemblance to the sailor played by Lev Sverdlin in By the Bluest of Seas, a hero long among her major dream men.

A pregnancy had even happened once before, the previous summer. Then she'd miscarried, early, among mosquito swarms, dazed with relief and physical misery. She'd concealed her condition from Magga but the miscarriage she couldn't hide, needing bed rest and hot water bottles, extra napkins. There to help, the dvornik, also the vital source of a powerful insect repellent home-brewed from a tree bark base, had given a satisfied grunt at the news.

"God's will," she'd said.

"Well," said Musya.

"You took something?"

"No! Of course not."

"So. God's will."

Since then she'd tried to be careful but her means were limited. In fact she had no means at all. Boris disapproved of contraception. Legalized by the Bolsheviks in 1920, abortion was once more a crime in 1941 and had been for the past five years. Her friend Fanny often spoke of being through with babies despite her man's wish for more—but how the woman's will prevailed here Fanny never said and Musya refrained from asking, lest her curiosity confess her need to know. Fanny was never any better reconciled to Boris Kotz, she'd barely greet him when he entered the room. Musya hadn't dared risk the older woman's disapproval by admitting that his second marriage was no longer a one hundred percent chaste one, and hadn't been all year. She couldn't claim that he'd forced her, no one would believe it; although he was larger than she. But he was soft; he wheezed; she could have knocked him over with a hard shove. The whole situation was deeply embarrassing. The night before their departure she'd told him the news, she thought the pregnancy was about three months already advanced. He'd been ecstatic. He'd always wanted a big family, he told her. She looked at him now, pointing out the window at a passing smokestack, happier than she'd ever seen him. He was joyful. He was a man who'd impregnated two sisters.

He mystified her.

Musya didn't care whether they ever returned to the Jewish Autonomous Region. She doubted they would; after all, almost everyone who moved there left within a few years. The climate was awful. She knew she'd miss Fanny and her other friends but she could always write to them. She'd miss the many children who'd joined her in the fields but she'd been seeing much less of them since the new school had opened. While the instruction was in Russian, the teachers were Jewish and kind; Sender loved it and Anton was enrolled for the coming year. But every place had schools.

The treacherous waist-deep mud puddles? The under-stocked shops? The long wait for a table at the one decent restaurant? Even longer, the bakery lines? It was hard to think of aspects of her life in Birobidzhan whose loss she'd regret. She'd miss tea and gossip with Fanny and Magga and the drafty cinema with Kitty (and the boys, since Boris had relented—he'd even joined them for a few weekend matinees); by now the old features that arrived in town were new to Musya, too. And she'd miss, very much, seeing what the State Yiddish Theater did next. She'd finally seen a few productions and the place impressed her.

She'd miss her sister's grave, her visits there—weekly now, sometimes more often.

The letters on the board were fading: needless to say, Boris hadn't replaced it with a marble obelisk.

She'd miss the bright blue Bira and its noisy winter coat. Of course there'd be other river views in her life, and Odessa had the sea; but since the day it first surprised her, she'd felt a connection and a kinship with this particular river that she sensed would be hard to replace. More than a comfort, it had been almost like a secret lover. In her bag she'd even packed a fallen pine cone from the wooded bluff that overlooked it, a memento of their rendezvous.

A chill ran through her limbs and her face went hot at the thought of what awaited her in Odessa. She pictured encountering Leon Flohr in the railway station, by sheer coincidence he'd be standing there at a news kiosk, idle and alone, amazed to see her, amazed at the effect the unexpected sight of her was having on his numbed, half-frozen heart. Then he'd see the husband, and then he'd see the children, and then he'd see—she'd been so weak, so changeable, so unworthy. He'd never speak to her again. Almost no one would. Old school friends would look at her and be disgusted. Worst of all was imagining how her mother and father would react to her pregnancy—and worse even than what they might say aloud was the thought of everything they'd keep to themselves, having deemed Musya too lost and gutter-bound to hear it. A few months would go by and then, in all likelihood, she'd be back in Birobidzhan, ostracized by that set of friends. But wherever they went she'd feel mortified. Should a miracle occur and Boris find work in the western territories, her situation would hardly improve. He'd still be her dull, homely, preposterous husband and her mistake would still look like her choice. The shame was crushing, unbearable; nauseated, Musya wanted only to close her eyes to everything and sleep.

Her nephews chattered noisily, non-stop. This was the greatest day of their lives, no question, outstripping even the Saturday of their first cinema double feature (Circus and Volga-Volga, two old standbys that seemed to return every few months). This adventure had everything for them: motion, machinery, novelty, views; they cried out at the sight of grazing livestock; their first railway bridge crossing occasioned panic, terror, ecstasy. They'd never been anywhere. They adored books and stories that took place in wild nature. Now the wildest scenes they passed held their minds in clutches—a single glimpse was insufficient. Boris had to make solemn promises, Musya, too. Between naps, she'd begun to enjoy herself. Yes, by that lakeshore they'd camp, up that stream they'd paddle, across those craggy foothills they'd climb to reach the lands beyond.

The journey west was slowed by delays and many diversions onto sidings outside stations or even quite in between, virtually nowhere. According to what Boris could learn, this was for the sake of the heavy freight cars rushing raw materials—lumber, ores, phosphates, fuel—from east to west in support of the German war effort. A true partnership, he described it. No one else in the world would give them anything.

Sender Kotz asked why not. An hour's stop among birch trees in a glade refreshed by breezes and sunlight; passengers had climbed down to lounge and wander on a slope above the track, many going barefoot. The men had rolled up their trouser legs. The six year-old's question seemed more idle than urgent, more indulgent than sincere; maybe, already, Musya reflected, as she watched the breeze raise a silver cloud of midges and shake it out above the grass like a sheet on a laundry line, he didn't expect Boris Kotz to have an answer. She didn't expect one herself.

Indeed: "Because—the other countries won't help Germany because it's war. This is what happens in war. These are called the rules of engagement."

Sender dug his toes into the grass. "Papa, why does fascist Germany hate Jews?"

"European Jews," Boris said. He was startled. "Jews in Europe are very different. Where did you hear this?"

"In school. Is it true that Jew-hating is a German fascist cure for sadness?"

"I don't like that school," Boris said to Musya. "I've never trusted it."

"It's a good school," she told him.

"Propaganda," he insisted. "Reactionaries. They've been infiltrated."

Anton gave a screech. He'd caught a toad, a very small one. It got away.

Disheartened settlers from the Jewish Autonomous Region filled a large share of the passenger list. Most had been on collective farms at which equipment and seeds had failed to arrive when due, if ever; for everything was needed elsewhere, among fields deemed more important. They'd had to give up hope. Some thought they'd try Palestine next, it seemed more promising at this point. Others thought like Boris Kotz to move west with the Ukrainian border and then ever westward, as the Soviet Union stretched into territories already Jewish, already civilized; the prospect of bringing healthy socialism to Western Europe and a conquered Britain drew them. War made them restless and at times fantastical. Late into the night they'd gather by the carriage samovar to dispute over plans for the administration of Paris. Too tired to spend much time in conversation with the other wives, Musya missed the singing and the bayan tunes of her journey out. She slept in her own bunk with one arm as usual around each nephew, her dreams uneasy.

The first sign of real trouble met them at Omsk, about halfway to Moscow. Here a man boarded who didn't look well, although he was an official, bound for the next station along; he made reports on Siberia's supply lines to the German forces, this was his position. He'd been all across Poland and back a dozen times. He appeared to be about thirty years old. Catching him by the samovar, a crowd of passengers plied him with sweet tea, maybe some wine, and started to talk, hoping to draw him into conversation. The official, who had a grayish-yellow pallor and a tremor in his hands, drank thirstily without relieving either symptom and kept mum as their voices buzzed around him. Musya felt herself growing bored with this dull, unattractive and sickly man who had nothing to say; but other, eager faces pressed near his shoulder. Strawberry-tinted droplets clung to the sparse brown beard around his lips—which parted in a sudden laugh, high-pitched and violent, it surprised her, surprised all of them:

"Historic Lublin! Ha! He wants to modernize historic Lublin!" The official was laughing at Boris, who crouched among the younger men near his knees. "What an ambition. Understand this, my poor fellow—Lublin is an open grave. Every other Jew is dead and gone from Lublin. And the rest, you know—you are all Jews, yes? So then you should know, someone threw a fence around a few historic little streets in Lublin and put the Jews inside—like herding them into a little pen, yes, crowded together—and locked it behind. No food comes in—no one comes out—modernize Lublin! Oh, dear!" He laughed, almost screeching, then moaned. "A beautiful ambition, really beautiful." Now he slurped more tea. His wet lips and the rattling train parts in motion made the only sounds: the listening group was stunned, silent, motionless.

Boris rallied first. He was angry. "What are you talking about? Who is they—who did this?"

"Who?" The official goggled his eyes; it had to be wine, he had to be drunk. "Who? The Germans, of course. Your Germans, they do not fool around when they want a place to modernize."

"But the Jews." Boris spread his hands in argument. "What is this you are saying? Lublin is a Jewish city."

"Not anymore!" With another piercing shout of laughter the official reared back until his head and shoulders thumped against the wall; he seemed to like the feeling and did it again, harder, and again.

"He's crazy," Boris said almost to himself, then looked around. "This man has gone mad. It's obvious. You are mad, Tovarisch," he finished in Russian.

"Mad!" The official shot to his feet and stood, teetering, he loomed over Boris. "I am the madman, you call me the one—when you men are bringing your women and children to the mouth of Hell? You say I am the crazy one? Let me tell you my friend, from what I have seen I should be crazy—better, no mind, no memories, nothing. Let me not remember a single forest, let me not remember what a ditch is, what it looks like filled the way." He stopped, his eyes wide, blinded by horror. Or madness. He stood panting, a repellent figure; the crowd drew back. "The way I have seen," he finished, raising the little tea glass whose rim clicked against his stained front teeth. Finding it empty, he dashed it to the floor and Musya heard the woman whose set it came from give a single plaintive cry, dismayed, although by no means had it been an heirloom, nor even expensive, they all knew this—still, something she'd have to replace. It was a shame.

Unaware that he'd offended the madman looked around, blinking his surroundings into focus. His gaze fell upon Musya.

"Go home," he told her. "Turn around and go back where you came from. Walk if you have to—better you should run."

Her heart began to pound with alarm and confusion. She watched her husband clamber to his feet and extend a plump white hand, palm up. "Sir," said Boris, "please be so good as to compensate our fellow passenger for the damage to her glassware."

The officer stared at him. "Her glassware?"

Boris gestured at the shards of glass around their feet. "Yes, the piece you have broken. It has some value. You may come here among us as a representative of the state but that does not entitle you to engage in wanton destruction of our belongings, I think?

You find me amusing, sir?" For the officer's stare had narrowed as his smile—his teeth were very bad—grew broader.

"Yes," he said. "I find you very amusing. The historic madman of modern Lublin who called me a madman, yes, you are a funny man. Here, for your damages." Without looking he dropped some crumpled notes onto Boris's palm, a hundred times too much; a few fell to the floor and were snatched right away, he'd so forfeited the car's consideration, much more completely than a simple madman could have done. "You people are out of your minds," he said in parting, his tone really genial. His exit inspired chattering relief.

He'd frightened them.

As the hero of the moment Boris lingered in conversation at the center of a little crowd while Musya returned to their berths. Little Anton had napped through the entire episode but Sender hadn't, he'd trailed her up the corridor, he'd heard everything. She found him in tears. He wanted to do as the crazy man had counseled—he wanted to go home.

"But we are." Watching their reflections in the window, she rocked him in her arms and kissed the red curls on the top of his head. "We are going home. Odessa is our home, your mama's and papa's and mine. It's a very nice home, you'll love it so much there. You'll see all the ships, remember? Just like I've told you." A long blue twilight gently erased the features of western Siberia as she comforted Sender with strings of words he'd heard her recite many times, lists of sights and names of streets and remembered café menus, she crooned them until he was calmer, until he fell asleep.

From her mother's letters she knew it would be different in Odessa now. Much had changed. The work regulations had tightened again and her mother no longer sewed at home all day, she sewed at a factory instead. At night she still made some dresses for the same old private clients, the widow Tsigal primarily. Musya's father had resumed doing the fittings and deliveries; otherwise he seemed to work as a waiter at a hotel but this detail remained sketchy. In her old home her parents had barely half the space they'd had since the little house had been repaired (barely) and re-divided; there was a family of three inhabiting what had been the sisters' little bedroom. According to her mother, who didn't care for many people, the neighborhood had grown extremely crowded. Refugees, *bezhentsy*, Musya remembered this Russian word she'd used. People seeking refuge from the war in the west, from bad conditions there, from things—she thought of the official's jaundiced eyes, starting from his head in horror at the sight of his memories—unreported; none of it had made the newsreels, this was for sure. Triumphs excitedly narrated over scenes of giant weapons on parade, their escorts a hundred thousand marchers strong keeping perfect ranks in perfect tandem: this was what Musya had witnessed of recent history. Now it occurred to her to wonder whether Boris, with all his frowning concentration on papers and pamphlets and pointless correspondence, not to mention his simple access to the world of adult men, had gleaned hints of danger that he hadn't seen fit to share with her. Did he know better than to have led them on this journey? When at length he reappeared, all his praise collected, she asked him point-blank: were they safe, going to Odessa now?

"Of course we are," he answered. "How can you wonder? That man was a lunatic, just as I said—couldn't you tell? He was raving."

"He said he'd seen things."

"Yes—because he was crazy. Crazy men see things, my dear." Bustling about with no aim or effect, Boris started to dig through his shaving kit although he'd already shaved; he was in one of those moods where his touch bred disorder, Musya recognized it. She leaned back against her old travelling bag half-protectively (it had all their paperwork inside) and watched him up-end the kit's contents onto the berth. Spare razors flashed. He claimed to be looking for tooth powder. "I don't doubt he's seen some atrocious things—it stands to reason, in a war zone, not every sight is going to be picturesque. But to fall so completely to pieces like that in front of civilians, in front of women—really, if this is the sort of character they're putting into responsible positions these days, I almost despair." She sat and listened as he fussed and unfolded well-rehearsed gripes and spilled hair oil on the blanket, briefly cloaking the compartment in synthetic lilac fumes. There was no doubt in her mind that he was frightened almost witless but she didn't say so. In fact, far from compounding her own anxiety, she found his alarm strangely reassuring: if he felt afraid, there could be little or no actual cause to. This husband of hers was always wrong.

He'd been wrong about Birobidzhan, which was no Zion, Soviet or otherwise. He'd been wrong about farming, at which he'd proved a failure. He hadn't become a field scientist by making written applications. If he really had an eye for hidden value in a bargain, it hadn't been the abracadabra to private wealth he'd sought. His admiration for German management principles looked to be somewhat misplaced; his idea of moving his family to occupied Poland was almost certainly a bad one. And once—if not twice—he'd married the wrong woman. If he insisted, Musya decided, on continuing west from Odessa then she would divorce Boris Kotz, keep the baby, keep the boys and send him on his way alone. That night she slept soundly. She awoke refreshed, calmer, her entire being lighter; at the washbasin where she arrived humming tunes the other women remarked on her good cheer. One of them suggested that she'd been loved in the night. Musya burst out laughing and walked away shaking her head.

They'd intended to tour the Moscow landmarks but with all the delays en route they needed to rush for their train to Odessa. On a packed crosstown tram Sender and Anton shared a sweaty seat grip and craned their necks to snatch window views while Boris argued with the large-busted conductor over their fares. Hulking gray buildings, overhead wires and windows reflecting more buildings and wires were all Musya could see past the heads of the other tram passengers, none of whom seemed happy or pleasant; the glamour she'd found on the Muscovites' faces at the time of her journey out had gone missing. Two years before they'd been much kinder, as well. Then she'd had eager help with her six enormous parcels and her bag; today none was offered, and the little boys were left standing. Sender made a disappointed noise: he couldn't see anything, he wanted to see Comrade Stalin.

"No." A man standing beside them who didn't look down said, "No, you don't."

The boy started to respond but Boris hushed him. The tension in the tram had become a solid thing, the silence leaden.

Enormous queues streamed from every tea kiosk and counter café in the vast central hall at Kievsky station. The Odessa train's departure was delayed. Needing provisions, the Kotz family had an unpleasant wait. Drunken soldiers muscled through the lines trailing obscene insults. A woman close to tears tugged Musya's sleeve and asked her a question she couldn't decipher, she could only gesture her regret. Along the edges of the hall and even in the middle of the floor lay luggage heaps and sticks of simple furniture on which impossibly wrinkled old people and women with babies wrapped in shawls were perched—bezhentsy, refugees, here they were, observed in their eastward flight. No wonder the lines were so long: they were stalled here, forced to live in the Kievsky station, people in transit with nowhere to go, nowhere to bathe themselves. The volume of a patriotic anthem blaring from loudspeakers set along the high cornice peaked suddenly, then plunged and faded; in its place a sound like waves at the seashore rose and rose with a rush the gray color of walls as she felt her knees float off and her stomach give way.

Carried to an antiseptic side room full of steel and white tin and white cloth and ailing women, revived with smelling salts and strong sweet tea, Musya remained ill and faint until their train was actually in motion and all through the next day she slept; perhaps, she guessed, after two weeks on the rails she hadn't been prepared for solid ground. Hard, immobile Moscow had defeated her. Boris and the boys were almost silly with relief to have her awake and talking again. Outside was Ukraine. They were already south of Cherkassy, the following evening they'd be in Odessa. Four together on one bench in the sitting car they passed the night embraced.

Near dawn the shriek of brakes awoke everybody and the long train ground to a halt. On either side were fields, a bit of ground fog, a distant farm with one light burning, no sign of a station or town. The sun came up. The provodnitsa left to investigate and didn't return. Insect cries in the tall grass outside became audible. Nothing else happened for hours. The samovar went out, the water ran low. People shared what provisions they had. Children who climbed out to play alongside the tracks returned complaining of boredom, nothing but grass and a wheat field, no sign of life from the farm buildings, no animals: dull terrain. Around noon with a great slamming of passage doors the conduct-ress finally reappeared and in mute and frenzied haste made straight for her cubbyhole. A minute later she emerged with a travel bag, seized a small oil can off a shelf, dashed to the exit door, leapt down and looked right, left. Then, as fast as her bad knees about which she'd complained constantly would carry her, each footfall trailed by a tiny puff of oil droplet cloud, she ran away. Moving to the windows on that side the whole car watched her squat determined figure cut a groove through the green wheat and disappear among some distant farm buildings. This was the second sign of real trouble.

"Outrageous," said Boris. "What are we to do for shaving water?"

The train started up again soon after. Without topping quarter-speed they made laborious progress for less than an hour before they reached another halt, briefer than the first. The iron groaned, the floorboards shook—but now with a series of thuds, jolts and tooth-vibrating creaks the engine reversed and they began to crawl backwards. What for the children Anton's age represented an extraordinary thrill was for the adult majority quite dismaying. Hungry, thirsty, they'd planned on buying food at station platforms along the way, they needed to reach the next station. Here instead, forced upon their view, were the identical distances—unpopulated and empty of ripe sustenance—they'd already laid up and counted towards their goal; only like a poor novice handwriter, the train retraced and spoiled its copy. And why so unpeopled? Where were the farm workers who should have been tending this wheat? The laziness, the incompetence, the flat indifference to the common people's needs: wasn't this what socialism was supposed to have solved and replaced? Yet here it was, all of it, as ever, thriving. Beyond disillusioned, a carriage majority felt frankly abused and would not accept reprimands from self-styled better socialists when offered.

Musya listened tiredly and peered out at the landscape. It was odd: half a day from home, she would have thought she knew these latitudes. Early summer and the wheat was green but the daylight seemed tarnished, autumnal. She gave another sigh. Her youth was gone.

A great jolt sent luggage spilling to the floor amid cries of pain and outrage. The train rocked, sat motionless for a few moments, then surged forward. From the wash and welter of emotions one—relief—rose uppermost as the sights they'd reversed through rushed past, now for the third time, properly. "Is that smoke?" someone asked. An amber tone to the middle sky had become apparent. A large fire, it must have been, ahead of them to the south, no doubt as well the cause of these delays. Soft blessings for the firemen and the people affected echoed up and down the car. Offers of help, kindly smiles and soft laughter bubbled as the taller passengers lifted others' bags and parcels back into place. At the next station everything would be explained and made well.

But at Voznesensk, instead of a platform's worth of food vendors with portable stoves and kvass barrels, they rolled up to chaos. A solid line of men, not all of them in uniform, some armed with guns, others holding lengths of wood, confronted a frantic crowd pressing out through the station doors towards the tracks. Above faces contorted with panic, dozens of fistfuls of cash were waving like raised torches. Announcements or commands too entwined with shouts, static, sobbing pleas and whistle blasts to be decipherable thundered from loudspeakers. Half the crowd must have been dressed in its best clothes: Musya saw a pretty purple hat get knocked right off a woman's head and vanish, followed closely by a child in an immaculate sailor's blouse who tumbled from his perch on someone's neck and reappeared boot-stained and howling. The passengers who'd planned to step out and stretch their legs, get a shave, shop, visit the station washrooms, instead kept their seats, no one moved. The train idled and shook with unseen activity. At length the first railway employee they'd seen since the provodnitsa's flight, a station commissar with bulging eyes, a rip in her skirt and a sweaty, furious air entered from the passageway and barked at them to make more room. Boris stood up angrily:

"This train is fully sold—you cannot mean to board more people."

"Shut up!" said the commissar.

"What's going on?" someone else shouted, everyone shouted. "Tell us!"

"We are at war!" she bellowed back. "At war, I said. Germany attacked the Soviet Union last night."

"It did not," said Boris.

"You, zhid—I told you to shut up! Shut up!"

"Sit down, Boris, please," Musya told him, pulling at his cuff.

"They didn't, Muschka." He sat. "This didn't happen."

"All of you be quiet and listen!" The commissar produced a crumpled twist of yellow paper—Musya's heart sank: a telegram—and without bothering to flatten it out and read them the message—she only shook the thing like the stump of a baton—began: "It is my duty to inform you as citizens of the Soviet Union that your motherland was attacked in the night by the lowest forms of pig-fucking life ever to crawl from a male whore's wormy asshole."

Four or five seconds of dumbfounded silence ticked past before Boris said, "There, I told you—nothing about Germany."

The commissar lunged and stabbed at him with the corkscrewed telegram, shrieking: "You want to hear me say Germany? You want more about Germany? Let me oblige you!" She delivered his shoulder a last swat and drew back. "Germany! Broke the peace pact, without reason or warning—Germany! Has attacked and overrun our western border—Germany! Bombed our cities in the night, from the air, a cowardly sneak attack on Kiev, Sevastopol—" Odessa! Everyone shouting at once—was Odessa all right? "In flames!" she screamed at them. "Do you understand? Savages are coming from Berlin to kill you and rape your mothers and eat your children! Now make room."

Down the car she went, shoving, swearing, pointing. Musya's little family squeezed close on top of their luggage; Boris held the hatbox full of dishes in his lap. "That is," he griped, "a libelous exaggeration. They are not cannibals." His German grammar was packed away—fortunately, Musya thought.

The sitting car was so completely full when the train finally left Voznesensk that she didn't see how the sides wouldn't burst open and spill everyone out. There wasn't room to drop an apple on the floor. The newcomers had crammed themselves into every spare inch of space; from the platform they'd brought all their panicked outrage and din, much amplified in the closeness, along with a great many bags and personal effects although far fewer than any of them had intended to carry aboard. No one trusted the handlers in the baggage car. What they'd kept they held close, very: their valuables, Musya realized. At first they took little notice of the "original" passengers whose midst they now occupied. It took them nearly an hour to recount the day's shocks, losses and hardships, somewhat competitively although no clear winner emerged, no single individual could claim to have suffered or lost more than the rest. They'd all been shocked; every one of them had pushed and been pushed, harried, crowded; no one had escaped without paying at least one substantial bribe. Enough that some of them should have been placed in sleeper compartments, surely—yet here they were in the sitting car with barely room to sit down. It was outrageous that the railway hadn't added extra cars, even extra trains with departures on the hour: the demand was there, but where was the leadership? Where was the will? No wonder, if this was the best that could be managed, no wonder calamity had struck. And now, against the imminent onslaught of an armed force historically unprecedented in destructive power, they could look forward to being defended by the same Red Army that just a year ago had almost lost a land war with Finland. Was the next outcome even in question? Ukraine was done for and Moscow would not be far behind—Moscow's luck had run out. Napoleon on horseback didn't signify anything in this modern age. Proof bloomed from points all along the southern horizon, where smoke pillars rose thick and fixed from the ruins of airfields and fighter planes by the thousand wiped out in the overnight bombing raids, dimming the daylight. "We've got no planes left—we can't pursue—we can't retaliate—we can't engage." Such a hopeless situation faced squarely required men and women of reason to set aside patriotic idealism in favor of rational action.

They chose to flee.

"To the ships," Musya whispered. Sender had been tugging at her collar, he didn't understand where all these people were going in such a hurry. "Odessa's harbor, remember, has ships. They want to sail away." She thought they had the right idea, frankly. Athens, Tangier, Gibraltar, Chicago—enticing place names studded the swirl of conversation. Musya felt her own anxiety soften and assume the form of something more like pleasurable anticipation as it occurred to her that for once in his life, her husband might not have blundered: if only through an amazing accidental coincidence, he was taking them to the right place.

But Sender was still confused. "Why don't they want to stay and fight the German cannibals?"

"They're not cannibals," Boris insisted.

Musya explained. "They're not fighters, these people. They're only people, just like us."

"I'm a fighter," he said. Anton agreed, they were both ready to fight for the motherland.

"Little boys." One of the new arrivals looked down at them with a melancholy smile. "Little boys."

"So we're little—at least we're brave!"

Musya heard grumbling: Sender had a ringing voice when he chose and his retort had carried. She pitched her own voice to match and told him, "People can be brave without fighting. They can be brave and go far away to a new land, a new life."

"We're not going anywhere," Boris snapped. "This is all—it's ridiculous. Temporary. A complete and very stupid misunderstanding."

Someone screamed—a woman who kept screaming that she could see the Germans, they were coming, a whole army of them. The entire car was gripped by a horrible panic until someone called this woman very stupid for mistaking some late-day light effects for the German army, especially when she was looking out a window on the wrong side of the train, the left-facing east. Naturally the Germans would be coming from the west.

Now Musya and everyone else with seats on the right-hand side turned to squint out their own windows. Past the rushing train's light-stream reflection on the ground outside lay a yellow glare laced with elongated eye-straining shadows. What would the advance line of the German army look like? They were too young, none of them knew. But what resembled what it might? Everything. Tractor barns, wooded hillsides, power stations, fences, all rocky outcroppings, anything on wheels or in motion: it was fortunate, she reflected, that her fellow passengers were only armed with fear and fancy or else they'd have left nothing but craters behind. The view spilled by inscrutably. Towards dusk the scope for optical confusion grew so wide that most of the adults stopped looking entirely—at least they resolved to stop—but the children kept on, crying out their sightings in thrilled voices, provoking their elders to take yet another glance into the gray-green soup where every pale floating fleck might have been the face of an enemy infantryman.

With nightfall, the train went lightless through the dark, only a dim blue lamp burned in the reek by the lavatory door. Conversations, crooning songs to infants, even arguments and angry outbursts drifted lower and stuttered to a close. They rode in silence for a quarter hour or two. Then came peeping tears, whimpering, whispers ending in a woman's cry: "Oh please, someone on the other side, please change seats with us, please—my child is so frightened!" This confession from the west-facing window seats sparked more just like it; not only children wanted to move to the less exposed flank. But the only offers to switch places came from a few people standing in the center aisle, the most exhausted and despairing, clearly.

"Should we move, Mama?" Keeping vigil, Sender Kotz had his face almost pressed against the window glass.

"I'm not—" But Musya wouldn't correct the slip, he was under stress. "Move? I don't think—" She stopped herself again as he resumed:

"Yes, you're right. Here is better." Which left Musya shaken: for he hadn't been talking to her. She'd intruded.

Although if the dead had it in their power to help and protect the living beings they'd left behind, she welcomed her sister to try. However vast the land beyond the grave, how many of its citizens could possibly match Liza's organizational gifts? In this situation the first Mrs Boris Kotz would have had every child in the carriage sitting by the east-facing windows hours ago, maybe every child on the train.

With a sigh, Musya took another surreptitious sip of tea and bite of bread roll. Hunger and thirst were general by now, she knew; some people had no provisions at all. Her conscience goaded her to share but pregnancy gave her such an appetite that she couldn't afford generosity—not with two growing boys along, too, this was for sure. Stuffed with jam roll, Anton lay across her lap, fast asleep, mercifully. Pressed like a sweat-dampened bolster along her left side, Boris was just as unconscious; although he was awake. Now and then he twitched. Short groans rose from his shirtfront; from his mouth came fretful smacks and clucking sounds; while a nostril—she thought his right one—put forth biting insect whines with each frequent sharply indrawn breath. He was steeped—she recognized it even in the dark, maybe more easily in the dark where this state of his was most familiar to her—in his own discontent, afloat in a swaddling bath of self-regard; immune to facts, anaesthetized against physical reality, especially hers; unaware of crowding her on the bench while she attempted with no help from him, none whatsoever, to feed not only herself but the greedy life with which he'd burdened her womb, he sat there taking up space, consuming oxygen and winning arguments against the authorities in his mind. She could almost hear the ring of pompous triumph in his inner voice. Then she heard his stomach gurgle. This enraged her and she dug her elbow into his ribs. He cried out:

"Gefangen!" As she stared he shook himself and gulped. The effort sounded strenuous. Now she felt an impulse to be gentle, and when he asked, "Are there any bread rolls left?" she gave him the last but one from the bag. He thanked her and ate without speaking.

Exhausted by humanity, Musya leaned back and waited for sleep to find her. The air by the ceiling of the car was slightly pale with a violet tint. The crowd in the aisle dozed on its feet, a jostling wedge in black and walnut tones. She hoped she wouldn't need to use the lavatory again for several hours—at which thought she needed to, urgently; but she ignored this. Turning to the window she could see the sky, starless with an orange cast like dying coals or unwashed carrots or her husband's funeral suit, its black serge rusted. As she tried to pinpoint the shade, the color field itself appeared to shrink. Then she realized that it was really filling—being filled—by row upon row of pitch-black text or insignia that scrolled—that flew, in formation—from right to left across her view, from west to east and south across the sky. They appeared to hang nearly motionless as their route and the train's ran parallel, a synchronization that lasted long minutes: German bombers. She held her breath, waiting for someone else, maybe Sender, to spot them and raise the alarm, but no one did; waiting for a bomb to fall, maybe close, maybe too close, but no bombs fell. The carroty sky showed clear again. Whatever it was she'd just seen, Musya wished she hadn't. The terrible thing was that she'd wet herself a little and there was nothing to be done but ignore it. With a determined frown she closed her eyes and began composing a letter to Birobidzhan:

> *Dear Fanny, Trusting that this letter finds you and your family well, I send Greetings. We have our health, all four, and can't complain even though we rode the train into the war. Bad luck for us. What will be left of Odessa when we arrive, I wonder? Maybe not as beautiful as your Baku, I can't say for sure, only that I loved it. Boris still has his dyspepsia. I know you don't like him and maybe you never will. For me, he feels like the work somebody assigned me for this time being. We aren't so free to choose our occupations—true? Or false? You tell me, Fanny. I have important news to give you but I will save it for next*

time for later my next letter save it for save it...

Anton shook her awake. She heard bells. The daylight was blinding yet hazy, the haze was even inside the sitting car and the stench of it was horrible, toilets and rot and smoke from a conflagration, everything had caught fire—wood, petrol and cooking oil, houses and bread, chemicals, dogs, rubber, everything. She peered at the four year-old face, alert, cheerful and jam-stained as usual.

"Where's your father?" Her voice was a horrible croak.

"He took Sender to peepee in another car."

The train, she realized, was stopped. The crowd had thinned. The windows glared. "And where are we now?"

"In Odessa."

"No," she said. She thought it couldn't be true, not possibly. Odessa was sea breezes, park gardens in flower, sandstone balustrades, romance. Not stink, heat, and incredibly loud hammering, metal on metal, that rang out from a dozen directions at once; her head ached worse with every blow. Maybe she was sick and in delirium, dreaming— Musya almost wished she might be.

But she wasn't. Boris and Sender returned, they'd found some cool tea that she felt a little better after drinking. She'd been asleep for many hours, often snoring, they claimed, through many detours and delays. The nation had begun to mobilize which put civilian transport down among its lowest priorities: their train had stopped and given way to every Red Army mule cart. And now, yes, they'd reached Odessa, the station was just ahead, close; but the tracks had taken a hit in the bombing raids. They were waiting their turn to approach on one of the sets left intact. Those who were willing to walk through the rail yard had already left. Others chose to wait though it could be hours. Musya, too, she told them: she preferred to wait and ride into the station like a civilized human being.

"Yes? You're sure?" Boris asked.

He wanted to get off now, she could tell, but she told him, "Yes, please, let's wait." Her left foot descending, touching the platform in a polished shoe; then the whistle blasts, the bustle, the marble floors gleaming, the soaring, echoing rotunda: how many times in the twenty months since she'd left Odessa had she pictured her return? And never once had she not pictured the station. She couldn't let it go so lightly. "I need to change my skirt." The lavatory made a brief reprieve. She returned to the seat.

Bang. Bang. Bang-bang. Painful vibrations began to dig through her sinuses and cheekbones.

The truth was, Musya didn't want to leave the train at all. To step outside and face the glare, the pounding, the smoke, the smelly decay, the signs of destruction that were sure to be everywhere: she just didn't feel up to it. She wanted to step off onto a clean and orderly station platform, find the nearest large bag of licorice and lemon drops and proceed to suck them, alternating flavors, until this war with Germany was through.

The sitting car sat in the Black Sea summer sun. They sat inside it and felt the temperature climb. Not one single circumstance among the hour's many dire ones improved. Musya could list them: stench, stronger; hammering, louder; hammerers, more numerous; glare, harder on the eyes. Almost ten minutes had passed.

She climbed to her feet. "Fine. Let's go."

(7)

They had a great deal to carry and the immense rail yard wasn't easy to cross. Empty boxcars and carriages, some blackened and smoldering, littered the crisscrossing tracks with maze-like effect. Vast numbers of civilians and soldiers and railway workers were busy telling one another what to do but none of them seemed to know the way out. Twice, lost, the little family walked in a torturous circle.

At last reaching the back edge of a neighborhood, they entered the city through a fetid alleyway. Musya didn't recognize a thing but Boris did, his family lived not far from the station, near the Privoz market. This she recalled, for the two families had met at the parents' flat before Liza's wedding. Now the way there detoured around bomb craters and skirted impassable throngs. People, livestock, bicycles, handcarts, wagons, motorcars and trucks of every kind; she'd never seen the like of this in Odessa, not even on May Day. The congestion, ruin, noise and dirtiness after only a day of war shocked her, and shocked Boris worse. "This used to be a very nice neighborhood," he kept telling them.

The last turn led down a very pleasant street indeed, old but well-maintained, its sunlit length cooled by bordering shade trees. Potted flowers bloomed on many window sills among the twinned ranks of golden-brown buildings. Always the successful merchants—not the most successful, obviously, but good solid local successes—had aspired to live here, Boris said.

"Why can't we live here, Papa?" Anton wanted to know.

"Because in this family we make our own home. In an honest place."

The parents lived in tall white-fronted building at the next corner. There was more foot traffic here and quite a lot near the front door, which stood open. Boris came to a stop on the pavement and they drew up beside him. Sad-faced people filled the front yard up to the threshold. A young couple, the girl bent with weeping, said some goodbyes and came out to the sidewalk where they passed the family from Siberia without a word. Those left in the yard continued to converse in solemn undertones and frown. There'd been a death—someone fairly young, Musya sensed. *Poor Boris*, she thought. Between the Germans and this, what a homecoming.

A big man taller than the rest appeared in the doorway. "Uncle Falk!" Boris hailed him in a scratched voice. The yard crowd turned and stared.

"The schmendrik brother," someone said. "The brother with the sister."

"Ah." The big man stepped towards them and Musya recognized the wine merchant who'd bankrolled Liza's wedding party, a man full of joy he'd been. His beard was grayer now and his manner might have been scoured of gladness with steel wool. "The pioneer returns. Welcome to you, Boris."

Another voice rang out: "Boris! Where's my money?" Some angry laughter followed that Boris struggled to ignore. He stammered something at which the uncle raised beefy hands in a pacifying gesture all around. They weren't related by blood, Musya remembered; this was the mother's sister's husband. He looked at her and dipped his massive head.

"Your sister, the late bride—my condolences."

She thanked him. "Could you tell us what's happened here, please? We've just arrived and know nothing."

"Your nephews?" He deflected, studying the boys. "I'm glad to see them. They look like good Jewish warriors—strong."

"We are," said Anton. A spark of pleasure in life flashed from the wine merchant's sad gray eyes and he grinned:

"Good. We need more of your kind here. Boris, your brother is gone from us. Samuel. He was on a night job in the second warehouse when the first bombs caught him. There was nothing left."

Boris said, "Samuel." Musya recognized the name of the one Boris liked least of all his siblings—the Fat Prince, he called him. Also Samuel the Piglet: "Samuel—gone?" He seemed both surprised and apprehensive, as if half-suspecting a cruel practical joke that might conclude at any moment with this brother jumping out from behind a tree to pinch him black and blue as in childhood. "Did he still live in Odessa, then? I thought he moved to Kherson."

"Kherson. I tell him his brother is blown apart and he stands there and talks about Kherson."

"I only—"

"You haven't aged, my friend."

At his command they left their luggage inside by the staircase and, squeezing past mourners and unconcerned tenants in about equal number, followed Uncle Falk down a hallway much narrowed by room-hallway hybrids with flimsy partitions or blankets for walls. Boris kept exclaiming at the alterations which he found entirely for the worse. A door near the back opened on a nicely papered room hung with dozens of mirrors in small frames. Sunlight poured in through two windows and fell first upon three large canvas-draped objects near the sills and then across a long zakuski trestle before it reached the room's human occupants. Of these there must have been fifteen or so including a pair of elderly beggars in black, gaunt, desperate, their arms extended towards her:

"Ah! Musyu!"

"Mommy! Daddy!" Thoughtless, forgiving all, she leapt into their dear old embrace.

But they kept it a brief one in this house of sorrow. Musya recognized most There was

Boris's sister whose three pale-faced children watched their ruddy Birobidzhan cousins with undisguised alarm. Ignoring everyone and everything else, Sender and Anton were tucking into the meat salads as if they'd never been fed for a year; Musya heard actual growls. The grandmothers alternated between piling their plates higher and pulling them close enough to suffocate. Finally Musya's mother spared her a second look.

"You've gained weight," she said.

"Yes, well." Musya felt heat on her face and a heavy lock on her tongue. "I've had no exercise since we left—usually I walk everywhere."

"You've always had a tendency to gain."

"No—I mean, possibly, yes. In the past."

"Your sister had a gorgeous figure."

"She did, Mama, that's true," said Musya, a little distracted by the size of the Kotz family which looked daunting to her but could have looked larger. A third brother, the eldest, was absent, he'd been siring children in America for years. Betrothed but still unmarried, Samuel, the youngest child, had left no descendants:

"Thank God," said the sister. She had a big bust. "Thank God he didn't live to marry that woman."

"Thank God," her mother agreed.

Boris objected. "You two never stopped complaining that he hadn't married yet."

"Be quiet," his sister said. "You don't know anything."

"This is my welcome?" he said. "This?"

She rolled her eyes at him. "We're so sorry, Boris—we asked the Germans to wait and not kill us until you'd arrived but they wouldn't listen."

He ignored her. "What was Samuel even doing at a warehouse in Odessa when he was supposed to be in Kherson with Cousin Benya?"

Musya heard her mother groan. "This man. This man."

"I know," said Uncle Falk, who was helping the boys to seafood zakuski they hadn't been able to reach. "He's the same as ever. Not an iota changed."

Her mother groaned again. "One daughter lost to him wasn't bad enough."

"Yes?" The sister's voice rang like a shot across the room. "Yes? Better my brother than that gonif Leon Flohr."

"He's no gonif!" Musya cried. Then she stood mortified. No one asked who they were talking about; the whole room knew. How? She felt naked.

Her father wiped his nose on an ancient white handkerchief and said to her gently, "A little yes, Musyu, your friend Leon is. Maybe more than a little."

Forgoing the argument, she hurried to embrace and comfort this man whose age-milked eyes streamed fresh tears every time he looked at his grandsons. Despite being sweaty, rumpled, two weeks unbathed and now food-streaked and studded with poppyseeds they were beautiful boys, seeing them through a grandfather's eyes Musya felt proud—a mother's pride, she thought it must be very like. The child she carried was so unnecessary, so wrong! She couldn't say a word about it, couldn't bring herself to try. She wept in shame, soaking the father's thousand-times mended old jacket right through the lapels.

At length she felt a light hand pat-patting her shoulder: Boris's mother offering a sympathetic smile and sweet tea in a glass. Slightly more than Musya's height but smaller boned, her attractive, still girlish freckled features stretched taut and stained by grief, gray hairs frizzing past the confines of a bun with chestnut traces, otherwise extremely neat in every particular, she terrified Musya. Here was not only her mother-in-law—bad enough—but also a woman who'd just suffered the loss of her youngest child, a son; what could anyone say to her?

"My condolences," she managed. She didn't even know the woman's name. "To you, Mama Kotz. And to your—mister."

Here she gestured weakly towards where the woman's husband sat testing the button threads of a suit vest with a midriff surrendered to corpulence. He hadn't moved from his seat on the long scroll-backed sofa in the entire time they'd been there. He might have been watching his wife but it was impossible to tell, his spectacles were astoundingly thick and his features slack as a man's struck unconscious by a blow. His big busted daughter sitting beside him clutched one of his hands in both her own. Musya took and drank the tea gratefully. It had never occurred to her before these moments that she had another family to contend with—for life. She didn't feel ready.

Her mother-in-law called her a good girl. "To stay in that place and take care of my Boris, it's good of you."

"It's no trouble," she lied, ignoring the ninth or tenth glance at her midriff. Just then the woman gave a start and moved away:

"Ah, careful of my babies, don't wake them!"

Musya felt profound relief. She'd lost Mama Kotz's attention as Sender and Anton, glutted with food, had begun to tug at the mysterious canvas sheets by the window to see what was being cloaked. She kept birds, Musya remembered; these were singing finches at which their grandmother let the boys peek. Musya had rarely seen them so impressed, their mouths hung open. Hidden claws skittered. The cages were large and sounded very full, to judge by the prolonged drumrolls of fluttering. Boris approached but declined to look.

"Mama, those things are too much of an extravagance. It's absurd, this is even more than you had when I left—you're not a grand duchess, you know."

The scolding only made her smile. "You know I love my birds, Boris."

"Yes, more than you ever loved me—get away from there, Anton, don't touch that. Birds are dirty." At this his mother started to object but it was Musya's mother who seized the floor:

"Anton?" she said. "What is this Anton? His name is Anshel."

Blinking in surprise, Musya exclaimed. "Ah! I thought so!"

"His name is Anton," Boris said.

"My daughter named him Anshel."

"We agreed, Liza and I, to change it."

The mother gasped. "You dare? You dare to say her name? My daughter whose mind you stole to feed to your Zionist Moloch?"

"I'm not a Zionist!" he cried. "I've never claimed to be a Zionist. I am a thinking Jewish socialist. And at the time, when we changed it that is, I thought a Yiddish name was not appropriate."

"Not appropriate." The mother's lips parted; she'd lost a tooth on the upper left side since Musya had last seen this angriest smile. The black gap made it no less intimidating. "Is that how you say things in your reports?"

His mouth trembled. "My reports?"

She said yes. "Yes your reports. About your neighbors, about my daughter's friends."

Boris breathed loudly through his nose. "That correspondence, those letters—you wouldn't understand," he said, fatally. "They are analyses of present conditions, my contribution to a community of other men in and outside of the regional soviet, all of us thinking along the same lines." The mother's laugh at that was awful.

"No," she said. Boris was wrong. She could understand very easily; for nothing in this world was more commonplace than the way men had of liking to meet in community, carefully apart from women, in breeding places for malicious gossip masquerading as thought; also well known was the way men cared to parade before one another, she said, inviting envy and idolatry when not wholly engaged in acts of brutal violence and wealth extraction, reducing the cultures around them to rubble, ever-intent upon backstabbing one another over small pieces of property. It simply wasn't hard to understand: the ways of men ruined everything,

But even worse, the mother continued, were the ways of men such as Boris Kotz, who sat and did nothing but write letters.

"You—you." Gripping her gray shawl closed with one hand she raised the other and used its long bony forefinger to aim before firing point-blank at him: "Letter writer!" Then she spat, sprinkling his shoe toes, something Musya had only seen her do six or seven times and never indoors. Rushing at her grandsons, the mother enfolded them in a convulsive hug. She kissed Mama Kotz on both cheeks.

Then she left.

Trailing behind, the father turned on the doorstep, raised his arms in a helpless way and let them drop. To Musya he looked to be made of old washed-out patches, so insubstantial that a needle and thread could have pierced him through at any point. "Come to see us, Musyu," he said. "In our home. Bring the little ones." She said she would. By the time she thought to follow, he was gone.

Once again her family had contrived to leave her alone with this uncomfortable other family.

Musya gave a quick and anxious look around. Sender and Anton, familiarly covered in crumbs; Boris, trembling and livid, intimately known to her; then there was a group of strangers. The room felt ominously quiet until the wine merchant spoke to her:

"Your mother is a fine woman—I always said so."

"It's true," Mama Kotz said equably. Her mekhteyniste's furious spirit had left the curtained finches in commotion and she'd been making hushing sounds, stroking their cage bars through the fabric; her babies. "A very fine woman."

"Fine!" Boris almost shrieked. "What are you saying? Didn't you just hear how she insulted me? Worse than insulted."

The wine merchant fixed him with a granite look. "Your conscience is your own, Boris."

The woman by the cages hummed and said, "That's true."

"Stop agreeing with him!" Close to tears, his face red and twisted, Boris shouted at his mother. "You always take his side against me! Who is this man that you should take his part against your own son? What is his hold over this family? I'm sick of it!"

Uncle Falk ate a grape. "You're the one who came to me for money, Boris—not otherwise."

"I'll pay you back your filthy loan—that's not the point."

"No, maybe not," the older man drawled. "So what is the point?"

"Leave my mother alone!"

"Be quiet, Boris." From the sofa, piped from deep within thick fleshiness, the father's voice, almost feminine, came again—another command. "Stop talking."

Boris put on a sneer. "Oh, you're helpful as always—thank you, Papa."

"Papa said be quiet, Boris." The sister was getting involved. "No one wants to hear what you have to say."

"In front of my own sons, you all insult me!"

The sister said, "They can't help what kind of man their papa is."

"Quiet, both of you," said their father.

"I knew it was a mistake to come back here!" With dark looks to spare for the entire company, Boris saved the most accusing one for Musya. She returned it levelly:

"This trip was all your idea, Boris," she reminded him.

"But what choice did I have?" he barked. "Tell me! None!" He grabbed his head in distraction and stamped his foot; hair came away in his spongy hands. "Boys, say good-bye to your grandparents—we're leaving." These words provoked a general outburst, every corner of the room rang with objections, some jeering: where would he go? "To a hotel, of course," said Boris. Two days into a war, when already there hadn't been a decent hotel room to be found in Odessa for months? "Then we'll sleep in the train station," he told them.

"No!" It terrified her: stranded among the moving crowds beneath the sparkling rotunda, the four of them hunched on a luggage pile like a bezhentsy family, she couldn't tolerate the idea. "This we can't do, Boris."

"Well, I'm leaving anyhow!" And he hurried from the room.

The sister made a disgusted noise. "And he lives. He survives."

"Be quiet," said her father.

Musya blinked at the empty doorway. A few seconds passed and Boris didn't return. He wasn't going to. He'd beaten her—this was her first thought. In the race to abandon this excruciating situation, her husband had passed her and won. He'd cheated, using old grievances as shortcuts. Now Boris was free, while she would probably be asked to help clear the buffet table after the sitting. Injustice had prevailed here.

She felt a tug on her sleeve and another on her skirt.

"I don't want to leave." This was Sender. "We don't want to go before we see the harbor and the ships and the steps, you said we'd climb the big steps."

"And cinema," added Anton. "You said."

All this was true: she had promised sightseeing and new first-run features in abundance. More to the point, no one here (the unfriendly young cousins of course excepted) would think of parting with these boys now that they'd been restored to their rightful perches in the family's broken bosom; already Mama Kotz had pulled them to herself with both arms, she held them close. Musya sighed.

"Let me talk to your father."

She found him out front, pacing and stripping leaves from a bush beside the walkway; each leaf he plucked he shredded and let the pieces sprinkle to the ground—in crisis, he littered for comfort. He was muttering under his breath. Musya glanced back at the threshold where an assortment of mourners and tenants hung about enjoying the show he made. She let out another sigh.

"Go back inside, Musya," he said sullenly. She didn't move. He continued, "Your sister was right—Odessa is rotten. She knew."

Musya smiled. "Liza didn't really appreciate the life here, no."

"No, because it's decadent and full of mockery."

"Maybe so." She watched him pace and rip three leaves into bits. "Boris, about Leon Flohr—"

"Oh, I never believed that," he said, surprisingly. "That was just a rumor. Gossip."

"Well, yes, it was gossip, but—true gossip."

He didn't seem interested, really. "So you knew the man, that stands to reason."

"Yes, I knew him." Thinking hard, she spoke carefully. "In a bed."

He stopped short and gaped at her. "You told me you were a virgin."

"Yes, I know I told you that, Boris, and I meant to tell you the truth, I really did, but." She waited. The flow of words to her lips had given out; she licked them, tasting salt. "I didn't. I didn't tell you." She watched him nod angrily.

"Typical!" He grabbed off two handfuls of leaves at once and crushed them in both fists as he resumed pacing. "Just typical."

"But this was a beautiful summer in Odessa when it happened," she continued in a pleading tone. "This is my point in telling you."

He laughed mirthlessly. "Your point. Yes."

"Let's go to America, Boris. Please. Your family knows what to do, they'll help us. We can go to your brother at first. And think—if we go soon, our baby can be born in America. Safe. Please, Boris."

"My dear, do you have any idea what they do to socialists in America? They send them to prison labor to dig drain lines and pick cotton with Negroes."

"Not all of them, surely." In fact she'd read somewhere that Hollywood was full of socialists.

"No America." He was adamant. "Your mother is a demon, by the way. I mean this."

Upset at the toppling of her escape plan, Musya only shrugged at this observation. "She's been disappointed in life."

"She should watch her tongue!" He snatched at a whole branch and tried to yank it off the bush but it resisted him, rattling its leaves. He cursed and called it a beast. Laughter rose from near the front door and someone called out:

"Denounce it in a letter!"

"Shut up!" He wheeled on them: "Do something for your country and then criticize me—vermin!" The laughter turned riotous; he hadn't changed at all, apparently. Musya felt glad the boys were still indoors while their father set such a poor example. She might have been back in the snow by the Jewish cemetery, breaking up a fight about a sled ride out of turn.

"They're only teasing you to get a reaction, Boris—don't listen."

"I want you to know, I never discussed your sister's activities in a single letter—not once. Whatever she might have told your mother that this demon witch has turned to poison against my reputation here, the fact remains that Liza was never in jeopardy, never implicated, never named, not by me, not ever."

She stared. He amazed her, this babbling infant man. "What are you talking about now, Boris?"

"No one understands me." His shoulders slumped. "I need a career—I need scope for my abilities—I would have been content to farm but there was too much mismanage- ment—I never wanted to return to town—I despise city life—I can't live as a clerk—I need more time to devote to study and science—I have important contributions to make—I bound myself to family life too young." On and on he went, the words streaming out of him with every sign of inexhaustibility. The message was clear: Boris Kotz pitied himself.

The message was too clear. Musya lost interest. First, a breeze distracted her. She raised her chin. Tugging at the edges of her senses, teasing them, were the components of something like one of her husband's equations, June plus Odessa plus Home: honeyed sunlight scattering dappled leaf shadows like coins onto pavements, new dresses, passing faces; Yiddish shouts, Yiddish jokes, Yiddish curses, Yiddish bargain- making in the open air; organ notes high and low rolling in from the funnels and whistles of steamships at harbor with the Black Sea's warm seducer's breath—an atmosphere perfumed with fuel, floral greenery, ozone and brine. Each breath took Musya deeper than the last into the recognitions that flooded her. Back, she knew, across the surface stretched a net of sirens, grinding engines, smoke and sodden ash, panic—closing her eyes, she left it behind her and sank. Boris was right, this mess was only temporary.

"Are you listening, Musya?" She blinked and frowned at him. He said, "I think we should go to Kherson."

"But why, Boris? Everyone says that Kherson is very dull."

"There's an export trade there, my father's cousin is involved in it. Samuel was supposed to be."

"You mean—black market?"

"Black, red, brown, what does it matter?" He pressed. "It's a means to an end, that's all. When I have valuable goods from the east in my possession, why not use them to advance my program?"

"Your." She thought she'd never found him so intensely irritating. "We can't sell the tiger skin, Boris, it's Anton's favorite thing. And I refuse to go to Kherson. Our families are here, everything is here, in Odessa."

They started to argue but were interrupted when a noisy brown truck with a canvas-draped bed pulled up at the curb right next to them. Two men got out, Red Army soldiers, not young. One had a sheaf of papers in his hand; both wore sidearms. They were locals. The one holding papers spoke:

"Samuel Kotz."

"He's dead," said Boris.

The soldier glanced at the top sheet. "Not last week he wasn't."

"Yesterday," Boris told him. "Or the night before, in the bombing raid."

"And you are?"

"His brother."

"Age?"

"Twenty-nine." In fact he was over thirty. "What's this about?"

"It's about time for all able-bodied men to stand up and defend their good motherland from that cocksucker Hitler, comrade." This was the other one. The first began quizzing Boris: name, home oblast, work, military status. Musya glanced back at the house. The loiterers were gone from the doorway, evaporated. And Boris kept talking:

"I have no military status, naturally—I'm a scholar."

"Scholar of what?" The other one.

"Of many things, many branches of science. Geology. Soil."

"Soil scholar! Good. Time to get dirty. Pack a bag and come with us."

"He's not on the lists," the one with the lists objected.

"Close enough." Against the other, objections didn't work.

Ten minutes later Boris climbed into the truck bed where a few figures looking as ill-prepared as his own slumped already, his traveling bag, never unpacked, in hand. Most of his family was out on the walkway, their farewells fairly stunned and in no case tearful; his sons were ecstatic to have a German-fighting father to boast about and share their warrior blood:

"Be brave, Papa!"

"Of course," he told them. In truth he didn't expect to see combat; far more likely was that he'd be attached to a command or supply unit for his administrative skills and technical know-how, he said. Ten minutes past his conscription, Boris saw a bright future for himself in the Red Army. He kissed Musya like the rest on both cheeks and embraced her warmly, his last embrace.

The truck pulled away. Suddenly Boris popped his head out across the back panel to call:

"Musya, dear—write to Magga and tell her not to send the Manchukuo dishes yet!"

An exhaust cloud full of dust dimmed her final view of him.

Turning back towards the house she caught her sleeve on the woody branch Boris had tried to snap, he'd only bent it outwards. A tough oblepikha bush, Mama Kotz explained, helping her free. Once its berries ripened in orange clusters wild birds would flock to her yard again as they did every year. It was quite thorny and Musya wondered how Boris had escaped without getting scratches all over his soft hands.

(8)

Little Anton had always loved loud noises. At the railway crossing in Birobidzhan he'd strain to get closer to the engines and carriages rumbling past; they'd had to hold him back, many times. Anything that roared attracted him. The greatest day of his life had been the one that sent a stray spark into a shipping crate of Chinese fireworks set too near the tracks—sadly, at mid-morning, but Anton hadn't cared. At four, his favorite instrument was trombone, his favorite piece of music the 1812 Festival Overture. The first night they spent in Odessa there was a bombing raid. Anton didn't want to hide in the cellar with the rest of them, fearing he wouldn't be able to hear the explosions; but he and they could hear perfectly. Dozens of neighbors, few of whom had dressed for bed, guessing what was to come, cowered along the crusty limestone walls in the light of a single storm lantern and watched the laughing boy cavort and dance with his antic shadow. At least one of them would die happy, this was the consensus view.

The next night he was excited again but halfway through the attack he got sleepy. Musya took him into her lap and he fell into a deep slumber. Every concussion sprinkled them with limestone dust; they tied handkerchiefs around their mouths and some covered their whole faces. What was there to see? Musya carried Anton upstairs to bed when it was over. The next morning he woke up complaining of itchiness, thirst, bad dreams. For two days the bombers didn't come. When the city alarm sounded next, Anton who'd been coloring a picture with oil crayons jumped up with an angry shout, stomped down the wooden cellar stairs ahead of practically everyone else, went to a corner and sat down cross-legged on the floor, facing the wall. Then nothing happened. Hours of stillness passed until the all-clear signal came. Anton hadn't moved or made a sound. He might have dozed. The following night they were forced to encircle and drive him into the cellar, he was strong and fought them, insisting that nothing would happen again; but they could actually hear the plane engines overhead, many. The storm lamp trembled and shook on the table and white dust fell in sheets. The train yards again, someone said, maybe even the market. People groaned. Then Anton raised his voice:

"Stop it! Ostanovit! Make it stop!" He punched her. "Make it stop, Musya!"

"I can't," she told him.

"Why not?"

She rubbed her upper arm, it stung, and became aware of a quiet, questioning space in the cellar's atmosphere. The other children present, they had the same question. Already during the first nights of bombing it must have been asked, when they'd had to huddle underground in a frightening cave long after the fright had ceased to be fun: *Why?* The adults who'd had no answers then were listening, too, they wanted to hear what she'd say. The whole room was waiting. Would she do better? "I can't because I can't." She couldn't. "None of us can. We're only people."

He started to cry, at top volume, rhythmic ear-splitting sobs without cease. At the next raid his sobbing started with the first strains of the city alarm and never stopped for three straight hours. While phosphorous bombs flattened whole streets of industrial warehouses in Peresyp, here across town in this cellar Odessans were really suffering. Rude ire and evil looks threatened to become the family's lot also by day; the ones with the wild child, they heard. Uncle Falk was consulted. He brought wine, a case, his sweetest. They started feeding it to Anton at dinnertime, further sweetened with fruit juice, which made him gladsome and hysterical: bombs or not, by ten at night he'd be unconscious.

Now loud noises made him jump. His reckless curiosity, turned more fitful, felt more desperate. Cheerful smiles still beamed from his bright gray eyes but so did moody looks, so did suspicion. Anton had gone behind a shutter, he was looking out from dimness. This had all happened in nine days.

Biased or not, in the Kotz household it was Papa's judgment of his grandson's state that was held to be conclusive: "He misses his father." This was what they'd say, out of deference to the old man's age and state of health and not because they believed it. Even Papa Kotz didn't believe it, this was Musya's suspicion. The boys were fond of him, he taught them dominoes and droll sayings, sent them on errands around the house and paid them in coins they cherished. Medically certified with some kind of organ trouble he hadn't worked in years and didn't move much at all during his present bereavement; he kept to the parlor sofa, right where they'd first discovered him, often making it his bed at night. The world's lightest sleeper, he didn't mind being roommates with the songbirds, he found their chatter restful. He liked to have a small plate of nosh within reach at all times and was a connoisseur of fresh fruit which he peeled expertly, a real showman with his silver-bladed knife. Musya found reminders of his son in him: the loud nostrils; the chronic low-level petulance, much like a child's; the tendency to be wrong. Maybe Anton missed Boris a great deal but his problem was with bombing raids—the problem was the war.

Despite his medical exemption Moishe Kotz (he preferred Papa) still kept some books and wrote a little business correspondence for his brother-in-law, the wine merchant, who described him as a "personal accountant" and treated him with affection. Uncle Falk was a daily visitor, at least: most days he stopped in more than once, usually staying for a meal—he'd often brought the food. That he was the patron of the household and its head in all but name seemed to be known and accepted by everyone. He had keys and always entered after two quick knocks, never waiting.

Falk was there listening to Comrade Stalin make his first address to the nation since war had befallen them. Instead of a mere tarelka the married couple owned a cabinet radio, very handsome. The speech had been broadcast already, all day; a recording and not a good one played. The room was hot. It was July. "And about time," said Falk. "Almost two weeks without a single word—where has he been? I say on a bender."

"Please, this is our profession talking, Falk, admit it," the wine merchant's accountant argued softly.

"I know what I know, my friend. Here, wait—listen!" Falk commanded the room with an upraised palm and even the finches' racket faltered. "This part." Dry, monotonous mumbling with an accent like a load of gravel piled on top: Musya hoped they wouldn't broadcast the speech again today, she greatly preferred music and hated fighting. "Right there, you can hear it. Drunkard's phlegm."

"He says the German fascists are cannibals." Sender Kotz sat close to the radio, enthralled for the third time through by his leader's speech, feeling addressed personally. At six, he took it to heart. "He calls them cannibals."

"They are," said Falk. "Famous cannibals."

"But Papa kept saying they aren't."

Falk scoffed. "When did my nephew Boris ever meet a German in his life?"

"Papa had a letter from Germany," said Sender. This was true, Musya chimed in and told how her husband had been too proud of his return envelope with the German postmark for the rest of them ever to forget its existence.

"He said it came from an advanced thinker," she added.

"So?" Falk wasn't impressed. "As if you can tell a man's diet from his signature."

Mama Kotz stirred over the mending in her lap. "I think the only cannibals these days live in terribly deep tropical jungles. Not in Germany. Modern Germany is just like here."

Falk dipped his chair seat towards his sister-in-law's and spoke with warmth, his bristly gray beard parted by a fine smile: "Baila, my dear, please look at the facts. First of all, Germany is not modern and it's not just like here. You complain when we have short-ages? For years after the last war the Germans were past shortages. They had nothing, no food, zero. An entire population starving on boxed sawdust and clay to eat, we know this, the whole world knows this. They should be feeble. Yet somehow all at once they rise again, millions strong, and conquer Europe in a few months. How? Cannibalism. Only a nation full of cannibals could do that."

"He's making a lot of sense, Mama" said Papa Kotz.

The housewife and hostess smiled, her eyes still on her work. "If you men say so."

"No, I think it isn't true, it's not, it's only a figure of speech," argued Musya, feeling strange. What compelled her to try and defend Boris Kotz against too lopsided a defeat in an argument he wasn't there to lose? Was it the pregnancy? She wondered. "It's only to say the worst thing possible about the other side. Cannibals. Fascists. These are insults."

"Exactly," said Mama Kotz. "So much of this war is nothing but talk. It's only name-calling."

No one leapt to agree before Sender pursued his theme again. Though his eyes were big with anxiety these days, they hadn't put him on alcohol yet. "But if we're in occupied territory and the Germans enslave us for their princes and barons." He looked more confused than frightened at the moment. "Will they try and eat us or not?"

"Not right away," Falk told him. "Not if we can keep them drunk long enough to eat them first." That this was an attempt at humor he tried to indicate by twinkling his eyes; but Sender's frown was unliftable.

"We've got to fight them," the boy insisted. "We've got to harass and destroy them, Comrade Stalin says so."

"Quite right—and we will, we have the weapons. It's easier to destroy a drunken cannibal that a sober one: remember that."

Papa Kotz stirred uncomfortably. "Who says they'll get this far?"

"Finland." The wine merchant told him. "Finland says so. The boychik is right, he's been listening. We should be prepared for a long occupation."

His accountant said, "Maybe not. You hear the speech—he says we have the Americans on our side now. Maybe it will be over quick."

"That's what I think," his wife agreed. "Because there's no reason for it, none at all. My Samuel died for nothing."

"Don't worry," said Falk.

"I'm not worried!" she yelped. "Really, I'm really not at all worried. I don't think they'll get here."

"So maybe they won't or they will." He patted Mama's knee through her mending. "Either way. Don't worry."

Which was easy for Falk to say, Musya wanted to grumble. Easy, she meant, since the wine merchant had the wherewithal to make the most of an occupying force. He had contacts and resources in rare combination: he had influence. The shelves of the Kotz household larder (a padlocked closet in the flat's sliver of a kitchen, happily private) were stacked with smoked and potted meats and fish and pickled vegetables and bottled fruit preserves from England, Sweden, France, all of his supply. Uncle Falk knew people—not the General Secretary-now-Premier, of course, but some important types. Wine was a good business that way. Without question, he didn't need to know Stalin to know how to get out of Odessa by ship, paperwork-wise. The Kotzes' busty daughter was gone by the end of July, thanks to his help. She and her unfriendly family would join her brother in America.

No one talked about following. Falk's wife, Baila's sister, was sick. Her husband kept her in a sanatorium, one of the nice private ones with planted grounds on the way to Arcadia Beach. He sat with her for two hours every weekend. Their marriage was child-less. Musya couldn't discern whether the complaint was in the wife's lungs or nerves or both; whether there was even cause for hope was never clear. The case was plainly serious and the situation bound her family to the spot. Sometimes his sister-in-law would ask whether "they" had announced any plans to evacuate the patients from the sanatorium. Falk would always answer, "Nothing. Silence from the charlatans."

And with that it would end. Few discussions in those days were much better or longer or more informative. The bombing raids had made nighttime sleep all but impossible. People went around in a fog. No one wanted to be living in the middle of a war. Yet here they were.

In addition to her caged singing finches, Baila Kotz kept some chickens set aside in a communal coop; her treasures also filled most of the dovecote that stood nearby, down in the courtyard. Inside four walls formed by the adjoining buildings of the city block, a long rectangular space overlooked by their rear windows and the sky, otherwise floored with garden plots, fruit trees, spots for play and ball games, benches, water pumps, and the flagged paths crisscrossing among them, this was a private realm in the old style, sex-segregated. Elsewhere men ran what they ran; women ran the courtyard.

Cool in the shade of blue-green lilac bushes two stories tall they'd sit and watch other women hang laundry. Every so often a faint lilac after-fragrance would reach them from the last bright blossoms withering as contentious blackbirds shook the branches. Flame-bright with sun, their family's laundry occupied Baila's customary stretch of line. Others present had their own lengths and segments. The rest of the women were using what spaces remained in a nervous, piecemeal fashion under a many-eyed watch. Laundry theft: from freakish rarity the crime had lately turned commonplace. The newcomers, the bezhentsy were blamed. Uprooted, tossed up among strangers, these people had no reputations to lose; almost inevitably their morals decayed; as a bloc they formed a natural bad influence. And they were getting worse and worse, all the established tenants said so. And this was all over Odessa—by now the state of the city was almost cause enough to join the general exodus, Baila Kotz agreed.

"If I didn't have a home," she said. "If I didn't have my lovely comfortable home, everything would be different." What kept her in Odessa was the sweet familiarity of her own rooms, she admitted it. Others present said yes. Yes. She'd summed it up for many of her friends and neighbors.

But these remarks and their like hurt Musya to hear. Not that she could contradict them: the Kotz home was exceptionally pleasant, the family lived very well there, very true. She wished she had a home of her own to cling to just as sensibly. But—and this was key—she didn't. She had no such ties, none at all, here nor anywhere. For Musya, any fairly pleasant place to live would do: "Just not in a war zone," she'd stipulate.

Down in the courtyard they'd met an unmarried Jewish girl from Kiev named Roza, who smoked. Musya declined cigarettes: she had no money at all and could not afford a smoking habit. She liked Roza, who was skinny and thin-faced, nervous, intense. A big reader: "The Germans want to exterminate us," she'd say. Roza was fed up with waiting to find out when she and her sister and her sister's in-laws were going to take ship from Odessa. Weeks had passed already and the seas weren't getting any safer. What kind of evacuation was this? Roza had heard, she said, of people opting to go overland, escaping south by foot to Stamboul and she was ready to try that, she really was—if she could find such a walking party she would sign up to join in a heartbeat. The prospect of a sea voyage terrified her. Even worse: "What if we're delayed in the harbor 'til after dark and the planes come again?"

Musya made sympathetic sounds. In truth, being sunk and drowned in a fiery bombing raid was an off-putting prospect; but she thought she'd have risked it, herself. She was desperate to escape by sea. "Why do the Germans bomb the port and ships?" She really wondered. "Why don't they just let the people who want to leave, go?"

Roza explained. "Because they expect to rule the world and they're trying to cut the workload in advance. It's only efficient management. Why wait to exterminate us when they can do it now?" For no more did Hitler and Ribbentrop want Ukraine's Jews to show up as bezhentsy hanging onto their undesirable lives in the next Nazi conquest along. With foreign refugee populations so notoriously difficult and expensive to govern, best to keep any from spreading. The girl from Kiev squinted at the sparkling lines of laundry and smoked. She said, "Understand, it's like running a business to them. To us this looks like death but for Germany it's what's cheaper." Two days later she was gone, destination Marseilles. Whether she made it, Musya never knew.

Roza's place in courtyard society was quickly filled and filled again by a steady succession of unmarried sisters, adolescents comical and poetical, aging spinsters and other female eccentrics local to more or less faraway places. That summer it felt like half the population of the continent was trying to get through Odessa to the sea. It made a human flood. Streets already narrowed by sandbag installations were heaped with household goods in transit. Groaningly overfull trolley cars squeezed along. Every side-walk, park and passageway was jammed; shops were selling out in raucous sales; queues spilled past the entrance doors of public offices. Scuffles escalated quickly into scrimmages and Musya hurried her nephews past a few near-riots. Getting a berth on a ship wasn't easy, she explained.

Unlike the Kotzes and their neighbors who considered the city too dangerous for sightseeing, Musya felt safe enough. She only found the sights unpleasant. A month of bombing raids had left the blue summer skies permanently smoke-stained, high noon a gluey haze. On every corner, peering around at their dim surroundings, stood people who'd never set foot in a city before, much less a great one. *Odessa!* While they waited anxiously to leave, here was their chance to say they'd seen it. Their multitudes that filled the Richelieu steps like some encampment cheated her nephews of their downhill climb; the famous panoramic views from the top, lately altered to include dawdling transport fleets and ruins smoldering near and far along the Black Sea shore, were still impressive but these weren't the sights and this wasn't the city Musya remembered or wanted to share. From the teeming quays below came cries of aggression and panic to punctuate the roar of machine engines violently enmeshed with man-made haste; not inviting. She took her nephews' hands and turned back from the shore. Inland, at their goal, her favorite cinema, a place like a palace, the longest line yet was crawling; but the feature title on the signboards made them groan:

Волга Волга!

This famously lively old musical, said to be Comrade Stalin's favorite, her nephews had seen not once but twice already before in their young deprived lives.

"Musya, you said there'd be new pictures!" Sender was in tears now, that disappointed.

"I didn't know," she told him.

It had been very kind of Baila Kotz to part with some pocket change to send her grandsons and daughter-in-law for a day at the cinema. Since they'd skipped Volga-Volga, Musya handed back the funds but her hostess laughed and told her to keep them, her pleasure. At this rate, Musya calculated, returning the soft bills to her empty purse, she'd be able to buy their way out of Odessa in about a thousand years. She waited and waited to receive her husband's military pay and papers but nothing came, the Red Army sent her nothing. Boris never wrote, which was unlike him. He'd said he might telephone but that didn't happen. Samuel, according to his father, had been the one for the telephone; when he'd lived at home he'd been called to the communal box constantly, a line of people waiting their turn had trailed down the hall at his heels like a fixture. The box, Musya guessed, was out of order now, she never heard ringing. She had no idea where Boris might be. By now compared to Odessa even Kherson seemed like a good idea, she'd make the crossing happily and join the black market as its best new shop girl if someone would only post her a ticket plus two for the boys. But no tickets arrived. Bereft of employment and cash—as usual—she was stuck.

Day by day her pregnancy advanced. No one else knew. Boris hadn't had a chance to tell; they'd never told the boys. A few times during their week of acquaintance she'd come close to telling Roza, they'd discussed other intimate matters, lovers; but in the end she hadn't. Admitting that she'd gone to bed with her dead sister's husband would have been easier had he been a handsome and successful man. Or might have been easier; she'd never know. It might have helped if he hadn't owed money all over the place—if he'd even been in the least bit esteemed or fondly remembered she thought she might have spoken. Her tongue was stilled, instead, by the weight of his unpopularity turning to shame inside her: this disadvantageous mating embarrassed Musya to the core.

It didn't help that of all available opinions about Boris Kotz, his mother-in-law's was probably the worst. "Your sister married beneath herself," was a typical remark. Musya's father might make a protesting sound—after all, the man's sons were both standing there in the room—but the mother wouldn't be deterred. She'd only kiss the boys again, harder. It was astonishing. More caresses than her daughters had received from her in their whole lives combined, she produced for her grandsons within five minutes every time they met and didn't stop. She adored Sender and Anshel, as she insisted on calling him (he answered to it readily, leaving Musya to guess that her sister had used the original name around the home more than once or twice). Determined to fit them for new clothes, the mother was forever requiring the pair to stand undressed on top of the work table while she stuck them with pins in careless haste: this part, by contrast, Musya remem-bered very well from childhood. She still pinned lavishly. Sailor suits, of all things, she'd decided to make for both. "At least you look like my beautiful Lizaleh and not your father," she'd tell them.

The streets around Musya's old home on the city's former outskirts were narrow and muddy as ever. The house felt even smaller now; and these were no longer the outskirts. In the course of its expansion the great city had come and gone, ingesting nearby towns it passed through, leaving no visible improvements indoors or out, only less space and more crowding. The mud smelled worse than she recalled; surfaces and inhabitants alike seemed dirtier in general and shocking instances of filth such as she'd never seen during her childhood were everywhere; and dead animals were everywhere, dogs and cats, their small hard hush spotting gutters, alleyways, trash heaps. Musya wished she could seal the boys' eyes as they walked, she found the entire scene so revolting. Her parents agreed, they complained. They'd always been poor and lived simply, their neighbors the same, it hadn't been bad here. But this was poverty all around them now. They hadn't lived in poverty before and they disliked it.

"You could leave," she told them. "There's an evacuation going on at Odessa harbor, many people are leaving."

Musya's father, who had not adapted well to the latest labor discipline rules, clapped his hands and laughed. "Good! Let them go. Who needs them? Let the population go back to normal so I can get a seat on the streetcar again, please." Showing up at the same workplace at the same time every day just didn't suit him. As a waiter he had neither thrived nor stuck. Which was bad, because he'd been cautioned twice already against being unwilling to maintain a job: "flitting" was the term. "They're right," the father said. "It's true. I am—I'm a flitter." He seemed perfectly cheerful about it. Now he found positive aspects to extoll in the advent of war to Odessa, leading as it must to a collapse of the city's bureaucratic controls. He'd be off their lists. "I'd like things to go back a little to the way they were before," he said, sounding confident that he'd soon be free to return to private enterprise and the life he enjoyed, keeping fairly rich housebound old women in fresh made-to-order antique couture.

The man wouldn't dream of leaving.

She ought to pay a call on the widow Tsigal, he told her; Musya's old customer always asked for news of her. "Don't get a baby," Musya remembered and resolved not to go.

"Visit her soon," said the father.

Musya nodded. "I will."

"Bring the boys. She'll love to see them."

To this she also agreed, at the same time thinking it was even less likely to happen with the boys in tow. As the heat, the tension and the swelling in her ankles all increased, getting between any two points in the city had become a chore. The boys were miserable on the overcrowded trolleys. Without them along, a family visit would have been simpler and far less arduous for Musya. Only her parents had made no secret of their lack of interest in seeing her alone: "Don't deny us the boys!" they'd said. As their mere daughter Musya had lost all appeal for them.

Soon the father took his grandsons downstairs to see a litter of puppies. The moment the door closed behind them, the mother told Musya she looked fat. "They have too much food in that house," she added in a disgusted tone.

It was true, Musya told her, they did. Another truth she knew was that the father would never have the final say on any subject of importance, not around here. She took a lungful of breath and said, "Mommy, really, with the war now, don't you think it's time to leave Odessa? Maybe as a family? Maybe we could travel together, you and Daddy and me and the boys. Soon."

"Soon? How?" The long face showed no emotion. "They're taking doctors, businessmen, Party members, big shots—this isn't for us. I sew dresses, they're going to ship me to Tashkent like a film star? Otherwise we'd need money."

"You don't—don't you? You must. Still. Unless." Musya floundered. Her mother saved tins full of cash, she hid them everywhere, Musya had always known this. "Were you robbed?"

Some emotion appeared: fury. "You could say that," came with a snarl. Who'd done it? There was a dramatic pause that Musya considered might have been the envy of the film stars from whom her mother had stolen it. At last: "Your father. He gambled it away. Lottery bonds." He hadn't bought them too often until one time he won a prize. Then he'd started buying more. In the end the habit had outgrown his control, bankrupting all of them.

Musya felt stunned. "He took all your cash money? All of it?"

The familiar frown lines lingered, etched deep, as the mother sighed and nodded. "What this family could have used was one good man."

Somehow she found the energy to object: "Boris isn't a bad man—he really isn't."

"Never speak of that charlatan to me. That—correspondent."

Musya hurried to drop Boris and revisit a more vital topic: departure. "It would hardly cost a thing to walk to Stamboul, Mommy. It can be done in four months." She knew this cut it close given the facts of her developing condition but as Roza had said, more than once: There was always Bulgaria. "We could find a few other families to walk with and go before the weather turns cold."

"Are you crazy? Have you looked at your father? He can barely walk across a room."

According to his wife, the man had been destroyed by Liza's death; losing both daughters to Boris Kotz and the Jewish Autonomous Region had gutted him, there was almost nothing left—he was a suit of clothes that kept moving from lottery to lottery. Musya didn't think he looked that bad: "And I'm," she said, "here. I'm right here in front of you, I'm not lost. He didn't—you didn't lose both daughters." A brainstorm drove her to add, with hands clasped: "You have one daughter left—why not try to save her from the German army? Walk with me, Mommy, please."

The mother said, "You're so selfish, Musya. Listen to yourself. It's not only you—we're all in danger. Everyone." She wrapped her long-fingered hands around her daughter's upper arms, gave her a firm shake and then let her go. "You should practice eating less," she told her.

(9)

Arranged protectively around the city's landward edge, three concentric rings of Red Army artillery were firing and being fired upon. Day and night in every weather the sky rumbled. With summer's height came Odessa's annual parade of late afternoon thundershowers. The heavens gave another growl: would it be downpour or destruction?

Looking up from the courtyard floor Musya spotted a daytime star piercing indigo, smoke haze, pollution; maybe a planet. Baila guessed Mars. They were tending the doves, a pleasant activity. The dovecote floors were swept, the pink-throated birds freshly watered and fed were burbling with mass contentment. She could never leave her birds, Baila said.

Musya rolled up the top of the feed bag, pinned it closed and sighed. Further down the courtyard two women had brought out some carpets to beat while they chatted, th-*thwack*, th-*thwack*, their thudding sticks never quite in tandem. Did they plan to pack up the carpets and carry them away, she wondered? Or was this only housework that they planned to do again a month from now—six months—every year? The sky to the west let out a long deep cough. She pictured stowing away in a carpet, rolled up inside like a fruit jelly center and spun free, dizzy and alive, onto a wharf in Marseilles. This wouldn't happen.

She said, "I'm going to have a baby." Surprising herself—she hadn't intended to tell Baila, not yet. "No one else knows—except for Boris. His baby, your son's," she added. The birth would be in January, she thought. She couldn't think of anything else to say. Her mother-in-law, openly shocked, asked why she hadn't told sooner and Musya said she didn't know. A sob swelled her throat. "I don't want to be a burden!" she managed, then burst into tears. The doves raised a protest: because they required calm and cheerfulness in their tending, Baila had explained this already, she said, Baila whose bony arms waved before they offered an embrace of trembling stiffness.

Later that evening the Kotz family doctor came to make a special house call and confirmed that Musya would be fine, plus one, around the turn of the year. He wished her well. For his own part, the doctor had reestablished his family in Kherson where he'd join them when Odessa fell, he'd get out at that time; meanwhile he'd stay with his practice. A light-eyed man with aged-looking papery skin and the jitters, he failed to stir Musya's imagination as a doctor should have done—she felt really disappointed. She heard him unpacking syrups and pills for Papa Kotz in the next room, there was always something new to try to get a little more relief. Doctor and patient conversed like old friends:

"Tell me, am I fit to travel or not?" demanded the sick man on the sofa.

"You'll never be fitter. Even so." The doctor administered a resounding pat to some swollen body part. "Never try it, Moishe. It will kill you to travel."

Mama Kotz's voice rose, sharp with worry. "You think to travel, Papa?" He grumbled something in response. "Papa?"

"I said it's nothing!" the old man bellowed.

His doctor laughed easily. "Baila, your husband is an Argonaut at heart, always voyaging after new worlds to conquer." This remark, so wildly inaccurate, left everyone speechless. Then she heard Sender contribute:

"Yes—like how Papa is!"

Seconds passed. In the pooling quiet, the boy must have started to look around him. From the bed in the next room where she'd lingered in privacy, still half-undressed, Musya listened and pictured his wide gray eyes encountering, like a language barrier, a uniform facial expression indicative of the contempt his family felt for Boris Kotz.

"Our Papa," he explained. "Mine."

Tears burned her. "Boys!" she called, sitting up. "Sender—Anton—come help me with my hair!"

She'd taught them some simple braiding which they enjoyed although they weren't very good at it. Brushing they didn't like so well. Now she brushed and they braided while she explained what the doctor had found: the prelude to a new more-than-half-brother or sister for them to play with, an actual living baby. Which news they must never repeat to Musya's parents, not ever. She swore them to secrecy and bought their silence with the promise of a second cinema outing.

In the Kotz family home the prospect of a new grandchild aroused enthusiasm more abstract than keen. Musya could understand. There were already two, after all, neither one provided for materially, encamped on the premises; two growing boys were enough for any household in a city under siege and on the brink of major shortages. The mother-to-be kept herself and her nephews busy at housework and avian care, all day long they helped to earn their keep. The boys still enjoyed some esteem but Musya's stock had fallen and kept falling, this was perceptible. "I didn't know you liked my son so much," Papa Kotz had averted his astigmatic face to say to her, for instance. The Kotz family knew the truth about Leon Flohr and now Boris and now they just thought she was sex crazy.

Acting on a courtyard rumor that the siege had turned up a treasure at a local cinema, an authentic cache of all-new feature films which new management had determined to show, Musya hurried with her nephews to the next scheduled half-price matinee, arrived exhausted, read the marquee, and stopped in her tracks: it was ЦИРК!

"Tsirk!" she cried. "Ugh," said Anton. Three times they'd seen this one. His brother was happier, Sender enjoyed mammoth musical production numbers with dance. But they were the victims of false rumor, maybe even of clever false advertising. Indeed, a large and disappointed crowd had begun to resolve itself into one long ticket-buyers' line. So what? people said. So what if Circus was five years old, after all, it was good and they'd already come in this weather and what else was there to do? "At least we know before we go in—at least they didn't wait until we were sitting in the theater to tell us," one voice rose to say. True, this was very true, others agreed.

Musya voted not to stay; Anton, too, he didn't want to see Circus again. They were not unanimous: Sender planted his feet and glared down at his little brother. "You liked it before!" This was true but Anton denied it and now they had an argument. "Why are you lying, Antosha? You still like it—just be honest!"

Anton stamped his foot and shouted at his brother: "Don't tell me what to do!"

"Sender, please, he's four years old, of course he's forgotten what he thought six months ago." She was trying to broker peace but contention was chronic between them these days and she felt worn out—no less than theirs, her nerves were frayed. And this film wouldn't help. There was too much suspense in Circus, she felt she couldn't face it; she wanted more of an escape. Of course, in the final reel, human representatives in native dress from every people of the Soviet Union would smilingly cradle the same sweet black baby that a backward and intolerant America USA had chased Lyubov Orlova out of the country for having, unwed and white as she was. Far from being a comfort, the story in prospect only served to remind Musya that she wasn't going to have a sweet black baby. She'd have Boris Kotz's baby, a creature with whom no man or woman on Earth would greatly sympathize.

Hearing someone call her name she looked around. A young woman, fairly well-dressed, held her in focus with bright brown eyes and approached, a bit unsteady in heels, smiling. The boys fell still and watched her. With that brownish tooth she was perfectly familiar to Musya, she was one of The Geese, the old school friends. Her name? Forgotten.

"Musya, is that you?"

She mustered the brightest smile she could and exclaimed: "Yes! But—is that you? Yes!" Then without pausing she surged forward to clasp the other woman to herself with effusive warmth while thinking harder. No name came. She let go and stepped away. Still nothing. The woman was extremely thin.

"Are these your children, Musya?" She admired them. "Your boys?"

"Oh, no, they belong to my sister. Belonged."

"These are Liza's boys?"

Musya felt worse and worse about this situation. "Yes."

The Goose was full of sympathy, she'd heard about Liza's death. But about its aftermath, not so much, apparently: "And you stayed in Birobidzhan to take care of them until her husband remarries—he's taking his time, isn't he?" This was what she'd heard.

"Yes." The front of Musya's mind was entirely dominated by a picture of her proud, fantastical Mommy producing this lie to raise against an age-old foe, social embarrassment. The geography and sequence of events were clear: while Boris Kotz was permitted to marry a second daughter in the Jewish Autonomous Region, back in Ukraine the mother pretended that it never happened; such was the woman's shame at her own role in the outcome. "Yes, it's taking forever," Musya said.

"You look." The familiar nameless gaze paused at her midriff. "Very well, Musya. Very—healthy."

Sender spoke up in a loud voice. "Mumeh Musya's going to have a new baby. At Novyi God." Then he slapped on a nasty look and raised it defiantly in her direction. Poor Sender, he never acted like such a poor sport in normal times—Musya thought this even as she felt enraged and delivered her response through gritted teeth:

"You've seen that picture three times before."

He shouted. "I want cinema!" Anton shouted that so did he, Cinema! Which made, Sender kept shouting, two against one. Before Musya could protest he crowed that babyish Anton couldn't be expected to remember his vote of five minutes past. She was beaten.

"And where is your husband, Musya?" At the first quiet moment, her former friend inquired.

"Oh, he's in the Red Army now, they took him. And yours?" she thought to add; but too late, Anton was already in full cry:

"Our papa's in the war! He fights cannibals!"

The Goose blinked quickly and looked at Musya with grave compassion. "So you're waiting for both of them, Liza's husband and yours. For news or—home leave."

Musya said, "Yes, it's been a little difficult."

"Where are they stationed? Together?"

"Who?" said Sender.

Musya ignored him and nodded. "I should think so, yes. Although I don't—we don't know. No one knows, there's been no word at all."

"From neither?" Frowning concern, kindness itself: the name began with an A; almost certain of it Musya shook her head back and forth: no. "How terrible." Now she agreed. Every sound she made, every instant that passed took her further from good faith, further from the truth and closer to the appearance of purity; her shame harnessed to her mother's made a powerful team. Of course, manners dictated that she ought to ask one word about the other woman's situation—what kept her in Odessa, what kept her so thin, what maker and season her shoes represented, anything—but Musya couldn't stop to display decent manners, she couldn't risk the exposure that lurked in a polite exchange. She had to keep going if she meant to escape humiliation—there was still a chance she might.

Sender tugged hard at the arm of her blouse just then. "Who's with Papa? Who went with him?" He asked so eagerly, Musya's heart flared and silenced her for several moments, at the close of which she couldn't think what to say. Her lips parted as she only stood there but nothing else happened.

"Your." More kindness, the knifeblade figure bending to help. "Her husband, my friend's—your mumeh's husband is with your daddy—yes?" she finished a little uncertainly. The two little boys answered with frowns, not pleased at the interference.

"No," said Sender.

"That's enough," Musya told him. "Please. I'm trying to have a conversation. But yes, it's true, my husband," she told The Goose, "is his daddy—their daddy—I'm sorry—my sister's husband is mine now. Because—we're married. I married him. My mama said to," she added. Looking extremely shocked, the friend of her youth wobbled and might have dropped from her high heels onto the pavement had Musya not caught her by the elbow.

The woman twitched away. "But—good then! I wish you happiness," she finished hurriedly.

Musya stammered some kind of thanks and said, "We'd better get in line before the tickets sell out."

"Oh, I'm not going." The other blushed from breastbone to hairline for emphasis. "I mean, I've seen Circus too many times before."

They parted awkwardly. Nowhere to be found in Musya's memory the missing name remained, which didn't help matters; in fact, she reflected, of the four or five girls in question she could name only two in full and another in fragments. She'd never once written. Had they kept in touch, the old gaggle, while she was away? Did they still share scandalous news with lightning quickness? She might never know. With luck, all of them might escape to different places, flight dispersing their chance to breed rumors around her.

Back at the Kotz family home, current events continued to intrude on daily life. Kherson, their sibling city further up the Black Sea coast, was reported to be under heavy attack, things didn't look good. Papa Kotz had more than one favorite cousin living in Kherson; and his doctor, sadly misinformed, had sent his mother, wife and children there for safety. The next news didn't take long to arrive: Kherson had fallen—fallen first, that is—to the enemy invaders. Papa reclined and grieved on the sofa with a bowl of walnuts to hand. Now and then he'd say, "Those sons of bitch cannibal Germans are eating my family." When his doctor failed to arrive for the first of two weekly visits he waited fretfully for word; the hour and day for the second came and went as well. No word arrived and there were no further house calls. No one they talked to ever saw the Kotz family doctor again. Exerting himself somewhat, Moishe Kotz knelt to rearrange things in the cedar wood bookcase; he moved his wife's complete novels of Gorky to one side and lined up every one of his medicine bottles on the empty shelf. There from his bed on the sofa he kept them in view all day long and all night. His nerves were affected now.

His brother-in-law the wine merchant counseled patience, deep breathing, optimism. The family doctor was no great loss—in Falk's view the man was a charlatan. Of course the doctors at the official clinics were no better and those at his wife's sanatorium might have been actors in costume for all the healing they'd delivered. "We're on our own in this life," he'd say. "The sooner we accept that fact the better off we'll be." Like any healthy man of business he despised Soviet bureaucracy, resented its extortions and loathed its hypocrisies. Fine wine being a Party member's prerogative, he'd seen these people in their native element for years. The good ones never lasted, the inferior devolved and the real scum rose, inevitably, to the top posts. He was ready to see the whole sorry crew get thrown out, he said. "Wash the muck of his ideas off a German and you'll still find a capitalist underneath—for all his crazy philosophy he believes in letting men use their talents to create their own wealth." And after all, he said, would it be such a great loss if this experiment in so-called Socialism in One Country should crash to its natural conclusion now, in 1941, before its voracious failure consumed another generation or (God forbid) two? Come what may, he was open for business to any and all interim powers—and their competitors; ready to serve an occupying force, he was equally well-prepared to support a long and determined resistance, he said. "I'm on my own side," he said.

Baila Kotz claimed to spend half her waking hours telling Falk to lower his voice. It didn't work—at least not well enough. A young man with a terrible scalp, peeling everywhere, appeared at the flat one night near the end of August to report the wine merchant's arrest. This young man was a clerk at the wine shop and had witnessed the whole thing. Three police, NKVD thugs, virtually silent, and a long black car: Falk had been shouting, reeling off highlights of his customer lists, naming men in high places—he was under their express pro-tection, he said; he knew their wives, too. He was still shouting when the men shoved him into the back seat and sped off. No one could believe this had happened: Falk hadn't been arrested in almost four years and by now—especially now—the authorities should have found better things to do. Papa Kotz shook his head in perplexity and wonderment:

"With the Germans three kilometers away how do these assholes have time to pick up Falk?"

His wife cautioned him about the rough language in front of his grandchildren. Musya said she didn't mind: having grown up in the heart of a railway town in Eastern Siberia the boys had heard much worse, very often. "Well it's my house," said Baila. She was on edge, grinding her teeth, clangoring silently. Musya registered Baila's state but was still made miserable by the older woman's snappishness. Her own nerves, by contrast, felt as though someone had taken a blade to them—her nerves and her hopes alike, sliced right through. Without Falk and his connections, there was no getting out of Odessa and no safety in staying.

Unstrung, she sat a little slumped between the boys who were both squirming, denied exercise again by a day-long spate of alarms and bombardments. Peering past the birdcages out to the long late high summer twilight, she could see nothing but a few shapes floating in a violet-gray soup, shapes and the prickly-petalled starbursts of passing headlamps. Baila followed her gaze.

"It looks like a winter sea fog."

Musya said she agreed, it did—a winter fog larded with salt, explosions, sirens, house fires, pulverized streets, the occasional scream, she didn't say. But the situation was horrible.

In the next moment two sharp reports sounded on the flat door which flew open and Uncle Falk with a bruised face strode into the room. "Those stupid pig-fuckers!" he shouted. Baila Kotz launched herself from her knitting chair and threw herself against his chest with a high abandoned groan. He gathered her into his arms, lowered his bearded cheek to the crown of her head and let his eyelids fall. One eye was bloody, turning black. Musya threw a curious look at the sofa where Papa Kotz had his medicine shelf under an exhaustive survey; now he took his glasses off, polished them. Seeing which she sniffed. Here were her in-laws holding her in low regard for her relations with her legal husband—and this was how they lived! These Kotzes!

Sensitive and more conscientious towards the old man's feelings, Sender gave his grandfather's shoulder a nudge. "Papa Kotz, are the pig-fuckers the same as the assholes or different?"

The wine merchant laughed and sat down to table with an appetite (he ate little, however). His old influence had kept its juice, he said. Only an enemy downtown had used a recent unmerited promotion to exact some illegal justice. The real bosses were fleeing which left half the top-rank places vacant, naturally the scum was seizing its day—all over Odessa one saw, he said, the same thing going on in the higher circles of organized crime as in the party committee and ministries. "Not that there was any difference to begin with," he said.

"Please," said Baila Kotz. "Please stop talking."

With Falk's safe return, those around him relaxed. They'd had a needless fright; now all the dangers facing them looked flimsier. What's more, they were lucky, in the Kotz household they felt this—luckier than the common herd, they might be lucky enough to remain alive in their comfortable home. Even the danger of being informed on grew less as the city continued to empty around them. The Black Sea Fleet was doing wonders: some streets in the Kotz neighborhood had lost nearly every resident to the evacuation.

"Poor planet!" Musya's father laughed. "Having to take in so many Odessans—I wish it luck."

The two of them were spending the afternoon together at the Privoz market, winding their way through a racket of hammers and saws at work in the bomb-damaged sections. The big guns boomed further north today, emboldening many to visit the place. Despite a number of more established shops and family stalls being shuttered, the vast complex remained amazingly well-stocked. There was a lot of business being done in what had become a messier, more chaotic setting. Every price was astronomical so the labyrinth of aisles rang with outrage and bargaining in a confusion of tongues. Musya waited while the father picked through some beehive heaps of shoe leather being sold off a dirty plank table.

"Daddy," she told him suddenly, "this is like Birobidzhan."

He cast an agreeable look around at the squalid state of a beloved landmark. "Yes? Is that good or bad?"

Terrible, she said, of course it was. "Because Odessa is a great city. It should feel like one. Not like a place someone built yesterday." She thought of Kitty, the dvornik's daughter, with her pink face and fantasies. "People dream of life in a great city like this, but if they saw it now they wouldn't know why they ever bothered."

"But this is what war does. It won't last."

"What if it does? What if it destroys Odessa?"

Now he laughed. "Destroy Odessa! Never. There's too much money here, too good a harbor, too much for these maniacs to fight over. Please, not until war is destroyed will such a city as Odessa be destroyed. Don't worry."

She wasn't inclined to put much confidence in his opinion. "So you think it's safe to stay?"

"I didn't say that," he answered slowly. "Staying isn't safe, no. But Odessa's never been the safest place. And we're still here, aren't we? We've stayed and we're alive."

She had to agree: they were alive. A thick-necked man standing near them raised a slurring voice: "Like a wound," he declaimed, "speared in the side of the Western world, Odessa spills humanity onto its waters."

The father chewed and nodded. "Very true," he said, walking on. From an old woman at a brazier he'd bought a small bag of roasted chestnuts of very uneven quality and now they were splitting them, father and daughter. Back at the Kotz flat, where no one would mention news of Musya's pregnancy for fear of the reaction, the mother was fitting sailor suit pieces to small boys' bodies. At this moment, everyone was alive: Musya and her parents, Sender and Anton, Baila and Papa and Falk and probably Boris, too, plus Kotzes in and en route to America; and the child Musya carried was quick, sometimes restless. A sizeable group, but what its existence proved about anything remained to be seen.

"It's in God's hands," the father said, surprising her. "I leave it there. I recommend you do the same."

Musya said she'd try. In truth she thought these hands of God were only more of the man's weak excuses in life. She asked him why he played the lottery so much; the question annoyed him although he laughed again. Popularity, excitement, he won more than he spent—she rolled her eyes at him.

At times she'd force a stop to the chatter of her worries by concentrating firmly on how powerless she was to help herself. Even Falk's wife appeared to have a more active will in the disposition of her own person: she'd simply screamed when anyone had made the slightest move to make her evacuate her Arcadia Beach Line sanatorium, screamed and screamed until they'd just let her be; along with a few patients being ministered to by a skeleton staff, she'd remained put. Sixteen years of silence and separation lay between the sick woman and her sister Baila Kotz. A complete break: in all that time they'd never met or spoken. Musya had learned of this ruptured bond right away from the courtyard's kibitzers, for whom of course it was staple fare; but inside the Kotz family circle she heard no hint of the estrangement. Always Baila spoke warmly of her poor sister, sympathetically—even now:

"The poor woman doesn't know what she's doing."

"But couldn't they have given her an injection?" Musya demanded this a little violently but she was really upset. Among her very few remaining hopes had been one reliant on the evacuation of Falk's wife in her hospital bed or her straightjacket—either way onto water, a sea voyage to safety that might prompt Falk to follow with the rest of them in tow. Here, finally, the order had come, the transports of mercy prepared and the sufferers loaded aboard; at this moment those who could move their arms were waving good-by to Odessa's much-photographed shore. But not this one. The essential sufferer: "How could you let her decide if she doesn't know what she's doing? How could you allow her to make such an important decision?" The facts were actually dizzying. She sat down on the nearest bench.

Baila went away and came back with a handkerchief soaked and cooled at the courtyard fountain. "My sister has always had a strong personality. Sickness doesn't change that."

Musya wiped her brow and couldn't help asking: "Is she insane?"

"She has many problems."

"But is she a crazy person? Because if she's insane and she wants to stay in Odessa, isn't that—doesn't that make it more sensible to leave? For everyone?"

"Please don't upset my birds, Musya." Ending it, Baila spoke quietly. Word of her poor sister's persistence had come in a note delivered by Yankel, the wine merchant's dandruff-prone clerk, a nice young man beneath his surface problems, Musya had enjoyed their little chat while out of the corner of her eye she'd watched a gladdened mother-in-law smile at the tidings in her hand. Mama Kotz had been in a cheerful mood ever since, her step notably springy, so happy was she to prolong her best excuse for resting in place.

As for her husband, he was even happier not to be bothered. These days he was reflecting mightily upon his eldest son, the popular one, Samuel who'd finished life in smithereens. There hadn't been a thing to bury. Now there weren't enough clippings, not enough photos; Papa had them scouring the flat for every scrap of paper linked to his Samuel. The sole Kotz to go in for athletics, he'd won a pile of red and gold ribbons at running club meets and had appeared in published lists to match. The old man kept everything in a heap within easy reach of the sofa, ceaselessly sorting and mingling it with smears and crumbs of nosh. His appetite hadn't failed but his clothes hung loose on his sinking frame. He mourned his son, whose body returned to him piece by piece in memory:

"Falk, on the edge of his earlobe, a little bump." He'd waited until his wife was out of the room, she abhorred these discussions. Strange doubts had descended to prey on the old man's mind, worsening his insomnia. With a glance at the door she'd left by, the wine merchant nodded.

"I remember it. On the right ear."

"It looked like a little pearl."

Falk rubbed his face with both hands and combed through his beard with all his fingers. "Exactly. A pearl."

Anton, drunk on three sips of wine, burst out laughing. "A pearl on his ear!" He began to jump around and shriek, again and again: "A *pearl on his ear!*" Papa Kotz gave a roar and aimed a slap at him but only succeeded in toppling his own bulk from the sofa onto the rush carpet. This produced a tremendous sound from the very foundations of the building along with a quavering cry from Baila Kotz who rejoined them in haste:

"Papa!"

The wine merchant's tone was calm as he and Musya helped Papa Kotz off the floor. "This pischer, empty-headed as his father. Just ignore him, my friend—you remember how." Falk was trying to avert a more terrible scene but he was angry, all three of the older adults were angry at Anton for this behavior. Of course they were angry at Musya and Sender, too, if only for being there in association with Anton—if not also, that is, for being a burden in their own right. Anton they wanted to beat, however. Her strength fully occupied with the upper torso, Musya could hear Baila snarling after him as the wine-fueled four year-old kept up his chanting just out of range. All around the room Anton scurried until his big brother managed to grab him, then he struggled with his legs kicking the same air that he pierced with screams: Falk's wife in her echoing ward could have learned something here, Musya considered. Now the finches screamed along while Sender held on and begged through sobs for Antosha's life. Heart-wrenched, Musya realized that he felt all the room's hostility, this poor little boy, nothing spared—not even the anger, bitterest of all, bitter cold, at his absent father. Whose family would never forgive Boris Kotz his comparative persistence, multiplied as he was in children born and unborn when the son universally preferred had died issueless. That Mama and Papa imagined their non-existent grandchildren as being far superior to the actual models, Musya didn't doubt. Their freezing scorn of reality stretched like a permanent ground frost beneath all the Kotzes' many genuinely warm and loving gestures. Sensing only the chill, Anton put up mad attacks. Sender felt the cold's full force and petitioned it for mercy:

"Don't hurt my brother!"

Vexed and groaning, Baila left a single swat on Anton's tough behind and turned away. Then she ordered them to bed, while it was still quite early—Musya, too, was told to go along with the youngsters. Craving rest she went gratefully, trailed by Papa's melancholy voice in retrospection:

"My Samuel never acted so—not once."

Soon Musya shifted comfortably in her nightdress, propped the Russian book's spine against her otherwise inconvenient convexity and began to read aloud from the story of Treasure Island. Under the bed, behind his box of filthy postcards she'd found a stack of Samuel Kotz's old A.C. Grin adventure tales; but this gift from their father was always the little boys' favorite. Curled alongside her on top of the featherbed they listened closely, correcting her every mistake. After so many readings they must have had it by heart. She fumbled another word, her mind was wandering. Into their windowless little chamber through its transom light ajar, Papa's droning voice came in splashes. Still talking about his Samuel: "No fool." His Samuel: swift, canny, cunning; nobody's target. Could any attack have been sneak enough to catch such a man with his back turned? What his father thought more likely was this: word would come.

"Oh, Papa." Baila's voice sounded weary. "Don't."

The old man growled for silence, he had more to say. Enemies? His Samuel collected them—plenty. Debts? When had the boy not owed money—big money, usually. His son: never one to miss a chance, he'd always had his reasons. Was he really lying dead under rubble? Or was he lying low—wasn't that more likely? Word would come. The truth about Samuel's survival was being prepared for them. All it required was their presence at home to answer the door.

Fifteen, Musya thought to herself; fifteen men on the dead man's chest in the old pirate song. How many would Samuel's chest fit? She pictured a battered and padlocked box, somewhat bloodstained, with herself and the rest of the Kotz family balanced on top, their limbs knotted, contorted, herky-jerked. A feat impossible were the dead man's chest to move even one inch—but it wouldn't. Neither would they.

With his fretful, restive, worrying mind, Papa Kotz had been Musya's likeliest ally in her campaign for the household to decamp all at once for the nearest ship and leave Odessa. At any moment, she'd thought, he might have hauled himself off the sofa and plunged them all into motion. As hopes went it hadn't been much and now it was gone. His bleary attention halved between his medicine shelf and the door of the flat, the old man kept vigil. "Who knows?" he'd say in response to practically everything. Water was rationed, not always running, since Odessa's reservoir had been captured; the city's defenses might be crumbling. "Who knows?"

"Stop watching the front door, Papa," his wife pleaded. He was causing her heart-break, she said; but she watched the same way from long habit. Indeed, Papa snapped at her:

"You watch for yours and I'll watch for mine."

Musya dwelt just as much as her hosts on that front door. In her mind's focal point it flew open repeatedly to admit something tall, forceful, uniformed. Compulsory evacu-ation: her frustrated hopes had conjured an imaginary policy and an armed patrol to match. At every stray moment she pictured a man, full-lipped, with bushy russet-colored hair and a thick moustache, striding up the front path and down the hallway, raising his freckled knuckles to knock, knock, knock—a stranger. Inside the flat, breath would quicken as Baila Kotz hurried to admit him, a sensitive, discerning man with maybe an old injury somewhere about his powerful physique. Once his eyes met Musya's sparkling brown own it would be all over with him. A probably green-eyed man in love at first sight who'd cry at her:

"But you must leave, you should have left weeks ago!"

"Months," she'd correct him gently.

"Months—you're right! And now you must leave. Red Army orders."

Her in-laws would protest, refuse to budge; crazed with disappointment, Papa Kotz might even bellow insults at the man in uniform. Meanwhile Musya and the boys would be packing. "It's the law," she'd explain. "We're following the law."

In another daydream she had a civilian savior. Slender, poetical, dark, soft-footed, a tumble of black curls veiling quick restless eyes narrowed by cigarette smoke into permanent slits—a gentleman gangster, or an artist, maybe a censored musician—Musya pictured him clearly but he could have been anyone. His image would flicker into difference before her eyes. Outward form was less important than the shape and flavor of the soul in this case, as she only looked for the sign, the word, the telling gesture to reveal it of a man that he could be her romantic hero.

For example, anyone sufficiently heroic for her requirements would surely leap without hesitation to offer up his seat to a pregnant woman on the trolley. This was the smallest of tests yet not a single able-bodied man in today's car had passed it. Heavy with child in the center aisle crush, small nephews clinging to her skirt, Musya stood and counted the vacant glances of men who sat, sparing themselves. She and a woman standing nearby with both arms full of parcels traded wry grins: The city's men hadn't changed. All the same, this had the feeling of a nadir. They'd grown demoralized, she supposed.

Her feet hurt.

Of course the news was always awful—the real news, that is. The radio reported triumphs but the truth always seemed to seep though each new batch of whitewash. Word did come. One retreat followed another. This war was being lost. As order collapsed, a stink of uncollected garbage welcomed oceans of wounded men to the city they'd been defending. A temporary amnesiac with a brilliant past, perhaps, the future hero of her heart could be raising his bandaged face to the sun among those fellows sprawled on the sidewalk; or maybe, like a chrysalis in gauze, the one in store for her would soon be hatching on some nearby casualty ward—an eventual man with an eye-patch, a limp, and a steam yacht.

Before the sadly dull and speckled looking glass that had hung in her childhood bedroom Musya stood fixing her hair. She'd been hoping her mother would wash it for her as she'd used to but there wasn't enough water. Like everyone else in Odessa she looked tired, unwashed, worried. She was worried that her pregnancy might show. In the room behind, "Whatever side wins—our life," the mother was telling her grandsons, "won't change. We won't be any less poor, we'll still have bad light and cockroaches, your grandfather will be helpless as ever. So their side kills Jews—our side does, too. Both sides kill Jews, they all want us dead. Which side wants it faster—who knows?"

"Mommy, please don't talk like that."

Sender Kotz who had bigger hopes to dash was objecting anyhow. "We need to fight for this side, our socialist side, we need to defend the motherland." Hunting allies in his campaign for permission to volunteer on the front lines of the siege, he must have been counting on this grandmother's support, since a good part of the local Red Fleet had gone inland to fight there, too. "And I have the uniform you made me." He argued in vain. The grandmother dismissed the idea utterly. As Musya well knew, the woman's patriotic sympathies were ever as meager as the output of her sink taps today; it was simply that for boy children she had always considered naval dress very elegant. Sender pleaded. "Children can be heroes like anyone else—our country needs us!"

"If your country needed you so much then why did it kill your grandparents?"

Musya turned from the mirror, she'd heard enough, and spoke the first thought on her tongue. "You look thin, Mommy." It was true, but an understatement. The mother's face was gaunt. She watched its shadowed planes shift into a show of displeasure.

"That makes one of us," the mother said.

Hunger? Anxiety? Illness? As the frown grew harder, the resemblance to Liza's final face became really unnerving. "Do you eat enough, Mommy? I thought you had food here." A glance showed her plenty of food. "You do."

"Is that all you can think of? My daughter the glutton? Food—food—food!"

"*Food! Food!*" Anton shouted. "*Food! Food! Food!*"

"Listen to him, these terrible manners he's learned," the mother continued. "And this one who wants to run away and kill himself in bullets—and you, Musya, look at yourself, you're shamefully fat!"

"*Fat! Fat! Fat!*"

"I'm not fat!"

The mother threw back her narrow head and scoffed loudly. "Ha! You've been gorging yourself!" Musya watched the huge eyeballs roll in their sockets and hated them. She hated her mother's eyes.

"I'm not fat," she said. "I'm going to have a baby in three months."

So jolted in her seat that she knocked herself against the work table, the mother cried out and exclaimed: "Whose?"

"*Whose! Whose!*" the little boy chanted. Musya shouted over him:

"*Whose?* What are you talking about, whose? My husband's, of course!"

"His—you." Here was illness, this look now. "You can't." A look ill with shock, horror-sickened. Musya felt a little staggered by it. What had these people expected her to do—resume her virginity upon marriage? Remain a celibate for life? Like a heat wave off a house fire, the scale of their presumption almost blinded her.

"Of course I can—he's my husband, remember? You told me to marry him—you told me to!" The first drops from a deep rain-colored reservoir of tears that she'd just happened on inside her own heart emerged and slid down Musya's cheeks, cooling them. Tears of woe: "You made me do it and it's all your fault!" This she had the relief of shouting before the mother stopped her with the hard grip she put on Musya's arm:

"He forced you? His—he forced himself on you?"

Suffusing the mother's ravaged countenance, stilling her outrage, was a bright blaze of hope, unmistakable. Tears clogged Musya's throat for another instant and in the next drained away as she considered her response. However slanderous and appalling and completely untrue, this lie her mother trembled to hear might be worth telling. There was still—she didn't know whether it was a living presence or its scar—a chance or the ghost of a chance of escaping Odessa, all of them, alive. If such a chance existed, if it hadn't decayed past revival, however, without the mother's dynamic energy it was defunct. They wouldn't go anywhere without this iron will, this self-fueled rage, this ruthless cunning.

And Musya—how could she face what lay before her without the mother lending her fierce wild strength, her refusal to bow or compromise, her self-abnegating drive, her untapped hoards of cash (for there were more—there had to be!). What the mother wanted to hear was a big lie, yes, but when weighed against all that Musya stood to lose, what did it matter? Where was Boris? Her ridiculous second-hand husband with his soft stuffed curves and his sweat trickles—where was Boris Kotz (quite possibly nowhere!) that she should stand up at her own risk to defend him? A normal human young woman desperate for fresher air and he'd had charge of the single open window—practically he had, yes, forced her. His sons watched now for signs of meaning: the confabulation had taken a strange turn into parts unrecognized and their gray eyes swept her face, her twisting lips, for clues. What had their father done? Their wonder was full of fear.

"Of course he never forced me. Boris is my husband and I—I love him." Now Musya felt ill and ready to cry again and knew she looked it—already not at her best, she was a wreck. The mother didn't care:

"Get out!" The command came underlined by the long bones of one arm with finger pointing at the door. "You are not welcome in my home—get out of here and don't come back!"

At this moment the door opened and the father walked in. Gray stringy hair and an ancient suit: he was carrying a paper bag. "I found figs, big ripe ones, expensive but not too bad," he announced while embracing his grandsons who'd run to him, they wanted another visit to the puppies downstairs. One of his boot soles was tied on with twine. He looked around and kept his mild brown eyes wide with innocence. "Is everything good here?"

"I told you not to wear those awful boots again—how many times have I told you?" This was his wife.

"They're fine in dry weather."

"I'm throwing them away!"

"But they fit me. Musyu my darling, you look well."

"She's pregnant." The mother.

"Oh!" He blinked rapidly. "Since when? You didn't tell us? The puppies went away, my sweeties, they left us," he said, then began to exclaim in his way. What news! Why hadn't she said something? So went the theme of his warm embrace, he'd crossed the tiny room to wrap his arms and his comforting smell around her but it was too late. Guilt had already engulfed her. Past comfort, she wept. He soothed and patted and said: "So it's—Boris Kotz is the father, is he?"

"Yes!" She jerked back from him. "Daddy, thank you, yes!"

He said he hadn't meant anything, he hadn't thought before he spoke too hastily: these sorts of excuses he delivered with the same smooth ease which she'd forgotten and now recalled in a flash of pure aggravation. His one talent, the mother had often said so, this knack for oozing out of range of any blame. Musya glared, indignant and sore; her anger struck jelly. He was exhausting, the mother was right about that, too. Even as she told him, "I don't forgive you," she recognized the spark in his eye that said he didn't believe her, that said he knew her weakness. Already diverted, his attention fell on Anton tugging at his sleeve. "My Russian grandson!" he said.

"Where did the puppies go, Zayde?"

"Tashkent," he improvised. "Off to Tashkent to be great stars of the Soviet cinema—dog stars." When? They clamored: when could they see the film? In the future, he said. "The future will be great."

A harsh laugh penetrated the attractive patterned curtain behind which his wife had withdrawn from view; this was a second sleeping alcove. "Don't lie to them!" Indeed, as Musya considered her old home's current dimensions, they weren't so greatly shrunken as to preclude houseguests: while Boris might have represented one too many, she and the boys might have stayed here all along, she needn't have been among strangers. Only the mother liked the extra space.

Musya said, "Daddy," and moved to him impulsively, raised her hands to his chest, lowered her voice to a whisper and started pleading: "Daddy, let us come to you, let us stay here. It's better—it will be better for us—safer—and when—after the baby I can come back to the business with you, our old way." He looked alarmed.

"You know I can't decide," he said.

"Decide what?" the mother demanded—he hadn't whispered. "I told her to go!"

"You're the liar!" Musya screamed at the curtain. "You lied about what happened to me—you never told people here how I had to get married and how you told me to. What happens if they believe you and not me?" From behind the pattern of peppers and leaves came the answer with a scream:

"Then it will be your own fault!"

The father used a sidestep and a firmly hooked arm to catch his angry daughter in a half-embrace. This was too much drama and overreacting, he assured her. "We all know the truth," he said. "An honest young wife and mother-to-be—that's you, Musyu."

"Yes." Emotion wobbled her lower lip as she wiped away tears. It felt so good to be defended. "Yes, that's right."

"That's right. The good wife who belongs in her husband's home," he finished.

"Now." The mother really finished: "Go there now. I shun you—I shun you, Musya!"

"I shun you worse, Mommy!"

The father said no. "No shunning in this family. Leave that to the dog stars of Tashkent."

Empty words, Musya thought them; but her nephews seemed relieved to hear a joke and laughed immoderately. From this gray crumpled grandfather she guessed they'd inherited his allergy to seriousness. Escorting them on their cityward return by trolley, he made the whole car laugh at stories from his Party café waitering days, which had been brief and apparently brimming with lapfuls of soup. He presented Sender with a thimble from his pocket—antique silver, he claimed. Musya knew it wasn't but didn't say anything. As for his wife's wrath, the father had no explanation and nothing to suggest beyond the cure of Time, slow but certain. "Poor Boris Kotz, she blames him maybe for our Liza." This was all he'd offer. With his shoes too dirty for visiting such fancy mekhutonim, he said goodbye and left his grandsons and surviving daughter at the oblepikha bush. She watched him bend to stroke an orange cat before he disappeared around a corner—her last sight of him.

His words echoed. *Poor Boris Kotz*—poor Boris: naturally. How else to think of her husband? In the little bedroom alcove Musya and his sons were sharing he'd left behind, in something like ten minutes, a litter of papers, books and effects that kept collapsing as often as she stacked it. She picked up his German grammar. Inside the green cover was an envelope containing a typewritten note, brief, pinned to a factual correction in sixteen numbered parts across three pale blue pages which Boris had written and sent to the author of an article about rhizomes, as she recalled him explaining in tedious detail, a scholar of rhizomes who had returned it; everything was in German, the whole corres-pondence, Boris having managed his end from this grammar that he'd never really studied and a dictionary missing random pages. He'd said the note was thanking him for his ideas but she'd never had confidence in the accuracy of that translation. Her poor husband: these past weeks had shown how much Musya's enduring disdain for Boris Kotz had in common with everyone else's—nobody but his sons had liked him more than she did; hers was a loving fondness by contrast and default alone. In what other sense had she loved him? For looks, personality or comfortable companionship he held the lowest ranks going, this she knew intimately; every day brought some moment when she was glad to be free of his presence. She could almost feel the man standing next to her as sometimes he had near bedtime. Frightened, weak-eyed, clumsy, unfit: where was he now? Surrounded by strange men he'd annoyed, probably—lost among men.

She sat among his papers and wept for him.

A wailing scream pitched strangely low drew an anxious crowd to the courtyard. Musya hurried down to find it parting to let her through, for the scene in front concerned her. Anton and Sender, both were crying, but quietly; Mama Kotz made the noise. Her chicken coop was empty, the door half off its hinges, the ground before it strewn with blood-smeared feathers.

"No more eggs," Musya thought aloud. She and her nephews ate them at every breakfast: a bad loss. And she pitied the simpleminded birds, for how they must have suffered the sensations of their last bad fear. The dovecote looked fine, she could hear its inmates pacing, calling uneasily—and no wonder. The warm courtyard air was saturated with the smell of roasting bird flesh that poured from kitchen windows high and low in every quarter. Musya's mouth watered with hunger, then nausea. She cried out: "This is a crime!"

"In broad daylight," somebody marveled.

"They should have flown." This was Sender. "They should have flown away."

(10)

By the end of September 1941 the leaders in Moscow had decided to give up on Odessa. The siege had dragged on for two months, the defense was going very poorly, they'd lost important battleships in the harbor, they had bigger fish to fry; there were enough reasons that no one could blame them. It was a hard place to defend. As for the population: after all the jokes, all the folk legends, all the dance numbers and soulful nostalgic ballads and bitter tragicomedies and Ilf and Petrov and Babel, what remained to be said? Indefensible, that brawling grab bag of crooks and characters would survive just fine, going its own way as always, on its own. Who could fault Comrade Stalin for his faith in its people's resourcefulness? This was the message Odessa should take from the Red Army's withdrawal, said the father-in-law. For two weeks the troops who'd survived to return from the siege went straight aboard Black Sea Fleet transport ships; thousands more of the city's civilians joined them, heading for Sevastopol, heading east. "Now we'll see something," he'd say, hugely keyed up, excitedly noshing from small plates gemmed with spoonfuls of luxurious larder contents. The glistening pickled and imported delicacies of Falk's former supply were serving the Kotz family well as markets city-wide ran short of food with a sudden vengeance. This was the start, this retreat, of the next fight, said Papa—the real one with real fighters defending them.

Hope lay underfoot, in the pale limestone from which the top half of Odessa protruded. Quite as substantial below ground level if all its cellars, sub-basements, tunnels and catacombs were accounted for honestly, every smuggler's hole included, the city also straddled uncharted miles of natural caves and lightless drip-fed waterways winding back to the sea. That's where the resistance would root itself, Papa Kotz said, down in the deep parts, where the most intrepid men had always risked everything over the most illegal contraband—Samuel's underground, his father claimed. Here Uncle Falk demurred and said that Samuel had never been that big-time a criminal.

"Be honest, Moishe, he was a dabbler not a crook." His face purpling, Papa called this a lie, his son had never dabbled one single day; and Falk apologized. It was true, he admitted, that they were burying weapons in the floors of wine cellars all over the Moldovanka. Good men would resist while other men fled.

Those left behind digested the news that it wasn't the German army alone standing poised to occupy Odessa. The Romanians had a bad reputation of their own, no question. Notoriously weak and inbred, spiteful, depraved, mental primitives, these particular allies of Hitler's were specialists in cruelty, famous blood-drinkers; on the other hand, Baila Kotz remembered, fond memories from her youth, Romanians were excellent musicians and dancers. Compared to the Germans they likely hated Jews somewhat less. Who didn't? Thus the swift emergence of a consensus view that it could have been worse. They could have had nothing but Germans come.

Musya's nephews talked incessantly these days of their duty to join the resistance fight in the catacombs. One dawn Musya woke with a gasp to find her right side warmed by the younger one curled there as usual but her left side exposed to a chill. Afraid he'd run away to enlist, she couldn't move or cry out, the fear of having lost Sender was paralyzing. Then to her joy he returned, half-asleep on his bare feet, and crawled into bed again, his hands damp from the washroom; he slept instantly.

For another hour or two she lay awake trying to imagine day-to-day life underground. She thought it might be preferable to their current existence. Maybe Sender was right: they could be like old Leichtweiss in his robber cave, make the rocky place charming with candles, carpets, décor, before launching increasingly bold sallies against the mighty and unjustly powerful: in their day's case, against Fascism. Musya pictured herself joined to the resistance in a major role—the very one, from the standpoint of Soviet history, that she might have been conceived and born to play. But Fate lay toppled, its wheels spinning, derailed by biology. She'd grown too swollen and lumbering to do the underground's cause any good; each day the tunnels down which she might have squeezed numbered fewer. Too pregnant, too conspicuous, unfit to fulfill her true heroic destiny; she'd been diverted, demoted, sucked into the ranks of the powerless, left to drift and bob like a piece of cork in a human sea of small children, ill people, the elderly, the indigent, the somewhat mad, the terrified, lost in a world of the weak who lived at the mercy of encircling armies: it was too bad for Odessa—too bad for the continent!— that what Musya might have been, she wasn't.

Here and now, above ground, she had her sister's children to raise.

Next bedtime, no storybook. Instead she asked her nephews if they heard the news about the pair of hero brothers living in a cave beneath Odessa. No? Apparently, in the midst of laying in supplies for the coming resistance they'd stumbled on a hidden hollow knee-deep in gold, mostly coins. The young brothers had boy hero names—Jim and Tom—and an aunt, Mumeh Tamara, sending down baskets of food to their gang at the end of a rope. Their life was an adventure saga in the making, Musya said she really thought so: only last week, for instance, they'd reported finding a sealed underground chamber guarded by six human skeletons.

She'd always liked the name Tamara.

"In uniforms?"

Jaded and indifferent to treasure, Sender wanted to know what the skeletons were wearing. Armor, she said, very old armor. Anton said, "I want armor!" Musya did too, she thought. As for what the skeletons were guarding, what lay behind the chamber door, she said they hadn't looked yet, the seal appeared unbreakable. Now the race was on to find the secret password combination before the Romanian fiends did. Dynamite, she explained, would be a last resort. Even in the heat of battle Jim and Tom led with their intellects.

"Like your papa," she added.

Bedtime came earlier from then on, welcomed. Also by day, after breakfast, after lunch, they'd retreat to their tiny room to add details, plot twists, discoveries. The hunt for the key to the skeleton chamber turned up pearls the size of grown men's fists, sea snakes with sopranos' voices, a party of witches on a group vacation led by Baba Yaga, and a mysteriously abandoned underground lab with blueprints for a death ray pinned around its walls. Anton loved death rays. He grew calmer and Sender, less restless, stopped talking about running away to fight all the time. The story was a cave. It sparkled with the furnishings of their imaginations.

Outside was mystery. They could only guess at what was happening with the war, facts were in such short supply. Fortitude had replaced the day's events as the subject of news bulletins, when they could get them. The airwaves were mainly given over to bursts of Tchaikovsky that swam to reach them through a gray sloshing noise. One morning they caught a broadcast announcing Rosh Hashanah, a day of importance for people of the Jewish faith, the newsreader said carefully. All Jews of the Soviet Union were encouraged to observe this and other High Holy Days however they wished; for unlike the victims of their fascist enemies, they lived in a nation that always celebrated freedom of belief and the cultural autonomy of its diverse peoples. A klezmer band recording came on then and ended after twelve bars in static. Papa Kotz gave his throat a skeptical clearing. "Gut yontif," he remarked. The family returned the greeting in murmurs. Was this real, a new day in history? Or was it a trick? They had no way of knowing and nothing more was said.

The streets, too, had turned uninformative, yielding little but rumors and their contradictions—which might have been part of a grand strategy, according to Falk. "The less we know, the less there is to conquer," he'd say. Now more than ever the wine merchant stood as the household's primary link with living reality. Falk's contacts in high places, though fewer, still required and repaid cultivation. Not only did he continue to make sales, but he'd added a vigorous sideline in liquidations, buying out his best-stocked customers and competitors alike as one by one they fled Odessa for Tashkent and other pseudo-Oriental nowheres, as Baila Kotz called them. Her lover's turf was actually expanding. And if certain cellars he decanted into his warehouses filled back up with crates of explosives, this wasn't his business, he said.

Baila wouldn't let it go. "Promise me you won't involve yourself!" She clutched at his sleeve; he laughed comfortably. All at once Papa Kotz roared and shouted:

"This family is already doing enough—more than enough!" The rest of them stared at the old man trembling on his sofa. Bits of walnut dusted his damp chin. "We should all be heroes?" This he directed at his wife who moved her shoulders and looked away, fixing her eyes instead on the sheeted cages rocked by commotion and slow to still. Hard breaths fluted through Papa's nostrils.

"My old friend," Falk began.

"Water! We need water," Mama Kotz interrupted. The taps in the flat were running dry, she needed Musya and the boys to go down to the courtyard pump. She hated to go herself because her heart broke there. It wasn't only the ruined chicken coop or the newly hateful neighbors, those killers. Fearing the worst, she'd emptied her dovecote and shooed its occupants away with a red rag tied to a broom handle. But the doves wouldn't leave. Too tame, whenever she appeared the old flock would materialize in a swirling veil of lilac-gray and land with muffled drumrolls at her feet. Encircled, soul-pierced by their fluted cries and cooing, she'd sway weakly. She still fed them. Falk knew where to find seed.

Of course they could only hope there'd be water service in the courtyard in these times. Rationing was awful. This late dry afternoon a dribble darkened the stone gums of the fountain lion, while the mud ringing the pump base had a promising shine to it. They had a bucket and cork-stoppered bottles to fill, with any luck. The expert pump primer raced ahead with his little brother—Anton enjoyed helping work the handle which could lift him off his feet on a good upswing. Musya trailed behind in a wing-beaten breeze as Mama Kotz's doves flocked to her familiarity and hovered in mid-air confusion, disappointed in a false mistress. At length the birds settled in scattered groups on the paths and flagstones, on the dovecote roof, among the benches where some young women she didn't recognize conversed quietly—about her, she guessed from the way their glances flashed. Though the place was otherwise deserted, human noises spilled from windows up and down the towering courtyard walls: bursts of laughter, an argument or two, even orchestral music which had to be playing on something hand-cranked, since the power had gone off again. She couldn't name the composer. She could hear pipes wheezing emptily as her nephews worked the pump's long clattering handle up and down. Musya hoped they wouldn't need more hands today. If her baby turned out to be a little girl she would raise her to always be friendly and never unkind to other girls: she'd just decided this when the pump let out a deep underground groan like an organ note followed by a loud gush of water with the usual mineral tang, she was close enough by now to sniff.

The boys hurrahed. At that moment the ground rocked. Then an enormous roaring blast of sound obliterated all other sensations.

Musya staggered forward, knocked her shins against the pump base, reached for the handle, cried "Stop!" Doves wheeled everywhere like tossed ashes. Again the earth shook, this time with a duller sound, repeating: three great thuds. "Stop pumping!" She couldn't hear herself, couldn't hear her nephews' screams although she could see the screams distort their faces. Innocent, innocent boys, so innocently they'd pumped a hole straight through to Hell. Any second now cracks would appear and a fire-bottomed gulf splitting the courtyard in two would swallow them, empty benches and empty chicken coops tumbling behind like matchstick fragments. Musya pulled the boys close and waited to see fissures in the mud where a last mouthful spattered.

More thuds boomed. The ripe daylight dimmed in an instant. Musya was certain that the pump had triggered this, its mechanics or friction sparking some fuse to a huge secret cache of explosives, quite haphazardly—all before a single fascist enemy had even set foot in the city. How could the resistance have been so careless? One freak accident involving an old yard pump and goodbye Odessa: it was discouraging. She felt hollowed out, too numb to care. The pounded earth shuddered and echoed. The sky spun loose and as dusk came on with an acrid rush countless dogs began to bark and howl. The girls from the bench ran past in a stumbling knot of dark wool, white hands, panic and pigtails. Screaming was general. Raising his head from her shoulder, Sender screamed again at what he saw.

Musya turned to look and also saw. *The Lord*, she thought. Booted in black clouds, the Lord stood over Odessa, and not alone but with an army whose columns filled the eastern sky with their gigantic sapogi. The Lord had come to save the Jews; it had to be. The child in her womb heaved its limbs. She cried out and turned away, her eyes squeezed shut, her heart pounding with terror and elation.

Winged things buzzed overhead. She listened for their song, then recognized their engines—Soviet, not German this time.

When she looked again, twenty pillars of coal black smoke were rising into a mass too dense for autumn's sun to penetrate. The billowing shafts flickered redly in places, dissolving in places, swelling in others. All the havoc was centered on the port, a safe distance from them, she realized; even so, here came a dense slate-gray drizzle of soot and a smell of burnt fuel strong enough to choke on.

Musya struggled to her feet and drew the boys to theirs. In a voice whose firmness surprised her she told them to start the pump back up again. Though it had a new dent from where she'd dropped it on the path, the bucket didn't leak. Fresh and oblivious, the water they kept gulping out of their cupped hands preserved the taste of life before a few minutes ago—it came from a time already past conceiving, when to stroll and laugh in a sunlit courtyard had been possible. "Drink more," she nudged when their thirst flagged. "Fill up, all you can."

They returned to Baila Kotz with arms and wrists strained sore by their errand's accomplishment. Offering barely a greeting and no thanks, she locked the door behind them. A tremulous forefinger signaled at her lips for silence.

"Papa needs to rest."

One side of her pale flyaway hair had come loose and hung past her shoulder. They stood uneasily in the rear of the flat and watched her at work in the kerosene lamplight, she was spooning mushroom caps from a can onto a small overfull plate. Sender raised his rosy eyebrows at Musya; she raised hers in return, at a loss. This was his grandmother.

He took a deep breath. "What happened? Bobeh? There was smoke and noise."

"Nothing happened. Go to bed." He argued, of course, so did Anton, that it was too early. "Don't talk back. Go to bed." Baila spoke without looking, then returned to humming something tuneless. The edge of her spoon scraped the bottom of the empty can again.

In the front room they found the finches cloaked and rustling softly. An incongruous dustpan filled with mirrored glass shards lay on the dining table, a few new vivid blocks of patterned paper on the walls accounting for its contents. Flat on the sofa lay Papa, a damp cloth in folds across his eyes, his breathing labored, his silver fruit knife clutched in one swollen fist. A cloying camphorated smell circled up from the brown dregs in his medicine glass nearby. Falk was gone—in search of information, Musya guessed.

Footsteps raced up and down the hallways and the street outside, where angry terror-stricken voices shoved past the blare and shriek of horns, brakes, hard-pressed engines. The flat, meanwhile, drifted on the current of its private dream, enchanted into somnolence: in here it was always bedtime. "Your grandmother's right," she told the boys, and sent them to change into sleeping clothes.

Back in the kitchen—she'd brought the dustpan but stood unsure where to empty it—Musya noticed soot sprinkled on the dancing surface of the near-full bucket. "I'm afraid this might be the last of the fresh water," she said. The older woman threw a look that way and made a peeved sound; the dent looked deeper in the lamplight, unfortunately.

"What happened to my bucket?"

Musya walked away without replying, set the dustpan back on the table, and joined the boys behind their chamber door. There among the bedcovers the topmost concern was for Jim and Tom's safety. Could even such intrepid heroes have survived those blasts? "Of course they could," she said. "That's what heroes do, they survive."

Sender Kotz had doubts. "What if they opened the skeleton chamber and it was a trap, someone put explosives there?"

"What if," she countered, "Jim and Tom put the explosives and someone else tried to open it? German spies, maybe?"

"Boom!" said Anton.

When at last Falk returned with the truth, Musya slipped out front to hear that on the eve of the Red Army's full retreat from the city, the Soviet leaders had decided on an aerial bombardment to destroy whatever the next occupiers might have used to defend Odessa in their turn. Anti-aircraft posts, bunkers, heavy equipment, fuel tanks, supply depots, naval installations and docks: gone in flames. Meanwhile the last defensive troops, thirty thousand men with their guns and ammunition, had boarded the last transport ships out, tomorrow they'd be within sight of the Crimean Peninsula. In Odessa the ruins at the port would burn for days.

Papa Kotz didn't care. "The tunnels." He pressed, intent. "Under the city—what about the men down there?" "What about them?" Lamplight leapt off the wine merchant's smoke-blackened brow, so close he'd gotten to the flames by the rail yard. "Good luck to them," he said and returned to his story. He'd tried, he explained, to reach his wife's sanatorium but the roads to Arcadia Beach hadn't been passable. Baila Kotz, perched on one arm of the sofa, kept untying and retying the sash of her brocaded dressing gown, tighter and tighter. She couldn't understand why he'd attempted such a thing.

"Why on earth—what good would it do?" she asked him.

"I'm worried," he said.

"Of course you're worried—we're all worried. Who isn't worried?"

"I didn't say you weren't. I said I'm worried."

"And you're so special?"

"Did I say I was?"

Musya was ignoring the old lovers' quarrel, trying to think. The port, the roads, the trains: gone. "But what if we need to get away?" She might have been the sound of an unimportant object falling off a table, the older people's notice was so blank. She knew they'd heard her but she asked anyway: "Did you hear me? How do we get out?"

A white smile flickered strangely in the murk and soot stains as Falk began to answer. Baila spoke before he could: "And go where, Musya? To live on what? Air? My son left you with nothing—where on earth do you propose to go?"

Papa grumbled, his confusion pitched high: "Mama, what is she talking about? She's leaving?"

"No one's leaving, stop it." His wife's voice snapped back in Falk's direction: "And you—what did you propose to do with my sister if that place would even release her? If she'd even let them? And how could you take care of her? You're never home."

"Naturally I thought I'd bring her here."

Baila gave a cry. "Here! You know she'd never come here, she'd rather die than set one toe of her foot in my home, you've heard her say this—my God! How could you!" Distress propelled her from their midst; kitchen drawers and cabinet doors started to slam and samovar parts began clattering. Falk raised his voice above the din:

"Because here is safer!" Then he sighed, and Musya felt his weariness, his nervous strain, and the kindness he was mustering for her sake as he smiled again and told her: "My dear, you're in the safest place you could possibly be, you and your boychiks. Don't worry. Nobody needs to go anywhere." The household, he suggested, ought to spend the next few days indoors, not displaying too many lights—but they should expect the situation to improve. After all, with the Moscow gang gone, capitalism could come out of hiding. He predicted "some changes, yes and some mess. Some rough patches. And then some good old-fashioned money. Real work for you, my friend!"

The old accountant grunted, his thoughts among the catacombs. His jaws worked tensely at some phantom nosh.

The next day, on the sixteenth of October 1941, the Romanians took charge.

(11)

Yankel Weissbein was the name of Uncle Falk's clerk, the one with the dandruff problem. The whole family had taken to Yankel, a very junior clerk of seventeen whom Falk appeared to be employing almost exclusively these days to replace himself as the Kotz household's lifeline. According to Yankel, who plainly worshipped him, since the Romanians' arrival the wine merchant had worked without ceasing; he ate on his feet and slept at his desk or in the cab of a truck that took him to every corner of Odessa, everywhere he'd stockpiled and hidden inventory—casks and cases underneath floors, behind false walls, tucked away in a few synagogues even. He'd lost some to theft and others to bombs but the bulk was intact; he'd been particularly lucky in his champagnes. When the city's freshly arrived ruling class called for a glass to celebrate (they disliked vodka, for a happy change) Falk was there.

So, as Musya saw it, to the fascist victors he supplied wine, and to the Kotzes he supplied Yankel Weissbein.

Three or four times a day Yankel's shy double knock signaled another delivery of milk, groceries, birdseed, sewing thread, sundries—and news. Without Yankel they might not have known anything. In this first week of occupation they hadn't ventured outside to be killed in the street. That others had, many others, they'd heard enough gunfire and screaming to know. Although they had electricity again the radio was dead in the absence of transmissions. Even so, the old man's mood was better than Musya had ever known it. This was more of Yankel's doing. He'd managed to supply some new medicines in green and brown bottles to nearly fill the dedicated shelf, save for the one Papa lay pouring sips from into his glass. His wife's jaw tightened and her nostrils flared whenever she raised her eyes to this sight. For now, she was restraining herself. Soon one of two things would happen: either she'd speak up, sharply, or Yankel's knock would sound first. They were sealed off from all other possibilities.

Or so they hoped.

Musya excused herself and returned to her packing.

Locked indoors, they'd nonetheless managed to wind up in a different place. Named for the land beyond the river Dneister and bordered by it on the west, the Transnistria Governorate was a wedge-shaped slice of Ukraine that had the Bug River for its eastern border, the Black Sea for its southern edge and Odessa for its future capital. The territory appeared to be Romania's reward for abetting the German fascist program; indeed, a lot of Romanians, close to twenty thousand of them, had died trying to conquer Odessa. As the victors took possession they also grabbed a certain measure of revenge against their prize and its population. They looted and pillaged and shot unlucky people—people unlucky enough to encounter them. The first few days and nights had been the kind of public murder spree which, according to Papa Kotz, was normal in war, very much to be expected.

Unfortunately, the Romanians hadn't come to this occupation so alone as hoped. Some of their German friends (or bosses, or rulers, or chaperones, nobody knew) were also along. Wearing lightning bolts on their black collars, fascist Germany's men moved swiftly with what appeared to be a single purpose. They killed Jews.

Where Musya planned to go next, what removal she was packing for with every exit sealed, she hadn't decided. Heading south by foot still teased her with possibility. She thought five or six weeks of walking might still remain within her power to do. But every step of the way—and how much more when the time came to stop!—she'd need strong, capable adults on hand to protect and care for her and the boys, and later the baby; she'd need rugged spirits, dogged fighters. Instead she had no one.

Consider Yankel Weissbein, whose poignant, tottering struggles with boxes that Baila Kotz hefted with ease had become a joke in the household, the young clerk overmatched by the tiny housewife and grandmother. Poor Yankel: he had brothers, some male cousins, too, she'd learned, but like the rest of his family they'd scattered. She'd questioned him about his friends, particularly the more athletic ones, but he didn't appear to have any. Nearly crowded out of his communal housing place by a large clan from Bessarabia who'd arrived sometime that summer, he slept in the kitchen on a cot he shared with the unmarried great-uncle, head-to-toe. Yankel said he didn't mind because it was only temporary. The Bessarabians had their eye on a much better place they planned to take over next. While Musya thought she could probably count on Yankel's devotion to her welfare, until he could defend his own corner of a room—or at least his own cot—she could only doubt his usefulness.

As for what she had to pack, a few sweaters and wool jackets completed their entire cold weather wardrobe. Boris had been sure they'd find better quality in Lublin so they'd left most of their winter clothes in Birobidzhan. Added in Odessa were the boys' sailor outfits and a few second-hand maternity smocks, the parting gift of a courtyard neighbor who'd left in August. A few pretty skirts blouses and dresses would fit along with the rather fragile shoes to match; she'd wear her walking shoes, the boys their fairly new boots. For towels and bedding they had what Boris hadn't taken: not much. Not for the first time, she eyed the good summer blankets presently humped on the bed where the boys lay fast asleep in a morning nap—they'd complained of noises in the night and hadn't slept well. Maybe the Kotz family owed Musya some blankets to replace what her husband, their son, had carried off to oblivion. These were Baila's blankets, though, and Musya wouldn't take from Baila. She didn't want Baila to have the satisfaction of an honest grievance.

Mother-in-law troubles made good conversation, Musya knew. Time and again she'd laughed along or groaned along with some beleaguered woman's story of her life as the bride to a living woman's son. Full of insult and injury, these were stories for telling, sharing, trading; the warmth of other women's sympathy helped heal the wounds recounted. Now here was Musya with one of her own—a megillah—and no one to tell. As follows:

A few nights before, in the darkest hour of the night, she'd been awoken by Papa Kotz blundering in, noisily confused, a shocking entrance. Baila called him back right away and he retreated; his wife was sending him to bed in his own room, the bedroom they shared. It occurred to Musya that he might have forgotten where it was. He'd left her door ajar. The panes of the transom light were burnished and pulsing with candle flames. Falk was in the front room. Musya felt a shock—she heard him sobbing. Then Baila's voice:

"Tell me again what you heard. Please—try to pull yourself together and just repeat, exactly—"

He choked, strangled: "Everyone, I told you, everyone!"

"Please—calmly."

"Calmly!" Passion and grief, Musya had realized, were wringing the wine merchant's throat. He let out a breath that sounded of saw blades. "Calmly, yes, calmly. Calmly, they came in the night and shot everyone in the sanatorium. They took them outside and shot every last one of them. Except for the ones too sick to get out of bed—them the bastards shot in their beds and threw the bodies out the windows. They're still there, bodies all over the garden. Do you understand me? My wife is dead—your sister is dead!"

"But." Baila Kotz started to argue. "How do you know this? How can anyone know this? If it was as bad as you say and everyone was killed, who was there to see it happen?"

"Of course there were witnesses."

"What witnesses? Who could even witness such a thing and not try to stop it? What kind of people are you even talking about? Witnesses—I don't believe a word from such witnesses, never!"

"My love," he said. "Please."

She burst out again: "It just isn't possible! Who would ever do such a thing?"

Up by now with her ear at the crack, cold in her bare feet, shivering, Musya bit down harder on the edge of her fist. With evident reluctance, Falk finally answered: "In this case, Germans. Some crazy outfit they call their Einsatzgruppen that goes around doing such things. Killing huge numbers of civilians. Mostly Jewish ones. And the sick, the afflicted, as a kind of sideline."

"But why?"

"Baila."

"It doesn't make any sense. I refuse to believe this—it's simply incredible! Who kills sick people in a clinic? This can't be."

"We've known this was coming." Musya's chin nodded: yes. She'd known. Roza had told her: *They want to exterminate us.* Roza had known—and the madman on the train, the one who'd seen Lublin. He hadn't been mad at all. He'd known what was coming. "Let's thank God." Heavy with sorrow, Falk's voice kept on. "It must have been over quickly for her. They moved fast."

"Nothing happened!" A whispered shriek: "Do you hear me? This didn't happen!"

And Falk hadn't been able to budge her. Baila's mind was made up. He'd even offered to go find and bring her the man who'd brought him the news, the man who'd heard it from a living witness; Baila wouldn't allow this, she didn't want that sort of man in her home. No: she wouldn't listen and she wouldn't believe it and she would not begin to mourn. "What should I mourn—why? And you shouldn't either," she'd said; Musya had heard this with sick horror, shaking.

"I don't have time to mourn," Falk had answered—truthfully, by Yankel's account. Odessa's busiest wine merchant hadn't found time to visit the Kotz household again, either. Appalled, Musya guessed, by his grief's reception and no doubt guilt-ridden, too, he stayed away.

Not far from Arcadia Beach, his wife lay dead on the cold ground. Murdered, unclaimed by her family, unacknowledged, unmourned, she lay shunned. Her name stayed unspoken. Pity for this dead stranger whose name she didn't know enflamed Musya's heart. Wild defiant fantasies possessed her. In life she became the woman's champion, her rescuer; in death, contriving to retrieve her corpse, she prepared it with her own hands for burial. She denounced Baila Kotz—that coward, that sick fantasist, that terrible sister, that cold-blooded adulteress—before witnesses, she said it all, kept nothing back. Towering speeches, rageful and tear-streaked, wound through her mind and repeated themselves from the moment she woke until far into the night; in fact she was surprised to have missed last night's noise, certain that she'd barely slept, half-doubtful that the boys hadn't dreamt it while she'd lain wakeful, drama-tossed. Her lips would purse, her breath race: there was a kind of pleasure in it, naturally, and a pull towards abandon. Whole phrases escaped her lips once or twice a day, at random, beyond her control. She was losing her mind.

It had to end. From a stack of her hostess's hand towels Musya took two and packed them. In her own home Baila Kotz was free to sit and knit and smile and hum and feed her finches as if nothing had happened. Musya wouldn't speak, she wouldn't speak because she was a guest and a daughter-in-law, dependent and much younger; from sheer tact she hadn't spoken, wouldn't speak. But she couldn't stay much longer because by degrees, unstoppably, the passing hours transformed the meaning of her silence from deference to moral weakness to collusion in the older woman's insane pretense, shared guilt she refused. Something had happened. If no one said so (and Musya couldn't) Baila would win and her sister rotting in the ivy bed would cease to be. And then? One death forgotten, erased, one body replaced by a figment: one and how many more? Which of them would be next? Breath burbled musically as Sender and Anton lay dreaming, sweet warmth rose from them. Musya studied their sleep-dampened curls for a few moments and then stole a bath towel.

She'd go to her parents first, of course, if only because they were the only people she could ask for money. In this newly capitalistic Odessa no less than in the Odessa before, it would take money to live. She had, as usual, none. With perfect clarity her mind's eye showed Musya a memory or a vision of her mother's long-fingered hand cradling a dense roll of chervonsty and roubles, small denomination bills stained and mostly tattered, the roll more like a wad of fabric scraps than a thing of any use; it was cash, though. Her mother hoarded it, she always had, never coins but paper money rolled up tightly and hidden in places some of which Musya's father couldn't have found, very secret and intimate places whose violation he'd never have dared, no matter how aflame to gamble, not he. Just enough to bribe her way into a temporary room and provisions and safe passage out for herself and their three grandsons: this Musya must have, she'd tell her parents. She was prepared to plead even tearfully—but not very. She'd keep her dignity, knowing her logic to be sound. Because when they considered, she'd explain, what she'd have earned for herself had she stayed in Odessa, she wasn't asking for the moon at all. In the two years since they'd forced her onto the train to Birobidzhan she'd no doubt have become independent; she might have married well; she might even have gained some kind of fame and prospered. If, instead, she was indigent, helpless and pregnant with her sister's husband's child, the fault was theirs and no one else's. Unless it was their idea to blame her for being too obedient? She hadn't wanted to go. And now, she'd tell them, if they refused to give her any money then they'd have to give up their second sleeping alcove to their daughter and grandsons; she'd leave them no alternative but that.

Another set of stretches to relieve the tension in her lower back worked even less well than the set before. She tried taking deep breaths and pacing, although there was barely room to take a step. More words unspoken: a hundred times by now she'd pictured the coming scene with her parents, fixing and perfecting every detail of her case, attacking every argument of theirs in too many undelivered speeches to count; only she could feel the weight of them, a cumulative drag. Her skirt and sleeves might have been hemmed with lead. If she'd only had one friend, one other woman to confide in and laugh with, her burden would have been immediately eased, Musya thought. Roza, Fanny, Kitty, even Magga: she missed them. The few letters she'd written them in Birobidzhan had received no reply. She berated herself for staying aloof from old connections since she'd been back in Odessa. Among The Geese she ought to have made a better effort, certainly, she should have found the nerve to come clean with them. With the widow Tsigal, too: for even to hear again about the mirror-like polish on the Liberator's riding boots, what a comfort! What's more, one of these friends might have given them shelter, a room, a corner, anything—a little corner in a room no bigger than this one would have been fine. But there was nothing.

She hadn't seen either of her parents in a month, not since the day of the shunning. Whether she'd be allowed by her mother to enter their home, yes or no, was a troubling question. A simple telephone call might have settled it, only her parents lived four houses down from the nearest telephone box to which her mother would have ignored a summons in any case due to her belief that spies listened and put everyone who used telephones under suspicion. Musya possessed one encouragement, though, a tangible hint that she might be welcome again in her old home. It had arrived by post about a week after their argument, addressed in her mother's handwriting but absent any note: a hard-bound book, the one from Moscow in which her schoolgirl poem appeared. It was heavy but she planned to pack it. Now, again, she opened to the facing page translation:

Кто будет любить меня?

Musya smiled, but sadly, as she considered that the hours she'd spent writing down a single Yiddish poem based on her childish looking glass romances might have been her life's most productive hours, if physical evidence stood as the standard of measurement. The plain truth was that she'd accomplished nothing further. A life more obscure than her own was hardly imaginable and yet she'd set her course for stardom, once. Here stood the record of her youthful dream, the string of handsome suitors each rejected bravely, firmly, in favor of a dazzling career; her plan for life announced in print, to state approval—the highest. For there he was among the opening pages, an appearance in two paragraphs by the General Secretary himself. Musya ran her eyes across his praise for this collection and these Young Soviet Poets, he'd predicted greatness for them. She'd planned to go far and instead she'd crashed. Now, from the wreckage, her girlish question echoed like an urgent cry:

Who, exactly who, would love her?

Love her enough, that is, to assume the part of savoir, protector, shelter-giver? If not her parents, if they shunned her still, then who? Penniless, married, accompanied by three young children—one inconveniently unborn—fathered by an unpopular man: how many suitors might she expect? Not enough to reject a single one, she thought grimly, packing the fat anthology away in her traveling bag along with the boys' favorite storybooks. Yankel Weissbein had supplied the newest of these, Jules Verne's tale set beneath 20,000 leagues of seawater. A Yiddish book from his own collection: she'd told him he was too generous; he'd blushed and run a hand through his lank brown hair—an unfortunate nervous habit, sparking the usual avalanche.

And yet, every person had flaws. As flaws went, furthermore, better a flaking scalp than a foul breath or a tendency towards gaseous wind; better dandruff than drunkenness, or wife-beating, or slothful disorder or an addiction to lottery bonds, Musya thought. Upper body strength was nice but no match for a kind heart in a man; when it came to really desirable qualities, she thought, a little shyness and a love of reading divided the better men from the brutes. No question, of all the men in Odessa she might have been opening the door to once or twice a day in this week of bloodshed and hazard, Musya was lucky that it was a man like Yankel Weissbein and not some bestial murder-minded degenerate; only, specifically, nice, polite Yankel, seventeen but mature for his age, Musya thought, and plainly, blushingly devoted to her. So he wasn't perfect, so he needed work: at any age, what man didn't? But with the right woman and family to care for, the right woman guiding, shaping, shampooing him, Yankel Weissbein might go far.

Her thoughts were on destiny when she heard the telephone down the hall start to ring.

This was almost unprecedented. The box hadn't worked since July except for one brief span, a few days at most, of frequent bells and long excited queues to call out. Musya remembered Papa Kotz as he'd been then, starting up at every ring to fix his myopic gaze at the flat door; panting, he'd gesture for silence. The knock never sounded, no calls came for their household. Then the service was gone again—until now. She heard the old man let out a loud, hoarse cry. The boys stirred but didn't wake as she hushed them, fixed their blanket. Curious, she slipped out, pulled the door shut behind her with a gentle click and turned to face the scene in the front room. The ringing was louder here.

"It's him! It's him!" Tremors of excitement muffling his shouts, Papa Kotz strained towards the door he couldn't reach—he'd tumbled halfway onto the floor again. "I tell you it's him! Answer it!" His wife's knitting lay on her chair in a neat green heap, she'd been knitting socks for Yankel with some nice wool he'd brought. The bell had caught Baila Kotz tending to her finches and appeared to have frozen her solid. To her husband's cries she was reacting not at all. One hand encaged in a flurry of blue and white feathers and bright orange beaks, Baila stood with her back to the door; then she jerked with a little scream as a furious pounding began. Somebody knocked with all his might. "Ah!" cried Papa Kotz. "I told you!" Now he noticed Musya and waved a commanding limb: "Answer it! Hurry!"

Already headed that way at her own pace, Musya sighed. "You know, your grandsons are asleep," she remarked in a fairly low tone soured by the knowledge that whatever she said would be ignored. She couldn't wait to be free of these people. The strange ringing continued and rose in volume as she turned the latch and pulled open the door: Yankel, naturally, but completely wild and unlike himself. The young clerk seemed ready to dash through and collide with her but he stopped on the threshold and started to shout, spewing words in her face, across her shoulder. *Never!* she thought. Incoherent with panic, disheveled, tear-stained, short, perspiring and smelly, shirt half-untucked, hair a greasy dusty mess, he looked about twelve except for the pimples she'd forgotten, this person she'd been picturing as a lover and life-mate not two minutes ago. *Never, never, never!* her mind roared now at the sight of him, leaving her a little dizzied as she excused herself to move past in order, her vague gesture explained, to go answer the telephone, she left him to continue his shouting inside the flat and drifted towards the bell.

The unswept hall was deserted, its vacancy amplifying the thumps and hurried footsteps behind the doors and partitions she passed. Her own thoughts amazed her. The shock of disillusionment gave way to relief—she felt she'd escaped herself. And poor Yankel, he'd escaped something, too, something dire in her. The fault of pregnancy, its unhinging hormonal effect, this had to have been, she decided, picking her way through some rubbish on the floor. She found herself remembering the times she'd been summoned to the box downstairs in Birobidzhan and forced to face the ever-present male population that lazed and smoked in its vicinity: always only Boris calling from the chair factory for some cause never so important as he'd claim. This bell she approached now sounded strange, cracked and uneven, a sick bell. The hallway stayed empty, no one else cared to answer it, Musya guessed. She lifted the receiver and spoke:

"Allo?"

All she heard was din, throbbing street noise. Engines and heavy wheels, a sea of them, whined and labored amidst a roar of human crisis. She heard sudden warnings, shouted commands, then a few loud sharp explosions, screams, panicked animals,

animals racing, windswept screaming, many children.

She'd heard enough and hung up. The telephone rang again instantly. Braced against fright, she held her hands clasped at her chin, held her breath. The instrument kept up the same crazed, blighted, ragged ringing as before. From what felt like an enormous distance away came a familiar voice raised in a querulous bellow: her father-in-law. Her eyes snapped wide open. Could the incredible truth be that he was right? Was this call coming from his son—from Samuel? Not alive, as Papa Kotz believed, of course not; but otherwise, and elsewhere, and connected by wires to them, telephoning from chaos, a dead man whose afterlife was a war zone. Cold terror shook her; even so, a simultaneous surge of resentment stiffened her posture. Once again these Kotzes had managed to land her in a mess. She'd never even met Samuel and now here she stood, a virtual stranger, about to bear the brunt of this haunting which he must have intended for immediate family alone. It was ridiculous. She wiped the sweat off her palms onto her smock.

Before she had the receiver halfway to her ear she heard the scream—a girl's, directly down the line, a piercing scream of agony and fear. The voice had a familiar quality and for a crazy split second Musya mistook it for her own, her voice, as if she were actually screaming in terror and hadn't realized it yet. But this was someone else whose scream continued in short high-pitched bursts; Musya could hear *pop-pop*-popping in the background, gunfire, between the pauses.

"Allo! Allo!"

Trying to shout into the receiver, she could barely make a sound. Now the scream turned deep and frenzied. The other snarled and howled as if she were struggling in the grip of a gigantic pliers; Musya pictured two machines, one to grip and one to tear off pieces. These screams, these were the noises she'd thought were coming from animals in the call before. This was torture, she realized. She heard a horrible rending of cloth, bone, sinews followed by a full-throated shriek and then a crack—she'd flung the receiver away from her. Having bounced off the wall it dangled around at the end of its cord for a few seconds, keening. Then the screams stopped. Musya reached down.

"Allo?" She held the receiver to her ear and tried again. "Allo?"

But the girl, the gunfire, the chaos were gone. The line appeared to be dead. Her pulse slowed slowly. From the Kotz household came the sounds of a typical commotion. Musya peered around the corner of the hallway at the entrance door which stood unlatched and outlined in a bright morning's silver. Needing a respite, she decided to go outside.

The front walkway was dusty, trash-strewn, half-hidden by dead leaves. Late October in Odessa she knew as a time of rich harvest scents and golden light. But today the nasty nose-wrinkling aftermath of a bad fire sickened an atmosphere otherwise close, glazed, oily. Mama Kotz's oblepikha bush had ripened on schedule, however. Luminous orange berry clusters tossed among its branches under a rattling assault of sparrows who cheered as they fed.

Trails of dusty sand snaked along the otherwise lifeless and empty street. Looking up and down, every building, every floor feigned vacancy but she sensed people everywhere, watching her. *Hiding,* she thought. An object in the gutter caught her eye and she went closer. It was a dead dog. Not a street mongrel but a pet, small with soft wavy brown and white fur, some kind of spaniel, she thought, killed by a motorcar. Blood stained its white muzzle. Although she wasn't especially fond of dogs, Musya felt heartsick. Someone would be brokenhearted, maybe a child had loved this little dog whose death had come with pain; now she wanted to cry. As she watched, one tan-colored curl rose and fell in a ground level breeze. Beneath her feet she felt rumbling—wheels approached.

Startled by a hissing noise at her back, Musya spun around to see its source gesticulating at her from the doorway of the Kotzes' building. She'd wandered further than she'd realized; now she hurried back as if in obedience to the stranger, a tiny gray old woman she'd never seen before who seized her, tugged her in across the sill, and shut the door behind them with almost comically surreptitious care for quiet. Then the old woman reached up and slapped Musya on the arm. She wasn't much bigger than Sender but her hands were like iron knots. Musya rubbed the sore place.

"Excuse me? Yes?" Then, remembering, she softened. "Was that—did you happen to lose a dog?" But there was no communicating with the other who kept up a furious hissing through gums without a single visible tooth, an old woman spraying wet wordless fury. Her state was dire: filthy, smelling badly of urine, clothed in a tattered assortment of various forms of feminine nightdress, children's winter wear and small men's suits. Seeping bandages wrapped her ankles and more bandages, brown with old blood, bound her swollen feet to a pair of mismatched slabs of wood, clumsily hewn from an old broken desk, it looked like. By no means did she resemble a woman with a lap dog; on the other hand, the world abounded in eccentric old women of unexpected means, Musya knew this very well. Now the stranger held a finger like a talon to her sunken lips, signaling Musya to hush. This was really the worst sort of person, a bullying old woman. "You hush," Musya told her. "You hush."

This earned her sore arm another slap and a hard shaking before the old woman sank into a crouch and fixed the street door with a look narrowed by apprehension. Her damp whiskers glistened. She was prepared to flee—where? Musya wondered. A woman looking so poor, dead dog or no, an old woman with no teeth to sell couldn't buy her way out of trouble. And she couldn't hide because anyone could smell her. This old woman had a future. It was no more uncertain than everyone else's future, really: what happened to her could happen to all of them, Musya saw. Any further she couldn't see. Outside, a collection of engines approached, wheel-borne on the rasping asphalt. The old woman hushed her and hushed her, kissed a quick blessing over her round pregnant belly and shoved her back from the door in the direction of the Kotzes' flat. Then she hurried over to the staircase and started climbing flights as fast as her bleeding wood-shod feet would take her, each step sounding down the stairwell like a rifle shot.

Back at the in-laws' flat, it was immediately apparent that Yankel Weissbein was fighting for his life. He straddled a small space before Papa Kotz's sofa, his arms spread, his face and neck flushed, his hair actually standing on end, and shouted at the old couple, clearly not for the first time:

"You must pack some things! We must go! Quickly! Please!" he added. But he'd lost Papa Kotz who, noticing his daughter-in-law's return, cried out:

"So? It's him? He's coming?"

Yankel answered in her place. "Papa, sir, there was no one, the lines don't work, I told you. This is only electricity, broken wires sending signals—please, get up and get ready, you must!"

"He's right," Musya told Papa Kotz. "There was no one, only noise."

He stared at her for a heartbeat or two. The truth was there, he saw; furious and bewildered, he wouldn't accept it. "You're lying! You didn't listen! You stupid tramp!" His wife, standing behind the sofa, threw her arms around his shoulders and wailed:

"Don't excite yourself, Papa!"

Rumpled and pale from sleep but listening alertly, the boys huddled by the bedroom door. Musya went to them, asking Yankel, "What's wrong? What's happened?" His brown eyes, she noticed despite herself, blazed like a romantic hero's—exactly like, even if the left lid drooped.

"We must leave," he said.

Sender Kotz explained: "The fascists are going on a rampage, Musya."

"Yes," she said. She'd packed almost everything. "We'll be ready in five minutes."

About twenty-four hours before this, on Engels Street, the Romanians' new military headquarters had exploded, a huge blast that took out their top general along with close to a hundred other souls. The night had been spent pulling bodies from rubble, a major operation loud enough to disturb young children in their beds two neighborhoods away. According to Yankel there were a lot of German naval officers mixed in with the Romanian military dead and other bodies, local civilians, cleaning ladies. The grand old building had previously housed Odessa's sizable and well-funded NKVD force. Now an entire wing of was gone: which was a terrible shame, Baila Kotz insisted, bemoaning the loss of such beautiful architecture, an ornament among the views from Alexandrovsky Park. Of course no one normal had gone any closer for years, at least not willingly; but the loss was a shame, and with the opera house in ruins, too, said Baila, really a tragedy.

Flitting between doorways, closets, and drawers the grandmother had assembled a thin pile of stuff on the dining table: a pair of gloves she'd never worn, a spare saucepan, some candles, string, a woven basket with a lid, a box of light bulbs. "But this is everything you should leave!" Yankel cried. He asked where she kept the suitcases. Warm clothes, food, water, essential things: these were his orders, to tell the Kotz family and limit them firmly, if necessary. Money and portable goods they could sell, any jewelry, any gold and silver they should bring. Falk had ordered Yankel to be firm and even to shout, he'd explained; but above all, to make sure they packed fast and moved speedily.

The reason for haste didn't matter a great deal to Musya. She felt any reason would do when it came to doing what should have been done weeks ago, months ago. They were leaving Odessa today, finally: good. She might never have questioned why.

But why was exactly what Baila Kotz wanted to know; and it wasn't enough to ask once, or ten times, or to hear an answer ten times more. She refused to be satisfied, no reason was good enough. What had it to do with them that a bomb had gone off across town and killed a bunch of misfortunate and mostly fascist strangers? Less than nothing, was the answer to her best calculation; through no fault of her family's had this happened. A loud grunt came from the direction of the sofa where the husband sat intent over note paper.

"Those shitheads, they know who did this—they just had the same thing happen to them in Kiev. Our bastards left the place ready to blow on a timer, *eyns tsvey dray* boom. Maybe this teaches them not to move into a secret police building."

"It's still a real shame," said Baila.

Intent on his single idea, Papa Kotz at first refused to leave the flat. But Yankel poured out an extra dose and persuaded him to write a note they'd leave for his hero son Samuel to find. Beyond his dog-eared clippings and his medicine bottles the old man claimed to have nothing to pack. He labored at this note, littering the rush carpet with crumpled drafts. Yankel he ignored except to press him for details:

"So? How far from Khosary is this place?"

It was to the young clerk's country cousins they'd head in one of Falk's delivery vans with Yankel at the wheel. A day's drive north would take them to obscure little village where the wine merchant was certain they'd be safe. Yankel said the place had a midwife, a good one, his aunt's friend; Falk had asked about midwives specifically. He'd thought of everything.

Almost.

"But he knows I hate the country!" Baila Kotz looked ready to weep at the prospect of her own sufferings from hay fever. Yankel told her it wouldn't be bad, the season was far advanced. Baila shook her head angrily. "That's when it's the worst, when the weeds dry out," she said. Alone, she was sorting jars and cans from the pantry closet into carriers, having refused all help with the task. Musya sat in the knitting chair for once and watched. She had an idea that she ought to rest every part of her body as deeply as possible right now. She'd packed everything she intended to take and so had the boys who, much like their grandfather, were using the time to quiz poor Yankel for details about their destination: they wanted to know about the village, the crops, the dances and costumes, the animals. Chickens, he said, there were many chickens, which pleased them. Baila scoffed: country chickens were poor ones, not the top varieties like they were used to; they'd see. "I'm sure this will all blow over in a day or two," she added. "I don't know why we need to leave at all."

"Please keep packing, Mama Kotz. Quickly," said Yankel.

The older woman raised her voice to pierce: "Can't you see that's what I'm doing? If only I had some help here!"

Musya closed her eyes; she'd rest them, too. A country village in winter: cottage roofs thatched with snow, windows rosy with firelight, work boots steaming on the hearth.

"Yankel." She spoke abruptly and looked at him. His shapeless mouth twisted at her. His eyes were perfectly round, terror-widened. "Yankel, when we leave here, on our way out of Odessa I'd like to stop and see my parents. Maybe—I think they might come with us." She watched him manage a smile.

"Oh, yes," he said. This was in the plan, Falk had specified a stop and a place for her parents, too, Yankel looked happy to assure her. "He thought of you, Musya."

Baila rejoined, "He thought of us all. Why he didn't think to come here this morning himself—that's the question."

"A daily visitor." Papa's tone was abstract. "No more."

"He has the inventory to protect," Yankel told them but the couple continued to gripe, almost as if they suspected Falk of being whimsical, hyperbolic, or simply in a rush to be rid of them; but this was their own pretense. No one could doubt the genuine urgency. With all the wrath they could muster, the occupying forces would rampage all over Odessa; the word for the day and the days ahead was reprisals. Officially the blame was being cast for the loss of blood, in the first place, on Communists. "And you're a party member, Papa, sir," Yankel reminded him.

This was true: Boris Kotz had boasted about it sometimes, Musya had never understood why. Denied his own membership, he'd claimed it was harder for Jews in his day than his father's. Now she watched Papa shrug. "That was for business." He sounded annoyed.

"But." Yankel gulped and cast a sidelong look down at Anton who sat on the floor singing number rhymes to himself, a strapped and buckled satchel clutched in both arms. Musya didn't know what he'd packed in there, Anton was being mysterious today. "But they won't stop with Communists."

"Of course they won't." Even Baila Kotz had to acknowledge a certainty. Today would be bad, tomorrow would be worse: these sorts of things, Falk had said, tended to get out of hand. His clerk had never known him to be wrong, not once. Baila laughed at that; but she was packing. From her husband came a cry as he crumpled another sheet of notepaper and threw it to the floor where it bounced into a corner. He didn't know what to write, he shouted, he couldn't think. She soothed him brusquely: "Just say *Inquire Khosary*. We'll leave word there—it's the best we can do, Papa."

"And," said Musya, "you should address it to my husband, too—you can write, *To Samuel or Boris*. He might come home first, you know."

Behind the thick lenses Papa's eyes blinked rapidly. Then he quivered all over and said, "Ah, yes, good idea."

Baila Kotz started to hum. Having arranged all her bags by the flat door, she turned to the first of her three great finch cages and went to unhook it. The rest of them looked at Yankel, who was drawing breath like a racer preparing for competition. An outburst of liquid birdsong filled the room. The rest of them looked at the old man who finally cleared his throat.

"Mamaleh, I don't think—"

"Of course I'm bringing my babies—you can't think I'm leaving them!"

Without further hesitation Yankel Weissbein dashed across the room to the window, fumbled briefly at the lock and flung it open wide. Then he wrestled the cage from Baila's hands, tore the wire door off its hinges, tipped the cage outside and shook it, banging it against the sill. Now the room echoed with screams: the finches', Baila's, Anton's—the clerk, too, was screaming as Baila pounded her fists against his back and tore at his head with her fingernails. Musya called Anton until he rushed to her embrace, he hid his face against her chest which stung, her breasts were sore. In the confusion of freedom a few birds had flown back into the room and Sender was on tiptoe with his hands up trying to catch them. Still under attack, Yankel grappled with the empty cage which knocked hard against the window frame, he couldn't get it back inside. From his sofa, Papa Kotz kibitzed:

"Drop it on the ground, stupid—just let go!"

But a final tug produced the cage and all Yankel's weight with it. He reeled back from the sill, knocked a shrieking Baila to the floor, stepped on her hand accidentally, then stood helpless, panting, as she wailed and rolled back and forth. She rolled onto her side.

"Mama, don't," her husband told her. "You can get more birds. They're everywhere." At which Baila sat up with a viscious scream and called him an alteh kaker. They were both right, thought Musya, watching Sender approach and kneel beside the grandmother. He was a kind person.

"Bobeh, don't cry."

The clerk touched his shoulder. "Help me," Yankel said.

"Yes," said Musya. "Help Yankel."

With the extra pair of hands the other caged finches were soon evicted. A few strays still beat their brilliant blue wings against the corners of the ceiling while a few more darted back and forth through the open window and voiced inquiries. Their mistress lay sobbing on the floor. Yankel Weissbein bent over her, pleading:

"He told me to do it! I swear to you—he told me I had to dump the songbirds, he said there was no choice. But look—look, Mama Kotz." He hurried to empty a bag of seed onto the floor beneath the window. "We'll leave it open," he said, moving to help the sobbing woman rise; but she twisted away from him. Another five minutes passed very painfully for everyone present as cool air filled the room.

At last Baila sat up, nursing her fingers, making a hesitant fist. "You've broken my hand," she said.

"If you can do that," said Papa Kotz, "it's not broken."

Musya was thinking warmth might become a problem; so too the means to procure it. Of silver or gold she possessed not a molecule. The wedding ring provided by Boris when she'd refused to accept the gold band from her sister's dead finger was what he'd called a "modern alloy" and weighed as much as a few feathers; he'd put the other in his wallet to keep. Baila Kotz, by contrast, wore fine rings and owned several more, also bracelets, brooches; the neighbors had talked of some notable pearls, Musya remembered. A present not from her husband, they'd said. Into her mind sprang a sudden image of her mother-in-law's slim hands with their many and impressive rings plunged to the wrists in the wine merchant's bristling gray beard.

She frowned. Falk was old, even extremely old but still handsome, exceptionally handsome, she'd always thought so; he was a widower now, too, his life had changed. *He thought of you, Musya*, she remembered. Maybe his old habits had grown distasteful to him lately and maybe as this happened—as inevitably it must with the stale habits of a man whose mind and flesh remained vigorous—his thoughts had turned elsewhere, maybe to a younger woman, a connection by marriage, for instance; an attractive young victim of the worst luck so far yet still full of spirit, admirably so. Of course this might have happened, Musya thought, and felt herself tremble a little as she stood to leave the Kotzes' flat for the last time. Had there been clues? Something in the wine merchant's words, in his glances? Sadly she'd always been too distracted to notice his deeper intentions, if so—of course her simple artlessness might have charmed him most of all. Bags in hand, she turned and gave the front room a parting look of slightly regal fondness.

"You forget something?" said Papa Kotz, and nudged her past the threshold when she shook her head. Hid note to the dead man lay atop the console radio, the customary place, she'd gathered.

The boys had their small bundles, too. And Sender Kotz, she noticed, was also struggling to manage a hatbox by its strings: "Papa's dishes," he explained. Musya rolled her eyes. The Manchukuo samples, of course. It was typical. Her husband, nowhere to be found, gone without a word; evidence of his doomed investments, always to hand, inescapable. On the verge of telling his son to leave the box behind she stopped herself. Even now it might be possible to sell these dishes—or barter them, if it should come to that. Something of their own, apart from the Kotzes' stash; Baila had assured her husband nearly a dozen times by now that she'd brought everything, the jewelry box, gold, all the cash. He was restive, coughing and throaty, shifting from foot to foot, unused to standing, Musya realized. They waited behind the front door of the building while Yankel fetched the truck that he'd concealed in an alleyway. Papa complained of the wait and his wife snapped at him to stop; then she wept afresh, refusing Papa's handkerchief. He ran the handkerchief over his face and recurred to the previous scene:

"Who are you calling an alte kaker? What does that make you, then—eh?"

Musya was shaking her head at Sender to discourage one of his helpful answers when a harsh blasting noise filled the stairwell. High up near the skylight someone peeked down at them and hushed them as loudly as could be. Recognizing the old wood-footed bully, Musya waved a satirical salute and saw another wet cautioning hiss descended through the pale daylight like a Novyi God streamer.

Baila Kotz, her tears evaporated, hissed back and fluttered her rings with rude derision. "Trash," she remarked. "That's what lives here now. Trash from the worst shtetls in Bessarabia. I'm not sorry to be leaving—really, how could I be?" And she snorted at Musya's objection:

"She's only trying to warn us, to keep us safe. She thinks it's dangerous outside."

"Is it?"

Sender sounded more enthusiastic than afraid. How bored he must have been, the thought struck her—how bored they'd all been! Cooped up in that flat for what felt like forever, faced day and night with the same handful of faces all growing steadily paler, the same fabrics getting dingier, the same smells gaining pungency, they were fleeing the familiar turned hateful and, yes, dangerous. It was dangerous inside that flat, bad for their health and sanity, they all sensed it. The unknown felt safer.

Then Musya remembered the dead spaniel. "It's a little dangerous but you've got all of us to protect you," she told the boys. "Just don't wander off, whatever you do. Stay with me."

The little brother stamped his foot and declared, "I want to go in the tunnels! I want to go with the fighters in the tunnels and fight!"

"You can't fight, you're too young!" the elder snapped. "You think the resistance wants you? They don't!"

"Yes!" Anton insisted. They both needed more sleep, really. Musya tried changing the subject:

"What's in your satchel, Anton?"

"Mine! My dynamite!"

"Liar!" Sender cried.

A hurried knock startled them all and Yankel reappeared, red-faced and out of breath, his hands making signals for quiet. A GAZ-AA from Falk's delivery fleet was idling out front. "You took long enough," said Papa Kotz.

"Everyone," the clerk answered, "please make as little noise as—"

Anton broke in. "Yankel, I'm going in the tunnels to fight, drive me to there."

"I'm going there myself, sweetie," Yankel whispered. "We'll go and join the underground together, stick with me. But right now we're going to be quiet as a mouse— all of us," he added, peering at them through his frazzled eyebrows with a warning frown for each. "Please be careful." This was superfluous. The deserted street at his back crawled with rapid gunfire bursts and screams of pain and fear, some distant, others less so. Without a doubt, in the hour since Musya had stepped out of doors the current local situation had deteriorated—but for whom?

"Are there so many communists left here?" Musya wondered half to herself. She'd thought most of them must have left on the transports weeks ago.

Papa Kotz said, "Maybe it's our partisans, maybe we're fighting back for once."

"No," said Yankel. "No."

"Then I don't think." Quavers deepening her voice, Baila Kotz stepped back from the door, she was ready to stay now, she'd changed her mind, no matter how many penniless Bessarabians life threw at her, she'd rather return to her flat, close the windows, lock them, lock everything; she backed up and babbled until her heels met the bottom board of the staircase and she sat down on a step with a small thump. From there she watched, gasping, as her husband with an enormous noise of breath hoisted two carrier bags in either fat white hand and strode outside with them.

The sight of Papa Kotz exerting himself had a galvanic effect: Baila caught up an armful of things and dashed after him with Anton, eager to stash his precious satchel, almost at her heels. Grabbing more bags than he could carry, Sender set off at a strenuous shuffle.

Musya and Yankel Weissbein were left alone by the front door. She had an idea that he'd planned it this way. She watched him run a hand through his sweat-dampened hair, watched the fresh dandruff sparkle. She prepared herself to hear him make a declaration to her. He said, "This, now—they're killing Jews now. It—I'm sorry. Today could be a massacre."

"Yes." She felt a tickling feather-brush of horror that her disappointment swallowed whole. "Of course," she said. She tried to catch her breath which had left her. She felt foolish, too, and pained, a little bruised by anticlimax; knowing that she shouldn't be feeling any of this, she'd begun to feel guilty as well. Gray splotches swam across her eyes and she heard herself ask, "Do you really think so?" He could only nod: of course. Trying to ease his way with a flattering tone of voice, she'd probably shocked him. Now she had to sigh. What he'd just told her sat between them and loomed like a large pile of boxes over which she was expected to exclaim at its size or wonder aloud what the boxes contained; when she didn't care. She didn't want to know that she might be killed at any moment, guesswork of this kind did her no good, it was unhelpful. Who would love and protect her? One simple answer, a name, maybe a vow, was all Musya sought. A spasm of irritation at Yankel's role in their present misunderstanding prodded her ribs from within. But why blame? What had she expected? "When I was seventeen I thought everything was a big drama, too," she told him. Already the others were hurrying back for their second loads.

Papa Kotz eyed her. "You can't carry?"

"I can carry," she said, hefting her old traveling bag.

"Mumeh Musya." Sender tugged her sleeve. This was his emergency voice. "There's a doggie—I think he's hurt."

"Ah. Yes," she said. "That doggie has seen better days. I'm sorry."

A gray canvas tarpaulin raised on a frame covered the truck bed where Musya would sit with her nephews, her back to the cab, on a featherbed among the luggage piles. She preferred it this way, she told Yankel, who was uneasy with the arrangement. Falk had told him to put Papa in the back but Baila wouldn't have it, she wouldn't let Papa out of her sight. The boys preferred it too and Musya felt comfortable, she felt fine, she felt really well, unlike the old man whose blood pressure, he said, was in the stratosphere. Warm and almost better than well, she felt, to think that the wine merchant had given thought to her personal comfort. Yankel lingered beside the truck, retying the tarpaulin string nearest her shoulder. They wouldn't suffocate. On either side between the canvas and the truck bed walls ran open strips of view; but they should stay low. He apologized again for not being able to seat Musya in the cab; she told him again not to worry, he wasn't responsible for the selfishness of his elders. They were whispering but she hoped Baila heard this. Yankel frowned wildly at a point near his left elbow and said, "I may be only seventeen but I have the feelings of a man."

She answered quickly, "Of course you do." Sender added that he, also, had the feelings of a man.

"Pashli—pajalsta," grumbled Anton. The manliest of all of them, Musya thought, he was impatient with their Yiddish feelings. Her ears, sorting all the while through volleys of gunfire, judged the worst to have increased in nearness and intensity. Anton was right: they should go.

All at once a jarring fusillade approached at terrifying speed and was upon them. Musya drew back with a cry and raised her arms. Then she recognized the old woman with wood on her feet, she was making a wild rush on them. Yankel stood in her way and got shouldered aside with startling force; now the old woman seized the side of the truck bed in her dark yellow talons and pulled with all her might as if to tear it off altogether. It flashed through Musya's mind to suppose that the average motor vehicle in Bessarabia might tend towards decrepitude and be fairly easily dismantled by human strength alone.

"She can't come! What is she doing? There's no room! Tell her there's no room for her in here!" In the truck cab they sounded outraged.

"Little mother, don't hurt yourself." Yankel Weissbein was trying to reason with the frenzied old woman. "Stop this, tell us, what do you need?"

Her, it transpired, when the GAZ-AA stayed stubbornly intact: Musya. She wanted Musya to stay, she wanted to rescue her and prevent her from leaving. Tears poured down the dirt-creased face in grimy sheets as she wailed—but so quietly! She was still being careful not to make noise as she implored Musya to get out of the truck, to come back inside, to stay, to avoid danger.

To Musya, staring back at it over the old woman's head, the entire block already looked like a model in miniature, a segment from a city on a tabletop built for imaginary occupants. Squinting more closely at the corner property in which she'd been trapped with her in-laws since June—an entire war so far—she was surprised that she'd never noticed its exact resemblance to a box packed full of ant poison. She'd never go back inside that place; her head shook back and forth: no. "No. I'm sorry," she said. The old woman lowered her face into her withered hands and wept. Accompanied by the sound of someone leading a tired cart horse, Yankel helped her back from the curb to the front door.

"Some farewell party," said Papa Kotz.

Yankel Weissbein marched straight back to Musya. He spoke. "Remember what I said."

"To keep our heads down, yes," she answered.

"No, I meant. When I—what I said. As a man." Two lightning sheets of green-gold fire flashed—his brown eyes had depths.

Musya said, "Oh, yes. Yes." She reached to touch the young clerk's hand—his eyes were truly admirable—and pressed it with her own; as she did she felt her racing heart with perfect timing give a leap into winged flight. Her outlook improved magically. Here, just now, a little late, was Yankel's declaration; while there, a little too absent, stood the handsome and powerful Falk, directing special care her way. Giddy, she caught a glimpse of what could be: master and man, age and youth, battling for her favors.

Anton groaned. "Pashli!"

(12)

The truck bed vibrated and rattled, the grinding gears made jolts, the wheels bounced on their shrieking axles as if the roads were paved with jagged teeth. On a few occasions during Musya's summertime idyll with Leon Flohr she'd ridden with him in trucks making mysterious deliveries. That had been pleasant but this would be awful, no featherbed on earth was thick enough to make a difference. Resentment of Baila Kotz deepening on pace with her developing nausea, Musya tried to wedge herself more firmly between nephews, luggage, some carrier bags. In the dusky light beneath the tarpaulin the boys' eyes gleamed; they'd been starved for changing views too long and now they were gorging. Two neat russet-colored heads bobbed and swiveled and floated too high. "Down," she told them, sparking gripes.

This wasn't their only disappointment. Trucks went too slowly, Anton complained, slower than walking. At points he was right. When he could, Yankel drove fast, but only in bursts. The main streets appeared to be full of obstacles and outright obstructions. Several times, engine squealing, the truck crept backwards to passed-over turnings and took them instead. Clamor and shooting were constant, sometimes off to the right, then the left. Their route stayed evasive.

From another short shady cobblestoned lane—mercifully short, Musya's shaken brain stuttered—they emerged onto a broad tree-lined thoroughfare. From her luggage nest she couldn't see below the second floors of the buildings which were grand in the Odessa style, grand like Paris, people said, nor above the lower branches of the trees, still leafed in spots. In floods of light the golden leaves were dancing. Musya raised her head to peek, she risked it, and thought she recognized old Vorovskogo Street. She'd shopped here, could picture a coin purse she'd bought here: long since emptied, long gone. But the street endured, the sandstone balustrades of its deluxe flats festooned with straggling geraniums. Elegant streets such as this had planted and nurtured desires in her that events hadn't satisfied. That she'd been a citizen of the Soviet Union the entire time hadn't helped. Being married to Boris Kotz had simply added a layer of disaster. Yet if cities and countries could change hands overnight, a woman's life could change course. She was only twenty-one. Who knew but that she might not return to this street one day with a man—a wine merchant, perhaps—at her elbow and keys to her dream rooms on a ring.

When the truck veered further from the curb, Musya could see a few facades. At one window a young woman holding a liquor bottle slouched in a bright red wrap, makeup smeared, dye job poor, a blond against nature. Next door, men mixed military sand tones with their partners' garish print dresses on a crowded balcony where they were all craning their necks at some sight down the block. Musya heard a piano. These people weren't fleeing Odessa, they weren't hiding among its back streets and catacombs. Possessed of the good flats, they put on a show of it. They were, Musya realized, the winners here. Sinking back among the carrier bags (one of which had already started to split, the corner of a tin of sprats in oil was pushing through) she raised her eyes to the collective riches of the turning leaves. Life in the countryside—for a season, a year, two years, why not?

Picking up speed, the truck barreled into a wide intersection. There it braked hard to a shuddering stop. Boys, bags, heaps skidded forward in compressed confusion. Musya's head took a bump on the cab's back window frame; the nephews' two were fine, her fingers checked. In the cab Papa Kotz was moaning—was he injured? Dying? But his wife's voice sounded hollow not with shock or grief but fright:

"No! No! No!"

Traffic continued to race past. Over an uproar of motors and horns laced with sirens and screams came quick shuffles of machine gun fire. A tap on the cab window: Yankel, white-faced, signaling through the dust-gray glass: *Down*. Then his hand across his eyes and a slow headshake: *Don't Look*. Musya nodded. As the truck edged forward, she slid down to lie as flat as she could and settled her nephews close on either side, saying to shut their eyes tight and pretend it was bedtime. Naturally they bargained: in exchange for compliance, a hero brothers story, a new installment they demanded right away.

Musya nodded and began. "One day, Jim and Tom were exploring for new caves." Just then the truck wheels jumped and jolted over a hard obstruction, at which the split-sided carrier bag gave up the spirit and spilled its contents across her legs. "Stay down," she ordered. One glance, once she could finally sit up far enough to see past her own abdomen, sufficed to reveal the situation: her legs were half-buried in cans. Smoked fish, mainly. There was nothing she could do about it now.

She glanced through the gap and there was a man floating above the road, three or four meters away, she could see his striped pants cuffs, his pale blue socks, his polished oxblood dress shoes, defying gravity—an authentic wonder. Curious, she leaned a little closer to the gap only to see another levitator pass, this one in rough brown trousers that were stained and torn open to show bloody knees, black blood; this one hadn't left the Earth to its own rotation so effortlessly as the first. She had a confused notion that both men were capitalist scientists whose conquest of weightless flight—an awesome discovery, truly an attainment to the power of ancient gods—gave them command of the scene and of all the people on this stretch of road, at least, if not throughout Odessa. The next flying man to appear had lost his pants entirely, lift-off had stripped them down to his ankles from which they hung inside-out like a rotten peel. The bare legs, still as ivory, were splashed with ink-black hair that grew denser as she dipped her head to see it thatch and curl into a cushion for a manhood thick, purple, half-concealed by a shirttail. Musya's eyes grappled with this sight as it receded. Immediately in front of her now was a dead woman dressed for work on a cooperative restaurant serving line who'd been hanged by her neck from a streetcar wire with her own uniform belt.

A sharp elbow nudged and Sender asked, "What happened?"

"No! Stay down, don't—nothing happened. Keep your eyes closed." She could see they hadn't looked, hadn't seen, but she covered Sender's face with her folded shawl. Wool-muffled, he went on:

"In the story, Musya, what happened? They went exploring for new caves, you said."

"They found one," she answered quickly, "very deep." Far below everything, her lips continued, the deepest cave they'd yet discovered was full of flowers. They grew from the rock, profuse without sun, a cave garden of thick freckled colorless petals and leaves—the color of rocks—and honey-scented, fertilized with everything that drained down deep, seeping from Odessa's heavy body. The cave flowers stirred and all together turned their pale blooms towards Tom's lantern flame.

She began to vomit and barely reached the side before she could spew over it. Small cans tumbled everywhere in the truck bed. Crushed between the metal and her choking bulk, poor Anton kicked and struggled. Finally she spat, wiped her mouth on a sleeve, and stole a glance up the road ahead, then another behind at the tracks that partnered the parallel wires of her old streetcar line. Dead hanging bodies were strung up along the route as far as she could see: she could have counted dozens. Under a few, the living had collected to lament, to howl, to clutch dead ankles, to collapse and huddle in the road. Most were unattended. Clearing the panicked sidewalks like some great segmented insect came a line of men with stepladders.

"I can't breathe!" Anton used his fists now. His face was cherry red. She apologized and reached to gather him to her aching breasts—almost in time. He dodged her and spotted something, legs bleeding through long underwear most likely. "What's that?" he cried.

She caught and pulled him back, saying, "Nothing." Conjecture came in hot breath to her collarbone:

"Malokhim!"

Angels—this was almost to laugh at. "No."

"Where? I want to see!" Excited and curious, Sender reached for the shawl. "Where are they?"

"No! They're only traffic guards," she insisted. "Boring. But we can't look at them, if we look they'll get angry and they might stop us. We have to keep going—don't look!" She settled Anton beside his brother and covered both their heads with the shawl. "Don't you want to hear about the cave flowers?" They did but grumbled anyhow, for they liked the sight of guards. Thinking of the peppermint balls she'd stashed away weeks ago, Musya turned to reach for her bag and caught sight of something outside that made her stare.

A woman, a very small one, had been hanged fully clothed in costume. An odd costume, it featured a structured bodice atop an old-fashioned mermaid's tail skirt and it looked familiar. Musya puzzled over the blue bead-trimmed fabric and then she recognized the style, the cut: absolutely, this was one of her mother's dresses—definitely one, that is, of the dresses her mother had sewn and her father had sold to a client, one of his miserly age-shrunken old women who now, still wearing it, hung there in the weak sunshine, tiny and terribly stretched, with one foot stuffed in a house slipper and one foot bare, yellow and blue. It was so very familiar, Musya thought she herself and not her father might have sold this dress, years ago; she even thought she recognized the widow Tsigal whom she had failed to visit. But the purplish dead features wouldn't come clear no matter how she strained her eyes before face, dress and woman had passed out of sight, gone behind the next victims. The slipper had looked new.

"The cave flowers turned their heads all at once towards the light," she continued in a firm voice. "And Jim was so surprised that he dropped the lantern on the ground."

"It was Tom's lantern—not Jim's, Tom, his lantern," Sender complained. "I want to look!" Anton, too, he wanted to see more angels.

"No looking. Tom dropped the lantern." She paused as the story paused to choose direction. Did the lamp oil spill and catch fire, were the hero brothers quickly surrounded by kerosene flames—or was the one flame snuffed, leaving them in total darkness? Would there be conflagration in the garden, the cave flowers aflame, twisting in agony, uprooting themselves from the rocks, fleshy petals blackened, burst stem walls piping on the boil? Or lightless limitless blackness and a rustling in the hollow chill, rustling that would become a rushing wave of sound and overpowering sweet, sweet scent as the lonely, carnivorous cave flowers advanced?

Musya didn't know, she couldn't decide. She lay back in the truck bed. At the next slight curve the full sun fell behind the hanging bodies and cast their shadows one by one across the tarpaulin roof—eyns eyns eyns—as if through fence palings. In the truck cab Baila Kotz's voice sustained a single wailing note, a violin and siren hybrid. The lantern shattered, what came next? And why hadn't she paid a polite call on the widow Tsigal as her Daddy had told her to, weeks ago, when she could have done it easily? The old woman might have waited, expecting her visit, might even have laid in some chocolates for old time's sake. Seized by regret, Musya Kotz kicked restlessly at the juddering cans. The future was changeable, no outcome was certain; a single day, an hour, one action, one remark dropped however carelessly inside the past could change everything. A timely kindness might have tinkered with the clockwork of all time to come and prevented the worst from occurring—but she'd withheld kindness. "The lantern broke," she said, "and the flame—"

Sender nudged her with his knee. "But you said they had electric torches."

"Did I?"

"Yes." He sounded less puzzled than exasperated. "From the crate."

"What crate?" She was mystified.

But Anton also remembered. "You know. From America."

The Americans—she'd forgotten all about them. They were allied with the Soviet Union in the war. This was supposed to have helped but didn't appear to be helping. She still didn't recognize the crate. "Tell me," she said. Shouts came from the road as Yankel made a sharp turn; the tires jolted over the tracks again and they entered a side street. The plot filling her ears with unsequential detail was barely familiar. Of course, sometimes the boys took the telling of the Jim and Tom saga upon themselves and sometimes her attention wasn't the closest. She wondered what else she'd missed. She felt grateful, in any case, to the United States of America for the electric torches with which both heroes were equipped. A deep breath, and she was able to begin again: "So Tom switched on his torch—"

"Jim! Jim's torch! Tom's is broken."

She really frustrated them sometimes. She pulled both boys closer as the truck bed bounced and banged hard enough to make the heavy luggage jump. Gears pounding, not braking at all, they raced through the foul smells of a tannery precinct and then left, right, down narrowing streets lined with low, poor, crumble-roofed dwellings. Geese raged in a long yard. The cave flowers proved friendly and hardly more carnivorous than Jim and Tom themselves, really. They spoke Yiddish, Flower Yiddish, Musya explained. Intrigued by the ways of humankind, and maybe grown a little bored with life in their lightless cave, the flowers were eager, once they'd learned of its existence from the hero brothers, to join the war above, lending what help they could to Odessa's underground resistance. Suitable for service on many sorts of missions, these versatile and fragrant allies could, for instance, disguise themselves as congratulatory bouquets and upon delivery to various high-ranking officials among the city's fascist conquerors, devour their recipients.

Here the ride turned too rough for storytelling. Down one dark, stenchful alleyway after another the rattling truck pitched as Yankel sped steadily. Rotten plaster mapped with stains streamed past. At the first open spot the truck slammed to a halt. People were near, voices, activity on a poor street. Musya's stomach was heaving from the sudden stop. She looked for some water. Yankel came out from the cab and spoke, amazing her:

"We're here, Musya. Your parents' house."

A wild survey showed her nothing familiar—almost nothing. Obscurity and mud: "How on earth did you find it?"

"I know every street in Odessa and every suburb." Pride made him blush. "It's my talent."

A great one, she told him. Falk's sending Yankel to drive made perfect sense now, because a more out of the way corner to live and grow up in she couldn't imagine. Had the street always been so narrow? A thin crowd seemed like a throng passing. Panicked and hurried, struggling for footing, shouting and shoving to make way for its babies, its old folks, its bundles and handcarts heaped with suitcases, a population squeezed past— no one she recognized. Who were these people? They eyed the truck, showing teeth, desperate and covetous strangers. Yankel helped her down onto the muddy road and across to the door of the little house where she promised to hurry. He returned to guard the steering wheel. She hoped neither parent would have much to pack.

Except for the drunkard in the cellar, once a soldier, who remained to moan the refrain of his eternal marching song, the house appeared abandoned. Newspaper sheets, cabbage leaves and all sorts of rubbish choked and slickened the little staircase up to her parents' room. She picked her way carefully, in time to the cracked old voice coming through the floorboards. *The Red Army is the strongest*, she didn't think so, feeling chilled. Her parents had left Odessa without her, she thought.

But a call came in answer to her knock and Musya stepped inside. She paused by the door. The mother was sitting at her work table, not sewing but reading, she held a sheet of paper in her hand.

"Oh, it's you," she said.

They looked at each other. Musya thought her mother might be quite breakable, she was so emaciated. Neatly combed and dressed and deathly thin, she sat reading old letters. With an unpleasant sensation, Musya recognized her sister's handwriting, black and spiky. "That's my greeting?" she said.

The mother frowned. "What brings you here? I've shunned you, Musya, I told you this."

"If you shun me so much then what made you send me the book with my poem?"

"Because I don't want it here. I don't have room for it, as you can see."

Musya glanced around at her old looking glass, her old bookshelf, quite full, her old things taking up space around the curtained sleeping alcoves. "So you couldn't send my gramophone? That's much bigger."

"You want the gramophone? Take it."

"I do want it."

"Then take it," said the mother.

"What's wrong with you! What makes you hate me?" She raised her hands to her face and realized that she was clutching a can of sprats, Swedish, in oil. "Mommy, tell me. What did I do so wrong?"

A sigh. "Musya, you're too excited, sit down."

"I can't sit down, there isn't time—where's Daddy? We have to go, please, I have—there's a truck outside, we're going to the country. Please, get your things, only what you'll need, warm things, food. Daddy, come, get up!"

Nothing happened. "He's not here," the mother said. "And I'm not going anywhere until he gets home."

"So when will that be? Where is he?" A shrug, another. "When did he leave?"

"Six days ago. He went to get food. It was lunchtime, he was hungry." Her mother glanced again at the letter in her hand, its closing lines plucked a slight smile from her features before she folded and returned it to its faded blue envelope. "He found one of his old women to take him in and feed him Turkish delight, no doubt. He'll be home soon enough. You're free to wait."

Musya's breath got shorter as the room began to buzz. Six days. She thought of Falk's visit, Falk's wife. Six days ago the Romanians and their Einsatzgruppen friends had just arrived in town. It would have been a bad day to go shopping—so bad, it didn't seem possible that anyone with a brain, especially one in a Jewish head, would have attempted such a thing. She moved across the room; her hand reached up and drew aside one sleeping alcove curtain and then the other, pepper-patterned one; she moaned at vacancy. Immediately she began to listen for her Daddy's footstep on the stairs, any second now it was bound to come, he'd be picking his way through the filth and probably exclaiming in a mild undertone at the waste of good cabbage; already the wait was unbearable. Six days the mother had had of this wait. As for the shopping he hadn't brought back with him—she looked around.

"Have you any food here?"

"I don't need food."

This was where Anton got his stubbornness, inherited, exactly from this woman. "Mommy, get up and get your things together and let's go, we have to leave right now." She looked for a traveling bag and found one under a bed, dragged it out and swatted at the moths that rose from the carpet sides. "Here—what do you need?" Her mother hadn't moved. "Please, Mommy, don't you understand? You can't stay here, you can't wait for Daddy any longer. There's a massacre outside—it's reprisals."

"It's a pogrom," said the mother. "Be accurate, Musya. This is a pogrom."

"It's—what? You know?"

"Of course I know. I have ears and a window, I know what a pogrom sounds like. Here we are." She smiled an especially bitter smile. And Musya, noticing the black gap where a tooth had been, was struck by its actuality. Her mother was no longer young. Her mother was mortal. Her mother was right: here they were, in the present moment.

"Please come with us." Her childhood voice, she couldn't help it. "Please, Mommy."

The mother refused, almost gently, still firmly. "No. You go along. Take care of my grandchildren."

"Come be with your grandchildren! And your daughter—your living daughter and her baby, too—we all need you. Come take care of us."

"Don't be silly. And Musya, whatever you do—don't die in childbirth. Please, for my sake. And yours. My aunt died in childbirth and it's the worst death for a woman, so painful and such a waste."

"Yes." She remembered now this great-aunt, this story; the memory had been absent from her mind but it was all coming back to her.

"Promise me."

"Yes, Mommy, I promise not to die in childbirth." Desperately she added: "You should come, Mommy, and be there to help me when—I mean, I won't die if you're there, Mamenyu."

"I couldn't do you any good. What do I know? I sew terrible dresses."

"Did you know, Mommy, they're hanging people from the streetcar wires? Women, too?"

"It doesn't surprise me."

"I don't want you to stay here—I don't want someone to take you and hang you from a streetcar wire."

With a last shrug, the mother turned back to her work table. "Hanging is quick. It's not as bad as what happened to your poor sister."

"But Liza died in bed, with her family beside her—she was so ill, Mommy."

"No. Before. What killed her."

"Tuberculosis killed her," said Musya.

"Betrayal killed her." Emaciated hands ran across the heaped letters as if the mother kept reading with her palms. "Your sister was a woman of faith."

Outside a horn bleated: Yankel. This was taking too long. "Mommy, let's talk about it on the way, you can bring your letters and we can read them together—please, we have food in the truck. You need to eat something."

There was something corrosive in the look turned on her now. "How can you think I would leave your father to go with that family of devils?" Musya stared at this. Devils? The Kotzes—and she knew her Kotzes by now—were tedious, obsessive but woolly-brained, lovers of comfort, rather lazy and selfish people. Devils they weren't. Her mother was raving. "Devils and destroyers!"

"But I thought you liked them, Mommy. You always said they were very respectable."

"Don't you dare throw my words back at me, Musya!"

"And don't you dare criticize, Mommy, when you gave your daughters to that family, both of us—you did that, Mommy."

"I did that." The enormous eyelids slid closed and she raised a wrist to her forehead. "Yes."

Musya glanced at the wall and noticed that Vera Kholodnaya's old publicity photograph had faded considerably. "Mommy, we don't have time for dramatics now, please."

The mother's hand slapped the work table. "Do you know what kind of man your husband is? The man you let, the man you allowed." She stopped and gestured at the pregnancy. "Have you any idea?"

"What kind of man?" Musya almost shouted. "A silly man—a ridiculous man! My sister's husband, the father of her children. A terrible housekeeper, a terrible planner, a terrible man to have for a husband in an emergency—what do you want me to say? He has his good points. He's kind. He's a gentleman," she added, using the Russian word. Never had she felt more certain that Boris Kotz was dead than she did at this moment as she struggled to speak of him as if he were still alive. Her eyes stung with tears for him, for herself, for her children. "And a good father—he is!"

"Do you have any idea how many people your good gentleman helped send to prison? With his letters, how many good men and women are dead because he denounced them by name?"

There was no time for this now. Letters, her mother wanted to talk about letters—letters were the problem, that at least was true. Out from the past, dead Liza's words had crawled like biting insects; Musya pictured the squirming black syllables scabbed on her mother's brain where they bit and fed. She wished she had a match, she could burn the whole heap. "Mommy, please—let the past alone."

"The past is all I have."

"What? Mommy, you have me—you have your grandchildren."

"His children." A large teardrop rolled down her mother's starched linen cheek. "The children of a murderer."

"But Liza loved Boris Kotz, she was very nice to him before she died, really, she didn't accuse him of murder, she didn't say any of this."

"Of course not. She forgave him. She said he couldn't help it that he'd lost his faith."

"But—faith is difficult."

"How would you know?" her mother demanded harshly. "When have you ever shown any interest in God, even a biseleh—never." Recalling her vision, on the day of the harbor detonations, of God and his jackbooted angel troops straddling Odessa, Musya stayed quiet. Her mother kept on: "Your sister was a good woman, Musya, not like you or me. She believed and she acted according to her beliefs. She could do that. Not me. I can't believe anything, I don't have that ability. I'm all head—I just know things. And you, you follow your moods, your whims, your—your appetites. But your sister Liza had faith. She believed."

"So? So? Look what good it did—look where it got her. A grave in Siberia with not even a stone—a wooden board, Mommy, that's what Liza got for believing." And if not for her sister's faith, Musya herself would have had an entirely different life—maybe in America, she thought suddenly. If not for God, she might be in America, a free woman.

The mother said, "At least she kept her honor."

"Excuse me? I don't have honor? I'm a married woman, too, Mommy, you should remember, it's thanks to you that I am. You don't like your son-in-law and mekhutonim, blame yourself. You could have called me home."

"I couldn't go against your sister's wishes! And she never expected you'd give yourself—it was you, Musya, you were the one, you could have done differently, you could have chosen—"

"To what? To live the rest of my life without ever having a man again? No thank you!"

The mother was disgusted. "Oh! Musya! You and your men!"

She heard another call from the truck horn. They could have argued forever, she knew. "Are you coming with us or not?"

"I've told you." It was as she'd already explained, she'd wait there for her husband to return, she couldn't leave before he came home. Musya practically slammed the tin of sprats onto the work table and stepped back to blow her nose. The mother studied the red and white lettering. "Is this from that crook?" she said. "That so-called uncle?"

"Falk is no crook, Mommy, he's a respectable businessman and he's saving our lives. He's a fine, good man with a heart of gold."

"Oh yes?" The mouth so like Liza's twisted. "Don't tell me he's gone after you now. And in your state—what, his wife's sister isn't enough for him?"

Too angry to speak, Musya advanced on the mother to kiss her goodbye, a rough kiss on her hair parting, on her scalp that smelled sour. The hair was mostly gray and thinning. She was over fifty years old, her marriage and her daughters had come to her late in life. Perhaps she ought not to have had them, especially the husband; she'd often said so. But there they were or had been. She'd had them. She was a wife and mother.

Who said, "Don't forget your gramophone."

"I won't!" Musya stomped across the room and took her old reward to herself from its place in the corner into her arms. It made a cumbersome burden. "Zay gezunt, Mommy," she said.

"Zay gezunt, Musya. Good luck to you."

Safely negotiating the slimy and treacherous staircase took every bit of her attention. At the bottom she wept, great wet heaving sobs that roused the drunkard below who roared out, she couldn't tell what, the noise bore no resemblance to language or song. As she made her way to the street her thoughts were swirling. Then she remembered the dress, the one she'd spotted earlier that day, her mother's handiwork—she'd meant to ask whether the widow Tsigal had ever ordered one in peacock blue with emerald lining the train. She'd hoped to hear no, that someone else had bought that particular item, some other client. It was too late to hear this, now.

Musya stopped short. The landscape seemed to keep moving for a moment before returning to her side with a bump. How could it possibly matter whether it was some widow other than the late Lev Tsigal's who'd been murdered and strung up by the neck from a streetcar wire? Could it be worse if it weren't? It couldn't. For something that happened, worse wasn't possible. The very worst had reached its limits here and now enclosed them. With sudden forceful clarity Musya perceived that something like a huge iron bell had been lowered over the scene and the city around her by the evil done in that single death alone, that murder alone—and it had not been alone. Iron walls in space were amplifying the city's panicked screams and cries for help but they'd never let a whisper escape Odessa: no, not one. Nobody could hear, no help would be coming. Even worse, at any moment some giant fist was liable to strike the bell and pulverize the brains of every creature trapped inside with sound waves; the suspense itself was painful. Musya had to urinate badly. She'd reached a late stage of pregnancy and this was a problem. Why was she carrying a gramophone? She opened her arms and the gramophone dropped and shattered into fifty pieces on the hard earth.

Anton screamed. "MAMENYU!" He stood on the featherbed, shaking and crimsoning, his brother's arms around his knees.

"I'm coming!" She waddled carefully through the wreckage, stopped and turned right to visit her favorite old squatting spot in the shade of the raspberry bed, then headed for the truck where Sender asked first:

"What happened? Where's Zayde?"

Where was her father? "They'll follow us, as soon as he gets home," she lied quickly, raking the street with her eyes for a sight of him. Other men weren't the same, they had sawdust where her Daddy had sweetness; charm trickled from the shambles he made of things, other men's shambles couldn't compete, really. She couldn't be interested. Up and down the muddy road, other families were on the move and she didn't care to know where or in what direction. Wrapped in dark wool and panic sweats, they had the look of people being driven from corners. She'd have traded any of their lives, singly or in bulk, to have her father standing in front of her for one more second of life, certain though she was that he'd have been no help at all. He'd have been a comfort.

But now came the sight of a figure almost as welcome, stumbling out from the little house into the road, waving her hands to stop the truck in time: "Wait!" cried Musya although Yankel was right there, he'd left the wheel to help her back into the truck bed. The mother seemed to make slow progress, the crowd didn't help but she could barely walk, a terrible limp contorted her usual hurry. She had no coat on, no bag. "Mommy, what's wrong? Where are your things?"

Tears, shockingly, streaked the mother's cheeks, genuine tears she almost never shed. "I fell on the staircase! Oh, my knee, my knee—I slipped and fell almost the whole way down!"

A red flood of fury made Musya shout: "Your stairs are so bad? Can't someone clean them?"

"Your father isn't here to do it."

"What?"

"He's been cleaning them."

"Daddy—Daddy was the dvornik? He is?"

"For a while, yes."

This shook her, the humiliation. In the next moment it didn't matter. "It doesn't matter, Mommy—get in!" She watched the mother swat away Yankel Weissbein's helping hand. "Where is your bag?"

"I'm not coming with you." Sender and Anton gave siren wails of protest but their grandmother was sorry, she couldn't change her mind, she couldn't leave today. Shifting onto her sore knee, she winced loudly and held out her fists. "Take this," she told Musya who didn't reach. She didn't move at all. So the mother dropped what she'd been holding into the truck bed, it looked like two rolls of cloth strips or ribbon; but it was cash, worn to threads cash money rolled and bound tightly with red string. Then from her skirt pockets, from her waistband, from the neck of her dress she produced more of the same, over a dozen rolls in total to tumble there among the cans of fish.

"Mommy."

"Don't argue, Musyu!" The pain pulling her features into one ashen grimace cracked the mother's voice. "Take what you need and go. Get away from this terrible war."

"What's the hold up?" Papa Kotz's voice heralded his head's appearance in the window of the truck at which he'd obviously labored to place it so as to be able to see them. He looked like a sick man. He greeted the mother, adding, "Please, get in."

"Not today." The tone said never.

He cleared his nose and throat and said, "Suit yourself. She says she's not coming," explaining now to his wife that this was the hold up, the mother wasn't coming, what more could he know?

Musya heard Baila Kotz exclaim in an aggrieved, baffled undertone, "She can't do one normal thing? Where's the husband gone as usual?" Then the voice rose to call with surprising sincerity: "Please come!"

But Musya's mother wouldn't.

Her grandsons she blessed and kissed, then she blessed Musya and kissed her, stroking her hair. One more, two more cans of food she accepted, no more. She blessed Yankel and kissed him on the forehead because he'd be driving the truck. She stood waving their exhaust cloud from her lips and watched them pull away, then started back across the road with an agonized, creeping gait as the child in Musya's womb somersaulted and held out its arms in her direction. Musya resolved to insist that these parents begin to live according to an honest budget and hire some housekeeping but she never saw them again.

The boys had scampered to collect the money rolls, a now-transfixing hoard. From the mouth of Anton's satchel where they decided to stash it, fiery orange glints pierced Musya's tears. He'd packed his tiger skin, as she had suspected. She'd feared it for a nuisance but now she felt glad to have it along. Of everything they loved and wanted, everything they thought good, they should be bringing as much as possible to the countryside, she thought.

Lulling herself with the speed at which they passed she watched narrow streets give way to wider ones. Not recognizing anything now, she realized why when Yankel next braked. This he did a little sharply at a broad intersection of several streets and open spaces. Pale brown dust clouds swirled as the truck advanced a few inches and stopped, advanced and stopped again. The noise produced by all the engines of heavy machinery, all the tire treads and boot leather laboring in the vicinity combined to rattle the tarpaulin fittings like coins on a brass tray. Odessa's outskirts had changed since Musya's time among them—they'd spread outward. These were the new outskirts. And it was here, just inside the far edge of Odessa, that the victorious armies had stopped and massed.

"We're going right across! We're going right across!"

Yankel's firm tenor surmounted the groaning dismay that rose over his passengers' view through the windscreen. One hundred percent confident in the young clerk's driving skills, Musya tried to relax but her in-laws' case of nerves was contagious. The springs inside their cab seat kept up a jagged squeak of tune that was like a fever symptom in her ears. She peeked outside. Scattered groups of men filed past through the traffic, at moments obstructing even the sidecar motorcycles' swift and wasp-like progress. Tanks and monstrous ammunition trucks made their separate ways. Beyond this hellish stretch, Musya guessed, would be what must have been here before: they'd find vegetable patches, brick kilns, muddy ponds, pigs in farmyards. Yankel inched forward between one and the next group of soldiers, their sand-colored uniform cloth blending with the dusty air to the point of invisibility. Elsewhere passed uniforms black as ink bottle spills. And then there were men who weren't soldiers but civilians—just as she and all the other ordinary people had become, who'd follow commands not as citizens or professionals but for personal reasons alone, including fear of public execution—prodded by the rifles of uniformed men, gangs and gaggles of civilian men shuffled across the scene.

Since she'd forbidden them to cut the wrapping string, the little boys were busy guessing at their wealth, their heads kept low. "If we have enough," they traded saying. Anton would put it all on a motorcar he could sit up in, while the elder brother had his mind on dry goods, bolts of silk and wool especially. "And if we have enough left over," he elaborated, "a custom-fitted belt-waisted camel's hair overcoat from London England."

Ten—eleven—Musya broke off counting swastikas to laugh. "For the Ukrainian countryside? It will be ruined in five minutes."

"No," Sender corrected her. "For the future. The future will be great, remember? Zayde said."

She remembered. It had been unseriously said as usual; but this might have been one time when her father's mockery was badly misplaced. In fact the future might be wonderful. If the wine merchant was right and getting rid of socialism helped move the whole Ukraine forward into the modern world, they might all live better and longer in better and prettier clothes—Musya liked camel's hair, too. If her family lived, that is, through these terrible hours, was it so useless to hope? Wasn't it better to hope? Was improvement impossible? Might not all the meanness and mess of today added to history's finally add up to things getting better in general for everyone—Jews, too?

A cry rang out in the truck cab followed by a roar of coughing. Papa Kotz had nearly choked on his own excitement by the time he could make himself understood:

"Samuel! My son! There he is! Samuel!"

Musya peered through the cab window past Baila's head but the windscreen was an impenetrable glare. She could make out a few wavering dark blotches that might have been human figures.

"They've got him! Samuel! Samuel! Over here!"

The window by Musya's head filled with his bulk as he leaned across his wife to shout from the driver's side. She heard him pounding, kicking in his seat as Baila screamed at him to stop:

"Moishe, stop it—Samuel is dead!"

"Fuck you! He's standing ten meters away from us—Samuel!"

"Ten meters! With your eyes?" laughed Mama Kotz. "Wait!"

But the old had found the truck horn to set it braying, a loudness notable even in the encampment's armored roar. The truck heaved forward and braked again to the sound of men shouting angrily at it from the surrounding traffic. At last Yankel Weissbein raised his voice:

"Papa Kotz, please, stop, you'll make me have an accident!"

"Go get my son! Go get him—he's there! There! There!"

Her stomach heaved with alarm at the sound of Yankel's door clanking open. When he presented himself at the side of the truck bed the clerk looked older; the day's action had aged him and improved his jaw line, she thought. The sparse hairs she'd found so unsightly were actually signs of a beard. Her fingertips twitched. He said, "There's another tarpaulin behind you, Musya. We may need it." She couldn't think why but she nodded: all right. She sensed that his eyes wanted to stay and rest on the picture she made, she and her belly and her boys on their can-covered featherbed. She felt him flinch at the pounding fist Papa raised to the cab roof for emphasis:

"Yankel, son of a bitch, hurry up!"

Musya said, "Is it really him? Is it Samuel?"

He raised his sparkling shoulders and dropped them. "I never met the man. Get the other tarp out boys and stay down, all of you. I'll be right back." But all three of them moved to kneel at the side of the truck bed and watch.

Up ahead, more than ten meters, more like twenty, one of the civilian gangs had paused in the road or possibly beside it, there was no curb or other demarcation that Musya could see. The men were simple laborers who wore their caps pulled low. As she watched, one of them raised a cigarette towards his lips and had it slapped away by a dust-colored soldier, he'd just materialized there with an angry sheaf of papers in his other hand. "Him! Him! On the left!" Papa Kotz shouted from the cab at Yankel, who'd made his way up to one edge of the group. The soldier who didn't want smoking was on the other side. Yankel's gaze kept bouncing between the collection of men and the truck cab. "Not him—him! With his back to us—there's a pearl on his ear, him, yes—yes!" She watched Yankel tap one of the taller civilian men on the shoulder and receive an expressionless look. Yankel said something and the man trained his cap brim in the direction of the cab window. He was a handsome and violent-looking middle aged Jewish man with fleshy earlobes.

Sender said, "He's nothing like his photographs." This wasn't precisely true but the man looked very unlike Samuel Kotz. Now the old man's voice came, pitched high:

"Is it him? Is it?"

They heard Baila answer: "Who are you asking, Papa? Of course it's not him!"

"It's not him." The words, quiet, hollowed out, carried. The stranger had turned right away from Yankel, in his situation he had bigger fish to fry. "It's not him! It's not my son! Weissbein, come back!" The old man was shouting again and in his agitated disappointment he gave the horn another squeeze. At the sound, the wrong man and all the other men looked around at the truck. "Get back here!" Papa ordered Yankel again.

They saw the clerk take a step to return. Out of the sand another man in uniform appeared and blocked his way. Yankel was small. His arms moved as he started explaining, trying to pass. The other soldier with the papers came around and began to shout and shake his papers at Yankel, demanding who knew what? A man in a black uniform walked up to the group and spoke. The civilian men who'd all flinched at his arrival stepped back and drew closer together. Yankel stood alone, face to face with two soldiers in sandy brown, one in black.

"Romanians and now a German," Sender breathed. He knew all the uniforms from studying every picture paper he found. "Yankel's dead."

Musay said no. "He'll be fine," she insisted, wrapping her arms around Anton's head. "Be quiet." After all, what could one Yankel Weissbein matter to one German fascist so far from home?

Yankel was moving his arms again, he was arguing, trying to persuade. One of the Romanians gave him a shove but he stayed upright, kept talking. Another shove he dodged. Then he made a run for it. Was he running to the truck? The trio stopped him, knocked him down this time, sent him sprawling in front of the civilian men. Musya could only see his feet now, one worn boot gouged the dirt, and his shins bare above them. Baila was knitting him socks—green, she remembered. The German in black nudged one of the Romanians with an elbow and took his rifle, aimed, and fired at the ground, twice. Yankel kicked and went still.

He was dead at seventeen years old.

Moments later Musya was hanging on with all her strength as Anton fought to break her headlock that kept him from seeing and breathing and Sender fought to leap out and attack Yankel's killers. Sender she had by the waist. Their struggles were desperate. More than anything she wanted to fold both boys into her own flesh and imprison them there, safe, with her baby—she'd wish to be huge and misshapen and them, safe. "No!" She couldn't stop saying, "No! No!"

"No! No!"

Baila's voice, a moaning echo, reached her through the glass. The old man she could hear blurting obscenities more and more steadily. Then Baila asked: "What are we going to do? Papa—what do we do now?" Sender kicked; Anton kicked; Musya strained her ears for signs of an answer. She heard a low rumble that must have been one because Baila replied: "Are you crazy? You can't drive this!"

He could, though. Papa Kotz insisted that he could because this was the genius of Henry Ford, any man could drive the vehicles he built. From the passenger door of the GAZ-AA Papa walked around to Yankel's and was puffing for oxygen by the time he arrived, even though he'd gone the shorter way. Musya glimpsed on his face the look of someone getting pieces carved out of his body while he attempts to complete an unrelated task.

"Little boys," he groaned. "Lie down. Be still."

Anton subsided immediately and Sender stopped at least to snarl at the grandfather: "What about Yankel?"

"Yankel did his best."

"I hate you!" Saying this, Sender started crying.

The old man grunted. "So hate me." He managed to climb back in and after a short rest even managed the ignition. Once more the truck rolled forward.

"But you have no idea where you're going!" Baila cried. "How are we supposed to get there?"

"I can find Khosary," he told her.

"Can you? Can you?"

Huddled in a sobbing heap, indifferent to the route, the other three bounced on the featherbed as the truck scaled a curb, swerved, clanked its gears and picked up speed; it left upset in its wake, angry voices and the biting insect whine of shots. Papa Kotz kept going, kept speeding up when his wife said to slow down; up and down across another sidewalk curb they clattered. Then a sudden, hard, almost sickening left turn plunged them into narrow shade. Almost at once they stopped. Why had he turned here? The driver didn't answer his wife as she pointed out that there was nothing here, no road, only walls, a blind alley. The engine died and revived. Papa started looking for the gear to reverse.

About three weeks later they were sitting outdoors with the Ukrainian countryside all around them. It was a beautiful day, cold but dry, almost cloudless. Pale blue above, pastoral browns below, stamped greenish-black by scattered pine woods, like every other part of the Ukrainian countryside they'd visited by now this stretch was also icy, desolate and greatly strewn with battle wreckage. Not a shop or a restaurant in sight, the only dwelling in sight clearly a poor one, probably abandoned: all as usual. There was even another Red Army fighter plane crashed nose-first halfway across another unharvested field: melons this time. It hadn't snowed but the tilled earth was blindingly crystalline, frostbound. Anything left on the frozen vines was inedible. In fact unless this plane had fallen down in a scattering of ration cans as the other had done, there was nothing edible in sight.

Her mother-in-law's voice broke into Musya's thoughts about ration cans. "I just wish I didn't feel so powerless," she heard her say. She turned her head and stared. At her shoulder, Baila Kotz's swollen but still admirable profile was lifted to the low sun. Sunbeams gilded the clouds her breath had made. Still in earrings—the woman amazed her. Thanks to her the rest of them were still alive; Musya said so. Baila made a noise, obviously pleased. "Alive—such as it is. Such as we are."

More breath clouds rose from her raw lips, glowed, and dissolved. What was being lost here, lost with every breath, Musya wondered? Water or strength, matter or spirit, they lacked any means or method to replace it. Conversation was a squandering but they had nothing else to do. Under better circumstances the Ukrainian countryside might have suited them but as it was they felt alien, unwanted—and were. No one wanted them. They had nowhere to go. Baila was very right: their claim on life seemed little. Where once they'd enjoyed shelter, warmth, cleanliness, regular meals, modern conveniences, today the Kotz household made do with seats in an oxcart. Homeless and without a country, they'd become citizens of the elements. Cold, wind, rain, sleet, snowy nightfalls, slow sunrises and the brief, brief miracle of noon were their new country.

The days were short. This one was far advanced and still no sign of snow, which in one way was a shame. "I don't feel powerless, really," Musya said. "I feel angry."

"Oh. Anger. Yes." Baila ran a piece of straw between her gloved fingertips; these had stains. "Yes, at everybody."

"Everybody," Musya agreed.

"Even me?"

Of course not, they told Sender Kotz. He'd been listening—the ones who listened weren't the problem. He sat across from them with the back of his head to the sun reading Jules Verne for the thousandth time in the light. He had a rosy halo.

His little brother, huddled against Musya's lap, head pillowed on satchel, was out cold. It was a little more possible to be angry at Anton who'd managed to reach and plunder his grandfather's very last medicine stores, this despite all Musya's vigilance. It was even possible to be a little angry at Baila Kotz who'd promised to keep an eye on him while Musya took a little sleep because that was when it had happened. Most certainly it was possible to be angry at Papa Kotz for letting it matter so much and becoming so enraged at the theft—of course he was the victim but his anger had been too much, a cause itself for anger. Slumped in his corner seat, the old man let out occasional snorts to mark his entrances and exits from the conscious stage; he'd had to take a double dose of what was left. At the other end of the cart Mrs Drobitz was still going. Nobody wanted to be angry at poor Mrs Drobitz but it was impossible not to be.

Three screeches.

Screech. Screech. Screech. Pause. Screech. Screech. Screech. Pause.

Repeat. For hours.

By now her vocal cords must have been stripped. The screams emerged like flute notes bounced off porcelain and struck with painful resonance between the eyes. In time Mrs Drobitz would wind down—in a long time. They'd had a rare spell of quiet before the old man's latest tantrum managed to set her off again.

Sender looked angrily at Papa Kotz and used his penetrating voice to say, "Everything is his fault." Papa twitched, maybe coincidence, and a gleam from the silver fruit knife he'd pulled on Anton escaped between his fat chapped fingers.

Baila said no. "That German contributed."

"Not as much." The grandson was not backing down from this. All respect was gone. "He should have known how to reverse."

"But he didn't—okay? He never learned how."

"Everybody learns that."

Screech. Screech. Screech.

"Fine," said Baila. "Mister Expert." She still defended her husband at every occasion but not always energetically.

When awake and stimulated Papa Kotz spent hours of breath on laying blame for all the family's present misfortunes at the doorstep of poor dead Yankel Weissbein. In his view, Yankel was the one who'd piloted their rapid course into the jaws of death. Imagining his own driving skills to be superhuman maybe this Yankel had been cocky and cavalier with their lives, said Papa; as if the young clerk, now dead, Papa continued, had set out to impress someone, a loosey-goosey young married woman for instance, he'd driven them like a maniac right up the ass of the Romanian army while expecting to survive; he, Yankel, said Papa Kotz, was lucky the rest of them hadn't been shot dead, too. The old man kept remembering points during that day's ride when he should have insisted: he ought to have taken the wheel himself far sooner than he finally had, he said. Sometimes he demonstrated with his blue fist in the air how to operate a real Henry Ford gear shift. Sometimes he cursed Yankel. This was hard for the rest of them to hear and everyone preferred him asleep, it wasn't just the tantrums.

Screech. Screech. Screech.

The whole family missed Yankel, Papa included, Musya thought. Anton missed Yankel especially, there'd been a real love between the two. Anton would never have stolen the medicine if he hadn't missed Yankel so much. She heard a voice say, "I don't care if your husband dies." It was her own voice, she'd said it.

"He'll outlive us all," answered Baila Kotz, arching her throat to the sun.

The woman combined personal charm with a talent for survival, that was the thing. It was an unexpected talent rooted in her affection for soft living that could pluck special considerations and benefits from any situation. In the terrible hour of Yankel's murder, under arrest as unregistered Jews but left unharmed, even allowed to unload and bring their luggage thanks to Baila's entreaties, they'd been sent by bus and not marched across town to Slobodka, a formerly decent neighborhood. Most of the buildings there had been knocked flat by bombs during the summer's siege and the rest had been bulldozed. Not one roof was standing. Now the whole place started to fill up with thousands of Jews, thousands and thousands, many thousands with no luggage at all, no food, no water, no blankets. Fences and armed guards encircled Odessa's new Jewish ghetto of Slobodka. Realizing she'd arrived early and just in time, Baila had immediately tracked down and claimed one of the few remaining partially sheltered nooks for her family's use. They'd even had provisions. Even so, but for Yankel's spare tarpaulin they might have died there. Thousands had, killed by the stubbornly wet and cloudy skies of 1941's unseasonably freezing autumn.

In Slobodka Musya tore the bottoms of her shoes on rubble, walking up and down the ruined streets. She'd seen people sitting bareheaded, completely exposed, as if their misery were casting airtight walls up around them. The next day they'd be there still, stone dead. She'd found no sign of her parents.

"Why didn't they pack better?" Baila would grumble about the doomed ones who came begging to her almost-sheltered corner, drawn to some degree by the swift notoriety of Mama Kotz and her amazing canned and bottled provisions, like the Ali Baba's cave of the place. She'd needed less than a week to bargain their way out of Slobodka. It took more than cash and some jewelry; Baila knew how to get things from people; she was sharp, watchful, intrepid. She knew how and when to point at Musya, too, and demand consideration for a mother-to-be. "Men are superstitious about pregnant women," she'd explained. "None of them wants your death on his hands—they'll move you along. And the rest of us with you." So far she'd been right.

Marked for transport to farm labor, the household had been bound towards Khosary, of all places, only this time in an open oxcart, one link in a long creaking oxcart parade. As modes of travel went it was slow and uncomfortable—bumpy, smelly, entirely unenclosed. Shivering on wet straw they'd begun to cross the Ukrainian countryside. Their route had changed and changed again; orders countermanding orders, the parade split into segments and dissolved in mysterious departures. Much more often than the oxen, the men driving the carts had changed constantly. There'd been soldiers, some local civilians, other prisoners. Not a single one had really known how to drive an oxcart. Were they driving in circles? It would begin to explain, Musya thought, why the sights had begun to repeat themselves. But of course they weren't going in circles now. They weren't moving now.

"Please. Please, try and calm yourself." Baila leaned across Musya into the falling light to address herself to Mrs Drobitz, who screeched twice more and paused. "Wasn't he— isn't it possible to think of this as—maybe it's for the best, you know?" She puffed a helpless cloud. Mrs Drobitz kept screeching. "I mean he was off somehow—there was something wrong with his wits, wasn't there? Wasn't he a little off?" Baila looked at her to confirm that Mrs Drobitz's little son had been strange and slow witted.

Yes, Musya tried to explain, yes he had been but it didn't matter. The boy's obvious extreme slow-wittedness did nothing to make it less horrible that two days before yesterday he'd been blown up in front of his doting mother's eyes when he stepped on a land mine and now lay visible to them in frozen pieces. He'd climbed off alone to relieve himself in the field. A leg was closest, Sender with the keenest eyes said the right one, less than ten meters away. To Musya it looked extremely close and to Mrs Drobitz it looked too close to be borne, clearly. Her wits were gone. Robbed of everything, all she had left was her alarm which she seemed determined to sound and would with her last breath.

"All I'm saying," said Baila, "is to suggest that with his problems he'd have so much trouble in times like these, at least now Baby won't suffer."

"Yes," said Musya, trying to drag her weary eyes away from the sight of Baby's leg. She and Baila were getting the afternoon sun but they had the leg view. However much everyone inside the oxcart would suffer from a covering of snow she couldn't help hoping for one; but the sky stayed clear. The big crows seemed to have cleared off for the day. In the oxcart they'd never heard his mother call her little boy anything but Baby; she'd never answer now when they asked what he'd been named. So Baby he was to them. The sound of his death had brought Anton's bombing raid panic back with a roar, all noises upset him now. He wouldn't have gone for Papa's medicine if the effects of panic hadn't made him desperate.

This had been a first-time experience of land mines for all of them and only one person had been willing to risk an encore. An all-but silent man had travelled with Mrs Drobitz and Baby—that is he'd sat next to the pair, not speaking, ever since the two families had been loaded together into the cart at some transit point. Balding, bearded, slits for eyes, thick lips pushed a bit to one side as if smeared by a thumb, all day long while Mrs Drobitz cooed and babbled with Baby he'd stared blankly. While the oxen thieves, roving deserters, took Mrs Drobitz and raped her underneath the cart he'd only groaned once or twice. When Baby blew up he'd held an arm across her shoulders. Just after dawn on the day after the explosion this man had cleared out, his steps down the pink road mincing and quick as Mrs Drobitz's voice, still fresh then, chased him safely out of view.

Screech. Screech. Screech. Pause. Repeat.

She must have been thinking how foolish it was to have given in, how foolish to have chosen life when eight hours later the point of life would be gone, dead and in pieces.

For Musya and the rest, Baby's fate turned their oxcart into a locked room, if not a prison cell. Crossing the field to squat near the tree line was out, they dared creep only a few paces away and felt shameful. There was no changing the dirty straw in the corners which stank. Where they sat a single terrifying monster menaced them from every direction at once. It was the Ukrainian countryside. Foraging for anything was out, hunting for wells or clean streams in the woods for water was out. And the household's days of being well-provisioned were long gone. Musya narrowed her eyes in the direction of crash site.

Baila said, "Please stop thinking about those ration cans."

"But we need them. We have no food, no water. Once we've eaten the rations then we can use the cans to melt snow in for drinking."

The older woman almost laughed. "Yes, we'll melt it on the stove."

But Sender still thought they could manage it. "I'll go," he said. They both told him no, he wouldn't, his going was out of the question. "Then send Papa Kotz," he said. Baila said never. Her daughter-in-law she also wouldn't allow:

"I refuse to watch my next grandchild get blown up in a melon field."

They'd all heard this before. Even the baby gave a recognizing kick, a proud and restless unborn child. As she pictured the first sip she'd take from the gleaming can, Musya's mind kept working. At night when Baila wouldn't have to see, then she'd creep to the fuselage and start feeling around on the ground with her hands in the moonlight. An electric torch would be better, of course, but in the oxcart there were neither lights nor matches. Trying to memorize what looked like the best route didn't work because she kept changing her mind. A sense of the hopelessness of all effort overcame her. Then she decided to cross the field on the following day at mid-morning when she'd have the sun at her back catching every last can in its spotlights—the same decision she'd reached three days straight now. This time she'd really do it, Musya thought; tomorrow. Then she pictured her cold body lying there with all its torn parts for the boys to look at and realized that she could never go.

She turned to Baila. "What is your sister's name?" she asked.

"My sister?" The older woman smiled and wiped her nose on a rag. True to her prediction, she'd been tortured by hay fever in the Ukrainian countryside. "Goldie. My sister's name is Goldie. My sister—my sister, Mrs Drobitz, I'm telling about her now."

There was no effect at first; screeches accompanied the story of a pair of beautiful sisters who'd also had a little property to sweeten their hands in marriage. Catches, they'd been, when the wine merchant had been still a clerk—an ambitious and handsome one, considered a Jew with a future in 1905, a big-time year. They'd spent it at school, in dreams—young girls. There'd been an arrangement on Goldie's account, after which Falk had come calling.

"He was for her and then he met me. In those days it was already too late. And my sister was so lovely—I wish I could show you. Beautiful as the seven worlds they called her." Burnt for campfire kindling by a transit guard she'd insulted, Baila's photograph album had been a bad loss, worse in its way than the fur coat she'd forgotten at home in

Odessa. The other fur she'd brought but it was long gone, too. Her tale continued.

Having taken place her sister's marriage hadn't prospered. Goldie who'd never been strong nor especially well couldn't carry one child to term. Her fragile nerves had deteriorated. Her loved ones had drawn closer together. "Your Boris is my husband's child, that one I'm sure of," his mother said matter-of-factly. By now the patriarch himself was snoring. "They're too much the same person. The rest, Samuel especially—who can say?" Here she gave a shrug. Her own marriage had been a test of patience while her sister Goldie, Falk's wife, had been jealous to the point of insanity. They'd always had to sneak around. And then Falk always disappeared whenever he felt like it. "And then he never came for us all that time in Slobodka, I sent him a hundred messages."

"Maybe he's." Musya hesitated.

"Dead," Sender supplied. "The Germans might have got him." The grandmother thought no.

"He's not dead." The reddened eyes leaked tears. "That man's faithless heart has been the tragedy of my life."

Musya looked around at the spacious dusk-swept Ukrainian countryside through which the air temperature was plunging straight downward. That was her mother-in-law's tragedy? Falk's heart? So what did that make Musya's tragedy? "What about this?" she wondered aloud. Nothing she could recall from her life before now felt as bad as hunger and thirst did at present.

"This?" Baila echoed. For a moment they heard nothing, no sound at all. The moment lasted, prolonged, a soft caress of silence in the heart of a war zone.

Mrs Drobitz had fallen asleep.

"Thank God!" Sender sighed.

Baila said, "Yes. This is actually quite pleasant." She was right.

In a little while the young moon would rise to make the landscape glow and many stars would appear through its silvery mists, countless stars. The present cold and solitary scene breathed peace. Having a doctor on hand would have been nice but except for Mrs Drobitz the Kotzes were once more alone with their privacy. The cart's last driver had left with the oxen and the thieving rapists, taking Yankel's tarpaulins; the rest with the stamina had run off once he was gone. There hadn't been a doctor in the lot, anyway. Musya heard something purring, not loud—motors, more than one, not airplanes, not too close. Anton slept on, fast asleep. For a few more moments she thought about how nice it would be if they could just sit there in the oxcart for as long as it took the war to finish and pass away. Such quiet was blissful.

PART TWO

OBODOVKA

(1)

For over three hundred years, reliably, there had been Jews living in the Ukrainian town of Obodovka. It was a good-sized town and at the time of the last tsars as many as three synagogues were being maintained in its Jewish quarter. North of Odessa, halfway to Kiev, Obodovka stood near a wide, calm stretch of river where two small rivers met and two major roads crossed there. Benefitting from the excellence of its situation for commerce, Jews ran most of the booths at the town's celebrated Tuesday bazaar; among their many other business concerns were a lumberyard, inns, and a shop that sold artificial coral to jewelers wholesale. Fertile and picturesque, the place had also attracted a family of Polish nobility, the Sobanskis, who'd built a mansion rather like a palace there, surrounded it with gardens and forested parks and filled it with art, books, music, balls and house parties: Europe came in carriages to Obodovka and returned to Warsaw, to Vienna, to Paris and London with endorsements of its excellence, its charm.

A good place to visit, a fine place to live prosperously, like the rest of the hemisphere Obodovka was greatly changed by the new century's wars. Once again the great powers sent men to fight over the rich Ukrainian land and reduced it to famine. The Revolution introduced more combatants—Reds, Whites, Poles, Cossacks, partisans—more famine, more change. The tsars were out, the nobility were out, market days and small trade were out. Stately homes like the Sobankskis' stood empty, looted. People starved when they weren't like Musya's grandparents, all four, slaughtered. The pogrom times had returned. Bad men and thieves prowled the countryside, stirring things up; armed gangs roved. In May 1919 came a widespread rumor that Obodovka's Jews had attacked some Ukrainians. Within days a band of armed Ukrainian peasants appeared, rounded up every man they could find in the Jewish quarter, marched them to the market square and machine gunned them dead, maybe three hundred men killed and buried in a mass grave. The town handled the burial.

Even then, Jews kept living in Obodovka. Though much reduced in size, completely stripped of wealth and nearly manless, the Jewish quarter still existed. It even started to grow again. Children orphaned by the massacre lived on at Obodovka in an orphanage established inside one of its emptied-out synagogues by the new Bolshevik government's bureau for aid to the victims of pogroms. As they matured the orphans settled nearby to swell the Jewish quarter's population; and other Jews settled there in what remained a beautiful riverbank town on a crossroads. There was even a synagogue again in Obodovka when the next war broke out. Five weeks later the town's decimated Jewish quarter was sealed off and declared a ghetto, marked for wrapping in German barbed wire. The surviving Jews inside wore the regulation yellow patches and began to cope with scarcity.

Next arrived word that they'd changed hands again. Taking its victory reward in Ukrainian land, fascist Romania and its Transnistria Governorate had assumed control of some hundred German-built ghettos and concentration camps in the territory for its own uses.

In Obodovka, for a time, nothing happened. Then with great suddenness its streets filled with oxcarts, foot traffic and misery. Jews, transport after transport of them, had begun to arrive from the south and west, from Bukovina, Bessarabia, from Romanian territories. To the five hundred people already captive and struggling inside the ghetto were added nine or ten thousand more. Winter came.

The town's Jewish population had peaked.

Mr Asch was their resident historian. He'd lived in the Jewish quarter of Obodovka since the early twenties when he'd arrived from Europe in response to the man shortage. He was tiny and knew everything about Napoleon Bonaparte. That mass grave and massacre of 1919 had also held a special fascination for him; he'd found witnesses who'd speak—very few though, he said. He never had found a woman. Before he died from typhus Mr Asch enjoyed recounting facts about this place that the Kotz family had reached at the end of a brutally prolonged passage through several other Transnistrian transit points and ghettos. By now they qualified as connoisseurs and Obodovka was a death trap.

Fire damage lay on a fair share of the housing stock that survived; the lucky crammed in there. Among various barns, stables, sheds and simple lean-tos were none with a functioning roof; all grew crowded. People slept in every corner of the Jewish bath house, inoperable for lack of fuel. The weather was wet, frigid, unrelievedly. In puddles, buckets, teacups, all water froze overnight. What little wood wasn't needed for shelters was too wet to burn. No one felt warm in the Obodovka ghetto that first winter although an approximate warmth could be achieved in small groups if its members huddled fully clothed under every available blanket with every scrap of stuff they could find piled on top. They slept in their coats, losing a coat to theft could be fatal. Keeping clean was almost impossible, clothes washing out of the question.

Spread by diseased body lice, typhus fever in its epidemic form had been leading bullets as the cause of European war deaths by a wide margin for centuries already when it returned to Eastern Europe and Ukraine in 1941. Typhus killed civilians and soldiers, striking closely confined populations hardest; the imprisoned would always suffer. The female body louse keeps her eggs warm for hatching by laying them in clothing seams; once hatched, the new lice start feeding on the human in the clothes. If that human has typhus then the feeding louse sickens and the contagion starts coursing through its louse body in brown-red torrents of infectious excrement that climax in its death—an event all too often delayed until after the sick louse has moved on from a feverishly hot or stony cooling host to a more temperate human, one who soon after scratching typhus-ridden feces into the red part of a new louse bite itch will contract typhus. Head pains, weakness, rashes, fever, delirium, stupor and death form the progression at its worst. The odds of survival fall sharply with age: young children would tend to recover, while the seasoned, middle-aged fighting men of Napoleon's Grand Armée never stood a chance. The typhus they caught in Poland and brought east to Ukraine reduced them by multitudes and kept their emperor from the Russian throne as surely as the Russian winter ever did, Mr Asch insisted. Now the same thing could happen again. "Our deaths will kill them!" he predicted—his last coherent words.

Of course all Transnistria was a death trap but at the close of December when the Kotz family arrived, months after the first big transports, this ghetto really stood out. The number of unburied corpses lying around outdoors was phenomenal. Frozen, naked, grayish, hideously gaping, hideously hair-tufted, hideously gnawed in spots like poppy blooms: these were the still people, as many euphemized them for the young. Sender and Little Anton since the day of Yankel Weissbein's death had of course seen too many still people to count but never so many collected together. The streets Musya would remember stood locked in something like an old postcard view of those Tuesdays in a lost Obodovka: hectic throngs collected for a market fair lined up along fences, here and there a bare limb erupting from its heap as if hastening to a cut-rate sale.

"No one here knows how to stack a body?"

Papa Kotz was managing to look around for a change. Epidemic typhus fever the family knew all about from an incognito doctor who'd examined the old man behind a blanket curtain on the way. What was wrong with him was uncertain, of typhus Papa only had the stupor, nothing else. The old saw was apt, said the doctor: a sickness imagined brings worse suffering than a sickness diagnosed. Papa said very little these days, all complaint. But none of them were impressed by any part of Obodovka—except for the scenic views, which were admirable. "But aren't the views here nice though, Papa?" His wife tried to keep him engaged but he relapsed into his symptom with a low cough.

Their first full day in Obodovka, one of rare sunshine, found the Kotz family house-hunting. It would be a challenge. Even with so many dead by now, the living had nowhere near enough room in this ghetto. Some had more than seemed fair, naturally, that would always happen where some were faster, earlier, luckier, more aggressive; back in Slobodka they'd had more than must have seemed fair themselves. Here they'd come late and less well provisioned. They'd spent the previous night outdoors tucked against a cow shed wall beneath a low projecting eave—sheltered, yes, but the comings and goings, the noise and dreck and urination of the people crowded inside the shed had prevented rest. Always liking to do better, Baila Kotz had performed another mustering of the family's every last resource and advantage to put on public view.

Needless to say, impossible to deny, they had along a mother-almost-to-be which might count for something with someone. Baring her head to the sun (her hair remained an asset) Musya nodded at a reminder to look healthy: it wasn't hard, she was a little weak but well, her nephews likewise. After two months' rough living the boys looked shaggier, with pointier faces, almost fox-like with their red coloring. Baila had them wearing their sailor suits. About poor Papa Kotz what could be done, not much except shake out his overcoat and spit-smooth the hair to his scalp, he'd never again do more than vaguely resemble a presentable man.

Mama remained another story. Her shawl arranged to display all the good things she'd managed to keep at once, including a well-tailored blue skirt, she went underdressed for the cold; her last best shoes she'd saved for their ruin in the mud of these morgue-like streets. For women her own age, family women to engage in conversation they should all be on the lookout, they knew. "One sympathetic person, we only need to find just one," Baila liked to say. The important thing, she'd told them, was to look pleasant and well-bred. Posture was key. Shoulders back, chin tilted skyward, she and her example led them by ladylike steps up one filthy lane and down the next through a reek of latrines, between dwellings identically overcrowded, past the fire-blackened remains of a small synagogue, past snowed-over garden plots where equally makeshift encampments battled corpses for the space—a losing battle it looked like. Maybe it was their nakedness but in Obodovka the still people showed more vital force. Bundled up in layers of rags, the men and women circulating past in sunshine-elevated numbers met Baila's famous charming greetings with a few blank stares, some flinching hostility; most reacted not at all. These people were hungry. Hollow eyes fixed on the ground they were scanning, scanning for mouthfuls of potato or bread miraculously dropped there and missed. Musya hoped no one would find anything in her vicinity because fights over food scraps could be horrible, even fatal, they sickened her. That the streets had been picked bare was more probable, though. Singly and in packs, minnow-swift, children slipped through every layer of the scene. Some carried water, others had armfuls of clothes or bits of wood or looks full of secrecy. Children found everything first.

At the house thresholds, clusters of invalids coughed and shivered, fluttering what blanket scraps they wore. Some shared their scraps and some had none. Some had caretakers beside them and some invalids were nearly dead; their caretakers, the saddest of figures, stroked their hair and hovered and held them to the healthful light but they were taking their last sunshine. The other sufferers in the flock, noticing their moribund companions, would stand a little straighter, act surer of recovery, only to slump listlessly again as worry and disease reclaimed each one's thoughts. Typhus wasn't alone, a death trap like Obodovka offered plenty of dysentery, pneumonia, starvation—many causes of death were on assortment here, many ways to be murdered.

Some people, for instance, had walked their feet off. Musya and her family had been lucky in this regard. Forced marches were the norm, routes hundreds of almost unsheltered kilometers long were common. Forcing Jews to cross Ukraine on foot in freezing temperatures was a common form of murder in Transnistria. Many died marching while blisters and frostbite hobbled the survivors who'd starve, unable to forage; or else their toes would fill with pus, turn septic and fall off and soon they'd die.

The doorstep invalids outside what Baila deemed the best dwelling in town had their eyes on one of these walked to death people: a young man, emaciated, who'd been laid out on the front path in a long bleached linen shirt. Almost from the Dneister he'd walked, someone mentioned. His furry-faced head was wrapped in the arms of a girl who knelt there, dark hair loose, ribcage hard-worked by the violence of noisy grief. The invalid band shifted as a figure emerged from indoors, a well-clothed but unhandsome woman close to Baila's age who with every sign of impatience went and stood above the obviously inconvenient pair. Instinct quickening her step, Baila moved forward to greet this patched rubber boot-wearing stranger and to call her Sweetie in proper Soviet Yiddish:

"This is your clean home? From before? What a shame these times are. What can we do to help you? Let us try, Sweetie," she offered. "So sad and terrible when such things happen in a nice home—this is her brother?"

"Her husband." To her scowl the Sweetie added crossed arms. "She says."

Making an appropriate noise, Baila mirrored the homely woman's disapproval with her mouth and brow. The woman thought them good enough for conversation: this was an important hurdle cleared. Baila turned topical, pointing past the young man's gangrene-blackened shins to the bloody louse smears on his linen: "No matter what killed him that shirt will have to be boiled or at least frozen. Of course I long for carbolic soap but there's none left anywhere."

The propped bust rose defiantly. "We're only freezing now. We can't do more."

"Of course not. All you can do is what you've been doing. You can't work miracles."

A stubborn frown: "We've come pretty close."

"Of course you have," Baila soothed quickly. She looked down and brought her fingertips, her last gloves, to the girl bride's heaving shoulder. "Miss, please, it's time we undress—"

The girl broke in with a foreign-sounding shout: "Ers nit toyt! Nit toyt!"

Sender Kotz agreed. "She's right—he isn't dead."

A glance passed between his grandmother and the Obodovkan Sweetie who added, with an eye-roll, "These people, where they come from no one knows anything, no more than a child." Backward cultures: she and Baila Kotz agreed that the Romanian fascists had sent them some real specimens. Sweetie reached down past the girl to touch the good shirtcloth. "If you don't take it someone else will," she told her. The girl slapped her hand away and she slapped back, first automatically and then with intent, again—the girl flinched from it, her close embrace shifting her burden, the still young man—who suddenly twitched and kicked the air with one of his murdered legs. Oaths escaped a collective gasp of breath, people drew back, an invalid toppled.

The girl on the ground gave a triumphant cry while Baila screamed, a low note like a saxophone's and not very loud since frost had wrecked her vocal cords.

"But I told you he wasn't dead," said Sender. "She told you and I told you."

Her mouthy grandson would have received a smart answer except Baila screamed again. This was a wilder scream suggesting causes deeper than the present fright; more rooted in the many bodies heaped around in view than in this sole one kicking, maybe, it expressed the situation. Screaming must have felt like a relief and maybe like a hard to quit one, thought Musya, too tired to scream. She thought she was too tired to go mad for that matter. Remembering poor Mrs Drobitz, she hoped sincerely that her mother-in-law hadn't worked up the energy to lose her mind. Maybe Baila had remembered Mrs

Drobitz too because with a catch of breath, she stifled the unceasing screams the situation warranted and burst into speech. Out spilled homespun cadences and phrases of the kind she'd never used back in Odessa:

"Oh lady," she said, "It's so hard losing everything! I'm like you, my family's like you, we're not used to this low life. I kept a beautiful home—not a palace, but nice. My husband, a family man, a man respected throughout the business community of Odessa. His heart broken by the loss of our son, our treasure, killed by a fascist Nazi bomb. My grandsons, these, look at these faces—scholars, good boys. Soon to have a little brother or sister. We don't come here empty-handed."

"I've got nowhere to put you," the woman said to that.

"Not a single corner?"

"Not now." She gestured at the ground where the young man's revival continued. He clawed the gray mud with both hands.

"I see." Baila's tone made clear her willingness to wait for what must happen soon, she didn't need to say it openly. This was good breeding again. As her gloved index finger brought its tip to one Chinese red earring she flashed the matching bracelets, her cinnabar set. Concealed on her person she carried a few more pieces of jewelry and the last of the cash, which being Soviet wasn't the best value. Silver and gold, the Kotz family heirlooms were long gone. Charm was their gold now, Musya guessed.

Sweetie accepted a bracelet, a token, to hold a place on her waiting list. Her hard bosom drooped as she employed an arm to point their way up the road to the ghetto's "next most respectable" place: "Krutonog's. Tell them Tauber's house sent you special. Now you should excuse me." For with her own hands she had to help the girl lift and carry the young man back indoors: no one else had the strength and to leave him where he lay would look terrible, she said. Sender wished he could have volunteered to help but he had bags to carry. Papa wouldn't keep. Burly at four, strapped into his satchel, Anton managed to plod along too but every stop left him asleep on his feet, leaning into Musya's thighs. The old sled was missed. From one minute to the next, of course, they missed all sorts of things they'd formerly owned or enjoyed.

The widow Krutonog was thirty-five, faint-prone, twice badly married, the second time abandoned. Childless and wary of children, she allowed the Odessans' gentility to outweigh their encumbrance by youth and made room for them. The sailor suits helped the family's cause here, no question. She accepted Soviet cash, as it happened. As for Tauber's house, the good report so expensively procured there carried no weight at all at Krutonog's. Three decades the widow had been keeping rooms To Let in Obodovka's Jewish quarter and she kept them now despite the extreme difficulties involved in the enterprise, especially since she was a kind woman who pitied everyone, the toll on her emotions these days was extreme; only the koorvah running Tauber's house—who could prove no relation whatsoever to any known Tauber, living or dead, by the way—Widow Krutonog would never pity. On the whole, she said, the neighborhood hadn't been good for a long time.

Often expanded, hung out front with a Lenin House sign but the name never took, the inn called Krutonog's remained a ramshackle collection of wooden rooms, dormitories, cubicles, cubbyholes, closets, ladders and lofts, indifferently plastered, mostly earthen floored, full of bugs, draft-riddled and damp throughout, wired extensively for electric light but very short on bulbs. Beyond a street door nailed all over with sheet metal, an uneven passageway zigzagged front to back through a dozen jumbled eras of construction, reaching its modern apex in Widow Krutonog's new tiled kitchen with steam boiler of 1931. Even here not one window was more than half-sealed for winter. A few glimpses of exquisite cloud-furrowed distance wavered in the crooked windowpanes between outhouses, sheds, tents, fence posts stripped of wooden fence and left aslant, clotheslines sagged by frozen garments, smudgy wisps of campfire smoke. There was a corpse heap in the withered kitchen garden. Somewhere inside was an old kitchen, too, with a clay floor on which people had established themselves in the most cramped conditions, at night they made a dense carpet of restless sleepers and all for the sake of nearness to an old brick stove they barely lit for lack of anything to burn. Of course, conditions in every room and cubbyhole and loft at Krutonog's were cramped. People lived in the bends of every hallway. Children slept on shelves in the empty linen cupboards.

In the old inn's new kitchen its landlady quartered with her female dependents. The baking table slept one or two. Widowed and otherwise bereaved in the summer's invasion that had hollowed out Obodovka's population generally, these women never went outside. Behind a glass office door, curtained, the favorites and their protector kept a private retreat. They had some comforts. In the Jewish ghetto by law they weren't allowed to run the electrical appliances but coal enough to run the steam boiler was scratched up with fair regularity, gentile townsfolk would sell bits of coal through the barbed wire—food, too. The prices killed, though, the widow said, and what she earned on resale to her tenants wouldn't buy a feather—it was wartime, yes, she agreed with Papa.

"And these people they've sent, you wouldn't believe some of these Jews, these primitives. Half the time I can't understand a word they're saying," she told the wife who said yes, exactly.

Woven throughout with Russian anyhow, the Yiddish the two women spoke as respectable Soviet citizens had been modernized, they knew. A national policy of the Bolsheviks' had stripped its alef-beyz of several characters, the ones derived from Hebrew, and all its Hebrew words had been prohibited and dropped from public use. This on the whole meant that the language of Jewish religious life was absent from this Soviet Yiddish and people Musya's age who'd been taught to recognize its sounds as backward didn't know how to speak it; while the elder Kotzes's generation could call up the basics from memory more or less complete. But the Jewish captives from the west in their thousands spoke their unfiltered Yiddish in strange accents full of bizarre idioms that added too much perplexity. Vastly outnumbered, the natives were inclined to grow clannish.

"We've been lucky," Baila said. "Under the Soviets—we advanced." The dependents murmured but Widow Krutonog agreed:

"True, that's what I say. Just look around you." Indeed, Baila Kotz recognized in this new kitchen her immediate housing ideal but the landlady was sorry, not an inch was vacant. The room was full up. "Also," she continued uneasily, "your girl will soon—I think about the mess." Baila told her not to worry, they'd been promised an easy childbirth.

"And the mess isn't so much," the Odessan grandmother soothed.

"We'll see," said Widow Krutonog.

What she had in mind for them was no palace, she admitted. But it had a bed and it would be private, their five or later six alone, this for a substantial sum she guaranteed. Potato "parts" from Krutonog's supply would be included but tenants were responsible for getting their own bread and extras. For now they'd have a brief wait, the widow explained, during the eviction and clean-up after the current deadbeat occupants. A tall, light-haired Krutonog dependent and housemaid who looked like a fighter, summoned, received her benefactor's orders and went to accomplish these tasks.

The wait was more than relaxing. After the family's ordeal, the two freezing and filth-ridden months of it and its indignities, to sit unharassed in a clean warm sunlit room was a staggering comfort. Musya fell fast asleep, she thought they all did, too briefly—the girl who'd come back flushed was too efficient. Kindly, though, she hefted Sender's hatbox of dishware for him and Musya's bag, too, and led the new tenants back to the quarters she'd just cleared for their occupation—the family's home for the rest of the war, as it turned out.

(2)

Papa Kotz went first. It happened not long before the baby was born, less than a week. From the start he'd hated life in the cubicle. Its discomforts made him restless. Whenever his stupor lifted he complained of breathing problems. He'd go stand in the corridor which was narrow so the people who lived in the other cubicles couldn't pass; sooner or later it always ended in a shouting match. Then he took to the thresholds where he'd find some invalids to argue with about blood sugar, kidney stones, trusses. Improbably, he began taking walks. One day he announced another need for air and this time he never returned.

"You're starving me." His parting words he spoke to his wife, who denied it.

"You're not starving."

"I'm starving. You're starving me." This time she didn't answer: they'd been through it before. He fumbled on the pair of eyeglasses she'd plucked from a corpse for him. They were missing an eyepiece, he'd complained. He cast a look around—he couldn't stand their cubicle.

He left them.

A cell, he'd called it—which it was, a squarish wooden cell. Lined with unfinished boards behind an exterior of plastered clay, it had a dirt floor, no ceiling, a miniscule window cut close to the rafters. Tin, thatch, shingles, cardboard, for all its layers the roof leaked anyhow. Flanked by others just as leaky, their cubicle had more recently housed indigent travelers and was part of the inn's former fruit canning shed. No trace of sweetness remained. Drafts assailed them but left their neighbors' stenches undispelled. Only slightly fitter for human habitation than a barn stall, according to Baila, who felt she'd been cheated by two landladies in one hour, their place had neither lock latch nor door. This wasn't unusual: beyond the new kitchen virtually no interior door at Kruto-nog's remained on its hinges. With every piece of furniture broken up and burned for firewood, doors stood in for tables, beds, benches, biers. The Kotzes' door, however, was both missing and gone. In Baila's eyes entitlement to a door came with the tenancy; she complained but nothing happened. With the widow in charge sensing more chervonsty in the picture than Baila wanted necessarily to show, a waiting game developed.

A bare light bulb in the corridor outside sufficed them for now. Papa Kotz complained nightly about sitting around in the dark. The bed was nothing but a rope frame and a mattress stuffed—not recently—with oak leaves. It slept four or Papa Kotz, whose sleep was too restless to share. He'd huddle atop their spread out luggage in his coat and sleep badly. For a daylight hour or two he'd take the bed where he slept even worse; he complained of the mattress, its deafening rustle, its dustiness which drove him from the room each day when they flipped and brushed it. He missed his old sofa but who didn't? What could they do? According to his wife he'd always been a restless sleeper, a claim he disputed. As recently as middle age ten hours sleep uninterrupted had been routine with him, he said. Now every hour or two he needed to get up and piss—or try to. The family's chamber pot was a badly dented zinc bucket for which Baila paid extra. Some people had brought their own, which mystified her:

"Who travels with a bucket?"

"I would," Sender said. He was keeping a mental list of what they should bring "next time." Bucket. Hacksaw. Matches. Salt. Leather strips and tools for shoe repair. Fingernail brush. More matches. More socks and gloves. Another bucket: "Two buckets—that would be better."

His grandmother demurred. "Two of anything would be better, no?"

"Not two of Papa Kotz," he shot back.

This was so far beyond the usual fond bickering that Baila caught her breath and looked sad. "What kind of little boy has no respect for his grandfather?"

"I'm six. Not little. I work."

It was true, he worked hard every day. Since the old man couldn't be trusted with something so valuable as their bucket—his stupor came and went—Sender always accompanied Papa Kotz on his trips across the yard to empty its contents. This was dirty work, too dirty for Musya to do in her condition. When it was Baila's turn, Sender went along most of the time. Sometimes he took his little brother for a walk, not too far. Inside the cubicle he managed many tasks and cleaned like a junior housemaid. Every day he helped shake out the family's clothes and check the seams for lice he'd pinch to death and nits he'd pick. Above all, he sewed, helping Musya put their wardrobe in repair while she combined the unsalvageable pieces into infant robes and blankets. Of needles and thread he'd packed plenty on their way out of Odessa.

"Your grandfather worked," said Baila. "All his life he worked, he was a hard worker."

"I never saw him work one minute," the grandson persisted.

"You don't know."

"No you don't know!"

"Be quiet," Musya said; and in fact a silence fell. The draft-rattled corridor windows provided daylight with the cubicle's own little ticket stub of a fentster contributing a faint square gleam. They could see well enough until dusk when they'd have to stop. Her father's thimble clicked. Sender was patching, Musya was tearing; they missed scissors. Along with Papa's silver fruit knife their only pair had been confiscated on the road. Musya's thimble had vanished.

The silence didn't last. "He goes and looks at the koorvah!" A piercing note in Sender's normally pleasant voice sparked Musya's concern. She thought he might be feverish but he said he felt fine. Meanwhile his grandmother looked askance at him and his announcement.

"What koorvah? At Tauber's?"

"No." He described a tent, a woman within, and the goings on outside. Baila shook her head.

"What kind of place is this place? Koorvahgrad, maybe." As the man's wife she'd have to see Papa peeping at the show with her own eyes, she supposed with reluctance. She'd spent three hours already that day out and about in the ghetto procuring food; every day it took longer. Her younger grandson lay asleep in bed, feverish, difficult to leave. She felt worried and tired. "What next?" she said.

Musya whose heart throbbed strangely in sympathy said, "Let me go." Maybe it was nothing, she said, not worth Baila's trouble. The walk to the tent was a short and safe one; she'd take Sender along to show the way. No, Baila didn't like it. But now Musya insisted—she wanted a walk. Pacing up and down the corridor for exercise wasn't enough. It didn't help that the old fruit canning shed's windowpanes offered almost full-scale views of the corpse pile in the kitchen garden through their mercifully numerous cracks and ripples. The sky was solid cloud, the day uninviting; but Anton's sleepiness and fever felt like monsters chasing her and now nothing could stop her, she had to get out of there. She needed a walk and begged close to tearfully for the permission granted her at last:

"So go. And if it's too bad don't tell me."

Once outdoors, Musya tried hard to be glad. The achievement of her wish to be there left a glow quick to fade. The cold was piercing. Though mildly picturesque, the latest snowfall struck her eyes as a fresh mortal hazard. The gutters were frozen, the outhouses full and nailed shut. Foul splashes from emptied buckets lay all around. The atmosphere stank. Icicles menaced. No pavements, barely a road; no trucks, no cars, no carts, no animals; nothing but footpaths paved with icebound clods: to walk was to stagger along. The human crowds were dense as usual. Hunger marked every living face, starvation many still ones.

Not for the first time, her thoughts turned to the still people's survivors. Of all those friends and kin left behind to walk past their pitiful nakedness day after day, how many took to other routes, she wondered? How many stopped going out entirely? Then again, how many still people still received visits from loved ones? Here and there a face had been cleared of snow by someone's hand, a lock of hair brushed free.

Always short of breath these days, Musya called a halt. They'd come to a narrow plot of land with a marshy aspect. A barbed wire boundary like the tangled, balled up leavings from a hairbrush lay across its further end. The snowy view continued into blond willow groves, winter river mists, bruise-colored hillsides: another admirably scalloped vista, the place could really boast of them. Nicest of all, at this particular moment the view was empty of persons living or still; only unsuffering nature. A deep inhalation stirred the unborn baby to kick her in the bladder. To have a baby would be fine. What Musya was wondering now was how long a life bereft of its older brothers would be bearable. She thought not much longer than the time she would require to carry their bodies outdoors, go back to the cubicle, lie down in a corner and die. She watched a band of waterfowl flash across the landscape trailing bugle calls. Of course, she realized, much better to lie down in the snow than go back inside just to be dragged out again as dead weight, less wasteful of other people's energies and probably faster, too; altogether more thoughtful.

"Don't die," she told Sender.

"Why should I die? Don't you die." He bent and finally made a snowball, threw it, not far. He tried again, an attempt to look vigorous. She wasn't fooled. He said, "Even if I get typhus disease I won't die, Herr Asch says so—I'm too young. And Antosha's younger so he's even safer." As if he'd convinced himself the next snowball went twice the distance and the whoop he gave was genuine; pure health.

They continued past a few gap-sided barns and warehouses jammed with groaning humanity, the absolutely penniless. If her parents had been shipped to Obodovka they'd be in there, Musya assumed. All her mother's sewn-up cash remained tucked among folds of tiger skin inside Anton's satchel, pillowing his burning head today. If epidemic typhus killed him, she planned to burn this satchel with all its contents in the kitchen garden as a funeral offering.

Beyond a string of empty paddocks lay their destination: another open patch, this one a waste ground. Bright rusted machine parts poked out of snow drifts. Shabby men stood about. The sky was low here, milk tea colored. The place was scattered with lean-tos and tents; Sender pointed out the koorvah's. Pitched at a distance from the rest it was inconspicuous, squat and small, almost too small for two. But a live fire smoked among the bricks of a little cooking shed just outside its flap: not the worst set-up in the Obodovka ghetto by any means. The smoke obscured things.

Musya strained her eyes. "Is he here?" Sender couldn't tell. At least a dozen men were visible. Not until a gust of cold wind cleared the view did they spot Papa Kotz, his humped shoulders distinctive. He didn't see them, he was facing the little tent—watching it, Musya realized, exactly like the other dozen men in the dumpyard were doing. She took a closer look herself. There was nothing to see. The tent's pale canvas sides were opaque. Maybe the canvas was moving; maybe not—not enough to tell. This was a determined but witless pastime her father-in-law had found for himself, she judged.

Then the tent did heave and a man exited in an unsteady adjustment of jacket and trousers. Like branches tossing in a wind the men on watch all crackled into animation; she watched their faces flare nakedly, their feet almost do dance steps. She nearly missed the next customer, who'd dashed from concealment behind the door from a half-dismantled truck—the koorvah's waiting room, she guessed—and dived right inside the tent, no chitchat. It was quite the cottage industry but at the same time frightening and uncanny. And what to tell Sender who asked, naturally, what the koorvah did inside her tent to the men who went in, and why other men were watching? Natural questions that deserved natural answers, real ones. However, quite simply, Sender was too young to know these things—he was too young to have seen this. This Moishe Kotz, indubitable father of her legal husband, Boris his son, had landed her in yet one more predicament. She thought of poor Mrs Drobitz's ordeal beneath the oxcart. Then she'd told the boys the men were hurting Mrs Drobitz, strange bad men. How to explain the same thing undergone voluntarily? How to understand well enough to explain? She couldn't. Of course, she realized, children always saw these things—some children.

She said, "The koorvah stops them being afraid. She makes men feel braver."

He considered this reply. "With magic? Like a witch?"

"A little, yes." Witchcraft: she pictured business drying up and the koorvah's tent home taking flight like Baba Yaga's on a giant pair of chicken legs, off to the next ghetto. "And psychology. Witchcraft and psychology." This customer was louder, he had a call like a weak steam whistle. "And exercise." And the men who stood watching shared the spell at second hand, she said.

Back at Krutonog's, Musya left nothing out as she reported her observations. Mama Kotz agreed that there was much to pity here and plenty to find humorous. Yet she was also incensed; she called the situation shaming. Hard, she slapped her husband on his arm when he returned that day, an hour behind them. "You better not go in to her!" She kept slapping Papa.

"Of course not!" He turned from her blows which struck his back instead with sodden, unwell-sounding thuds.

"A woman sick in the head like that to begin with and who knows what else—shame on you."

"She has problems," he conceded. "So leave it alone."

"You leave it alone. Seriously." Baila turned from him with a disgusted air to attend to the food she'd dished onto four Manchukuo import china dessert plates; small portions. The family would wash their dishes with snow later on. The main and only course was the usual potato peelings which would have been perfectly fine with salt, Sender was right about that, salt was missed. Tonight's rare bit of onion which would have been delicious with salt smelled delicious anyhow, like food. They'd offered it first to Anton but he'd pushed them away. Now they watched Baila take thirds from one plate, divide among the other three and put the empty plate aside. One plate for Sender, one for Musya, Baila took one which meant no nosh for Papa—zero. He whimpered when the truth hit.

Then the anger came. "What can I do? What do you expect me to do? After my life!" He thumped himself on the chest. "The way you had me live? What about my shame?" Baila kept chewing. "I've lived on crumbs!"

"You did okay," she told him. "What more do you think you deserved?"

His jowls were shaking like they'd never stop. His tears overflowed. "You're starving me."

"As usual," she agreed that time. "Says the fat man."

Anton sat up quickly in bed, flushed, unseeing. Then he turned and vomited again. Papa Kotz went and stood looking down at the puddle drain darkly into the earthen floor where it left behind a little pile of matter: canned wiener sausages. He groaned.

"That fucking Weissbein."

Was it true? Did his wife have it in for him? Or was this just another argument in the life of a long-married couple, with two sides and justice on both? Papa was right: being starved was no good. And his wife was right: if Papa wanted to eat, he ought to provide more. He said he couldn't; she said others couldn't but did—why couldn't he? The expenditure of useful energies required for koorvah-watching was debated: he claimed it was nothing, "less than nothing." He kept going to the dumpyard, kept coming back empty-handed and hungry. "All over this place I see they're starving the old men," he reported. His kind was endangered—he sensed a conspiracy. His wife while denying her involvement in any such plan might feed him two or three twists of potato peel in a day. Where he was concerned, her attention to what passed for the family's larder was fiercely prohibitory. One night he took some food and she woke up and beat him with the water pitcher—red and white enameled tin, it had belonged to Mrs Drobitz, after Baby her foremost treasure. The episode left its handle slightly loose and Baila wept about that the next morning. A broken pitcher they couldn't afford.

Musya knew in her soul that if Boris Kotz had been along, she and he would have argued just as cruelly as his parents did. Theirs were not love matches. Trapped in close quarters with the ones they hadn't chosen, the Kotzes weren't unusual. Recriminations of the most intimate kind rang out day and night from every corner of Transnistria:

"You made of me a laughingstock!"

"You made me old before my time!"

People hadn't been happy for years. By 1942, to no one's surprise, Love's dreams weren't coming true in many homes of the former Pale of Settlement. And now the happiness people had hoped for would never be theirs because human happiness had died. This was a major problem, this death of happiness. People mourned angrily.

Before he went Papa evidenced a slight relapse. Strange to see, it was a nervous stupor that possessed him this time around. He was unresponsive but twitchy, with swollen fingers returning again and again to every pocket in his clothes for a forgotten crust or carrot or for his lost fruit knife or for nothing; he might have lost his mind by then, Musya supposed. His fingers, his face, his whole body looked swollen. Where the rest of them kept their nails filed short his had grown out like gray talons. What the old man's fate would be she could not find it within herself to regard as a subject of interest—not then. Anton was in danger. He lay there. They rubbed him and rubbed him with dry towels to keep the circulation going as recommended against gangrene; they spoon-fed him some lemon preserves that he choked down. Yes, there were hidden provisions. Baila had kept some and Sender had too, all along, in secret from each other; they'd held back, planning for the emergency of birth when Anton's typhus intervened. To earn his beating Papa Kotz had consumed a stray tin of sprats caper-stuffed. How much was left in reserve Musya hadn't been told. Poor Papa, in his upset and general misfortune he'd vomited the stolen contents right away; then, swaying above his own mess on the corridor floor, he'd let loose with a howl which had been much complained of. The rest of them had cleaned up in a flash before anyone suspected the family's hidden resources.

"A bisel," he pleaded. It was his last day. "A brekl." He'd lingered indoors because it was snowing hard outside. Their backs were turned to him as they tended the sufferer. Baila said no. He came around the bedside to see their faces. They weren't looking at him, just a few busy glances. "You're starving me," he said.

He'd been gone a while when Baila had a premonition. She remarked on it but did nothing. An hour later they sent Sender Kotz outside to fetch snow in the pitcher. He returned snow-dusted, his feet dragging, his face troubled. He seemed to want to spare them.

"Papa Kotz is still people now," he said.

It was true. Outside, not right out front but sitting propped against the small fence two doors down the old man had come to rest. It was clear he'd been partially buried in snow until someone happening along had disturbed his stillness to steal his hat, shoes and trousers. Across his legs—purplish and pale, fat, strangely hairless, studded with ulcers like plum slices—fresh snow was collecting; the shoulders of his fancy overcoat remained thickly mantled. From the fringe encircling his bare scalp strands of unwashed hair some long as a woman's hung past his ears and down his neck which was grimy in death. His ears looked enormous. His crippled eyeglasses were gone.

With a couple of handfuls of snow his widow rubbed Papa's nape clean. "Which way to the koorvah?" she asked. Musya pointed: sad to relate that had been his direction.

Baila turned around and trudged back to Krutonog's with Musya following—as she'd followed her out to begin with—uselessly. Their trip had been quick, that was good. Children lived in fear at Krutonog's, where a rumor ran wild among their number about child-snatchers bent on selling them as house slaves to Ukrainian peasants. According to Sender the giant old inn was supplying all the local slave rings; with no doors to lock safely against them, lurking perpetrators had their pick of children left unwatched. How much truth there was in these ideas Musya didn't know but she'd hated leaving a six year-old boy alone with his sick brother and frightened. They'd had no choice: to identify a corpse for sure took two adult people. In reality it should have been Papa making this pair—but his had been the body. Already here was an example of how life would be more difficult without the old man. She pictured the care that went into working up schedules and daily routines in their cubicle and counted how many lay broken tonight. He'd had his small but significant share of tasks and his social uses as well, Musya supposed. Intangibles. What would they do with Papa dead? It was a mild one, maybe, but a catastrophe no less.

Vastly relieved at their return Sender leapt up and threw his arms around them, an awkward embrace given Musya's bulk and his grandmother's inattention. Her newly-widowed eyes raked the cubicle through frantic tears.

"How could I have him back inside? Where could I put him to lay him out with no door? Who could even carry—it's impossible!" Baila groaned, hating social impropriety. She paced a somewhat random track around the narrow cubicle, then stopped. She'd reached her decision. "He'll have to stay there."

"Well, of course," said Musya. Sender agreed. What could they do?

"My poor husband!" With that, Baila sank down on the edge of the bed next to Anton who looked a little better—very little.

Dizzy, still breathless and numb from the cold, the hurry, the shock of recognition, Musya leaned back and pressed her palms against the wall. The boards where she stood had been faintly warmed by a kerosene heater in the next cubicle—very, very faintly. Sender came and joined her, they always encouraged one another to exercise. He started doing leg lifts but she stretched her back only. As her breath began to steady and she felt the unusual surging sensation in her limbs and head surge unabated, she thought she might be entering labor; however there was no pain. There was simply too much to see, to hear, to experience in the world, she couldn't take in more than a morsel of it; even in their tiny cubicle the objects of perception were too numerous and pressing.

Life overwhelmed her.

For several moments alive was all Musya was. Life surged through her. She felt no sorrow, no fear and no discomfort. Her hunger pangs even changed character: now they signaled the anticipation of a square meal and not its denial—she'd eat again, she knew. Signs of recovery she'd missed she noticed now on Anton's face. The gloom in her eye had lifted to reveal a glimpse of hope, sharp, bright, fleeting; she pictured chasing it up to the barbed wire only to watch its escape, effortless; pure spirit. Hope would always get away here.

Baila sat shaking her head back and forth. At last she sighed.

"His poor trousers."

A moment later Anton stirred and the same thing struck all three: a momentous realization.

They lacked blankets.

"His overcoat!"

(3)

After she'd been in labor for about an hour Musya understood that she would probably die and she became furious. The sound volume she'd been trying to suppress for the other cubicles' sake—or maybe propriety's sake, she didn't know, she'd just stopped caring—shot up, doubled, tripled; she screamed with all her might. Even in Birobidzhan she'd have had medical care in a clinic of some kind. Instead, her cries protested, in this Ukraine where Jews were hated she found herself brought to childbed in hazardous squalor.

They'd been at Boim's when she'd gone into labor. Dealing with Boim could make anyone angry enough to scream, labor or no labor. He was an infuriating notable person-age at Krutonog's where he squatted in the center of a skylit room beneath a cloak of piled-up tattered fur coats. He came from a tough part of Romania where everyone who hadn't either been murdered by now or marched to a Transnistrian death trap of their own probably rejoiced to be rid of him. A criminal operator, a wife-beater (which no one could prove, he said), allegedly a pimp, Boim had enterprise. His wife had died and he'd sold their baby to some Ukrainians, this he admitted freely. Between his chamber walls a pile of garments, there had to be a thousand, rose waist-high and halfway up the open doorway; on this elevation he squatted in his furs at eye-level with his customers—higher in Musya's case—who were kept to the threshold. To find any item in the heap however deeply buried he employed an infallible system, a family trade secret: Boims had always dealt old clothes on the side of their crookery. A lineage of experts, he boasted.

Boim sat on a door laid crossways atop the merchandise that also served him as a kind of desk. The bare light bulb ablaze above his shaggy head indicated their arrival during business hours. Sender knew the place: he'd been along for Baila's attempt to get warmer stuff from Boim in exchange for the sailor suit Anton had outgrown. It hadn't been much and the creature had laughed cruelly—taking it, though. No doubt he'd done very well with this exquisite masterpiece of hand-tailoring; Baila could picture, she said, the illiterate local babushkas delighting in one lucky grandson's second-hand class. She'd hated Boim for his cruelty, his stinginess, and for the studied lack of respect he'd shown her. His condescension had been slap-like. "A creature—an animal," was how she'd described him. Now face to face with its wild yellow eyes and the hair on it thick and coal-colored, Musya could be more specific: Boim had the face of a hungry wolf. He was also tubercular and alcoholic. He crouched, looking down at her, and took a pull on a vodka bottle without moving his eyes from her face. Then he spoke.

"What you want?"

"Mister Boim—" she began but he stopped her.

"Ask me if I live here."

She blinked. "Do you live here, Mister Boim?"

"You call this living?"

"Ha ha," she said.

He grinned, a nasty sight of stumps. "You heard that joke before, girlie?"

"Only about a thousand times," she told him.

"That's right, that's right—you're a city girl."

"That's right," she repeated.

"Odessa."

"Yes."

"I know yes," he said. "Where's the other female of you? The old bitch who stopped feeding her fat husband—hey, you two are next. Better be careful."

Musya frowned hard. "Mister Boim—"

"Ha," he said. "Ha ha. It's my turn now to say ha ha. To you, Miss Odessa, ha ha." She waited. Mr Asch was still alive then and living in the same room he'd occupied at Krutonog's for close to twenty years; she wished they could have paid a call on him instead. But this trip to Boim's, she reminded herself, was to help Baila so Baila wouldn't have to do everything. Once more she tried:

"Mister Boim."

"Ha ha."

Sender thought this was enough. He raised his chin and started: "Mister Boim, my grandmother and I saw a little girl who works for you run away with my still grandfather's overcoat and we want you to give it back to us. Please."

Boim stared. "Who is this feygele?"

"Answer his question, Mister Boim," said Musya. "Where's our overcoat?"

"What overcoat? Listen, I got many little girls work for me, many people got many little girls work for them. Little boys, too. You, little feygele boy, you want a job maybe? Work for me? You do okay, it don't matter."

"I don't want a job, thank you, I want my grandfather's fancy brown overcoat. And the girl works for you." Sender pointed. "She's right under there, watching us." Indeed, to Musya's surprise a nondescript hump in the giant clothes heap twitched, shifted and split apart to reveal a pair of dimpled hands and a pinched set of features, female, very young. Sender said, "Not you, no, the other. Her." And there was another one.

Musya felt unwell. "Are these your children?" she asked.

"Not mine," said Boim. "They work for me. That don't prove an overcoat. What exactly do you city retards want here?"

"Justice—we want justice! Give us back what's ours!" This was Sender; she had to signal him to quiet down. At times he was so like his mother.

She explained, "It's Italian wool, Mister Boim, imported, excellent condition." At which Boim barked so hard and full-throated a laugh it landed him in a coughing fit.

Musya waited, wishing the encounter more speedily concluded. She wasn't comfortable. Halfway up the steep staircase to Boim's domain a rush of water had escaped her. *What next?* she'd thought, still climbing. Now Boim took a pull on his bottle, corked it, and from some recess in his tattered pelts produced the makings of a cigarette. The man was too much: only a criminal could sustain a smoking habit in the Obodovka ghetto. He was the first she'd seen up close. Fascinated despite herself at the display of sheer wherewithal she watched the process through to the match sparked on a thumbnail and the first unsteady puff. The tobacco burning in her nostrils made her stomach lurch.

"For my health," he said.

"Do you have our overcoat or not?"

Clamping his lips around the cigarette paper he leaned aside to plunge one arm up to the shoulder in cloth. When he sat up again, a brown wool coat trailed from his fist. It was covered in stains, bad ones, she could smell from where she stood, and had a ruined lining. "That's it," Sender said; the Mogen Dovid patch, his work, had been removed but he recognized the shadows of the six points and the remaining button, the label.

"Fake," said Boim.

"It's imported from Milan," the boy insisted doggedly.

Boim eyed the garment with distaste through plumes of smoke. "It's a piece of shit. Probably made in Bulgaria."

"You're a liar!" Sender accused. "And you sold your baby."

"So what? Somebody bought. What do I need a baby for?"

"You're a bad man."

"Okay Mister Perfect, have it your way. I'm bad and your coat is Italian. As for its excellent condition, if you say so, I say again, have it your way." Boim lay Papa's overcoat across his knees: traditional dealing. "So, what do you give me for it?"

"Nothing—it's ours! You stole it from us!"

"Sender!" Musya couldn't finish. Pain seized her. Cramp kept her bent and breathless. At last she straightened up, panting. "Oh dear," she said. "I'm having a baby now."

Sender pushed her arm. "Then let's get out of here!"

"This won't end good." Boim spoke unemotionally. "I can tell you."

"I'm going to be fine, Mister Boim."

"Don't get your hopes up, Odessa girl. Your chance here is poor." Infection would get her if shock and blood loss didn't get her first—she knew. The clothes merchant continued: "Hey, you got nighties—nice ones, two or three, no?" Boim shifted on his hoard and sent his yellow gaze darting at Sender Kotz. "You, Princess, tell your bubbe, don't waste, I got cash for her. Bring me these nighties today, clean condition, tonight, whatever. Cash money."

"Mister Boim," Sender asked, "why are you still talking?"

Musya stepped closer. "Please give us the overcoat, Mister Boim. We made a mistake—we should have taken it faster. Sooner—much sooner."

"That's right," he smiled, satisfied.

"So we lost it for awhile. But now we really need it back—more than you do."

"Wrong," he said. "Not more than me." He gestured around. "Where would I be if everybody took back? Sitting my ass on the floor with nothing to drink, that's where." In reply she screamed at him:

"Give us the overcoat! Give us one fur—one! Give us blankets! Help! Why won't you help us?" She kept it up, really haranguing him. "You don't need all this!"

"Yes I do need!" Boim scrambled on his haunches and thrust his face at Musya. "I need every bit. Don't tell me what I need, girlie. I'm a sick man. You think I can afford anything? Look at me—how long you think I'm lasting without my investments? I need what I can get my hands on. Now excuse me and get the hell out of here. We're closed." He reached up, pulled a string; his room went dark. There he sat, his mouth marked by an ember, growling.

"MOMMY!"

Musya screamed again. She heard a suggestion from Baila to quiet down a notch, followed by one of the Krutonog dependents saying it didn't matter. The other dependents agreed. They'd most of them assembled to stand around the cubicle and in its open doorway, a collection of amateur midwives and childbirth enthusiasts; the landlady herself kept away. All along Baila Kotz had been courting the beneficence of the new electric kitchen—groveling, she said—with little success. But once her recent widowhood supplied the missing spark, ties had formed. Until then an object of resolute disregard, the impending event in the Kotz cubicle became one of passionate interest inside the new kitchen. Pumping hard, Baila did her best to keep the level rising until now, come the event, the interest flowed back their way in woman helpers, fairly clean bedding and towels and basins of hot water. Not for everyone would Mrs Krutonog have consented to light the steam boiler.

They were lucky.

Musya kept screaming. She didn't feel lucky.

Where was her own dear mother? Where had she gone? Never more necessary, would she appear? The possibility that she might be close, there, inside the Obodovka ghetto tormented Musya. The horrible barns, half-reduced to frame and open to every other particle of the cold wet elements preyed on her thoughts constantly. Now she felt her screams extend to pierce their ruined sides: she called out to the mother.

"But I told you," Baila said. "I told you."

As far past their gaping wagon-sized doorways as she'd dared penetrate, Baila had looked in the barns, where she said people had jammed themselves in, impossible to tell how, on top of one another; they were stacked up to the lofts where they started again. She'd looked, she said, and asked who there was to ask, deciphering their shtetl Yiddish. So far gone with typhus as most of them were the coherence was spotty but the message consistent: from Odessa was nobody there. Likewise among the halls at Krutonog's, on the weekly bread lines, in the frozen carrot garden, by the fence where the townsfolk came to trade for food, no one had seen Falk nor any melodramatic, limping, razor-thin specialty dressmakers from Odessa anywhere around.

"Don't give up hope," urged one of the dependents and the rest agreed. They were they were on rare good terms with each other today, Musya had noticed; but it was true. Many reliable accounts existed of the most improbable reunions inside Transnistria. Sundered loved ones of every kind, parents with children, sweethearts in pairs, indeed entire families who'd found or been found by one another—all talking at once, the dependents reviewed some major examples. To hear them tell it the deported host had been pulled from its homes into an elaborate game of hide and seek sprinkled with miracles. Musya knew these stories already, she screamed.

In truth they'd been a private comfort.

She'd always hoped. Back in the rubble heaps of Slobodka she'd expected to find the mother at any moment. Since then, each new transit point and stop no matter how ghastly had thrummed with promise. Everyone healthy enough had seemed to feel the same; she knew Baila searched for Falk while she'd looked for her parents among the anxious crowds of eager-asking strangers with their treasured photographs to show. From Baila's album before it went in the fire she'd given Musya one to aid her search, a group portrait from Liza's wedding to Boris Kotz; spring 1934. Her own likeness was poor and the parents' unrepresentative; her whole family looked stiff, even heavyset. The image had seemed worthless for the purpose, she'd put it away—now it was the only one left. Her sister looked like a child in it.

Boris had never changed.

She grew agitated and called for Sender: he was in charge of the photograph. Was it safe? They told her not to worry. But Sender was gone, they'd sent him to sit quietly with Widow Krutonog and a buffer dependent. They'd set up a little bed for Anton by the steam boiler. Musya fretted. It seemed to her that Sender Kotz could do a better job delivering a baby than all these women; he was patient, efficient, clean, sensible, in all respects a more advanced person, she felt.

Someone told her to push.

Musya saw the world as a huge red sun speckled with black; the black spots were newspaper offices, all abandoned. She groaned and the vision faded. The women murmured, they were a wall of flowers: this was so much better, she thought. The woman flowers would multiply their leaves and blossoms to make a soft bed to catch her baby's fall; and beside it her burial place. "Bury me," she gasped. The rest wouldn't come, she couldn't ask for her dead body to be buried anywhere at all—her only wish, her last mortal desire. Yet even of this she'd be cheated. Her words had been murdered. Furious, she screamed.

At every stop on their road to the Obodovka ghetto she'd heard the same stories and the same kinds of stories. On one side were happy ones with unlikely reunions and near-death escapes and unexpected acts of mercy, kindness, charity. The rest were at least as numerous and they were like nightmares. The fascist invaders were cruel: no surprise, everyone had expected it. But the reality shocked. The reality caused unbearable mental pain. It was mass murder, nothing less. Jews died horribly, brutally murdered. Since

Slobodka she'd been hearing of atrocities committed all across Odessa—she'd witnessed the scene at the streetcar line but there had been more in those days. One massacre followed another. Musya had looked for her mother, picking her way through rubble, past corpses, past clutching fingers and hoarse, blind-eyed pleas; she'd looked for her in every group alongside every road; at every transit inspection she'd watched, alert; in cattle sheds turned teeming barracks she'd searched with no scarf tied around her mouth and nose to cut the reek of dysentery because she'd wanted to be seen, possibly recognized by her mother. She'd never stopped hoping. At the same time stories reached her. There'd been a series of stable massacres people spoke of, where Jews had been marched into Odessa's empty livestock pens and horse barns and shot on the spot—a use for the space, the Einsatzgruppen called it. Hearing this, she'd think: *Mommy was there.*

Near-witnesses told of the four warehouses filled with Jews from Odessa, locked inside. One warehouse, the most crowded, held women with children. The killers made holes in the walls for their machine guns and then on command stood outside shooting into the four interiors until all the Jews were dead. This happened a short march from the city, in Dalnik. The next day, just to make sure, they came back and set the warehouses on fire. Many people spoke of the woman who'd escaped through the roof with her hair aflame to meet a bullet death after all: Musya's mother? *Who else?* she'd think.

Even so she'd hoped to see her in the next louse-check line or find her sitting in the next oxcart, the mother with her mother's lap for a daughter's head to rest in, an embrace that banished pain. Like tempest waves, love and loss and longing for her Mommy crashed through Musya's soul.

They put a folded cloth in her mouth to bite down on and demanded she keep pushing.

As for the father, all she had was guesswork. One of the firing squads by Odessa harbor seemed likeliest, the timing would fit. While there, he might have been doused with gasoline and burned alive instead. He might have been hanged, thousands were; he might have been locked in a basement to starve. Far from impossible, the mother might have guessed right and he'd found an old woman to shelter with, a customer; Musya pictured a camphorated wardrobe shelf his hiding place. He might have been rounded up and deported into the countryside too, she supposed. She'd never track him down, any given description being pointless. Her Daddy was typical. He was vague, a bit of a clown. He slipped through life. He had some nice smiles and a few that were just fatuous. He cried easily, never for long, and garbled song lyrics. His physique wasn't impressive. He looked unimportant. He liked to wander. If someone were to demand his rank, position, profession, degree or his seat in the synagogue the answer wouldn't vary: none. His home village hadn't existed for decades; meanwhile his name was almost laughably common. A better photograph than they possessed wouldn't have helped since the man had never resembled his photographs, he'd managed to hide his true appearance from the camera every time, it was like some kind of trick of his not to leave a record. Too bad that his last remaining daughter would shortly die, murdered, by the deliberate withholding of modern medicine from those they'd imprisoned, by fascists. Maddening.

Now he had another grandson.

Apparently the birth had been quick; the Krutonog dependents all sounded surprised and a touch disappointed. They led a dull life.

(4)

Musya lay in bed for a week waiting to die. A new convert to the charm of small boys, the widow Krutonog kept Anton with her; he was said to be much improved, showing an appetite. Sender went back and forth between his brother's bedside and Musya's. So did Baila, making progress, she said. They were close to being almost assured a corner in the new electric kitchen in her latest report.

"Eat a smoked oyster," she urged Musya.

"I can't." It was true—she loathed them. Now that the family had a little salt she preferred to stick with potato peels.

"Try just one. It's meat, it's what we have!"

The point wasn't worth arguing so Musya did try one smoked oyster from the tin. It was delicious. Her eyes watered. "Poor Papa Kotz," she sighed.

With a quick look, Baila asked, "Why poor Papa?" Musya said she didn't know. There he was, photographing fatter in a fine suit, spectacles in hand so that myopic eyes peered back at them from 1934. His widow, stroking a single fond glove tip across his face, said, "Don't let him fool you. He led a comfortable life—until the end I mean. Socialism was good to Papa. He had his imported food and English cashmere socks. His radio programs he liked. To Papa that's what mattered most, his comforts."

"And Samuel mattered," Musya said. "He never stopped talking about his hero son."

A subtle eyebrow rose and dipped. "When Samuel was alive on the other hand, not so much. Then it was his no-good wastrel son. Then, they fought." Baila made a pained face, remembering happily. "Like roosters! Every day! No, Samuel was my pet, not Papa's. I was the one, I never stopped talking. My handsome son." Adoration lit the look she gave the groom's side as her fingertip returned to trace one edge of a thimble-sized glare in which a few symmetrical gray marks floated: a clean-shaven man. Musya barely recalled him.

"I wish you'd hired a better photographer," she said idly, then gave a wince as the dead man's namesake yanked at her sore nipple. Every time she started to relax it was this way, a sharp reminder in one form or other would come from her baby: there he was, no forgetting. She'd had him.

The next Samuel Kotz.

"Eat," said Baila.

"These were Papa's favorites," Musya answered. Her heavy heart sagged with pity for the old man whose sea lion tongue had lost the bite of brine forever.

"That's how come I hid them so well," Baila said. "Be assured. If I'd let Poor Papa get another hand on what we were saving then we'd have nothing now. He'd have left us with nothing."

"No," Musya disagreed. "Because then he'd still be here."

"Even worse!" Self-abashed, the widow dipped her pale gray head. Musya watched an insect cross the red-flecked parting in the hair which like her own was thinner, braided, pinned close. At some transit points and camps in Transnistria, to prevent epidemic typhus every Jew received a haircut down to the scalp, man woman and child without exception. It didn't work. She and Baila had been happy to have missed those stops but now Musya wasn't sure. Hair would grow back; meanwhile it was no advantage. "Ah, well. Poor Papa," Baila resumed. "You're right. It was hard at the end for him. But out here like this in a place like this was no place for a man like Moishe. I'll say it—he was soft."

And yet, Musya thought, he'd also been enterprising. He'd found community in Obodovka, there among his kindred peepers. Even in silence, the men gathered at the koorvah's tent to watch must have known themselves to be in company with one another. Which must have been a kind of comfort: she pictured some universal brotherhood of the carnal imagination—a sisterhood as well. For the number of fantasies she'd watched unfold across various blanks in time and space, Musya deserved her own membership. Deeply, in a way beyond marriage she and Papa had been bound: he'd been a dreamer like she was. Blame him for Yankel's death she always would but for his primary flaws she forgave him. He'd been a little rough but always a gentleman. He'd left them, not to be a burden in the end; he'd stepped outside. "I only wish you hadn't starved him to death," she answered. Decked in snowflakes, Papa slumped across her own conscience, unbarbered, windblown, still. "The worst part was how he knew what was happening."

Baila nodded a sad downturned face. "True. He suffered. But how else could it end?" Raising her eyes, she gestured around. The raw plank walls of their cubicle glistened with frost. "I mean, this isn't a set-up to keep us alive."

"No," Musya agreed.

"One generation makes way for the next."

"I suppose."

"These are the choices."

Musya gave the last word to her mother-in-law and ate some more nosh. At her bothered breast the next generation squirmed and suckled. Her baby was rose-colored with black fuzz and vaguely human features. Pronounced a handsome male in good health at birth he'd proved himself robust and what mothers called a good sleeper in the days and nights since. He'd barely cried. He seemed like a perfectly nice and even somewhat superior baby; Musya found him very interesting. Yet if the onset pangs of a death she feared—the lingering one that follows childbirth—were only a few hours away for her, how much more fragile was this life she'd given! It couldn't survive her own for very long, she knew. Doubtful of its surviving that far, Musya waited for infant mortality to befall them first. Inside a frozen little rag cocoon with wind-whipped ragged ends he'd be piled among the rest in the kitchen garden. Born to be snuffed out, the creature satisfied its momentary hunger while her body lived; she did her best and steeled herself against attachment.

She didn't care about the baby's name. She listened to the chuckling sounds it made as it fed, her eyes at play among the black feathered curls on its rosy eagle-egg skull. The nostrils puffed. Samuel was the name Baila wanted. Musya's first choice, had she cared, Samuel wouldn't have been; she'd have preferred Zev for a name—or Nemo, on which the boys were insisting. Yet Baila's choice felt almost right.

"Samuel Nemo Kotz." She named him to herself. Dimly, a pair of white shins twitched to a stop in a distant road. The baby's all-seeing gaze swept her.

After he'd lived forty-eight hours the crowds descended and began to circulate across the open doorway. Their tiny cubicle became a destination for inquiring, restless, busy-body types from up to three or four dwellings away. People in general wanted to see for themselves that something good had happened in the Obodovka ghetto. A few took heart, Musya could tell, at the authentic mother and child tableau revealed when their tattered curtain wall was parted but most remained skeptical. She remained skeptical. Time would tell.

Much more vitally the Kotz family's standing received an immediate boost. This feat of survival reflected very well on their breeding and hygiene—and highly also on Krutonog's. The landlady's hand in the success of things thus far was advertised; her reputation buoyed, she grew more generous. The hot water kept flowing. Clean diapers hung from a new laundry line supplied with pins. And the incredible boon of a small chest of drawers had made the premises feel and look far less mean.

An unlikely air of luck, comfort, even prosperity pervaded this busy time. It seemed the more Musya's family received the more they were given. Salt, matches, biscuits, candles, aspirin, thread: precious commodities were almost showered on them. Some person they'd never met brought them a blanket. A few offered baby clothes. A very surprising gift that arrived one night without explanation while everyone slept was Papa's overcoat—crooked Boim was presumed to have grown a conscience. Everyone seemed to bring advice, largely contradictory, Musya felt too distracted to consider any of it in detail. The chatter and the traffic wore her out but Baila was determined to maximize their visitor numbers. She said they needed to inculcate fondness and habits of giving within as wide an audience as possible. The family's resources weren't infinite. This baby would need backers. His grandmother had become especially concerned to promote his future welfare among Obodovka's religious "high-ups" as she called them:

"They take care of their own, those people," Baila said

One day came the news that Samuel Nemo required a dangerous sounding surgical procedure because of tradition. The foreskin that looked fine to Musya and Sender Kotz in fact had to go. "But he's only a baby!" Musya complained.

Baila was adamant. "That's when they do it. And it's got to be done this week."

"No! Can't we at least wait until we get out of here and we can have it done in a hospital?"

"Hospital! These people's babies don't know from hospital circumcisions. We're in the middle of nowhere."

Sender corrected this. "Mister Asch says we're on a major crossroads."

"I don't want to become religious," Musya said unhappily.

"No one's asking you to," Baila replied. There was zero choice involved and no point in argument; in a sense it was Odessa all over again. The older woman ruled the roost.

As her strength returned only little by little Musya felt weak. While tiresome guest tides ebbed and flowed at the doorway her eyes would wander to the wall beside the door. There on sunlit days a sight refreshed her without fail when icy sunbeams pierced the dusty pane of fentster glass overhead, and a little square of silvery brightness inched across the boards; its transit could last the length of a double feature, even longer. A dense mechanical drone would replace the intruding chatter as her own thoughts took the lead, liberated.

Often on her mind was Boim and his unexpected change of heart. A wool overcoat was valuable property. On these frigid nights his survivors were preserving their extremities thanks to the return of Papa's to the family's possession. Repentance, people said. Musya sensed other motives. This had been a substantial gift from Boim, one that examination rendered progressively more intriguing. Could it be that in the wolfish clothes merchant she'd developed an admirer? Without effort she pictured Boim fur-clad, driven to clamber down off his hoard and creep downstairs with his bundle, keeping close to the walls on silent tread. How his combusting gaze must have raked her sleep-cloaked face and limbs arranged there so innocently among innocents, the poor lovelorn criminal; a sick man, she remembered. Who could say? Underneath all the hair and funk might be a better man, too.

She managed a turn around the cubicle, every day a few steps more, several more. Her back muscles welcomed the difference: she was lighter. Still Musya had nothing attractive to wear although her baby was dressed nicely. He was handsome and looked good in everything. She pictured showing him off on walks outside once the weather improved. What would springtime do to the Jewish ghetto of Obodovka, she wondered? After the still people were buried—when they stopped piling up—when there was less freezing to death and starvation, less typhus—for the strong ones left alive, would there be the usual sense of life feeling better again? Would the rebirth of pleasure occur? Or would life never feel better again?

Musya felt her eyes enjoy the way the little patch of fentster light contracted at the knots and gaps it crossed, seeing it made her smile. Wasn't this already pleasure?

The bris took place on a bright morning in the major rebbe's quarters down the street while Musya stayed behind in bed, weak and unneeded. Practically everyone in the old inn had gone along for the show, joining the baby's usual audience. Left to sit with the mother, a bored Krutonog dependent dozed quietly. Rare privacy enveloped Musya and her secret friend the sunbeam. Nobody talking, advising, fussing at her, making demands on her mind or her body: this too was pleasure. But the savor was limited, brief. Short on comfort, the little tab of light conjured only worries today.

For example: what if Boim's heart hadn't changed so very much? He wanted her—maybe—but maybe there was more he wanted from his investment. A healthy male baby to a man with his connections might represent a windfall. She could picture hers getting passed through the usual fence gap in exchange for tobacco and vodka. People liked babies. For all she knew the rebbe's band had its own designs on him, a trade in babies for protection. And if an extraneous grandson were the price of the family's security, how long would Baila Kotz hesitate to pay? Especially when she'd be buying a better chance for Samuel Nemo's survival, too. The Ukrainians could feed him.

All at once, powerfully, Musya wanted her baby back in her arms. Every atom of her missed him so much she almost let out a cry. Then, because if she'd lost him the regret would ruin her life, she almost groaned; but her throat was shut by the recognition of disaster. Getting him back would be just as bad. Loving them couldn't end well when babies were born Jewish in Transnistria. She hadn't meant to long for hers to live, she hadn't meant to care enough nor hope to hold him in her arms forever but now she did: she loved him. In an agony of nervous tension she slipped out of bed past the slumbering dependent and with eyes averted from the corpse pile view began to pace her old accustomed track up and down the canning shed corridor.

Baila Kotz came back a little flushed with wine and triumph: no hitches. "Only they weren't so crazy about the Nemo," she announced. Sender had also gone along to the ceremony. What he saw there shook him and he was never willing to talk about it. His new brother returned red-faced and hot with recent tears but at least outwardly calm again. From the cradle of her arms Samuel Nemo looked up at Musya and studied her features; his eyes were gold, green, gray, quizzical, his eyelashes fused into spikes like marigold seeds.

It wasn't her fault. "I'm sorry," she told him.

Later on, speculation said a curse must have been on that bris, so many people who'd been there died within a month or two. Among the first was Mr Asch, a bad loss, they all felt it. For one thing he'd been an admirer of Baila's and a few onlookers had treasured hopes of witnessing a match there. Baila felt worse and worse herself, her head ached.

Three days after the bris came the very first, when the big rebbe who'd officiated at it dropped dead. With a few decades of renown among certain Hasidim in Bukovina behind him, expelled and driven east under violent and inhumane conditions from a life of books and armchairs, this elderly man's continued survival had stood as a sign to the adherents who'd accompanied his every footstep from their home community; they'd felt the presence of divine protections. The rebbe had gained fervent new followers along the way and even more within the Obodovka ghetto where they set him up as a blessing. The story was that the sacred vow he'd made not to die in this captivity had left him invulnerable. Not only that, they said, but the rebbe was more vigorous than many a healthy younger man. Such energies yoked to an older man's wisdom had elevated him to a natural judgeship among the petitioners who filled his days with their complaints, problems, disputes to settle. In fact it was in the midst of mediating a conflict between three family members claiming the same pair of boot soles that he keeled over.

The rebbe's too-unexpected death devastated his people who by now were many. They'd become confident; at the same time, they'd hedged their bets. They'd done so much, sacrificed so much to keep him alive; they'd kept him in every comfort possible so that he'd never shared the very worst conditions. Had this been a sinful hypocrisy in them? The decisive error in a test their faith had failed? Maybe like Job he ought to have been kept outdoors where all the elements could get him. Rocked by grief and speared by self-rebuke, the rebbe's people read their doom on every wall that had once enclosed him. Doubt took everything he'd left behind. Their morale collapsed and typhus claimed them like scythings into sheaves. And people who hadn't been his largely agreed, the timing was tragic. Just when some badly needed internal authority had begun to develop in somebody's hands, bang, it stopped. Now the place just seemed cursed and full of anarchy again.

"A deeper hellhole," Baila observed.

Mr Asch was gone, still, piled outside. His room at Krutonog's was being stripped, its shelves emptied and heaps of books, notes, maps, thirty years in the collecting pillaged, undefended. Since the cold had dug in with iron claws people were desperate for paper to use as insulation; others wanted something to read first before wiping with. The widow Krutonog looked on and groaned.

"I can't control them!" In his fever's final days she'd spoken of keeping the room and its library intact in her old tenant's honor "like at Gorki Leninskie." Sightseeing tours had been the landlady's passion. "The history, think of it—all that knowledge lost!"

Baila shrugged. Her mood was grim, her eyes pain-shadowed. "If knowing history can keep a draught out then it's useful for once." Back in the cubicle they'd had sheets of old chink-filling paper from Mr Asch some weeks previously.

Widow Krutonog died soon after cracking a back tooth on an ancient piece of hard candy which some accounts had as a ground nut shell and others as a piece of gravel left by the Ukrainians in the dried beans they'd sold her. But it was candy. In the crack, painful enough, an infection grew and spread. In the middle of her kitchen floor she collapsed and had a seizure, soiling the tiles. She recovered only long enough to produce out of hiding a glass medicine bottle sealed under Kerensky and dose herself to death on the contents. Like the rebbe's flock, her dependents went to pieces and typhus fell upon them. Contrary to sense, their quarters grew more crowded: line jumpers swarmed the new electric kitchen. Maybe Baila and the Kotzes should have been next, maybe next but one—it didn't matter since they'd lost their place entirely. Anton remained welcome, of course:

"But we could use you here," the grandmother told him, her voice starting to shrill. "Now that you're feeling stronger, you've got to start working sometime."

Anton eyed her angrily. The other place was warmer and they fed him there. Musya didn't blame him for preferring it but she was staying out of this.

"He's only four," said Sender Kotz in his unhesitating way.

"Old enough to help," Baila insisted.

Anton pointed at Musya. "Make her help. She only lies around."

"So? You want to be lazy like her?"

"Yes," he said.

"She's not lazy," said Sender. He'd get protective like this, all at once, his voice rising. "She's taking care of Samuel Nemo, don't call her lazy!" He wept.

They all wept, everyone in the ghetto. The relief—momentary, essential—made weeping commonplace among them; tears flagged health as well as grief. Everyone grieved who could. At the same time they felt repulsion. Overwhelmingly from elsewhere, they'd been through a lot of death before Obodovka but then they'd kept moving. Now they were stuck with it: death at its ugliest, piling up and up and up around them. Its toll rose, too. The impoverishments caused, the unmoorings were inescapable. The weak too often survived the strong who'd overexerted; the weak succumbed to hideous fates, difficult to watch. Nothing in Obodovka was pleasant to watch. From the full spectacle which included groans and screams and odors various but all alarming to the viscera, the deep instincts, the natural response was to flee. But they were locked in with it. The only way to cope, really, was to assume personal immunity. Death was for other people, the ones marked for victims: this decided, it became a pastime to seek and catalogue such marks as appeared surest—signs like the telltale pounding headache for which there was nothing to do but recline and rarely get up again. The bewilderment of people going into death was what would stay with Musya from this time. They lay down to rest their aching heads always intending the position to be temporary. When at last it wasn't, when the head refused another raising, the result was clear, the fact established: after all, they weren't unlike other people, other victims. Again and again with each beat of blood in the threads of their feverish eyes they watched their big belief get blown to smithereens, Musya saw this every day in a dozen fixed gazes. *To me*, the dying people lay thinking. *To me this can happen.* They were shocked and left bewildered.

One bright afternoon a neighbor walked Baila back into the cubicle from outdoors, she had her by the elbow and was doing most of the walking for both of them. This neighbor was a strong woman but three weeks later she'd be dead. His pale face stricken, Sender Kotz followed clutching the bundled food he and his grandmother had just bargained for at the fences. He said Mama Kotz had walked into a corner of a house. Musya couldn't take it in, she was staring at the bundle which even in a young child's hands looked pitifully small. Her disappointment rushed like a loud wind through her head and boomed among the hollow vaults of her appetite. The voracious baby heard and raised a brief cry, hushed with a quick unsatisfying breast. "What's wrong? Is that all you got today?" she said, just before her eyes adjusted to the sight of a wound on Baila's forehead trickling blood. "What happened—what house?"

"It could happen to anyone," the neighbor said. Baila swayed against her.

"I was seeing double."

"For what?" It was all Musya could think of to say. "What made you see double?"

"You'll be fine." The neighbor's hips shifted, transferring weight. "She just needs to lie down."

Baila said she'd rather stand, thank you. The neighbor held her fast and insisted: just for a few minutes, she said, a little nap, a little rest. From the violence of Baila's refusal blood trails set off from her wound in all directions, one tangling in an eyebrow. At last they persuaded her to sit on the bed, the edge, and be cleaned up and bandaged with some linen stuff left over from Samuel's delivery. There was a small cut, a scrape and a tender bump like the end of a spring eggplant. The neighbor, no nurse, excused herself and went away.

"We'll never see her again," Baila remarked more accurately than she could have known. Sitting had calmed her. "That's what happens when you're too much trouble—people make themselves scarce. Ah, well." She began to lean back, caught herself and plunged forward too quickly; dizzied, she fell on her side in a faint.

"But what about our food!" cried Musya.

Managing the sufferer from her outdoor clothing into bed, they discovered her chest below the collarbones to be a mass of red spots: typhus for sure, Anton said. He sounded unconcerned. "She'll get better. I did."

"But she's old," Sender argued. "Like Mister Asch."

"No, Anton's right. He was much older," Musya said.

Daylight waned as the family watched Baila sleep. At last with extreme boldness Musya got up and screwed in the light bulb the landlady had supplied for the birth; they rationed it desperately. The moment she awoke Baila told her to take it out again. "Why waste?" she murmured, shielding her eyes. The renewed gloom made Musya feel like they were being drowned in a mud puddle.

"How long have you been sick?" she asked. It must have been some days, the symptoms were advanced. Baila said yes, but she'd managed the worst with a little bit of aspirin at a time. "So take some now!" Musya cried; although she felt a pang. Since it had come among the gifts after Samuel Nemo's birth, she'd counted on that as her personal aspirin. "Take two, please."

"No. Save it." Wincing and rolling her neck, Baila swallowed. "I should have saved it anyway."

Difficulty swallowing: a sign. "No," said Musya. Eyes hard to focus: another sign.

"I'll be back on my feet in a couple of days." They all said this.

"Yes I think so," Musya agreed. "You will. You have to be." What would they do without her? "What would we do without you?"

"True," said Sender. In answer Baila only hummed, then she was unconscious again, just like that.

"But." Anton shifted on the bed. "Without her we can go back to Siberia."

They looked at him. The broad freckle-blotched face, calm with simple conviction, told the story: Anton believed they were still making a visit to his grandparents. "You think," Musya asked him, "if Mama Kotz goes—goes like Papa Kotz did, then we can go home?" He nodded, he did think this. Then he broke apart in tears she blinked away. "But we're not here because of them," she tried to explain.

Anton began to look angry, challenging. "Then for what?"

"It's because we're Jews!" Sender threw out his arms. "I told you this! I already told you."

"But for what? How come we're Jews? How come we can't stop?"

"Because we can't," Musya said. "We're just Jewish people."

A wail split the air: Baila. Her head tossed on their makeshift pillow. Now the baby who'd dozed off woke with a furious cry. Baila wailed again, tears began to stream down her flushed cheeks. Then she started coughing.

She coughed for ten more days.

One terrible moment led to the next in the freezing cubicle. In the precious hours between occasions for panic the little family lived in hope. They even had moments of happiness and how could they not with such a healthy highly entertaining baby in their midst. What's more, the worst might not happen. Recovery from epidemic typhus was more the rule than the exception, statistically, Mr Asch had said so. Despair paid regular visits, true. Baila stayed in bed. She coughed, coughed, coughed, choking on some inflammation, and made it difficult to sleep; she'd wake herself up with her coughing and groan. Her fever kept climbing, she shivered and shook the whole bed almost to pieces while the rest of them were trying to sleep; at the same time, she'd become a heat source. Lying alongside her heaving ribs in the midnight hours of frost they could begin to feel very grateful that Baila was burning up enough to drowse them. For all sleep was blissful—indeed, bliss and better moments might even have predominated on some of these terrible days and nights, time-wise, as their hearts performed a frantic counter-struggle.

"Don't touch me!"

This was one refrain. As if they were torturers, Baila would slap at them but her wiry arms were strengthless now and easy to evade. She had to be helped to the bucket and hated being changed. At times she went blind for a few hours. She didn't want to hear reading aloud, all language hurt her ears.

"My babies!"

This was the delirium which began to come and go. They'd stopped flattering themselves that they might be the babies—she always meant her birds. Doves, finches, chickens, Baila recognized their distinct voices and called them by name to feed from her twitching hands. The tips of three fingers had gone dark with gangrene despite all Musya's attempts to massage her circulation into shape—Baila hated being moved, being touched. She couldn't swallow aspirin, not even crushed, Musya felt sorry for trying. She all but refused food and water and then pleaded in tears for sweet lemonade.

They finished the last of the secret provisions without her. The collection of empty jars and tins made a building block set of sorts, the boys raised skyscraper cities from it on the earthen floor.

One night Baila's cough subsided enough that they all slept through to mid-morning. Musya woke at Samuel Nemo's squirming to find the cubicle at its brightest, too bright for her mother-in-law's eyes, she thought immediately. But from Baila although she could feel there was fever and breath, shallow, she heard no complaint, no cough, nothing. She sat up carefully, opened her chemise to the baby's hunger and stared. The end of Baila's nose had turned an inky blue-gray color and so had her earlobes. The silver fastenings of her earrings stood out strangely now, like fish scales. To judge by the state of the fingertips (worse) this development wasn't reversible. A great beauty lay defaced here.

As Musya's teardrops fell among the poufs of a grandson's curls, her thoughts returned to the transit camp doctor who'd examined Papa Kotz for typhus. A middle-aged man with a mild palsy and a worn-out look: "Short of boiling your clothes, what's the best way to avoid it?" he'd answered them. "Go west. I recommend Paris." Typhus lived here in these eastern lands; ten million Russians alone it sent to their graves in the epidemic of 1918—changing the course of history again, Mr Asch had used to quote Lenin's say-so. All this Musya recalled, wondering. How could a preventable disease dangerous enough to affect history every time it got loose have been allowed to attack another human population in this modern era? That doctor, he'd had an alarming theory: "This time it's a weapon. They're using it as a form of germ warfare to kill Jews." Even so, he advised the Kotz family not to take it personally. Scientists at Hitler's fascist laboratories were at work on a vaccine, he said, that would enable the Nazis to finally infect everyone with epidemic typhus but themselves. "Then they can wade through the sick masses, shooting. Like they enjoy." The doctor's tremor increased the longer he spoke to them, Musya remembered now, he was really shaking at the end. She'd been left intrigued but unpersuaded. Would a comelier, firmer man have been more convincing? As it was she'd heard his theory, she'd listened. It was a speculative thing—a story about the future. Were its premises correct? Would it prove true?

Who cared?

Accident or plan, she thought the difference didn't matter. Jews were dying of epidemic typhus in Transnistria in 1942 because their captors willed them to be filthy. This was a crime against them—mass murder, no less. At Obodovka they were even forbidden to use wells because the authorities called Jews a typhus risk. The ghetto's failing, overtaxed wells had been sealed up and rationed water deliveries imposed.

Baila Kotz ought to have lived to be an old, old woman with a cage of singing birds beside her clean warm bed and never one body louse, ever, on her clean old body. Instead, here she lay in her prime not only doomed but disfigured, facing a most squalid end. And the worst part? Musya sighed: all the parts were worst. Another terrible part then was that they still possessed a hand mirror, a very good one, good enough to be a luxury at any time and a treasure in Obodovka; and Baila used it every day, even more than once a day now in her illness, even when she was blind. Framed in fine tortoiseshell, it was an object of sentiment.

The dying woman's eyes fluttered open and fixed themselves on some alarming thoughts. The orbs drifted, staring nowhere: here was the bewilderment. The last sign. Musya said good morning.

Baila blinked and said, "Do you think my sister will forgive me?"

"Oh. I don't know."

The stare turned tragic. "She won't."

"She might."

"I was with her husband on their wedding day—before and after."

This was news. Musya gave a low whistle. "I guess you really liked him."

"He was a pig," Baila said mildly. Then she asked for the hand mirror: the next terrible moment had come. Musya handed it over and watched the sick woman hold the glass above her face and slant the tortoiseshell from side to side. "Will Goldie forgive me?" she asked again. She wasn't reacting; while the longer Musya stared at the earlobes and nose with their blue stained tips the more clown-like they looked to her, as if they'd been darkened with berry juice at some impromptu picnic amusement for children. How would the two little boys take to this new effect? What if they laughed? Musya reached for the hand mirror.

"Did he give you this?"

Her grip loosened readily. "I can't see in it now, the room is too bright."

"Yes." Musya tucked the hand mirror away. Later that afternoon she'd trade it for a week's worth of hot water and food delivery plus a little light housekeeping—even in the midst of domestic tragedy and disarray Krutonog's provided services but the costs were stratospheric. "So it was a gift, your hand mirror, from Uncle Falk?"

"Oh, no, I bought that for myself," Baila answered and paused. "With money he gave me." Her gaze grew bewildered again, but in a different way. "I was a pig, too, Goldie, I was. That's why it happened with us, we were the same—and you were better, Goldie! Can you ever forgive me?" She reached for Musya, her voice rising. "Can you? Please, please forgive me!" Her grip on Musya's chemise threatened serious damage. The boys would be bursting from sleep into tears in this commotion, the worst start to a day.

"Of course I forgive you, I forgive you—my sister—Baila," she said, hushing the boys as they woke.

A gasp of relief triggered Baila's cough again but she managed, "You do? You don't mind?"

"Of course not. What's to mind? Why should I? It's only a man." While she signaled the boys not to mention their grandmother's new face they hurried out of bed, away from it, not at all inclined to laugh as she'd feared they might be. "You're forgiven."

"Everything? You forgive everything?"

"Well—what?" She had an uncomfortable sense of taking on more than she ought to. Poor dead disavowed Goldie, rotting in an ivy bed on the way to Arcadia Beach—where was her say? "What do you want?

Sender hissed through chattering teeth. "Just forgive her, Musya!"

"We did disgusting things, Goldie."

"So? Fine—okay. Live with your conscience."

"But I can't—I can't forgive myself! Please! I can't live like this—tortured. Oh!" She'd just wet herself, Musya could tell. "Please, Goldie—help me! I'm all alone, my family went back to Siberia—don't leave me, Goldie!"

As if leaving were something any but the dead could do! Musya felt savage. "I'll stay," she told the delirious woman. "But on one condition. You give me your hand mirror."

"Oh. No, Goldie, please."

"Yes. The one you bought with my husband's money—otherwise I'm leaving and I won't forgive you!"

"No! I'll give it to you—please, take it! Take it!"

So the time went with them: another terrible moment adding its tally-mark to the latest waste of valuable daylight that had been better spent procuring food or water or cleaning or improving their position somehow. Inertia could be fatal when rapid deterioration was the rule. They'd begun to fall behind and almost to starve since Baila had taken her walk into the side of a house. She'd been their provider. Now she consumed them; almost.

"Thief!" Cough. Cough. "Liar! Thief! You tricked me!" She wanted her hand mirror back.

This was inevitable. Musya tried again. "I had no choice. We weren't managing."

"Because you weren't." Cough. "You're lazy. Papa always said you were a lazy nafka and he was right."

"Yes? Really?"

"My poor husband."

"I see."

Musya glanced across the cubicle at the girl who was listening with rapt attention while pretending to sweep. The same athletic-looking dependent who'd helped them move in; she'd kept her place at Mrs Krutonog's demise. Her name was Elkie. She was eighteen or twenty. All girls gossiped.

"The way," Baila went on, "you looked at all the men."

"This isn't interesting now, Mama Kotz."

"And between you and your sister." A coughing fit. "My poor little son. His—his poor little babies!"

Elkie let out a breath and shook her head.

"You don't—she doesn't know what she's saying half the time," Musya offered.

Baila said, "I know a lazy nafka when my husband sees one."

This was too much. "When did you get so crude? Why are you so crude now?"

"My poor husband. My." Cough. Cough. Cough. Cough. "Poor husband. My poor husband." And there she got stuck for a while, repeating a single phrase interrupted by coughing. "My poor husband." It would go on all night.

"Guilt," Elkie guessed in a whisper. "Over how she starved him to death—it's still on her mind."

"I hadn't thought of that," admitted Musya.

"You Odessans," Elkie breathed admiringly.

Then they were alone again.

"What does she want with us?" Baila disliked having a "strange girl" around. Elkie vexed her.

Musya repeated. "She helps with the housework. Her name is Elkie. She also brings our water since we can't get it ourselves."

"But I've always done my own housework."

Musya frowned. "You told me you always had a girl in."

"Only to help," Baila said. "She must be costing us a fortune."

"No. It doesn't matter." By now any lucid argument was welcome. The disease had reached the stage of advanced prostration with Baila. From where it had burrowed into chambers deeper than before a cough jerked and jolted her limbs without ceasing and denied her rest; just to lie there in bed was exhausting her. When she was awake her mind mainly wandered. Glad for someone else to hear her latest Elkie news, Musya whispered: "I think she tried to kiss me!"

Baila grimaced. "Don't go in with that. The men don't like it."

"I don't know. It's so strange." She really thought so.

"It's not nice." The sick woman's head moved on the pillow. "How do I look today? A little better? Show me—no, tell me," Baila remembered. They were one another's hand mirror now. Musya returned her practiced answer:

"You look beautiful." She used her memories. "Beautiful as always. Very thin, too thin." She ran her eyes again across the mask of red spots and blue-blackening splashes. "Your face looks thin."

"I look better with a thinner face. All women do."

Musya disagreed. She appealed to the well-swept floor, where the boys were erecting a train station: "Sender, do all women look better with thinner faces?"

"Yes," he said.

"I still disagree."

Baila coughed. "Well, that's one thing you'll never have is a thin face."

"What are you talking about? I've always had a thin face, I have a thin face now!"

"You have a round face," said Sender. No, Baila said: it was square. They were both wrong, she told them. Anyway it was normal to gain a little during pregnancy around the face.

"I didn't," said Baila. "And I never went up more than two dress sizes, either."

Musya shook her head. "You're delirious again." This was their last conversation. Baila asked to have her nails filed and Musya said, "Later."

She squeezed a few drops of cold water onto Baila's cracked blue lips from a wet cloth and wiped her brow. It was the next day. The fever had spiked again and the lice were on the move, she could see a dozen creeping down the hairline; beneath the blanket they'd be teeming. Every one a killer, Musya supposed. There was nothing to be done. Samuel Nemo shifted comfortably: they'd fashioned a sling from a shawl and she wore him tied to her front. Her hands freed to tend could do so little that it felt like nothing. Mostly she touched, straightened, stroked; she sent healing energies through her palms into her mother-in-law's suffering body; she told a vastness that she pictured, "Bless this woman. Heal her." She'd never prayed so consciously before and felt a frowning disappointment when nothing changed.

Very likely Baila might linger but not recover. Krutonog's was full of invalids who'd come through the worst of epidemic typhus and now lived on in bed—a living death, really, with the gangrene, the stupor, the ruined senses. Gangrene was slow. As Baila's advanced the sweet whiff of it had become enough to bother them, bothering Baila herself most of all. Even with the gangrene Musya hoped she'd linger—only in a state far other than this one, not scorched by fever, not shocked at rapid intervals by the cough going off in her chest like a steam piston. A long painless lingering amid fumes of mentholated ointment procured through miracle she wished her: not this. But even this she'd take. She couldn't bear to lose her.

She said, "Please stay with us, Baila. Please don't leave us alone here." To her dismay the swollen eyelids fluttered wide, the wide reddened eyes met her own: she hadn't meant to wake Baila and she filled her look with apology. A voice croaked, unrecognizable:

"You stole my towels."

"What?" Out of nowhere, the terrible. "Your—what?"

With an ugly jerk of her shoulders Baila sat half-upright. "You stole my towels!" It was insane, they'd had this out months ago. "You stole my towels!" They'd finally agreed to be grateful for the theft since Baila had managed to leave all the other towels behind along with a fur coat. Not bothering to answer the charge Musya took the shoulders in her hands and pushed towards the mattress. Nothing happened at first. From so little substance the resistance surprised her. They seemed to struggle. Then Baila fell back and took several loud short breaths. After the last one Musya waited. Baila was still.

"No!" She gripped the shoulders hard this time and shook. "Move, Baila! Breathe!"

Sender was on his feet, Anton behind. Baila's head bounced around, knocked against Samuel in his sling. He shrieked. Musya let go and Baila dropped lifeless into a puff of coppery dust that rose from her outlines and hung there for a brief eternity.

It must have been around lunch hour, a terrible time to die, quite wrong. Better they should wait, Musya thought confusedly, and try this scene again at night, some other day. Another chance, another five minutes she wanted. Soft squeals of upset reached her from across the bed: she held out her arms and Anton rushed to hide his face against her ribs. Sender hesitated. His tearful eyes were enormous, his mouth stretched.

He panted. "Did—did you kill her?"

She denied it angrily—she felt angry. "Am I fascism? Am I Jew-hating? Try heart failure killed her," she told him. A moment later his arms were around Musya's waist and his face pressed close. She gripped them: boys all around. Boys encircled her, Boris's, Liza's and hers. Another deathbed to bind them all faster—here it was. And here she'd done everything wrong. She might even have killed the woman, in truth. Another domineering woman. And they hadn't chanted, there ought to be chanting. Musya knew no chants, no mystic tongues. Only mixed ones:

"Proshchai, Baila—proshchai, Mama Kotz! Proshchai, Odessa Mama!"

Half-maudlin, half-mocking, the farewell cry burst from her throat. To Musya's ears it sounded hideously crude but she couldn't stop, couldn't help herself. The place bred typhus and typhus bred crudity, she guessed.

"Oy, Odessa Mama!" She raised her voice to a shout. Maybe Baila would sit up to scold her. "Oy, proshchoy! Proshchai proshchoy, Mama Kotz! Proshchai, Bobeh!"

She nudged at the boys to join in at random. Samuel was howling. They'd wake the neighbors.

(5)

Elkie clucked her tongue. It was an annoying thing that Elkie did sometimes when she disapproved. In this instance, as if really to break the quiet of their concentration, she did it again and added, "What a waste."

"You already said that," said Musya. While Anton watched sleepily, still in tears, she and Sender were turning a badly-stained white bath towel into long strips.

"This never works," said Elkie.

"It will," they told her.

Nightfall was close. The neighbors had retreated and the management had been apprised. Here was its representative, specimen of strength enough to manage two of Mrs Kotz's size single-handedly from premises to resting place, was her practiced estimate. Elkie carried bodies out in pairs routinely, she said, to make fewer trips. Why not? And thus employed almost every day, often twice, some days even three times, of the scene out there she had to be acknowledged as the expert present. So? She reiterated:

"I've never seen it work—not once."

They'd stripped Baila down to her underclothes first—silk, naturally. Every other scrap she'd been wearing Musya chose to burn, an extreme solution still smoldering in the kitchen garden. Then like a prakkes filling for large woolen leaves they'd wrapped Papa's overcoat around her into a bundle as tight as they could make it. This they intended to bind with strips of bath towel knotted tightly enough to scare away the most determined scavengers—the usual interference and exposure would not occur in Baila's case.

The young housekeeper called their plan fantasy.

"That's silk! She'll be naked as the rest by mid-morning. Especially if you put her in the street."

Given the high and oft-expressed regard mutual between the deceased and the late Widow Krutonog, they might have had a spot in the kitchen garden. Which cost extra, for the privacy; but the privilege to purchase was special, reserved to the names on a list—select. The elder Mrs Kotz certainly qualified. These facts Musya had learned only today, with mild interest; at heart her interest was nil, her desire to keep Baila's dead body in view from the corridor windows being negative. Instead she'd decided to reunite her in-laws by the fence down the lane where Papa Kotz remained slumped in slightly out of the way solitude. Once the ground thawed out they'd have a better chance of being buried together; until then the old couple would be company for one another, in Musya's mind—Sender's too. "Of course," he'd agreed. For a little longer they'd stood and watched Baila's wool skirt smolder from blue to ash, letting the semi-pleasant fragrance of cloth smoke fill their nostrils. Then the two of them had gotten busy.

Stripping. Ripping. Wrapping. Knotting. Planning. Forgetting.

Musya gave a start. "Her earrings!" She'd put them down somewhere.

Elkie patted an apron pocket. "Safe. Don't worry." Musya didn't exactly like it but preferred not to speak. The forward young woman was making herself indispensable, she supposed. A sense of weary unease overtook her brief effort to imagine where the situation might be headed. She tied another knot.

"There aren't enough strips," said Sender.

He was right, unfortunately. Elkie exclaimed, "Are you people crazy? More waste?" as Musya went for another bath towel. Jostled in his sleep, the baby on her chest hiccupped and slept on. "This will never work and you'll be out of towels for nothing—stop!" They were too busy making small rips in the edge with their incisors and spitting out threads to reply.

The project of the stiffening bundle made a helpful distraction, clearing space around horror for calm. At times, Musya remembered, she'd hated her mother-in-law; for weeks on end, back in Odessa, she'd thought her evil and mostly insane; she'd never have thought back then that even a tepid rapprochement could occur much less what they'd achieved by the end. Baila and she had made a good partnership. Musya dabbed at her tears with toweling. If only, she sighed, if only Boris Kotz had taken after his mother instead, she might have had a loving marriage.

Liza might have been happier, too.

But that hadn't happened. This had happened.

A towel and a half had to suffice: Elkie needed some daylight to carry by. The banded strips were fairly dense though far from the mummy-like effect they'd sought. The knots were fiendish. Bunched like pale gray twigs, shins and feet protruded from one end, a bud of sparse locks and scalp peeked out the other. Then Baila was gone. Beside her husband in the snow Elkie had laid her. Papa Kotz had toppled halfway onto his side, Sender reported, where snow drifted around him like a bath. His grandmother had sunk out of sight in it.

"That won't last—they'll find her," said Elkie, who stood slapping snow from her mittens and arms. She'd come to work for Widow Krutonog in 1935 as an assignee from a state orphanage; chances were she was barely Jewish, if at all. The landlady's death meant she was on her own. People left without family in the Obodovka ghetto often failed to thrive but Elkie was managing to do as well as the situation permitted. Elkie's boots, a size large, were good ones. Though missing a tooth or two, she ate enough to keep up a considerable strength in her limber, athletic frame. By Krutonog's management then and now she'd been deemed indispensable. Her cheekbones made interesting planes. She was a hard worker.

Musya blurted out, "Please—keep those earrings, Elkie." The girl still had Baila's cinnabar set in her pocket. "You've done so much for us today. We'd have been lost without your help." This was true: she'd even flipped their mattress for them. "You've earned a reward."

Strangely, Elkie's eyes narrowed and her mouth got tight. "You thought I planned to keep them without asking?"

"No—what?"

"You thought I'd steal them?"

"Of course not!" Really Elkie did extremely well. Not only was she employed with many varied occupations to fill her days, but she made her bed at night in Krutonog's main supply room, immediately behind the steam boiler. "I want you to have them, that's all."

"For what?"

"For—because—I don't know. I think they'd look good on you."

Elkie's face twisted and her voice emerged full of sarcasm. "Yes? In my pierced ears?"

"Oh." There must have been no piercers in the old state orphanage. "Well, to wear someday then. Please."

Although Elkie let herself be prevailed upon to accept the offering, soreness lingered to shade her moody goodnight. Soon the Kotz family, winnowed by one, lay down alone again. Minus Papa's overcoat and his feverish widow their bed was very much colder. They lay freezing. Killed by the briefest bereavement on record, Musya guessed, they might be dead by sunrise, like moths starved by eating moonlight. Another teardrop trickled itchily around her nose. The salt would sting but reluctance to expose a single fingertip to the air overrode everything—until Anton sat bolt upright and demanded a Jim and Tom story. They hadn't had one in forever. "I'm cold," he added. She wiped her face, drew a quick breath to reply and then couldn't through her chattering teeth. Instead she watched Anton reach around for the satchel he used as a pillow and begin to unstrap it. A few of her mother's red thread-cocooned currency rolls hit the floor, small earthen thuds in the dark.

The Siberian tiger skin saved them.

Back in Odessa, the hero brothers who hadn't stopped combatting the city's fascist conquerors for one single moment all winter long were almost out of bullets. It was time for a quick visit to their secret underground ammunition depot. So they set out—when what should befall them but an earthquake, a mild one but messy enough to send them on a detour, then another. The way sloped downward. The hours spun past. Far off course among tunnels unknown to them Jim and Tom performed an expert reconnaissance, unafraid, sure-footed, patient, seeking clues, finding none. Their calls echoed identically from every direction. At last, one wrong step: the ground gave way and they crashed through the ceiling of a vast, dimly lit cave into a huge pile of moldy linen, dried skin and bones, bones and more bones. Landing miraculously unharmed, they untangled themselves and stepped free from the wreckage and decay to find a tall thin bespectacled man standing there in sandals, a fez, and a long striped robe. Introducing himself as the caretaker, he welcomed Jim and Tom to the Chamber of a Thousand Mummies.

"Ten thousand." This was Sender. "A thousand isn't many."

She objected: of mummies it was. The boys disagreed. "So by the time of the story there are many more but there were a thousand when they named it," she offered.

Sender was uncompromising. "They should change the name, then. Be accurate."

"Yes, Musya," Anton agreed. "Change it."

"Tomorrow," she said.

The next days were hard: cold, lonesome, frightening. Also dirty, as the hot water delivery all but stopped. With diapers to wash, this was disastrous. Leaving Sender occupied with a stack of mending, Musya slung the baby tight and took him along—she planned to confront management. Anton hurried first and she followed up and down the cold crowded passages, their way slowed by recognitions and greetings, pettings, condolences. She felt not at her best and shy as a result, shy and disappointing. At her destination she arrived in a state of fatigue and walked into an uncontainable shock that spilled from her in speech—a murmured astonishment:

"There are men in the kitchen now?" It went unheard. In the tiled room which echoed with a crowd's voice as usual, the difference was jarring. A couple of men: the younger one couldn't walk, the other could with a crutch. He looked mean. Anton went straight to the legless one who gave him an affectionate welcome. This young man had hard candies, his lips were bright with them. Soon Anton's would be also. Musya raised Mrs Drobitz's empty tin pitcher and addressed the room generally. "I need hot water now and more delivered later, please."

"So pay," said the mean man.

"No, that's included for us."

"Not anymore." He was sitting next to Widow Krutonog's old place in the business corner. Occupying the place itself was a former dependent, not young, who kept her gaze fixed on the man's bearded lips like she'd been deafened by love: this was the late landlady's late first husband's niece.

"But we have diapers to wash."

"No one told you to have a baby."

"But—I did have one." Her argument wasn't any good, though. Baila Kotz might have managed to secure an extension of privilege from this sort of man but the task was beyond Musya's powers. She parted with cash, probably showed too much left in her handkerchief and had a strong feeling he pitied her when the legless man spoke up from his cot in a drawling baritone:

"You ought to do as the Chinese do and hold your baby out the window to make his toilet." He'd seen firsthand, he said, the young kept naked below in simple shift dresses and taught from infancy to relieve themselves upon request. It was all in the training— their mothers used praise, smiles, encouraging voices. "The Chinese even fertilize their flower beds with their babies' shit."

"I haven't got that kind of window," Musya told him.

Yet she left intrigued. Stopping by the cubicle later on, Elkie found her holding Samuel Nemo by his sides over their family bucket and said, "He's too young to learn."

"He's smart," Musya countered. "Will you sweep today, maybe?"

"Maybe later." The housemaid paced restlessly and plucked at the clothesline. A new transport had arrived, had they heard? Musya hadn't.

"This water isn't hot," Sender complained.

Elkie ignored him. "They're staying at Tauber's."

"Who are?"

"The new ones!" Elkie's exasperation left Musya confused.

"So you're working both places now?"

"No I'm not working both places!"

The reason for replies so snapped, Musya didn't care to spend any time learning. "What happened in the new kitchen? Who are those men?" she asked instead.

"They're smart guys," Elkie said with a laugh.

"They're brothers?"

Now an eye-roll. "So they say. But the one in bed is the gunsel."

The Yiddish being strange to her, Musya frowned. The explanatory thrusts of the housemaid's vigorous finger-show made sense only little by little. Sender looked on fascinated at the pantomime until Musya gasped:

"Does the niece know?"

"She doesn't mind, she says some men like both." Elkie knew all. The so-called siblings were specialists in the black market art trade who planned come spring to quit the ghetto, return to work in Kiev and grow rich again on their interrupted wartime profits. For now they'd found a warm indoor harbor at Krutonog's from which, all too successfully romanced, the niece planned to make a third at their escape, a sort of outlaw bride. "But she's not going anywhere." So Elkie concluded. "Not all men like both."

"Can we escape?" Sender Kotz with his glowing face sounded so hopeful. "In the spring?" Elkie told him of course not but Musya said maybe, prompting Elkie to ask why Musya always contradicted every word out of her mouth. A urine spurt missed the pail almost completely but saved her from having to reply: she beamed at Samuel Nemo, her good baby, her princeling.

Deep below its fascist-occupied streets, Odessa's hero brothers followed their attenuated host on a tour of his strange domain. An oil lamp he held up on a long hooked pole shone hollows in the gloom. Ten thousand at least, they estimated, peering through the lamplight flickers at the miles of pale brown antique winding linen wrapped and rotted, gnawed and trailing from thousands upon thousands of long-deceased people in mummified form, leaned, stacked, piled in great heaps like the one that had provided so brittle a cushion to their fall. Was this a burial-place, asked Jim? Had some ancient tribe peopling Odessa's limestone heights made mummies of their dead and left them in this chamber? Their guide said no. These were imported. The dead of Egypt's empire down through its Roman days rested here, far from home. *We rescued them*, the man said.

Next, food became a problem: scarce, unreliable, bad. The term of delivery secured by the family's hand mirror had long expired and now they owed Krutonog's. What Musya could afford to pay against their debt purchased little. The denominations her mother had saved were really very small; not only that, once uncurled a large share proved illegibly faded. Soft as old cotton, though, these bills made a small supply of toilet wipes each worth infinitudes more than any face value it might have possessed, so blissful was a basic comfort here. With the remainder—the decipherably former legal tender—needful frugality urged that Musya should stop enriching the middleman and instead resume Baila's daily circuit of the places at the fence where local goyim brought food to give away sometimes or else to sell and barter. At the very least, Musya ought to have been waiting on what passed for a queue at the weekly bread distribution when the Romanians tossed sacks of loaves over the barbed wire and the starving people tore them open. Always Baila had carried home the better part of a loaf from that bruising fray which often left her no more than disheveled. Tough, to be sure, she'd also used her head.

Economize, bargain, compete: the winning formula was known—but not many people could follow it. Some tried and failed. For everyone else, what needed to be done wasn't possible. Either too young, too small and weak, too elderly and frail, too enfeebled by illness, too despondent, demoralized or insane, too encumbered with invalids, babies and children, too fearful of leaving loved ones and property unattended to breast the ghetto's hectic human currents and join the fight for survival, they remained tied to their inadequate shelters, overcharged for every mouthful, squandering on exigency.

Purse-lipped, snorting, Samuel Nemo squirmed and fretted. Her milk was too thin for him, he was missing nourishment. Again and again she sang him Lyubov Orlova's bittersweet Moscow apartment lullaby, the cakewalking cadence and American language refrain stuck in her head these days:

"*Scleep mye baby—scleep.*"

"Don't sing that!" Anton, suddenly in tears.

The time was broad daylight. The floor was like playing on ice, though, so he and Sender were huddled in bed. The tiger pelt heaped on top looked to Musya's tired eyes like the only object of color in Transnistria—she could see its fieriness throb through the clouds her breath made, prisms flickering in every hair. The family hadn't eaten in one day.

"What's wrong?" she asked him.

"Ya pomnyu!" the four year-old shrilled. "Ya pomnyu! Tsirk!" He remembered—the little black Jimmie song had made him remember back to Odessa, that day, the last time they'd seen Circus—when something dire must have happened because Anton could only wail at the memory.

The other two tried to pinpoint the traumatic event. Musya pictured the day. A dry blaze of dust and heat that rose off the sidewalks and left her legs sweat-slicked: she remembered mistaking the sensation for discomfort. She remembered her old school friend, the Goose—but not a name, even now. She remembered thinking the auditorium seats needed upholstering badly. And as might have been expected from such fly-by-night operators, the feature had been missing parts of every reel except the last one, so the crowd forgave. The program returned to her entire, with its long matinee prelude of newsreels. One by one the several hate-filled madmen operating in peak positions of limitless power at the time had filled the screen with their gestures, their armies, their swelling throats.

"Hitler?" she guessed. Anton shook his body: no.

Sender went next. "The prices." The wails leapt octaves and became a whine—this was closer.

The tickets, Musya recalled, had come a bit steep but not steep enough to prepare the public for the concession prices. People had brayed with affront. The long glass counters had been busy, though: the amount of cash around had amazed her. Denied the frozen chocolate balls they'd loudly fancied, the boys had been forced to content themselves with sugar buns, one apiece from a paper sack of three. Musya remembered now. Poor Anton: after only a bite or two he'd lost his grip and dropped his on the floor. And she'd told him to leave it there because it was dirty.

"But I gave you mine!" she cried. "I gave you the rest of mine!"

"And they were stale," Sender put in.

It didn't matter. Anton mourned his lost bun.

Sender had his own moods, deep gray funks that should have been harder to detect than Anton's since the older brother's tears for the most part flowed silently; yet they were just as obvious. The focus of his brooding thoughts was less so. Until one day while shivering through a lukewarm sponge bath he broke down and told her: it was Papa Kotz on his conscience, weighing there with all the old man's former body mass and more. Sender believed he'd helped murder his grandfather.

"But his wife was killing him already—she didn't need you. What more could you add?" Musya reasoned with him. "You're only a little boy."

"I should have protected him."

"You couldn't."

He clutched his head through wild rosy curls. "I was so mean to him!"

This there was no denying. "You were angry." She rubbed his neck dry with the last towel, trying by touch to console him. "With good reason you were angry. He understood—he did."

"I should have fed him. One bite even." Tears rolled down his clean pink cheeks, too pink. "One sprat in oil. Where is it now? I don't have it—I should have given it to him instead."

His chest was pricked with red spots. All they'd had to eat in half a day was one small potato. Dizzy and half-dead with fear and grief and hunger, all she could do was keep arguing the point. "To take one drop of oil away from his grandson, that would have made him a bad man. Which he wasn't."

"No," Sender agreed. "He wasn't. I am."

Somehow the energy to forgive themselves had gone first. Guilt feelings attacked the little family like fever, each to stay its own mysterious duration, impossible to hasten past or think away. Musya was far from immune. She spent hours of time falling over and over again into the gulf, the dim-sided gaping abyss, between what she'd actually achieved and what she ought to have done at Baila's sickbed from first to last. Especially the last haunted her. *Am I fascism?* She reflected on herself and had to laugh. *Am I Jew-hating?* Claiming the high ground while there she was with her hands practically around the woman's neck. Yes, she thought. She was fascism. She felt hateful, like a hateful person.

Across the planet, according to Jim and Tom's torchbearer-host, wherever modern medicine had failed to completely catch on there were living apothecaries and healers and sorcerers who cleaved to the wisdom of millennia and followed its recipes down to the last arcane letter. For this breed, almost without exception, mummies stood out as a source of key magic potion ingredients. To prolong life and extend virility they sought, from the cadavers themselves, dried tissue and bones to be purchased whole or pre-ground to powder; brains and organs scooped from the jars entombed alongside the cadavers were in even higher demand. People also cast fortunes with the knucklebones and teeth and wrote spells on the wrappings. In truth, the last authentic mummy's brain had gone under the pestle to make a headache cure for Napoleon Bonaparte. By now the Nile Valley's organs were nearly used up. Even its mummified cats, in their multitudes so long the reputable charlatan's first resort, had been depleted, the sands almost picked clean of them. Demand was bound to outstrip supply, with the defenseless mummies rushing headlong towards extinction, at the mercy of rapacious miracle peddlers from every corner of humankind, a resource to be used up and lost, forever, gone. *Remember, these were people,* the brothers heard. Once living, then mummified, now endangered, they deserved better than oblivion. The man in the fez, he explained, represented a secret society pledged to protect and preserve them. Why Odessa? Its climate, catacombs and harbor had made it the natural choice. For decades now a steady flow of mummies had been arriving in the holds of Mediterranean ships, packed among brass tea sets and bales of dried apricots, rowed ashore after nightfall, ferried down underground channels to the great chamber's loading dock and left there to be processed and stored.

The hero brothers offered their congratulations. The man and his society had cornered the market. Until the fascist invaders were driven from Odessan soil, they could set up in business and make serious capitalist wealth catering to the global mummy trade.

But their guide shook his head: it wasn't like that with his secret society. Preserving mummies intact was its members' genuine mission. Their plans were far-reaching, their goal ambitious. They hoped someday to see every mummy in this chamber be adopted into a Soviet family or cooperative flat of good standing, there to be cared for, its linen bands to be dusted and kept free of beetles, each mummy given its place in some quiet corner of a busy room, a stranger welcomed from another time on the same planet. This was their dream.

Sender Kotz in low spirits took a cynical view. "People won't keep those mummies. They'll sell them to witch doctors right away." Musya nodded.

"That's what Jim said."

Sleep blessed them brokenly. Night and day blending, the hours passed much alike, each with its piece of sleep. At one awakening Musya had a surprise and a sharp cry escaped her—the baby's cue to set up his tormented engine noise with both lungs working at full blast. While his brothers, inured, were asleep again after a few whimpers, the complaints that issued from the nearest cubicles were loud and prolonged. For a change she didn't apologize nor did she try to hush anyone. First the shock was too great, then the horror. Paralyzed, she couldn't do anything.

Papa Kotz's overcoat was back. Neatly folded, lying at her feet—on top of them, she realized. Signals alerted her body to move, her legs to jerk the feet out from under; she flinched and stayed still. Her feet felt warm. Next, she groaned.

Poor Baila!

The snow drift tomb trampled, the proud still woman stripped naked: pity, aching pity struck and spread across the horror of it like blood into a fresh bruise. Poor Mama Kotz at her finches' cages, a petite well-dressed figure framed against a clean sunlit window, chiding Falk and Papa over some less than tasteful exchange, saying *You men!* with her smile—for all that charm, to end murdered and dead on the cold ground, just like the sister from the thought of whom she'd fled. Could that really be all? Or did another chapter follow? One set in a different, better place—another past, perhaps? Where Goldie and Baila, still practically schoolgirls, were busy fastening their long frocks and pearls, disregarding their father's impatience, too caught up in fizzy girlish surmise to obey and finish faster; it's the night they'll finally meet a young man rumored to be tall, intelligent and terribly handsome, with a promising future in wines. This time around, Musya hoped, he'd get the right sister.

Still, here on this Earth, unequivocally, Baila Kotz was dead and couldn't feel the cold.

Musya rocked in place and clasped Samuel Nemo, calmer now, to the fading warmth between her breasts. The overcoat was folded into a neat pro-fessional square she'd recognized at once: the gift again was Boim's. Poor Baila—poor old clothes merchant, too! He really had it bad for her, she guessed. From any thought to reciprocate senti-ments her quick imagination recoiled—for now. He was a bad man in a time more evil than he, this was all she could honestly say as she reached for the overcoat to unfold and add it to the tiger skin warming the little boys' sleep. A final shock jolted her: what fell out of the wool folds, a terrible nest of long white worms or snakes Musya took it for, proved to be no more than cloth: the towel strips, unknotted, eight of them, practically a whole towel.

For the reconstruction they decided to reuse the steely tough russet threads they'd saved from the mother's cash hoard. Elkie found the Kotzes hard at work, all three, upon her latest late arrival with their water in the bucket gone cold. "I'm sorry," she said uncharacteristically, and handed over some small boiled potatoes, more than usual. Musya felt her mouth fill with spit. Each boy got one potato right away. They were so hungry but their eating pace they kept slow—they knew what happened to gobblers from having had to help clean caper stuffing off the floor in Papa Kotz's vomit. A lesson learned. Musya chewed slowly too and examined the housemaid's demeanor, a new one, heedless, dreamy, stunned.

"What's wrong with you?" She was thinking it had to be the brain. "Did you fall?"

"No. I'm in love." For the first time Elkie noticed their needles, the thread, the toweling, the overcoat on the bed. "Where did that come from?"

"What do you mean you're in love?" It wasn't with her, this was clear. Musya was surprised. "When have you had time to fall in love?"

Now Sender spoke up. "At Tauber's. I told you."

She remembered. As the one who emptied their bucket when she didn't come in time, Sender had spotted Elkie loping away from the building one afternoon, hot water pail in hand. He'd reported following her to Tauber's which she'd stood outside staring at for several minutes before returning to Krutonog's where she'd delivered the now-tepid water—to their own cubicle. "But you didn't say she was in love." He'd said she was lazy.

Elkie frowned. "So your family's been spying on me?"

"We pay for hot water," the little boy insisted.

"I'm entitled to leisure time," said Elkie. "I work plenty. You don't know."

"I do know," he said.

"Can't you bring our water hot before you go to Tauber's?" Musya asked. "Please, Elkie." She didn't care who the girl loved, or how, or why—if she felt a little hurt at being less preferred, the relief felt greater. "I don't care who you love, it doesn't matter to me," she began again, trying to be nice.

But Elkie bristled. "No, you don't care, do you?" Before Musya could think of a reply, she added, "Don't worry. It's no one you know."

"Who do I know? I don't know anyone." A depressing argument threatened. "I only hope you'll be very happy—like you deserve."

"I am. Thank you." Appeased, Elkie sat. Instead of standing up again and sweeping, she tilted her chin Anton's way. "Him they'll feed in the new kitchen. You can save his share for yourselves." Musya was doubtful but Elkie pushed the idea: "Take what you can get while you can get it. They like him."

"Is it safe?"

She was thinking about the men. Elkie said of course it was safe since the men were for each other—and the niece, she added. As for unsafe, Elkie deemed few things in the Obodovka ghetto more dangerous than this gift of an overcoat—if, that is, she'd guessed its source correctly: Boim and his thieving pickers. "I told you so," she added.

Musya dropped her eyes as if she were about to blush, satisfied to reflect that Elkie with her cheekbones wasn't the only lightning rod for romance in the locale. Weeping into his thick black whiskers the clothes merchant pined for her, Musya Kotz, for her love Boim longed hard enough to keep sending her a love token that had substance and worth. Possibilities were everywhere. She gave a quick shrug, smiled. "I don't know why he keeps sending this."

"Because he's trying to buy you," Elkie said.

"With a coat? Don't be ridiculous." The overcoat remained filthy and old.

Elkie said she wasn't being ridiculous. "You don't want to owe him."

"It's not owing." Sender spoke forcefully. "Not when it's our coat."

This was true but Elkie disagreed. "It's owing when Boim says so." She told Musya to wake up, then lowered her voice dramatically. "He plans to get you in debt to him and then run you in a koorvah tent—it's one of his sidelines." She finished in whispers: this was classified stuff, top secret.

Musya stared. The wolfish man's villainy had pierced her midriff like a sword—a sneak attack. She said, "That will never happen."

"That's what they all say," Elkie said.

A day later Sender fell sick with typhus. In the throes of a soaring fever he became convinced that Musya was about to leave him alone and run off to meet men in one of Boim's koorvah tents. "Don't go to work! Don't go to work!" he begged her. He screamed at the pains in his stomach and head. She couldn't get him to swallow any aspirin, the little they had left was going to waste. He fell in and out of stupors. Three times it happened as she sat there keeping watch that she heard Sender scream when he was unconscious: she could see he wasn't screaming yet the cubicle rang with screams. Each time the phenomenon puzzled her until she realized that the sound came from her baby whose hunger was rage-like. Sender choked on food, threw it up, coughed it out— the cough had started.

Elkie came in with the pail and Anton was with her, he'd been getting his meals in the new kitchen. The housemaid dumped a handful of potato peels onto a plate—it was all they'd get today. Elkie blamed shortages. Musya sighed and asked about the mattress—it needed flipping.

Elkie couldn't help, she had to go. "Eidel needs me."

"Who's Eidel?" Musya met Elkie's stare. "Oh." Before she could think of anything to add, Elkie dashed off. At least she'd brought the water while it was hot this time. He wasn't due for one but Anton's squirmy, uncomfortable look and the way he kept tugging at his trousers decided Musya on an immediate sponge bath. He resisted her, why was soon clear. All around and on his genitals were sticky candy-colored marks. She looked up to meet his vast gray unreadable eyes, full of distance and disturbances glowing like constellations. "I'm sorry," she told him.

Day and night stopped alternating and the night stayed.

"Samuel Nemo!" At the top of his choked, cough-stripped voice, barely a whisper, Sender lay screaming. "Be quiet, Samuel Nemo, please!" He was such a nice person. The baby cried some more. Then Anton started in about the shmek again. The almost brim-high contents of their zinc pail produced a nauseating smell, he was right. Musya's monthly bleeding had decided to return in force which did nothing to improve the situation. What could she do? As if she were nearing the end of a losing game, she was trapped in the cubicle with their slops and no way to empty them. She couldn't risk letting Anton out of her sight but she couldn't leave Sender on his own. The baby was at too great a risk of being snatched and sold to Ukrainians to ever be left unattended. Her options were zero.

Then Elkie was back, empty-handed this time. She was there for Anton, acting as an emissary from his friends in the new electric kitchen: the little Siberian boy who loved sweets was wanted there. Musya refused and rebuked her:

"You said that gunsel was safe!"

To Elkie's credit, the story of the candy stains bothered her, no question. Then she said, "Children aren't affected by things like that. They forget the bad."

"He's not going there again, you can tell them."

"You're being a fool."

"Tell them!"

Elkie went away.

Musya went to empty their bucket. Anton hurried before her down the path. She hurried before Samuel Nemo suffocated beneath the layers of shawl and wrap she judged barely sufficient for five minutes' protection from his freezing solid. The cold was annihilating, like being pounded between two red-hot slabs of iron in a gigantic machine. Yes, worse than Siberia, she reflected. Somewhere among all those visits to her sister's grave she must have passed through lower temperatures—but back then she'd had vigor, fed on the regular rich meaty fare of Magga's kitchen. She thought about food constantly. Fat dumpling skins filled her mind's eye with shimmers. Her footsteps slowed.

"Further, girlie! Further!"

She continued obediently down the filthy trail between the banks of filth and snow to the emptying spot ordained by the invalids around the steps. They were bullies and cat-callers, smokers of tobacco. They said she was Boim's new girl. She ignored them, kept her mouth shut, wept stupidly.

She stood blocking the open doorway as Anton shouted at her. "Otpusti menya! Otpusti menya!" He wanted to go back to the new electric kitchen, he said. He was hungry. He wanted cognac.

"They give you cognac there?"

"No!"

Musya hadn't thought so, she'd never smelled it on him. One more time now she stated the facts: he wasn't allowed to visit that place anymore, no exceptions. He appeared to subside and found a seat on the luggage pile from which he scowled at her. The next time she turned her back he was gone.

From that point Anton came and went. Sometimes he brought food with him which Musya wished she could refuse. She ate for her baby's sake. Her milk in his mouth she pictured having the consistency of steam. He fussed, fretted, sneezed, squinted balefully, writhed and kicked; every few minutes he slept to the count of one hundred, no more. His reedy repetitive cries tortured his feverish brother. Despite some improvement, five times out of ten he'd miss the pail. Motion soothed him occasionally. Back and forth across the cubicle she walked with him, her footsteps darkening the frosty floor. She could feel the strength in her draining away into the baby's care; it wasn't replenished. *You'll be our ruin*, she'd think, kissing the crown of his noisy head.

Sender babbled. He was an easier patient than Baila had been, easier than Anton for that matter; it was easier to rub him down, sit him up, even draw him to his feet to stand and keep the circulation going. Musya refused to risk gangrene with him.

She rubbed his palms and fingers briskly. From their pillow his hot stare had strayed past her shoulder and fixed there. His voice came like a kitten's:

"Mamenyu, kiss me, they put me in the oven with my brother Shadrach, it's so hot here—they burned the laws, Mamenyu."

Caught somehow in the middle, Musya dropped the sick boy's hand and went to stand against the wall in the fentster's weak beam. Not only she gave up her place, but if Liza's ghost had come when called, Musya wanted nothing to do with it. These days she never held her sister blameless for their situation, she whose faith was so superior to Musya's frivolity—she and her kind, the violent enthusiasts, the ones who caused wars with their gods and sacred tales and revolutionary parties and hot red stares.

Here they were, the rest of them, trapped with the results, near death.

It was another in a string of stormy nights with the electric power fitful. As the hallway bulb rattled on and off the Kotzes lay shaking from fear as well as cold, hunger, fever, furious infant tears—a swirl of causes shook them. After a long time away Anton had stumbled back empty-handed. "*Nothing?*" she'd shrieked. The eruption still pained her throat. He'd crawled into bed with them, a small boy-sized alcohol fume. No woman on earth could have done him less good as a mother than she, Musya decided. She thought the end was near.

Relatively, they'd done well. Other cubicles on the corridor had emptied faster. But the Kotzes had run out of advantages. Poor and weak, they were done for. They lacked the resources to prevent their own murder by starvation and hypothermia. The crying baby would never let them sleep which would rush things. If they couldn't sleep, they couldn't rest; if they couldn't rest, they couldn't work; and only work could save them. Fortunately there existed a way to stop Samuel Nemo's tears, almost foolproof: put him face down on the tiger skin. He was so happy that way he'd start to chirrup.

So it was now. The cold and dark remained fierce but the calm held bliss. Liberated from her chest, the baby splashed happily among the gleaming stripes. He drooled when he was happy. Of course he'd die of cold unless she returned him to his bonds; tied against her heart, he'd survive not much longer. So it would be. They were too helpless, too friendless, too many. Musya let her thoughts drift back to buttered vegetables, heaps of them, great quartered cabbages and treasure chests of peas.

Her eyelids flickered. Molten light blazed and shrank to reveal a candle burning on the chest of drawers. She hadn't thought their family owned another candle. Magnifying the oily glare that pooled and spilled among its folds were the myriad silicate filaments of a Siberian tiger hide; empty folds. Her baby was gone. She'd lost him to the creature or demon, she guessed, crouched atop their luggage in the candle's glow. The size of a child, shapelessly cloaked in many garments, it had Samuel Nemo bundled in its grasp and was rocking him, whispering to him, stroking his head. He stretched and cooed, then his voice box twanged: contentment.

"Good Pretzel," the ghetto demon said to him.

Musya raised herself slowly, slowly. At one elbow was Sender, unconscious, his breath a rasp; at the other, the demon's side, Anton was awake, unalarmed. He had his eyes on their visitor which now began a quiet kind of incantation, it sounded like a little girl singing to the baby in a quiet voice. They listened. An almost tuneless nonsensical song about this Pretzel who enjoyed falling asleep in the sun.

Musya asked, "What is it?" She'd brought her lips close to Anton's ear as he lay there calmly. "Do you know?"

He nodded. Pretzel's kisses smelled of milk, they heard. Anton said, "Hello, Hodeh."

A pause. "Hello." A little girl. She took up her chant again. The baby scooped candle-light with rose-tinted starfish fingers, he kicked happily in Hodeh's arms.

"And why is the baby Pretzel now? Who is Pretzel?"

Anton knew. He said, "Her cat. She always talks about her."

For the first time Hodeh looked up at the bed. She had a small, thin, dirt streaked face and obsidian eyes that shone in flashes through a matted tangle of dark curls; she seemed entranced. She went back to kissing the baby's forehead. "Good Pretzel," they heard again. Then Sender groaned: more agony. This time he worked himself into a sitting position, into the light he said was blinding him. He tried to shield his vision and fell back from arm weakness. Musya put the freezing cloth across his eyes again. This time he surprised her with a novel request: he wanted meat.

"A little piece of meat—just a bite—a bisel—a little bit of fatty meat," he babbled now.

"It would be so nice," she agreed with him. There was nothing she could do.

"Please!" His voice was rising. "Please!"

At this, Hodeh climbed down off their luggage, returned the baby to the tiger skin and left her candle behind, still burning. She was gone. Startled, rather saddened, Musya didn't blame her. In this family the atmosphere of crisis was so unrelenting, the state of want so desperate, even a small child could perceive the wisdom of immediate flight. It was like they were already rotting, like poison. Sender moaned for meat; this time his brother answered:

"Soon, don't worry, soon—it's coming."

As she bound him to her chest again the baby kicked and fretted, wanting his fur combed and his whiskers smoothed some more, maybe. "What's coming? Don't tease your brother, Anton."

"But it is. Hodeh will bring it."

"Who's its? Whose it?" Out of his starvation daze, Sender waking to their dialogue: "Who?"

"Hodeh." Anton sat up. "From Boim's. She was here. She thinks Samuel Nemo is

Pretzel."

"Her cat Pretzel?"

"Yes. She was petting him like a cat—she loves him now."

"Oh, thank God," said Sender. "Thank God." Perpendicular again, he kept a smile intact through a long coughing fit and a swift return to slumber.

The two boys were speaking from a childish play-world, Musya thought. There could be no actual cause here for jubilation. Even should Hodeh return, it wouldn't be with meat—there was no meat to be had in the Obodovka ghetto. She suggested they blow out the candle to save for tomorrow night's lightless edge of extinction and prevailed against Anton's wish to keep it burning. Hodeh could get many more candles, he said:

"Hodeh gets everything."

"How? From Boim?"

"No." He turned evasive, stubborn. "I don't know."

Was there some kind of plot afoot? Was her own honor involved? Musya couldn't guess. "What have you heard?"

"Nothing." He wouldn't say more, Musya's energy was finished: the conversation was done. Curled up together, they lay shivering in a nighttime darkness that showed no inclination to lift. Dawn might have forgotten how to arrive here in Transnistria. Dawn might have stopped bothering. The end—theirs alone—eased nearer. Then came Anton's bony elbow shank to her tender ribcage as he crowed, vindicated: "What did I tell you? I told you so—I told you!"

At her return Hodeh stubbed a toe on their chest of drawers and hissed before she got the candle lit again. There lay a small package tied in a napkin. With the first aroma Musya felt her mind and all its senses receive fresh coats of paint. Red, green, brown, enamel-bright, jewel-bright, life's return flooded her at the revelation, with fat congealed among the fibers and parsley shreds, of Sender's wish come true; probably mutton. He ate and was saved.

Following the chips of living fire in Hodeh's eyes to her own bosom, Musya didn't hesitate.

"Would you like Pretzel again?"

She undid a few knots, freed the baby, held him in her two hands. She smiled at their new protector and offered Samuel Nemo to the little girl's sad ecstasy.

(6)

Hodeh was a thief.

She stole everything. Boim employed her off and on but he'd finally had to let her go for good, she stole from him. He was sorry to lose her. He'd already tried to realize some value for her but the Ukrainians wouldn't buy, they said her face was too pointy. Sad for them, the locks on their doors and windows couldn't resist her. The camp fences failed to contain her almost nightly. She stole supplies from the Romanians. She stole from everyone. Out of their family she'd had Musya's thimble and the blouse top of Sender's sailor suit which she wore near her skin; they'd thought it packed safely away but she'd been through everyone's luggage. She returned the thimble. Musya's mother had been an expert seamstress and the suit held up well. Hodeh and the three boys would wind up sharing it in sundry combinations until the war's close and beyond.

She was probably nine years old when she came to them. The boys knew her from the hallways at Krutonog's where she relaxed when not on the go moving merchandise or tramping outside after more. At Boim's she'd slept in the clothing pile where Musya must have glimpsed her; whenever Boim fired her she flitted, settling on hallway shelves mostly. Everyone welcomed Hodeh because she could always get food. At the same time, wherever she went people hurried to gather all their valuables and sit on them like anxious hens. She made those who owned things uneasy.

Hodeh stole and stole and kept things in secret hiding places. She could move soundlessly; she could run across the top of an uneven board fence at speed, erect or in a crouch; she could carry milk stolen from the udder in a stolen can spilling hardly a drop. She'd arrived at the Obodovka ghetto on a warm autumn day with no one but a grandmother who hadn't lasted. Before then she'd had parents and siblings about whom her memories were not the best. To Musya it sounded as if they'd always been poor, persecuted, disease-ridden. Yet Hodeh's life as a little girl before the war had been happy, radiantly so, because of one love, one bond, one black and white animal.

Her Pretzel: she'd had to leave her behind. Hodeh's hurt never ended. She missed her cat.

During her final week in Boim's employ she'd been tasked with returning the folded overcoat to their cubicle. Dead of night, frost on the stair rails, moonlight playing everywhere; only the baby hadn't been asleep. He'd rolled his head and crooked a shaky arm at her with a little noise, a mewling one. His mother wore him strapped to her chest that night so Hodeh started haunting them, desperate to hold the creature in her lap. When the chance finally came she was smitten. Samuel Nemo's tufted hair was black as Pretzel's; he was about her size and weight; like Pretzel he didn't bother with human language, having better sounds at his command.

To Musya's great relief their new protectress was willing in all ways to care for Samuel Nemo as a human baby, one to be water-bathed and held above a toilet pail and powdered from the sprinkle-canister of talcum she'd quickly procured for his rashes. He was at his calmest with her. To Sender she was a model nurse as well and later a close friend, practically a sister. She took Anton in hand. She was a good listener. When Sender's head was burning and his poor scalp was crawling with lice and Musya groaned how much she longed to crop his hair and give him some relief had she only been able to, Hodeh was back within an hour with a pair of scissors, very sharp. On the other hand, she never cared for housework and she was no laundress either.

It wasn't an immediate co-tenancy. Hodeh circled them for close to a week before moving in. She had her own place at the foot of the bed; the baby went back and forth. She taught him to purr.

Spring arrived. Right away there were problems in an abundance that was itself discouraging: here the survivors had been living for winter's end and then nothing really improved. Life in the Obodovka ghetto got no easier. Many felt betrayed.

First it smelled worse—much worse. The filth everywhere stank, the dreck-stuffed latrines stank. Death stank. There weren't more than two thousand Jews left alive in Obodovka; two out of ten, perhaps. Long before the ground had thawed, uniformed Romanians went through every dwelling and structure in the place with checklists and tags. At several points along the barbed wire edges of the ghetto they'd marked out grave-pits with posts and white string. Everyone remotely able-bodied was assigned to one and sent there every morning to dig with what tools could be found—none, for the most part—until nightfall. Whole days of work produced nothing but scratches in the leaden topsoil. The Romanians said to dig faster and threatened to shoot all laggards and shirkers. One day gunfire rang out, long, sharp machine gun volleys. People bent over and clawed at the dirt with all their might, yanking up roots in their fists. Next morning's pace was slack again: word had already spread that the targets hadn't been laggard pit-diggers at all, but escapees from Krutonog's, caught in the act—the gunsel, his brother-lover and the moonstruck dependent, all three. It meant more grave space to dig, almost three bodies' worth.

The labor was punishing and some people dropped dead, prompting others to complain that the exercise had begun to defeat its own purpose. Gasoline, came the call: only gasoline fires could soften the ground for the grave-pits. At last the Romanians turned up with gasoline and handled the frost-burning themselves. Over the billowing red and black flames about a dozen sand-colored soldiers stood guard, a few conversing, a very few making jokes. Most stood alone, solitary and unimpressive figures with dull, slack-jawed faces. Of the Romanian side in the war this wasn't the cream, to be sure; but their guns were in good working order and that was that.

After being fired the charred earth stank and left the pit-diggers covered in tar stains from scraping muck out of ankle-deep trenches all day. By midsummer they might have been up to their waists—far too slow, in the authorities' view. One chill morning the imprisoned Jews waited with soil-blackened hands at their pits, only to see their replacements arrive under escort of arms with pickaxes and shovels, wheelbarrows and ropes, tarpaulins, barrels of quicklime. The newcomers kept scarves and kerchiefs tied in place across their mouths and noses; to a man their eyes were furtive and appalled by the sights, the smells, the heaped-up remains. Decomposition slicked their way. Every few steps another hairy-faced nightmare with limbs like a spider's would run up to them begging for food scraps. The work gangs had no food to give. These men—prisoners of war, local conscripts, the lowliest soldiers—unfortunates all, dug the pits deep, dismantled the corpse piles, dumped and buried the dead until they ran out of ground for the purpose and threw the rest one corpse at a time onto reeking bonfires. They had the worst job anyone had ever heard of: *Those poor men*, people said. Fifteen days it took, back and forth through the gates each dawn, each dusk with but one half-holiday: people felt embarrassed. It pained them to be discovered in such squalor, it pained them to be found incapable of caring for their own dead. Some tried to join the work gangs only to be repelled with curses, kicks, rifle butts.

Granted, the would-be volunteers also hoped to escape the ranks of able-bodied ghetto inmates tasked at this new juncture with remedying the state of its outhouses. Frozen excreta, they'd learned, thawed unprompted at ten times the speed of Ukrainian topsoil. Yet again there were hardly any shovels. People improvised while their humiliations mounted. Not all troubles come from heaven, they told each other.

"How did you get a shovel?"

Musya heard this question from someone different every day: Why did she always have a shovel? For again and again her shovel was stolen when she put it down; two or three times she'd had a shovel snatched directly from her hands. The next morning she'd always have another. Then she'd wield it with equal ineptitude: Musya was a terrible shoveler. People were confounded at first, until they knew about Hodeh.

One afternoon a man thrust his way over to Musya and grabbed the handle of the shovel she was using. Instinctively she pulled away. He pulled back; she hung on. The man pointed with his other hand and asked angrily:

"Excuse me, girlie, but were you the one who painted that red stripe on this handle?"

She glanced at it. "Why would I waste my time doing something so stupid?"

"Shovel theft is a problem," said the man. They were both speaking through kerchiefs. "I don't like people stealing my shovel."

She frowned. "Where did you get paint?"

"None of your business."

"I remember now, that stripe—yes, I did paint it."

He scowled and gave a furious yank. She let go; he teetered. The treacherous slop at their feet was no joke to fall down in; she almost hoped he wouldn't. Seeing him keep his balance was the greater disappointment, though. Of course he had parting words:

"If I ever catch that thieving girl of yours around my stuff I'll brain her. Just like I would a rat—bang!" He demonstrated in the air with his shovel blade and splashed away.

Furious at herself for trembling visibly and even spilling tears, Musya stood there until an abrupt whistle blast commanded her to dig again. She sighed, rolled up her sleeves, and reflected that for all the life-giving things she provided their family, Hodeh also brought some trouble along every time—supernumerary, like a little taxation.

The final latrine was mucked, eventually, and close to the last body in ashes. The hideous labors of April had been accomplished and the strange work gangs no longer came with their sleep-filled eyes leaking fright and disgust. The Obodovka ghetto's streets belonged to living Jews again. Then it was impossible not to feel a measure of gratitude to the authorities for having forced the issue.

Except at Krutonog's no one felt grateful. Their kitchen garden corpse pile the work crews wouldn't touch: too far from the road, the troop commander said, and by no means too big for a few Jews to handle. The old inn's empty paddock was a natural small mass grave site—just come up with a few shovels and make it two point five meters deep; no less. This, the officer advised, was what happened to hoarders of privilege. They could bury their own, he said. Malicious, they called this at Krutonog's. Who had they to dig? Not one living soul in residence was fit, not since Elkie had run away to live at Tauber's. As things stood management could barely keep up with the manual side of the business, all they heard were complaints. They couldn't hire. First the labor pool was nonexistent with every able-bodied Jew employed as a dreck-hauler; that finally ended but then no one wanted the Krutonog's job. So their corpses stayed—theirs, management's, people said now—their responsibility. For hadn't they promised dignified earth burials? With prayers said, and grave markers? They had; and in every case they'd extracted payment in advance. Now people wanted refunds. Management asked for more time. Meanwhile any hope of putting the kitchen garden to its intended use and planting food there hung suspended as planting season came and started passing. Which meant less to eat: trouble.

When Sender and Anton, their health quite recovered, joined other little boys and girls at play in the nearest roadside field, Musya could hear their voices as she poked around the cubicle, cleaning, tidying. She couldn't launder as she'd have liked since the wells remained sealed and water was dear. What she managed to rinse she pinned to their indoor clothesline. Samuel Nemo's tufted head flashed chrome-silver as they crossed back and forth through the fentster beam—like the Odessa harbor light, she told him. His interested gurgle gave way to a familiar nasal call: quickly over the bucket she held him, cooing praise. When he was finished she swung the bucket across the threshold—she'd take it out shortly—and gasped.

"What's needing here is leadership," she heard.

This was Boim, startlingly present in her corridor. At first glimpse she'd thought someone must have let a wild animal into the building—he'd given her a kind of primal fright. He was so hunched and shrunken, so shaggy and grayish. He stank.

"Real leadership," he continued. "Not these females who run the place into the ground."

"I'm sure they do the best they can." Musya had no idea why she was defending management which she despised. "They haven't got the easiest job, after all."

"Sure they do. That's exactly what they got."

He scuttled closer, a better lookout through a less cracked windowpane his pretext. His head's incongruously balding crown reached no higher than her breastbone. Even swathed in the piercing reek of rotting corpses she had to take care not to inhale him. Her thoughts darted from one old daydream to the next. She'd had a series that featured the old clothes bandit. Taming, grooming, reforming him, making him taller, convincing him to release his child thieves and his koorvahs from bondage—hours spent in being more insane than imaginative, she thought now, as he continued:

"Someone with some kishkes and kerosene." His beard squeaked across the humid glass as Boim tipped his chin at the garden prospect. "Nice view. Listen, you want maybe to get put in a different location? I'm talking someplace good."

"Oh, yes!" She spoke thoughtlessly. "But how?"

"How?" A brutal cough forced him to pause. His chest sounded like a washtub crammed with dirty dishes, she thought she could hear his sclerotic organs moving around in there. He finally said, "How is I'll make it to happen."

"Oh, well, no—really, thank you, Mister Boim, but we're fine right here."

"So you're crazy?"

Musya was honest. "I don't want to owe you."

"You already owe me."

She sent a stern look down at him. "What are you talking about?"

He spat on the plank floor. His phlegm looked like a cockroach. "Don't play cute with me, Odessa girl. You know. That thick coat I give to you—two times." He held up two claws. "For what you think, for nothing? I got news for you in this case. You work for me now."

She said, "I've got news for you too. Forget it."

He bristled and his shoulders squared. "You're the forgetter. You forget who the man is you're talking to. I'm not one of your brats. I'm on the top here. I run the important businesses here that I don't expect you to understand how it goes. But when I invest in you, I want my return."

"Mister Boim, you don't want me, I'm not koorvah material."

"Hey," he said. "Sure you are."

"You're crazy."

"The work isn't hard," he insisted. "You could do it. You carried plenty that shit barehand—this is easy compared."

"I don't think so." She stared at him aghast. "I don't think it would be so easy to lie in a tent all day while strange men—"

He broke in. "Not all day, not all day. I'm not making you the main one. But I need girls to fill in. She can't work all hours."

"So, listen," she told him. "You made a bad investment."

"I don't like taking no for an answer," he replied.

The moment marked an impasse. In Musya's view, they'd fought to a draw—equals, equally unrealistic. Indeed, Boim's picture of her future revealed fantasy-making no less far-fetched than her own mad plans for his redemption. She wondered if he'd brooded many nights and how far into them. A man, a woman: he and she were as equal as two piles of ashes.

"I'll give you the coat back," she offered, peacemaking. It was spring.

He said, "You'll give me the girl back." She blinked. He meant Hodeh.

"I won't."

"She's mine."

"She isn't!" Her voice cracked under the rush of emotional heat: "Hodeh came to us freely—she was never yours, you never owned her!"

"You joke, girlie? I'm selling her out the back fence if her face don't look like a can opener."

"She's a pretty little child!"

"Say what you want," Boim conceded. "You're doing all right off her."

"I don't know what you mean," she said, glancing around.

Boim drew himself up. Strange to say, something of the man she'd imagined him to be appeared there, flare-like. "I said don't play cute with me!" His mouth was raw, red, blistered. "I'm a dying man," he declared. "You think I care if I hurt you? You think I care what happens to your brats? You can't outrun the moon, Odessa girl. You owe me."

He didn't really want Hodeh back, of course, only what she stole—a share of every-thing. He demanded eighty percent. "You're dreaming!" Musya cried. When he stood firm, she argued. "But how would that even work? I mean—of two eggs—what is eighty percent of two eggs?"

"Both," he answered. "Both eggs. She should steal more. Steal five. See? Easy."

It was a terrible arrangement, fraught with problems. Hodeh worked for Boim and they got his leavings. Far less than they needed was normal but this was too little again. They spent a dismal week or so while the corpse pile went nowhere, still. This forced Musya out of doors even though hunger made her feel sluggish, dull-witted, lazy. On the front path she looked up from Samuel Nemo and his straps to a pale blue sky. A few cloudbanks floated there, yeasty and indigo-shadowed, they were passing. The planet spun underfoot.

Strength gripped her elbow and Musya didn't fall. She heard her own voice leap with recognition: "Elkie!" The handsome housemaid had caught and steadied her. "Are you back?"

A blush showed her cheekbones to full advantage as Elkie said no. "Still at Tauber's. This is Eidel."

A light brunette, slender with actressy manners, she appeared to be around Musya's age; but Eidel wore a distinction beyond her years, mainly conferred by the paired earrings from Baila Kotz's original cinnabar set. In fairness they flattered her. Eidel's eyes were a pale shade of green and inexplicably hostile.

"Are you pregnant again?" she said.

"No—no, of course not!" Musya felt unprepared, too soft for this—whatever it was. "It's only the fresher air. And I'm hungry."

"You're hungry?" Elkie was surprised. "But Musya, I hear you have the biggest thief in Obodovka working for you."

"That's." It wasn't exactly a lie. "An exaggeration."

"Not a lie, though," said Eidel. She was clever; born in Ukraine not too far away, as it turned out, she had certificates and high marks. For now, Musya sent a narrow look at the girl's earlobes, right and left.

"There are bigger thieves around here," she said. "Plenty bigger."

"Not really," said Elkie. Eidel said, "These were a gift." Musya shrugged.

"Boim has Hodeh back working for him now anyway," she added.

Elkie exclaimed, "Good—better her than you!"

Something in the tone of this made pretty Eidel cast them both a look. *Trouble*, thought Musya. Yet Elkie's words fixed themselves in her ears and dripped acid on her conscience: the truth put so starkly smarted intolerably. It was true, she'd traded Hodeh's labor to Boim for her own debt; and as Musya saw it now, Hodeh's free childhood had gone in exchange for her own meaningless nicety. Selfish, selfish—the mother was right. As if a tent weren't good enough: with daggers of looking glass, self-hatred stabbed her. The wound was illusory, the damage was done.

"I wish I could be the biggest thief instead," she told them.

All three made way for a woman who sucked her teeth nastily in passing. The couple from Tauber's lobbed a few ripe curses at her back even though the woman had a small child by the hand. Krutonog's was even worse than she remembered, Elkie said. Premises, management, both in shambles; leadership nil; the tenants belonged in a pigsty. As for the kitchen garden:

"Why do you think I left, Musya? That would be my job too—oh, yes."

Musya's eyes had widened because of course it was Elkie the corpse-hauler who'd have carried out all those burials promised by management. Digging, hauling, liming, covering, pounding in the pricey grave markers—she'd probably have worked alone, too.

"My God, Elkie, you were right to leave! You're better off at Tauber's."

"That's not," Eidel said, "why she's at Tauber's."

"But Elkie," Musya persisted. "What do you think will happen—who will bury them? No one?" She'd overheard people guessing that management would opt out of removal and go the full exposure route instead. Natural decomposition hastened by crows, rats, insects, maggots, worms and weather—who knew how long it would take? Already, now, was too long.

Elkie thought neither. The corpse pile wouldn't just rot and it wouldn't be buried. "Someone will burn it. They need the garden," she explained. As for who'd bring the match: "The one to take charge will do it. The new leader."

Exactly what Boim had said, Musya marveled to recall. Two who would know: yet seldom had an event seemed less likely than the emergence of a leader at Krutonog's, where any leftover stamina after the work of basic survival went straight into suffering.

Though fewer, the people there remained overcrowded and underfed—starving, really. They were really many fewer and all were grieving. Many had loved ones lying still in the kitchen garden; even those who hadn't, even those like Musya and Sender Kotz who prided themselves on wiser choices, even the non-bereaved (if any) were still suffering from the painfully self-conscious shame the muffled work crews had introduced across the Obodovka ghetto through their horror-stricken grown men's eyes. While elsewhere that shame might be lifting now that its visible causes were gone, purged, at Krutonog's it weighed on unabated, heavier all the time. That they were people who lived this way felt shameful, insupportable. They detested themselves. Even worse they detested the people around them who were so inferior to the dead in every aspect—looks, morality, everything. They lived, each one, locked up with private griefs but had no privacy. Choking closeness with detested strangers bred no dreams of communal betterment, there was no idealism here. They knew any leader would be hated as a matter of course: who'd aspire to that?

Sure enough, a few days later a leader arose and it wasn't from Krutonog's. The leader turned out to be the neighbors. No more, it proved, than they wanted the smell anymore did they want their own kitchen gardens to be pillaged by the starving ones next door come harvest time.

They arrived, gray and determined, on a cloudless morning. She'd just finished bathing the baby when Musya heard their voices outside, they came up through the back way. Six men and women half-masked by the requisite kerchiefs, two bright red cans of kerosene: *More, more!* With arm gestures the rest exhorted the ones who did the dousing. Within ten minutes Musya and the boys were in the road out front, part of a crowd: Hodeh hadn't been home when they'd evacuated in haste, no preparation, they'd never drilled this. Anton had grabbed satchel and tiger skin, Sender their sewing kits and a few other things, Mrs Drobitz's tin pitcher Musya had. Her arms were full of baby otherwise, she'd been too rushed to tie his straps properly. In the air above Krutonog's mossy old roof they watched sparks dance, sparks shot in volleys off the fiery innards of the coal-black smoke that poured from the direction of the kitchen garden. A hellish stench had spread. They'd be lucky, she agreed, if the whole place didn't burn down: there'd be nothing they could do, they couldn't put out a fire with water from a sealed well.

If Krutonog's went, Musya reflected, the family was probably doomed. Clothes, books, bedding, dishware, even their shoes, their every tool of survival gone; their photograph, the one from Liza's wedding, lost—they and their line would perish without record. And it would be her fault, for leaving that last, singular treasure behind in her rush. The stiff young faces blurred even as she tried to recall, one by one: her mother and father, her sister, her in-laws, her husband. She'd never see them again. Never would her children either. No one would. Regret made her lean dizzily against the pushing rows behind her which pushed back. Then a thought flew in and beat its wings around her mind that this photograph had been too precious—its loss had freed her from incessant care. In the next moment she exclaimed with the rest as an especially bold red flame cleared the roofline with a noise like a windblown flag. There was scattered applause, an atmosphere of holiday.

The onlookers hung on and shivered in smoke-cooled sunlight until the diversion fizzled out. Krutonog's was spared except for an old shed at the back of the kitchen garden that caught fire and went up in seconds—and the corpse pile, which was almost obliterated.

With the photograph safe in her hands, Musya sat blinking away tears of relief. Their bed like everything else was unharmed. The cubicle was dim. Through the polluted glaze on the corridor's cracked window panes brown drips trailed horribly.

Footsteps approached at a run and Hodeh entered. Boim was dead. The smoke had got him, she said. It had trapped him on top of his hoard and choked him to death.

"He's dead," the little girl repeated. "Boim is dead."

"Good," said Musya. "Good."

The boys agreed. Hodeh took up Samuel Nemo to scratch under the chin. He loved this.

(7)

Aroused by the day's events already, Krutonog's erupted into action at Boim's demise. Its crazy-cornered halls were possessed by a form of gold rush fever; its stair ladders groaned. The cloud of immolation smoke had caught the clothes dealer napping on a high-watermark inventory with no more than a crawlspace between the open skylight and the merchandise below. Hundreds upon hundreds of garments vanished in an hour, less, as the living absorbed what the dead had relinquished. Suits, coats, shirts, woolen dresses and underwear, child's frocks, nightgowns: no more Jews would freeze to death at Krutonog's during the two more winters they were to spend there. Of shoes, sadly there'd been none: Boim had exchanged every pair of shoes he acquired straight through the fence for vodka. However decrepit, they had market value in a Transnistria low on shoe parts—buyers came from all around.

As for the hoard's former proprietor, a few volunteers burned him in his clothes and half his furs because no one had ever seen so much vermin, they threw him onto the coals of the immolation site with the chunks of ash and glowing bone. The fire was still hungry and caught right away. Through fur and fabric it raced until it reached the man himself—Boim, so hollowed out by disease and so alcohol-soaked that he combusted with a gruesome pop.

The next morning three unfamiliar men entered at the front door and took their way straight to management: the neighbors again, people guessed; not quite accurately. Although one had helped burn the corpse pile and all were from the ghetto, yes, with the same yellow cloth badges, these men were gendarmes of the Ghetto Council. This was a new entity in Obodovka, formed by the forcefullest of winter's survivors for the purpose of improving order. Blue gendarme badges would appear in a week or so; for now the Council's representatives walked anonymously. Their business at Krutonog's proved twofold, to match the violations charged. First, the major failure to secure community property—for those clothes had come from every part of the ghetto, not Krutonog's alone—followed by improper corpse disposal—Boim's, that was. Business, charges, violations, all were serious, the officials stressed.

To management this scolding came as the last straw. Right away they chased out the gendarmes with cutlery and turned the heavy bolts: entry was barred. The gendarmes, never identified, left. Being a Krutonog's business strategy of almost constant recourse, another emotional lockdown might have escaped notice except that this one coincided with its own inevitable discovery—in truth, only the festival of rags that Boim's death became had delayed it—as a stampede of tenants who'd paid earth burial fees met at the unyielding door to demand restitution. They sought significant cash refunds. Their voices rose and their fists began to pound. Thick locks held firm.

This was the scene when Musya arrived in a mood of annoyance. Because Anton was late returning to begin his chores, her own time had to be wasted. Many days he woke up first and had his breakfast in the new electric kitchen where she chose to assume lightning wouldn't strike twice—not since women had resumed command there. Now he appeared to be locked in with them.

"But he needs to come home, please." She gave the door another rap. The crowd had let her through once she'd assured it of her claim to nothing but a small boy. Again she bent to the keyhole and shouted: "Anton! Come out of there! We need you at home."

"*No!*" she heard him shrill.

"*He's better off with us.*" The usual tone from a voice Musya recognized too well. Anton was the favorite of an original dependent who'd helped nurse him out of typhus back when Widow Krutonog and Baila Kotz had been alive—better days. Through seniority in place this woman possessed standing her wits didn't merit. "*Better in here than with the nafka shnur.*" Her words carried remarkably well through the locked door and lingered buzzing at the keyhole. The crowd massed in the hallway regarded Musya the slutty daughter-in-law with new interest.

She said, "Can't someone help me? Please? Won't one of you try to help?"

"Best to leave him for now," said someone she didn't know but nods all around and murmurs agreed. It looked unanimous. "He's better off."

She turned and stormed away.

Noon found her balanced on the knobby untended grass outside the kitchen windows, her anger intact. She swiveled her hips with unusual vigor to rock the baby slung on her chest, calming herself. Through the half-sealed kitchen windows Anton peered grayly down at his older brother and little Hodeh who were standing on tiptoes to see him, beneath the sill. The girl's dark hair was brushed and braided, she'd allowed this liberty to Musya who on her own behalf had begun to train Hodeh's nimble fingers in certain higher braiding skills the boys had resolutely failed to master. Musya felt almost presentable.

"Come out, Antosha!" his brother cried.

The round red head, emphatic, attractively cropped, shook no. How would Anton ever escape strangling someday? Musya wondered. She wanted to do it herself. She watched him throw a look across his shoulder into the dim interior and then one, two steps down he was gone below the sill, out of view. Someone must have called him, she guessed.

"No—he's coming!" Sender dashed towards the back door (also bolted within and possibly nailed shut, opinions differed) where men stood knotted in debate. "Please, let me through—my little brother is coming from this door." He tugged at a jacket hem. The owner reached behind and swatted air. Otherwise nothing happened. Musya called him back.

Hodeh hadn't moved either. Sure enough a bare minute passed before Anton climbed into view again, now with his jaws at work on a mouthful of something. He added more. Sender staggered off his toe tips and gasped.

"They have tinned cookies still!"

Hodeh gave a soft cry. "The locked pantry—he's in!"

Anton, chewing steadily, remained impassive. Musya shouted at him through the glass:

"You can't live on cookies!"

Elkie and Eidel wandered up through a curious throng attracted by rumors of unrest on the premises. While the siege developed, most people took the opportunity to inspect the ruins of the burned-down shed and eye the blackened, not quite circular circumference of the former corpse pile, mercifully heaped with some rotten burlap sacks that concealed what lay there still, charred, undigested and stinking. Eidel's nose was buried in a perfumed handkerchief, a sweet perfume, not to Musya's taste at all. If Krutonog's was such a dump, she wondered, why did the girl hang around?

Elkie cocked a wave at the kitchen windows. "Good day, Tovarisch!" They'd always got on well; Anton waved a cookie in reply. "Mandelbrodt! He's got mandelbrodt!" Eidel exclaimed, darting forward. Her eyes began to search. "A ladder—can someone find a ladder?"

Hodeh spoke up. "There are no ladders."

Eidel looked around at her. "I suppose you would know."

"I do know," said Hodeh.

"I hate it here," Eidel said. Returning to Elkie's side she repeated, "I hate it here so much." Making sympathetic sounds Elkie caressed her friend's shoulder blades. As Eidel returned the crumpled silk to her nostrils, Musya's cloyed.

"It's easier to ignore the smells," she pointed out.

"So you go ahead," said Eidel. The silk—not real—stayed put.

"Did you get any clothes, Musya?" Elkie shifted the subject. "From Boim's room?"

"Oh, no, we kept out of it, we didn't get anything."

Eidel's bay leaf-colored eyes slid in Hodeh's direction. "I suppose you needn't bother."

"Antosha!"

Sender's shout drew their attention back to the new electric kitchen window and gasps were heard all around.

He was eating an apple!

"They're really going crazy in there," Elkie said wonderingly. Then a man from the group by the steps approached them and spoke.

"You girls need to step away from the building," Another foreigner, his accent said. "And take those kids if they're yours." They did nothing but stand and look at the man, an anonymous stranger, so he added, "I have authority to order you. Authority from the Ghetto Council. I'm a gendarme. Do what I say."

"What's a gendarme?" Sender had come up, asking.

"I don't have time to tell you," said the gendarme.

"It's like police." Eidel's tone was unfriendly. Her eyes were on the gendarme.

He countered, "It is police."

"But if you're police," Musya cried, "then help me! They've got my—that little boy, in the window—he's supposed to be out here with us—I mean, with me."

The gendarme squinted. "The one with the apple? That's your son?"

"My sister's," she began, then decided better to simplify. "My son, yes. He's mine. He's four years old, five soon."

"He looks okay." The thatching of beard hair and grime above his shirt collar heaved convulsively as the gendarme swallowed saliva, Musya realized. Like anyone else, he was starving for that apple.

She said, "He's been kidnapped."

"He's better off," the gendarme answered, casting a look at the group of them. Eidel erupted:

"Who are you to say that? You have no right! Who are you to judge? This is wrong!" Her swiftly tearful voice cracked; Elkie held her shoulders. The gendarme growled some kind of curse.

"The two of you—go back to Tauber's. And you." He pointed a finger from Musya to Hodeh. "Your girl is a thief."

"The whole world is one thief!" she retorted. "Do your job—rescue my son!" Eidel applauded loudly and Musya said thank you. This felt good.

"Step back, ladies!" the gendarme bellowed. They said no, they asked why. He rubbed a hairy wrist across his eyebrows and turned away to spit. "Why? This is the point—you don't get to ask why." It didn't matter. Elkie who'd slipped off was already back with the explanation. The latest women running Krutonog's had just sent out a credible threat to blow up their decade-old steam boiler and thus make an end to themselves, their kitchen, and their ordeal by petty harassment—the ultimate protest. "Your friend is correct," said the gendarme. "Any second now this whole wall could explode, maybe. They've invoked fakakta Masada. Group suicide."

"What!" Musya was staggered. "Anton! Anton, come out!"

"Masada with a steam boiler." Eidel seemed impressed. But Elkie didn't think they'd do it. "No one left in there has the nerve." The gendarme agreed but his orders stood.

"Move along, ladies. The bigger the audience, the worse these crazies act."

Anton waved them goodbye with the apple core as the little party joined a general movement at walking pace past the burlap sacks, the burnt stumps of the shed, the ever-straining laundry lines. Near the brick campfire circles a larger stable showed signs of continued habitation but another stood vacant and the tents had gone, leaving a bare rutted flat. Just beyond rose some patches of verdant hillocky growth. They picked one and sat down to watch, they were still within sight of the kitchen windows. Hodeh took Samuel Nemo and lay him under some dangling stems in the sun where he kicked comfortably. His brother Sender pulled off a few leaves.

"Can we eat this?"

"No," Elkie told him. "Never eat that plant. It's grasspea."

"We could make soup," Musya suggested.

"Especially not in soup," was the answer. "Widow Krutonog told me a lot of people got sick from trying to eat this plant all sorts of ways in thirty-three. Leaves, roots, seeds, it's poison no matter what."

Musya didn't understand. Even by current management's standards the irrespon-sibility of this was striking. "But she kept it there? Instead of planting something that isn't poison? You couldn't try strawberries?"

"You think I was the gardener, too? Anyway it didn't matter since people stopped trying to eat grasspea."

"But what made them start in the first place?"

Eidel jumped in. "For the same reason as now, because there was no other food. People were starving all over the place then. That's why I'm small, that's why you're small, Musya. When we were children the whole Ukraine starved." She tipped her chin at the stripe of distance visible, a leaf-carpeted river valley. "This part like the rest. I should know." It was true: although Eidel wasn't short her build was slight. And she knew her locality, having family roots in a village not too far away, on the Lviv road, Musya knew the whole story by now. Eidel could have called herself lucky since the rest of that village had perished by suffocation in sealed freight train cars back in August, by all accounts. She'd been teaching school at a collective farm settlement near the Polish border when Germany struck; in flight, capture, and incarceration alike, she'd revealed an uncommonly strong gift for coming through. Nevertheless she cried for a while every day and never called herself lucky. "This is twice in my life I've starved—twice!"

"I don't remember starving before," Musya said. Although she didn't either, Elkie's memories were too few to deny it had happened. She believed, as she often said, that children forget the bad.

"I didn't forget," said Eidel. "I remember every minute. I'll remember every minute of this, too. And I can remember people making the soups from the grasses, and going out to help pick."

"And this?" Musya asked. "This grasspea, you remember that it's poison?"

"Grasspea I don't remember," she admitted.

"It's poison," Elkie said. "Widow Krutonog knew. She told everyone."

"But!" Musya wanted to slap someone from sheer impatience with this account. "Instead of telling people she could have just dug it up and planted something else—something edible! Thirty-three? She had almost ten years."

Elkie nodded sadly. "The neighbors wanted to fine her. At first."

"They should have! These women—" Musya began but broke off, startled by a noise. Another loud dry crack jolted her nerves before she identified the sound as a piece of old stable being snapped off for use as kindling wood. Within seconds the first reports became a fusillade as an instant mob hurried up full of hands. Fire was slower than scavengers so desperate. Of course the stable boards belonged to Krutonog's but none of the Krutonog's tenants who looked around at one another said anything; in light of the clothing situation that kind of protest was bound to lead nowhere. What stopped the gendarmes from intervening was anyone's guess. In quick order the stable become a flat square of earth littered with splinters and nails and some grooves where the walls had been.

By contrast the new electric kitchen remained fully intact, its position unchanged. Its windows occupied the same row in space as before. Yet the longer it lasted the more the structure resembled a mere collection of brushstrokes on a blown glass bulb—a view of itself applied over trapped air.

A shande, Elkie called the last armful of kindling's departure. "And a waste."

Sender agreed. "And the gendarmes don't do anything."

"What do you expect? When socialism is dead here? Reflect!" The schoolteacher in Eidel was showing. She'd taught political theory to her share of six year-olds, generally tough pupils. "They're not here to help you. They're here to serve our new bosses and safeguard their interests, that's all. Police are nothing but lackeys of the bourgeoisie."

Elkie shook her head. "They'd have protected that poor stable just now in that case. Krutonog's management is the biggest bourgeoisie around here."

"Not anymore." Eidel drew a loud breath through her nose and said, "Take a whiff. That's the smell of a big bourgeoisie turned into lumpen-proletariat. It's no wonder these women are doing this. If they intend to regain any class status, then suicide is probably the only way." Musya said she agreed, it made sense. Elkie said it wouldn't happen.

"In one million years they never will." She looked at Musya. "Don't worry." Nearby on the grasspea patch Eidel frowned.

Musya looked at the clouds again. There were three overhead, three silly clouds lined up like fingertips, one two three prints on the blue, very small, discrete, downy, wind-wisped on one side like top-feathered chick heads. What kind of clouds, she wondered, were these to gather here when every other decent self-respecting cloud—thunderheads, hurricanes, pillars of fire—kept its distance? Maybe to call them clouds was a mistake. Witnesses drawn to be in the sky above the worst thing on Earth when it happened—what were they, really? Demons? Insane dwarfish demons disguised as silly cloudlets, were they waiting for Anton in red and brown bits to be tossed up across their laughing faces? She thought possibly, yes. She felt time shrink past eggshell thinness into membranes thinner still; the end appeared through a blood vessel veil.

At Hodeh's cry her eyes flew open. "There—look!" Hodeh again. Hodeh's forefinger pointed to a spot near the kitchen foundations where sod was tossing. As they watched, a square trap door heaved on its hinges and finally swung clear.

Up into the daylight Anton climbed. In his brown sweater that sprang new holes as fast as she and Sender could darn them and his short pants grown baggy and frayed he started towards them, his steps determined, his expression a displeasured frown. He must have come from the kitchen through the secret root cellar, Elkie guessed. The rest didn't breathe. The situation felt more delicate than ever. Marking the limits of danger from a blast, presumably, the gendarmes were back in conference over battering rams. They'd come up with a fence post to use but the wood was rotten. Pure chance tossed a moving glimpse into one of their eyes as Anton marched past.

"Hey, it's the hostage! The apple kid! Where'd he come from?" Someone else must have pointed because the gendarmes rushed over and disappeared one by one like giant ants down a hole.

The little clouds had started crumbling in the blue, a beautiful blue, Musya noticed. Three friendly forms soon to be a cloud field—she'd misjudged them badly. Now seeing them go she felt contrite and her contrition felt like superstitious dread. After all its basic kindness she'd defamed Nature, accusing it falsely—she'd seen demons when there were only benevolent vapors. Demons!

"I'm sorry," she told the sky. It waited. The first crashes burst from inside the new kitchen, the first screams and peremptory shouts. "Thank you for your help." There'd be some injuries but no explosions, then or later: the steam boiler was preserved.

Anton evaded hugs and kisses. What were they doing, he wanted to know. They'd been having fun without him, he accused Musya especially. She denied it:

"We thought you would blow up—how much fun could we have?"

"It wasn't so bad," Sender said. "We got to watch them destroy the stable, Antosha. And then we found this plant that's deadly poison to eat."

"Grasspea," Anton said. "I know. It kills the legs. Hello, Pretzel." He knelt to pet his baby brother.

"That's right—the legs," Elkie remembered.

Musya looked down at him and made two fists. "Were you going to tell us, Anton— did you plan to tell the rest of us about grasspea?"

"I don't know." He shrugged. "Yes."

"Did you bring any mandelbrot for other people?" Eidel asked.

He hadn't. "I ate them all," he said.

Eidel nodded. "And this is the reason I don't miss teaching—not for one minute." She climbed to her feet and shook poisonous seeds from the folds of her skirt. "The child's mind in its natural state." With little more being said, she and Elkie went off in the direction of Tauber's.

Closely, over one shoulder, Hodeh marked their progress, her mouth compressed into a crooked line. At last she turned and held out her palm. Anton reached for his waistband and poked around in a hole he found there. What emerged was a brass key. Hodeh gave a nod of satisfaction as her fingers closed on the prize.

The Ghetto Council's solution to the Krutonog's problem wasn't half so radical as management had feared or the tenancy hoped. There were no charges brought, no trials, no hangings, not even any expulsions from the new kitchen; the same women kept the same sleeping spots among the tiles—all save one. Anton's special patron found herself evicted and the prime alcove within the glass-paned inner sanctum was cleared for its new occupant, a widow of late middle age whose figure suggested cement poured and hardened in overflow. This was the new management. With several bags and two bearers she arrived on the arm of her married son who proved to be a big wheel on the Ghetto Council. They'd been deported from a town near Bucharest. Here he'd found his mother an attractive situation and gotten her out of his wife's hair at the same time. He had drive but his mother had more. To a good deal of moustache and beard she matched thick brows whose charcoal gray awnings shadowed languid eyes of unnerving night-creaturely brightness. Her basic menace was such, every faction obeyed her. With unerring results she could add subtract divide or multiply any set of figures faster than a machine and she loved a game of chess; she drank tea without ceasing, had a deep fondness for sex gossip, kept a strict no-work shabes and always wore a wig on her head; she preferred the wig askew. She never smiled. People called her the Ernste. After hardly any time at all at Krutonog's she'd learned every detail of the place—every tenant in every corner, every rent, every debt, every earth burial refund sum owed and exactly to whom (most took their payment in credits for better bread, hotter water). Later the Ernste knew every leaf and flower of every plant in the remarkably fecund kitchen garden. She always knew everything about the place except for why, every so often, some nice bit of food would go missing from her locked pantry shelves.

(8)

The small chest of drawers that had improved the Kotz family's lot beyond measure was a battered survivor from an early low point in Soviet mass production, birch veneer over cardboard and tin, no good for burning. Rickety in the extreme at delivery the chest had stabilized with time cold and damp; its top although tilted leftward was the family's flattest surface. Tin gleamed through veneer strips worn almost away and reflected the candlelight—low, nearly guttered, the candlewick looped like a big darning needle.

The stifling night ticked with heat release and wood beetle jaws. Musya blinked a few times and propped herself on her side. The last one left awake, she'd dozed off mid-story, lost for words, some time ago. The others, Pretzel too at Hodeh's shoulder, slept on, sleep-tossed, twitchy, plagued by fleas and sweaty closeness. Flurries of candlelight swirled about in the feather-mirrors of mosquito and moth wings. Discomforts abounded here along the old fruit canning shed corridor, true; but the night held some satisfactions. The absence of neighbors on one side remained a luxurious balm. That set, never friendly, always grieving, had recently packed up their sad noises and kerosene heater and fled the rent. Better still, they'd left its long-detached door behind in the empty cubicle. Warped, stained, splintering, scavenged and scoured it served the Kotz family as a table-of-all-work and leaned in idle hours against one corner of the space to make a little privacy around their bucket.

A flapping shadow drew Musya's eye that way. The wedge formed by the corner and the tilted door suggested the mouth of a cave deep past fathoming. From its darkest point a pale spot wavered into notice. She watched the spot assert itself, blaze paler and swell, then elongate and grow an army tunic half-tucked into loose trousers. Next came limbs, shoes, hands, fingernails and a thin-haired head to scratch fretfully as the spot stepped into the straining candlelight. Its spectacles, smudged with dead fingerprints, flashed. It was her husband.

Beyond acquiring a uniform slightly phosphorescent pinkish hue, Boris hadn't changed; he hadn't aged a day, as usual. She'd forgotten until his appearance now that he'd dropped some weight in advance of their trip west. He'd been determined to appear in trim, less for the Odessa crowd than for the German allies among whom he'd planned to seek employment. Germany's physical culture, he liked to say this instructively, led the world. To herself she always pictured an earlier, pudgier Boris Kotz, Musya realized—exactly the one in their family photograph; her sister's husband. This more recent model wasn't that bad, truth be told. But what did he want of her, here—now? Some renewal of her wifely duties? The prospect alarmed her, although he'd never made demands before. His long lips drooped. Musya's right fist clutched her sleep chemise closed at the throat; she wasn't breathing as Boris stepped closer.

He ignored her completely and went straight for the chest of drawers. There he stood in a fret. Hands and sleeves the color of bone marrow moved restlessly among the pools of light on the tin-patched surface. This she recognized: he'd lost something. Boris was always losing things in all his stuff. His blocky back was turned but she could see right through to the objects scattered there: the piles of books, Mrs Drobitz's tin pitcher, a hairbrush and comb, the dying candle on its plate, and a small ornamental pine cone that came from a wooded bluff on the edge of Birobidzhan. Seen through the gauzy glow of her husband's midriff the brown scales on the cone appeared to be fluttering like fern heads or underwater weeds. A chill slipped into the atmosphere and felt almost pleasant.

"It's not there, Boris," she whispered; waited. "Boris?" He seemed deaf to her. She thought he must be looking for his German grammar whose onion skin pages especially his father had favored as toilet wipes. Long gone, some in handfuls, they'd outlasted the book's green cloth covers which after serving Papa briefly as a rain hat had dissolved into fibers and pulp. It was a shame, but there'd be no learning the German language during this family's course of confinement in the Obodovka ghetto.

Maybe it was something else he wanted. One drawer after another Boris pulled open and rifled while she could see the drawers never moved, he went through all their belongings ghost-wise. They had more than many had, for sure. His search dragged on. "What do you want, Boris?" She sensed a desperation in him. Was it his dishes? Had he rooted out a way to make his Manchukuo import scheme succeed beyond the grave? And what was the hurry? Was the man only small-fry there, too, answering to a bigger spirit's time clock? Poor Boris Kotz, he was probably still writing unanswered letters.

On the other hand, he'd fathered some excellent boys. Rosy ectoplasmic light rays played across their perfect slumbers—except Samuel Nemo lay with gleams between his lashes, wide awake, purring, pillowed on tiger skin. "Come look at your new son, Boris," she urged.

The father only scratched at his scalp again and moved towards the luggage pile. Musya shuddered. Ghost lice—horrible thought! Shouldn't death relieve exactly such earthly troubles? But was Boris even dead? Maybe he wasn't. This visitation could just as well represent a message that he lived, that he was very much alive and not one iota less annoying—witness the possibility. Was it even a hope? She watched him swarming back and forth across their bags like a tinted spotlight.

The candle faltered and flared its last. In the dark, after a short pause the heat came down thick again. Dead or not, Boris was gone.

Every detail of the encounter remained so vivid in her mind the next day, she felt compelled to tell somebody. Of course the children were out—they'd be furious in the first place that she hadn't roused them in time to see for themselves. Musya passed the morning basting Mogen Dovid stars and empty number patches for Sender to sew on beautifully; with the windfall of jackets and coats occasioned by Boim's asphyxiation the call for this service had skyrocketed. Theirs wasn't enterprise so much as strict necessity, for they worked on Krutonog's behalf in exchange for lodging these days. Krutonog's supplied the patches; the ghetto authorities would ink in the numbers.

At the earliest opportune hour, leaving Hodeh in charge, Musya hurried down the road to Tauber's where she found Elkie and Eidel sharing a back wall bench in the sun. They looked glum and unreceptive. The Ghetto Council, they told her, was establishing classroom instruction for the ghetto's school-aged children and Eidel had been drafted as a teacher. She dreaded the work:

"There won't be any discipline at all. No support, no supplies. Pedagogy, forget it." The early mornings wouldn't help. Musya said it sounded bad to her but also less boring than housework. Incorrect, Eidel claimed: "The boredom of a teacher's life is beyond anything."

Elkie said, "You could teach a class, Musya. At least the little ones."

"No I couldn't," she answered truthfully. "I don't know enough."

Eidel nodded. "Yes. The training matters."

"Listen, by the way." Elkie kept up with all things Krutonog's. "You'll have to make the little girl stop with the stealing, at least for a while. They've got a big crackdown planned." Musya felt offended.

"But how can we live if we don't steal?"

"I'm only telling you. Oh, and you should take that empty cubicle next to yours before they move someone else in. Just change. It's bigger and it has a dugout." Under the firebox, apparently, the top rungs of a ladder lay concealed. "It goes to a little hiding space under the floor. There's a few of them around—people had them put in after nineteen."

Mr Asch's pogrom massacre, Musya remembered. The firebox was a low wooden frame full of sand where the departed heater had rested; the neighbors would leave a door behind but never that. *"You care more about kerosene than you care about me!"* How many times she'd heard their heart-sore voices, their dying starvation cries.

Elkie continued: "We almost used it when the Germans invaded but Widow Krutonog fit us all in the secret root cellar instead. At least it used to be secret."

Musya sighed. "I don't want to move," she said. The trouble and mess involved in moving house even so slightly made gray roaring sounds appear in her head. The thought of tackling Hodeh's habits went just nowhere.

As for Boris and his apparition, which she described in detail at her first chance, the couple spoke with rare accord: she'd dreamt it. Dreaming that she was awake she'd imagined the entire scene.

"This ghost or whatever you think you saw could only exist in a story. Or cinema, maybe," Elkie explained. "Tales of superstition," Eidel added. Musya said she supposed so.

They were too rational.

"But say it really did happen," she persisted. "Would it mean the person was more likely dead? Or alive somewhere?"

Eidel decided. "Alive, actually. Because astral projection is real, it's been observed experimentally. All it requires is the proper conditions and technique to produce the phenomenon."

"But my husband." She didn't know where to begin. "I don't think so."

"Maybe Nazi scientists have him," Elkie said. "Maybe he's being dematerialized in a Nazi experiment."

"Or maybe we've caught up—maybe the Red Army is testing the technology on its own solders," her friend Eidel suggested hopefully. An instant later her pretty features crinkled in distress. "Oh my God! I can't believe I have to teach again!" And with the heels of her hands she pounded on her own blue-veined temples. "I can't stand it!" she moaned.

Elkie caught her wrists and petted her, comforting. Musya glimpsed another passerby disapproving of the tableau with a look she returned sneer for sneer, in solidarity with her comrades: these two girls were all she had for friends now. "At least you have each other," she said impulsively.

It was true: together Elkie and Eidel did well. To experience a career crisis was a luxury in Transnistria.

A few minutes later Musya was heading back to Krutonog's without the answer she'd hoped to collect. Lab-manufactured astral travel made a poor substitute for a visit from the afterworld. Because Nazi science or no, if her husband Boris Kotz lived, nothing changed; her lot as a helpless unprotected female prisoner with children remained exactly the same. Whereas with Boris a dead man's shade, she'd be a widow. A widow was something, a real identity, one not uncommonly buttressed by higher status and benefits; a widow was respectable. Musya's legs pumped the folds of her loose black skirt into swirling motion. No longer this helpless shucked partial thing exposed to every sort of grief by the quotidian facts of separation—but a secure, independent, experienced adult able to fend and to choose for herself, that's what she'd be in widowhood.

She detoured past the fence where Papa Kotz and his widow had spent their last long months above ground. By the time she'd finally steeled herself to visit the place, winter had been halfway to spring and she'd found a good-sized corpse pile where the old couple had once slumped alone. They'd seeded it, she supposed, and she guessed they'd gone along when the whole heap got carted off by a work crew team for burial; she hadn't witnessed the last event. The gravesite no one could tell her. She paused on the roadside by the natural declivity that might have reminded the old man of his soft old sofa. Its summer blanket of grasses had been picked almost bare. A wayward clover blossom remained to be pinched off and chewed for its hot green sweetness, slowly. Up and down the road the view looked similarly plucked and gnawed-on. Sure enough, weak shuffling footsteps grew louder from three directions at once as street-combers who'd spied Musya grazing closed in. Their hunger came to crowd her elbows, they were after the fodder. She left them to it.

The way to Krutonog's was brief and at the front path she decided to keep walking, she wanted to move more. The skirt was a bagatelle, the loose black cotton cut to flounce, a relic. She'd gone café dancing with Leon Flohr in this skirt. And she'd pulled out Baila's old black shawl to wear above her pink blouse although the day was warm— she'd dressed herself in wistful trappings. Her mother-in-law: there was a woman who in the brief time she'd been left to enjoy its advantages had really made widowhood count. All the way up to the nascent third-act romance that expired with Mr Asch on his death-bed's good horsehair mattress: whatever Baila's calculations might have been, she'd made the old historian happy before the end. The love he'd come to Obodovka seeking so long ago he'd finally located, a good man's reward.

For Musya instead of reward there was the same old refrain. Who would love her? She wondered, looking around, how many good men were left alive to love inside the ghetto—useful, that is, as well as decent. To be loved by a starving street-comber of notable kindness and virtue wouldn't be the best, it wouldn't help. Other healthier-looking men stood conversing in the shade of house eaves; a few others even wore handkerchiefs on their heads and took solar rays for pleasure. Underfed, no doubt, these men managed to live without hunting for mouthfuls of food at all hours. They were hungry but they were eating. A man such as one of these, a careful comfortable man with connections enough and even some privilege, the perfect match for a youthful yet not under-seasoned widow with a heart made for love: which one would he look like? Better yet: which would she choose?

"Hey, you. Miss." The well-built older man spoke to her by her birth name from Odessa. He stopped her in the road. "Look at you," he said. "A maidel mit a klaidel." The line without the tone of a sweet talker, the speaker not completely harmless-looking to Musya who was small: she eyed him.

"Yes?"

"You remember me? Your papa's friend?" She didn't, really, and frowned. He said, "Pompoms." She stared harder.

"Oh—yes!" Now she remembered him, he'd kept a little kiosk among the Privoz market's trimmings and haberdasheries halls. A dark-skinned man, fond of nougat. He was Armenian.

"I've forgotten what they call you," he said.

"Oh—I'm sorry—Musya. It's Musya. Kotz, now," she told him. Her smile flashed. "I've forgotten your name too, actually."

"Golbus. Mister Zaim Golbus."

She nodded; a curious name. She asked, "I never knew you were Jewish."

He paused to reach into his garments for a handkerchief. "Unfortunately, I am," he answered. Now she waited through the time it took him to blow his large and sadly grimy nose and return the horrid rag to his front trouser pocket where portions showed through several holes. He was uncared for. He was about to speak but Musya's tongue went first; she meant well:

"Did you lose your wife, Mister Golba—Golbus?"

He followed her gaze to his thigh and understood. He gave his pocket a tug, then tweaked a few more low points in an attire very poor in general. "Oh, no, my wife is here but we always had servants, she can't do anything."

"But how do you live then?"

"We keep a girl, a moyd, she takes care of my wife."

"I see." She stared at complications and left him to continue.

He cleared his throat. "Listen, my dear, it pains me to bear you this news, only with my profound condolences, the fact is, your father passed away. He is no more."

"He—what?" She felt a furtive pang. The old annoyance.

"Your father. Your daddy. I saw him die. Back in Odessa." About a week before the fascist headquarters bombing this had happened, Golbus explained. Already then there were daily round-ups of Jews, mass executions. Along with about forty others, the father and he had been plucked from the market quarter and lined up near the south gate by some Romanian troops under German command. "They started marching us in the direction of the harbor. It was a death sentence, we figured. So we go march, march down the road—I'm no marcher, I wind up in back. Then ahead of me I see your little father, my old friend." Golbus clutched his rag-stuffed pocket in a large emotional fist and continued. "All by himself, he walks along with the group but outside, way outside. The Germans see him and shout, they're saying to get back in line, threats, who knows?"

Her daddy hadn't known, Musya was sure of that. "So they shot him then?"

Golbus shook his head. "He got all confused. The next thing that happened is one of their Nazi trucks went past at high speed and ran him over. He died instantly—almost instantly. I'm very sorry."

She was taking this in. "So—he was in the road?" Golbus nodded. "And there was no firing squad? I thought." She trailed off. She'd pictured gunfire, always.

"Don't ask me," said Golbus. "After what happened to your daddy there was a lot more confusion and a few of us in the back got away. I took off and ran home to my wife. We knew about a secret cellar where we hid with some neighbors until the dvornik's wife snitched and a round-up got us. This time either, no firing squad. Maybe to save bullets after how many they used on the dvornik. Whatever that was they did to Slobodka, that's where they put us instead."

"Oh, I was in Slobodka." She smiled conversationally. "I didn't see you there."

"We saw you," he said. "In fact you talked to us one time. I thought maybe to tell you then but then I decide no, I don't want to upset you so much it could hurt your baby."

She nodded, lost for the moment in that wasteland of rubble strewn with seated corpses. "Thank you."

"Did you ever find your mommy?"

"No," she said. "No."

"And your baby—is good? You had?"

"Oh, yes, he's fine. A little boy. Samuel. Nemo. Kotz."

"And where is Samuel?"

"He's home—I mean, where I live."

"Who with?"

"With—the girl. I keep a girl too, actually." Her wits were clouded by discomfort and by something else, she supposed it must be the beginnings of grief. She couldn't think what to say; assuming she ought to ask a question, she couldn't frame one. Did she really want to know more? She wasn't sure. "My poor daddy," she said.

"I don't think he knew what hit him. Actually."

"No, that sounds about right." She gave Golbus a quick glance. What she'd recognized by now as his hostility perplexed her. Her next remark was inane. "He always complained about the traffic in that part of the city."

"Your father thought the world of his little daughters." The Armenian glared at her. "It tore him up inside, losing them the way he did to that informer you both married."

"My husband is fighting in the Red Army, Mister Globechuck."

"Golbus."

"Yes, sorry. Golbus."

"Therefore all the more reason," he resumed, "if that insect is still alive for his wife not to be palling around with pervert girls and walking the streets giving grown men the glad eye." The blush rose so fast to her cheeks she felt singed. He continued, "For your good father's sake, honor his memory and try to have a little self-respect why don't you?"

Without leaving her time to find the words to defend herself the pompom man dipped his head and walked off. Musya stood in the road. He'd left her encircled by a closer kind of barbed wire, a fence of human eyes. Regarding glances of every sort—intercepted, felt, imagined—stung her wherever she turned; men especially were watching, they watched and judged. What were they seeing? What had they just witnessed? A respectable gentleman displaying an uncordial lack of all the decencies to a young woman wearing a pink blouse, that's what. Not even a handshake: she felt badly misread and disastrously misrepresented. Musya wasn't a person to be spurned in the road yet now strangers would think otherwise.

As she hurried back to Krutonog's she kept her eyes downcast. To dull the painful consciousness of being marked and graded from every side she thought furiously about the wrong just done her. This old Golbus had dealt her a big ball of insult. No offer of help, no invitation to meet again, only rejection and a public spurning she didn't deserve—but what sort of woman, she wondered, deserved to be spurned in the road? One who worked in a tent for someone like Boim? Or one of the pompom man's pervert girls, maybe? Koorvahs and perverts deserved better, too. There was nothing special to this wrong she'd suffered, the wrong was the same for any woman it befell to be treated like something unclean.

Her poor father. He'd have defended her with all his gentle heart. Daddy: he'd understood Musya like no one else in her life ever had—maybe not better but more comprehensively, because he'd seen more good in her. Poor man, no one to take his arm. He'd drifted out of the doomed herd into traffic, typically, a flitter to the end. He'd tell her not to put such stock in other people's views that they spoiled her own outlook; don't mind gossip, he'd say. The mother may have been right to call him the Soviet Union's most feckless husband and father of children (his son-in-law perhaps excepted) but as a life philosopher Musya's father had been all practicality, no nonsense. Don't try to change other people, he'd say. Time heals all wounds. Don't cry, he'd have told her;

and she didn't cry, not yet.

A hanger-on acting as dvornik stopped her just inside Krutonog's metal-clad door to tell Musya she was summoned. The Ernste, in the new kitchen, immediately: "Go straight through," she was told. She carried on down the zigzagging halls feeling more or less numb. Pink Boris as its harbinger, this day was beyond anything. At the threshold of the big tiled room she announced herself:

"I haven't got much time, my children are unattended."

A deep growl of a voice amplified by a resonant rock-hard-sounding chest cavity rose to jingle in the corners of the walls. "Sholem-aleykhem," said the Ernste.

"Yes," said Musya. "As I say."

There was a pause. "That thief is with them." Again the Ernste had spoken and now paused again to sip tea from a glass. She didn't offer any. She occupied an armchair placed outside the frosted door to her quarters; on the tea table at her elbow was a chessboard arranged in a game. Other chairs were nearby but Musya wasn't invited to sit. "You running around again?"

"I was paying a call, a social call." She glanced around. The room was full but the normal old hubbub was missing. Former management, two or three housemaids of extreme youth and a handful of male lackeys made nothing but murmurs as they watched the Ernste at work.

"You go see those nasty girls." The wig dipped on the right today and rested on a woodsy brow. "You know what I'm talking about. At Tauber's. Those girls do nasty things to each other's places."

Musya denied this. "I think they have a romantic friendship, that's all."

The Ernste grunted. "Believe me, you don't want to try and sleep at night near this friendship. Very wrong. And not romantic. I know these things, the good people they come to me and tell."

"I see." Musya let her gaze drift to the windows. Down the yard, four or five figures knelt among the grasspea patches—she raised the alarm the moment she realized: "Those people, they shouldn't be doing that—they'll be poisoned!" They were browsing and harvesting. She started in on the hazards but they were nothing the Ernste didn't know quite well already, she said:

"That plant grows like crazy. They pick every bit and it comes right back." She signaled for a fresh glass of tea.

"But they'll be crippled—grasspea poison kills the legs!"

"With God's help they'll be spared."

"God's? Just dig it up and God won't have to do anything."

The Ernste asked Musya not to tell her how to manage property. "I know what I'm doing better than you. And I don't want those foul girls on the premises."

The murmurous background volume spiked. Musya objected for everyone: "But Elkie is a friend to Krutonog's, she has many ties here, she grew up here, she—"

"She's allowed. The other stays out."

"Fine. May I go now?"

The Ernste relaxed in her predecessor's armchair and replied, "You give me problems. Too many problems for one little matchbox rent. For what you keep so many children?"

"What? *For what?* They belong to me!"

"Not the thief."

"She's—I've adopted her."

"You could send her out to work. The bigger boy could also go—he does good work on those patches." The Ernste tipped her bristles at an example or two in the room. She was right: as cloth humiliations went they were oddly becoming. "He's yours?"

"Yes, mine, my sister's—yes. And day-work is out of the question. He's just seven years old!"

"And the younger one." Now the new electric kitchen hummed. "The people here would take him."

"No!" She looked around again. "No!"

The Ernste was inexorable. "Then you have this little baby you can't be bothered to care for." She overrode Musya's objections. "I hear he's healthy, that's good. Healthy for now. For how long, who except you can say? His chances could be better like *that.*" The finger snap was a rifle shot of a noise; her hands were hard. "Good people come to me and tell me such sorrows, such losses they've suffered, lost loved ones they pray to replace with a nice baby—I'm talking about good families with better mothers."

"No thank you. Really," Musya said. "My family is fine, we're managing fine on our own."

This the Ernste contradicted: "You're stealing. Your managing is stealing. You live on stolen food and comforts."

"Should I drop dead?" Musya asked. "Should my family die? Would that be better? Should we give up stealing and die instead?"

"If that's your choice," the Ernste replied. "I just told you other choices you can make. But from this day on the stealing ends—period."

Musya said fine. "Fine. We'll manage without. We'll be fine."

The wig rode up atop its brow like a tortoise's shell crossing some undergrowth formed of skepticism. "Fine? Yes? How? You'll find another tent to work in?"

Once she understood, Musya was outraged. "I never did that!"

"No? You're on the list."

"What list? You people have another list?" But it was Boim's list, apparently, located among his effects, on which her own name featured as Odessa Girl with asterisks; genuine, the Ernste produced it from a handy reticule. "He approached me, yes, but I turned him down completely." She was blushing at the ridiculous asterisks: Boim's strangled poetry of ardor. "I don't belong on that list."

The armchair's spring coils gave an irritated squeak. "That's what they all say," one of the lackeys supplied. Musya threw out her hands:

"So maybe it's true!"

"It's not true," said the Ernste. "If only it were." Amidst ripples of pious agreement

Musya stood silenced and apart from these people, none of whom—least of all the Ernste—honestly thought she'd ever worked in a koorvah tent; they knew better, only her morals were their momentary sport. Their leader carried on: "It doesn't matter how you decide to manage, there's bound to be just as bad trouble with men."

"Oh," Musya said. "Now I can't have a man?"

A loud interrogative noise pretended to escape the Ernste. "She asks? What, your little baby came without using one?"

She cleared her throat. "I'm a widow."

"Maybe, maybe not. I'm a widow," the Ernste added. "As for you—no men on the premises."

"Fine."

"In fact I want you off that corridor. Those stalls aren't meant for women and children. For you I'll find a much better situation in a real inside room with a couple nice families you can help doing their housework."

"No!" Musya observed a general flinch from the ricochets and kept her retort pitched at peak labor pain volume: "We're staying where we are—you can't move us! I refuse! No!" She felt an attack of hysterics coming on that would put Eidel's poor tantrum to shame.

The Ernste must have felt it too because she brought the interview to an immediate close. "Then go live like animals. Go, with your so-called family, be happy." She dismissed her.

(9)

There was Romania, there was the Ukrainian town, and there was the Jewish ghetto of Obodovka.

The Romanians were an occupying power and as such it was their business to make their presence felt. They used violence. Women weren't safe with them, girls and young boys weren't safe either. They were cruel, quick to pull triggers, paranoid; though brutish they craved luxury and commandeered all the best housing and provisions. And stables, since a few of their officers rode; the horses displaced they slaughtered for the meat, they were meat-lovers. On the edge of town they'd erected garrison barracks and built a military prison nearby, both fairly small. It wasn't much of an operation. There was no airfield. But the troops saw action almost every day because the surrounding countryside was infested with armed Ukrainian partisans, mostly ex-Soviet army, many deserters. Inland from the river the craggy ground was full of woods where trained guerilla fighters surrounded the occupying forces and seemed to aim at them from every tree, every rock cleft and shadow.

Meanwhile, in Bucharest, men and women of good will reported to the comfortable committee offices of charitable organizations, and worked up relief programs for the Romanian Jews marched there so cruelly to starve in Transnistria, philanthropists happily unaware of the scenes just then taking place in different offices in Bucharest, where men in uniform sat at long tables deliberating over the same Jews' enslavement. Good fertile land but at present a ruinous rearguard battleground, Transnistria would plummet in value if the labor question pending there were settled otherwise, the winning plan's backers claimed. The imprisoned Jews must labor.

Obodovka sprawled along its riverbank. Inland lay a high road with some public buildings and stores flanked by networks of chalk lanes that meandered past grass banks, cottages, well heads, empty paddocks and kitchen garden scarecrows. The under-populated town had its share of sons and fathers in the Red Army. Plenty of others were still in the neighborhood, attached to one or another of the partisan bands that kept nomadic quarters within the local landscape's rich array of feathery reed-roofed inlets, abandoned hunters' shacks, vine-curtained limestone caves and similarly picturesque elements; sneaking back to town for news, sex, baked goods, changes of underwear, they'd find its streets deserted. Very many Obodovkans, men and women, boys and daughters, had perished during the Axis powers' sweeping ground invasion. One year on, at least one result of fascism stood out: Obodovka needed laborers. From all the daily tasks undone, like great weeds, up grew want, dirtiness, misery, all from short-handedness. Plots of land, shops, cottage trades, manufactories sat idle or nearly; no money was coming in. The occupation drained resources at a barely manageable clip and its soldiery was prone to drunken terror sprees that pushed the damage toll much higher. Complaints went nowhere. The town's links to their partisan foes were no secret to the Romanians who'd restored all the local Soviet police torture rooms to full operation. Tortures came and went as mourning over last year's dead continued, life after life, toll upon toll; incessant hurt dulled suffering; the time was gray, irreal. The energy to go on without help was lacking and communal spirit nowhere to be found. The experience of having lived so near the Jewish ghetto during its first winter when eight of ten died there left all kinds of scars locally. Many people had carried pails of boiled potatoes to the barbed wire gates and given them away to the starving Jews locked inside but many more had not, for instance.

Behind the barbed wire, the Ghetto Council was not everyone's idea of a worthwhile institution. Among its opponents one group believed that gendarmes and kindergartens were beside the point and that every organized waking effort ought to work towards gaining liberation. Some people speculated openly that more mass death and anarchy inside would force some set of hands—official, popular, partisan, whose didn't matter—to clear away the fence-wire and let the Jews walk free; they trumpeted visions of an easeful liberty that the beautiful riverine landscape surrounding the place did possibly too much to foster. Allied with these dazzled theorists were others who opposed the Council on various grounds, some temperamental, others more practical. Those doing regular crimes, for instance, wanted no kind of police in the ghetto. And then there were the ones keeping watch for a leader to step out from the crowd or ride up from outside on a motorbike possibly and take all the actualities in hand—a hero. A small secretive body of self-interested middle-aged men was not what this faction of the heart awaited.

Most Jews in Obodovka didn't care greatly what happened so long as conditions improved. On the whole they had no energy for politics. Even the urge to escape wasn't general. No one much wished to give up a roof overhead during wartime. In rejecting calls to cast themselves upon the mercies of the Ukrainian countryside, Musya's family was one of many that could call upon recent first-hand experience; indeed not a few felt safer behind a thick barbed barrier keeping out the local population. By this settled majority the Ghetto Council wasn't held in any serious regard at first. Its plan for schooling the ghetto's wild children was vague on details and its gendarmerie's blue cloth badges drew jibes enough to splash its entire law-and-order effort with comedy. Obedience was a laugh and resistance a farce when both sides were abject, weaponless, and tagged alike with the same yellow badges. But circumstance and nerve soon put the Council in charge and left it entrenched.

First charity arrived in its usual way, late for the crisis. Kitchen gardens and fruit trees were already bearing when the first installment of food relief marked in Bucharest for Transnistria's Jews reached Obodovka. It was welcome, of course. So was the cooler fresher water from the wells unsealed around that time: typhus cases had grown rare enough. Death rates from every cause had dropped. Now thirst itself was beaten back and almost vanquished. No thanks—none of it—to the Ghetto Council, which wasn't involved until it took over. Those pushy men, as some people said, put themselves in charge of receiving and distributing the new hunger rations, they set up an office and everything. Another day, out of nowhere, they regulated the ghetto's fresh water use by posting regulations in Yiddish on all the wells. These new rules were widely ignored but the appearance of print made the Council's authority surge. No one else had thought to write anything down: who'd have dared? That the Ghetto Council had to be cooperating with their captors in exchange for primacy, immunity, signboards and paint was a fact people begrudged less and less as little by little their comforts increased; no one else wanted to run the place, really. When the gendarmes came to arm themselves with sticks they heard very limited ridicule. By then a fixture, they were kept busy among the ghetto's frequent vicious conflicts fueled by pure overcrowding. An enormous loss of life had left still too many for the space.

The crowded ghetto with its Council, the emptied-out anemic town, and the occupying forces of a hostile power made three. To complete the picture were two vast absences: Germany and the Soviet Union. When the war ended, one would control Obodovka and Ukraine and no doubt also Romania which could hardly be expected to hold its own against either army. Nazi or Red? This was the question mark whipping the troika. An uncertain future clouded every present motive save for short-term gain. Those in positions to issue commands knew themselves to be the most vulnerable; today's collaborators could face next year's firing squad. Grief was endemic, many actions unreasoned. The conditions for disinterested sympathy were absent and kindness would be hard to find—yet people talked of miracles. All anyone could be sure of one hundred percent was that no matter what happened, whichever side won, the Jews wouldn't be wanted.

The fence-wire stayed. High summer glowed. Inside the Obodovka ghetto people admired the views while standing in line for food or baths or drinking water; nothing moved like clockwork. One morning new Council signboards appeared, damp black script translating the latest from Territorial Command—new orders. Between the ghetto and the town the barbed wire gates were to be unlocked; passage in and out had been established. New policy took flesh across Transnistria.

As the Ernste explained it to Musya, yes, strictly speaking forced labor was slavery but would she prefer death? This was the choice, one of two. As for slavery, "It's honest work," she said. "It breaks up the day, gets you out of the house." She said everyone at Krutonog's should count their blessings, because thanks to her son on the Ghetto Council she was contracting her tenants out to the softer, better situations in town while the less fortunate got sent to the margins—the fields, brickyards, building sites and worse where the hard labor happened. "What, you'd rather carry sacks?"

"I'd rather get an exemption, please," Musya asked again. "I have a little baby and children to care for."

"Not so special. Women have children in life. Take your baby along—people like babies."

"Of course I'll take my baby—I'll take all my children then—all of them."

"No," said the Ernste. "For your little children, for that girl especially, a little school is good. Keep thieving fingers busy." Merriment danced in the eyes that peered at Musya over the rim of a tea glass. There was power in this new dispensation for the Ernste as well as profit; she was well content and there was no arguing with her.

Musya tried one last time. "And my Sender should also be in school, he's much too young to go out to work."

"What? I should send the apprentice without the master?"

Sender tugged Musya's skirt. "But I want to work!" Musya said no and he insisted. Debate ensued. At last the Ernste declared:

"Enough. He goes, you go, both. No more argument. You should thank me and instead you argue."

"You believe I should thank you for sending us in slavery to Ukrainians?"

"Yes," the Ernste said. "You should. By rights I should give you nothing, no work and no food either. What I get is sent for Romanians only, not you Odessa Jews. I share with your family because in my kindness I won't watch you starve—so yes, you should thank me. But you won't, you have no gratitude in your heart." This was true: Musya wouldn't thank her. "And while you're at it, you should spare some thanks for our Regina-mamă— and all blessings be on her."

"Who?"

The Ernste blinked away some tears as outrage replaced other sentiment in her eyes. "Who? Our Queen Mother, Elena. Who else makes them send food to the Jews here?"

"She's the mother of their King Michael," Sender added helpfully.

Musya laughed. The backwardness! "You people still have a king?"

Tea splashed to the floor. "Of course we have a king! We have a very good king and a great royal family. You Russians would still have one, too, if you weren't a bunch of godless savages and murderers." The wig had slipped, was practically a blindfold. The Ernste reared back and hollered, "Get out!"

"I never murdered anyone," Musya protested.

"Out!"

The arrangement was for room—their same cubicle, they hadn't moved—and a minimal board for the lot of them, including Hodeh, in exchange for day-work in the town where Sender's skills with a needle along with her own were to be put at the disposal of a goyish Obodovka fallen very far behind on its mending and alterations. In the town as in the ghetto, the loss of skilled tailors had been notably complete. Sender Kotz was a valuable asset, as some people preferred a man's tailoring always. The board—thin potato gruel or millet, soft onions, an occasional hunk of sour black bread, some powdered milk, almost nothing else—would be the family's share of hunger ration which they'd receive from the tiled kitchen. In town they might get something to eat where they labored. They might also be struck or beaten, kicked to the ground, abused. Any assailant could act with impunity since they'd have no more rights than a stray dog.

Back in the cubicle it was nearly nightfall. By what light remained Sender rearranged his sewing needles by size again in a precious felt strip. The next day would be their first in the town and he was too excited to stop fussing with the kit they'd share. "You should have your own kit, Musya," he urged again.

"We're sharing," she repeated. The sharp scissors they were leaving home with Hodeh, just in case.

"But you have your sewing needles and I have mine."

"Yes."

It was a fact that the birthday gifts he'd received in May had included three sharp smooth-eyed needles which Musya had gotten in trade for some coins of Hodeh's procuring. Which sorts of thefts she hoped were through but it was impossible to know, Hodeh kept secret hiding places after all. "Every time you steal for us," Musya had told her, "you put Pretzel in more danger. Pretzel can't live outdoors, not in the rain, not in the cold and snow, but that's where they'll put us. They'll put us out, Hodeh." The girl had reached back for her black braid to gnaw the end of it, thinking hard before she answered. Two weeks on she hadn't really answered yet. Save for one single, vital exception, neither had she brought anything else into the cubicle from outside. The one thing Hodeh couldn't stop stealing was eggs—chicken eggs mainly, but other sorts found their way by her efforts and offices into the hands of the Kotz family which sucked them for their vital nourishment. All Hodeh would say is, "Eggs come from trees." Uneasily, Musya wondered what she'd do to entertain herself and Anton between the time school let out and the end of a twelve-hour workday. They'd be much on their own. And according to Eidel the classrooms wouldn't be ready for another month at least.

"Do slaves get uniforms to wear?" Sender asked.

"No. We won't have uniforms."

"We should."

"Maybe." Musya was indifferent. She lay there depressed. Her friends wouldn't be slaves: Eidel had an exemption to stay in the ghetto and teach while Elkie had one from Tauber's where she did everything; Tauber's had Council influence equal to Krutonog's. Granted, both young women would be hard-worked every day but Musya envied them. For the Ernste was wrong: going out as a slave didn't feel honest at all, it felt polluting to a degree that dreck-shovelling had never approached, not even with a lost shovel. Then she'd labored mechanically, one among multitudes set on a single task, the smallness of her part corresponding to the little that it mattered to her; then she'd retreated to the sheltered precincts of an unsullied, scentless, dreaming selfhood. Already in prospect this bondage to the town cut deeper, it cut her off from refuge. She couldn't be indifferent. Slavery was too personal to be denied.

"Will they give us new names?" Sender asked.

She sat up. "Why should they?"

"They did in Babylon. They changed Daniel's name to Belteshazzar."

"They wish this was Babylon," she said. "In their dreams. Don't worry—you're Sender Kotz and that's final."

Sleeping poorly she kept watch for Boris but he didn't appear. They'd been abandoned, she supposed, they'd sunk too low for the astral plane to even bother. At dawn a loud rattling one-note electrified bell sounded: this was the new work bell. Sender sprang up, flung off his nightshirt and leapt into his sailor suit trousers; for the occasion Hodeh had relinquished the blouse to match. One year on, the sleeve and trouser cuffs were a little short but the fit was otherwise very roomy, Musya saw with sorrow. He told her to hurry, they shouldn't be late on their first day. She had Samuel Nemo yanking at her nipples and snapped, "Who cares?" Then Anton turned a sore red and screamed at them not to go. He lay down stiff across the threshold and kicked the gray floorboards, howling and shrieking. Hodeh sat quietly and chewed her braid; she was frowning but she nodded when Musya asked, "You'll stay, won't you? You'll take care of him?" Poor Hodeh: domestication had to be robbing her young life of zest. Without the baby to pet all day, Musya feared she'd leave them.

The bell clanged lengthily as she and Sender sucked an egg apiece. Now everything was noise and haste and they couldn't get out of the cubicle. Anton swatted and kicked and obstructed. Sender knelt down.

"I'll find you a job, Antosha. Don't worry—I'll ask the people. They'll give you one."

"A big job!" He was relenting, no doubt bored already.

"Of course," his brother said. "Big and important."

The corridors and then the ghetto lanes were thronged as every dwelling emptied itself into a dewy sunrise. Strange armed men roamed among the council gendarmes while councilors with checklists directed traffic. The workforce they'd mustered was large but otherwise unlikely to impress the employers of Obodovka in its favor given the general state of raggedness and emaciation, the bleary eyes, shivers, odd bald spots, sores, staggers, reeks sharp and stale. To Musya's astonishment, the worst-off captives had turned out, too: street combers and grasspea pickers, pregnant women, the elderly infirm, none exempt. And crop-headed children were everywhere, frail limbs sagging from their swollen rectangular trunks they shuffled along, necks bowed like withered saplings, work-bound. Not one looked as healthy as her children, Musya thought. Before a tall new gate hung with signboards swelled a human flurry. Here each worker would receive the same day's ration, a single raw potato which many bit into at once, the pain in their gums making tears run down their faces. What she and Sender got they pocketed to save in case they found themselves near a stove.

Space yawned wide around the sorry crowd that stepped into the strange Ukrainian town and divided into details, one line following the right-hand road and another swerving left. Men blew whistles. Shouts came: someone else had fallen, the strangeness was dizzying. Musya had a slip of paper, their assignment. Pointed straight ahead by a bayonet, she and Sender crossed the intersection towards a pair of men in street clothes. One also wore a wooden boot, the other an eye patch; both held shotguns. As the half-blind one reached for her paper he barked some incomprehensible command and sharp-edged recollections of her failure to learn more Ukrainian when her sister had ordered her family to try made Musya grimace. The guard scowled at the slip, thrust it back into her hands and signaled her to wait with the rest of the group. She recognized several faces from Krutonog's.

Quiet fell. They stood and looked at the ghetto. This side of the gate had more signboards on it, warnings mostly. Behind the tangles of barbed wire, crack-plastered house walls rose to shingled roofs and some dark clumped bushes stood picked bare of leaves save for their topmost branches. The start of a lane ran down to the corner of a well. The dust that lay thickly on everything had begun to throw off sparkles in the stronger sunlight of another hot, dry day. What did the townspeople see, standing here? What had they been looking at for close to a year now? What the signboards told them to see, in angry letters faded to gray and pink beneath the summer dust, was a place forbidden, dangerous, off-limits. They might have believed it. No one else was around but the Jews and their guards. Soon the road was empty, the group marked for labor in this quiet corner of town waited alone. Insects sang.

A small boy appeared from a side street. He was a handsome child ill-clad in nothing but a worn-out blouse with a rose pattern. The blouse ended halfway to his knees; his legs were filthy and his feet were bare. Sender gasped at the sight of him and grabbed Musya by the skirt:

"That's Little Lev—Little Lev, he was kidnapped, Boim sold him. Lev—Lev!" The eye-patched guard raised his voice for silence and took the slip of paper Little Lev handed him. He peered at it. The boy glanced at Sender and then looked at the ground. His blouse trembled and his bare toes curled in the dust. The guard pointed at a woman from Krutonog's upper floor and a pair from the old kitchen and signaled them to follow Little Lev, who turned and left without a backward look. Rents in the fabric fell away from one shoulder blade and a buttock to reveal grime, red welts, bruising. Sender cried after him: "I'll mend that for you, Lev—come look for me!"

"Quiet, child!" A woman with a brown headscarf and two rings left, good ones, hissed: "Be quiet—don't make trouble for people."

Musya said, "The little boy is his friend."

"Who cares about little friends when they could blow our heads off for talking?"

"I hope they do," Sender told the woman. "I hope they blow your head off first."

Musya hushed him. "Eat your potato."

"I'm not hungry."

Perceiving discord the infant Samuel Nemo complained through his nose. She jiggled on her heels to coax him back to sleep. By now a few more children little better clothed than Little Lev were approaching. Terrible to see, all of them were shoeless. Even if no more than the remnants of shoes tied together with rag strips such as Musya wore, to wear less in the ghetto was considered not only dangerous, it signified the most grievous extremity, far past help—so with the overnight lunatics who'd invariably take to the streets bare-footed. "These, too?" Musya bent to whisper: "Kidnapped?" Sender's nod was tentative, he wasn't sure about the newcomers. All held notes which they presented to the guards: claim forms. By twos and threes the group shrank as the children led people away.

The Kotzes' shoeless escort was a small, emaciated boy in a ragged undyed tunic and trousers set. His scalp looked worm-ridden; his widely-spaced features were dotted with sores. He limped badly. They trailed him to a turning at a narrow graveled lane bordered by wooden fences. Once the guards were out of sight, Sender hurried to catch up and question him.

"Do we know each other? You're Jewish, yes? From back there—inside?"

Their guide in his Yiddish answered, "I'm not allowed to talk to you." He seemed to be Sender's age, maybe a little younger.

"But do you know Lev? Little Lev? He's a slave here, too, he's a friend of mine. Do you know him?"

"I don't know anything."

Musya asked, "What happened to your leg?"

"A wolf," he said. "A wolf ate my leg."

"But it's still there," Sender objected. The other boy went silent.

After the ghetto, the most striking aspect of things out here was their cleanliness; for despite the Council's best efforts the ghetto remained heavily filth-strewn. Too many people and not enough caring, people said. Too many: another big change from the ghetto was that in the town of Obodovka there might be too few. The lane emptied onto a chalky, unpaved cart road, bluish white in the sun, lined with low-slung dwellings, empty paddocks, untended fields. The place seemed abandoned, all but given over to weeds and brambles which in the ghetto would have made green soups for days. Field nor road, Musya didn't see anyone. No dogs barked. Only here and there when one of the sprawling cottages with their deep eaves and rain barrels released a curl of chimney smoke, or a window curtain twitched, she glimpsed occupation.

The white road dipped between high banks overgrown with blue honeysuckle, noisy with bees; then it climbed again and they emerged at a bare farmyard bordered by a double row of whitewashed stones. They followed the boy past a single large tree and a dark blue house front. A steep, massive roof bristled with lightning rods leaking rust stains down its tin facing. There was a chicken coop that looked empty and an over-grown garden plot profuse with squash blossoms. Unseen, something animal that rotted there fed a loud insect feast like some intoxicant. The boy led them onto a glassed-in porch that ran along the back part of the house. Inside it was hot as a furnace and reeked, being stuffed full its entire length with unwashed laundry, bedding mostly, heaped and stacked as high as the bare rafters. By the door where they stood room enough had been cleared on the floor planks for a small worktable and two low wooden stools. A drawer in the table held thread. The boy retreated to the doorway.

"You work here," he said.

Sender gave another look around. "But bed linens aren't very interesting."

"I remember you," said the boy. "And your little brother who had the fever. You cried."

"He lived," Sender said. "He's all better now. He needs a job, too—have you got another?"

"You cried and cried. You're a veyner."

"I said," Sender said, "have you got another job for my brother, please."

"I haven't got anything. Don't ask me. Veyner," the boy in the doorway added.

"Don't," Musya told Sender softly. A more pitiable bully had never existed, she thought, than this one. She tried smiling at him. "Even a name you don't have? You've got a name—you must. Our names are Sender and Musya." His spotty frown deepened and he shifted on his sore leg.

"Russvelt," he said.

"Liar," said Sender. "Liar, that's not your name."

She put one hand on Sender's bunched shoulder. "It could be. If he wants. It's a good name."

"My father owns America. He killed Hitler with a fountain pen."

Smile and fingers gripped in place, she said, "Please give him our thanks."

"There's a dead girl in the garden. I have an airplane," he answered. Sender breathed hard but limited his reply to a stare. Almost at once the other boy's gaze grew vague and drifted from them. He limped off without another word, twitching his chewed-up head away from the bold attentions of two orange butterflies that trailed it out of view: a little madman. They'd seen plenty of his sort by now. The theft of working wits was a common form of murder in Transnistria: its victims, driven insane, abandoning self-care, fell subject to every sort of fatality. Others who got too close were too often dragged down with them; fears of contagion were real; even mad children were shunned. Their madness was a peril. The false Russvelt's departure left Musya relieved.

"Some people are much worse off than we are," she sighed.

But Sender turned on her with a face full of tears. "I don't like that boy—I don't like it here! I want—what about Little Lev? Why can't we go find him?"

"Stop," she said, looking around. "Because we can't." Only a step from the exit the space was airless. Under brown paint chipped down to blue and white another door on the opposing wall stood closed. Some gardening tools were rusting in a corner. "Eat your potato."

"You eat it!" With that he yanked the thing from his white trouser pocket and threw it at her, missing wildly. Neither of them saw where it landed. They guessed it had to have gotten lodged among the torn piled-up curtains and sheets, the innumerable ragged blanket folds, the actual mountains of bed quilts with gray cotton wool dripping from leaks which they now began to search.

A human noise from behind found them up to their elbows in separate heaps. The interior door was open and there on the porch stood a woman of fleshy build who exclaimed, possibly in pleasure, at the sight of Samuel Nemo strapped to Musya's front. She squinted when she smiled. *Our owner*, thought Musya. A tallish black-haired woman going gray with a round, pleasant face, a small flat nose and eyebrows plucked to arching wisps, she was old enough to have a few children in upper school but in fact she was childless, although not unmarried, they'd learn. Over a tight blouse and skirt she wore a double apron heavy on the hand embroidery; on her large feet she wore black house slippers. She had thick calves, a well-defined waist, a fairly deep bust. In her mouth among the good teeth were some very brown ones and some flashing metal; her lips remained parted at most times. She asked first if they could speak a little Ukrainian and Musya shook her head mutely. The woman tried again:

"You understand Russian? Ah, good, it is good—most do not."

"I am—we are from Odessa," Musya said.

"Ah." With widened eyes the other nodded. She looked them over, especially attentive to the sailor suit which as Musya realized now was disgracefully yellowed and stained, she felt like a fool for having hoped to impress with it. And yet the Ukrainian woman was impressed, this was apparent. She praised the work. "Yours?"

"My mother's."

"She is here also?" An eager tone. "With you? In—there?"

Musya shook her head back and forth. "Nyet. Nyet."

Deep-set blue eyes shuttered in sympathy, then opened smiling. "And the baby is yours?" The woman started forward but paused as something rolled around her feet. "Ah," she said. She stooped, picked up the potato and put it in an apron pocket. Musya heard Sender draw breath to speak but then nothing else came from him. She hadn't looked on the floor either.

At this moment Samuel Nemo made a familiar noise. Musya, with a firm "*Pajalsta*," crossed to the door and stepped into the cooler air outside, unstrapping the baby with practiced speed as she went. Naked beneath his best shift, he relieved himself at length on a kitchen garden bed overrun by weeds that lay along the porch foundations. She spotted the leaf and fruit of a wild strawberry plant in the mix and took care to hold him away from that patch. He squirmed and chortled in her hands as she murmured the accustomed praise for keeping his urine arc gentle. "The Chinese technique. A labor saver," she explained to the Ukrainian woman who was looking on from the doorway in surprise. Only pronouncing the word delivered a sharp reminder that she and her nephew were labor, the labor, this woman's to command. Were they allowed to come and go through a door without her permission? Ought Musya to have asked? The woman might even punish her, punish all three of them; although it appeared unlikely from her response:

"Ah," she said, impressed again. "This is the higher thinking."

Musya who'd learned survival at the side of Baila Kotz didn't hesitate to force whatever advantage was here. She smiled. "Could we have some water, please?"

As she led them to the yard pump, the woman described their position. The goods on the porch, she explained, had been sold or abandoned by departed townsfolk and were destined for resale. The primary family in the farmhouse was her own, as was this cottage trade in second-hand bedclothes and rags; the patronymic was Babiak and her name was Oksana. She had a handshake firm and brisk—a trained Party comrade's, in fact—and she herself would supervise their daily quotas while doing everything else around the place, practically alone, although there was a houseful of women in residence; the few old men they'd brought along were no more. The house kept one maid-of-all-work but had lost all its seamstresses. (Here Oksana cast a disquieting glance at the garden.) The porch mending had piled up until it was urgent—good bedding was short and dearer each day now. Her customers included Romanian officers. Her prices weren't cheap. She decried the cut she had to give Obodovka's mechanized laundry on which she depended to collect, wash, package and deliver the finished goods, they were practically robbing her.

Back in the sunlight, "You have—animals?" the overseer asked. To illustrate she scratched her scalp a little, then her collar bone. "You understand?"

"Oh—yes," Musya said. "Yes, we do. Of course. We have them."

Sender also understood. He offered in recollected Russian: "The most common is the flea."

"What did you expect?" Musya said.

The woman bobbed her head and for a moment or two appeared downcast. "It is very difficult," she said. "Even for us—out here. It is not easy."

"Of course it is not." Sender volunteered it before frowning Musya would speak again. "You are under fascist occupation just as much as we are."

"Well," said Oksana Babiak, somehow delighted. "What an intellectual family."

The boy who called himself Russvelt reappeared as their escort back to the the ghetto near sundown. Half the sky was the color of chicken fat, the other half blue. Released from their close stitches the Kotzes were blinking. They had about them some berries and vegetables from the garden edge bundled small to evade detection. The little fantasist limped doggedly, breathing hard with a wheeze in his throat. His scabs were blackish in the dim blue light. When Babiak's was well behind them Sender tried him again on the subject of Lev, he of too little rose-patterned blouse. ·

This time Russvelt had more to communicate. "He's dead. He killed himself today. He jumped down a well."

Musya told Sender not to believe it. He said he didn't. "You should be ashamed of yourself for lying so much, Russvelt," she added.

He turned and his pinched face made ugly wrinkles as he screamed at them: "You only wish it was me! You like him better but he's dead! I don't care—you'll see! You'll see!"

And he ran off, leaving them to find their way without him. At the intersection where they'd started they found a small sea of weary Jews being squeezed back into the ghetto at rifle-point through the gate's excruciating paperwork. They witnessed threats, blows, collapses. The scene was violent and frightening. Musya held Sender to her side and hung back but her consternation roused Samuel Nemo to his first full-throated crying fit of the day. Seeing a soldier turn, scowl, advance a step, she hurried them into the crush, she burrowed them into its side. Groans rose all around them. People wept from fatigue and the hurt of blisters and sprains, people were shaking, people were weeping and shaking both. Many had turned monocolor: from their matted heads to their rag-wrapped feet some were the orange of brick clay, some coal-blackened, others the chalk white of road dust. Red-rimmed eyes peeked through, dull and afraid. People whispered.

Who wasn't returning—who hadn't made it through the day? So many. Familiar names: Golbus, a woman named Golbus; the pompom seller's wife, Musya supposed. She concentrated on keeping two green peppers safely hidden from the human press. People complained about her. "Can't she stop that baby crying?" a few asked until someone retorted, "The baby is human—let it cry." His mood contrary, Samuel Nemo hiccupped and fell quiet. The crowd inched forward.

Hodeh met them in the road out front of Krutonog's where her fervent kisses sent the baby into a blissful purr. Glum and nonchalant as he listened to his older brother tell how close they were to securing a big job for him, any day it would happen, Anton said no thanks.

"Work is for schlemielen," he told them. Then he ate all the wild strawberries when Musya's back was turned. He was desperately jealous of what he mistook for their freedom of movement amid fun and luxury; in which regard it might have been a mistake to return with sweet berries on the very first day, she acknowledged this. Next morning's departure filled him with heartsickness over this renewed abandonment. He was difficult to leave. Musya felt awful. Maybe Anton should join them at Babiak's after all, she started to think.

Back at their intersection Sender Kotz watched desperately for Little Lev who never appeared. The Russvelt arrival was late again and their escort to Babiak's conducted in the silence of a soreness unabated; one last "You'll see!" was all the boy would utter and that in parting at the porch steps. The sight inside felt deflating. What they'd done the day before had seemed so much but by morning's light not a dent showed. They sat down at the table again, unplucked threaded needles from their stopping points and began stitching by hand again. They were due a sewing machine. Oksana Babiak had offered one for their use as soon as someone to carry it out to the porch could be found. She entered mid-morning, not with news of the machine but of matter far worse—a dead boy, a Jew, down a well. His corpse had been hauled out on a hook overnight by soldiers working with electric torches; where they'd taken it, she hadn't asked. But the odd-job children who died were commonly taken away to the outskirts, the town maintained a common plot there.

"Maybe it isn't true," Sender said. "Maybe it's not him."

Sadly, the news continued: "People here are all talking about it today because he was the most handsome one. Little Angel, we called him. The Angel."

Sender wept onto his stitches.

"Careful," said Oksana. "That is silk." Yet more urgently she sought to console. "But listen, this is my idea, I think this can be good for you." The Angel's place was vacant, she explained, and she knew the affected family well. "So maybe I move our stinky boy to their place and your younger comes here, Muskah. Work for the little brother." She smiled down at Sender who sniffled and blinked uncomfortably.

"But you said." He paused. "Yesterday you said no openings."

"But that was yesterday." Oksana answered smartly. As they hesitated, she urged, "We can take him, I think, even to sleep here."

"Where does the boy sleep you have now?" Sender asked.

She pointed outside, saying, "The nice birds have all gone."

Musya asked, "Your boy—the one who calls himself Russvelt—he sleeps in a chicken coop?"

"His name I do not know," Oksana said. "He is not a good one."

"Probably my brother cannot come to work here." Sender's voice shook with the effort to be firm. "He needs to go to school. For education." His eyes shot Musya's way, a wide gray signal flare for help as Oksana's face dipped to one side and she recalled:

"But yesterday you said you wanted work for him."

"Yes—it is true." Now Musya tried for an authoritative tone as her head filled with panic. Images flashed there: Anton ragged and shoeless; Anton being whipped, his freckled skin bruised; Anton sleeping in a fouled nest. "School is most important for Sender's brother. He is a scholar, you see. He dreams—like his father he dreams of a career in science."

"In field research," Sender lied more accurately.

"Yes," Musya said. "So he must study always, always."

Oksana accepted this. "Such brains in this family," she said, before her thoughts returned to the suicide. Her voice grew sad. "That poor well."

On the fourth day some Jews from the mechanized laundry arrived to pick up the finished mending and found it a struggle. This would always be the pattern with them, to come irregularly but never before the accumulated load surpassed the strength their workplace hadn't yet soaked from them. In lye steams and chemical heat their hands and skins grew spongy soft, their hair fell out, their chests were ruined. If they'd shown up at Babiak's one day or two sooner every time their lot would have been bettered but this adjustment wouldn't happen. They'd raise the cart shafts onto their shoulders with difficulty and deep choking groans: "We're half dead from working there," they told Musya.

"Yes," she agreed. Half, in fact, looked to be a low estimate, and it was only the fourth day. "I'm sorry." There was nothing she could do. To work more slowly and send less for them to wash wouldn't help. Compared to the occupying force with its uniforms, blankets, linens and underclothes, her contribution to their plight was negligible. Even so, as the pair plodded off she resolved to take more care over her stitches—less, she knew, for any fraction it might shave off the launderers' workload than to cut her own chances of sharing their fate should her work fail to please; she'd trade some quickness for security. Sender's stitches, of course, were infinitely careful and precise—and fast. The sewing machine would be for her use, she needed it more.

The next day Oksana asked, "Why so slow, tell me?"

"What about the machine?" Musya said.

"The machine? It is coming. For this work a machine is no good anyway."

Musya blinked dizzily. Her fingers ached. "So—not coming?"

"Sew a little faster," Oksana said.

The nightly cram before the ghetto gates continued to buzz with news of fatalities. One notorious detachment assigned to the riverbank wharves saw Jews sent to move barge loads drowning almost daily. In the brickyard Jews lay crushed beneath a stack collapse. Like Baby Drobitz they were exploded by mines and live ordnance while toiling on roadworks and farmland. Soldiers and partisan snipers alike had adopted them for target practice right away. Night after night the ghetto filled back up with people, pain, grief, exhaustion, and fear—fear of tomorrow. Sleep perished. The living lay clenched stiff against the first notes of forced labor's harsh iron music: what rattled Obodovka's Jews awake each dawn was an electrified death knell.

Sender Kotz was laughing when he returned to the porch one morning with his hands full of wild onions that dripped from the pump. For the fresh air and exercise of his foraging skills, Musya sent him outside whenever she could. Yet she needed his needlework if they were to make their daily quotas and he'd been gone long past his time. The irritation this had caused her was instantly forgotten in the pleasure it gave her to see his smiling face again, always her favorite among his faces. He looked healthier, the vegetables were a godsend. He told her what was so funny was the Babiaks' maid-of-all-work. "She's afraid to death of Jews!"

Musya took a bite of onion. "So she's dead?"

"No, she ran away—screaming!" His delight peaked in high cackles. The tale spilled out more calmly once he'd bent to his work. Young Russvelt was involved, of course, with his claims to powers of invisibility and mind-reading he had Sender in thrall. Concerning the maid's peculiar affliction of fear he'd promised a show and he'd just delivered spectacularly. The two of them had happened on her in the yard. She'd been standing there not doing a thing, her eyes lost in the empty spaces. On silent tiptoes they'd crept up behind her and waited—all true, it was all true, Musya realized with a sensation of shipwreck among strange legends revealed in prodigious life. All the graffiti and slurs she'd shrugged off, all the rude caricatures, all the bad make-up on screen had been more than greasepaint, more than noise. It was genuine. Odessa had never felt further away; modern socialism might as well not have existed. Far from accepting the equality of all citizens, the backward types around here believed Jews to be monsters of evil with creaturely attributes and for this reason held them in an abject crawling terror— a peasant terror. The fascists might have brought some decorative innovations with their coils of barbed wire but basically nothing had changed in three hundred years. At Obodovka the old-fashioned frights remained uneradicated. "She turned around and spotted us and then she screamed and pulled her apron up over her face and ran back inside."

"How old is she?"

He guessed, "Your age." So the maid was about twenty-two and basically a savage— but also clever. For this explained why their work-harried owner was doing double-duty as their overseer. Unable to force her will past her maid's refusal to enter the porch, Oksana Babiak had been stuck with them; brandishing primitive notions alone, her maid had outwitted her.

Musya was still pondering this state of affairs when Oksana herself arrived. She was drying her hands on a dishcloth and looked vexed, her eyes darting around. Her color was high. After they'd counted off the morning's work tally she looked right at Sender.

"Do not bother my maid, you, Zenderkaz. Please, I cannot have it. She is bad enough," she told him. "You and the other boy, him, too, the stinky. No more bother the maid time. Keep away."

"We were not bothering her," he answered stubbornly.

"She is bothered however. She is in her bed where she does not work, she stays who knows how long there?" An exasperated breath. "Listen, believe, for this today I blame the stinky, not you, Zenderkaz. But if you do it again—"

"Not the Stinky," Sender said. "His name is Russvelt." Of course Oksana rolled her eyes at this silly fiction, just as they had done.

"Do you have any sort of papers for him?" Musya asked. "I mean, when you got him, what was supplied?"

"What are you talking about? This boy was never for me—he came along with one of the old lady dames who lives with us now. The soldiers took the house she was in for their officers—but they don't take the boy because they do not need him, they have better boys. So he is here." Oksana shrugged. "I use him but true, he is not good."

"So his—the old dame who brought him—maybe she knows his name," Musya suggested, then watched the bright and dusky stripes change places on her damask headscarf as Oksana shook her head:

"She never talks now. No words. Anyway people talk too much—I talk too much—so do you, both," she finished in a clumsy, mixed manner, half-smiling, dead serious and sly, too.

Musya asked, "Do you have ownership papers for us?"

The woman's face went naked. "I have what they gave me."

"But why did she scream?" This was Sender, he'd pursued a different line of thought entirely. "Why is your maid so frightened of us? Why did she run?"

Here was perplexity. "She is—because of Jews. She is frightened."

"I know that but why?"

"It is her way." A hard effortful squint creased the hairsbreadth brows as their owner thought and spoke carefully. "Because it is her belief that she should be. I think for family reasons. Many people have this."

Musya elucidated for the boy with his sheltered Birobidzhan upbringing: "They think we have long hairless tails and drink babies' blood."

"Not all have long tails, no one says that," Oksana objected before her blush returned and she started to leave. In the doorway she turned to say, "It makes no difference. Belief is only belief. I am running a business here. You two do good work so far. But keep away from my maid—I mean it. And try if you can sew a little faster."

(10)

Samuel Nemo fretted for Hodeh's embrace sometimes, there was no denying it. Even as he rolled contentedly in the long cool grass his features would tighten and twitch to the verge of protest; he felt a lack. His mother wasn't enough, she reflected helplessly. Then she caught her breath at how long she'd paused between stitches. In search of her place on the soiled linen her eyes swam, strained weary and stung by puffs of ammoniated breeze. The uncertain sunlight wasn't helping.

Although she'd longed to try it, sitting outdoors to work had lost the charm of novelty quite soon. In fact between insects and glare, the lingering stench and the ground level dampness, it had failed to be pleasant at all. There was also the newly uncomfortable fact of exposure to any passing view. All told, there were zero reasons not to take their work back onto the glassed-in porch—zero save one. Musya raised her eyes to the long yard where a giant's crazy quilt of mixed bedding aired its appalling stains. The inroads she and Sender had carved upon the impacted heaps of work had led to their making a nosed-out discovery: the bundled remains of a newborn child. At least it was probably newborn and with any luck stillborn. It appeared to have been very small and terribly leaky. The find had thrown Oksana Babiak into tears over the bestial subhuman shrewdness of her supply base, country townsfolk, one of whom had managed to foist their own mess and a legal dilemma onto her far-from-unburdened shoulders with this thing; she spat, she said, on the character of everyone involved, she made a spitting motion and dried her eyes. The smell of rot was unbelievable. They could only do their best to air the affected stuff first before mending. "It would not pay to wash it twice," as Oksana said.

The sky was clouding with a yellow cast. Though hot, the sun's strength to disinfect was waning steeply as the days grew shorter. Their return to the ghetto each night took place in deeper dusks. Musya glanced out towards the white road. Empty: a relief. Very often since becoming an object of interest to her work gang guard, the one who wore the wooden boot, the armed collaborator, she'd had warning in the distinctive slow thump of his approach. Other times she'd looked up to find his rough garb and stubble and fever shine already in place at the edge of the road, his regular spot; she'd have missed his arrival because he hadn't made a sound. At the sight of her surprise a brief amusement would make him waver, mirage-like. Spotting him out there one day, Oksana had smiled and said, "You have an admirer, Muskah." Usually he was alone.

A wild ripping rattle of stalks and leaves heralded Sender Kotz's exit from the garden: he burst out at a run and staggered onto the grass beside her. Russvelt pinwheeled out from the undergrowth next and collapsed nearby. They were panting fast, Sender exclaiming:

"We saw the girl—I saw her feet!"

"They moved—her feet move I tell you!" Russvelt with his nonsensical lies, when everyone knew better.

"Please," Musya said. "I told you to stay out of that part. Leave her alone. Leave her in peace."

There was a dead girl in the garden. It was true, a fact of the premises. She'd been a seamstress there and then unfortunate. When soldiers marauded, girls didn't always survive. And sometimes as their bodies lay unburied, decomposing, being devoured by whatever crawled or flew and hungered in such otherwise unvisited nature spots, they wound up becoming objects of awesome fascination to small boys.

Musya mostly kept out of the garden. Now it occurred to her to ask Sender, "What about her shoes—did you see?" He said there weren't any. Shot through with frustration she kicked the ground and regretted it at once: like much of the rest of her body both feet itched painfully. "Are you sure? Go look again," she urged, the wish already fixed in her mind by desire become need. She yearned for it to be true: "Maybe when—maybe her shoes fell off someplace nearby."

Even a pair of slippers, she was thinking, would be a vast improvement over the rag-bound broken boots she wore, so cumbersome, so prone to soaking. They'd come complete with holes from Mr Asch's trunk for Baila Kotz whose grandson refused to go back for a second look around. Russvelt volunteered but returned moments later with a denial that didn't convince Musya at all; of course the seamstresses might have gone as badly shod as the child slaves around here, she admitted. Overhead clouds kept gathering. The western sky had begun to droop so their sunset would be smothered. All around was green—green leaves, green grass leaves—but it was blackening beneath her eyes, gangrened by the mood afoot.

From the very first, some people had been too broken to return to forced labor from one day to the next. In what ghetto-sheltered rests they had to call their own they'd stayed, unable to move for brokenness. For a time the broken rested unharassed while malingering enjoyed a heyday. If nobody actually checked, went the logic, why bother? Should persecuted Jews force themselves to killing labors on an honor system?

Rebels and shirkers multiplied to blatancy lounged in sunny corners with card games; the women laundered together, hung clothes together in back gardens. It was an idyll of some days that crashed to an abrupt conclusion with the arrival of armed men—chapers—who shouted commands, wrenched arms and delivered rifle butt blows and beatings. In Musya's case, what marked the end was a sudden booming thud of footsteps down her corridor. They'd sounded to be coming at a funereal pace: not so. A close floorboard cracked before their curtain rasped aside. The wooden-booted one filled their open doorway. He'd acquired a pistol that was strapped to his leg; his short jacket sleeves revealed black-furred forearms; his wrist bones, stark white, stood out like cufflink studs above his short gloved hands. Musya sat exposed to view on their bed breastfeeding Samuel Nemo, bare-breasted, she'd had her blouse off to mend and sat with a towel draping her shoulders. This was unfortunate—she hoped not too unfortunate. The whole thing was such a shock that nobody moved, they were all paralyzed. The chaper had a long look at her bare breasts: rashy and bitten red, milky and full, too. He licked his lips with a thick tongue. His lower eyelids twitched. He put off a rancid smell that reached them revoltingly—Musya leaned away and tugged the towel around, hiding the baby's head. The children moved, too, slight motions, there they were, dressed for wash day in their underwear, present again. Taking in the entire scene for the first time, the man saw a sort of barn stall full of children and revolted in his turn flinched back. Only then was it apparent how far into the cubicle his bulk had carried.

Then he turned mean. He snarled and shouted and pounded on the plank wall for Musya and Sender to dress themselves, hurry: Back to work. They'd missed almost three days at Babiak's where Oksana raised their production quotas by twenty percent which felt like a hundred. A day after sinking the next laundry cart to its axles in soft ground with the results, they'd found the putrefied baby. And the collaborator with the wooden boot had Musya to look at now when he passed by to stare. He'd circle all day now.

Only for the moment they'd seen the last of him. Bad weather threatened. Daylight failed in a hurry and almost went out in a series of chill gusts that snatched at the scattered bedding and sent some flying into the dimmer corners of the yard where Russvelt helped Sender chase it. He was much with them, having proved himself so poor an errand boy that his labor was almost never requested much less forced by any-one at Babiak's. He appeared to speak and recognize nothing but Yiddish. Moreover he stank, looked poorly and limped. He was a wreck of a boy and a liar about everything. Here he came with Sender Kotz, they made a two-boy pack mule with their great load of captured bedding: and what was it now? "I killed the wolf with my bare hands," he was saying.

"But listen," Sender replied, his voice tight. He told Musya, "He says he sleeps in a fireplace room under a wolf skin. But tell him."

"He's lucky—I envy you, Russvelt," she said, her own worries enough while there remained quantities of bedding to fold and return to the porch and far less mending than ought to have been completed by now as well.

"No." But Sender persisted. His delicacy strong as steel wires, he slung a loaded look at the chicken coop. "Tell him—tell him we know." Russvelt followed the full indication; Musya saw him recoil with embarrassment and shrink, almost turn hunchback. His scabby features tight with pain and greenish in the half-light, he lurched a little distance off from them and sneaked a fist to his mouth. Then he was chewing. This prompted his friend to shout: "No! Are you doing it again? I told you not to eat those—he's eating grasspea pods!" Once more Musya found herself addressed. "I told him not to."

The abundance of this plant in Obodovkan yards retained no more power to surprise her. "Please don't eat the grasspea plant, Russvelt, it's poison."

"No it isn't," he answered. She closed her eyes and kept herself quite still. Then he added, "But I like it."

"*It's poison!*" Kotz voices rang in sharp-edged unison but made no apparent impression. Musya heaved a sigh, enlisted despite wanting no part in Sender's helping care for this hapless house slave, this Russvelt, another doomed friend of his. She counted also Little Lev; then poor Yankel Weissbein who'd been friend enough to share his Jules Verne tales, shared forever; and odd Mendel from the playfields with the collection of theater magazines and the father at hard labor, he'd seemed like a weak link too. Poor Sender: she felt a heart-pang as she wished they could be living someplace with a better pool of friends for him. "Better boys," she murmured.

Russvelt looked up at that. She met his hard mournful recognizing eyes. Then she examined him more closely. He'd survived this long while the boy with the angel's face was in his common grave.

Musya turned and told Sender, "Grab him." She took the other arm and together they ransacked his rags to recover all the grasspea Russvelt was carrying, seeds and pods and leaves, even some roots of the plant he'd gathered. For a change he hadn't been lying, he did like grasspea. His legs were permanently weakened by it but somehow not killed, he continued to manage.

A few fat raindrops and then a sort of fistful struck them—hailstones, she recognized—but then nothing more. Now it was Russvelt sneaking a glance at the old coop, his thoughts on shelter. Musya grimaced and her arms tightened around Samuel Nemo who kept up a squall, having taken a hailstone to the forehead. She kissed her baby. Another child would be suicide. *That poor well*, she thought. All she could do she had done. Sender tugged at her sleeve, his fingers pleading, his face pleading, tears in his eyes; she felt he was the better person and allowed this conviction to persuade her into speech. "Listen," she said, still uncertain—when a passing thought that two boys would be better protection than one urged her on: "Spend the night or two with us, Russvelt. See how we live, sleep a little, get warm. It's not so bad in the ghetto where we are." To her eye Russvelt looked skeptical and surprisingly disinclined to accept but Sender was nodding eagerly, taking up the case: her part was done.

Fierce regret seized her immediately. Whether their resources would stretch to support an additional life in their cubicle was of course not in doubt—they couldn't. Even more panic-making was the chance she was taking with this boy specifically. For Oksana Babiak maintained a meticulous tagging and tracking system; what could go missing from her inventory on the porch was zero, she claimed. Yet Musya had begun pilfering stock. Throughout this ghoulish lot especially were items their proprietress had missed, while the abundance of scraps not worth saving except to sell for gun rags held steady, offering other chances. A patch here and there Musya pocketed along with stray lengths of thread, sometimes handfuls of loose batting not too rotten: little by little she'd made a collection for piecing together by corridor light sometimes, when she wasn't too tired. So far it was about the size of a hand towel. She thought she'd make a bed quilt that she pictured very often. Now fears of being reported for it at Babiak's filled her mind instead. Russvelt was crazy and she'd never be able to trust his silence. Terror snatched her up, shook her a bit, tried out a few different grips and then dropped her. A little boy might blab: so what? Another worry was all it was, a minute addition to the crowded worry field through which she'd rush between work and childcare and sleep and wandering thoughts and blank bouts of forgetfulness. Another worry she'd barely notice.

But then Oksana shocked her. It was the end of the day.

"Of course he cannot go with you, he belongs to the lady dame. What nonsense!"

"But. He." Musya waved an arm at the chicken coop, the sky. "Rain is coming."

"So? There is a little roof. He will be fine, like before. Why do you care what is not your problem?"

"Just for tonight, let us!" she pleaded. Why? She couldn't help herself—being denied sparked her. "The little boys, they have their hearts set on it."

"Oh." A puff of air. "Boys. Their hearts."

"They are young. Please," Musya tried. A little rolled-up stack of gingham lozenges sat in her pocket like a ruby stone aglow.

Back and forth the neat graying head kept up its refusal. "You have the heart, Muskah. The too soft heart. I know how this is—what happens. You must be harder. Another little boy child is not for you now. Do not collect."

"Yes, you are right," Musya said. "But should this one die?"

The Obodovkan woman made a face, called this a crazy remark. "Listen," she began. A pause lengthened. Musya sensed crumbling. One big flaw in hard-heartedness: people were show-offs. Maybe the striving Party side of Oksana Babiak couldn't resist a demonstration of capacity. "You," she called across the grass at Russvelt—then paused again, long enough for Musya to recognize her own hesitation echoed and likewise repressed. Why did they hesitate? Why choose the harder path and then regret? Why did they keep choosing that path? They were both women. Was that all? This was such a problem child who struck so many unattractive attitudes—as now, jut-bellied in a ripped tunic, sucking the dirt from an idle hand's worth of fingernails. Women were supposed to care for children. Who else would do it? "You, little stinky boy, you have a new sleep-place. Here. Muskah, you tell it." Indoors, just off the front hallway, a little stove used for drying boots and icy overcoats had a bench Russvelt could occupy. But before he set foot inside he'd have to wash himself. His lady boss ordered him onto the porch to await the hot water she'd bring him.

"Hot water!" The little boy's fingers popped from his mouth like a cork, his joy was overflowing. Now joy and haste to obey turned his first step into a stagger, almost a tumble. There to catch his arm in time, Sender held on:

"Don't you want to come with us?"

Russvelt tried pulling free. "No—not back there, no! Are you crazy? Here is better."

"But you're a slave here."

"So are you!"

"Not as much as you!"

This Russvelt disputed. A little Yiddish interlude of strife featuring hot tears and some shoving went on under the quizzical eyes of Oksana Babiak, who requested translation.

"They argue about slavery," Musya supplied. "Which is the bigger slave of yours."

Oksana dismissed this with a flipping hand. "I do not call it that," she said.

Musya wondered. "You call us—forced laborers, then?"

"I call you workers." The birdwing brows leapt and hovered. "I had Jews to work here before—I am paying somebody still—how is this different?"

"But I—we—before, my family. We would not be working for you. Not even for pay."

"No?" The offense was unfortunate. "You think you are too good to work here, for me, in this work? Maybe—I think you are a little proud maybe."

Feigning distraction, Musya raised her voice to scold the little boys for fighting: a harmful hypocrisy, this, as she was far more concerned with escaping one of her own than ending their dispute. All to the good she considered any rift between Sender Kotz and this bad influence of a Russvelt. But trouble between herself and Oksana Babiak she couldn't afford. This time she skirted some.

Alone, she and Sender headed back to the ghetto at dusk. Under close overcast skies weighted with nightfall, a little day-lit landscape lay trapped as if inside a shirt box. The now-familiar lanes dipped, unevenly muddy. Of the wooden boot there was no sign save a few stale tracks to be seen. Sender plucked a stone off the road and threw it down again. "Why wouldn't he come? It's better where we are—it is!" he declared.

She agreed and she didn't; she kept quiet at first. From different compass points came voices poking spikily at the subsiding sky, still distant enough to confuse with what ears bracketing plans to bargain down the wholesale price of artificial coral from the Jews up ahead would have heard when they still passed here, the calls of drovers and farmers. Tonight there'd been no herds in pasture, no harvest to cart home from fields only dotted with the burned and rusted carcasses of war machines. Through the strangeness of history, these shouts and oaths tonight drove Jews from scenes of killing slave-work back to that same market quarter, now become a prison and a death trap.

"He'll be sleeping by a warm stove every night now, your friend." When Sender didn't speak, she added, "I told you he was lucky."

On their arrival at Krutonog's she went to pick up their food ration. The Ernste told her no.

"No rations today. It's a fast day. No eating."

"What? What fast day? Why?"

"The fast of Gedaliah. On this day we mark the Jews' return to exile in Egypt."

This meant nothing to Musya—nothing at all. Egypt was the Sphinx, some pyramids; Moses, sure. All she wanted was one piece of black bread. "Nobody told me."

"You're supposed to know."

"But I'm not—I don't care," she said, her mind puzzling. "Why did they go back to Egypt?"

"It's a long story," said the Ernste. "But let me tell you in case it comes as news. Next week Yom Kippur we have another fast day. Our day of atonement, we fast."

"Yes," said Musya. "That figures." A glance or two around the room showed a bare scattering of lackeys, many fewer than normal. Most of these appeared enfeebled. The rest, she surmised, were out putting food in their mouths.

"And that day by law no Jew in Obodovka will work. Thanks to my son." The motherhood of the Ernste was in full bloom of pride, for through a triumph of righteousness allied with skilled diplomacy the Ghetto Council had gained a concession. A mid-week holiday: Musya was glad. But tonight's problem remained.

"I must have food for my children," she insisted.

The landlady tut-tutted. "You're supposed to put aside a little snack for them on fast days—I know, I know, you didn't know." She counseled Musya to try asking at Tauber's kitchen. Hunger rations were always in play there, and the people didn't know enough to be frum.

Indeed, Elkie spared her a couple of handfuls. Musya wrapped the food up close as the two of them discussed the reputation for fanaticism and carryings-on that the old housemaid's place just kept earning. Yom Kippur maybe, but other fasts weren't enforced in the ghetto.

"Only at Krutonog's," Elkie said. They were in her room at Tauber's, a narrow one whose ceiling sloped steeply—it was under some stairs, practically a closet, in fact, but clean and freshly papered, with a chink of window-light and an oil lamp, Elkie's treasure. The lamp had a glass chimney and sat on its own wall shelf. The close air was perfumed with paste, sweat, flowery chemical scent, lamp oil and underclothes. A temporary order lay imposed on Eidel's stuff which tended to escape its stacks and carry-alls and hooks and run riot otherwise. Even so, when the girl herself entered there was barely room for three.

Eidel threw an irritated, red-eyed look around. "What are you doing here?" she asked Musya.

"She's on a visit." Elkie had ducked onto a corner of the mattress where she sat in a crouch. "She's just going."

"I've had the worst day," Eidel answered. Her gaze with its autumnal bloodshot returned to Musya and flashed with obscure disfavor. "By the way," she said, "if the parents and guardians of the intelligent children don't send them to the classrooms then our entire instructional program will be damaged. You undermine any chance we have of conducting a comprehensive unified pedagogy."

Musya stared. "What are you talking about? What classrooms? You said it wasn't starting yet."

"We started almost two weeks ago."

"But nobody told me—why didn't you tell me?" Musya asked Elkie. She felt hurt.

Her eyes sliding sideways, Elkie shrugged and said that Musya hadn't been around to tell. "You're supposed to know," added Eidel.

"How? I'm not here all day like you two!" She could hear herself, loud, full of pain, the slave complaining; she felt close to tears.

"But it was posted by the gates. And by all the wells and wash houses, there were notices," Eidel said.

"Ah." This explained it. "I stopped reading those."

Elkie said, "Really, Musya, you've got to read the printed notices."

The next morning's second work bell caught her out of time. Unable to escort them there herself and rushed as usual, she left Anton and Hodeh combed, dressed and good-luck kissed for their first day at school. She'd told them exactly where their attendance was expected, just down the lane, and had secured their promise not to disappoint her. She hoped they'd go. Making believable claims to having joined certain of their truant peers in spying on the classrooms since day one, they said they'd seen enough not to want school educations. People sat in rows or circles, they said, to recite alphabets as if they were stupid.

"So what? Sit in a row, sit in a circle—just go!" She'd implored them. One day, they'd finally promised they'd go to school for this one day, just to try it once and make her happy.

After one step outdoors she'd have turned back and called a bad weather postponement but she couldn't reach them, retreat was impossible. The crowd behind was far too dense and squeezed around the doorstep as the laboring residents pressed reluctantly into the terrible cold rain. The ground was churned-up and treacherous, too slick for shuffling, they could barely creep. Every little step in the cold watery mud sucked the rag wrappings looser around Musya's tattered boots; the water got in and the mud clung like plaster. Just beyond the gates she remembered too late to look for the school notices, she'd missed them again.

The low dissolving cloud banks poured rain onto Obodovka. The trees looked faraway like mountain ranges. Rain bounced off the branching roads and turned them to knee-deep streams down which Jews trudged into liquid obscurity. Occasional slender silver-gray walls of rain blew in and closed off portions of the view to create haphazard highlights. Not far away, wetly vivid in the mud, lay a cloth star with a single point of six left untrodden. A bad loss for somebody: she could see it was amateur work, nothing like what her family was known for. Rain slammed down harder, the gray screens of it twisting. There at the crossroads stood the wooden booted man making a return appearance with his long gun. Although he frightened her as always, that he was no better dressed for the weather than half the Jews at Krutonog's caused Musya a certain malicious satisfaction to see. He looked like a drowned dog. She approached. Malice was in the air, it sizzled in the raindrops bouncing off her face and his. He smirked down at her and spoke some crude coaxing insinuations, all mockery. His fellow guard gave a nasty guffaw and a bad Russian translation:

"He says you miss him when he went away, you cry, did you?"

"I did not," she said. The wooden booted man kept a twisted grin on his face. He swayed as his working knee buckled and jerked upright. "He looks sick."

"Samogon bender. Famous for them."

She nodded. In fact the moonshine vapors streaming from their overheated wet skins made both men smell combustible. She wondered: had goyish Obodovka kept some ancient feast while the Jews at Krutonog's fasted? If so, there might be leftovers at Babiak's for lunch like twice before and thus the day might be redeemed from its miserable start. With a more positive air she said, "So, we reported. We will go now." The morning routine had become this informal: the guards kept track by sight, the escorts stayed home. Russvelt came when he felt like it but on a day such as this they'd never see him before noon. She touched Sender's arm and moved off a step.

The two-footed guard said, "Wait."

"Wait what? I'm cold." She was. Her head and shoulders thinly covered since she'd put all her other wrappings into Samuel Nemo's; her chest bulged like the nose of an airplane.

The guard said, "How do we know you will go where you are supposed to?"

'Where else would I go? Why?"

"That is what we don't know," he said. His wooden-booted comrade snickered, he'd understood the universal tone: Man wins cheap trick argument. "That is what we want to find out."

Tar seemed to be drizzling with the downpour across her view of the nearest Romanian soldiers. She made out a featureless dun-colored man-high mass laced with bayonets, like a memorial sculpture. "I go every day to my work—our work—that is all we do!" Loud enough only to wake an infant, her voice sank into a sheet of rain that swept across her face. She sputtered. "We are leaving."

Cold mud numbing her feet, weighting her steps, she went along in a slow hurry. Samuel Nemo couldn't be comforted, this had the sound of one of his long cries. "Keep in front," she told Sender. He whimpered, softly, afraid. "Keep going. Be brave. Hurry."

Trading jokes, spitting occasional mouthfuls of rain into the rushing brown gutters, the two men trailed them at an easy pace as the wooden sole found all the hard spots, it was the drunkard's uncanny luck. Where the road ran past a low-lying sunflower field she heard his boot slap, elephantine, four times into the muddy ground. Then he was upon her, speaking. The other drew up, out of breath, listened, agreed. "Yes," he said, "Get rid of baby."

Without a word she untied the sling of wraps. In the rain the knots were almost impossible but her chilled fingers solved every one with untrammeled speed, desperation inspired. She told Sender, "Take Samuel Nemo to Babiak's, get warm. If I don't come then go back and give him to Hodeh. You and Hodeh will be in charge. Do what she says. Go." What else could she say? Rain battered her breasts through a thin blouse, the men were in a hurry. "I love you all. Don't cry. Don't worry. Go! Don't run too fast with the baby!" Her loved ones: stubbornly she watched them turn into a shrinking blot among raindrops. The men gave her another shove. She ran from them but made it very little distance before the unwinding of her rag boots tripped her up. By the time they got her to the ruined truck one leg was barefoot.

This was the first time she was raped while being held captive in the Obodovka ghetto. Before the war's close when she was free to leave there would be others; there would even be a pregnancy, fortunately a very brief one that ended in a miscarriage, her second in life and harder than the first, bloodier. The rapists were a mix of locals, deserters, Romanian soldiers. One gave her a bad rash and others some parasites but nothing incurable. This was lucky. Survival was lucky. Every time, starting with the first time, she thought about the dead girl in the garden—the girl she might become, might be tomorrow. Fear in the nearness of death took her sensations along with her strength; she'd feel little while thoughts came and went. She noticed things. That first time her eyes followed the fine mocha-colored piping on the pigskin of a vain cripple's gloves. She despised him: the burn of drink not enough, he'd required the encouragement of company. Already middle aged, he didn't live much longer and never raped her again, he dropped dead in the street, done in by the combined effects of alcohol and a battlefield amputation that never healed properly. The other rapist she outran more than once, he had no wind capacity at all.

But not every man could she outrun. Every time she remembered Mrs Drobitz's ordeal, that long night between the oxcart wheels. Nothing so bad as that poor woman had endured was happening, nothing so excessively drawn-out and crowded, Musya would note. Her children were never forced to watch or listen, a fact she kept in mind with gratitude. She'd hear herself making a noise like an animal being kicked over and over—a sheep, maybe. Released but still caught in the twisted metal ribs of a ruined truck, like living wings of screaming flesh her cries vibrated, amplified, self-appalled. Her situation was bestial but the men's was no better. What were they doing raping a poor short starving young Jewish mother in the middle of a war zone? Who was organizing their time? Was there no better use for them? The sad uselessness of these violently cruel men would come to her with their semen, every time a fresh form of pity would take shape in her breast for this man with no reason to live: *this poor man.* Then with a pop like a thin bladder his separation from the rest would evaporate. She despised them all. To a man these were sheer opportunists, arming themselves to prey on the weak, raping; cruel and empty, with their violence they took advantage of an accident in time. Here where civilization had existed not so long ago, when they might have been merchants or farmers and she might have been selling them gloves at a polished counter, history had advanced backwards. Sinuous curtains of bone white rain chased each other down a field. Mortal life was grotesque and full of brutality, physically miserable. Men did everything to forget. A few wept when they'd finished, tucking themselves away. A few tried to kiss her. Humanity was broken.

Just before Babiak's where the road dipped last a wide puddle had formed, knee-deep, deeper, practically a pond. She knelt in the middle to clean herself. The men hadn't followed. A grey mud bath seemed to be on the boil around her hips but the water was freezing. When she emerged her last half-boot was gone. Her lunch potato, however, was not. On bare feet she walked down the farmyard and onto the porch. It stank still and Sender wasn't there. She chose the garden shovel from the rusty tool pile by the wall and went back outside. A brief search took her to the dead girl in the garden whose body she proceeded to heap with wet earth. Her shoveling technique was perfect, unrecognizable. Muddy clods full of roots gave way to her, piling up to be patted flat in the pouring rain. She found no shoes, no slippers. When every part of the dead girl was hidden she returned the shovel to the porch and entered the house through the chipped brown door.

A dim passageway, Russvelt's droning voice: she followed both to a little stove-warmed alcove full of boots, overcoats, shawls drying on clotheslines. Here was Sender Kotz, too; and in the folds of a threadbare old fur piece his brother Samuel Nemo slept quietly, safe. Seeing her safe Sender wept. Russvelt joined in. Weeping and amazed they gaped at her appearance. Thinly dressed, shivering, dripping water, very mud-stained, she chattered her teeth at them when they asked how she was. What could she say? Her eyes fell on a pair of valenky with a neglected but sturdy air; sure enough, good materials, intact. She put them on her feet. With some padding they'd fit and she'd manage to run in them, wrapped in rags they'd stay fairly dry. Warm and dreaming, the baby was better off staying where he was while she went to fill the morning quota, Musya said. She left the boys with glowing faces.

Lunchtime quota-check found her sitting alone on the porch at the little work table. "Where is Zenderkaz?" the overseer asked immediately.

She kept her eyes on her work. "Today is his holiday. A holiday for Jews. We celebrate the return to Egypt."

"I thought your holiday comes next week."

"A different holiday."

Oksana Babiak frowned. "Big?"

"Very."

The woman murmured some syllables of impatient Ukrainian but her notice was shifting to the laborer at hand. Her look turned close. "It is well with you today, Muskah?"

"Musya."

"Yes. So. You." Save for the felt boots on her feet Musya sat naked under the meters of unmended bedclothes from which she'd improvised a bundled robe and headdress. Her blouse and all the rest were outside in the mud and rain where she'd thrown them. This Oksana noticed too. "Is anything wrong? Did something happen?" she asked, turning back from the window.

"No. Nothing happened."

"What is it you are sewing?"

"A tunic. Maybe some trousers." Coarsely cut from old blankets with the dull scissors, the simplest design, almost prison garb, double-sewn with rough padding like a snowsuit.

Oksana said, "With my inventory? In my old valenky? Stop—you cannot do this. Stop."

"No," said Musya.

"No? Yes! I am telling you stop—I order you to take off those valenky and stop what you are doing."

Her needle dove, disappeared, reemerged. "And I say no. So kill me."

"Are you crazy? What?"

"Kill me if you want. Get a gun and shoot me."

"I do not need this kind of talk today," Oksana said. As an overseer she had many problems and projected little authority. She took an experimental sniff. "The smell out here is better, yes?" But the next sniff she regretted because it really wasn't. She brought a hand to her mouth.

Musya, however, agreed. "Yes." A bad smell couldn't help itself. She continued adding stitches to a seam as the slave-holder watched. "Please," the woman said to her. "Stop sewing. One minute, please." She slipped her needle through its stopping place and pulled out the lunch potato. It was a bad one today but she forced herself to keep chewing, to swallow. She looked up at the shadowy eyes in the neat round head, then took another bite, observing a widening alarm: "And that smells rotten!" She admitted that it was and Oksana Babiak, smacking the potato from her hand onto the plank floor where it rolled into the corner and almost like an animal found its way behind the mud-caked shovel blade, issued an angry command: "That is enough—come inside!" The voice was injured, bruised; the woman had limits and she'd just struck one, maybe several. Musya, by contrast, was sitting somewhere past the idea of them—limits didn't apply where she was. From the outside they looked slightly comical, like someone running away. She remembered: "Do you have feast foods? Have you been feasting here with your people?"

"Is that all you people can think about? Food?"

At the opposite end of the corridor from Russvelt's nook was a workroom containing a large amount of sand-colored fabric, some weak natural light, an inadequate string of electric bulbs, and a draught that tended an empty brazier stove. Musya examined the two elderly motorless sewing machines from the Podolsk factory. One had a treadle but the smaller hand-powered model was portable, they could have used it on the porch all along; she could have screamed except the overseer reappeared with a bowl of warm fatty borscht. Both boys got the same.

The house was in a giving mood. It yielded up a wooden box crib for Samuel Nemo along with a woman's dress plus underthings, worn but clean: "From before," was all their owner would reveal about the provenance. She had the dead girl she'd buried to thank, Musya supposed, dressing gratefully; a good turn returned, maybe. Fed and clothed, her swollen breast squeezed between her baby's fists, she was finding it hard not to weep. Her limits ached where she'd passed them. She was returning.

A last concession: the valenky. "We are not bad people like you think," Oksana Babiak said from a seat by the cold stove. "We know things must be hard for you people inside that place."

"Yes," Musya said, ready for the lunch break to end. She held up the bundled parts of her tunic project. Would she be going too far? The thought crossed her mind. Not at all, she decided. "I will finish this today. The cloth is already cut," she said.

Oksana let out a breath through her nose: a laugh. "All workers steal." She spoke grimly. "I accept it. I accept it." She made it sound like a small coal handed into her palm. Musya waited. For a rarity the woman's mouth was shut upon any view of her stained teeth. A faint moustache danced as she worked her jaws around, deliberating. At last: "You do what you need to do—but for Zenderkaz today is half a holiday only. He works now."

Of course Sender didn't mind, he got to use a machine which he enjoyed although for certain tasks he always favored hand stitching. Fed, warmed, from a daze of relief he'd emerged nerve-shattered, furiously talkative, unlike himself. They splashed back to the ghetto at day's end through his detailed musings on the design and production of uniform shirts. Musya paid less than full notice. The rain was now an oily drizzle. From a low hill's height above the field she could make out the upended truck bed, rear wheels to the sky. A fresh pregnancy fear assailed her, sloppy and half-soft though the two rapists had been. A few broken sunflower stalks remained pointed wildly where they'd dragged her struggling off the road, blind bird-ravaged crowns tipped in the mud. Here was where, to satisfy strange men and keep them from harming him, she'd given up her baby—the same baby who bounced along past the place, snugly tied to her chest again, beaming. If he was the same, that is. At moments she thought Samuel Nemo seemed changed, newly distant. If he knew what had happened it had to have changed him, she thought. She told him for what felt like the hundredth time, "I'm sorry."

Sender's voice rose. "Are you listening, Musya?"

"Yes, but I'm not interested in epaulettes."

"But they're very interesting," he began to explain again.

In line at the gate the baby squirmed and complained. Was he more eager than usual to be handed off to Hodeh's kisses? Musya couldn't tell. From the cubicle she set off right away for the wash house to try and get the putrefaction off her newly-made outfit. At this hour the task was partly guesswork when a single flickering light bulb barely cut the gloom; electricity was getting scarce on top of the bulb shortage, she'd heard. Between sniffs she was keeping her mind intent on the project she'd conceived—one tunic set, at least one, for each child, even Russvelt—and what its completion would entail, the subterfuge, the brazen thievery, the stolen labor. It was so hard losing everything. The heels of her new boots scraped in the grit on the floor, for a wash house the place was filthy, the whole ghetto was filthy and would never get cleaner.

She was bent over the small Manchukuo plate of hunger ration in her lap when Anton said, "You forgot to ask us about school today, Musya."

Coming up from a daze she looked at him. Her breath caught. Anton appeared to be her sister transfigured and returned to youth, but a youth with none of Liza's pinching discontents. Then Anton was her father on the verge of a good punchline; and then Baila Kotz, his grandmother: the dazzling people. Enmeshed in ghostly candlelit resemblances, the contours of his freckled and commanding face were extraordinarily beautiful to Musya. And what if this had never happened? What if she'd never seen him again, never witnessed this gathering of the dead at their most beautiful—lying dead as she might have been tonight in a disused Ukrainian field? She couldn't let it happen. That to his young life's excess of grief she should contribute one more grief was a thing she couldn't allow—not when she pictured him grieving, a true orphan; not when she pictured him troubled, gloomy, riot-prone, growing from a bigger boy into a grown man; one whose stormy eyes looked at women's bodies. What would Anton be without her? Maybe not so good.

She couldn't die. It was that simple.

(11)

The Ghetto Council's standing took a nosedive when the authorities cancelled the next seventh-day rest after the famous Yom Kippur holiday: which made one gigantesque week's forced labor during which the first hard frost struck. The morning landscape looked covered in bread mold to every horizon. Slick roads printed with pale blue tracks snapped underfoot. Ballooning breath clouds collected at the gates where fights broke out constantly: the cold upset people. Their lunch potatoes weren't big enough and the Council was blamed. The gendarmes defended themselves with their sticks. Now it took almost as long to get out in the mornings as it did to get back into the ghetto at night. Rumors spread of people toppling over dead while they waited, more bad deaths to pile with the swelling numbers of suicide reports and worksite fatalities. At last more gates were opened, easing that particular crisis. The Council was quick to post claims of credit which Musya tried too late to read, all defaced as they were, barely a word remained legible through the invective slapped there in red paint. Yet even the invective resisted her comprehension at times. Other people's need to make marks and leave signs, other people's minds were all alike to her some days, off-putting and alien.

She could sympathize, then, with Hodeh and Anton's hatred of school, even their disdain for literacy. At other moments she envied them so much a tremor would grip her, she wanted childhood back that badly. What were they complaining about? Why? She found it difficult to listen with any patience. Aleph-beyz songs, all learning-minded songs they derided. They'd sing examples that charmed her—that is when she could bear the sound of them because at other times she agreed, the songs were horrible. Their rhyming melodies would burrow into her brain and beat there like super-diabolical metronome pendulums, regulating her steps, her stitches, her thoughts. Education was horrible— words and the letters that made them were horrible, she agreed.

But all this horror was probably necessary. Every morning the Kotz family cubicle walls witnessed the same scene played to the same conclusion: for what had been at first a piece of trickery wound up built into their routine. The two unwilling students would promise her to go to school once more; she'd promise that she'd never ask them to again. Some days it was barely more than automatic, an exchange of promises recited like mezuzah prayers. More often Musya doubted their hatred's sincerity. They really liked school but hated to admit it more, she guessed.

At the same time it seemed to her that they were indulging her with kindness. When they always shared a bit of food with her, when they stopped fighting at her show of tears: to see the children display such good hearts under her custodianship gladdened her and awoke a little pride. Frequently however Musya wanted nothing but to be left alone and the world never left her alone. With the kindness some intimacy was always being demanded of her, often unbearably; she was always turning something like a naked breast to some attachment in a way too far beyond her control. Before bedtime she'd sit immersed in secret needlework while Hodeh and the boys entertained themselves and the baby, their pet. Her attention adrift among colors, patterns, dreams of rescue, she'd speak aloud without meaning to sometimes, half-nonsense that Sender proved especially adroit at fielding as normal conversation. She appreciated his kindness most of all. But what he knew felt also like too much. Musya would have preferred to leave him behind in school with the other children sometimes.

Instead his days continued with hers, six of seven passing in the skylit workroom where they labored on another and newly revived Babiak's sideline, sewing uniform shirts to supply the local Romanian garrison. The original business had lapsed with the contract's passing to competitors, all of whom had troubles of their own filling orders when so many seamstresses around Obodovka didn't last long. Already stocked with materials, Oksana Babiak came back in as a subcontractor at profits near one hundred percent—if only it hadn't been for labor expenses, she griped. What she paid for two Kotzes she wouldn't divulge, she only called it enough; and while she complained constantly about being shorthanded she never bought anyone else. She was a cheapskate. Every day at least one rotten thread disaster stopped her obsolete machines and left her slaves sitting like castaways among meters of desert isle-colored fabric.

Intrigued by its challenges, at first Sender enjoyed uniform shirt-making. Musya did not, she never did. She considered the work repetitious and boring and tricky in the worst combination; she claimed to have preferred mending rot-stained bedsheets. On the other hand, uniform cloth made excellent quilt lining. She cut liberally and pilfered much.

Between frosts an enormous flock of birds swept through and ate every last berry seed and piece of grain in sight. Sender gleaned a last black and white garden squash. It was only half edible. After that the land stopped supporting life for the next seven months. They had nothing left to sell. Only hard work and human kindness could feed Musya's family now—most Jews in Transnistria, the same. No one's plight really stood out. Bucharest's charity persisted through shifting war zone channels, easy prey to corruption. As a second winter set in and their allotted hunger rations usually failed to reach Obodovka's imprisoned Jews, their dependence on the local powers was total. Even more than before they held the status of commodities: human labor. The Ghetto Council, the town and the garrison combined to run a compulsory system. All Jews who could work, worked. Those who worked, ate. Those who didn't work had to hope someone would share. And many people did share. Some were so unsparing with what they had, they kept too little and gave too much away, they shared past their limits, shared their way into graves—actually into the trenches that by order of the Territorial Authority had been dug ahead of time this year. Starvation killed the kindest, Musya heard this all the time.

One rest day she left Samuel Nemo asleep in Hodeh's lap and slipped out to visit the wash house with a load of clothes. On the road in the pale weak sunlight she was recognized by a tall, bearded, barrel-chested man: it was her father's friend from the Privoz market pompom counter. He spoiled an impression of vigor by leaning heavily against a short-faced girlish person wearing a lipstick color popular in 1935 and a large spherical bosom across which some cashmere shawls were pinned. The situation wasn't difficult to interpret but the man supplied answers anyhow, once she'd hailed him:

"Hello, Mister Geldus."

"Golbus," he said. "Like before. And this may I present is—this is the girl who took care of my late wife. And now me."

She wished him comfort from his loss. The moyd kept mum as Golbus spoke emotionally about his wife's extinction. A bucket line in a gravel pit: Musya remembered hearing talk. Her eyes wandered from Golbus's teary eyes to his threadbare striped trousers and the champagne satin showing through the rips—he had to be wearing the dead woman's satin bloomers underneath. "Her weak heart failed," he concluded.

"I'm very sorry," she told him again. "I hope you're managing all right without her."

"We'll be dead in a month," he predicted. "That's if we stay. Without food. Without my wife's rations."

She asked, "You don't work?"

"I can't work," he answered. "And she's needed here, with me." His elbow shifted on her shoulder to indicate the moyd, on whose part Musya sensed zero regret over not being part of a work gang. "Starvation or suicide we're looking at here, once we've sold everything I've got left. And suicide I refuse."

Musya nodded. "Yes, I agree," she offered readily. "The suicides are cheating." The couple looked at her. She thought about this man's eyes watching her father's body go under the wheels. The same eyes, warm and selfish, were on her body. She asked, "But you keep saying if—all this if you stay—so you'll leave?"

"You bet we'll leave. We're out of here." The moyd had a startlingly deep voice and thick shoulders. Golbus shifted to caress one with his hand.

"That's right. The first day the river freezes hard we'll go. It should be this week." He glanced up at the daytime moon and nodded sagely, a notions wholesaler pretending to expertise in weather science.

Musya wasn't impressed. "How will you even get to the river? We're locked in."

"With all these gates now? They don't guard them for shit. People leave every day. It's safe now." Whether this was true Musya had no way of knowing; her circle of acquaint-ance was not the largest. She was far less convinced than the moyd sounded, definitely.

"So you leave—then where will you go?" she asked. They said they'd find a farm to feed them, the collective farms returned to village farms might need someone, maybe a chicken farm—they'd find some farm and work on it in exchange for food. She said, "But if you can't work now, how can you work on a farm?"

"I can work on a farm," said Golbus.

"I see." She did. It was perfectly clear. The ex-pompom man was bribing someone for his rest, his comfort, his girl. Maybe his wife had kept more than her shawls and an old tube of lipstick; he might have been left with some means to run through whose end might be close. On a work gang his likelihood of survival was small: everyone's was. "Good luck," she said.

She never saw Golbus or his moyd again. No later word came, no gunshot reports, no torture stories. They might have made it through. Forever she'd picture them hand in hand in silhouette against a pink-streaked frozen river dawn, one tall and unsteadily shambling, one stable and round. Their plan was appealing but not for her, this Musya had decided by the time she reached the wash house. She didn't need to take her baby and her children scrounging for work on a chicken farm. They got eggs, Hodeh found them in trees. Three young children and a baby: escaping, walking out, running away, an act by any name equally out of the question. She reached into the basin of slightly soapy clothes and pulled out the dead girl's skirt that Oksana had given her. She hadn't washed it before nor examined its construction closely enough, as grew more apparent now.

For inside the skirt a cleverly-fashioned double lining concealed secret pockets, at least six. Folded inside some small currency bills which were wet but salvageable, she found packets of needles and pins. Because all seamstresses stole; and because unlike her, Musya realized, the dead seamstress had known how to go about doing it. Maybe some well-informed peer or elder had taught her to sew these pockets, the way no one had taught Musya. On the other hand, what idea could be more obvious! She ground her teeth thinking over the vast amounts more of everything she might have come away with by now had the idea crossed her mind even once.

Musya left the wash house with her armload of wet clothes, still berating herself for blockheadedness. Cold air and pique hastened her steps; anxiety to start adding hidden pockets to everything she and Sender ever wore turned her speed careless and when a fast light figure in a purple coat crossed her path they collided, or nearly.

It was Eidel. She bent and returned some fallen wet things to the top of Musya's laundry pile. Her laced boots had high heels and just a few patches. "Look out where you're going," Eidel said, adding in a somewhat friendlier voice, "I've just been at a teachers' meeting on what was supposed to be my rest day. I can't help you carry that, I have a chronic shoulder injury."

"I don't need help," Musya said.

She kept walking. Eidel fell into step beside her and demanded, "Tell me, Musya, are those children of yours ever going to attend school or not?"

"What are you talking about? They go every day."

"No they don't."

A little black ink seemed to leak across her eyesight; her next footsteps reached uncertainly for ground. "They tell me they do."

"Well," Eidel said.

Musya reacted angrily. "Are you calling my children liars?"

"Excuse me? No—I'm telling you they're delinquents who don't go to school like they're supposed to."

Now she felt dizzy and abject. "They don't go at all?"

"They go when there's cake."

"There's cake?" How was this possible? And they'd never said a word. She ruminated fretfully to no point until they were already at Krutonog's, where Eidel left her by the path with admonitions:

"Get up earlier and walk them to school yourself!"

"Wait," Musya stopped her. "Have you heard about people leaving? Are people really planning to leave once the river freezes?"

"Yes. But they'll die," Eidel said. "They'll all die out there."

The first snow fell in the night. Not much, not more than ankle-deep on the road, it was still enough to crush the last dry remnants of field verdure and leave a geometry class harvest of triangles inked from bent stems to poke through. Drifts and shadows washed around dead armored cars, some familiar, some newly revealed, where they stuck out like city monuments. The altered view showed two wrecks in the white sunflower field: Musya saw one for the first time, the other she knew but now which was which? She couldn't tell; and the entire edge of the field looked like the spot she'd been dragged through—she'd lost her own traces.

They crunched past, she and Sender Kotz, and continued towards another day in Babiak's frigid NEP-era workroom. The two rackety old Singer model machines at their fastest produced no heat at all; and their fastest was rare. Chronically prey to encrustations of thread residue at their dozens of vital oiling points, instead they devoured maintenance time by fingers clumsy with chill. Daylight diffused by the snow-sheeted glass overhead fell greyly, warmthless. Halfway through the morning shift the overseer rushed in with news. Musya greeted her:

"Light the stove. Please."

"This is more important. Listen!" She'd been notified by house-to-house delivery—she raised the flyer in her hand.

"Did we win?" cried Sender. Oksana Babiak looked at him, puzzled. He asked her in Russian, directly, "Did we win?"

She was still puzzled. "Win what?"

He faltered a bit. "The war. Did we—is it ended?"

The woman let out a short laugh. "This war? No." Instead, she explained, hers was big news of a business kind. In short, Obodovka was the newly-designated primary supply depot for its section of military Transnistria. It seemed the ambitious commander of the local garrison had contrived to muscle a new prestige, a lucrative one, onto his own shoulders. To stock the operation the colonel would be needing uniform shirts by the dozen as quickly as possible. The order was placed. Babiak's former contract was restored and all its subcontracts remained in effect: a huge payday. They'd have to sew much faster.

"Hire more people," Musya said.

Oksana waved this aside. "No, listen, listen."

The next day they had company in the workroom. Also some heat: finally stove coals appeared under what Oksana called "the new tenant arrangements." On low chairs blocking maximum warmth from the brazier, three old lady dames with needle skills who'd been collected from their separate corners in the house and not given much choice in the matter, from what Musya could tell, sat where they'd been set to basting uniform sleeves and button sewing. The women didn't like this, or professed not to like it. Judging by their conversation's animated quality a little stove-warmed piecework made a welcome change in dull lives. Their leader was named Yelyuk. They were religious women, Ukrainian Churchers; they dressed in felt house boots and layers of old knitting, in multiple aprons and headscarves; they carried a strong smell, minty and spirituous, from the liniments they rubbed into their joints and the nerve cures they swigged out of brown bottles. They discussed while ignoring the Jews in the room for exactly two days and a quarter. That was how long they could resist a handsome male baby with a ringing laugh and authentic Chinese toilet habits. They'd never seen it managed so neatly, she gathered. Comfortable as co-existence soon became, conversation remained difficult: Sender knew even less Ukrainian than Musya did, while the old lady dames spoke dreadful Russian and of Yiddish not a word.

Presentation was key, so said Oksana Babiak to explain why she herself did all the ironing, folding, and packing. Also she had a personal method for disguising stitching flaws through steam. Sometimes while at work among them she'd play translator; she said a little conversation could improve morale. The Yelyuk woman was always ready to cross the language divide, always with something to say. In her opinion the boy tailor was very effeminate, for instance.

"Like a young girl—girly," Oksana supplied. The other two agreed but Musya shook her head—no. Sender Kotz was manly through and through:

"He is always right. You cannot argue with him. You have never seen anyone more stubborn."

Also feminine traits these, as the Ukrainian women were quick to point out. "It is the truth," said Oksana.

"I disagree," Musya said.

Also did Sender disagree. "I am not girly," he said. But Mrs Yelyuk said, yes, he was. "I am not!"

The Ukrainian women ate separately, in a room off the kitchen, at midday break, when Musya and Sender would make their move to sit by the stove with the box crib and roast their lunch potatoes on the coals. Along with these and their blackened skins something from the kitchen came as well, bread usually and cabbage soup, often with fat and occasionally meat threads. Oksana always served, the maid remained unseen. This was the grasspea cripple Russvelt's daily meal as well for which he joined them. He coveted bites of the potatoes that Musya had forbidden Sender to share. Most days Sender shared anyhow. They saved bread to take back to the ghetto at night to supplement the ration provided by Krutonog's out of its return on their labor. Sometimes there was extra from the Territorial Authority. Musya ate all she could at Babiak's.

"You are so demanding!" Oksana had complained. "I have never heard anything like it."

"I am hungry. I have a baby. I am working all the time here. Give me more soup." The Grand Duchess, Oksana started calling her.

With the production switch Babiak's had joined a different supply chain. Instead of dying Jews bent beneath the shafts of laundry carts came paying customers—or their representatives, more often. A wire cord ran between an old-fashioned pull ring at the trade entrance and a little bell mounted on the workroom transom board. One day the clapper sounded just when the girl was due to call for Huba's order, in fact she was a few minutes late. Up to her elbows in ironing for the colonel's order, a rush job for delivery in one hour, Oksana sent Musya to hand over the five uniform shirts for the week. Mrs Huba was usually ten shirts short of being able to complete her military order and her dramatic surge in production was puzzling them all. Had she hired someone? Musya was planning to ask as she made her way down a short flight of stairs to the half-cellar and opened the trade door. It wasn't Mrs Huba's girl but a Romanian camp orderly who'd rung. Dressed in a woman's fur coat sliced to fit and belted over his fairly small frame and uniform, years older than the colonel's usual delivery boys, he had a loose wet mouth and a shambling manner. His moist eyes slid around. He was somewhat insane. He spotted Musya, pushed her inside, overpowered her and raped her on an old desk. Neither of them spoke, they made barely a sound. This one was virile. Determined not to respond and not to resist, Musya thought mostly about the damage to her tunic trousers and the unwelcome addition of pregnancy fears: bitter thoughts.

When he was done the camp orderly staggered over to the trade door, scooped the shirts off the cold cement where she'd dropped them and grunted quizzically.

"That's not your order," she told him.

Just then the bell rang again in the workroom overhead and the iron door-knock sounded. The rapist yanked open the door and Mrs Huba's girl standing there screamed: she recognized him, Musya guessed. The girl stumbled backwards into the snowy yard; then, seeing the man's meaty fists full of uniform shirts, five in number, she screamed again. "It's her order," Musya said. The camp orderly seemed to understand. He thrust the shirts in the screaming girl's direction, edging his grunts with impatience, until she snatched them from him and ran away, her footing deserting her more than once. The girl's knees would be sore, Musya thought. The path in the snow was a poor one; Russvelt and the maid between them couldn't get it right. The bare trees were like cracks in a frozen scene the color of cauliflower, she remembered this color of brains, she remembered Mrs Drobitz.

"Close the door, you're letting all the heat out." She had to motion before the rapist obeyed; he knew no Yiddish. He looked worn out. He kept his distance as she crossed to the steps. "Wait here," she told him, and hauled herself back upstairs. She felt tired, sore, stained, bloody. Entering the workroom she announced, "They are here from the colonel."

"O my thoughts!" Oksana groaned. She had more shirts left to iron piled there beneath the hanging loop of light bulb string. "Why do they come early?"

"I will tell him," Musya said. She went back along the hall to the top of the stairs and called down at the rapist in Yiddish again with one hand raised, showing him: "You have to wait. Don't come up here." She watched the light-splashed eyes narrow in his bristly face before he turned his pelts to her and sat down on the staircase. She looked for any kind of weapon on the cellar walls between them but there was nothing. The garden tools on the porch crossed her mind one by one but she returned to the workroom to find Samuel Nemo fast asleep in his box crib by the stove. She received a sharp greeting from the overseer:

"What takes so long? What is this with you?" Mrs Yelyuk spoke up and called Musya a fantranizer, typical Ukrainian peasant nonsense illiteracy; but Oksana nodded. "I think so, yes. You fraternize. Jews fraternize."

"What?" Musya stared. "I was not fraternizing."

"So. Okay. Do not," Oksana said, ironing at top speed. The starch hissed again. "And what was that scream before? Was that my maid? Did she see you?"

"No. It was Huba's girl." Musya threw the big Yelyuk mouth a dark look as she returned to her machine. The old dame's face creased: this amused her, this reaction. Reacting was out, then, Musya concluded. She pumped the treadle into gear and backtracked a few stitches.

"Answer me!" Oksana Babiak, still. "What was she screaming? Why?"

"Who? The girl? I do not know," she said. "I do not know."

"Well—did they hire someone?"

"I do not know."

This answer frustrated everyone, Sender Kotz included. "But how did Huba's halve their whole deficit in one week?" he wanted to know. Musya couldn't tell him.

The two old sewing machines resumed their gentle drilling and the workroom its familiar, intermittently warm drone. Her feet rocked, the treadle clattered, and the chrome flywheel ran towards her as ever, eagerness in place, a sunshine spirit companion to her own: the flywheel sympathized, she felt. Meanwhile the indifferent needle deposited its tracks, stitches the faded brown of writings left to be unearthed in a ruined city. Here and there a line wavered: she was putting the thoughts of her heart onto cloth in a forgotten code, perhaps. Someday who would read them?

"Finally." Oksana Babiak to herself: her ironing was finished, the delivery ready. Steam-flushed, she prepared to take the stack down to the colonel's man herself and made a little joke: "Her highness has fraternized enough today, I think. It is time for someone else to get a chance."

One glimpse caught the woman going out the door. Then Musya looked back at her stiches. Her mind touched the treadle with its toe but nothing happened. Musya could only sit there, paralyzed though she twitched. Conflicting currents of alarm held her stapled to a silent place. To call out, to cry out a warning, to tell Oksana not to go, to tell her to come back: too late. She was gone. Now the time that remained to hurry after and stop her was passing just as quickly. Because warn her of what? And how, without disclosing how Musya knew what danger lurked ahead? For she didn't want to discuss it. *Poor woman*, she thought. Descending to the rapist's den, her weary arms full, all defenseless: if screams came, Musya decided, then she could always run to the rescue, no harm done; while if harm were actually done, no one could blame her. There'd be no way for anyone to know that Musya might have stopped it. And stopped what? How? The same way she'd stopped it before? Should she have been a more perfect slave and volunteered herself in her mistress's place? Should she have gone back for more rape? Harassed by these questions, she started pedaling her machine again. The wind-whipped sound of oiled steel parts in action stopped her ears. Time passed, as had passed all the many years there'd been to motorize these two machines and equip them with lights when it hardly cost a thing to do so, even Boris Kotz had sprung for it. Babiak's failure to do the same had angered Musya badly all along. She watched the needle cast another row of stitches, recording—what? No ancient heart songs now, she knew. Instead, second by second, were these present moments being inscribed. This seam she sewed was her confession: Say the rapist got worse and Oksana never made it back upstairs alive, she, Musya Kotz, would share the blame.

Not so indirectly, she might have just murdered her owner.

Then what would happen? Reassigned, sent from the comforts of Babiak's to a work gang doom in the slippery brick stacks or the chemical steams or the freezing water's edge, she and Sender would perish. Anton and Samuel Nemo might survive in Hodeh's care but the Kotz family was basically through. She had just authored their catastrophe with her silence, her selfish cowardice. The treadle banged in time to her pounding heart. Her poor victim: a woman wrenched from the prime of life into horror and whatever lay beyond—maybe nothing; in her own home, too. Teary-eyed, Musya pitched forward, cursed. A wrinkle on the seam had rucked up and got caught in the pressure papka. Minutes later the garment remained at a standstill when a voice surprised her:

"Please do not break my machine, majesty."

She looked up from the ridiculous tangle of cloth thread and steel and heard herself accuse: "'Why are these machines not motorized? And we need more light if you expect us to see!"

"There is a skylight," Oksana said. Not a thing had happened to her. She used the receipt folded in her hand to point up at the dim, snow-smothered panes. "It works fine."

Four days later the same camp orderly raped Musya again on top of the same desk. She'd tried to avoid going down to him, saying he'd seemed rough to her, not saying more. Not to be silly, Oksana had told her. That was only Cezar, the colonel's special man. He was a harmless idiot. This time he stroked her hair: he liked her thick braids, he liked her hair color.

(12)

She sat mending rips in her stained trousers when the work went dim in her hands. The corridor light was being blocked by an enormous surprise that stood in their doorway. It was top management paying them a visit.

"Sholem-aleykhem," said the Ernste.

"Are you here to give me an exemption?" Musya replied. She asked every other day.

"Don't expect a different answer. No," the old woman from Bucharest stated. She'd come alone. With carefully laborious use of a battered cane she stepped down into the cubicle. Now she was their guest. "Chair!" she said.

"Do you see a chair here?" Musya said. "You run the place. Give us a chair and you can come sit in it whenever you want."

"Less mouth from young women," said the Ernste, "would be good." She made for the luggage stack, the same seat Hodeh had deserted in a flash to go stand near the doorway at the wall's dimmest point. Seeing which, Musya wondered: Was the little girl stealing again? But why—and when—and where had the goods gone? There'd been no sign of increase around their cubicle, no extras, for sure. And what about Anton? Musya noticed he'd edged closer to the door as well. Her mind raced uneasily as their visitor settled with groans and grimaces atop the pile of bags and then examined her surroundings. "You should hang less clothes around," she observed. "It doesn't look nice."

"Are you joking?" Musya laughed. "I'm sorry—thank you for the constructive criticism." She put the mending down on the tiger skin and raised Samuel Nemo to a full breast that she bared with no effort at modesty, she only pulled her shawl back around as he nursed because the air was freezing cold. "Now you evict us, is that it?"

"For what I should evict you? I can't pay a social call?" the Ernste asked reasonably. "Tell me where is your other boy—my prime tailor."

"You need tailoring? He's at the well."

"It's late for the well, it's late for that. A young boy."

"What else can I do? You're the one who sent him out to work, you didn't think he was too young then."

"A talent is different," the Ernste said. "Never mind, I don't need tailoring. But here we see the trouble with you always, you can't control all the children you have."

"Of course I can control them." Now that she looked, in the dim spots by the doorway were no children, the other two had gone, they'd slipped off. Musya frowned and said, "What's your point?"

"Don't push your luck is my point." The tone and promptness scolded equally. "Maybe your so-called mother-in-law with her balbatische act made Widow Hard

Candy landlady before treat your family like something special. Not me. I never give special treatment to the mighty. What the good people tell me, I tell you: her husband was a low-morals nobody and so was she in her day. Even locked up here with him gone she got man-crazy."

"She was a good, cultured woman!" Musya cried, thinking of Baila's matching bound volume set of Gorky. The Confession, the Childhood, the Recollections of Tolstoy, the Untimely Thoughts: all terrible. "And she was not like that. And my so-called—what do you mean? Her husband is my son—I mean. No. Her son is my husband. Or was."

The Ernste raised her chin with an air of virtue. "Let's just say I have no reason to doubt my informants."

"I don't care about your kitchen gossip," Musya said. "Talk all you want, it doesn't change the facts. I'm a married woman with a husband from a respectable family. Dead or alive."

"Have it your way," the guest conceded. At another survey of the cubicle she observed, "So any man passing here can see your naked tsitskeh whenever he wants, is that the story?"

"Of course not." Beneath her shawl tugged tight the baby squealed uncomfortably. "We have a door curtain."

"Use it," said the Ernste. Once more she looked around, on the floor too this time. "You can't offer tea?"

Musya stared at this insane question. "Tea?"

"Yes. Tea. You can afford it."

"What are you talking about? I don't have any money left."

"Tea from a kerosene samovar by now, why not?"

"Kerosene!" Musya's voice cracked in disbelief. "We use no kind of kerosene here— we freeze!"

"Then where goes the money?" the Ernste asked.

Her mouth went dry. "What money?"

The old woman gave a more impatient toss of her whiskers and her wig slid right, exposing a feathery strip of scalp, henna, gray. "What money? The money they get sometimes along with the food, the money people give, what they throw. The people and the soldiers."

"What food? What soldiers?" Watching the quick bright eyes scan her confusion for signs of dishonesty made Musya feel outraged. "Tell me what you're talking about! Seriously—what?"

"You don't know what your children do here most days?"

"My children? Most days?" Her mouth was so dry! Sender was taking so long at the well—another worry. The younger ones had called Eidel a liar. The pretty teacher had it in for them, they said. "My children go to school."

"No, they do not go to school." A headshake too vehement almost toppled the wig. After a strange hesitation the old woman reached up to set it straight: she wasn't accustomed to using her hands, Musya realized, occupied as they usually were with her tea glass plus saucer.

"No? They don't? How do you know?" she finished belligerently.

The Ernste answered, "Because they stand at the fences begging for food and money from bus riders. They perform the Song of Youth from Volga Volga."

"I don't understand," she said. Something like a flowerpot had just tumbled off a sill inside her intellect—it had crashed on the ground but was still falling and crashing over and over again. This was the limit of Musya's reaction. And she didn't understand. "Is this true?"

"When I'm saying what I saw with mine own eyes—yes. How can you ask me if it's true when your boy is the only fat child in this Obodovka?"

"He's not fat," she objected. "His father was the same, it's the way his body is made."

"Other children starve. Not yours."

"No?" she asked. "And that's so wrong? All should starve? What do you want here?"

"What do you think? I want money."

Musya breathed out a laugh: she'd just remembered. *The Lumberjack!* That was the name of the wooden river ship in Volga Volga on which the number in question concludes. She could picture it whole. She felt wonderment. "They sing?"

"A Song of Youth, yes, from the Russian film. And the Internationale, one verse, like before. Your old friend Mister Boim used to run a child act in the same spot. Before those children died your girl used to manage them—when she wasn't thieving. Now she's got your younger boy up there with her along. Dance, sing, beg—they do well, it's very sprightly. Did you hear what I said? They're making a good parnosseh which needs to be shared with the house." Musya kept trying to object, to question; fruitlessly. Why should the Kotzes' living be any of hers? The Ernste answered, "Why? Why? Because do you think what I get paid for sending you to town is enough to keep your whole too-big family here? Of course it's not." Brooking no argument, none, she gave her ever-present black reticule a nudge with a soft boot toe. "You're a charity case on my books yet here you sit raking in cash money."

"Raking in!"

Musya couldn't let it go on like this. Her mouth was too hot and dry to say more. She gestured some excuse and carried the baby out to the corridor in search of Sender Kotz with the well water. Steps away, there he stood with Mrs Drobitz's tin pitcher clutched to his chest because they couldn't trust the damaged handle. His front was soaked with what he'd spilled while standing there waiting, the wet jacket would freeze solid overnight. He shivered, whispering urgently: "Are we? Are we evicted?" She told him no. Past his shoulder the other two lurked.

"The musical stars," she greeted them. "Here, take Pretzel." She held Samuel Nemo out to the little girl who darted forward. He sounded pleasantly surprised.

Hodeh tipped the point of her chin towards the cubicle doorway. "Don't believe her," she said.

"No, Musya," Anton agreed. "Don't."

Their non-cooperation was a given, she perceived. Basically indifferent, without troubling to respond she took the pitcher and carried it back into the cubicle. Water cups they had from Hodeh's old thieving days, a fact of which she was reminded when the Ernste wiped her furry wet lips on a wrist and announced, "This cup looks like one I recognize. I think I'll take it back to my kitchen with me."

"Be my guest," Musya said. How many arguments weren't worth having? Nearly all, she estimated. Here was another. She took some sweaters out to the corridor for Sender and returned with his jacket which she hung on the pripetshik, a section of plank wall so-called for the heat which had once escaped from their departed neighbors' kerosene heater in the cubicle next door, a phantom hearth. "Will you be staying much longer?" she asked.

The Ernste directed a long squint at her and finally asked, with a surmise so impersonal it might have been delivered from a burrow entrance, "Have you got something wrong with your mind all of a sudden? Your mentality? Is crazy a trouble you're having?"

"I don't think so."

"Because I don't need that in addition to your other troubles here."

"I think, I don't know what you mean. Why—why do you ask?" She felt so exhausted and she was hungry again, she never ate after dark these days. This old landlady hadn't brought help, she hadn't brought comfort—anything but. New wounds to add to the wounds unhealed: "So much for religion," she added vaguely.

"Religion? You reject your faith now?" The old woman stirred on the throne she'd made of their bags. "You're here indoors from religion. You're here from my charity, my religious charity, I told you before. Don't play games." Her soft boot stamped their dirt floor almost soundlessly. "How many times now I've said it? I want money."

"Yes, money!" Musya remembered. "I don't have any. I really." Her random glance was arrested by the sight of Anton's satchel. He'd evaporated from the room without it—quite uncharacteristically. When she hefted its surprising weight, both women heard the shifting scaly clink its contents made. They unstrapped the canvas flap and looked inside: small bills, coins.

Anton was hoarding cash again.

"That's what I'm talking about," said the Ernste.

"How much is here?" Musya wondered. "Wait—when you asked for tea, you said I could afford—is there enough here for a kerosene heater? Is there?"

A movement of shoulders. "Possibly, sure. I can get you one of those. It won't be the cheapest," the landlady was adding to their negotiations when a small bellowing form hurtled between them and seized the satchel strap.

"Mine!" Anton screamed and pulled. "Mine! You can't have it!"

Musya tried reason: "Anton, she'll give back the satchel to you! But we can use the money for a heater—to get warm, please, Anton!"

Nothing worked. "Mine!" They grappled with him until Anton lost his footing and let go—the Ernste had cuffed him in the face. He curled up and started to sob. She was telling him:

"Yours? Mine! This is mine. You live in my house. You work for me."

"I don't!" He sobbed. "I don't!"

"And don't cry. You'll get your share. No one expects you to work without pay."

"I forbid you to ever hit a child of mine again," Musya told her.

"You don't know how to raise children," the Ernste answered. Sender had hurried in to kneel beside his brother. Hodeh lingered by the doorway with Pretzel cradled in her arms. They all watched the old woman scoop cash into her reticule—all but Anton who stayed in a ball—before she handed Musya back the empty satchel and got herself upright. "You'll get your heat. And you, Song of Youth." She prodded Anton with the end of her cane, she wanted him out of her path. "And you girl, you'll come to see me in my kitchen, regular. I have other better songs to teach you. Yiddish songs."

"I don't want them learning religious songs," Musya said.

The Ernste said, "If you're not religious then what do you care? As long as it sells."

The little boy sobbed quietly on the floor.

"You wanted a job, Antosha," his brother reminded him.

Her boot steps squeaked on the lane's packed snow so Musya dropped another step behind the two children she was following in secrecy. At the gate she'd feigned an hour's indisposition and turned back to spy on their exit. Keeping up now taxed her vitality. None of them had slept well. Anton and Hodeh hurried anyhow—but not because they suspected her presence. Their speed signaled upset. In a direction exactly opposed to the one in which their schoolroom lay, the short, piston-legged pair was walking off angry steams. They were furious at Musya, whom they believed had betrayed, robbed, and sold them.

Attempting to counter their charges all at once, "And what about me?" she'd demanded. "Every day you told me you were going to school and that was a lie."

"Every day," this had been Anton, "you said we wouldn't have to go back again and *that* was a lie."

For a change she had daylight to see that though much improved from the previous year, conditions inside the ghetto remained very unsightly. Where the dead had been stacked, trash was strewn and waste-befouled. Worse, the habit of piling dead naked bodies outdoors appeared to have become engrained within the imprisoned population as little heaps of three or four were present, only in different spots this time. The bodies were much rat-gnawed, the ghetto's rat population had peaked. A brief time ago the Council had acquired and laid out oison and suicides had gone through the roof, she'd heard. This was where she left these two children alone six days in seven—this place.

They were heading for the Bulbe Fence, named for the pails of potatoes the charitable townsfolk still brought to its gaping wire strands. It was also the site of an active trade in valuables exchanged for food, medicines, sundries, tobacco. There were always two or three soldiers keeping an eye on the situation. The gate abutted a town road and outside was a bus stop shelter painted aquamarine. Being among the ghetto's busiest points also made the Bulbe Fence attractive to aimless restless able-bodied prisoners, a population which now, with the work gang chapers safely gone, began to emerge and drift up, the exempt and the reckless malingerers mixing in the yards and lanes.

A bus was idling in the road and a whiff of diesel fuel stained the air above a small crowd scene in the making. Near the fence on the ghetto side, atop some overturned wooden boxes that made a rough podium stage, a cherubic redhead in nautical costume and an awl-faced girl belted into an old man's overcoat stood hollering. They called people to them, called the bus passengers to come closer:

"Orphan children! Come hear the orphan children sing! Listen—we need your help!"

At the sound of Hodeh's voice Samuel Nemo stirred and muttered, yearnful. Quickly Musya cut behind a tall leafless hedge where through a screen of branches picked so bare they'd never leaf again she could peer at the performers—their upper portions, that is. People pressed around them for a view and other people outside the fence came close. One of these waved a carrot through the barbed wires—an offering for the orphan children, Musya realized. Then she felt a soft collision. The young woman who'd just walked into her shoulder stopped and exclaimed in surprise and apology:

"I didn't know anyone else was here!" Musya said it didn't matter. They traded remarks about her baby and the strength of his grip; the newcomer had a gentle, curious, kind manner. A not quite pleasant musty smell came off her patterned rayon wraps and skirts. "I always stand here," she explained. She was about twenty, missing some teeth, more than Elkie was missing. As they spoke she uncovered a headful of black curls worn short, she'd been cropped bald before in a transit camp or a typhus fever bout more likely, Musya guessed. The red-cheeked face showed signs of wasting. Yet she had a charm, she was pretty; she looked something like Anna Sten, dark and pretty and comical. She said her name was Roza.

"I knew a Roza. From Kiev," Musya said. Old fondness inclined her to friendliness. "Tell me, do you have a work exemption? How did you get it?"

Obodovka Roza stammered, "I have—I have—I work inside. Here."

Musya nodded. "You teach school?"

"No." Her eyes darted towards the makeshift stage; it was clear she wanted to enjoy the show in peace once it started. There wasn't long to wait. Hodeh counted three and then joined her sharp shrill voice to Anton's piercing one:

> *Vast and golden panorama, radiant road ahead...*
> *Youth impossible to number join their joyful tread;*
> *Like the sky is high inside you,*
> *Like the sea is wide within you,*
> *Take the path immense and great with joyful youth—hi-ya!*
> *Heave-ho—pull harder*
> *With youth-full ardor!*
> *Like the sky is high inside you,*
> *Like the sea is wide within you,*
> *Take the path immense and great with joyful youth—hi-ya!*

Of Dunaevsky's melody not many notes were left but all the bounce survived. The heads of the crowd kept time. It was a good number. From Volga Volga's bayan-laden river barge the children had even purloined and perfected a classic highlight: in a shock to her, because he'd never shown signs of being musical, Anton had learned the wooden whistle solo—the whistle was its own surprise—and he could play several bars with one nostril alone. Roza laughed at this, a nice deep laugh that shook her musty skirts. It was sex, Musya realized. The girl reeked of semen. The work she spoke of was inside a koorvah tent. Her lips moved between lyrics and smiles showing gaps and forgetful pleasure. All at once she turned and said, "They're good, don't you think? I like to see them."

"Yes," was all Musya could answer. "Yes, they do well."

She felt certain Roza must read her eyes and find—what? Barely clothed in pity, some shaming look, chipped from whatever it was that made the girl seek vantage points veiled by dead bushes in the first place, Musya feared. Embarrassed by her own embarrassment and stiffness she rocked Samuel Nemo with an excess of vigor that whirled her with him into open view where they were spotted immediately. Signaling another whistle solo from her partner, Hodeh sprang down, parted the onlookers and soon confronted Musya from a few steps away.

"Why are you here? Leave us alone!"

She objected. "This is a public performance, I think."

"It's still none of your business! We're not doing this for you now."

"Now? Were you ever? I must have missed that, I saw no signs." Samuel Nemo's struggles to be released early to his night carer's embrace gained strength. "Roza, may I introduce my adopted daughter, Hodeh."

"It's an honor," came shyly from the branches.

"And my Anton, on stage, the musician. You see—wait!"

With another spring Hodeh was there, yanking at her shawl knots. "Give him! Give him!"

"You don't—leave Pretzel alone now!"

But the little girl was too insistent, she'd had an inspiration. "Give him before the people leave—we need him!"

"Well I need him when you're done!" She let him go. He let out a rapturous cry as Hodeh dashed back towards the stage. A moment later he reappeared, lofted in her thin arms, a smiling baby star.

"Ah!" people said.

"Our orphan brother! An orphan baby! We need your help—please help the orphan children!" Hoden shrilled another eyns-tsvey-dray and the pair took up the Song of Youth once more. This time people chimed in, some clapping. Merriment spread. Then Hodeh was off the box again but still in full voice, she did a kind of speak-singing. She moved among the small audience with Pretzel in one arm and the open satchel in her other hand, following the fence line from face to face. The baby equaled revenue, unquestionably, Musya could see people dig deep.

"They're very talented." The young koorvah had come alongside her.

"Yes." She smiled. Her fatigue had lifted. She felt really proud. "Not from me I think."

They watched the satchel swallow a small loaf of black bread. "You're lucky to have children," said Roza.

Vast and golden panorama, radiant road ahead...
Youth impossible to number join their joyful tread;
Like the sky is high inside you,
Like the sea is wide within you,
Take the path immense and great with joyful youth—hi-ya!
Heave-ho—pull harder
With youthful ardor!
Like the sky is high inside you,
Like the sea is wide within you,
Take the path immense and great with joyful youth—hi-ya!

Our chances sail us past where seagulls fly to
'Til we rise up past the dark clouds—yes we break through!
O see our smiling friends down there,
A sixth part of the planet where
Our joyful destiny has filled the whole wide view.
Heave-ho—pull harder
With youthful ardor!
O see our smiling friends down there,
A sixth part of the planet where
Our joyful destiny has filled the whole wide view.

In our dreams we see a thousand things we wish for,
When we wake we find the courage to desire;
Wake up reaching reaching reaching
To the future future future,
When ripened joys will burst upon the bright unknown!
Heave-ho—pull harder
With youthful ardor!
Wake up reaching reaching reaching
To the future future future,
When ripened joys will burst upon the bright unknown!

(13)

Anniversaries approached and passed. One year since their arrival in Obodovka, a year since Papa went, then came a year since Baila. In between somewhere was Samuel Nemo's first birthday. No one remembered the same date and the family had nothing in writing that they could find. In the end they went with Musya's guess and held a song party in the cubicle by the lamplight Elkie brought to the event, with glasses of tea and good buttons for prizes. The Ernste donated the loan of glassware and samovar. The night was festive, the turnout large: since the Kotzes had acquired their kerosene heater people were friendlier. They felt less difficulty, Musya guessed, approaching less dire situations.

One day in the workshop she understood a Yelyuk remark to the effect that nursing mothers were barren. The other two lady dames by the stove agreed as if it were common knowledge here: nursing women couldn't conceive another baby while their breasts continued to give milk. Hearing this for the first time in her life almost knocked Musya off her work stool. Because Cezar the rapist hadn't left her alone; and then because one of the Babiak men on a stealth visit back to the homestead from his partisan shack in the woods who'd just bathed, fortunately, had muscled her from the hallway by the lavatory door one morning into the dining room where he'd raped her against a wall, rattling crockery until she'd thought the whole house must be shaking to bits but no one came to stop him—she'd feared pregnancy. This mammoth worry whisked away, her nerves collapsed like an unpegged tent. Her hands shook from wanting to applaud clench wave all at once. She sat and snapped her fingers quietly instead until Oksana noticed and ordered her back to work; prompt and cheerful, Musya obeyed. Cheerful she remained, admiring the landscape on their morning walk, all the milk tea shades among the white expanses of snow, field, rooftop, cloud, and the mulberry brown and gray stitching of trees. Always one or two loose threads of campfire smoke dangled in the wooded distance; some days they spotted puffs of gunfire. Eyes wide at the flapping echoes, Samuel Nemo bundled and warm bounced along on her chest, sharing her smiles, getting hungry; her amulet.

But then it turned out to be untrue. What she'd heard was bad information, a bobe-mayse she'd bought when she might have known better: Fanny's last two in Birobidzhan had seemed remarkably close and she'd sworn by breast-feeding. For Musya miscarried, a painful surprise that turned bloody and dangerous overnight. Her children raised the alarm and neighbors who'd been at Samuel Nemo's party hurried to help. The gendarmes arrived with a stretcher.

She woke up on a cot in the Ghetto Council clinic where hot towels and a single aspirin saved her life, aided by twice-daily cupfuls of watery soup. She received no other treatment during the ten days she spent there. Her condition in light of her husbandless status minimized sympathy. The other patients with the strength to talk shunned her until she missed her little fentster beam's companionship. Samuel Nemo wasn't allowed inside with her because babies carried disease. Her few visitors otherwise were far too many, everyone complained. The children were tolerable but Elkie and Eidel no one could abide, especially Eidel who criticized everything that went on. There were no doctors and no actual pay involved here, the clinic staff reminded Musya all the time.

Nine narrow beds besides hers were fit into a stuffy room; incredibly, four were empty. She lay between clean enough blankets, mostly asleep. Somehow her blood was growing back again as she dreamt of running late after the work bell. In her waking hours she often wondered, whether this terrible miscarriage felt better or worse for being a huge surprise. Would its arrival in fulfillment of a desperate hope have done much to improve the experience, or not? She couldn't decide. To have been the dupe of a bobe-mayse might have been nicer, with less day-to-day miserable fear; when that seemed so, Musya found herself even a little grateful to the foolish old dames. According to Sender the Ukrainian trio pressed him for details of her medical progress with unrelenting zeal, the ladies couldn't get enough gore even though they never understood what he was telling them. In her absence he kept working. Babiak's not only couldn't spare his labor, it piled more on Zenderkaz. For a few nights he slept on the boot-room stove bunk with Russvelt—his first time away from home with a friend, it was a great adventure for him that he recounted exhaustively on his next visit to Musya's clinic bed. Under Hodeh's supervision her boys appeared to be thriving, warmed at night by plentiful kerosene, by day productively employed and the Ernste kept happy. Now that Pretzel appeared in every performance the satchel kept coming back full. Even the baby failed to miss her, having made an effortless switch to bottle-feeding on a raw egg formula mix concocted by the new kitchen's infant health authorities. Hodeh carried him strapped to her chest with Musya's shawls these days.

The sickroom was stuffy, not warm, and it reeked from the chamber pots that were always being knocked over and kicked uncomfortably far out of reach beneath the crowded cot frames. The despair of the clinic staff down on its hands and knees reaching blindly was general. Their hygiene was not the best. The walls ran with cockroaches. Yet to achieve admission as an in-patient was almost impossible. When hundreds vied for every spot, no one could figure out how this so-called Musya Kotz from Odessa had managed it. They discussed the question all the time, patients and staff arriving finally at a joint consensus: there'd been a mistake. Her rescue ought not to have happened.

"So I'm a miracle," she told them.

"You're no miracle," was the reply. But they wouldn't throw her out too soon when she still needed bed rest, not in these heavy snows; they were good enough people.

Deep in the quiet of night came the hours Musya preferred to spend propped on her pillow-towel, wakeful. Across the room a low lamp flame flickered greenly in the stinking air. She thought about a doctor, a man of middle height or somewhat smaller, young and idealistic, with a soft well-tended beard, a pride of his—male vanity, she'd tease him. She pictured his arrival—he was always arriving, always noticing her presence in the room for the first time. The first glance they traded ricocheted through countless variations. They intro-duced themselves endlessly with shy looks and witticisms: she, the stigmatized but resilient young widow; he, a rebel with skills, a reformer with finely-tuned hands. He wore spectacles but not consistently. He found her, alone among the rest, advanced enough to agree with him that the ghetto clinic was a disgrace in every way a twentieth-century person could name. Linked in righteous thought, patient and doctor pledged to list each outrage in a letter to the Territorial Authority; this would be a working partnership. It was after bedtime and they sat in the next room sharing a wafer of desk lamp light. Shoulder to shoulder or knee opposing knee, trying not to press, distracted by proximity, trying not to kiss they kissed anyhow; although sometimes they waited. No matter, one or two strong blasts of passion later she and he were paired. Now their program of improvements sped forward. Cleared, cleaned, plastered, sterilized, outfitted with real beds and every one filled with a worthwhile and interesting case, the clinic would become a model of its kind. She and her doctor would run it, his name would be Zev, she decided. The cures he effected would astound.

Time passes. One day a visitor, a Romanian general making a survey tour of Transnistrian ghetto conditions, arrives with his suite in response to their eloquent letter, enters their clinic and exclaims at the cleanliness, the modernity around him. How was it done? This fragrant general with rings all over his large white hands asks to know. As Zev begins an answer for the translator present, the general's eyes fall upon the doctor's partner and won't leave her again—they cannot. He's been mesmerized.

Next? When the general pushed to make a plaything of her, what would happen? Would she flee? Or for the good of the greater number would she submit to his will? Fully alive in the scuttling darkness Musya regretted the good young doctor's heartbreak and wept tears at being the cause of his pain. She pictured him clutching his brow after she'd left; he'd sit awake by the light of their desk lamp, she loved the soft dense shiny clean hair on his lamplit forearms. She loved him. She loved him and love sank into her nights like a healing balm. Even lying there tormented by love's impediments, her body grew better, fuller, stronger.

By the tenth day there was no place Musya hated worse than the ghetto clinic but as the scene of her devotions, she abandoned it with grave reluctance. Doctor Zev would never find her when she was no longer lying there to be found. Despite its being wholly imaginary, she felt robbed of a good chance. Nor was she half as strong as she'd thought herself by the time she stood bundling on mufflers and shawls for the long walk back to her cubicle bed of oak leaves bagged in mattress ticking. The occasion was also a nightmarish one for the clinic staff since it was Eidel who'd arrived to collect their departing patient. The rude schoolteacher never spared them. Now she laughed at them sarcastically:

"Congratulations! Now half your beds are empty again."

"We do the best we can with what they give us!"

Eidel then called them troglodytes. She and Musya couldn't leave quickly enough for the clinic staff.

Everyone else being busy at work, Eidel had come alone. Especially Elkie was otherwise engaged, her friend explained, since Tauber's had turned up another suicide in another dark edge of the attics, the last of the poison cases it was to be hoped, dead for weeks already and surrounded by dead rats, a very bad clean-up. Musya said she could imagine. Although the day wasn't too sunny she had to shield her eyes with a freezing hand, in such dimness had she been dwelling. The cold felt interplanetary, the air without stain burned her.

"That's my limit," she heard Eidel say. "Rats. They terrify me."

She said, "You know, Eidel, I was attacked. A man—men, attacked me, they raped me."

"Of course I know that, " Eidel said. One arm through Musya's, she guided their shuffling progress down an icy brown path through the glare. "What did you think?"

"I thought—nothing. I mean, I wanted to be sure people knew."

"Of course they know. No one blames you," she added. "But you need to learn to avoid these things."

"Yes. Of course," Musya agreed. She didn't recognize any landmarks until they were almost at Krutonog's—under another meter of snow the Obodovka ghetto looked squatter, more backward and even more uninhabitable than she recalled. As for the tiny cubicle, she resumed her life inside it with a sinking heart. Romance dropped dead here from lack of possibility. Even the fentster light beam appeared extinguished—the sun's course had shifted in a year. No one was home. Eidel stayed to help get the heater lit. The match flame burnished her blonde prettiness. "What things?" Musya asked her. "Learn to avoid what things?"

Adjusting the wick, Eidel frowned harder. "Those things—the things that happen with men. When they attack. You need to learn to recognize the warning signals and avoid them."

"The warning signals," Musya repeated. "Of course."

"Well, you must know what I mean."

"Sure, but what good is knowing how to recognize a warning signal when you can't change what will happen?"

Eidel said, "Then don't walk around alone—try not to, anyway."

"When am I ever alone?" she complained. Eidel stayed barely another minute. The cubicle was slow to warm. Far too tired to housekeep although every surface was covered in a thin film of kerosene soot, Musya sank onto the rustling mattress and waited for the children to get home from work with her baby and some dinner. Ten days recovering from blood loss on a weak soup diet had left her with an appetite that wouldn't desert her for years.

Were the children glad to have Musya back? She thought they were probably relieved without necessarily being glad. They'd been in the midst of an adventure. She with her grown woman's body took up a good deal of room and made a grown woman's messes. Cramping, fun-stifling, smelly, troublesome as it might be, hers was a familiar, reassuring presence. She watched the three of them relax little by little, she caressed them as they came one by one and sat down and nestled against her and got up and left and came back again later. On top of a good dinner they gave her part of their sugar bun. Not a terrible homecoming, it raised big problems, too—problems that involved her baby. Samuel Nemo was probably glad to have Musya home again, she thought. But restoration to his mother's arms was less and less a relief to him as their reunion night wore on and his hunger increased. For her milk had been too long interrupted; he sucked, hurt, failed to raise it, turned furiously red and bawled; he kicked at her aching front, kicking away from her as if to propel himself through his mid-air world back to Hodeh's arms, where he quieted in an instant. The little girl soothed him: "Pretzel—there, Pretzel." There was his relief, there with his mistress.

Then came the matter of livelihood. Her contribution to the family parnosseh had barely been missed, Musya learned to her dismay; indeed they'd had quite a bit more to go around without her; she'd been revealed as a drain. By contrast, her baby's addition to the orphan act looked set to secure his family from exposure and want. The high-earning trio had got in tight with the Ernste whose kitchen was their second home. They'd also gained a degree of local celebrity. Wherever they went the baby was a draw, people wanted to meet and often subsidize him. Hodeh and Anton had even brought Pretzel to school one day where he'd made a terrific impression—sometimes they really did go to school.

"When there's cake, I know," Musya said.

She refused to leave Samuel Nemo behind when she went back to Babiak's, however, no matter how hard he kicked and cried. Her breasts' attempts at feeding him still failed. Grudgingly provided a cup of fresh milk which he drank very messily, he spewed. After that he tossed and screamed in his box crib without interruption until quitting time. She couldn't bring him back, Oksana said not to.

In this way her baby wound up becoming a professional beggar. When she attempted to object that she wanted better for him, the Ernste would have none of it.

"Better? This is better. I don't understand what your complaint is. He does well, the people like to see him."

She said, "Because I'm humiliated. You're teaching my children Purim songs and I'm humiliated, that's my complaint. Give me an exemption!"

The answer was no. "And those are the best songs." Her lackeys within earshot of the Ernste agreed—the season was sure to be profitable. Hodeh raised her eyes from the chessboard, the Ernste was teaching her the game.

"It's true. They're good," she said. Across her lap Samuel Nemo lay purring, half-awake, unbothered by Anton's efforts to learn wooden whistle tunes going on in the glass office behind him.

Musya reached for her regular objections and found them all strangely weightless, like papier-mâché fruit unfit for throwing. Under the circumstances it might be that all work was equally honorable, begging alms with song no less honorable than finishing sand-colored uniform seams by foot power. Whose battle was she fighting? Boris and his family no more than hers would have liked seeing the next generation take to the amateur stage with its hands out. The mother, the sister, the husband, her life's strict moralists with their hundred hidden clauses tucked among their hoards—they'd lived but partially. They'd missed the Jewish ghetto of Obodovka. With a year's worth of its events even the mother's bitter bleakness would have been hard pressed to keep up, her surviving daughter considered. As for Boris Kotz, who was he to judge his begging sons when he'd been on his own way to ask Adolf Hitler for a job? And as for the repertoire, if the people liked Purim songs then who was anyone to judge? They weren't to Musya's taste which she acknowledged hardly mattered: they weren't being sung for her, she was never in the audience a second time. Her sister, on the other hand, might be a regular. Liza would have loved the Purim numbers.

"I give up," Musya said. She did. "Let them play orphans."

She went off to enjoy some extra quilting time. Her family rented a small oil lamp these days and she'd curtained off a corner to illuminate and quilt in when the children went to sleep; she was joining them later at night now. One by one she'd finished the quilted tunic sets they slept in, she'd gone on a purloining spree. Lately she'd been adding to her patchwork bed quilt. Vigil hours that marked the sure ebb of intimate closeness between Musya and her baby, she passed absorbed in plans and happy accidents of pattern, color, shape. When Doctor Zev returned to her thoughts she pictured turning him away: he'd seek her out, she'd send him back to the clinic—their love's legacy, his duty.

A few days after returning to Babiak's she was sent down to answer the trade door. As she'd known he would be, Cezar the rapist was standing outside. At the sight of Musya he yanked off his sorry-looking camp orderly's cap to grasp in both fists. In his thin forelock the toothmarks of a comb, on his pallid skin an oily sheen that seemed to magnify the pores: he was in a sweat although the world was frozen. She had an outdated number 2 flat iron by the handle prepared to brain him with it should he advance. Instead he dropped to his knees on the snowy threshold, bowed his head and erupted into mournful burbling noises. Even if she'd spoken Romanian no more than a handful could have been words, Musya thought. Mucous and spittle ran in strings from the rapist's mouth onto the threshold, she hoped they wouldn't leave an icy mess. She looked at his scalp seething with louse bites. "What are you doing? Get up," she said. With the barest of delays he grabbed the doorframe and pulled himself to his feet. Seeing her grip get readjusted on the heavy flat iron handle he dipped his head again and shuffled back half a step. The look he fixed upon her through his brows and breath clouds was pink and sentimental. His mumbling dirgeful rant resumed with more imploring tones plus gestures: the rapist slammed a fist into his own chest, pointed a hand at Musya's midriff and lower, then crossed his short thick arms and rocked them, cradling emptiness, weeping. He mourned his share in her lost embryo. "I hate you," she said, realizing that she ought to have grabbed the number 1 iron since this one was too heavy to swing head-high; her arm strength was not the greatest these days. Her rapist paid no attention. His eyes rolled back as he fumbled at his collar; he pulled forth some trinkets on a rough chain—religious, by the looks of them. She spotted a hare's foot hanging there as well and wondered what it signified, which of the rapist's holy saints. It was his faith in play here, the repentance they did, she realized. He was sorry, Hristos made him be sorry for what he'd done to her quite often. She might have died. "I don't forgive you," she said. He kissed his trinkets and shed two more tears.

Then he gave her some money.

It was a substantial amount. Cash, folded; in her confusion she'd taken it for payment owed on the order she handed him—but that came in the usual envelope. This other was separate and hers alone, her rapist even backed another step or two away from her when she reached to return it. She didn't just let it drop to the ground, she held onto it. "This doesn't make any difference, it doesn't change anything," she said. He'd made her a figure of gossip—how else could he have known? "It wasn't even yours!" she told him.

"Iarta-ma! Iarta-ma!" His voice cracking, he sank down to his knees again.

She slammed the trade door on him, bolted it, and spent a minute standing motionless in the dim snowbound light. Then she divided the cash between two secret skirt pockets and made her way back upstairs to the workshop. Just as she was getting settled on her work stool again, the overseer came up and said, "Did he take care of you?"

"What?"

"The colonel's man. Cezar. He was going to give you something, a present. To show his sadness."

"His sadness? His nerve," Musya said, taken by surprise. The room shimmered, fraught with discomfort. No one had mentioned her long absence at all yet. "You talked with him about me?"

"He said you were together."

"Together?" Too loud: the lady dames in their wooden chairs variously twisted to lay greedy eyes on her. Sender's machine had stopped, he was looking around at her, too. "Get back to work," she told him. She watched his right hand return to the balance wheel handle, the machine before him spin and click-clack to life again. Keeping her voice low she asked a second time: "Together?"

"Yes, together." The tall shoulders shrugged. "Maybe not at first."

"He attacked me—always."

"He has a problem," Oksana acknowledged. "But he never hurt any girl. Not like some others. Do not worry. Listen, Cezar is simple, a good soul. Since the big church in town has services again he goes all the time. He loves the church."

She said, "I thought it was something like that."

"Yes, and now he gives you this present because it is their season in the church for this—they say Triodion."

"Triodion!"

From her seat by the stove came the Yelyuk cry followed by a speech. Musya barely understood ten words. The lead lady dame's voice as usual gained in volume what it lost in clarity after midday—a drinker, no question. Oksana shook her head impatiently as she translated:

"She is saying, yes, now before Pascha confession is time to atone. Your Cezar knows he will see the kingdom and not be going in eternal fire this way."

"My Cezar? No." She disposed of that. "What kingdom?"

"The kingdom of Bog in heaven. Bog will forgive his sins and he will enter with the blest."

"Bog will not forgive what he did to me," Musya said.

"Yes." Oksana agreed with the Yelyuk woman and they both disagreed with Musya. "He will be forgiven by the blood of Khrystos."

She insisted. "No. He will burn. What is she saying?" For Mrs Yelyuk hadn't stopped talking and now the other two dames didn't stop nodding their heads.

"She says," Okansa said. "He was led into sin by woman."

"I see." Musya kept an ear on the old lady's pronouncements. A word almost identical to one in Russian kept recurring. "Yes? What about us? Jewish women—tell me."

Oksana translated, "No, only that you—only that Jewesses like men." The old dame's voice rose. "Or anything. Men or anything."

"I see," she said. "May I please return to my work now? Would you like any work done today? Or is there more time to insult me?"

"Work, work, please, majesty," Oksana said. "Work."

But there he was, hours later, exaggeratedly dawdling at a distance behind them as she and Sender headed back to the ghetto under a risen full moon. Bluish light lay everywhere. The moonlit snow gleamed, its shadowed hollows like pools of sapphire. The stars looked pale. The cold was killing. Sender grew alarmed as Musya hurried them towards warmth:

"What does he want? What did we do?"

She said, "Don't pay any attention to him."

"What did he give you?"

"Nothing," she said. The rapist's footsteps kept pace behind them. "Only some money—Romanian bills."

They skidded carefully down where the road sloped. At the bottom he asked, "What will you do with them? The bills?"

"I don't know." This was true: she had no idea.

"If it's much money, you'd better give it to Hodeh."

"But it's mine!"

"Not really," he said. "We owe Krutonog's."

"I'm not giving it to Krutonog's," she said forcefully. Walking on, they looked behind and saw that the rapist had slowed his pace. Quickening theirs, she asked, "What would Hodeh do with it, then?"

Sender said, "She'll buy things we need. She'll use it to take care of us. But for what did he give you money?"

Musya said she didn't know, and added, "What else is he going to do with it out here in the countryside?"

Just then a sharp cry cleaved the frozen night behind them. It was the rapist, he'd stopped back there at the road's highest point. His cry came again, then another—these were notes, he was singing notes. He sang—not well although he wasn't talentless, she and Sender agreed—a mournful tune they didn't recognize, almost howling it. But not to Musya nor in her direction. He serenaded the view, the snowy expanses dappled with blue humped shadows, obsidian-edged where the fields ran down to the inland forest. Empty: Earth out-sparkling the pale stars. He sang at the top of his lungs, as if to reach every seat in a huge arena, as if the emptiness had invited him personally to fill it with sound. They could still hear whispers of his voice when the gates were already in sight.

Back in the cubicle Sender didn't wait too long to announce, "We have Romanian cash, Hodeh."

"Give it," Hodeh said. She followed the boy's eyes to Musya. "Give it."

"But it's—what will you do with it? You'll buy something?"

"Yes. Toys for Pretzel and Anshel. A man is selling them. Give the money, he might be gone after tomorrow." The little girl reached with her intelligent hand.

But Musya hesitated. "His name—his name is Anton."

Hodeh's shrug said so what. "He needs toys anyhow."

So the wheeled wooden horse and the rest came into their possession. Hodeh also bought a tin drum and trumpet but she managed to get the Ernste to invest some proceeds and pay for those. The musical orphan act's popularity only grew. At the Bulbe Fence they'd gained feature status on two separate bus routes, the bus drivers always stopped at Obodovka now so any passengers who liked could disembark in time for the performance—an authentic ghetto show. The Ernste always had one or two minions in the wings to field inquires, keep order and pay any baksheesh required; the drivers got a share, naturally, the regular armed guards got a share. What remained was plenty. Between the four walls of its cubicle the Kotz family continued to survive a winter milder than the last which saw the murder of Jews in Transnistria by exposure, hypothermia and starvation continue regardless.

On one of Musya's next free days she started out to visit Elkie and Eidel's room and was nearly there when she saw Eidel walking towards her. Musya stopped and stood admiring the astrakhan collar get bigger the closer it came. A recent birthday gift from Elkie, the black pelt's origins were cloudy but its quality was not in doubt, it was top of the line. Sender Kotz had done the job of tailoring the purple coat collar to fit it perfectly. His grandmother's cinnabar was also on view; somewhere along the line Elkie had negotiated the bracelet as payment from Tauber's to reunite the set. The teacher was on her way to meet colleagues for a little hard-earned relaxation. As for their mutual friend, sadly Elkie wouldn't be free to entertain Musya's visit at this time: the latest fight over food scraps there had left a bloody mess for Tauber's loyal housemaid to scour and tidy.

"Head wounds," Eidel said. "I had to get away."

"Those are bad," Musya was agreeing when an unknown woman plodding past stopped dead in her tracks beside them and drew in her breath:

"Wait," said the stranger. "Isn't that the orphan baby?"

Distracted by from Eidel's inexplicable amusement, Musya felt her mouth fall open. "This?" she croaked, slightly.

The stranger nodded, positive. "I'm sure it is, I'd know him anywhere! He just has something. It is him, isn't it?"

"Yes," Musya said. "Yes."

"I knew it! Oh just look at him." The stranger gave his wrist a gentle shake and Samuel Nemo blessed her with a smile. She was skin and bones. "Oh! This precious orphan. And you are?" she asked Musya. Her teeth protruded.

"I am." Eidel's right eyebrow arched sarcastically in her peripheral vision. "His carer. I care for him—today." A quick sidelong glance revealed a disdainful smirk on Eidel's lips. The strange woman however seemed satisfied.

"You're even more precious in person," she told the baby, moving away.

Musya called after her. "Thank you! Thank you," she told Eidel.

The schoolteacher snorted. "Far be it from me, Musya, to interfere in your family's profit-making."

"Profit! What profit?"

"Although I disapprove of course," Eidel continued smoothly, "as an educator here, seeing first-hand the bad influence our students receive when they see your children doing what they do."

"When they see my children do what? Work? Be talented? Entertain—entertain a woman like that, dying from hunger?"

Eidel said, "When they see them pass around a bag that people fill with cash and food gifts, actually." She said truancy was soaring and delinquency would soon become a major problem as the children of the Obodovka ghetto had been seized en masse by dreams of golden fortunes to be found in song-and-dance routines. "We can't make them stop practicing long enough to teach them their lessons."

"Why not let them practice, then? We welcome the competition." Musya gave Samuel Nemo a jollying bounce.

"You're impossible. Oh—by the way," Eidel said. "I hope you've given up that kerosene heater."

"No, of course not."

"You didn't hear about the family that got asphyxiated in its sleep? But this happened at Krutonog's, how did you not hear?" For there must have been talk, six lives lost at once was a newsworthy tragedy. Three of them children—they hadn't stood a chance in an unventilated cubbyhole. According to Eidel a kerosene heater was the culprit, its flame had devoured all the family's oxygen and left it nothing but a deadly gas to breathe. "Krutonog's supplied the kerosene and the heater. If yours is the same model you could be killed."

"I think mine is a different model," she said, thinking hard. "When did this happen?"

Eidel wasn't sure. "I heard about it a few days ago—maybe a week ago."

"And you only mention it now?" Musya's voice rose. "Maybe you or Elkie could have warned me before this."

"I'm sure we both assumed you would have known—it happened right next to you, practically. Don't blame me." Eidel began to move off again in the direction of her teachers' party. "You should try to know more things, Musya, for everyone's sake. Maybe pay a little better attention before your children start another dangerous craze. Some of our children, in fact quite a few, by the way, are actual orphans."

"Good for them," said Musya to the back of the astrakhan collar. By now her temper was seething. With what kind of friends was she saddled, she wondered, in these inattentive girls? She'd only seen Eidel by chance—would they have sought her otherwise? She doubted it. And as for her landlady, this took the grasspea negligence and stretched it too far beyond toleration. What might have happened? Musya could recall many nights when she'd burned a little extra kerosene to fall asleep by. More blood-curdling to contemplate were the ten nights she'd spent in the clinic while Hodeh ran the heater nonstop for Pretzel's perfect comfort. She might have returned to a lifeless family or maybe even worse, to an empty home with their dead bodies gone, already stacked and dumped somewhere outside the reach of anyone's memory. Misplaced. Then she wouldn't be so different from so many of the rest here, she realized; then she would number among the ones whose losses had finally added up to all alone. Eidel's precious orphans weren't even the half of it when it came to the army of solitaries patrolling these sad snow-banked lanes. Some were starving, some not quite, but they were all the living victims of loved ones' murders. The bleeding ends of violently broken human ties trailed their steps like ragged foot cloths.

So was this not pain enough? Was this not bad enough, that landladies should also see the need to provide health hazards in place of amenities?

Musya reached Krutonog's in a state of boiling grievance and strode straight through to confront management. She was surprised to find a man in the kitchen ahead of her, already complaining to the Ernste: it was her son the ghetto councilor who stood before his mother's armchair where she sat and drank tea, her manner calm. Under the circumstances he looked smaller than he really was.

"I tell you Mama, you have to stop this! It's irresponsible—it looks bad!" His voice cracked.

"The good people like it," the Ernste said. "The passengers enjoy some entertainment. Nu, I provide."

He groaned. "This again! Mama—nobody asked you. Nobody put you in charge of entertainment here."

The old Bucharester made a face. "Who said they did? Who needs them to? This is a nothing, don't bother."

"This is not a nothing," her exasperated son said. "It is very much a something when the fascist guards come and demand from the Ghetto Council a bigger share out of what your child act is earning."

"For what should they come to you?" his mother asked. "We pay them directly."

"They should come to us because that is the correct procedure, Mama, they do come to us because that is what happens. All transactions—"

"Excuse me. Excuse me," Musya cut in, not interested in these sorts of details. The son turned wild eyes her way and she noted the weak mouth showing as usual through a brown beard that had the fingers of his right hand tangled and possibly trapped in it. She peered around him. "I need to talk to you about the heater you're renting to us."

"Sholem-aleykhem," said the Ernste with finality.

Musya threw up her hands. "Sholem-aleykhem, sholem, fine" she said.

"That's not a rental, it's a loan," the Ernste continued. "It's on loan to you."

"Mama," said the councilor.

"But." Musya paused. "We paid—we pay you."

"The deposit on the loan. Plus interest. Plus kerosene. Of course."

"Mama—excuse me, Miss, you're interrupting a private conversation."

"I only get one day off to do all this."

The Ernste said, "It's called the shabes, you shouldn't be doing anything. This girl," she told her son. "She's the mother. The one with talented children—that's one of hers, there, the famous orphan baby. You don't recognize?"

The councilor glanced over Samuel Nemo's features, frowning. "Why would I—you think I go to watch him, you think I have time for your shows, Mama? I guess he's not bad."

Musya objected. "He's better than not bad."

"So that's it, Mama, that's what it is, I understand now." Red with emotion, the councilor yanked his fingers free. "You must think your prayers have been answered because you finally have the stage brats you always wanted, yours to control, yours to profit from—just like you wanted to profit from me except I could never do it, no matter how hard you kept pushing—no, no." He wouldn't let his mother disagree. "Not because I didn't have the talent, because I did, I was choking on talent. But because I hated it, and the harder you pushed me the more I hated it. No, it's true, I did! I hated every single hour I spent practicing, every minute of every audition was hell for me.'"

"Auditions," his mother managed to say, "are supposed to be hell. You were good. You could have been better than good."

"Not the way you pushed me.'"

Musya said, "I just heard on the street that one of your heaters killed some people here and I wanted to know, I wanted to make sure we don't have that same model. In my cubicle."

"No, you have a different one in there," the Ernste said. "Plus you got no door so don't worry."

The councilor added, "Mothers have ruined countless talents through over-pushing."

"We have a door curtain, though," Musya said. "And no ventilation—I'm not sure it's safe."

"Let God worry," the Ernste told her.

"Listen, this is the point, Mama—you have no business managing child talent, you're just not good at it!"

His mother narrowed hard eyes at her son. "You go tell your friends to mind their own business and try getting the rest of us some light bulbs and soap. And you." Back to Musya. "This catastrophe happened two weeks ago, no one stops talking about it for ten days and you hear for the first time this hour? Where is your head? On some man, I guess."

"For a woman with that many children she's fairly typical," said the councilor. "Exactly the ones who'd benefit most from having information absorb the least."

"Yes, please, soap would be nice," Musya said to him. "I can't wash all my fifty children with information."

He said, "If you don't like being typical then don't be."

"Quiet, both of you. Go keep shabes." The Ernste gave her an extra look. "Go home and pray."

"You pray," Musya said. "You pray that heater of yours doesn't suffocate us in our sleep because then no one will be getting shares from my children's labor, not you and not your son's idiotic council, either."

The councilor inhaled sharply. "You are a very disrespectful girl," he said.

"She's from Odessa,'" his mother explained.

"That's right, I am." Her throat caught on a burning coal, Musya blinked back tears. Homesickness engulfed her, gray-green shore-smashing waves of it; she drowned and kept standing there. Lost views looped on floating trolley rails ran through her mind's eye along streets of sculpted porticos and long window shutters—past shop signs, past plane trees, café orchestras, her Daddy's hand dipped inside a bag of chestnuts, the harbor light's insistent searching flash. Were all the good men dead? She almost panted for sea air.

The Ernste said, "Send your Anshel to me later, I have a trumpet part to add to Mu Asapru for him to learn."

"Fine." What was she fighting for, she wondered? But the man at her side cried out:

"Are you kidding me, Mama? That's my song—it was my trademark number!"

His mother said no, Mu Asapru was everyone's number, from God; an argument to which Musya left them. The unfamiliar Yiddsh ditty, unappealing to her from the first, did not improve on closer or prolonged acquaintance, in her view. Since Hodeh and Anton practiced it endlessly these days, she wasn't surprised to find them hard at work on the fast patter verses when she returned to the cubicle. *Seven are the weekdays, six are the misnayes, five are the chamushin, four are the matriarchs*—she'd had enough. Told to be quiet and keep shabes, the children appeared dumbfounded.

"Here?" Hodeh said.

Musya said yes. She was looking at the back wall of their cubicle, the outside wall, narrow, blackish, studded all over with twists of paper stuck in the chinks—a kind of library wall, she supposed. From the out-of-date books and historical journals that Baila

Kotz had coaxed from Mr Asch for the purpose much remained; the worst pages of Musya's old youth poetry prize volume filled other gaps. Even so the winter cold forced its way in at her as if each crumpled printed line were a twisting pipe to blow through. Damper drafts billowed in past the blanket curtain. Her panic subsided. Circumstances hadn't changed but their precarity seemed less. With the next really piercing gust relief surged in waves through her limbs. She sat down on the bed. Her children were grouped noisily around the little heater on the floor. Samuel Nemo sat among them on the tiger skin shouting parts of words and pounding the tin drum with his hands. This was also practice and even by shabes rules must be allowed, they told her. Practice was a necessity.

"Mu Asapru is a very hard song," Anton said.

"And this calling you Anshel, what is this?" she asked him. He looked aside with a shrug, his expression gone overcast in a way she didn't like to see, it made her heart ache for him and irritated her nerves at the same time. "Your name is Anton Kotz."

Hodeh popped her braid-end from between her lips and spoke. "This is better. She likes it better."

"The Ernste, she means," Sender said.

"Yes. But." Musya sighed. "I'm only thinking of your father."

"Papa's not here," he said.

The younger brother added, "Papa's a bad Jew!" Musya told Anton not to talk that way about his father and he jumped up and ran out crying. She sat in the cold breeze he'd left behind, the major villainess in the room. The baby cried. She didn't understand, Hodeh told her: Pesach season was near and this was their showstopper, a beast of difficulty requiring perfection. Then she left, the one who'd see Anton through his moods, the cubicle's calming influence. She and he made a good team raising Pretzel, Musya acknowledged. They'd nearly trained him to use the bucket by himself. While she sat there irrelevant, her worries phantasmal, her shabes sham: her interference wasn't needed in this family, at least not now. Now, clearly, the less she cared to meddle in its affairs the better for all of them—the faster she retreated to her perpetual daze, maybe, the better.

For where was her head? To her shame, the Ernste was right: these days and nights it was usually fixed on a man—a man she pictured coming to the ghetto as a special prisoner. Captured in his leather driving jacket, always brown leather, he was a dark-eyed curly-haired man with some initial face bruising and a brilliant smile. He smiled incredibly often given the conditions he found in Obodovka but such was his nature and his mission and, indeed, his crime: he was an inspiring leader of heroic optimism. He smiled especially at Musya. A one-man antidote to the Ghetto Council, he strode down every street and lane, through every barn and back garden, meeting people, making friends, organizing games, exhorting lay-about invalids to clean the steps and squalid footpaths around their own dwelling places. In the end they'd do it gladly, with song. Morose, lamplight-pale Doctor Zev would emerge to stand in the clinic doorway and watch the new man's followers parading past, his naked squint embittered, sardonic, not quite comprehending, his capacity for enthusiasm circumscribed by the hygienic walls of his clinic—a worthy, professional, limited man who still loved her. She pictured his eyes flying wide open, despair-blazed at the sudden unmistakable sight of her beautiful hair. Maybe already she had one arm hooked through a brown leather elbow.

Could Zev blame her? He offered clinic beds—ten of them—when she craved health and joy; he kept his corners clean, here and there he saved a life; but his rival stood for more. Dignity for imprisoned Jews, freedom from fear, release from forced labor, food enough for every captive—was that all? The sad young clinician laughed at her newborn outlook; stung, she left him laughing on his doorstep and hurried back to the parade. She pictured preparations for a dance, a great ghetto ball.

(14)

A cry like an animal's yelp, frightened and pained, came from close enough to touch. Musya looked up from the seam beneath her presser papka and blinked the workroom into focus. The silence was strange. Sender's machine was silent, still. She watched for him to raise his right arm far enough to grasp the manual drive handle and realized he couldn't do it—instead his cry came again, an agonized pain-strangled shriek. The voices of the lady dames were rising in wonder now. He tried again and it was the sound caused by a fur trap, she thought—helpless, inarticulate, doomed. Was Sender Kotz doomed? To her disbelief he was about to try again, already hissing through his teeth. "Stop!" she cried and hurried around to him. Droplets all over his forehead, his expression confused:

"Am I broken?" he wondered. She told him of course not but in truth she didn't know, she thought it possible.

"Try not to move," she said. One of the older old dames had gone to fetch Oksana Babiak in this emergency. Not Mrs Yelyuk whose knees weren't good, she never walked extra. That left her looking on in vocal fashion. "What are you blabbing about—stop blabbing!" Musya shouted at her to no effect before their overseer burst in, wiping her hands on a white dishcloth. She was heat-flushed, her bosom and the foiled crystal cross emblem on it dusted alike with flour.

"I have too much baking for this today," Oksana said. A scowling remark silenced Mrs Yelyuk momentarily. Next she eyed her machine labor's predicament. Signaling Musya not to speak, not to bother, she said, "Zenderkaz raise your arms please."

The left one, nearest Musya, complied fluidly but the right rose not even far enough to shake hands. She heard Sender suck breath through his teeth and Mrs Yeluk calling him a liar, this she understood: "He is not a liar—he always tells the truth!" she cried at the circle by the stove where the old dames refused as always to know Russian. The Yelyuk called out something else and Oksana Babiak agreed:

"Yes. It is cramp maybe." At which she took Sender's right arm in both her hands and raised it like a pump handle.

He screamed, he sounded slaughtered. Musya's shout of protest seared her throat and made her own ears ache. As the overseer let go and stepped back with an abdicating gesture, the palm of Musya's left hand pursued her through space; but never made contact. Nothing was said. Sender kept screaming. His hand stayed in the air, his arm seemingly welded there, jammed, his fingers gripped in a hard tremor. Now he wailed with pain and his tears had come—he turned his red wailing face to her and his sad little arm struck her side like a turnstile's embrace. "For what?" was all she understood him to say with any clarity. She held him fast. She'd failed him. She wept into his dirty hair.

"We need a doctor!" she cried.

A few minutes later she sniffed an unfamiliar liniment and looked up to find someone new on the scene. Another old woman—Musya marveled, so many had held on! The lucky ones, too strong to be dislodged, too canny and tough for the latest wave of assailants, heaped layers of shawls upon themselves, stuffed their carpet slippers with old newsprint and prowled familiar rooms. They were an army, unnamed, unclassified, undivided by nation, race or belief, these shuffling old women—so many, like the old newcomer, even looked the same, as if the sameness of the circuits through the years had worn them round and smooth until they looked like river boulders wearing kerchiefs. This one they called the Stara. Everyone deferred.

"The Stara knows healing," Oksana told her. "She is a wise woman. This is her home."

"Don't touch him," Musya said. "Do not touch him."

But the Stara didn't seem inclined to touch Sender. She looked him up and down with distaste. Musya she avoided seeing at all, she treated her as something invisible. Bending to the old woman's hidden ear, Oksana made something like a plea. For Musya she translated: "I am telling her, he is my best worker." The Stara made it plain she didn't care. She muttered and spat on the workshop floorboards as well. Oksana grabbed up a handful of cloth scraps and dropped them onto the spittle, then used her toe to swab, explaining, "She hates Odessa, the Jews there, the Odessa Jews."

Musya stared down angrily at the scraps she'd planned on taking away with her in a hidden pocket, angry at the waste, angry at herself for waiting too long to hide them. She was really enraged. Then she looked up. "But he is not from Odessa," she said.

"But Papa is—and Mama," Sender began.

She told them, "I am from Odessa, yes, but the boy was born far away, in the Jewish Autonomous Region." Maybe to Oksana the words rang a bell, the rest looked at her blankly. She continued, "In the Far East—Eastern Siberia."

"Siberia!" the room exclaimed.

The Stara murmured to herself and Oksana said, "Siberia they know enough people sent away there." Before Musya could object the Stara's bast soles slid forward and she lay her slate-veined hands on Sender's shoulder. There she performed a brief manipulation that released the frozen arm to fall back against his side. When he stopped writhing he thanked her. He could barely raise the arm at all now. The overseer gave this some thought and then said the answer was easy, they'd simply switch Zenderkaz to the treadle machine. His legs were too short, this remained true; but she had the solution: "The Stinky! He can sit underneath and be push power. You—Stinky!"

He'd been there, watching from the door, but he'd disappeared before the second call, taking a guilty look with him. For their overseer had tasked Russvelt strictly, and he should have been cleaning and oiling that flywheel drive every day. Instead—Musya reached and tested, she ought to have tested every day, too—the handle turned heavily, stiff. His friend had covered for his lapses, straining, straining. Not every child was cut out like Sender Kotz to be a hero of forced labor. He had it in him; Russvelt, no. Russvelt shunned forced labor and the likelihood that he'd willingly impersonate a human piston motor for several hours each day was nil; even so, Musya cooperated in a test, playing the grasspea cripple's part she knelt on the freezing floorboards and pushed the treadle up and down on demand. Sender's legs dangled before her. She kept flinching away—frustration and pain made him kick out spasmodically as he tried his hardest to operate the machine with his left arm alone. Russvelt hadn't swept the workroom floor lately either, Musya observed from her crouch. A certain Romanian general would be very displeased if he were to walk in and find her like this, she was thinking with some satisfaction when Sender cried out through his tears for rescue:

"Musya, vu zaynen di Amerikaner?"

Before she could say a word the overseer went first. "America? Do not waste your time to hope America is coming, Zenderkaz. Sew faster—try." But it was no good, he couldn't manage it. When Musya returned to her feet, her seam was ruined and Oksana looked despondent. But now the Stara voiced a suggestion that made the overseer's frown turn thoughtful. "The Velykden vyshyvanky—tak," she said. Quickly then she and the Stara led Sender away, taking one of the lady dames too although not Mrs Yelyuk who was invisible like Musya to the Stara, it appeared. As she was leaving Oksana told Musya to resume her work. "Sad to say," she added from the threshold, "if he cannot sew the Velykden vyshyvanky then I must replace you both. This is a business. You will go to the steam laundry."

"No, he can sew those, he can sew anything." Musya wondered what they were.

Sender clarified. "If I use two hands, however."

"I am sorry," Oksana said, turning to lead him away.

Moments after they'd gone Russvelt materialized and demanded to hear what he'd missed. She told him Sender had been transferred—she struggled to name where until the Yelyuk corrected her loudly: "Velykden vyshyvanky!" The boy whose appearance was much improved these days but still nowhere near good turned green with shock at this information.

"But he's Jewish! They'll kill him!"

She felt herself start to tremble. "What will? What are they?"

"A vyshyvanka's a bluzke. Like they wear," he said, pointing at the lady dames' blouses, the broad yokes embroidered with red and black roses and the like. Musya understood that much.

"And what is Velykden?"

"The Goyishe Pesach." But it wasn't the holiday, it was the workroom, Russvelt said. Where the bluzky were sewn, that's where they'd brought out the house icons and hung them, close to the Stara. "Their icons are cursed against us. Any Jew that sees them will die—he'll burn up! Oh! Oh!" He put a lot of fingers in his mouth and looked distressed. Remembering Maga's closet back in Birobidzhan, Musya smiled and reassured him:

"No. Sender loves icons." From across the room came low Yelyuk chuckling. *Popil*, Musya heard. Popil. Ashes. "My boy will not be ashes," she said.

In actual fact he was hired. As an embroider of Ukrainian-style motifs onto plain linen peasant-style blouses, he'd started work immediately that day. The idea was for the occupying forces to buy them as Velykden souvenir gifts for loved ones back in Romania. Sender could manage the work with one hand, it was only cross-stitching and the patterns were easy, he said. The only male and the only Jew, the usual language barrier further divided him from the girls and old women who shared his labors. There were now ten embroiderers, crowded into quite a warm parlor-like room devoted to this work, handing pieces back and forth—they worked out specialties. Sender had been filling in rose leaf after rose leaf with black wool all afternoon, with pauses for the Stara to wrap his right shoulder in her own concoctions of boiled birch parts and camphor. He claimed to feel already some relief as he and Musya made their way back to the ghetto that evening through a light snowfall. The rapist she guessed was at the church again, she didn't see him. She wanted to ask Sender so many angry questions that she let the snow bury instead, as if the unspoken left a trail of footprints to be lost. She'd never know how long his arm had been hurting, nor why he'd kept quiet when he had to have known what was harming him. *Get back to work.* She'd told him herself. She thought about asking him how to be a good person, a mensch like he was. Instead she asked about the icons: had he seen them?

He had. They were beautiful. But first he'd had to keep his eyes shut tight until the Stara moved everyone safely out of the way. "Except You-Know-Who didn't move, she said it was superstition." This was how he'd refer to Oksana Babiak, whom he had liked, from now on, she'd hurt him this much. "She laughed when nothing happened."

"She's very fond of you, really," Musya remarked. When he kept quiet, she added that at least they'd learned the truth at Babiak's. Icons didn't kill Jews. He said no.

"They say I might not be Jewish."

She laughed. "Of course you're Jewish!"

"Or else there's a bad icon, they say."

The snow made whispers as it fell. "Don't listen to them," she said.

He walked quietly for a few steps. Then: "They also say Siberia is where the saints go. I think that part might be true."

"Saints?" Paydays in Birobidzhan, drunkards lining the plank sidewalks, the occasional mud puddle drowning: all this came to mind. "I don't remember any," Musya said.

"But what about Mama? She might have been a saint—she looked like one."

Liza with her bloody chin, her heated gaze, here she rushed into Musya's memory, exacting vows. "Yes? And what about me? I don't?"

"No," he said. "Your face is too round."

In her curtained nook the oil light flickered. The lamp also smoked and none of them knew how to fix it: she'd asked Elkie once but then her mind had wandered during the explanation and she'd missed everything vital. She didn't want to ask again. Now her mind kept wandering and she kept pricking her fingers as a result, and every drop of blood she sucked from her fingertips seemed to spark her annoyance with Hodeh anew. Why couldn't Hodeh fix the lamp wick? Some afternoon, instead of improving her chess game, why couldn't Hodeh be the one to pick up a needle and sew a lot of colorful patches onto her own costume? Once in a while, why couldn't Hodeh act more like a moyd and less like the head of their household? She'd ordered the patches to be finished for the next day; but it was dull work and a drain on quilting supplies. Of course there was no point in arguing. Hodeh was about ten years old and girls that age won't be contradicted.

Musya sighed.

"I'm sorry," Sender said. He'd been dozing over one of Yankel's old books, away on an undersea voyage he must have memorized two years ago.

"Why? Don't be," she said. The other children's fascination with his freakish shoulder injury had been intense but brief; they had Transnistrian reflexes, signs of weakness bothered them like bad smells, even Samuel Nemo had made a strange noise at him. He'd left them asleep in bed to come sit with Musya because it hurt too much when he lay down. Costuming had been his job—he'd volunteered. Now the job was Musya's. She forgave him. "You aren't the one who decided Papa Kotz's overcoat needs so many more patches all of a sudden, this isn't your fault."

"No, but I am," he said. "They were my idea—don't you remember? For Pesach. We told you."

"For—yes. Of course," she lied. In her mind Sender Kotz had been sewing her a sand-colored dress skirted to dance in, with trimmings, this was what she remembered. Now here he was, crippled. That daydream flickered out. She looked more closely at the boy. "Did you—before—did you tell me your arm was hurting? Do you remember telling me?"

"I didn't," he said. "It wasn't hurting. Why don't you ever tell us stories like you did before?"

"But," she said. "When do we have time now? We're busy working as slaves and your famous brothers and Hodeh are busy being famous people around here. Everyone always working—we have a busy family."

The curtain flew aside and Hodeh stood there in her quilted sleep-suit, hair every which way out of its braid. "Less talk and more patching when famous people are trying to sleep," she said.

"Sorry, Hodeh, yes, Hodeh," Sender said.

Hodeh waited.

"Yes, sorry, Hodeh, yes," said Musya, adding, "Go back to bed. Go to sleep."

On his first return visit to the workroom Sender wore his right arm in a fragrant sling, a welcome sight to her. Better yet, he'd been sent to fetch Russvelt, whom Musya happened to be training on the manual bobbin winder at his old machine. The little house slave was proving a hopeless pupil, his digits uncooperative, his resistance to practical knowledge complete and very understandable considering what had happened to the last boy assigned to this work—with two healthy arms Russvelt barely got by.

He was even less eager to face the icons' fatal effect. "I choose life! I want to live!" he cried with his eyes on the exit. But the embroiderers, Sender told him, had cookies to eat, spiced ones they called medivnychky.

"Medivnychky!" Mrs Yeluk howled in her seat by the stove. The old dame felt painfully excluded. As for Russvelt, when he left with Sender he was certain the icons would kill him but the temptation posed by spice cookies outweighed even ultimate fears in this sorry boy's existence. Left behind again, Mrs Yelyuk groaned. "Medivnychky—o!"

"Your favorite?" Musya asked sharply. The old dame refused her a response and grumbled instead to her companion, the sole one left to her; the slow one.

Later came the story of how Russvelt, dragged before the alcove, had hidden his face at first, then peeked through his elbow crack and finally faced the icons whole. The natural zero happened. "They can't figure out what's wrong," Sender said. He meanwhile had been assigned to tutor his friend in cross-stitching, the other boy's survival having consigned him to vyshyvanky as well. Sender claimed swift progress but Musya doubted him. The chilblain scars that disfigured Russvelt's fingertips would make needlework too hard for him, she thought.

A day or two later she and Mrs Yelyuk said goodbye to the slow lady dame, called up, like the better workers before her, for Velykden duty. She tottered out; which left two of them. Musya wondered what the other had done to offend the Stara so decisively. Shunned for all to see and very sore from it—Musya knew the feeling but she came short of pity for this Yelyuk.

They never spoke. Stripped of her sycophants, resultantly bored, the old dame's new routine was to turn up late, seat herself by the stove she'd set roaring and attach uniform buttons with angry accuracy for two bibulous morning hours, then pass out, wake up long enough to go eat something and return to drink a little more before dozing the day away. Less and less present herself, Oksana Babiak grimaced at the sight but refrained from action, saying silence was gold. "Better she sleeps than talks." In fact she was far from silent, all sorts of snorts and incoherencies and song fragments were always escaping Mrs Yelyuk's old lips. Yet the relative quiet eased the way to forgetting she was in the room. Musya would be bent above her ill-lit work, her mind playing dramatic scenes of rescue from Yelyuk treachery; for in her imagination this monster of malice never rested from plots and slander. Sides were drawn, abuses suffered and eloquent denunciations thundered before Musya and her champions prevailed. Sometimes there'd been casualties. She had a hundred Yelyuk punishments in mind.

One day when her righteousness had brought the scheming old dame to get down and beg with both hands clasped for mercy, which she was just about to deny, it happened that the Yelyuk gave a snort like a horn call in her sleep. Musya looked to see the slumped figure already breathing quietly again and daydreams fell from her like paper wrappings in a mess to the floor, she saw a woman other than she'd pictured. The diabolical mastermind of her imagination was in life a tired, ailing, ill-natured weakling, disliked and abandoned by all the world. For several moments Musya stared at the strangeness of this revelation. She felt a heart pang. Not real: her daydreams were only that, all of them. She sat until she was numb again and then kept sewing.

Then the woman herself was gone. She came to the workroom one morning later than usual and never settled down to work, instead she muttered at the cloth and needles, rattled a hand through a box of epaulette brass, took at least one long pull from a brown-sided bottle and jammed the cork back in with an emphatic thump. Nerves boosted, she got the workroom door in her sights and made her exit through it. Hours later Oksana Babiak swept in with her arms full of blouses to iron, very merry, talking of a party in the bluzky room that day, a big reunion since Mrs Yelyuk had apologized. Musya asked, "For what?"

"None of your business."

The overseer smelled of wine. Her mood was blunt but talkative. From now on, she explained, Musya would be alone in the workroom. No one else could be spared. Originally a low-key sideline around the place, the Velykden vyshyvanky had exploded overnight. Oksana's wayward, reaching, Russian-purring Romanian colonel was behind the business once again. It seemed the holiday pay his troops were due to receive in less than a month would be far short what he had promised them, and they'd get no cash bonus—that had been an empty promise he couldn't possibly fulfill but he hated to lose popularity when he'd been drinking. All men were the same, Oksana said. After every big blunder they'd sit down on the nearest curbstone and cry loud tears to attract a woman's help. Her own idea had been this: to every man give something better than cash, namely a future heirloom for his sweetheart back home, all hand-made in the traditions of the Ukrainian countryside. The desperate colonel had snatched at this proposal. Despite what Oksana was charging him, he was lucky to have her, she said. The plain blouses, machine-made of course, had been in Babiak's storage for years since a long-ago bargain; lately bleached at the steam laundry, the cloth was good quality, Musya could think of many better uses for it.

"What about the uniform shirts?" she asked.

Oksana said not to worry. "Sometimes it is good if a shortage happens."

After that there was nothing for Musya to do but sew pieces together and stack the unfinished garments, her work orders being to take each one no further; no epaulettes. She had no one to talk to. The lady dames might have been crowding it still for all the heat she could induce from the stove with her meager fuel allotment. She was cold and her groin ached from pumping the cast iron treadle. Eyestrain tormented her in the poor light, half the string of electrical bulbs was nothing but burnt-out gaps and weak flickers. One day she noticed a faint gray gleam new to the mix—the day was sunny and the snow that blanketed the skylight had made April's first discernable concession. This finding seized her interest. Several times an hour she switched off the remaining bulbs to gauge the level of natural illumination in the room. The light grew more watery without seeming much stronger and soon a leak appeared. She found an empty jug to catch the drips. Back to sewing sand-colored sleeves, she let her thoughts return to their smooth tracks that ran among imaginary dances and meetings and rescues and intrigues and men competing for her love through song—these days she pictured a contest on the night of the ghetto ball.

The emcee was her old suitor the Romanian general, appearing in full regalia to sing a bass baritone aria out of competition and then to introduce the acts. Next on center stage was Doctor Zev, surprising her with a keen tear-wringing tenor voice; a mournful number. The ghetto gendarmes would perform in comic chorus. Pretty face framed in a shiny new flower print shawl, Obodovka Roza always got up and sang something heartbreaking. Later in the program the curly-headed rabble-rouser, they called him The Motorbiker, might lead a defiant sing-along. Even Musya got up, competed and probably won, even the son of the Ernste entered and performed his famous Mu Asapru. Otherwise it was taking hours to pick everyone's songs, the selections kept changing as she combed her memories of film scores and gramophone parties, the task grew almost tedious.

The drowning skylight's leaky frame dinged snow drips into the clay jug below. Musya pictured a blaze of day to pour through the panes and strike the floorboards—the jug erased, instead a light columnar and cloudy with gilded dust motes, a singular secluded radiance for standing in to exchange passionate kisses with a man. It was The Motorbiker. He'd come for Musya in the town, a mad step, it could only mean one thing. "That's right," he told her. Ghetto uprising: he'd finally incited one. It must have turned into a general breakout. Now he proposed to abscond with her on stolen wheels, he pressed her. She tried to pull away:

"What of my children?" she asked.

The Motorbiker gave a great shout of laughter and said not to worry, he'd known she couldn't leave them behind so he'd attached a sidecar. He'd thought of everything. His body like a beam of clean carved stone stood in the flood of sun growing hotter.

Musya had to take a deep breath. Not everyone could handle the excitement of a life like hers, she reflected.

The jug chirped on the dim floor. She tried to focus on her work but the imaginary spotlight beam had become a too-distracting optical annoyance. The unrhythmical drips compounded her distress until it seemed to her a terrible intruder would be standing there when she turned her head next. Murderous, vengeful, an angry ghost—yes, naturally, Baila Kotz in her blue skirt and her last brassiere, gangrened fingers raised to her naked earlobes, ice-cold curses blasting from between ghoul jaws frozen closed, she'd be there at the front of line. The periphery of Musya's sight blazing—the accusing dead turned the lights up high for their arrival, she could hear the filaments crackle and hum. She didn't want to look and stared instead at how her stitches veered from the seam line into a tangle of loops and spirals on the sand-colored cloth.

Her seat crashed to the workroom floor behind her. She didn't look back but hurried up and down strange hallways until she reached a door with the Yelyuk's voice behind it. Musya knocked and entered a heavily carpeted room too small for the dozen people it contained. Sender and Russvelt sat together by the wall, old newsprint covered the carpets immediately around them. White cloth splashed with red lay everywhere. The heated air made her head swim. She spotted the icons in their Ali Baba's cave: lit by a few tall candles, a glow of gold leaf and enamels like gemstones, bristling with spiky worked brass. A step or two nearer she could see how the candlelight crawled across long sad staring faces, stony sheet folds, silvery wing feathers, swords, tiny cities, unnatural hand gestures.

"Very nice," she remarked, shrugging at the disappointed faces of women and girls strange to her; even the two little boys looked like they might have been hoping for more. Between the icon alcove and Musya and the alcove again all eyes bounced critically. The Stara made a bitter remark; Oksana Babiak laughed but frowned:

"She says they got a forgery icon. What are you doing here?"

"I see," Musya said. "I am reporting a leak. You have a leak in your workroom. The skylight is leaking."

"Already? But it is too early for this—what is happening with our weather now?"

Musya looked at her. "I am sorry," she said.

Sender spoke up in Russian. "If you are not burning up alive, Musya, maybe you can stay to stitch blouses."

Hurt in her voice, Oksana said, "Zenderkaz will not talk to me."

"No," she agreed. She told the boy, "I have my own work orders, I must return to the uniforms."

"Listen," said Oksana. "Wait." She picked up a clipboard and started checking production figures. Inside Musya was wavering, undecided: because for all its drips, ghosts, chills and monotony, she thought the empty workroom she'd fled might be preferable to this one with its outward attractions such as warmth and living occupancy and light from a sealed window with even a glass shelf for houseplants. But the Ukrainians' malice against her lay too thick here, she could feel it in the way they were breathing; and the pungent mix of their liniments tightened her throat, revolted her viscera. She was ready to leave, really hoping not to stay when Oksana gave the results of her accounting:

"The Grand Duchess can go back to uniforms." At which she wept for disappointment, mystifying herself.

She wasn't gone long. Close to lunchtime that same day, back at her machine, she looked up at the sound of a step on the workroom threshold. Cezar the rapist stood there. She glanced above his head, she'd never heard the transom bell. Her eyes followed the wire to the hole in the far wall: normal. The rapist took a step into the room and Musya screamed "No!" In every language she'd learned to say it in by now, including his own, she kept screaming "No!" at him. From a third or fourth chain around his unwashed neck he wore a black wooden cross for show. He didn't advance but he didn't step back. She let her voice rise. Then Oksana Babiak appeared in haste and ordered quiet. "Tell him to go!" Musya screamed. She watched the rapist turn to Oksana with a shrug, as if he couldn't understand her behavior and welcomed the older woman's helpful intervention. The clearly semaphored reply was that Oksana could do nothing because Musya was out of her mind today. She turned to her:

"What is wrong this time? He is our customer."

"I will not stay alone in this workroom if he can get inside like that. I won't," Musya said. "Not alone. Send back the Yeluk dame."

The overseer barked a short, cynical laugh. "Never! She will stick like glue now. Listen, stay while I get what Cezar is here for. Wait," she told him, touched his arm and turned to leave.

"No!" Musya said. She went forward. "I will go with you."

Oksana was annoyed. "No, you go alone then. Tell Zenderkaz, he knows what. Do not take all day."

Biting her lip, Musya squeezed past and went. Fact: this woman, their owner, liked danger. For a moment the lately-threatened steam laundry seemed like a refuge, calmer and safer after all—but she'd seen enough bald crumbling skins by now to know better. Perils or no perils, they were lucky to be at Babiak's.

She reached the proper door and entered this time without knocking. Again she swayed in the smothering onrush of heat, again her eyes were dazzled by the alcove shrine, again she stepped closer. Her sister a saint: indeed, Liza's resemblance to these faces like tragic-eyed knife blades could not be denied. Several of the icons were quite worn and studded with old seals. She stepped back as one of the bluzky girls filled a blank spot on the alcove wall with an icon she'd had by her chair. It looked no faker than the rest to Musya's eyes. "If they can get this to work," she used Yiddish to ask, "what do they expect?"

Russvelt told her, "We think it's supposed to happen like a death ray."

"I see." To her surprise he was embroidering a creditable red rose petal. Musya nodded at Mrs Yelyuk and the Stara who worked opposing sleeves of a single blouse near the ceramic stove, their laps fused beneath the same gray rug. At least they looked back at her, at least she existed visibly this time. The door opened and Oksana walked in, hurried but perfectly all right.

"What is taking so long?"

Musya burst out. "Did he attack you?"

Oksana said, "Yes. His smell did." From beneath an empty chair she snatched a cloth bundle—the colonel's silk underclothes she'd mended with her own hands this time; once before Sender had helped. They came from London. Halfway out the door again the overseer pointed at the low wooden wall bench the two boys occupied with a little space to spare. Only now Musya noticed the cordon of white powder laid across the newsprint, encircling them: insect poison, replaced daily and occasionally supplemented with rags soaked in kerosene. "So, your highness," she heard. "Sit. Join us. Someone give her a vyshyvanka."

(15)

A new element appeared at the Bulbe Fence with the first breaths of spring: Competition. The orphan children weren't alone anymore, other acts started showing up to jockey for attention and cash; mainly children; mostly orphan acts, too, some few more authentic; but the worst garbage, all of them, Hodeh said. They didn't even play instruments. Which didn't stop their collecting a few coins every time—coins formerly marked for one satchel alone.

As the original orphans' daily haul shrank with dismaying rapidity, their big backer the Ernste was swollen with anger in its place. "My own son!" She almost spat. For the upstart acts were giving profit share to none other than the Ghetto Council—the very cut she'd denied "that syndicate" when her son had come seeking. These new competitors enjoyed a distinct advantage in having official ways cleared for their shows to go on. Twice as Passover neared, her trio had been swatted off the best box stage by gendarmes, mid-act. Their shins were green with bruises. The orphan baby had escaped fortunately unharmed.

Musya said, "I know maybe it looks like—maybe I haven't been paying the best attention, but I notice it when my children are in danger because you don't pay some local tax like other management pays no problem."

"I will not negotiate with extortionists! I will not be shaken down!" the Ernste thundered.

"Then they're done," Musya said. "My children are finished performing for you."

"We aren't." Anton spoke with his mouth full for which Musya rebuked him.

Ignoring them both, the Ernste darted a hand at her chessboard and said, "My son forgets who he's dealing with! He and his friends think they're such geniuses. *Sah*," she told Hodeh who growled, wrapped another loop of braid around one hand and scanned her decimated ranks with desperate eyes. The certain victor concluded: "They just geniused themselves into more trouble than they can handle." Checkmate in three, exactly how a mystery to Musya tonight as usual.

At Babiak's they'd set Musya to work on the white inner borders of a standard repeating keystone trim which was somewhat hypnotic. The vyshyvanky room was almost too warm, its air much too close, the occasional kerosene odor dizzying. She fought to remain awake and never lost a round unremarked by someone's vigilant cruelty: a syllable, a finger snap, a hiss would jerk her head upright again. The drowsy boys were more indulged—she was the focus of the room's hostility. Her trips to the lavatory continued to occasion trial and error tests to isolate the faulty icon that had foxed the fabled blasting ray. The Obodovkans took every chance to mutter at her meanly; she recognized many curse words by now. One day when their overseer was checking progress against quotas, Musya complained:

"What is wrong with these women? Where is their hate from? Tell them I am a respectable married woman, a mother, with a husband in the Red Army, a military wife." She glanced at Sender who nodded smartly.

"Possibly a widow," he supplied.

Oksana shrugged. "They know all that. But it is because you come from Odessa."

At the sound of the city's name Musya's co-workers spat and hissed with wrinkled noses. They had to be the biggest anti-intellectuals on the planet, she remarked—and ungrateful: "Without us what culture would they have in Ukraine? This?" She raised the vyshyvanka in her hand. "This trim design is from America. We sold it in Odessa first, a long time ago."

"You talk so much," the slave owner said. "But of course no, they do not care about your culture. It was the bread." Here the Obodovkans all started a clamor to be heard. The overseer continued, "Yes, ten years ago, there was no bread, no food here, for a long time. None. This it was not possible, it was not permitted to discuss this here in the whole Ukrainian Soviet Socialist Republic. For a long time." Her voice stopped, her thoughts distant.

"Holodomor." The Stara brought a foot down on the carpet. "Holodomor!"

Oksana nodded. "Yes, yes, Holodomor. The murder famine, it happened here. Who knows how many Ukrainians starved to even count the millions—and whose fault—who knows? These." She gestured around, ending at the Stara. "She says it was the Odessa Jews."

"The Odessa Jews never starved Ukraine," Musya said.

Now Mrs Yelyuk got the others nodding with remarks of which Oksana delivered the gist. "She says it is true. When Ukraine starved, at the worst time, she says in Odessa they had bread trucks and every Odessa Jew received two fresh loaves per day by special order."

"That is a lie," Musya said. She stared at Oksana. "What bread trucks? What order? This is a crazy story. You must know that—you were a Party member, you worked in the government!"

"I was never told everything."

"There were no bread trucks," Musya told Mrs Yelyuk and the Stara in plain Ukrainian. She was disgusted. "It's some bobe-mayse they picked up somewhere. In the gutter," she told the boys. Oksana, fielding more commentary from the room, told Musya:

"They say it shows in you. Because you are fat."

"They say—what?" The truth was, her release from the ghetto clinic would mark a permanent change in her figure. From that day any weight she put on stayed somehow— she thickened. "But I am not fat," she said.

"They say you are," Oksana said. "The only fat Jew they know here."

Musya remembered Eidel's theories about the years in question. She said, "The truth is, I am small. Because I did not get enough to eat, because my family had little, I am small." She frowned as a Yelyuk rejoinder raised a laugh.

Oksana said, "She says your family was probably too lazy to go to the bread truck."

"Ha ha," Musya said.

They disliked her after that. Her mocking reputation for grand duchess airs had transferred with her from uniforms; now she was branded a sarcastic bitch as well. At the same time, the Ukrainians had been made easier about having Musya in their midst. They seemed to accept her presence more as a tolerable fact than as a provocation to be met with curses. They stopped interrupting their own conversations to cast outraged looks across the room at where she was sitting. Attempts to unleash their death ray on her ceased and the young girls went back to studying their mystical prayer books. They all hated Odessa Jews, this wouldn't change; she would experience not the least soften-ing of manner on this account; their hate was always active. But once they'd exposed its source to her, the atmosphere relaxed, they didn't need to show it all the time anymore.

They were Obodovkans, a few made homeless by fires and bombing raids, the rest displaced from their rooms in what must have been the nicer more convenient part of town by the fascist occupation and its officers. The girls had lived-in as housemaids although at least one was also a distant relation of the old dame she served. On the brink of Velykden their conversation was all of hairstyles to wear to the church. At some point there wasn't room enough before the wall glass so Oksana Babiak hurried upstairs to her locked bedroom and back for a hand mirror. Musya recognized the tortoiseshell perfectly. So did Sender, who gave a cry and then said in careful Russian:

"Musya, where did she get that?"

She told the overseer, "Your—our—that was his grandmother's, her hand mirror, he means. She died."

Sender said, "It belongs to us. Tell her."

"Tell him," Oksana said. "Tell him he is crazy."

The room was listening. Musya said, "It is an heirloom."

"A real one," Sender said. "A real one, tell her."

Oksana said, "Do not insult me Mister Zenderkaz. Mister Crazy. I bought this fair and square, I paid plenty. It is mine and my heirloom now."

"No!"

"We understand that," Musya tried to interpose.

Sender said, "We do not understand! We want it back."

Musya went to Yiddish. "We can't have it back. We sold it anyhow."

"You sold it!"

"Stop crying. But we only wonder this," she told Oksana. "Where did you buy it when it was not for sale?" To her knowledge (and the lasting resentment of the dependents left behind) this hand mirror had departed the ghetto with old Mrs Krutonog's lovesick successor and those two terrible brothers; all three shot dead, their bags and all their possessions had of course survived them. Like battle spoils: "You bought it from a scavenger?"

"I got a good deal," Oksana said, blinking. "From my friend. The colonel, you know." An uncomfortable silence was broken by Mrs Yelyuk snorting twice. The overseer had indignant glares for everyone. "This is what happens in a war. Tak?"

"Tak." Musya and a few others murmured their agreement. But Sender wept noisily—he was exhausted. Oksana's brows collapsed and twitched.

"Tell him I cannot bring his dead grandmother to life again for him. Tell him I am sorry."

"He knows."

"Then tell him to get back to work." He sat and only sobbed—so tired. They all were, Musya realized. To almost everyone's relief, the room's activity had ceased. But Oksana twitched. She didn't like talking but couldn't have quiet. "She died how, this grandmother?" she asked.

"She was murdered," Musya said. A flurry of interest enlivened the scene and even Mrs Yelyuk couldn't help but admit some knowledge of the Russian tongue. Much to the Stara's annoyance, she half-dislodged the lap rug sitting forward to ask with a lick of her lips:

"Stabbed?" Oksana translated.

Musya took a breath. "None of your business," she said. After that they all did their best to ignore her. For now the old dame by the stove made some philosophical remark. Oksana nodded her agreement:

"Yes, the Stara is saying, she points out to us, that the first person born in this world, he was murdered."

"There is no way to know that," Musya said. "Maybe he was eaten by an animal. Or maybe the first person born was a woman."

"Nay, Musya." Sender's Yiddish was gentle, a trace sad and a bit embarrassed for her, too. "They're right. It's the truth. The first was Abel. The first son of Adam."

She took this in. The scientific principles of Boris Kotz: how clear their dull old recitation rang in her mind for a moment—and how hollow! How confident her husband's claims at pedagogy; how he'd boasted of having instilled true scientific thinking in his sons; how emphatically he'd compared the accounts of the prophets to Arthurian legend over a dinner she remembered, they'd all agreed with him. All stories, he'd called the world's religions. Her poor husband's mental fatherhood—all hollow. This boy had kept his mother's faith.

All she could do was nod and tell him, "Yes. Of course. I forgot." The Stara's next remark Musya understood clearly enough without Oksana's helpful translation:

"You godless Odessans, she says." The overseer hung the hand mirror from a nail near the icons, they looked at it every day that followed.

The Ernste kept her work, about trouble. When the Ghetto Council's gendarmes next swooped down to break up the Kotz orphans' performance, the Bulbe Gate guards rushed to their defense and drove off the gendarmes with rifle butts, inflicting no serious hurt but not fooling around, either. The stage remained shared after that, but the Ernste's act headlined.

Calamity struck just before Passover, five minutes before the westbound bus was due. Commerce through the Bulbe Fence wires was at a fever pitch. Secure against gendarme harassment, everyone's favorite orphans were ready with their opening number when they heard a wondering, laughter-streaked commotion start outside. Directly across the road, someone had erected a box stage very like their own, only taller and far sturdier-looking. On it stood a boy soprano, about Hodeh's age, warming up his voice, singing scales. He didn't miss a note. He sounded, as everyone began saying immediately, angelic. Every exemption holder in the ghetto crowded as close as the barbed wire allowed to listen better. The orphan trio found themselves looking down at the backs of gendarmes and even a few ghetto councilors squeezed in among them. The singer outside wasn't alone, other children were on hand, other acts; there was some adult management; a real production, Hodeh said. Another boy, this one holding a violin, joined the singer on the stage, the pair identically shirtless in outgrown black suits loaded with bright patchwork—another stolen idea. A couple of townswomen ran up and completed the costuming: a rusty homburg with long brown wig curls sewn into the hatbands went on each one's shaven head.

Moments later the Kiev-bound bus pulled up. The prisoners with a blocked view groaned and parted ranks, moving right and left along the fence for better sightlines, dropping a few potatoes on the ground in their haste. The soldiers on duty walked over to watch alongside the bus station guards who seemed to be in charge. The boys opened with Tum Balalyka and swung their forgery ear-locks in tandem a lot. Other Yiddish numbers lifted from the ghetto repertoire filled out their program. The preempted orphans had not hesitated to spend the show collecting dropped potatoes in the satchel Hodeh guessed their new competition would leave empty otherwise; and indeed the bus pulled away without a single look being cast at them, much less a coin. When one of the Council's acts decided to launch into their own stolen version of Tum Balalyka, one guard turned and fired shots overhead. No one tried singing again.

Three hours later the same set-up from town was back for the eastbound show. "Come out and hear the new zhidy!" the driver clamored at his passengers. By some accounts (not Hodeh's) the angel-voiced singer's rendition of Papirosn made stones weep. In the ghetto, the Bulbe Fence stage stood permanently mute: a shande, no question. But for now all anyone could talk about was the boy phenomenon and whether he was Jewish or not. Was he one of their kidnapped children? One of the sold? The young violinist was deemed definitely Jewish but no one recognized him either.

To the Ernste that mystery was less than air. What mattered was her enterprise—finished, kaput. Opportunists, imitators, plagiarists: she'd seen their parasitic ilk before, time without number. She blamed the greed of the ghetto councilors who were busy blaming hers. She couldn't blame the poor townsfolk, things were tough all over. "Welcome," she said, "to the world of Delusion," a world destined to pass, only not on this Earth, probably. She put her orphan act on vocal rest. Musya found this development encouraging. Maybe Hodeh and Anton could go to school instead; but it was the school holidays, they told her.

Passover came and went, then Velykden. Musya was back in the workroom alone, finishing uniform shirts, when Cezar the rapist attacked her again. Another soundless approach, another bestial rush: his repentance time was over, she guessed. She tried to scream but coughed, she tried to fight him off but found herself too weak. He used her clumsily, painfully, not really penetrating, struck her a blow on the side with his arm and left looking shamefaced.

It was a wet spring. At quitting hour in the terrible mud she could barely walk a short way, even using Sender Kotz as a human crutch wasn't enough. All her little strength had turned to pain. They'd never make it back to the ghetto—which meant they risked being shot just as roadside stragglers almost always were shot, mercilessly. It made more sense to return and seek shelter at Babiak's, however unwelcome they'd be.

But the rapist was behind them. In the long twilight he looked like a scorch mark lurking there. Musya strained her eyes to make him out and everything went dim. A sharp voice, Sender's, close to her ear, roused her:

"No! Stay back!" They were in the road, in the mud, no change. "No, Cezar, stay away—you always hurt her! Stop!"

The rapist approached to within arm's length and grunted at them. Musya's eyes fell to his holstered sidearm. She guessed he'd shoot them both dead in the road now, just a man doing his job. After all her trials, all her pacifist precautions, her rapist would be the last living sight of her life, after all. She wondered why she'd even bothered. "Please don't hurt my boy," she tried to say and moaned instead. His shouts came from a distance but Sender hadn't run away, he wouldn't, he held her tight and tried to shield her: he was foolish, she thought. The rapist tore him off and tossed him aside into some waterlogged weeds. Then he took Musya by the waist, lifted her over his shoulder like a duffle bag and started down the road. Back on his feet but barely able to keep up, Sender caught one of her dangling hands and clutched it, he didn't let go. Her cheek bumped against the rapist's rabbit fur coat full of stench. She watched the black wet-breathed fields pass upside down, the crescent moon become its own flailing reflection in a ditch. Her senses swirled and ebbed.

Hands woke her, many fingers: she was back at the ghetto gates among the returning forced laborers—formerly a small sea, now a simple throng collected each night by delay. "Put that woman down, you animal!" she heard. They were mobbing the rapist and he was panic-sweating, trying to drop her. Then he was gone and other arms were around her, holding her up on her feet, strange little arms, each like a marionette's inside its costume. "It's the Kotz orphans' mother," she heard. "The nafka, the funny one." Their murmurs disapproved yet people seemed friendly. They were helping her to walk. Sender Kotz should go fetch Doctor Zev, she tried to say. A blankness swept across her mind before she woke again, walking. The gate was still ahead. As a topic of conversation her life appeared to have passed. All talk now was of life inside, where the Ghetto Council had announced a grand reopening of the ritual baths in time for Pesach and then nothing had happened. The baths stood vacant, their displaced tenants proving bad neighbors to those who'd been forced to take them in. Then overnight the Council claimed the women's bath for offices and the men's side for meeting space: a major misstep. The talk now was of last straws. Aggravations. People said the place was so badly run. Dilapidated house fronts peeled, roofs were sagging. Why didn't the Council do this, why didn't it do that? Why didn't it fix or improve anything? Their captors' malice was evident—too evident. So what was the point? They were suffering enough without a nuisance bureaucracy—weren't they? How hard could it be to make a few simple improvements? The way things got done around here had these hallmarks: malice, waste, delay, incompetence. Wasn't it true? It was, Musya thought, it was all true. Her fellow prisoners in complaint: with a feeling of having escaped into a state of perfect safety, she relaxed and let them sweep her along.

She'd contracted pneumonia. This time of course there was no question of her being admitted to the ghetto clinic, such a mistake wouldn't happen again, lightning wouldn't strike twice. She lay in their cubicle. The chapers came once or twice and then left her alone. Her limbs were leaden. She couldn't lift her head, small hands raised her head from the tiger skin bolster and brought cups to her lips, cups of water, cups of potato soup, cups of milk—she thought she'd dreamt this. She craved salt but couldn't say so, from weakness she couldn't say a word for days. At times, reliving her childbed recovery, she waited impatiently for her mother-in-law to come open a secret tin and feed her something capered pickled or smoked, tears leaked from her eyes with the craving. She pictured seas boiling with sprats and the fishermen scooping them up for the cannery; beds of oil in the cans, silk-slippery, gleaming. She craved oil, she cried: Russvelt should come put the can to her thread-clogged chest for once, if he weren't so lazy. A simple rag wipe and a drop or two of oil would do the trick, her breath would run smooth as polished chrome. She lay wheezing and thought she was shouting for help; she moaned at the appearance of the gray looming shapes, tall as grave markers, that came instead to criticize and smother the life from her by turns. Who were her persecutors? Half-familiar names spilled down their fronts in shifting unreadable script: she lay puzzling and fell into unconsciousness. Sometimes in the dead of night she woke up sealed inside a coffin full of other bodies. The coffin rolled, lifted and lulled on oceanic swells, bound for the mummy caves of Odessa. There'd be more room for everyone, it would be such a relief, when they were nothing but dust and winding sheets, wrappings and bones. She craved dissolution.

Little by little her surroundings grew clearer and more consistently identifiable. In the Jewish ghetto of Obodovka, supine and strengthless, she woke and closed her eyes again, pursuing sleep as she'd once chased a streetcar just leaving without her. Small hands kept raising her head. She looked into a pair of eyes, bright, black, impersonally frowning: Hodeh's eyes returned to the cup at her lips. She choked a little, trying to say thanks.

"Don't die," Hodeh said.

Musya let her eyelids dip to say she wouldn't. It really was milk, thick and warm from the animal. "You're so good," she managed to whisper. "So good to me."

Hodeh explained, "They won't let us keep the room without you."

These days when the morning work bell drilled her dreams to smithereens she turned on her side, switched tracks and dreamed awake. A late spring or midsummer fête would be next for the ghetto, she'd decided; she pictured lights strung outdoors, trestle tables, a punch bowl gaudy with slices of fruit. She'd dance barefoot, she'd decided. On stage, an orchestra, her children featured, the Ernste wielding the baton; at the microphone, Doctor Zev. His soft beard gleamed in the footlights as he crooned a serenade. Down among the dancers, untidy brown curls slicked for the occasion, the Motorbiker would partner Musya from foxtrot to mazurka to rest; when before they could catch their breath the floor would be thronged for a riotous Romanian folk dance full of twirling skirts and scarves. Laughter would ring against the starry sky—life would be celebrated.

The sudden fall of a male hand heavy with rings onto Musya's shoulder would almost stop her breath. It was the general's. All this time, of course, she'd been forgetting him, or at least not remembering him enough. His steamy eyes, his trembling offers of perfumed handkerchiefs, his gifts of fruit and hard candies, all this she'd taken for granted, almost ignored, like a fool. The amorous old Romanian had it in his power to change everything, every one of their fates lay in his sensitive hands. He loved her, after all. He requested the next dance—the waltz—and she found herself spinning. An elegant flat full of white lilies in vases in Bucharest: why not?

But quite suddenly Cezar the rapist was there, right in their midst, cap in hand. The music stopped dead. Where had he come from? Where did such men come from? She couldn't keep a circle from clearing around him.

Then he'd raise his stinking arms and take the first deliberate steps of an ancient dance. She pictured the rapist with a bottle balanced on top of his head, squatting, kicking. A few people began to clap in time as the rapist danced before them. Where had he found a bottle in the Obodovka ghetto? What was he doing at her party? Would no one expel him—would no one actually kill him? There was only more clapping. Even the general, even her lovers, even her children, everyone clapped in time, everyone clapped for him. Barefoot, ignored, disgusted, she turned and fled the scene she'd conjured. Through the darkness beyond the dance, through an unattended gate, she ran towards the river she pictured in moonlight. Again and again she escaped to the water's edge. Sometimes the Motorbiker stopped her there in time and sometimes not.

Musya's amazing survival inspired the usual talk of miracles before the subject was exhausted and people left her alone again. Her recuperation was painfully slow, she had set-backs. For exercise she resumed her former pregnancy circuit, around the cubicle and up and down the old fruit canning shed corridor. She felt almost weightless but Eidel said she was no slimmer. Accompanying her steps, her skirt in his fist, talkative and intermittently almost coherent, went Samuel Nemo. Her baby walked now.

"We trained him," Anton had told her proudly. "He runs, too, but he falls."

"I could train him," she said. She felt excluded and vaguely ashamed. "To run—I'll teach him to run. When I'm better." He told her no, he and Hodeh would do it themselves.

Six days a week Sender Kotz reported to Babiak's where the uniform shirt concession had fallen through completely. Either the Romanian army had found other ways to dress its soldiers, or they were on their own these days. Likewise lifeless was the vyshyvanky market. But he'd seen priests from the local church pay several business calls, a big order for new cassocks might be in the offing. Meanwhile skilled needlework was always in demand. Fashion didn't stop advancing just because the shops were empty. Spring 1943 had arrived with new collections just the same, he said. As for the other children, still in their landlady's care and employ, they came and went from the cubicle all day long, often dirt-stained from helping the Ernste plant and tend the kitchen garden. Further down the yard the grasspea was in flower again, they reported.

The children also had a secret. They wouldn't tell it, they wanted Musya to hear for herself direct from the source. When they judged her strong enough, she was bundled in shawls and led by the hands into the loud sunshine. She winced and protested as they pulled her further into chilly mid-morning air that reeked of death, sickness, outhouses, garbage. The children tugged at her excitedly. Samuel Nemo scampered ahead down the path, then pulled up short and landed on his bottom with a bump and squall: Hodeh had him by a string lead tied around his waist. An invalid lounging by the doorstep laughed and said they'd need a chain for their bear cub soon. "He's not a bear, he's a cat," Musya heard herself answer. The sky was astoundingly large, any second her feather-light head would be swept up and lost in it. She looked down at the faraway ground, then back down the path to the road where a little girl Musya hadn't seen before was waiting, crop-curled and extremely grimy. Through several layers of ragged clothes her bare skin showed in streaks. She had a pale mouth lined with brown chancre sores.

"Sholem-aleykhem," said Musya.

"Aleykhem-sholem," said the stranger.

"This is Pearl," Hodeh said. "She lives in the old kitchen. Her family are rat-eaters."

Anton enthused, "They cook them on sticks!" Pearl acknowledged these facts with a nod.

Musya asked whether this was the secret. She wanted to go back to bed. But the secret was elsewhere, apparently, a walk's distance further. Pearl had a contact on the outside, they said, who'd told her the secret. So Musya fell into step behind the children while Samuel Nemo strained at his lead in front.

Spring had peaked. In the Obodovka ghetto, this meant mud, ankle-deep in spots. It meant stink and fly swarms and damp trash fires coughing up cold blue smoke. It meant green on green vistas glimpsed from a gray-colored place where so many branches stripped naked last year had failed to put forth leaves: they knew better this time, Musya supposed. Crows rattled among refuse piles, fearless of the sparse humanity that poked alongside after tidbits. Rejected even by the chapers, these were people driven from their own deathbeds by hunger pangs and delirious fevers. Yet more than one recognized the orphan children, greeting them with warm affection. The big blades of their terrible smiles cut Musya adrift. Frail, alien, ghostly, come from a different existence where health returned, where fruit trees flowered, she didn't belong here.

Even accounting for the work gangs' absence, the ghetto presented a depopulated look. Following Papa's old koorvah road they came to the barns, once teeming and stacked with prisoners, now half-collapsed, the other half gone for firewood. A few occupants remained, for Musya spotted horse blankets hung in place of walls, a line of child's laundry, a curl of smoke from a makeshift stove pipe. Set back from the road nearby was a dirt mound fantastically verdant with vines, stalks, weeds, wildflowers; like its several counterparts around the ghetto, the mound marked the site of a mass burial and its crops were avoided at this time. Further on where the koorvah tent had stood they found nothing, no one. Musya's heavy feet bore her mechanically past.

"Did Roza die?" she said.

No, Roza lived in a room now, at Tauber's in fact, the children told her. They knew everything about the koorvah's enlistment as a typhus nurse at the ghetto clinic when epidemic typhus had gotten out of hand again that winter; she'd survived it the first time and was immune. Musya hadn't known. Pretty Roza, pretty experienced Roza in white at work in the clinic by lamplight: envy surged through her heart and left it scoured raw with failure. She'd done nothing with her own life. Typically she'd had no chance to—she was always being sent far away from every opportunity to live.

The little party halted further on, at the edge of the ghetto. Fir trees and weeds almost obscured a section of looped-wire fence. Pearl gave a sharp two-fingered whistle call, then another. Some branches moved and another little girl appeared outside the barrier, fairly pretty, not shoeless. She wore a gray coverall and led a blonde three year-old, Musya guessed, by the hand. He was dressed in a sailor suit, the smaller in a set of two, considerably bleached, stained, and faded since the mother had sewn it by hand for her younger grandson.

"Is this the secret?" she asked again. That heartbreak encircled them was no secret, she thought. But again they said to wait, listen:

"Tell her, Waslyna."

Pearl prompted the girl, who took a long, suspicious survey of Musya's person and asked, "Are you even married?"

"Yes," she said. "You speak Yiddish?"

Pearl supplied, "She's from here with us. She got sold. Now she's a nanny. She's my friend, her name is Waslyna now. She's eleven already." Musya nodded, her eyes snared on Pearl's scabby lips, on her tongue, her gray-green teeth; she kept expecting to spot rat hairs or whiskers stuck there.

"What's the secret?" she asked.

The answer came in pieces. While they were talking Samuel Nemo reached and poked a finger on barbed wire, then the Obodovkan boy cut himself the same way only worse, no doubt for the attention. Blood drops added to the stains on the white blouse and his young nanny had to stop and scold him, at which his wails rose in volume and needed to be hushed—guards patrolled here sometimes, even these days, Hodeh warned.

She tugged at Musya's arm. The secret was told, it hung there. "Is it true?"

"I don't think so." Musya shook her head. "I don't see how it could be."

"But it is," the girl called Waslyna now insisted. "It has to be if the priest said it."

"Maybe he said." She could only shrug. "Who knows what priests say?"

Waslyna repeated, "It's for sins, he said, for killing the Krystos. That's why you're in there. Because the zhidy sinned."

"Don't say that!" Musya scolded her. "We're Jews—say Jews."

The girl said, "Jews, then. You're still being punished. You sinned. But you can repent and get baptized like me. You can change."

"This man doesn't know me, he doesn't know my family—what, my children sinned? Who is this priest?"

Waslyna said, "He's holy. Jews caused the war, too."

But Pearl, interrupting, said it was very simple. "Forget the war. They put us here because we're Jews. So if we stop being Jews they'll let us leave—we just need to get to this priest."

"You'll need the priest for water baptism," Waslyna explained. "Also he might make you apologize."

"When can we leave?" Anton wanted to know. "I think it's true—I'm ready."

So was Hodeh, who agreed, no doubt impatient to get home to her real Pretzel. "If it's true, let's just get baptized and get out of here."

"But I think." Musya faltered. Wondering what to say felt like staring into an impenetrable mist. What was going on in the rest of the world? With the war, even? She had no idea. Soon it would be two years since she'd seen a newspaper. Beyond gossip, speculations, the few random remarks Oksana Babiak dropped, she hadn't heard a news report. And even if she'd been handed a crystal radio set and the latest Izvestiya, what would she have learned, she wondered? One thing she'd never seen in the Jewish ghetto of Obodovka was a journalist. So what else was the world outside missing? She said, "Jews are locked up all over—here in Ukraine, in Poland, maybe all over the Soviet Union. It can't be that simple, that we could leave and go home if we all got baptized."

"Not all," Hodeh corrected her. "Not all Jews."

"That's why it's secret," said Pearl.

Musya said she needed to rest a minute and she took a seat on a protruding tree root in the shade. While near the ground the air was still, the topmost fir boughs were wrestling in a steady breeze. The air was so much fresher here at the limits of the ghetto. Pale blue, immense, the sky poured down cleanliness, sweet smells, space. The children waited. They couldn't get to the answers they sought, as if certainty were on a high shelf they needed her reach, her adult's stature. Their expectant eyes were on her as she huddled on the root. She felt frail, unprepared and outnumbered. Only the youngest ones didn't care and didn't doubt her. His hurt forgotten, Samuel Nemo sat on the ground poking a stick into a patch of sand; while the boy in the sailor suit, sniffling and envious, whimpered for sand and a stick of his own. Musya pictured her mother's mouth, the ever-present row of straight pins clamped between the scowling lips as she'd fitted poor Anton for that suit; he'd stood on the work table, wincing and yelping each time a pin scratched him. *Poor Jews*, she thought suddenly. How they suffered! Sold, stolen and robbed, starved and pricked, exiled from love, their mouths full of pins and rat bones—this poor people of hers. She said to Anton, "You remember that suit? It belonged to you."

He said, "No, mine was real."

In a few more days Musya was officially well. Her strength wasn't much but she did sitting work, the Ernste reminded her, and the Kotz family needed the income if they planned to eat. Leaning on Sender's shoulder at points along the way, she went back to Babiak's. He was delighted to have company again. Lined with brambles, its chalk surface invaded by long grass, the whole route looked like a major breeding ground for snakes in Sender's view. She wished she could have disagreed with him. But here and there amidst the neglect Obodovka was farming again. Strange to see, the sunflower field was under cultivation, sprouting crooked leafy rows that swerved around the weed-sunk wreckage of her nightmares. All the field hands she spotted were women. None returned the greetings Sender insisted on calling out. They walked with rakes balanced like rifles on their shoulders. Some spat.

The eight year-old didn't think much of the baptism scheme. Even if it worked, he said, once released they'd still be left with the problem of earning parnosseh—their living, that is. It was only as Jews that they earned their pittance now, he reasoned.

"When we're not Jews then You-Know-Who will have to pay us more and she won't, she'll only hire other Jews for cheap and we'll be stuck with nothing."

Even so, he agreed she ought to make inquiries. The other children would never be satisfied until they had an answer, Musya knew. Earlier that week she'd discovered them at daven in the vacant cubicle next door; Pearl, too. *"Khrystos, Khrystos, Khrystos!"* On their knees, chanting and rocking: "Practice," they'd called it.

Acting on a different plan, her own plan, she'd armed herself with the sharp scissors, she had them in a hidden pocket at her hip in case of rapists. She planned to kill the next one—especially Cezar. She watched for him on their walk but he didn't appear. The expectant sunlight glittered and the shady spots throbbed. Banks of blue honeysuckle rained perfume onto the road's deep dip where a host of black and white butterflies ignored the footsteps squishing past to feed on, entrancedly, from the slick, track-printed verges of its perennial mud-puddle. Up the slope to Babiak's stone border Musya labored before she had to stop. The place looked worse than she remembered, smaller, more run-down and rickety, cold and confining, rust-capped, basically poverty-stricken. Her spirits plummeted. No wonder working here had almost killed her—yet here she was again, giving her murderers another chance. What a mistake:

"I should have run away," she sighed, thinking of the moonlit river.

"Where to?" Sender said. "Where would we go?"

She couldn't answer, couldn't admit that her pictured flight had been a solitary one.

Here too there'd been efforts at planting, along the side of the house were young herbs and things, although the big garden had returned practically to nature, it was a buzzing thicket. The wild strawberry patch had spread, Musya was glad to discover, but the crop needed ripening. Not much was left on the side porch. Most of the old bedding had been sent for rags and what remained stacked there, its tags freshly inked, would be staying—another market whose bottom had dropped out was bedclothes, apparently. Continuing into the house they found the workroom empty, the sewing machines under dust covers and not a uniform shirt in sight. Instead the folding table was stacked with bolts of black fabric, a thin wool giving off a musty smell. Of course there was no ventilation. They heard footsteps; Oksana Babiak entered and said, "Ah. You are alive." Her frown turned critical. "You do not look bad." Musya said thanks and covered her mouth for the duration of a deep, demonstrative cough. On her side, she thought the Obodovkan woman looked not only worn and old with her brown teeth and her big front sagging, but oddly clownish, an effect of the reddened splotches around her freshly plucked brows. Her cheeks were red, too, rouged with broken blood vessels.

Sender pointed at the table and told Musya, "The wool for the robes, I think."

A mirthless laugh bore stale wine fumes to them. "Yes it is here. But now they do not want so many. Or they want, sure, but not to pay." Oksana sounded glum and put out. She walked over, tipped one of the bolts on its end and let it drop; dust made clouds and the mildew smell sharpened. "Six dozen down to one dozen—at most, they say. At most. These cheap priests, all they talk about is the poor, love the poor, the poor little poor. But what about my investment? When I am poor what will they do? Preach about me?"

Did she want pity? Musya didn't know what to say. She tried, "I am sorry. But I can begin sewing now. Is there a sample? A pattern?"

"I do not need you for this work, I have the Yelyuk, she has done it before, many years," Oksana said. "I do not need a house full of women who do nothing but sew. And boys," she added.

"I am sorry," Musya said again. Her blood ran cold all at once and left her trembling. Would she finally be sent to work at the laundry now? Certain death—but she couldn't die, she remembered. "Give me something else to do then please."

"What can you do? A fat sick girl with no breath—what? Tell me." The question floated there, dipping like a feather in an updraft. Then Oksana waved a hand. "Listen. I need a maid. I lost mine."

"Have you looked in the garden?"

The overseer's mouth snapped shut and twisted. Her head shook no. "This sneak? She ran—gone." The girl with the terror of Jews had decamped in the night, helping herself to the household petty cash along with some silver plate and an icon she'd been known to fancy—the objects irreplaceable as the maid herself was proving to be. Maids!

The war had drastically worsened an already dire shortage of these troublesome, flight-prone human necessities. Floors, beds, windows, night buckets neglected—an old farmhouse couldn't care for itself, Oksana said. During lulls such as this on the needlework front there was plenty to be done.

Musya sighed. Slavery with the addition of drudgery—it sounded bad. "Night buckets?"

"Of course." Oksana gestured around. "So many old tenants, too many stairs, what else?"

In truth, it sounded impossible. "Stairs?"

"For now, Musya," Sender interceded in his stubbornly indirect way, "for now you should ask maybe to work on tailoring with me. Until you are better."

Oksana snapped at them both, almost tearfully, "For now you should tell him—tell Zenderkaz he should go to his work."

"Tell her you are too sick!"

"Tell him—go!"

He'd already run from the room. Oksana went and lowered herself heavily into one of the chairs next to the cold stove. Being childless was sad for her, Musya realized.

She walked over and took the other chair. "I need to ask you a question," she said. "It is—someone told me. I want to know if it is the truth. Because I heard that it is possible, that Jews can leave the ghetto and go free, if they stop being Jewish." She watched Oksana turn and squint at her.

"Who went free? Who let them out?"

"No, I mean, I heard they could. We could. Go free. If we stop being Jews."

"How do you stop being Jews?"

Musya shrugged, her palms turned up. She pictured a little girl biting down on a charred rat's leg. "Baptism?"

Oksana laughed. "It would never work! A Jew is a Jew. You have Jewish blood."

"Yes I know, but—people convert. There are conversions."

Now the woman blew out air. She seemed more like her old self, more cheerful. "Back in your Odessa maybe. But here, now, no. You cannot change your blood," she explained.

Stubborness drove Musya to persist. "But what if they are children—say my children. What if I took them to the church here, to the priests? They like the poor, they love the poor you say. So these poor children, I could say—please to take them, give them some baptism, give them a room, a bed, let them eat, let them wash themselves. Let them live!"

"Listen," Oksana interrupted. "Priests, these priests, you do not want your children washing anything or in a bed anyplace near. We Soviets had plenty good reasons why we closed them down before, believe me. Now they are back, they are no different. Same cloth, worse smell." She frowned at the stacks on the folding counter. Her voice grew thick. "Forget priests—forget baptism—forget Jewish. Better you should accept, work hard, keep out of trouble, wait for what happens. Forget freedom. Free is not so great when life is bad everywhere. Come." She watched Musya cry for another moment. "You will see where we keep the mops and brooms."

<h1 style="text-align:center">(16)</h1>

The summer sun rode blue heavens in glory. The hills along the river rolled like limbs luxuriating, sated, blissful. Cool thick woods inhaled and sighed while ten million leaves, their black veins sunk in green translucence, trembled. A choral symphony of birdsong and muted gunfire was playing. A young woman walked the forest paths alone. Coins of sunlight fell and flashed on her bright auburn hair. She plucked speckled wildflowers to drop when they faded. Snatches of songs from her childhood escaped her in undertones. From a city of legend whose great harbor teemed with foreign ships she'd been swept inland; like some exotic cargo gone astray she trailed perfumes of strangeness. She was misunderstood. She'd been victimized. She glowed like beeswax in her innocence.

Across countryside as fertile as storied, galloping hooves churned. The horse was enormous and black; its rider, descended from princes whose derelict palace was near. He mourned his ruined patrimony and rode all day long to forget, shunning humankind. His only pleasure was bitter, for he found it in the beauty robbed from him—the landscape's sun-warmed prospects were all he cared for. In consequence he was called a madman.

Her mind had wandered. There wasn't time to leave the forest path and hide behind a tree, no time at all to run away before the pounding hoofbeats were upon her. The great shrilling black beast reared up. She gave a cry, fell to one knee. The rider made a calming noise and reined his mount sideways. The young woman crouched there saw one long, tightly trousered leg whole. The man wore a white shirt open at the collar—open quite far down his chest, actually. His head disappeared in the treetops. His accent was Polish, his voice tense with a pronounced tremble despite his efforts at control; she'd startled him just as badly as he'd frightened her, she realized. But maybe it was more. The dark pool of his face stared, wide ice-blue eyes fixed on her shapely mouth.

This was Sobansky.

One morning it had happened that while Musya was scrubbing the hallway floor at Babiak's, she heard footsteps pounding down the stairs from the bedrooms above. A man slung with ammunition belts and carryall straps appeared. She recognized the partisan who'd raped her in the dining room, months ago. Dropping some bags onto the wet floorboards, his features as before a darkish blur, he advanced on her again. She rose to her knees, slipped a hand into her skirt and grasped the sharp scissors hidden there: a short upward thrust to start, she was thinking. Her own heartbeat deafened her. All at once a third figure materialized like one of the angry djinn. Between tugs at his slovenly costume, Oksana Babiak scolded the rapist and hissed at the mud streaks his boots were leaving. He shouted at her for silence and she shouted at him to be quiet himself and go. To Musya, who watched from her knees, she explained, "My husband does not use his head." Then a moment passed, while the overseer's raw eyes moved back and forth between the two. The rapist breathed loudly.

"My clean floor!" Musya wailed. "My clean floor!" She hurled the scrubbing brush against his legs and knelt there, hiding her face until the couple had gone.

Although Babiak's runaway maid had performed frequent errands in the neighborhood, her replacement was never sent out likewise until later that morning—down the road to Huba's and back to collect on an old bill, then out again with cash to buy loaf sugar. Along with a corner snapped off and tied in a rag knot, Musya pocketed a small coin on both trips and spent most of an hour seated under a tree, at exquisite leisure, sucking a hard peppermint candy ball she'd swiped from the shop. Jews who worked at the laundry plodded by, bent under cart shafts, they didn't see her there. As for the overseer, she wouldn't meet this slave-maid's eyes for a long time.

So began Musya's errand-running labors. Her compunction nil, she stole money, food, piece goods, time—especially time. Oksana would mutter, nothing more, when she'd return late and light-handed almost at quitting hour. The lengthening afternoons invited exploration; the neighborhood couldn't hold her. When anyone warned of danger she agreed, Obodovka was dangerous, she knew. Occupying troops on patrol, the partisans' forays, occasional gunfire exchanges, still-unexploded live ordnance and mines littering the land were all constant dangers. And Cezar the rapist hadn't gone anywhere. He found ways to make himself visible although he kept his distance now, as if he sensed the danger she and her scissor points posed in their turn to him—her threat perhaps the meanest tendril of the danger that had choked the planet's surface like a crawling vine until every life was a shoot of it, just waiting to leaf and flower into murderous deeds. Avoiding the town unless sent on an errand there, Musya sought out lonely spots, for the only safety was in solitude. She began to haunt the alder groves above the riverbanks. A pretty waterfall drew her until the day she found a campfire smoldering near its base; she never returned. Another roundabout walk led her to an old Jewish cemetery in the woods, a low gray tumble of modest headstones engraved in Yiddish and Hebrew characters. She looked for Krutonogs but couldn't find one. On her next attempt she couldn't find the cemetery either, she'd forgotten how the path went.

To escape one noonday's heat she ventured deeper than before into another wood where this time a fragrance reached her. Roses, not bottled, growing. She followed the scent until countless splashes of red and white appeared through thinning trees. A great abandoned rose garden had married a wild forward forest and become a runaway, blowsy, bug-bitten bed of perfume and incongruous color. Bordered by grape vines and wisteria, the whole place resounded with birdsong; sneezing once or twice, Musya could barely hear herself. On the ground she spied a toy-sized spoked metal wheel all rusted and picked it up to carry. Baila's historian Mr Asch had spoken of a palace with gardens hereabouts and indeed some lichened rocks, on further inspection, proved to be a faun pair eroded by rain. Curious now to see the palace she pushed on, skirting some final roses and thorns, but soon found her way barred by a massive box hedge, its branches filmy with spider nest, which lost itself at either end in thicket tangles. Unwilling to retreat, she found a gap to crawl through.

The garden beyond was equally forgotten. A thick almost unbroken dry carpet of dead vegetation tossed where mice and other creatures skittered through it. Here and there fresh verdure climbed to flower against some crumbling ornamental masonry. Past gigantic toppled urns and long-dry fountain basins choked with generations of decay, she followed the ghost of a footpath to a padlocked gate in the barred iron fence that enclosed the present palace grounds. Just inside lay yet another garden, this one narrow, modest, pebble-paved, not long neglected. A few pot geraniums weren't even dead. Through the bars Musya had her first sight of the palace. Topping a line of yew trees along a disused tennis court, a tall stone watchtower lifted straight from an old fairytale rose complete with square-toothed parapet.

Enchanted at first, then drawn on by resemblances and recognitions, moved by nostalgia for Odessa, she started following the fence to catch more views of the golden-brown palace. More urns, missing their tumbled companions along a marble roofline lumpy with blackened moss; green water stain garlands draping cornices, columns, decorative portholes; big stone-framed windows that gaped or stood dusty and shuttered. In the murk collected underneath the major portico she spotted something gleaming—it was bicycles, twenty or so. Then a gate, chained shut, surmounted by cast-iron scroll-work. On an old plaque set into the gatepost she could make out the European name and date below: Sobansky. 1800.

Musya wondered at these sights for a long time. No one else was about. Insect choruses were screeching as the heat poured down. She thirsted but turned back. She was dirty and smelled bad, her tattered skirt was covered in seeds from the wild paths, her blouse and Mogen Dovid both dirt-stained. She didn't want to be seen in this condition.

Sobansky was indifferent to clothes. All the same he dressed beautifully. His was the simple elegance of stainless breeding. Sometimes he wore a monocle. He'd been a writer of essays, a chemist, a soldier, a student in Paris, a spy, decorated profusely, unjustly demoted, wounded and tortured. He had scars, many; sometimes they were even disfiguring but she didn't care, she'd tell him so with perfect truth.

She was adding stitches to her quilt one evening when Sender Kotz came in from the wash house with his arms full of wet clothes. He announced, "That man Drobitz is here."

Her thoughts had been happy. Now this—why? Musya grimaced and temporized: "Who?"

"The man with Mrs Drobitz. The man who ran away."

Impossible, she said. Such a person, such a nonentity—when so few survived, how could someone like that have managed it? Sender had to be mistaken, she told him. "It can't be."

"It is." He gave her a stubborn look. "It's the same man."

He was right. Mrs Drobitz's deserter was clearly recognizable when Musya passed him a day or two later coming back from the wash house. He was in conversation with some other men, a couple of them ghetto councilors, whose markedly respectful manner she chalked up to the superior condition of his shirt and shoes—a different, better pair, as she recalled, than the one he'd run away in. Seeing him again made her feel cynical, angry, unwell. She glared at him and their eyes met; he was watchful and he'd spotted her. With a blush she hurried past, back to her cubicle where Sender sat reading to the other children from the adventures of the American river town boy, Tom Sawyer. She interrupted to apologize for doubting him.

He lowered the book and asked, "What now? What should we do?'"

"Nothing," she said. They were powerless to change what had happened. To protest his survival would do no good, it wouldn't even make sense. They might as well have been back in the oxcart, watching the man run free. Samuel Nemo scrambled into her lap when she sat down; she held him and sighed. "We can't do a thing."

"But he's bad. We should tell someone."

"Just ignore him. Pretend he isn't here."

Anton shouted. "Keep reading!"

"May I please," she asked him, "have a conversation?"

He said, "No. You see Sender all day—have it then. Read," he told his brother again.

This wasn't out of the ordinary. Since her failure to secure their release through baptism Musya's popularity with her younger children and their friends had been stuck at a low ebb. She'd tried to cajole and charm them back to friendliness but it was the satchel all over again, they'd cast her as the villain, the betrayer. Sometimes they gave her the silent treatment. Sometimes they'd acquired hard candies and sucked them in front of her, not offering any—although Samuel Nemo couldn't help it, he'd always share a sticky taste with his mother. Him they forgave. Little Pearl still hung around and scowled at her like the rest. They wouldn't tell what they did with themselves in the daytime; she knew they hadn't been to school since Eidel still complained about their chronic truancy whenever Musya crossed the teacher's path. Which wasn't often: she saw very little, in truth almost nothing of her old friends these days. New friends she had none. Her solitude spread like oil on a pool.

One late afternoon she was surprised to see the children at the entrance gate, the baby dressed in their sailor blouse running to greet her. He. Happiness surprised her as he grabbed her legs and laughed. The other two were unsmiling, upset. Anton said, "Pearl is gone."

"Oh." Musya raised a hand to her hair which needed a wash and a good brushing. Weary from her day's labors and rambles, she'd have wished for a different conversation.

She added, "I'm sorry. Was it something she ate?" Death was sadly common here and this one came as no surprise.

To her shock they looked at her with loathing. Her heart felt wounded, pierced by icicles. "No," said Hodeh at last. "She's not dead. She left."

"You mean she ran away? Her family did?" This, too, was extremely common.

Wrong again, it seemed: the family hadn't run. A truck had come and driven off again with several families piled in back. There'd been tears but also smiles and cheering—an upsetting mystery.

Horrified, without listening to another word, Musya led the way at once to the tiled kitchen. Terrible memories trailed her steps, her thoughts. She entered crying out: "This is it, then—yes? They've begun to exterminate us! They're starting to choose!"

The Ernste sipped tea. "Calm down. Less drama," she commanded. "They've only picked some people to send east. To work. The Germans need workers right now, they have problems recruiting. This has nothing to do with me, by the way."

"But they were cheering," Anton said. "Who cheers work?"

"They shouldn't?" the Ernste replied. "When we should all be so lucky? Because once this group will finish some work, then it's home to Bukhovina, that's the deal. It's good for them."

But here a dark, contradictory look shot up at Musya through the wiry brows. A glance around the tiled room showed half a dozen minions in concurrence, nodding grimly: she hadn't been far from the truth. East or west, nothing good would come to Jews from a German summons in Transnistria. *Poor Pearl*, she thought. What a short bad life.

The children remained cheerfully oblivious. Sender was already saying their family ought to volunteer for the next transport. Three enthusiastic votes followed his; for "Yo! Yo!" Samuel Nemo was crowing. Of course they wanted a change of scene. After more than a year and a half—her baby's whole life—in the Jewish ghetto of Obodovka, how could travel not appeal? Musya understood but had to tell them no, which did nothing to increase her popularity. She exited alone.

Not far past the kitchen threshold a pair of men whose trousers were obscenely tattered stood slurping a bitter-smelling soup from cans. Forced to squeeze past, Musya kept her eyes lowered and deafened herself to any sniggering, an intruder in her own hallway. This foul indoor gloom with its filth-blackened surfaces was such men's rightful territory. They, as the fatally unpresentable, shared it with the dying, the bedridden, and those who mourned. Someone was always mourning somewhere at Krutonog's. Tonight's lamentations which sounded from every quarter seemed to increase the dampness of the old inn's walls; Musya hated this warm damp closeness that turned summer's lingeringly day-lit nights into torments. She might have voted for the east as well, or added her tears to the general burden—if the many compensations in her life hadn't kept her too busy to mind. She had only to take up her quilting again to lose herself in richly colored patches.

She'd found a new ribbon somewhere, blue silk, for his monocle. He changed it out immediately, said he'd keep this one always; she took the old to treasure. Occasionally for fun she'd slip the monocle into her own socket and squint into a round of dazzling green and gold distortion while he laughed at the faces she made. There was also a pair of dark glasses tied to the recurrence of an old eye injury—on those days she'd lead Sobansky by the hand to one of their favorite shady retreats, she'd be carrying a picnic basket in her other hand. He'd speak of his privileged boyhood, Ukraine's loneliest. Thwarted of human harbor, his love had gone into his pets, his books, his toys—one favorite toy especially, his painted train car. When one of its wheels fell off and got lost his childish heart had broken. And this was the wheel she'd found in his family's old garden, none other: "You were destined to," he'd marvel. He called it their talisman. She'd laugh and kiss him, from her fingertips she'd feed him another smoked oyster. They traded poems from memory. She loved to lie with her ear against his chest and listen to the rumbling music of his foreign stanzas.

Disappointingly, to ignore the man she knew as Drobitz and pretend he wasn't there proved impossible. He didn't want to be ignored. It was a rest day and Musya wanted to rest after standing in line at the well. Instead she heard herself hailed in the road outside Krutonog's:

"Hey, you with all the children—girlie!" The ghetto councilor son of the Ernste motioned at her to approach. At his right hand the man who'd changed hardly at all since his flight from the oxcart stood slouching. Same thick lopsided smear of a mouth, same small puffy eyelids leaking distrust; he'd kept a thin beard and expanded his bald spot. He was a fairly short man and did himself no favors through lazy posture, as Musya's mother would have put it. If he recognized the red tin pitcher she carried, he didn't show any sign. The councilor said to her, "This is my trusted acquaintance, Mister Fein. A landsman of yours. He's asked of me that he could meet you. Treat him with respect."

She looked at the man. "Your name is Fein?" He nodded. Was he lying? Anything he claimed would resemble a lie to her, she realized.

"He comes to us from the Golta Ghetto," the councilor said. "Where it's better."

"Is it?"

She was only being polite but Drobitz-Fein seized on the opening to expound in a practiced, treble-pitched voice. He appeared to have established himself as some sort of expert on Transnistria's labor camps and ghettos. The authorities were always moving Jews from place to place, adjusting their numbers; by now he'd been all over the territory; through some mix-up he'd even passed through one of the Roma camps, the memory made him shudder. His last stop before coming here had been at Golta, he said things were much better in Golta, organization-wise. To Obodovka he gave a poor rating but it wasn't the worst. Many places he'd seen were a thousand times worse: Bershad, Bogdonovka, Vapniarka—all worse. He'd had to be smart to survive. He gave her a long direct look and said, "I wasn't fussy, I admit."

The pitcher was full, cold, heavy. She said, "I was at Golta—my family was, before we came here. For a week. It was terrible."

"Then you weren't in the good part," he said. "Or else you don't know terrible." On the subject of terrible he was also expert. He'd seen murder happen over a mouthful of carrot. The Romanian fascists weren't fooling around, in his experience. They'd make people hand over all the gold they had left in the world for one loaf of bread that lasted their family a day, they left them with nothing. He said at Akhmetchetka they'd put the Jews in old pigsties where they'd starved them to death—children, babies, old women— by the thousand. From Bogdanovka where he'd heard they'd shot everyone, he'd barely gotten out in time. "I'm lucky to be alive, sure, but I used my brains, too," he said. She murmured something. He didn't interest her. The Ernste's son nodded, rubbing his hands.

"It's good when a man and woman meet," he said. "Even in a place like this, a little normal life should happen."

"What are you talking about? I'm a married woman, I'm not interested in a match."

"Who said anything about a match?" he argued. "This is Kohol."

Their community, as Jews living together, he meant; she'd learned it from the children. Kohol: this little society where she slaved for the councilor's mother and made a potential mate for his friends. She tried picturing how he must picture her place in it. Relatively pretty, relatively vigorous, unclaimed young womanhood, she made a problem to be solved. The councilor saw the blank after a sum sign; or spare change to be spent; or an empty hole, just that. Because holes could be treacherous for Kohol, maybe, she couldn't be left alone. Looking away in vexation she spotted Elkie's tall figure not far off, an empty water bucket swinging from one hand. Elkie had already noticed her—the men she'd seen, too. Now as her friend's eyes signaled distress the housemaid kept moving, all downturned lips and disapproving frown. Left chagrined, Musya watched her go.

"I'm sorry," she told the pair before her, "but I have so many children, I don't have time for other things." With that she excused herself and walked away, haste splashing her blouse front.

Sender was off somewhere with the others when she got back to the cubicle. She'd have to keep the latest Drobitz news to herself for a while longer, Musya guessed, as she set the pitcher down on their lopsided tin dresser top. The round of water within trembled and became a wishing mirror—a broken one that showed unwelcome memories.

At the transit point to which they'd been shipped with Mrs Drobitz after being ordered off the frozen oxcart, the Kotz family had spent two more nights outdoors. There'd been no shelter there at all. Hundreds of people huddled on the ground, in ditches, under blankets of grass, protecting themselves however they could from the cold, without a stick of wood to burn, without food and with nothing but ditchwater to drink. She'd knocked holes in the ice on top and scooped what was trickling into the tin pitcher. At last they'd been ordered half-a-day's walk to a cattle barn shelter where there'd been some potatoes and campfires. But on the day before that one a few trucks had arrived, empty save for the German soldiers who'd descended and begun to walk among them, pointing: *you, you, you*. Some of the people they chose could walk, the rest had to be lifted or dragged to the trucks. The dead who were many by then they left there on the ground for the locals to rob and strip, various locals came two or three times a day for the purpose and left naked corpses behind. Still people didn't feel the cold, they'd told the boys, she and Baila. The trucks that day, loaded with sick and elderly people, mothers with babies and young children, drove off at a walking pace while the rest of the chosen struggled alongside: just another relocation, people said. It happened constantly. The departed convoy had been out of sight for several minutes when a terrible burst of gunfire came from that direction: the trucks hadn't gone very far by the sound of it. Steadily and then in spatters the bullets' molten noise entwined with that choked screaming everyone knew by now; they all prayed to never make that sound, she thought, each one fervently, in secret. The next morning they were marched for three hours, many on frostbitten feet, to that precious shelter with potatoes; for the fascists wouldn't spare the trucks if it weren't to a killing ground, Jews otherwise did nothing for their numbers.

Why had her family been spared? They'd looked no fresher than the rest when the soldiers were selecting victims, she knew. There was no logic or meaning to what happened.

Inside her old travelling bag they kept the family's precious papers. She grasped its bakelite handle to pull it off the luggage pile and sat down to sort past her internal passport, the older boys' birth records and travel permits, the photograph from Liza's wedding, a German letter, until she came to the pair of pages she wanted. When the old Soviet Youth Poetry anthology had begun to make indifferent toilet wipes, she'd extracted them for safekeeping. Here was her name in print. The name she'd lost to Boris Kotz, true, but not her theme; she'd kept asking:

ווער וועט ליבע מיר?

The actor, the doctor, the rest—who would love her? The whole thing might have been a little silly but it wasn't too bad, at least not on this rereading. She skipped the final lines which weren't her own but the forgery ending of her nation's top leader, general, and editor.

Despite its mutilation, her poem was a comfort to Musya, who felt her bleakness start to lift. Here was a thing that she'd done: it existed, something to tell about.

(17)

Every day she could, Musya visited the Sobansky palace. She'd found a simpler route by a cart road, where she kept to the verge and ducked into trees or the ditch alongside when any kind of traffic approached. She'd followed the high cast iron pickets around the property enough times to know there wasn't an opening anywhere. The gates were always chained shut. Yet one wing of the palace appeared to have been in fairly recent use as an invalid clinic, to judge by the moldering wheelchairs piled up by a door; and, once, a long green motorcar was parked beneath the porte-cochere, alongside the bicycles. The next day it was gone. Nothing else happened. The palace hummed with shut-up stillness in the heat. Crows circled their homes in its turrets. Breeze-fluttered wild grass fringed its gutters and roofline. Locked within, her lover reclined behind broken shutters—in every room he dreamt of her. She caught the dreams and collected them like cloth scraps fragrant with happiness.

"You are not the best maid," Oksana told her.

"No," she agreed. The windows weren't looking good. She'd also left a night bucket splash on a baseboard that no one had noticed yet. She was leaving it there. A burst of laughter sounded from the icon room where Sender Kotz tailored at his seat among the girls and women; Russvelt was in with them, acting the clown again, Musya guessed. Cut off from the joke, distant as someone in another country, in another century, she received the day's errand list. On a bad day there'd be heavy bundles involved on a trip to the mechanized steam laundry and its mud-slicked approaches. Better luck would have her call at some of Obodovka's other homes—scattered, mostly smaller than Babiak's but equally full of women who maintained an active commerce in bartered goods and nervous antagonism—where more flourishing garden plots might be plundered. Then came an occasional stop at the unpicturesque Ukrainian church, where the priests were back in black but the pediment still wore a bronzed hammer-sickle wreath from its late usage as a workers' recreation hall.

Today's were the commonest, a handful of errands on what passed for the town's market high street. Here a string of dank little eating rooms and shops overcharged for what wasn't worth stealing, while a sand-colored foreign soldiery—whose barracks she never went near—supplied catcalls and menace. Jewish slave children and maids running errands like Musya's completed the scene on a typical day, for the local population made itself scarce and unfriendly. At the once-busy crossroads, civilian travelers were few, save for the sort who came on foot, begging, destitute wanderers of roads who risked the whims of the soldiery—people, even whole families like that weren't uncommon.

So Musya saw without surprise that two children had their hands out in the road near the cooking oil seller. What did surprise her, on closer view, was that the beggars were her children. Dressed in their worst most ragged outgrown clothes, Anton and Hodeh keened for help at the passers-by, adding a little Russian for effect:

"Pajalsta, pomoygi!"

She walked up and slapped Anton's begging hand. He growled and took a swipe at her but Hodeh held him back, they didn't want that kind of scene. Musya asked what they were doing there and he shouted anyway, "We're working!" He had his tin trumpet; Hodeh had the satchel which she'd clutched to her chest at Musya's appearance.

"How did you get out? How often do you do this?" Their mouths didn't move. "So where's Samuel Nemo? You have to tell me."

Hodeh shrugged. "Your lady teacher friend borrowed him for the classroom today, to show."

Musya was bewildered. "To show what?" They couldn't tell her for sure, only something scientific. A moment later their interest quickened and they shoved her aside.

On the approach was a well-dressed local woman who must have been there on some business she couldn't entrust to a child or a maid. When Anton blew an opening bar and the pair launched into verse one of Raisins and Almonds, she paused attentively. The recent bus service shutdown had made this a rare chance to hear Jewish song, authentic or otherwise, for no one performed at the Bulbe Fence these days. Musya watched people come out through shop doors to listen, make an audience. A woman in the chicken butcher's doorway called and signaled: Where was the ditina, the baby, the little one?

At once her orphan children ran through a dumbshow of dire illness—coughing, vomiting, feverish shivers, prostration. The blood-stained woman clucked her tongue and came forward with small bill currency that she dropped into the satchel. Others followed with coins, bread rolls, candies. No one was really in the mood for a full concert, Musya could tell. After a brief encore she approached the stars again.

Anton looked truculent. "This is ours. You can't have any."

"I don't want any," she said. "Are you still giving splits to the Ernste?"

"None of your business."

Hodeh said, "What's wrong with you, Musya? You look funny."

"Oh," she said. Dawdling in a field near the Ukrainian church she'd made herself a dandelion flower crown to wear to the palace. She felt herself blush. "Nothing. I'm fine. But I have a lot to do today."

They eyed her distrustfully. "Like what?" Hodeh said.

Her intention to scold them evaporated. Now Musya only wanted to be alone again. "A—a visit," she stammered, and with a vague goodbye she headed off, leaving her errands undone.

The sting of embarrassment didn't last long. Just past noon, heat had begun to rise and return from the white chalk road to the sky's violet zenith even as more heat poured down. Musya baked in between, comfortably, she'd always enjoyed the heat. Not like Sobansky, a man for coolness and shade. How funny he'd be inclined to think that last encounter, how droll—for he loved children, she realized. Indeed, he wanted fatherhood, as much as possible. He planned to educate his many children in a school and pedagogy of his own design.

Cloud shadows slipped across his haunts that spread themselves before her as Musya climbed beyond the last dwellings in town. On her right, winding in silvery segments past wharves and woods, the river they both loved followed the mists of its own breath to a hilly blue horizon. Away from its banks, like a quilt patched from velvets on a love-tossed bed, the land lay plush and wrinkled, a tumble of emerald green marsh and meadow grass, purple thickets and ripe golden grain fields swelling up to the blue-black walls of his ancestral forests. She smiled. *Your aristocrat,* Doctor Zev called Sobansky with a touch—more than a touch—of envy shading his ironic tone; for which she chided him. The truth was, they were all equally exiled and empty-handed, everyone she knew.

Somewhere past the foot of the hill a living man appeared in front of her. He'd crawled from the ditch, a ditch-colored man dressed in the ruins of a few different uniforms. Who was he? He could have been anyone dirt-streaked, hung with weeds, splashed with sores, stinking. Before she could move he was on her, forcing her down onto the road with hands strong as wire. The front of her blouse tore away. He had sharp teeth. She jerked away from his mouth, his fetid tongue. Road dust choked her. His knees battered hers apart and she felt his penis seek her blindly with its canine snout in every crevice of her, its attack forcing pain from her and sharp cries. Then as he started to thrust he reached wildly to grab a clump of earth; she heard grass stems squeak. He'd freed her arm. Quicker than thought she pulled the scissors from her skirt pocket and began to stab him in the head, the back of his head and his temple, one blow after another piercing his skull like a beak or a serpent's fang. "Ay—ay!" he protested, pulling back. She struck harder and scrambled out from underneath as he tried to shield himself. Some blood was trickling from his scabby hairline.

"Good!" she said. "Die!" Kneeling there to strike the fatal blow, she raised her weapon. Only now Musya saw what she was holding: a rusty cast iron toy wheel. The ditch rapist stirred his limbs, growling angrily. She felt fingers grasp her elbow and jerk her upright. Hodeh was there. The wheel dropped to the ground.

They ran. Hodeh led the way, pulling her at moments, shouting at her to hurry, the satchel streaming behind her from its strap like a pennant. Musya labored after her: "Wait! Where's Anton? Anshel?"

"I left him with Waslyna."

"But I don't like Waslyna!"

Hodeh didn't answer. They left the road and darted among trees. At a mossy rise they stopped to listen for the ditch rapist's pursuit: yes, he was somewhere behind them, stumbling and hollering. A shot rang, echoed. They raced on, Hodeh fleet and sure-footed, Musya less so. Her clothes were falling off. Up ahead the trees were thinner; beyond, a gold-leafed glow of wild wheat ripened undisturbed. They burst into the open where Musya gasped: in the middle of the golden field, like figures on an icon, two great horses stood at rest. Their riders, caught dismounted, cradled long guns. One gray horse and one red: neither man was her Sobansky. Now in fact she recognized Oksana's colonel, the big gray belonged to him. The other man was holding a limp dead bird, examining its breast feathers. The colonel gave a shout at Musya. Hodeh turned and ran.

She followed. Back among the trees they dashed, heading crosswise towards a blue-black line where the woods thickened. Thundering hooves and cries of men and horses combined with their headlong panic to disturb the forest birds whose shrill alarm, spread among multitudes, rose swiftly in a screeching tidal wave to drown all other noises; the pursuers might have fired shots, Musya couldn't tell. She was floundering through a thicket; then plunging through a fragrant twilight woven out of pine boughs; then skidding down a clay bank, splashing through a shallow stream and clambering up the other side. More woods, more running: Hodeh seemed to have a destination in view. Hearing Musya give a cry she slowed down long enough to ask what was wrong. Musya said it was nothing. She'd only exclaimed to find herself back in the old Jewish cemetery, to which she'd never discovered her way again since that first time.

Just beyond the last gray headstones, at the bottom of a short steep wooded slope, they reached a clearing. In yellow sunlight sparkling with gnats and pollen, loud bees tended carpets of wild flowering vines. Hodeh stopped at a grassy hummock where an otherwise invisible entrance appeared behind the curtain wall of stalks she held aside. Musya crawled through into something like an upended basket high enough for her to crouch in; warm and dry, with ample room for two despite its clutter. Hodeh had followed her inside. "We're safe here," she said.

Musya couldn't answer for amazement. Daylight filtering through the densely knotted roof struck gleams from collections of spectacles, some missing lenses, lined up in rows; medicine bottles, some with labels, arranged by color from brown to blue; a few pairs of earrings, none cinnabar; beaded necklaces, chains and good luck charms; watches of all kinds, for both sexes, none ticking; curios, sea shells, braided lengths of human hair in the keepsake style; brooches and lockets, some open to photographed faces; and keys, brass keys and iron ones, suspended from the vine-woven ceiling on lengths of thread (Musya recognized the sea-green STOPFTWIST reel she'd swiped from Babiak's and had been missing), dozens of house keys that danced in mid-air, turning and catching the light. She touched one and set it rocking. "Those poor people," she murmured. She thought of them missing their keepsakes and glasses and medicines, searching hopelessly; even the townsfolk robbed here she pitied. Among the keys floated wedding rings and signet rings, all sorts of rings hung there, one set with turquoise, one a small child's that spun in the current of Musya's breath. Down below, atop a tin box painted with Red Square views (Mrs Krutonog had missed this souvenir fearfully in her time, Musya remembered) the foremost treasure of the secret hiding place was easily identified: a tiny mass-produced porcelain black and white cat curled up asleep.

Hodeh broke the silence. "I haven't been here in a long time," she said. This was as close as she'd come to contrition, Musya guessed. Unable to scold, she pointed and smiled:

"It's like Pretzel?"

Hodeh nodded, picked up the figurine and kissed it. A thought struck her then and she took up and opened the tin, rummaged through it briefly, and produced something impossibly rare and valuable: a packet of German steel safety pins. She handed them over with a glance at the bare breast, Musya's left, that was completely exposed. Musya blurted an apology—she hadn't realized, she said. Her hostess gave a quick shrug and started winding watches.

Musya went to work with the pins. She hadn't realized, either, how badly the ditch rapist had mauled her. There seemed to be more rips than whole parts to her blouse and half her undershift was gone. Bite marks purpled her breasts and shoulders like the signs of some unclean disease; her cheek stung where he'd left another on her face. Her skirt, she noticed now, was bloodstained and her thigh was very sore. She had a wound there. Gunshots, she remembered. She didn't want to look. Closing her eyes, she sat and listened to the bees drone and the purr of many watches ticking now instead. A tug on her sleeve roused her. "You hardly did any pins yet," Hodeh complained.

She made another apology as the turquoise spun, winking blue. Was she bleeding to death, Musya wondered? Had she reached, right now, her final end and resting place combined? Dying here, to lie here forever, her tomb a woven nest dripping with dead men's rings and dead women's house keys, she felt her lip tremble as she said, "I'm sorry to spoil your hideout."

Hodeh frowned. "At least cover the tsitskeh," she said, taking the pins from Musya's hand. Then she looked alarmed. "The sharp scissors—what happened to them?"

"The sharp scissors!" Musya cried. She had them still. They'd caused her thigh wound with their points poking a hole in their hidden pocket to gouge her as she ran. The brown bottle section yielded a small dose of iodine, enough for the bite wounds as well. The remaining half-shift did for a bandage. Musya bandaged while Hodeh pinned. "What made you be there, Hodeh?" she asked. "You followed me?"

Hodeh shrugged. "We thought you looked like trouble."

"How? What trouble?"

With a sidelong glance, the girl reached up and pulled a wilted dandelion from Musya's hair. An instant later the jingling of horse tack froze them. Hooves thumped on loamy ground as the riders moved at a slow pace in the woods above the hollow. Had they heard female voices? There was a stalking air about those hoofbeats, Musya thought. She and Hodeh crouched statue-still in the nest below their hunters. Around them rings and watch faces twirled slowly, trading flashes in the dusty sunbeams.

She watched Hodeh catch up the end of her black braid and start gnawing it with furtive patience, black eyes fixed on the grassy door. Did her rescuer comprehend what that man had done to Musya in the road, she wondered? Or why he'd wanted her breast like that? She'd worked for Boim, she must have seen it all—but what did Hodeh know? Worse, what had she endured by now at the hands of such men herself? What assaults had anyone Musya knew endured, for that matter? Trapped among her own sufferings, she'd felt singled out; but of course she hadn't been. The same conditions prevailed for everyone weaker than a well-armed man in Transnistria. They were all in the same war.

Who knew what pretty Eidel might have undergone while fleeing the Polish border? And Elkie for all her strength was only an orphan girl. The vulnerable were prey and it didn't take much, even a paralytic gunsel had gotten to Anton and left him sticky, harmed and ashamed. Poor Anton, close-mouthed ever since when he wasn't on stage because shame worked to silence the innocent. She might never have known if it hadn't been her job to dress him. Sender and Hodeh dressed themselves, so gulfs that only confidence could bridge divided them from her. Maybe they were hiding things when they kept quiet. Into what they had of privacy in a place without privacy, whatever gem-world of private selfhood they'd managed to preserve, they could be burrowed deep. Maybe she could offer comfort but she couldn't heal them. Their hush she couldn't break.

Soon the men's voices reached the hollow. The big horses shuddered and jangled, at rest while their riders strolled in conversation. She heard attempts to sound out familiar words.

They were looking at the graves.

Hodeh left it as late as she dared. The hollow was deep in twilight and already gathering dew when they emerged from hiding. The horses were long gone, no search parties looked to be out, and the careful secondary route they followed back to the ghetto spared them any sign of the ditch rapist as well. Musya made it through a gate just being closed for the night while Hodeh slipped around to a certain gap she used; they arrived at Krutonog's together and exchanged a look that signaled major relief. The feeling didn't last. Waslyna from town was supposed to have returned Anton to the ghetto right away but she had not done so.

First he wasn't in the cubicle. Instead, planted outside in the corridor looking furious stood the one who'd told Musya not to walk alone.

"I've been waiting here for hours—where were you?" Eidel greeted them.

Before Musya could reply she had Samuel Nemo rushing out to clutch her legs, his voice at top volume. "Listen to me! Listen!" he shouted. She gave Eidel a look—her baby hadn't learned this at home. "I'm sorry we're so late. But you could have given him to Sender."

"Yes? And what if something were wrong and you didn't come home—what was a small boy supposed to do all alone with a baby?"

"I'd be fine!" Sender called from inside the cubicle.

Musya said, "But I did come home and what were you doing with my baby in the first place? He's too young for school."

A blonde impatient head toss. "In the first place, no, he isn't. And we only wanted him for an hour, that's what we paid for."

Musya stared. "You—who? How much? For what?"

"It's not true," Hodeh said.

Eidel grimaced sarcastically. "*It's not true!* I saw you take a cut from your landlady with my own eyes. Musya, our older pupils are doing a teacher-training unit on child development and I hired your baby as a demonstration. Their brains are very plastic at this age. Here, watch." She addressed herself to Samuel Nemo who kept refusing her. "Baby, yes, listen—listen to me. Pay attention. Yes. Now, count. Eyns—yes. Count!" A last refusal; then numbers one through eight followed in a messy rush that ended with him throwing himself to the floor where he rolled around shouting nonsense. This new behavior was really terrible, Musya thought. The teacher scolded him: "You made it to ten before, what's the problem?"

His mother had mixed feelings. "You took him for science?"

"Science pedagogy. We're training the older students to take on some of the class load."

"But why should he know how to count when he's only a baby?"

"Yes, you're welcome," Eidel said.

A few seconds more and Musya did feel grateful, even pleased. Her own baby, already counting. "Is he a genius?" she asked suddenly.

Eidel said no. "Not in the least, his development is perfectly average in every point. What happened to you, Musya? You look injured. Where did you get safety pins?"

"Oh, yes." A familiar agony of shame twisted her like wet laundry. "It wasn't a very good day."

Hodeh slipped into the cubicle and asked where Anton was. "He's not with you?" Sender asked.

Musya said, "Sender, where's your brother, where is Anton?"

His voice quick to show panic, Sender said he hadn't seen him. "I thought he was with Hodeh—where is he?"

"He must be in the new kitchen," Musya said to reassure everyone. Pain twanging through her back, she lifted Samuel Nemo to one hip and clasped him there. "Let's go get him."

"And what if he's not there?" Eidel said. "Do you see now why it's important to put them in regular classes?"

She wasn't staying to argue. "I'll try, but they just don't like school."

"They need school, Musya!" But she was already telling Eidel goodnight, as the family hurried off to the new kitchen with Sender anxious in the lead. Hodeh was fuming.

"We already taught him to count, why does she take credit?"

"Eyns-tsvey-dray!" the baby said. "Eyns-tsvey-dray!"

"Every little bit helps," Musya told her.

They found the Ernste drinking tea in the midst of a crowd and her domain decked with wildflowers, greenery tied to all the cabinet knobs. She greeted the Kotz family from her chair. "But where is Anshel? This is Shavuot, he should be here for the reading."

"He—he's not here?" He wasn't there. He was missing the Ruth Megillah. His brother gasped and plunged into distress, tears already leaking. Musya was trying to explain, the little boy should have been back in the ghetto hours ago. Now it appeared he was still outside.

"That's not good," the Ernste said shortly.

Her numerous company of guests made a worried murmur, for Anton remained a favorite of the tiled room. Unfortunately (for them and for the boy they called Anshel) Jews of any age caught outside the safety of the ghetto after hours were liable to be shot. Of course, even worse could also happen. The lead minion summarized and pronounced:

"Wise children have short years."

"Shut up." Musya spun around and snapped at her twice. "Shut up!"

But the woman persisted. "You should blame yourself. You don't take care of those children. You run around, you get in states—look at yourself!" Too late, Musya remembered her rips, her blood stains, her pins.

"She's right," the Ernste added, peering hard at her. "What happened to you?"

"Everything happened to me. What are you going to do about my boy?"

"I'll make some inquiries. For God anything is possible. Go back to your room and pray. We remember the dead in our prayers tomorrow—so start early. And you." She pointed a short brown finger at Hodeh and beckoned. "Satchel, please."

A few hours passed. Hodeh and Sender couldn't be deterred from mounting a search, which left Musya to wait in the cubicle with her hands full of quilt work she'd taken up to calm herself. Samuel Nemo slept, his sweaty limbs tangled in tiger stripes. Songs and sounds of implausible but authentic revelry penetrated the plank walls. Outside, out of doors, people were making a late night of it. In another life she might have joined them; in this one she sat alone. Lost through negligence—her own, ultimately—Anton might be. Sorrow swamped her. It felt too late to start praying. Her heart overflowed and she asked her sister Liza's forgiveness, and then the mother's forgiveness. "Forgive me," she begged their gray glowering thin-faced shades. They'd never liked her, she began to think. Certainly they'd asked far too much of her, making this a kind of spitefulness in them, a blow aimed at her true nature. Divided from Odessa and from her lover Leon Flohr, she'd been diverted from her destined path's ascent to higher, even highest happiness. But it didn't matter: if they'd only return Anton to her safely, she'd never cease to honor them and consider their dead women's wishes in all things, she promised. Musya pictured this which was her prayer calling their powerful spirits to meet and embrace. The universe shook at their reunion and one great bright blast of Providence sped from the afterlife to deliver their son and grandson from harm.

With Anton riding his shoulders, hobbyhorse-style, Sobansky arrived in the ghetto. Guards couldn't stop him. He'd found the boy trying to drink from a fast stream, perilously close to immersion, he told her. Anton clung fast until Sobansky with his own hands tucked him into bed beside the other children—a second father to them already, she couldn't help but reflect.

When Sender and Hodeh returned alone they found Musya smiling over her quilt patches, calm. She told them not to worry, everything would be fine: "Go to bed, get some sleep." A short while later a lot of footsteps and commotion came down the corridor. Recognizing Anton's loud voice Musya scrambled to her feet. Her heart pounded.

Who would she see? The doorway filled. It was only a man from upstairs with Anton in his arms, a second man from Krutonog's, and a third who came from elsewhere in the ghetto. The lead man set Anton down on the dirt floor of the cubicle where he promptly collapsed though his song continued, the words a nonsense, the tune a hodgepodge. He was roaring drunk. The three men appeared not too sober themselves. "Where did you find him?" she asked.

"He found us. He joined our party. He was already drinking." They handed over his bottle, they called it: empty, no label. Red wine. "He said the priests gave it to him."

She asked, "But why is he naked?"

They shrugged. They guessed he'd felt like it. He'd been dancing that way. "He wasn't wearing much when he got there," they said, handing over some clothes, no trousers. He was still clutching his tin trumpet. "He says he's been baptized," the first man told her. Anton heard and broke off his song to confirm this immediately:

"I'm baptized! I'm not a zhid anymore—I'm baptized!"

"See?" they said.

"Oh," she told them, "I'm sure it's not true."

"Don't spank him when he's been drinking," the second of them cautioned in a sentimental voice.

She said, truthfully, "I don't spank—I never spank my children."

The third man stood there peering in at them. "You hear a lot about this family," he said. Musya glanced around. Hodeh had vanished, gone beneath the covers, she guessed.

"Yes, well, goodnight." She thanked them.

"Proshchai!" Anton shouted. "Proshchai zhidy!"

"He already threw up, don't worry," said the second man, the kindest but drunkest of the trio; which made no move to leave until Sender Kotz added his shouts from the bed where he sat with the crying baby:

"Go away! Good night! Go away! Leave us alone!" The men dawdled off and Hodeh reappeared from behind the corner curtain. Anton staggered to the bucket and began to piss with wild inaccuracy. Musya hurried over.

"After today, no more Waslyna—that's final!" she declared to everyone.

(18)

Each part of her body felt some kind of pain the next morning when the work bell blared and she started to move. To cushion her wounds and blisters she groaned her way into a pair of stockings which Oksana Babiak happened unfortunately to recognize later that day. "Mrs Yelyuk was missing those stockings," she said.

"She cannot fit into these stockings," Musya said.

It was true. "Do not let her see you wear them," she was cautioned. More serious had been the errands she'd left undone the day before—a dereliction with consequences. The household was almost out of sunflower oil. Also the colonel had stopped by the previous night to report seeing Musya well outside town, running for no reason, she and some wood-elf child. After all the unsatisfactory service she'd given at Babiak's, this report marked enough. Her last errands had been run. "I cannot trust you," she was told. The way Musya felt, the loss didn't strike her as great. The complaints kept coming, though. "I do not know where you are, where you go—you look like you got into trouble."

"Yes," she said. She had.

"I am not surprised." The overseer continued her survey. "And what you are wearing is not good, you look too poor again."

"Yes. I need new clothes."

"You need!" the other echoed. "So easy for you to say." But a key from the ring in her apron pocket opened a cupboard from which she extracted some musty gray and red striped cotton fabric. She shook defunct lavender buds from the folds and handed it over with a gesture towards the workroom down the hall. "Make what you can of it."

Musya frowned. "I will look like a convict." She'd heard all about Babiak's old prison supply sideline. The cloth wasn't bad, though. In an instant she'd planned a skirt complete with hidden pockets; hers were empty today, Hodeh was keeping the sharp scissors again. Enough might be left for a child's tunic or two if she measured carefully. One of the unfinished uniform shirts would do for a top blouse, with a tuck here and there. She suggested it and the owner agreed:

"Why not? They will never pay for the rest of that order," she added grimly. The colonel had lost his budget and now he owed money to everyone.

"He could sell his horse," said Musya.

The woman shook her head. "No, he will eat it himself when it is time. Listen," she said. "This war has come close, east of here. Too close. The roads are not safe now, there are too many men going away from the war on every road. They run, they escape. They fought too much and you do not want to meet them."

"No," she agreed, a little startled by the sound of caring. She hugged the cloth to her chest.

"You understand," Oksana Babiak said. "If you are too damaged to return inside to your place then I must pay the authorities a fee that I cannot afford now. So no more running around all day for you." Deliveries and purchases were down anyway, business wasn't good. The household was having to sell valuables.

"You still have valuables?" Musya asked.

Of course they did. "The valuables are the last to go."

A morning or two later she and Sender Kotz were leaving the ghetto with the other laborers. Almost at the gate she heard her name and a man grasped her arm from behind: Drobitz who called himself Fein. "Sholem-aleykhem," he said. She asked him what he wanted. He said he liked her new outfit but what had happened to her face? He stared at the bruise the ditch rapist's teeth had left on her cheekbone; it was turning green now, the children said. The skirt and top blouse had taken hardly any time at all to make. She thanked him for the compliment and said she had a dog bite.

"I can't even count," he said, "the number of dogs I've been bitten by in the last two years."

Before she could answer Sender Kotz told him, "Too bad it wasn't more, too bad they didn't eat you."

He answered, "That's not very nice. That's not respectful."

"You're not going out to work today?" Musya asked him.

He said no. "I work in here, for the Ghetto Council. I organize, write letters, that kind of thing."

At which Sender exclaimed, "Oh, go sit on scorpions!" before he spat on the dust where Drobitz-Fein was standing, spun on a heel and stomped away. He was the picture of his grandmother, she thought. The man's puffed up eyes made slits after him.

"What's his problem?" he wondered.

"He hates you. What do you want?'"

He persisted. "I heard the goy priests in town got him drunk and baptized him."

"That was his brother—but it's only a rumor," she added quickly. "Not true. No one can prove it." It might have been true. Anton's story of the night changed with every telling.

"So both your boys have problems," Drobitz-Fein said. "And the girl is some kind of burglar."

"Maybe. What do you want?" she asked again.

"Plus a baby—no, wait." He took her arm to stop her. She shook away his hand. He said, "What I want, is." She waited. "You and me. Maybe we should get together."

Her mouth fell open. He was serious. "But you're the worst man in the world," she said.

"I am not." He bristled. "There are worse. What about Hitler?"

"What about Hitler?" she answered him. Shaking her head, she moved off. Again he snatched at her arm. This time he kept a tight grip. She looked around and was dismayed to notice Cezar the rapist standing among the armed guards by the gate, she hadn't spotted him for several days which had led her to hope he might be gone for good. But here he was, staring right at her and Drobitz-Fein who said, "What are you talking about, lady? What did I do that was so bad?"

She couldn't help turning on him. "How can you ask that? I know who you are. What about what you didn't do, like when you didn't try to protect your poor wife from those men at all—and then you ran away."

"Try so they could kill me? And I ran because I had a chance!" he objected. "So what, I ran—what was I supposed to do? I never wanted to marry that woman."

"What?"

"You thought that was a love match? Are you crazy?"

"Am I? Who cares? Mrs Drobitz was your wife anyway. She had your child, your—Baby."

He gave a kind of laugh. "Mine? That thing was never mine, it was from her first husband. I came along after. She had money, she needed a man, I was broke. Our families arranged it. I never wanted her, I had other plans."

"You? Had plans?" she asked furiously.

"Sure I had plans. I didn't want marriage, I didn't want that settled down life. I'm an actor."

With a sensation of being under bombardment, large sections of her inner life in flames, she said, "But you're not good-looking enough to be an actor."

"What, so you've never heard of a character actor? I'm versatile—and very talented, that's according to some critics who matter, not just me, by the way," he explained. "But it was my luck to get saddled with a dead husband's idiot child. And her. Don't get me started on that woman and her habits. And hey, don't act so offended when I know she drove you crazy, too. I bet you ran from that screaming of hers the first chance you got and never thought once of my so-called poor wife until you saw me here."

"No. We stayed with her. And I think about her every day, I do. We still have—we were with her until the end. When she died. Your wife died."

"Of course she died. She was out of her mind with wanting to—what else you think made me run? I didn't want to die with her." He shrugged. "So what happened? She came to Obodovka and what? The typhus got her?"

"No, it was." Halfway from the oxcart to the frozen field, still they hadn't been able to get Mrs Drobitz to stop screaming; Baila Kotz had begged her to be quiet when the soldiers kept shouting at her to stop but it hadn't done any good. Screech, she'd gone. Screech. Screech. A singular shining matter: "A soldier knocked her brains out with his rifle. They—her brain came out."

Drobitz-Fein's fleshy face clenched and went slack once or twice. "Well, what did she expect," he said finally.

"Let me go," she told him. "Let me go and don't ever talk to me again."

"You think that was my fault? That wasn't my fault—it had nothing to do with me! And what's past is past, we can't change it, we just have to keep living, people like you and me."

"Leave me alone!" She tore herself from the actor's grip and stumbled away from him. Between washes of tears she could see Cezar the rapist waiting, his face an angry demon red. She heard the other jeer at her back:

"You're not as good as you think you are, lady!"

The gendarme who was holding the work list today asked, "Lovers' quarrel?" The others laughed. She brushed past and collided with the rapist who stank badly as usual. There was nowhere to go, in the knot of men she was trapped where she stood as he stroked her hair and aimed furious looks back inside at the ghetto. When he touched the bruise on her cheek with his dirty fingers, the thought crossed her mind that he blamed Drobitz-Fein for leaving it. Then she remembered the rash he'd given her one time and screamed; but her voice came out broken, like wind through a torn paper flap.

"Let her go, Cezar! You're making us late for work." She felt a tug on her wrist and Sender Kotz pulled her free, out into the road. He hurried her away. A glance behind showed the camp orderly's uniform lingering among the rest, no closer. Still they hurried. Sender was upset that she'd even stopped to talk to Mrs Drobitz's betrayer. "Just ignore him! You don't need to stand there and fight with him like sweethearts."

"You too? Please," she said. "I told him to leave me alone."

"Don't talk and you won't need to tell."

She pondered this injunction in silence as the sunflower field came into view. Her arm was sore where Drobitz-Fein's grip had bruised it. "He's an actor, he says—did you know?"

Sender said yes, he'd heard that. "He played in The Dybbuk someplace. It doesn't matter."

"No," she agreed. An actor, in the flesh—she'd finally met one and this was how he was. She supposed it didn't matter. By the end of the day she'd almost forgotten about him.

At Babiak's all hands were busy with the latest sideline, embroidering export vyshyvanky. The overseer's colonel had returned from a brief home leave with orders placed by two shops and a wholesaler in Constanta. Musya joined Sender and Russvelt in the icon room for part of each day. Still on night bucket duty, she shared the other housework with the younger girls from the bluzke detail, this their punishment for sloppy needlework and general silliness, she gathered. Much of her time was spent outdoors where Oksana Babiak was trying to coax some sustenance out of the overgrown garden and vegetable plots. She wished Sender might have joined her in the sunshine sometimes but he couldn't be spared, he was their best. Her own labors were hard, back-straining. She bent to pull weeds, heaved spades heaped with earth, lugged pails of water around, all at Oksana's direction; and the overseer watched every sign of growth with nervous care which left not a mouthful for Musya to pilfer. Her hidden pockets hung empty. The sun beat down on her shoulders, the back of her neck, her kerchief-bound tresses.

Where had she been? Sobansky asked. He never saw her anymore. "You're seeing me now," she laughed. He looked pale and sleep-deprived, as if he'd been brooding. He said yes, these past nights had been unquiet ones. Steeling himself, he admitted that he'd thought she might have found another man—if not a new one, then maybe one of her old loves, the doctor perhaps, might have proved himself more worthy—worthier, that is, than he, a broken-spirited, occasionally stone blind, penniless aristocrat of a crushed old order. No, she said. She touched his mouth. No, there was no one else. Red returned to his cheeks, his lips—she watched him bloom.

It wasn't the first revival she'd led in him. Hurt almost fatally by women, Sobansky had bricked up his heart. But Musya had restored his faith in love—and he, truly, hers, she swore it. He made her want to vow things. They confessed to one another, enumerating all their own faults (hers was vanity; his, pride and quickness to anger) and every misfortune they'd suffered, down to the most humiliating. He wept over the indignities she'd suffered at the hands of other men, which he said had ennobled her—and more, in his eyes being raped had made her holy, such suffering bestowed holiness. "Even saintliness!" he cried.

She demurred. Who could call her saintly? Who, especially having known her sister Liza Kotz—and yet! Musya carried night pails of wet stink downstairs to dump on the bean patch. Saints did the humble things, didn't they? And when even one small tomato was missed, saints ate dry bread without soup for three days as punishment.

As for her rapists, when Sobansky spoke of what he called "those beasts not men" his lips paled to gray and his eyes burned with cold fury. She felt something implacable in him then that her own spirit could rest on, a comfort like an steel platform set down in the midst of muddy desolation. At the same time he frightened her a little. What would happen? All he'd divulge to her was that the Polish nobility could count on a great deal more support in these parts than most people realized. He meant she'd be revenged, comprehensively, bloodily. This his kisses vowed. Musya could stop fretting about what had already happened, past and future. She believed him. Sobansky held her to his hard, beating chest.

On the walk back to the ghetto that day she filled two hidden pockets with flowers to add to the children's supper. They'd complain every time, but in fact flowers were delicious and filling. From the roadside she favored margaritkas.

To the general lushness of Obodovka at high summer its Jewish ghetto presented a stark contrast. With every bush and tree long stripped of bark and leaves and mostly all the grassy banks picked clean, the scene inside looked bleached. The hard ground baked. Then footsteps trudged it into powder. Beds, cups, hair, teeth, all filled with grit; dust reddened every eye; dust clouds shrank the sun and chilled the rancid daylight. Viewed from the road, the place behind the barbed wire was cloaked in a yellowish smog. At the end of a workday the surviving forced laborers were slow to line up at the gates. They'd drag their feet and fill their lungs a few times before entering. Their numbers had dwindled steadily. Their labors still murdered them, for one thing; and a few more truckloads had been collected for worksites in the east from which none returned. Escape pushed the attrition rate higher. Aging badly, ill-patrolled, the fences were temptingly porous. Talk of running off to join the local partisan bands filled the air since a handful of fugitives had slipped back to report and recruit; tales of life on the run from cave hideout to cave hideout were in everyone's ears at some point. Jews had their own bands out there by now, armed and respectably deadly. The fascist enemy saw more losses all the time.

But when her bellicose children rejoiced at this, Musya wouldn't, she told them. When the problem was war, what good was more fighting? She'd argue with any man or woman, yes, she'd complain and battle for better treatment; but bloodshed was out. Her pacifism left her isolated, a minority of one in their cubicle where infatuation with the hero partisans was all-consuming.

"Hey! Hey—girlie!"

Just inside the entrance gates Musya glanced around to see one of the gendarmes scowl at her and point. She hadn't shown her work return ticket. Half the time—more than half—no one asked to see it. She'd lost a dozen of them. Now she fumbled out the latest and watched him prolong a spurious scrutiny. Other forced laborers filed past with a sound like bodies being dragged through the dust; their walking erect was some kind of illusion, she thought. A few steps away Sender Kotz waited. They both kept an eye on Cezar the rapist who stood in conversation with a few other soldiers just outside. He'd followed them closely, singing again, this time something military. The gendarme didn't notice. He coughed.

"Show your pass, okay?" he said. "Stop expecting special treatment."

"Your flies are open," Musya said. It was true. She snatched back her ticket and walked away. The man was short a few buttons; she might have offered him a safety pin for something in return, but he'd harassed her. Before she'd gone any distance at all Drobitz-Fein appeared, planted himself in front of her and made sure the gendarme behind was listening. He'd planned this ambush, no question. That morning she'd rejected him, he'd had all day to dislike it.

He said, "The officer is right. Everyone else shows their ticket—so what's your problem, lady?"

Sender was tugging her arm but she stood and glared. "Are you in charge now? Is this your ghetto? Or maybe it belonged to Mister Drobitz, before you married his wife—or excuse me, before your parents forced you to stop being a burden on their old age."

"Shut up," he said. Anger widened his eyes which she saw for the first time were the raincloud color newsprint leaves on sweaty hands. He said, "You think you're special."

"Of course I think I'm special, what's wrong with that?"

"She's special." Sender added his voice. "She is. Now leave us alone."

Drobitz-Fein shook his head. "You're not special." And with that he raised his left hand to her right breast and squeezed it through her sand-colored blouse; rather hard.

She slapped the hand away and he reached up to do it again. She heard Sender's angry cry before all other sounds were lost in the tumult of boot soles pulverizing distance between entrance and man. Cezar the rapist led a raiding pack; the gendarmes on hand couldn't do anything but watch as five soldiers descended on Drobitz-Fein, drove him to his knees and then onto his side in the dust and encircled him. Seconds later he was shrieking, begging for his life. The man who ran hadn't a chance this time. He wailed as they kicked him. She heard cracking—his ribs. She thought he might recover as men did from beatings. Doctor Zev and Nurse Roza would save him, possibly even reform his bad character while he lay safe between them in plastered traction. The men kept kicking. Musya staggered, she screamed at them to stop. Something horribly wet happened. Then an eyeball bounced out of the dust cloud and rolled, trailing crimson threads, almost to Sender's feet. He couldn't move to leap away, he was shaking too hard and further wracked by shrill distress cries that exposed all his bad teeth and his red gums. Musya saw he'd soaked his trousers. She swept him into her arms, held him close. More kicks thudded. Already the gray eyeball and its blood tangles were coated with pale dust and almost hard to discern. She hid Sender's face against her chest although she feared her shouts would deafen him. "Opshtel! Opshtel!" She couldn't stop shouting, her throat was on fire.

At last Cezar the rapist raised his arms in an odd motion and it was over. His circle of assailants expanded and dissolved, gone into the dusty air. He turned to Musya, made some sounds—words maybe—and bowed slightly at the waist, copying his colonel. Then he followed the other murderers out of the ghetto into the town road. The gates closed behind them. The rude gendarme dropped his stick, bent over and vomited. His partners stared blindly.

New footsteps raced up and Elkie said, "What happened, I heard—oh my God! Musya, what did you do?"

"Nothing," she said. The weight of the sobbing eight year-old boy in her arms was suddenly too much. "Please take Sender home. Don't look," she told him. He clung at first but then switched willingly; Elkie handled him as if he weighed no more than a pillow. He hiccupped against her neck.

"I wet myself."

"I don't blame you," she said sincerely, moving off with him to ask across a shoulder: "You're not coming?"

Musya said she'd be another minute. The gendarmes were still retching. Others choked and joined them, others wailed. She looked down at the dead man oozing, leaking stenches, half-jellied, splintering and split; the critics' darling. A man of folly. She screamed at his corpse:

"You should have left me alone!"

More people were arriving but no one approached. There was a lot of murmuring she tried not to decipher. Why was she standing there? She realized: Drobitz-Fein represented a link with her past—with Baila, with Odessa, with Mama. So few were left that she didn't want to leave him.

She watched an old man, or maybe a young man, creep out from the crowd, a sick bent barefooted man making crab-wise to where one of the dead actor's good shoes, tongue askew, laces surprised, lay in the dust. The man scooped up the shoe, held it to his chest and looked at Musya. His eyes begged her permission; for the left shoe was still on its sockless foot. She nodded. "Go ahead. Take it." He darted forward and complied with swift and horrible dexterity, then made off with his matching prizes. The section of crowd into which he disappeared surged a step closer, as if he'd fed it a growth pill.

Now came a small white butterfly to dip into view, descend to the edge of some spilled blood and rest there to drink. Its wings with their black button trim stretched and quivered. Musya laughed. She recognized this butterfly. It was Baby Drobitz.

The next morning she woke to feel her face touched from all sides by her sleeping children's breath. She lay back in happy forgetfulness, savoring a rare sensation of peaceful well-being for the few moments it lasted. Then she remembered the murder, the turmoil, ghetto councilors shouting accusations, curses fallen on the color of her blouse. That ill-fated pink: she sighed and stretched. The ghetto was awake, voices raised; someone banged on metal. The work bell hadn't sounded, this was the difference to the day. For it had to be past time, the morning was bright, not bluish, and her little fenster beam was on the wall where she never saw it anymore. A minute later Musya tensed as heavy footsteps creaked the floorboards outside; but today's chaper was the lazy one who only shouted down the corridor. They were late.

The day took its next unusual turn on the path outside Krutonog's. Enrobed in a quilted mulberry colored silk dressing gown, the Ernste was addressing a few dozen of her tenants. Without her armchair the woman of Bucharest looked like a chair anyhow, thick and upholstered. Spotting Kotzes she cried out, breath short, bosom heaving:

"Ah! You. Her. This one right here."

Musya was surprised. "Sholem-aleykhem! What did I do? I didn't break the bell."

"Yes, you did. And worse." The Ernste continued with the usual touch of pride, "To my son they write, the local authorities. For what went on yesterday, they say, we get immediate consequences. Punishment. Because of you, Miss Mouth—you and your men."

She stared. "What are you talking about? What punishment?"

The padded arms waved at her to look around, to listen. In the late morning sun, Musya could see the bright eyes shining with tears. It was remarkable. The Ernste looked at her and cried:

"My poor kitchen! Don't you understand? They turned off our electricity!"

(19)

By late summer of 1943, Germany's invasion of the Soviet Union had changed course and become a retreat. In the Jewish ghetto of Obodovka young children rejoiced while their elders hesitated, afraid this show of weakness might be only Hitler hoaxing his last living enemies into the open, where they could be reaped as if with scythes; unpersuadable, the most fearful made smothering sounds at every exuberance.

The rest wondered what could have happened. Pieces of answers reached them in the ghetto; news was more frequent now that it favored the Soviet cause. They learned that Krutonog's late historian Mr Asch had been right, his deathbed prediction proved true. At the same time it was murdering Jews and other victims in their prison camps and ghettos, epidemic typhus had struck the Germans, too, not so inhuman as they'd looked while invading Ukraine. They were human, they weakened and died. Their allied fascist forces had seemed invincible but not at all, far from it. Unlike the Grand Armée of 1812 they never managed to occupy Moscow. On that count their Hitler was no Bonaparte, everyone commented. And he seemed unable to learn—for after that failure he'd ordered his armies to stay in the east and attack the Caucasus. He wanted those oil fields. The Volga River city of Stalingrad stood in his way, guarding the Caucasus. There a great battle ensued and in the end it was the German fascists who surrendered. That had been back in January and Hitler's armies had been in retreat ever since.

The victory at Stalingrad was the biggest news to ever reach the ghetto, where it took time to really sink in and convice people that Hitler had lost the war. Considering how little resistance the Soviet Union had mustered initially, this outcome was staggering. There must have been miracles, people said. Others talked of Premier Stalin's genius. Or else it was simple, as Musya supposed: one man's blunders had finally outnumbered and outweighed the other men's blunders in fatal severity.

After more than two years, war didn't interest her.

At night in their cubicle, in town at her labors, in all the various lines she passed through day by day it was the same. The names of generals and battle-fields buzzed in her ears, empty noise. Loss by loss, the Germans retreated. They'd lost a big tank battle on the Russian border at Kursk in July. Now they were being driven back across Ukraine, east to west. She'd hear *Amerikaner!* and ask where? Always too far away to make any difference; and her heart which had raced a few beats would fall back to tolling the same slow hours. Every moment felt uncomfortably familiar. "Here we are," she'd say out of nowhere, to nobody. "Here we are again, waiting for the Germans to come."

"What is this you are saying?" Today it was Oksana Babiak who asked. Musya said it was nothing.

With her responsibility for emptying the old lady dames' night buckets, she'd known as soon as anyone at Babiak's that the Stara was deathly ill. What was in there was terrible, much too foul for the bean patch. Still deferred to, she'd dragged herself downstairs for a while longer but one morning sure enough the Stara woke up paralyzed; she died two days later, flat on the bedroom floor where they'd laid her for comfort, her dying eyes mocked by the latest fecal splash Musya's carelessness had left on the baseboard. She was thinking the view might have added impetus to the Stara's final ear-splitting groans which remained faintly present, tangled like blackbirds in the ceiling cobwebs. She knelt and reached across the body, her knees aching.

"Terrible!" The overseer complained through the kerchief tied around her nose and mouth, bandit-style. "The poor Stara."

"She had a long life," Musya said, wringing her wash towel into the basin.

"But she hated Odessa Jews so much. And here you are. It is a terrible."

It couldn't be helped, though. The surviving dames had tried but failed to assist in the preparatory rites—the smells, the seepage, in general the signs of a long lumpy blue and yellow living dissolution had left them too demoralized. Strung between nausea and tears, they drifted in and out of the bedroom to watch. Two watched the basin with particular jealously, for they were waiting to collect the corpse-bathing water, a local remedy for eye disease. With every drop Musya spilled on the floor she heard one of them wince at the cost to their sideline. The dead Jew hater's body released more gases with each towel stroke. Musya didn't need to wear a kerchief mask. A priest would come with men to carry down the corpse and set it on a bench in the icon room, a burning candle at its head. And there'd be more, there'd be food, breads of all kinds. This wasn't Russvelt's first Ukrainian funeral and he'd told the Kotzes what to expect. Bread and honey at the feet, bread in the coffin, food everywhere, spare candles and money, too—coins on the eyes and lips, more thrown in the coffin, small bills in the dead hands to pay off dead relatives' debts in the goyish afterworld: crowding close and staying underfoot, a small quick-fingered person could thrive. Here, death meant feasting.

They began to dress the Stara's body in her burial clothes, nothing but an old nightgown, the linen poor quality, easily torn. They managed to stuff on a pair of white cotton socks and soft slippers to cushion the dead woman's feet for the rock-strewn afterworld. They were binding the limbs with clothesline rope when Sender appeared. He stared at the rope and forgot what he was holding in his hand until prompted: "Zenderkaz brings us something?" To Musya he handed a sash sewn from white bluzky cloth with some striking roses embroidered in black silk; not his best work, rather rushed.

"For tradition," he explained. "For—her." It was to go across the Stara's chest.

"Excellent boy!" With this the overseer took a breath to hold and lifted a corner of her mask to blot tears. The lady dames, similarly moved, exclaimed at the workmanship.

Musya lowered her voice to ask why: "For what? She was a terrible person."

"But it's traditional," he said.

They turned to watch Mrs Yelyuk shove through the other dames' lamentations and blunder into the room, bellowing sobs. She held out a small dusty battered wreath of artificial purple flowers at which Oksana barked angrily: This was the best they could find? The wreath was key! "Terrible!" The Yelyuk retreated in a storm of tears and alcohol fumes.

But the whole thing was very unfortunate. All Obodovka knew the Stara as one of those women who spend years, decades, planning their own funerals down to the last candle. She'd drawn up menus; she'd collected fine grave linens in cedar chests; the local carpenter had her coffin measurements, she'd reserved his top-end model; her burial plot with its picturesque view of the old willow was already marked off with white stones—she'd visited often and kept the stones gleaming for years, twenty years. Then the linens burned up with her house in the German bombardments, the coffin maker got shot and the cemetery was dug up pell-mell to accommodate the small mountain of clients he hadn't lived to serve. If only the Stara could have held out until after the war, she might have retrenched somehow. As it was, all her plans went for naught. It didn't help to be in the midst of an egg shortage which left the bread crusts very dull. The honey was old and clouded. The mourning guests could only shake their heads over the state of the linens, although the sash was praised. The low point came with the coffin supplied by the military authorities (the best the colonel could find, he said), far from well-made and exceedingly narrow. She'd had to go in on her side, more or less. Coins slipped from the Stara's dead face and thudded, one two, onto the plain unsanded pine boards below. Russvelt wept.

Strange to see, blame for the debacle fell entirely on the Yelyuk head. The war received no credit; Obodovka's invaders might have been virgin schoolgirls in guilt when compared to the Stara's old crony and final corruptor. For hadn't her doctors warned that the next round of drinking strong liquor day and night would put the Stara in her grave? Yes, and so it had. And then there were the omens, like the black houseflies the young girls said had settled all over Mrs Yelyuk as she slept during work hours right there by the window, it was only a day or two later that the Stara woke bedridden. And before that an icon had crashed to the floor as she passed by, sustaining damage.

"I am innocent!" the Yelyuk wailed brokenheartedly.

No one agreed and no one would comfort her, not a word was said in kindness as she sat, slumped, unpitied, unkempt, sheets of tears glistening her plum-colored face. Tears dripped from her chin. Even Sender Kotz with his kind heart kept both eyes on his stitches. Musya alone met the shunned woman's gaze and saw hatred flash there—personal hatred wrapped around an idea. *I shouldn't have looked*, Musya thought. What would happen was immediately clear.

The Yelyuk woman needed a scapegoat. Within weeks, a tirelessly self-ingratiating campaign of innuendo, misdirection and subterfuge would raise the old drunkard (loudly reformed) one vital step in the household's esteem, just elevation enough to make her not its most disliked and stigmatized member. That place she'd exchanged with Musya, now branded as prideful, a food sneak, a thief and a lazybones. All true, but it stung.

Life inside the ghetto found her reputation at a matching nadir. Two solid years' worth of gossip had caught up with her all at once. The yentas who'd known and respected Baila Kotz, most of them long dead, had always been reluctant to buy the double schnur mayse. Their doubts survived them. Was there really any sister or even any husband in the picture—a Red Army soldier, no less? If not, then whose baby was that? Time had confused other identities. Resembling her to the highest degree, the other two boys were assumed by many to be Musya's despite her relative youth. It wouldn't have surprised anyone to learn she'd been pushing them out since girlhood by various fathers. She was said to have worked in a koorvah tent, after all. She liked men, old and young, had a taste for them—but a woman would do, witness her ties to the pervert couple at Tauber's. Good decent women disliked her. Her gait was far too provocative, with that long swinging braid. Her fatness came from food sources nowhere near normal or honorable. She employed a girl thief and was probably dealing in stolen goods. Her unschooled children went out begging. The oldest boy was the sheerest feygele. She'd had the one with the Russian name baptized, he was a goy now. Even the baby showed delinquent tendencies, he wouldn't end well. With such a mother, how could he? A mother who'd stood there and watched her fascist boyfriend and his gang of thugs murder a leading citizen in the road at her feet and never made a move to stop them—some mother. She'd led poor Fein along, led him straight to the tomb, then stood laughing over his dead body. Truth! He was looking at a great career had he lived to survive; time would have seen him lauded among character actors, an ornament to the Jewish race, another Zuskin. A shande! The man had beaten Death at every major death trap in Transnistria. If only he hadn't landed in Musya so-called Kotz's poisonous web. If only! What a waste! The regrets he'd left behind were fertile, they multiplied until she heard them all the time.

The electrical situation was enough to give her notoriety. Pitch-dark nights kept it fresh. Although the first punitive shut-off didn't last very long, only a day, others and longer followed. Blaming the ghetto's collusion with more than one partisan band, the local powers had been less accommodating lately anyhow, stricter on work quotas, tighter-fisted with basic supplies. Soap was nowhere to be found now, for instance. Now there'd be some infraction—a labor crew reporting short, an escape too dramatic—and the current would stop. As the original cause, Musya got charged with the sequels. Blame took the form of abuse, mainly abusive remarks, shoves, some spitting.

She could harden herself to it on her own behalf but not on her children's; for what they felt she suffered. Quite often they all four seemed to hate her. The family's comforts in general were fewer which didn't help. Lamp oil she considered the hardest shortage to bear since it meant less quilting. The season advanced, the sunlight shrank, shorter by a crow's step every day, people said. Chill rose from the earthen floor in the dark. Huddled restlessly with her angry children in their cubicle, Musya waited as everyone did for more than the dawn. Outside, sure as the sun from east to west came an army of Germans. How would it be? Would they arrive like a meteor shower, singly in violent streaks? Or would they retreat as they'd entered, massively, like a detached continent crashing down on a village, a family, a little girl's cat, again and again and again? Every noise in the dark was startling. Chased by too many worries across too many hours, sleep fled.

In fact she had nothing to fear, said Sobansky. "Not almost nothing. Nothing—true zero." He made a perfect circle with the fingers of a black-gloved hand. Thanks to her because he adored her, Obodovka's Jewish ghetto lay under the protection of secret forces, men armed and organized, fired by sympathy, ready. The Motorbiker was among them, he'd escaped the territorial authorities for good and made himself an ally of the hero Poles, their best mechanic and a leader of men to his fingertips. Brave, curly-haired suitor: she'd always known he was destined for something remarkable. He loved her, too. Rivals united by urgency, he and Sobansky had sworn a blood brotherhood. While other partisans lay plunged in unconcerned or sottish slumbers, Musya's own true champions roamed the night, ever-vigilant, guarding the ghetto that housed her. The Germans were in for a nasty shock.

Around Obodovka the beautiful landscape turned harvest colors but the harvest was meager. Experienced small farmers had been extinct with their fields there for over a decade, seen out by the giant collectives, if not removed to Siberia then they'd likely perished at home in the ensuing famine. Little know-how combined now with insufficient tractor fuel and fertilizer and indifferent seeds to make poor crops. Kitchen gardens yielded better but theft was rampant: neighbors, soldiers, drifters, roving orphan children all got a hand in at some point. From the plots at Babiak's what was left to preserve wasn't nearly enough to fill the hidden shelves cleaned and papered at the overseer's direction. The willow boughs of her frown bent ever further as if beneath a perpetual downpour. Her rapist husband and his partisan comrades had practically wiped out the bean patch in one night's visit. How would they live once the Germans came through again pillaging? "You eat too much" became Oksana's standard greeting to the household. She cut everyone's rations, Musya's most, after she found her pocketing an onion. "Eat what you stole from me all summer—eat your guilt," she told her.

Hatefully familiar discomforts crowded in, the season's one abundant harvest. Cold mornings and colder nights made Musya and her children cringe until they ached with stiffness. Their noses had already run themselves and their upper lips raw. Old chilblains on their toes and fingers throbbed in readiness for frosts. And they were starving, that old murder-torture renewed.

Hunger bit at her. It had a rapist's bite, a rapist's persistence. Cezar the camp orderly was back again, too. The incursion he'd led into the ghetto against regulations had earned him some brief term of arrest, the place beyond the wire being off limits to plain soldiers. The murder itself appeared not to be punishable, maybe not even a crime. He'd reappeared after a week or so with a shaved head and an attitude of proprietorship. As if the blood he'd spilled were a bill of sale and his prison stay the registration of the deed, he thought he'd claimed her, owned her. To do with as he would, to kiss, to grope, to follow closely, to ejaculate on, he'd procured her. Indeed, the rapist thought he'd earned her. His uniform was cleaner, he'd bathed—altogether Cezar the rapist's confidence was soaring. He dogged her like hunger pangs, ever-present, a visual stomach growl. He gnawed her like a bone.

And then he stopped. Overnight, waylaying her was out, following her at any distance and all serenading were out. He was still around, maybe more than before. He'd simply lost interest in Musya. Now that he had her, maybe she felt more like a burden to him than a prize. Or maybe his sentiments ran strictly to pattern, each conquest victim making way for the next. The rapist couldn't stay faithful. His attention had switched to one of the young girls at Babiak's, a nervously slim owner of mystical prayer books, whom he'd raped, Musya was certain, though the girl herself may not have known. For now at every bell she leapt up to preen before Baila's hand mirror on the wall. An apparent courtship of which the Stara might have approved—she'd always said Cezar had it in him to reform. The rapist brought the mystic bouquets, late-blooming purple wildflowers. Soon a small silver ring went on view. Musya felt the icon room's unkind attentions. Bouquets were more than she'd been known to receive from Cezar the rapist, with never so much as a sniff at a ring, a telling fact the Obodovkans observed at length. Spurned by her rapist, Musya should have rejoiced but she couldn't. That anyone imagined her to be jealous was maddening, yet another torment.

Through fog-bound dusks she and Sender returned alone to the ghetto, trying despite eyestrain and fatigue to keep their footing along with a sharp lookout. Minus a protector the blue-gray landscape teemed with threat. This was the desperate hour of gleaners and of thieves who came along after the poor harvesters; the whole defenseless world hurried homewards. Musya's thoughts were stealing towards the comfort of Sobansky's embrace when footfalls came quick down a side lane and skittered into the white road beside them.

It was Hodeh on the run. She stopped and said, "What's wrong?"

"You frightened us! What's that?" Musya pointed but already knew: feathering from the little girl's fist, those were carrot tops.

"You can't have any, I got them for the Ernste." She displayed the roots, a bunch of ten or so, mostly crooked, narrow and wan. "For her special sweet year tzimmes."

"Her what?"

Sender explained, "Tomorrow is Rosh Hashanah."

"Oh, yes." She'd forgotten, lost track, she'd had no idea—she wasn't sure it mattered and she didn't really care, not this year. Only her spirits sank at the idea of another obstacle course built from obscure fast days ending in winter. And Hodeh wouldn't part with a single carrot, the whole bunch was pledged to the old glutton from Bucharest. Their family had fallen too far out of favor to spare any remedy, even one bite, one measly tip marked for her traditional dish.

"She'll know," Hodeh said.

Musya gave it up and kept walking. In truth their family needed help that only the Ernste could give: their rations of millet and onion, their lamp oil, the kerosene for their stove, their very shelter were quantities she regulated. When she'd been fond they'd done well. She wasn't so fond now that her favorite might have been baptized, she couldn't feel the same towards him. The former infant Samuel Nemo was also no longer small nor quite so adorable. Maybe as a result, the children's begging income had dropped; their act kept getting chased off the town streets nowadays, biting into the new kitchen's profits. And of course there was Musya, fatal man trap and quencher of life-giving electrical current.

She held out that night's rations and asked for an onion less decayed. The answer was no. "This one is fresh enough for you, the destroyer of peace. And worse, a godless atheist," the Ernste replied, eyeing the carrots she'd accepted impassively.

Onion oozed in Musya's fist. "Yes? Why shouldn't I be a godless atheist?" she said. "I'm not like you people, I don't come from a backward place like you do—I'm from a real city, in the Soviet Union, where we're beyond religion and primitive superstition. I am a Soviet citizen!" Bang, stamp went her purloined boot on the linoleum tiles. "And we are still standing in the Soviet Union, right this minute." Three times more. "So I don't have to follow your religion, I don't have to obey your councilors or your fasts. And by the way, my boy's name is Anton!"

The Ernste sighed. "Poor children of such a mother. Shana Tovah to her anyhow. Get her out of here."

So began Musya's third year in the Jewish ghetto of Obodovka, where the barbed wire had been reinforced with fresh coils for the last time. Those who were going to run had mostly done so. The rest were staying put. From their original nine or ten thousand they were down to about six hundred souls. The place remained overcrowded, dirty, typhus-ridden, its dooryards scabbed with invalid clusters, its lanes the haunt of wild orphans whose hunger fur showed through their rags. Starving boys in gangs robbed and terrorized the invalids especially. A weakened, unconfident gendarmerie had no answers. The boys were vandals too and, when they could get a match, match-tossers. After a string of petty arsons, one night the old barns went up all at once taking a few more lives. The ruins steamed through the first snowfall. Much depleted, the forced labor gang lines gossiped and complained. People said it was too much, that on top of expecting murderous hordes of Germans to descend at any time they should also have to worry about being roasted alive as they slept.

Relief was general, then, at November's announcement of policy changes from Bucharest. Their Regina-mamă and her friends had been hard at work on behalf of Romania's Jews, too long lost to a Transnistrian exile that hadn't been fair on them from the start. Now, as winter dug in and the Germans fell back through Ukraine, relief programs were being retooled towards rescue. The young orphans, at least, should be brought home from Transnistria—or at least out from the path of immediate peril. The Ghetto Council drew up a list for the Territorial Authority. Soon came the day when the delinquent boys, their cooperation purchased with blankets and cocoa, boarded a truck marked with white crosses that rumbled off west pursued by cheering in the ghetto's streets. Councilors gave out handshakes and received congratulations. They'd finally done something right. A little peace of mind had been restored. Now those who remained could wait more harmoniously for the next decree. Plans sprang up for homecomings and reunions that gladdened the next few breaths—a happy change.

Six nights later during another black-out, someone was careless with candlelight and the house next door to Tauber's burned to the ground. Several families survived but now one lived at Krutunog's in the long-vacant cubicle next door. Having neighbors again was hard to get used to, Musya found. The wife made a fuss whenever the power was out and the Kotzes tried lighting candles, of which she'd been left with a panic phobia. In the daily gate line-ups grumbling reappeared. People mentioned those poor transported boys, so high-spirited despite the bloat and wasting effects of their hunger, not listless like the rest—maybe they'd been accused and dealt with unjustly. By whom? Who else but a Ghetto Council overreacting in typical fashion. Soft-living types were always the swiftest to act in defense of property and so-called public order. Words were spoken in public and private talk spread; corrosive doubts dug in. Mindsets inside the wires shifted, blown misshapen like snow shrouds on rooflines by new snowstorms.

Hodeh sat and gnawed her braid, Musya watched her sometimes. Many people wondered why this notorious little girl hadn't been sent away as a delinquent too. In fact her son had put Hodeh on the list but the Ernste had intervened, partly for her chess game. For the present Hodeh stayed but she brooded on her future. Because she was a child, her future was her past—she looked ahead and pictured her happiness, the life she'd loved and cradled, black and white and warm, purring, at home. She pictured and yearned but there were problems. Among the Kotzes she'd formed strong attachments. Hodeh's sensible wish that the family return with and join her and her cat Pretzel there had foundered on one misfortune: her shtetl had no name to guide them, she'd come from a place between places.

Where would Hodeh go? Where would any of them go? For the survivors of two years in Transnistria, painful bewilderment was common. Life went on as it had, just as diseased and degraded, nothing had changed except for the addition of an end-pointed prospect, a future elsewhere. The same snow fell in the night. The same swollen blood-filled supply aircraft dragged their belly shadows across it the following day. Only now thought followed the wings out of view; a beyond had been added. Out there—was what? Infinite strangeness and something obliterated.

Musya would let her attention drop back to the bridal quilt in her hands.

Most of the time at this point she pictured her life progressing towards a winter wedding ceremony. She planned the guest list, put roasted chicken on the menu and had her trousseau on the brain. One man had won her but others would fight—not fight, but vie for her in a display of talents bravery sympathetic appeal. Another day she was choosing which shoulder to cry on after the telegram finally arrived to confirm her widowhood, she could almost feel the slips of yellow paper in her hands, when a male figure stepped from behind a tree into the dim twilit road in front of her. Without thinking, she screamed. This kept happening. Strange men, familiar men, sometimes women, the overseer more than once, caused her to scream when they appeared unexpectedly. Musya herself was always startled most of all but no one liked it. Fortunately no rapist had determined to withstand it yet since otherwise she went without defense. Her many frights were terrifying and brief. Pleasanter ideas kept her preoccupied, like a bird with eggs.

One morning she got her face slapped hard for not taking it seriously enough that their Romanian colonel had been discovered in his quarters strangled to death with a Velykden vyshyvanka.

"It is very bad!" Oksana Babiak rubbed a smarting palm. She looked oily and desperate. Being screamed at again had also upset her. "Do not think, you, he was one of these big fascists. He was an entrepreneur, a nice man, old-fashioned. And he owed me payment late on three finished orders—what am I supposed to do now without him?"

"What do you think I care?" A tarnished ring had struck Musya's cheekbone and it stung. She'd never hit her hard before. "Do you not have your husband?"

"But they will kill my husband now! With my colonel, he had protection. Do you think he can hide behind trees really so well?"

The Obodovkan's worry on this point was not overwhelming her, Musya noticed. Bothered no question by the target on her rapist husband's back, Musya judged her more upset about taking a loss in surplus inventory. She said, "So you do everything for his sake? Your husband's?"

Anger returned to flush the pallid worry-slackened face. "And why else? Um? Because I am a whore? I am the fascist enemy's whore, you think? Bad woman, bad wife? Listen, do not confuse me with you." This time she poked Musya hard on the collarbone with a fingertip. "At least I can keep a man."

As it turned out, the colonel's demise dealt catastrophe to Cezar the rapist. For days his comrades even held him for the crime; and the good cell he'd occupied on prior trips to the stockade wasn't offered him this turn around. He suffered for his unpopularity and emerged dirty, broken—more like his old self again, Babiak's observed. Yet his passion for the silly Obodovkan mystic burned still. It glowed even hotter. There he'd be, haunting the snowy front yard, hugging himself in his old war spoil furs, a wavering mortal-brown smudge on the doubled front window glass. But the new colonel's new man had identical tastes. The mystic's heart was soon under new management.

"Poor Cezar."

Musya gasped at hearing this from Sender Kotz. "What?" She raised a hand but stopped herself in time, seeing him flinch and cower. Then she began to weep at what had been done to her. She was so changed. There in Russvelt's warm stove corner where they sat side by side stealing time she gave the little boy her sobs to hold as he wept his own tears and she held him. She pitied both of them. They were so damaged. She pitied Russvelt, too. And Musya could see how someone might even pity her rapist, who in the midst of this terrible war had lost love from his life. His poverty was complete. It was true, Cezar the rapist and former camp orderly was a poor man of a piteous kind. Her nose ran. She wondered, "Why can't someone just kill him?" She felt Sender draw back.

"You mean," he said. Their scrawny host stirred in his sleep but sank back right away, an expert sleeper. "You mean, like Drobitz?"

She said no, of course not. "I mean in fighting, in war. He's supposed to be a soldier—why can't he go die in a battle or something?" But of course, she thought, he wouldn't. The rapist was too low for death in combat. What a contrast, a true gulf, lay between his world and the one she and Sobansky inhabited, theirs so much more elevated and privileged—although not by wealth, not greatly. They both believed material things didn't matter. They were rich in moral gold, paid out to them by Providence in hours full of meaning and moment; full of zealous heroics, passionate embraces, laughter, and love of the arts; a life worthy of romance.

Doctor Zev, for example, after all this time was making a hard late run at her consideration. Betrothed to another Musya felt torn, she really did. A fallen nobleman wasn't a prince and these days a prince was no doctor, especially not a good one. And her former partner in model clinical administration was a great doctor, peerless. His flaw? The speed at which he'd taken up with her successor on site had left her feeling very replaceable. Was he truly sincere? And where was Roza all this time? Were they to be rivals? These were questions she'd never need to ask about Sobansky, her intended, her soulmate. Yet Zev's flashing hazel-green glance had kept house keys to her vitals which leapt at its return. She longed for the man whole again, her mind on how the soft white bulbs of his wrist bones emerged from his silky brown pelt. The wedding night towards which Musya quilted couldn't come soon enough—although her body felt bound in chains to her like a naked criminal, she longed to be touched. She pictured scenes of kidnap bondage rescue, the doctor exploring her bruises with his healing hands to their mutually embarrassed thrill. Meanwhile The Motorbiker revved his engines in the snow-packed road outside by moonlight. Yes, she had many heroes about her, many champions, she told Doctor Zev's gentle grin. "You give us life," he answered.

Luckily a fresh exalted mood was upon her when Cezar the rapist came up behind and attacked Musya where he'd done the first time. She screamed as she'd never screamed before and fought him away from her until footsteps came pounding down the cellar stairs and he ran. Bitter winds swirled snow veils through the open doors he'd left behind him. She dashed forward and set every last bolt. The girl mystic and her friend stood watching; they called her a bitch for leading the poor man on again. Balanced on the steps behind were the two little boys to whom she said, "I don't want him at my wedding, not as guest, not as entertainment—do not invite him!"

Russvellt hooted. "A wedding—a wedding feast!" He shook himself with glee and translated for the girls.

"Who'd marry her?" the mystic wondered.

The limestone cellar walls were crumbling, the floor strewn with rubble and grit. She never cleaned down here. They'd be surprised, she said. The girls laughed, they said she'd gone crazy, crazy. She shouldered past them up the cellar stairs. The Stara would never have permitted so much of their breasts to be showing, Musya knew. She squeezed through the boys' open-mouthed amazement at her revelation of a life she'd hidden from them. Sender Kotz trailed her. No, she admitted: there was no secret betrothal, there was no one.

"There's Papa," he said. "Papa."

She said, "Of course, him." That Boris Kotz was long gone from her thoughts as a living man she'd never say. "Your father is the reason why there's no one else." None of it true but nonetheless she wasn't crazy; that was just wrong. Only day by day love encouraged her.

Conditions improved when the annoying new neighbors moved out, shipped southwest towards repatriation with the latest round of Romanian Jews. Prominent amid the final transport were the Ernste and the household of her son the ghetto councilor. The old show business veteran displayed sentiment in parting with the Kotz children for whom she had bargained vigorously, irked to the last by Musya's steadfast resistance. She considered the orphan act to have a future and for Anshel solo had offered cash outright. With her contacts and under her management, a top juvenile could be booked on every Yiddish stage in Bucharest; she had a strategy and thought the Transnistrian ghetto background would really sell. Musya wouldn't do it. The Ernste who could never stand hearing no for an answer bared sharp front teeth before religion tranquilized her enough to complete the farewells. "Waste a talent and you reject God almighty," she warned.

"Yes, yes," said her son in a sour parting voice.

His mother took a final mournful survey of the act she'd leave behind. Her prayers would be with their whole family—who wouldn't be forgotten anyhow. She uncurled one knotted digit to point: up. "Every sparrow is reckoned."

Of course every kind of hardship increased at Krutonog's with the Ernste's departure—the hand-picked successors weren't so competent—but losing those neighbors at the same time was real compensation. Soviet and stuck there with her children, once more Musya could sit up late quilting; and the extra room next door found itself deployed as a guest accommodation in her latest bridal plans.

Where would the wedding flowers come from in the middle of winter? Here was conundrum. She couldn't fool herself, Sobansky didn't have a working greenhouse, she'd seen the empty frames. But what was there to prevent some distant relative in Warsaw from responding with a cargo-full of blossoms and a personal appearance—an interesting older widow, perhaps, to make a late-in-life love match for the Romanian general who still hung his devotions across Musya's hours. An ideal solution—she was glad to be rid of him but glad to see the general happy, too. Why not? He wasn't a bad sort of man in the end, barely fascist. Just too old and hidebound in custom, he needed someone from his own generational world, they could remember the good times on the planet better between them. Past banks of white flowers from her hothouse the gray-haired couple danced a first expert waltz while the room watched admiringly. Smoothing one white silk sleeve in the candlelight, Musya would turn and speak to the person beside her, they'd exchange perfect words.

Then all would dance and some raise toasts: Truly, they'd shout, this was the way to live while waiting for a German army to come! Behind their smiling eyes signal beacons flashed code, as each minute passed according to plan. Musya's wedding was the lynchpin, the cover—for while its celebration filled the frigid night above the general's rented hall with music and revelry, the rest of the Obodovka ghetto was to head across country by torchlight to Sobansky's palace. He'd thrown open its hundred rooms to the

Jews and put his disused clinic in his rival's hands to run. The Germans would never touch them there, not with the Motorbiker and the hero Poles successfully combining ragtag defensive forces until the Americans arrived to put an end to all the fighting. And Musya, a benefactor they'd never suspect, there she sat in her white dress sipping champagne and watching her wedding guests waltz clockwise while frightened Jews poured across her true love's marble thresholds, some bumping on the rubber tires of wheelchairs re-commissioned from his yard.

And after the Germans, after the war, maybe her family would stay in Obodovka with other Jews who'd reached the same decision more or less in favor of its beauty, its crossroads, its fruitful bottom lands, the gardens and grounds of its palaces. Soon, finding more work than hands, more Jews would flock there and a certain fame for charm would spread, one to attract artists, writers, poets, actors, pianists, maybe a film studio as a Jewish town became a minor city. Near the graves of the ghetto's dead they'd erect profound monuments. Americans would come to make records of everything and leave large donations. Sobansky's palace would become a college where Anton Kotz would study chemistry someday and Hodeh law; Mr Asch would have his name memorialized on the biggest lecture hall. For a change there would be learning in the Ukrainian countryside. They might plant vineyards.

So Musya was thinking one dawn as she and Sender Kotz were heading out to the day's forced labors. All at once Elkie appeared and pulled them from the line, out of earshot. "Not today," she confided, would there be laboring in town. "And no tomorrows. All those contacts are voided," she said. "It's done. Their last line broke already—the Germans are almost here."

Sender gasped. How terrified he looked, Elkie too, by this news. Which was truly untimely, having arrived both many days sooner than expected and dangerously late, long after the fact, Musya realized. For her part she'd been wholly unaware of its approach, though she'd known just as well what was coming. The bigger surprise was to learn the date, already February 1944. Beneath the sameness of the snows she'd lost time. Now everything that had been passing was done. Here they were, in the least safe place possible. Alarm, kindled, spread. The first sharp cries sawed through a cold fog with tones she recognized from previous massacres—pogrom voices, as her mother would have said. Someone trying to ring the work bell by hand was banging on it with a metal serving spoon or something of the kind. Every sign pointed towards a day soon to become one of the worst yet.

Only now she observed a lot of bags in the snow—Elkie's luggage. More terrible news: "You're leaving?" Musya asked dejectedly—at first. "Wait! Can we go with you?"

Elkie said, "There's no time, we might not get far enough. Listen, Musya, you remember what I told you before, about the room next to yours?" Her voice dipped low. "Under the firebox, that old dugout from after nineteen."

"But what about the secret root cellar?" said Musya. "We could fit more easily." But Elkie was already shaking her head.

"Too many people know—all those gendarmes were down there already, remember?

It's bound to fill up right away. But the dugout, I've been in it, we could fit all your children along with you and me. And Eidel. We could probably even fit more." The long cheekbones were left streaked with a brick-red blush like savage war paint as Elkie finished a little desperately, Musya could hear.

"Oh. Of course, yes," she answered. Now here came Eidel's purple coat, her black fur collar and impractical boots. Among her shawls the teacher cradled Elkie's oil lamp with its glass chimney.

"Please be careful with that," Elkie said. Eidel said, "I am being careful." Then she listened with her eyes darting around at the unsettled crowds as Elkie told her of their seats in Musya's dugout. "Good." She nodded tensely. A woman in another street screamed and kept screaming. "Good."

But Sender said, "Hodeh won't like it."

"Fortunately," said Eidel, "it's not her decision to make."

Musya was looking past Eidel's shoulder, she'd recognized pretty Roza coming their way with bags and bundles. She hailed her and the girl stopped. "Roza, how are you—how is work at the clinic?"

A pained puzzled frown. "The clinic? I haven't worked there in forever—I quit that job," she went on, seeing Musya's confusion. "A long time ago." Now Roza glanced uneasily at the rest of the group. "Please tell your orphan children goodbye from me, I need to leave now."

"No, wait. Listen, Roza." In a rush of sincerity, Musya entreated her rival. "We have a hiding place where I live with extra room—why don't you come, too? It's safer there. Come hide with us." She reached but the girl snatched away her copper-braceleted wrist with a rattle. Her big eyes darted back and forth between the two from Tauber's.

"I don't think so," she said. "Not if—no."

Eidel snorted. "Fine. Die," she said.

"No, Roza, don't die, come with us." But Musya couldn't persuade the poor girl from the road. Her yellow skirt left a long stain in the ground fog.

She felt a tug on her sleeve and Sender said, "Don't invite anyone else until we ask Hodeh."

"Ask me what?" All three costumed in beggar rags for the Obodovka high street's morning shopping hour, Hodeh came up with the two younger Kotz brothers t her heels. The boys' red-auburn ear-locks, grown long for professional effect, were on display. Hodeh was looking around. "What's going on?"

Everyone except Musya answered at once: the Germans were close—too close—and the whole Red Army to follow—a double rampage, at least—with the locals to add an unknown quantity. Hearing a pause, Musya said, "Hodeh, I've invited Elkie and Eidel to hide with us in that dugout next door."

"No," said Hodeh.

Elkie made a noise, then said, "We have supplies."

"How much?" Hodeh looked them over and her head went back and forth. "No. It's not enough for both of you."

"Of course it is!" Eidel cried. "This shouldn't even be a question—it's preposterous—Elkie—Musya, you've made this decision, the decision is made, yes?"

"Not really," she admitted.

Anton spoke up. "I don't want her in with us."

He meant Eidel, they all knew before he pointed. There was a grudge between the two. Eidel said, "Very nice. Very nice behavior."

Hodeh said it was decided. "She's out."

Musya made an unaccustomed effort to impose herself and said no, she wasn't. "You all like Elkie, you want her to be there, don't you?" A strong brave capable lamp owner: of course her children wanted Elkie around, they weren't stupid, their lamp was smoky and much smaller. "So, you want one, you get both. That's done, it's final. Yes wah-wah-wah. You want Elkie and her lamp, you get her friend too."

"I've got the lamp," Eidel said. "I've got the lamp."

In an urgent voice Sender told Hodeh that Musya was inviting everybody. "She already asked Koorvah Roza but she said no. Thank God."

Musya said, "Don't call people that. And if we have extra room—"

"Get her inside," Hodeh said.

Over all her protests they steered Musya back to Krutonog's. The old inn, so far indestructible, loomed. She cast a wild look up to catch some final glimpse of sky but the doorway eave had already eclipsed it. Next she found herself standing by the shifted firebox. The empty cubicle next door to hers was full of people with their eyes on a dark square opening in the earthen floor. The initial blasts of moldering fungoid reek from its depths had subsided to an ice-cold gush. She held a candle in one hand. Another set of hard uncontrollable shivers made her eardrums ring.

The others said the same thing again. "Get in the hole." They planned to hand items down to her while she prettified the space, she could whip up some comforts. The only way they could guarantee her silence, they said, was to have her safely underground. No more heartfelt invitations, no one else was to know. Elkie claimed to have already dug out a dirt toilet, whatever that was. "We don't have time, Musya, you've got to stop arguing," she told her. The rest of them would be very busy in attempts to secure every supply that would fit and carry whatever water they could there, right up to the last possible moment. Again they swore it wasn't so bad in the hole, they'd all gone down and had a look. Even Eidel said it could be worse. "It could be much more grave-like," she said.

Lost for the words to tell them that none of this would be necessary, that their present alarm had no future except as rescue would confound it, Musya said, "No." They lacked faith, the frightened ones, too little faith was their problem. The mother was right; again. She pictured that Odessan woman, more aged by grief, more hollow-cheeked with moral triumph, slipping into the empty seat of honor next to hers at the front table—found, miraculously alive and in time for the wedding, the whole mother, down to the tilt of her chin; she'd sat just there, testing the edge of the guest mattress, Mommy with her gray hair unloosed to stream around her long neck tendons. "Wait! No—no!" Musya the Golden Bride struggled in their hands. "Let's follow the rest of them—let's go—Sobansky will help us!"

Eidel stared. "Who?"

She said, "From the palace outside town—the Sobansky house. He'll hide us until the Americans get here."

An impatient shout broke from Elkie's throat: "Not this again! There hasn't been a Sobansky living in that house since two wars ago—she's seeing ghosts again. Musya, stop this."

"Really," Eidel agreed.

"No." Musya tried to move. She felt words fail one by one. "No of course not." Her children's faces all four began to look relieved. Freezing rot bubbled and boiled up around her.

She was climbing down into the dark.

(20)

Imprisoned Jews left undefended to face their mortal enemies marauding in defeat, they were lucky to have a hole to hide in. Pogrom after pogrom after pogrom for centuries and this was the best modern culture could offer. What sort of betrayal by the rest of humanity did their plight represent? Here was a problem for thought without limits. Realistically seen the situation offered no one to blame, only immediate peril.

From the lower ladder steps people more and more resembled grave markers for the way they stood around the edge up there. Touching bottom made Musya so afraid they planned to yank out the ladder and bury her alive that for a long time she wouldn't let go. At last, keeping one foot on the bottom rung, she got the candle lit. The dugout was even worse than she'd expected, far more soil-based. Stones and knob-ended roots stuck out everywhere. Dank irregular walls met at many superfluous angles. The roof at least was wood, wide wooden boards and a single thick crossbeam, all buried in the earthen floor above. The boards were sagging and a lot of rootiness and drips and icicles of rime were coming through the cracks between them quite naturally, she supposed, after twenty-five years.

"Musya, look!" she heard. Her children and the room above were vanishing as they pulled the firebox frame across the slot. Closed in alone, she couldn't find the breath to scream. "*Look—look!*" she kept hearing their voices. Shadows fluttered overhead against a brightness: in the chamber up there her children's hands were waving her attention towards a small hole cut through the firebox and covered with a piece of screen. It would show them night and day and nothing else. She called: "Yes, good. Now open it again." Her candle-flame lit up a bad dirt floor of uncertain dimensions. Big the place wasn't.

Having almost no distance to go the walls closed in swiftly. "Open it!"

But open or shut made no difference, Musya was still in the ground, alone with tenacious fears of abandonment and live burial that only company's arrival would quiet. Fortunately, some things couldn't be tossed into the hole, they required to be carried down.

First was Sender Kotz with her wedding quilt she'd requested and the collected tailoring tools they'd need if their family lived to make its honest parnosseh. He resembled a flower standing there cradling it all like a sand lily with its leaves. He said, "Don't put the sewing kits anywhere, just keep them out for me, I'll hold them." He had his own kit now, Morocco leather, a birthday gift from Babiak's.

"Just put them somewhere. We could be in here for days, Elkie said, maybe a week," she objected.

It didn't matter. "I said I'll hold them. Listen. I'm worried about Russvelt."

"Why? Russvelt is indestructible."

"He is not." At her shrug Sender continued, "I want to run to Babiak's and look for him, I'll find him and bring him back here. There's time and there's room."

"No," said Musya. "It's a terrible idea. And there isn't room." There wasn't.

"But you asked that Roza that our family doesn't even know and we see Russvelt every day. And he's my best friend!"

"You're not going anywhere." She wouldn't argue. "What does Hodeh say about it?"

"I thought it's up to you," he sniped.

"It is—and I say no."

"Then promise me." Now he'd take no refusal. "When we get out of here, we'll go find him and he can stay with us. Promise."

She tried, "No."

"Yes."

"Fine," she promised.

It was true, they had no room to welcome Russvelt. The former housemaid had exaggerated its spaciousness, in fact the dugout would just fit their seven. The traffic of a dozen feet in the chamber overhead kept sending clay dust showers from the cracks between the roof boards—the atmosphere inside was murky even with the top wide open. Elkie fanned a view clear in it and pointed at the screened hole in the firebox frame. Designed to let some fresh air through, it would just as vitally admit the warning smell of smoke once they were closed inside. Fire by arson was their biggest possible and not unlikely problem, Elkie warned. Should Krutonog's old fruit canning shed happen to catch they'd have no choice but to climb out and make a break through the nearest wall. Two hand axes, Tauber's greatest treasure, she set by the ladder. "No touching. Tell your children," she said.

Anton joined her next wearing the tiger skin he'd entrust to no one else around his shoulders like a Hercules. Unwound and folded, he put it in the center of the overcoat she'd laid as a floor rug and said, "That's my spot. Don't move it anywhere." He picked up an axe to swing around.

Musya was thinking back to Anton's tormented air-raid nights. When the loud noises arrived, this ordeal to come would be hardest on him, she feared, without the sweet wine he'd learned to rely on then. Trying to recall her role in any decision to dose him, Musya felt like she'd lived as a sleepwalker once in Odessa. Where had she been? She said, "Fine. But I'm not in charge of seating."

Anton knew that. He put down the axe and she watched him assume the uncomfortable look that said his business was still incomplete. Their eyes connected, his glowing. "Is Papa coming with the Red Army?" he asked.

"Possibly, yes," she answered without hesitation. "We'll see."

"And then can we go home with him?"

She nodded her head. A winter short on food had worn down the fattest child in Obodovka, he didn't look so solid as before. "Home?" she said.

"Yes, to Siberia."

She said, "Yes, but I want to go back to Odessa first."

"For what?"

"Because I want to see the ocean." It was true.

"For what?"

"I have my reasons. Then we'll go to Siberia."

"With Papa?"

"If Papa wants, of course with Papa."

"Promise."

She considered. Her thought took the shape of a newsreel map with moving arrow. Straight to Vladivostok and on to America—Musya crossed her fingers. "I promise." Even Boris might be willing to try America now.

They sent down her carpet-sided bag full of books and papers and most of the luggage pile, the Manchukuo dishware, the heater, the bucket. Mrs Drobitz's tin pitcher arrived brimming with cold well water. It was bothersome to have to keep ducking underneath the crossbeam. Every peek the others took left them critical of her arrangements. They and everything they owned would be filthy in two minutes. "I'm not finished yet," she kept saying.

"Mamenyu!"

The baby was teetering alone at the edge of the ladder. Her voice rose in horror as she went to catch him: "Mamenyu's here!" But he kept his balance and then insisted on clambering down by himself, every rung, while she kept her hands around his ribcage. Samuel Nemo was exhausting lately. Safe at the bottom he threw himself onto the dirt floor and rolled around until he was filthy. This took five seconds. She dragged him to his feet and he looked at her, handsome as a boy-god disguised as a penniless student of Torah, with the faded blue-trimmed hem of the sailor blouse he wore under Anton's old worn-out brown sweater touching his knees. His wide mouth was twisted, his big eyes searched her face. "What do you want?" Musya said, at which he burst out crying. She knelt to clasp him to herself and kiss him, her child from her body, a circumstance which amazed her and left all her anxieties increased. "What's wrong?" One of his ear-locks brushed her lips again. Mother and son, they were almost like strangers. She had no idea what might have upset him so much, usually Samuel Nemo enjoyed family activities, she knew that. The words he was sobbing she could barely make out as he clung to her and shook:

"I don't like! I don't like! No good—it's no good!"

At last she thought she knew. Samuel Nemo was afraid but had no words for saying so. He'd never spent an hour in school except to eat cake and fear was not in his vocabulary. Holding him, Musya made comforting noises until he grew calmer. "Mamenyu's here," she chanted. "I'm here."

"He's supposed to be up here!" Hodeh was firm in pursuit at the top of the ladder. "Send him back up—Pretzel, come up here, we need you."

The baby snuffled and moved to obey. "For what?" Musya objected, holding on.

"For asking people for things," Hodeh said.

She said, "Ask for them yourself, I need him here, I'm his mother." But he was pulling away towards the ladder and up—he liked work.

Parting with her baby's ankles Musya found herself alone again. She let out a scream when a dirt clump dropped from the ceiling to the floor beside her. No one responded.

Then no one liked her arrangements. Comfort and satisfaction were nil. Inside the hole was a muddle of shoving and cross-purposes. Listening up top for the Germans' arrival, Elkie told them every half-minute to hush down below but their voices kept rising disputatiously. Eidel wanted half the space for their couple, she'd claimed it and now she wouldn't budge because she didn't understand why everyone ought to be equally crowded. "Where is it written?" Eidel said. A moment later they all heard a loud bang.

"Grenade," Elkie said, swinging onto the ladder, "This is it." Dirt showered them as she pulled the firebox frame across.

Darkness, chill, decay: Elkie struck a match and held it to her lamp wick. The tiger stripes leapt. Eidel gasped. "Are you crazy? I don't want to be asphyxiated." They all stared at her. "We need light, we need heat," Musya said. But no: Elkie was reaching. Off went the kerosene heater lit only minutes before, they'd had hardly any relief but enclosure made it too dangerous. "I don't know why," Elkie said, "every time, Eidel, you jump to think the worst." Eidel replied, "I'm logical—I know facts—I'm sorry—can I help it?" Musya's nerves sent warning aches of overstrain. "We wouldn't asphyxiate that fast," she said. "That's what they all say—don't you think?" Eidel said. Musya said no, she didn't. Elkie said, "We need to get organized. There isn't much time." But what could they do? Everyone asked Elkie at once. Too small for both sides to be right, the dugout had no room for compromise. Either half was too much for two or it wasn't.

"The split is no good," Samuel Nemo observed unexpectedly.

Elkie was much more interested in laying out the principles and use of her makeshift latrine in the far corner. She'd rigged up an old door curtain to supply some privacy and she thought they could keep a candle end burning inside, at least by day. Correct use would still leave them very grimy and bothered by stink, there was no doubt about that.

All at once the Kotz family's share of the dugout didn't seem so bad since it was further from the dirt toilet. With the lantern turned down to its lowest blue flame the candle-glow behind the curtain strengthened alarmingly. Eidel said she felt sure the Germans would see. Elkie's disastrous response was to ask Musya's opinion at which Eidel cut in: "It's not enough to invite her gigantic family in here when we can ill-afford the oxygen—you have to put her in charge of our lives as well?" Musya objected. "Invited us? What are you talking about? This is our space," she said. "Actually," Eidel said, "it isn't." Then Elkie admitted that since the dugout at Tauber's was in such terrible repair, she and Eidel had been planning all along to use this one; just if they had to. "If you weren't using it. We've been saving supplies," she added. Musya said she didn't recall Elkie's saying a word about this to her and asked, "Did you?" Elkie said. "No. I'm sorry." But Eidel denied any cause to be sorry. "Why mention it? We had our plan. Presumably they had their own plan," she said. "Yes," Hodeh said. Wondering what Hodeh's plan had been Musya said, "Of course. Of course we did."

Into the momentary lull came four deliberate rifle shots.

Dozens of other Jews electing against flight from the ghetto had likewise concealed themselves inside the familiar fabric of their prison. Sadly, not all were well-hidden. There'd be a hunt, Elkie guessed. "And the more people they find the longer they'll keep looking." The dugout listened to silence for a few moments until Musya said, "Don't worry, they won't find us." Eidel said, "Don't you think everybody says that, too?" Before she could reply a spray of bullets overlapped another, closer, overhead: a hunt with machine guns.

A boy's high voice rose and whispered in stammered Ukrainian: Sender Kotz, a sinner, asking mercy one, two, three times, begging for it from a son of God. The foreign syllables grew quieter and spilled with smoother rapidity from his lips. The repetitions didn't stop. "He's goy too now?" Elkie asked. "You're goy, probably," Musya reminded her. The other children had begun to grow alarmed. "What is that?" Anton demanded. "Why is he doing that?" She said, "Oh, he learned it from a girl at work, it's mystical prayer." Eidel said, "It's superstition. Keep your voices down." Anton made a noise. "But for what? Ask him!" The quick chant ceased. "For protection, Antosha. You should say it too. It's the heart prayer," Sender explained. Eidel was scoffing. "It's famous. You say it to Lord Isus Khrystos all the time constantly and when you think of something bad, it makes it go away—it's not garbage, miss, it's from the Philokalia, it's older than Europe."

"Oh please," Eidel said.

"Can we say in mame loshn?" Hodeh asked. Sender said yes. "The language doesn't matter." Anton asked, "They really go away? Bad things?" Eidel said of course not but Sender disagreed. "I think the more people who say it, yes, maybe." To which Anton and Hodeh said, "Teach us." They'd made up their minds. Eidel thought it disgraceful and in especially poor taste given the circumstances; but her friend found it amusing, so long as they kept their voices down, to hear a Yiddish prayer said to the goy Lord Jesus. "Why not?" Elkie added almost cheerfully. "Our Lord—Jews' I mean—is their Lord's papa. It's the same family." Eidel corrected her. "The same backward delusion, you mean. Why not recite the multiplication tables instead?" The rest ignored this suggestion. Minutes later, with Samuel Nemo doing the best he could, the heart prayer dribbled from six mute mouths, a liquid thing of Yiddish tongue clicks. The impregnable front door of Krutonog's boomed under blows. No one was getting in that way. The Jew-hunters and their guns would have to use the side doors or come around to the back through the kitchen garden.

Elkie put the candle out.

This, now, was waiting for Germans. Compared to this, Musya considered, her waiting of the previous weeks and months had been nothing but time passing. She'd let it paralyze her all the same. When Germans were coming there was nothing to be done, no place to run safe enough; she'd learned this lesson. Any will she'd ever had to behave otherwise was long gone, she could no more run than Yankel Weissbein could now. Hitler had convinced her heart against which prayer words rang as when hailstones strike the bronze suit-front of a Party saint on a town square plinth, shattering against her unbelief in anything but German barbarity. Fact: here it was, almost upon them. And only emptiness remained when she thought of the wedding plans that had kept her from reality until today. Just that morning, only a few hours ago, she'd chosen the flowers— white lilac—and for the candles, very simple, some painted silver embellishments; she'd been so pleased with both decisions.

She and Sobansky had really mistimed things, however; and Musya couldn't blame herself so much. He was the one who lived in the world—a dreamer, granted, a typical Pole that way. Her usual smile at his national foibles faltered as she began to wonder what delayed him; for even a dreamer can take action. So why hadn't he taken the Obo- dovka ghetto into his palace already by now? And it was true, any big party night might have done as a pretext, nothing required her to sacrifice and give herself in marriage except that he'd wanted it. Or had he?

Her heart kicked the prayer off her lips. For here she was, Musya had to acknowledge, still as single and imprisoned as she'd been—jilted, possibly, abandoned even in her perfect dream by a man who couldn't love Jews after all, the old hates were too strong for his weak nature, maybe. One thing was certain: she'd never regret him again.

Samuel Nemo was hungry, he said. They all were, they whispered. And Elkie, bending to her stores, said, "Why not?" Everyone got a dry biscuit which all but Sender sucked on first so as not to make crunching sounds; his prayer continued, his biscuit untouched, slipped into his sewing kit. They heard a crash upstairs—a door, a door frame. "Keep saying the words!" he urged them. Biscuit crumbs flew as pattering quick chant resumed in every mouth, even Eidel was saying something. "The threes—the multiples," she explained. Anton said, "No! Don't confuse Lord Khrystos."

Musya sighed. How her sister Liza and their husband Boris Kotz would have hated equally to hear everything in this minute! She supposed on their behalf she ought to raise some strong objection. But she didn't object; only she found prayer grew tiresome. "Is this all it is?" she whispered to ask. "Just saying the same thing over and over?" "Self-hypnosis," Eidel said. The others hushed them and Eidel started on the fives.

Strange men swarmed the wooden halls in heavy boots and made the dugout's dirt sides thud in sympathy with the old inn's foundations. Stairs creaked, cupboard doors slammed, shelves and their contents crashed onto floors. Screams stripped by distance and obstruction to their bird-call cores broke out: the hunters had found someone. Musya pictured Germans, their eyes mad and pale, the knuckles of their meaty hands livid from gripping gun stocks; pot-boiled homogenous men. Where was Doctor Zev? Where was his sardonic mouth with its capacity to deliver incongruously soft kisses of the perfect duration? Left behind by his pretty nurse with a handful of patients, he'd play the Jewish hero now, she feared. Crazed with thoughts of injectable drugs the retreating fascists would converge on the ghetto clinic soon enough, no question. Always given to uneasy joking at the preponderance of brains over brawn in his own make-up, Zev was liable to overcompensate with some defiant rash self-sacrifice. That he believed Musya lost to him didn't help. He didn't know she'd dropped Sobansky, she hadn't had a chance to tell him. Removing his spectacles with a calm hand he stood in the clinic doorway to greet Death.

Her breath caught—everyone's breath caught. Footsteps overhead, very loud and rapid, the boot heels slippery, not in good repair, the floorboards told them. Dirt sprinkled them twice: there was the briefest pause at every cubicle, a continuation as if down a spine to the end of the canning shed corridor, a reversal and an exit. Quiet returned except for the rampage and screaming elsewhere up above.

They exhaled and Sender Kotz had time to say, "You see?" before a horrible burst of noise reached them through the ground itself. The secret root cellar was discovered. Worse came next from almost overhead. It was the kitchen garden where many feet thudded and screaming bodies crashed through snow cover to clawingly uproot the frozen grass. All this was bad enough but then horrified consternation swept the dugout: Eidel and the children recognized a voice, a certain Simon they all seemed fond of, among the youngsters' screaming voices. His name was a blank to Musya, after the rat-eating Pearl she'd mostly lost track of her children's friends. To Eidel of course he'd been a student and maybe something of a pet, she seemed so frantic. "Pray again!" Elkie commanded. "Pray or multiply." Their lips moved. Men were raping Simon's mother on the ground, they heard clearly. Then someone killed her with a blade. What they were doing to the little boy meanwhile was hard to understand. From Musya's point of view what this Simon needed was a doctor—and she knew a great one. He was a doctor in need of being needed, her green-eyed love. Zev was right: this was a day for Jewish heroics.

She climbed to her feet and said, "Don't worry."

One step cracked her forehead smartly on the crossbeam. In a fireworks show of hurt she staggered backwards to collapse against the wall. A few instants later she came to herself again, she was weeping. "Quiet!" she heard. Small dirty hands grasped at her mouth from all directions in the dark to still it somehow; moving her head to evade them was agony. "Quiet!" The others were upset with her but the pain was too much, Musya's sobs grew louder until finally Elkie crawled across and put her in a smothering embrace; the noise stuck in her throat as the housemaid's never-ending heart prayer thundered in her throbbing brain. Headfirst into a lightless underground sea of tears she dove and swam towards the depths until she burst and drowned. She floated there, one with grief.

"What is wrong with you?" The ground was still. Candlelight caught in her eyelashes, dazzling her. She was thirsty. Eidel's voice came again: "Seriously—what is going on inside your head? Don't you understand? Your children need you."

"My head," she rasped. She'd awoken alone, wrapped in a tiger skin on the freezing dirt floor. "Of course you need her." Now Eidel was arguing with her children who were saying no, they didn't. Musya felt terrible in every way. The little patch of screen was dim, the short day was almost done. Not a sound came from the kitchen garden. Death, its terrible mystery, weighed on the ground there—a stillness heavy, wet, sinking. "The little boy," she managed. "What happened to Semyon?" His teacher answered through a stuffed nose, "Simon. They cut his throat." Like his mother, then, Musya reflected. Would her own children survive her so briefly? Sitting up made her feel sick. The moment's rest she needed dragged on.

Next all was dark overhead. Behind the door curtain's orange membranous glow the dirt toilet already stank. And the still winter cold of the frozen Ukrainian land overwhelmed them. They couldn't use the heater, from her perch on the ladder Elkie kept hearing too many noises through the screen to open wide enough to offer the least ventilation. The children's teeth chattered, they were having a loud chattering contest; Sender's were so rotten he'd dropped out early from the pain. The baby's small teeth made a hair-raising sound, Eidel judged him the winner. Musya said she agreed, it was true. Her heart was breaking. She asked for a drink. The water was so cold. She told Sender to pull out her quilt from the luggage where he'd helped her store it for safety: "For you children," she said. To her surprise every one of them objected on the quilt's behalf. She said it didn't matter but wept anyway to see its colors exposed to a soiling such as this promised to be. Her unfinished quilt made a great lump over the four children's heads—a buried lump, it looked like every hope she'd ever had. Elkie told the others to let her cry. "Let her get it out—it's very nice work, Musya," she added in her usual tone for addressing speech-deprived invalids. But Eidel didn't hear it that way. "You were always sweet on her, weren't you?" Elkie denied everything and said, "Just look at this beautiful quilt, Eidel—you're the one who's always talking about handicrafts." "A lot of beige," Eidel answered doubtfully.

Around dawn everyone smelled smoke at the same time.

Was it Krutonog's? They all sniffed and sniffed. Elkie thought it must be coming from a few streets off. Eidel said maybe it was Tauber's. Elkie groaned furiously and said, "Can you please stop being like that?" The smell of house fires came and went for the next five days. And Eidel did not stop, she'd suggest Tauber's again and again. As they were to learn, Elkie cherished plans for taking charge there since management had fled. Eidel's guess kept her bothered. She fumed, "Twenty other places it could be and you have to pick that one." Certain hints Eidel dropped made the pretty blonde's motives clearer, as they disclosed a heart set on less Obodovka, more downtown Moscow. At the children's encouragement, Elkie countered with a plan to take over Krutonog's, why not? Forget about Tauber's which didn't even have a modern kitchen. "But I don't cook," Eidel said, "and neither do you." The two friends would bicker all day but Elkie's arms would be around Eidel without fail when it came time to try and sleep, affectionate kisses for two in the dark producing strange discomforts in the wakeful remainder.

The action continued overhead. It wasn't safe to climb out and fill a fresh water jug, not once. There was some full combat. Charging feet pounded, trucks barreled past, explosives went off and sent showers of dirt into the dugout; hunted Jews kept being discovered and murdered as German, Romanian, Soviet and local fighters rampaged over the ghetto in turn. As a diverting change from heart prayer everyone memorized the multiplication tables to eleven. Eidel was at her best then, a born teacher. During respites safe for talking she dominated every discussion. "Up there?" She said, "They're setting fire to paper files in offices." She'd seen a lot near the Polish border. "They're collecting women to fill brothels. A brothel is a kind of labor prison," she answered Anton. He never missed a word from Eidel's lips, unfamiliar or otherwise, and was always questioning and picking fights with her. Once the delinquent boys who'd been sent away for arson were the topic and Eidel said she didn't care about the witnesses, she called the fires accidents, the boys falsely accused, innocents stigmatized for their rambunctious youth, innocent young boys. Anton said, "They were not, they were firebugs and rotten criminals like the council said. Hodeh knows, she had to fight them off with the sharp scissors!" Hodeh said, "I did. They were after the sharp scissors." Eidel said, "You see?" "No," said Anton. Nobody but Eidel saw. Her voice grew impatient. "They needed tools—basic tools—but no one gave them any. They weren't rotten, they were failed by their guardians and representatives. This is what happens when you don't have socialism." It was easy to see why the teacher longed to go to Moscow, her friend Elkie said—because there were more crazy people like her there. Eidel called Elkie an obstructionist.

Nightfall brought rats to the room upstairs, many rats, many vocal and curious about the firebox screen, on the move, Elkie guessed, from burned-out former premises. They couldn't get in the dugout at all, she told Eidel. Down below, the little clutch of seven souls stayed hidden. Maybe in the night or maybe tomorrow, they'd tell each other, the fighters would at last move on from the Obodovka ghetto where their continued presence was mystifying, really. Had the local scenery beguiled them, as Musya suspected? Were they lingering over a chance to risk death in the Napoleonic winter battlefields of boyhood's imagination? Who could understand the minds of men still intent upon burning down buildings and killing more people at this point?

"We're alive. And they're alive," Elkie said. She meant the dugout's insect life and worms. Lamplight made their numbers come on strong. "We're all alive here so let's just try to get along with each other without screaming the roof off." Every many-legged thing their body warmth had hatched in the Ukrainian soil now crawled towards its source to poke with head or mouth or feelers through the dugout's dirt walls, plop down onto a person and keep crawling. Even the children objected to being so neighborly as Elkie now suggested. "What if they try to eat us?" Anton asked. Eidel said, "Of course they'll try to eat us. What? Worms and beetles eat flesh—I'm not allowed to know that? Ignorance never helps anything," she finished strongly.

Musya kept mum. Her usual bromide felt out of place: why shouldn't they worry—especially if they wanted the occupation? Misery could do with variety, she thought. The lump on her forehead still hurt and she was tired of life in a dark stink-filled burrow in Transnistria. Crawling insects made the situation worse—but everything that happened made it worse. Death stenches, all too familiarly penetrating, reached in from the kitchen garden. Rats' feet scrabbled at the firebox frame night and day now. And the three of them who could were menstruating in tandem—the mess was terrible, disheartening. They needed more soil for the latrine all the time. Eventually it happened that Anton was excavating from a wall near the door curtain, Hodeh assisting, when a portion came loose and spilled something into their midst.

A human skull.

A pile of bones followed, dislodged at the same time along with a lot of black beetles. It wasn't safe to scream. Samuel Nemo was noisily fascinated. Hodeh caught him up. "Quiet, Pretzel!" The bones with their bulging ends were just like the ones sticking out from the dugout walls on every side, she'd thought they were roots, age-blackened leg bones and arms bones and ribs; there were digits and knucklebones all over the floor that she'd taken for chalk pebbles. There were some hair strands but no sign of clothing or jewelry, no rings. "I never heard of a graveyard here. It must be very old," Elkie said, moving the lamp around. "No wonder there are so many insects." "And worms," Eidel said. "Elkie, you told me this was a safe dry clean place, you called it the best hiding hole in Obodovka—and you," she turned, "you were down here in broad daylight for hours arranging things, you never noticed the decay of dead Jews all around you?" "You were the one," Musya replied, "who said it could be more grave-like." "Well I was wrong," Eidel said. "Anyway," Musya continued, "They don't look like bones, they're not white." Eidel was exasperated. "Those bones you're picturing aren't naturally white, they've been boiled and bleached with caustic soda. Which I know because I was friends with a medical instructress," she explained to Anton. He said, "And how do you know they're Jews?" "Who else?" Eidel said. "Who else winds up in a mass burial in the middle of Ukraine?" Elkie said, "This was always the Jewish quarter. Maybe the ground shifted, that's why." Her voice trailed off. "The ground didn't shift," Eidel said. Sender pried a section of another skull from the wall by his head and spoke in a wondering tone:

"It's the mummy cave! The Cave of Ten Thousand Mummies, under Odessa—you remember, Hodeh, we told you." And he described hero Jim and his brother Tom and their guide the strange conservationist with his torch and his great heaps of ancient remains. Anton said it was better in the story. Eidel agreed that it usually was. "That's a rib bone you're holding. And that's part of a pelvic girdle. It's really not funny." The children kept digging out the oddest ones they could find, hoping to stump the teacher who named them all in Russian. "Don't pick at the bones, leave them be," Elkie warned. She had concerns about a possible collapse; but it was a case of some kind of skeleton fever where Musya's children were concerned, they loved to pull bones from the walls when no one was watching them. Elkie and Eidel blamed her, the mother, when a great sheet of earth fell around Musya's shoulders one afternoon and left her hair full of cockroaches.

Now she sat away from the wall, hugging her knees. Tears dripped down her filthy cheeks without ceasing. The possibility that her children would die here chose this time to feed among her thoughts; an awful carrion bird with a beak like a spider, it left her mind filled with disgusting chaos. Then every twenty minutes or so a special fear that someone would physically hurt them gripped her and hollowed her out with an acid or caustic soda solution—if she moved it would start to dissolve her. She couldn't move, couldn't speak, couldn't speak to them. Every memory she could make of them was precious but every moment now felt horrific, better forgotten. She preferred to watch the four of them asleep beneath her patchwork by the candle end alight. If she narrowed her eyes, the reeking dirt toilet that shimmered there became the icon room at King Nebuchadnezzar's palace. Then more vivid than dreams came two little boys in quilted suits hurling themselves down the sled hills of snowy Birobidzhan; the infant Samuel Nemo in the family sailor blouse raced on his impossibly fast short fat white legs to greet her at the ghetto gates; and next lay purring, his small feline self again, starlight in his eyes, in little Hodeh's lap; then she was back in Hodeh's Ali Baba cave-nest surrounded by floating housekeys. No one was speaking much lately, they were almost out of water. For six days straight the blood seeped from the boy Simon's throat and his mother's had been making its way through the soil towards the dugout walls. The rotten bones in their multitudes were highly conductive, she guessed, so that she expected to see it appear any time now on the wall nearest the kitchen garden, there by the glowing curtain, at first a trickle through the bones like honey glaze. Musya was certain she could see movement there.

"I told them not to touch the bones." Elkie sat up angrily. "But they're all asleep," Musya said. There was a definite disturbance in that corner, though. She gasped as her heart sank. "It could be my husband again!" Pink ectoplasmic Boris Kotz, he felt like the last thing she wanted to see. She watched a dirt clod tumble down the wall, then something of darkness slide out and stop—a big rat body. Would there be a transformation? Would it grow spectacles? She'd never know. Elkie sprang forward and hissed at it, "Shoo! Shoo!" and the rat turned and vanished. Elkie risked another candle flame and signaled to Musya; the others were still sleeping. "Where's the hole?" She'd picked up a skull to use as a plug. "We can't let them get in here, there's too many—they really *will* eat us."

A couple of leg bones served to brace the skull. It would have to be good enough, Elkie whispered, adding:

"Don't tell Eidel!"

Broad daylight showed overhead. The dugout had slept poorly in general and late.

Anton sat up, did some arm stretches, glanced around and said, "Who moved my things?" Musya said, "Don't worry. We had to borrow a couple of bones, that's all." He missed his femur. "And my best cherep—you took them. Give them back." "No," Elkie said. "Yes," said Anton. He climbed to his feet. "Yes—yes—yes!" It was bad enough being robbed, now he couldn't get justice—she understood completely, Musya told him. "But we're using them for something very important." "An emergency repair," Elkie said. Eidel said, "What's broken?" "There!" Anton slipped underneath Elkie's hand, yanked his big leg bone from the wall and shook it like a club at them. "This is mine! I'm collecting them!" Dirt and metatarsals tumbled around his boots. Elkie said, "Fine. We need another to replace it." "No!" Anton said. She told Musya to find one. Anton started shouting "No—no!" "He's out of control," Eidel said. Musya and her other children nodded helplessly. "Give me that bone and be quiet." Eidel held out her hand; to their wonder, Anton obeyed in full. Elkie was next. "Why do you need to take his bones?" Eidel demanded of her. Elkie said, "Because." At that moment they all recognized the sound of people walking in the ghetto, many feet lightly shod. Civilians. Earth drizzled from the walls and ceiling boards. A woman called out that she'd heard something inside there, sounded like voices; a man cursed in Ukrainian. It was the townsfolk.

Did this mean it was safe to emerge? Not one of them thought so. "Blow out the candles!" Eidel said. "No, we need them—wait," Elkie protested. "Just—oh you momzer, shoo!" Maybe the same big rat vanished into a slightly different hole. Eidel gasped. "Was that a rat? You swore they couldn't get in here—you promised!" They'd had the run of the place up there beside the kitchen garden and the sudden arrival of people was scaring them underground in great numbers, this was the situation as Elkie explained it, apologizing: "Woman plans, God laughs." Eidel scoffed. "Enough pseudo-religion—you lied to me!" "But how was I supposed to know what would happen?" Elkie said. "Then you shouldn't have promised," said Eidel. Her friend snatched the big bone from her hands and said, "Excuse me, I need to obstruct something. More bones," Elkie told the rest. "We need to block anything that looks like a rat hole—hurry!" she whispered. Skulls, scapulas, pelvic girdles were produced; lamps and candles lit the grisly work too briefly, they extinguished every flame with the first sound of civilians entering Krutonog's on their soft feet. At the emergency wall Sender filled chinks by hand with pats of dirt and Anton kept pressing as hard as he could at a scapula he was trying to embed there, until Elkie signaled them to stop: "It's not safe, the whole thing might collapse." They all drew back and Elkie swung herself onto the ladder to listen for developments. The wall in question broadcast a series of muffled squeaks followed by a lot of gnawing sounds. "In one more minute," Eidel said, "I am officially going to go insane." Sender said, "Oh, please don't." Voices exclaimed; they heard disgust, physical—the townspeople had found the kitchen garden. Some were in the old canning shed corridor, looking out at it. They'd picked a sunny day to explore the ghetto. The firebox screen was admitting plenty of light for the ones in the dugout to see a piece of pale calcified matter jiggle and vanish into the wall, to be replaced by something silvery, whiskered. Sender sprang up and pounded a piece of cranium over the spot. Dirt showered him as footfalls creaked the floorboards overhead. Not everyone had been dissuaded from the tour by the sights and smells of week-old massacre outside. These were some intrepid folk of Obodovka who were amazed and appalled to the point of amusement that anyone had ever lived this way, even zhidy. Elkie reached down armed herself with both axes. A gleam caught Musya's eye through the clay-fogged air: Hodeh ready with the sharp scissors. That left the weaponless to worry and speculate. For someone might get curious and shift the firebox back—what then? Or what if an intruder or two simply crashed down into their midst through the rotting roof boards? Would Elkie chop them into bits if they'd only come to sightsee? What were they doing up there, anyhow? Little by little, hard listening told.

They were stealing the chest of drawers!

It didn't take long, of course. To pillage the whole Jewish ghetto took not much longer. The Kotzes hadn't lost much besides Samuel Nemo's old baby clothes. Elkie was infuriated anyway: "They have everything in that town and they come here to steal our only furniture? Hey, get down, baby—no, go back." Without Musya's noticing Samuel Nemo had slipped across to the ladder and was trying to climb it, he was going after the thieves all by himself. Hodeh pulled him back onto the floor. "He has no word for fear," Musya explained. "Delayed language skills," Eidel said. Elkie said she thought it was safe to risk some candles. Before anyone could move, a fist-sized bunch of dirt and bones tumbled off the rat hole wall and two rats dashed through to chase each other round and round the dugout in crazy circuits, flinging themselves through space, slamming into everything and everyone, squirming through clothes, scratching faces, catching and swinging on braids, until Hodeh cried "Kill, Pretzel!" and there came an exploded squeak. The rest raised their eyes to find Samuel Nemo gripping the sharp scissors and a big rat impaled on their points. He had his little teeth bared at its fellow rat crouched there. They heard him growl and the rat vanished into the wall, the last rat they saw. "On the other hand, he has phenomenal motor skills for a two year-old," Eidel said. "Thank you," said Hodeh. "My friend taught him that."

They waited through one last night and then Elkie called it safe to emerge. They had not died in the war. Strange to see, when Eidel put her foot on the first rung of the ladder Anton rushed to throw his arms around her in a sobbing embrace: he loved her. "This always happens," Eidel said.

Musya found her old pine cone rolled into a corner of their empty cubicle. Sender was examining the dirt on her quilt by daylight, their sewing kits beside him—he'd never let go. "Don't worry, this will all come out," he said.

Elkie stopped short in the new kitchen doorway. Eidel, behind, peered around her and said, "What on earth?" Lording it over the premises from the Ernste's badly-listing old armchair was her friend's employer, the woman from Tauber's. "But you ran," Elkie said, dismayed.

"Just to the woods—the partisans showed us where to hide. What, I'm not allowed to survive a massacre? No one invited you in here," she told the pair as they stepped into the room. "I never liked you especially," she told Eidel. "Unless you care to make your-selves useful and cook this delicious dinner."

She gestured at the propped-up baking table where the rat in its skin on Manchukuo dishware with scissors no longer protruding lay presented on top. There wasn't another bite to eat in the place, she'd told Musya's disappointed family who'd headed there first. Earth had yet to be piled over the dead in the kitchen garden. As for the new baleboste's domain, it lay in shambles. The glass office shattered, every surface splashed with food waste and bad smells everywhere, torn-down cabinets and broken crockery heaped on the floor; but the sink taps worked. The stove needed one minor fix. Always superior, Krutonog's electric kitchen had beaten its rivals for good since Tauber's was a charred ruin, Eidel had guessed right after all.

Elkie knew. They'd gone to Tauber's first. She said, "We don't cook."

"They who needs you here? Get out and take your perversion with you."

"Yes?" Elkie took a step forward, gave a curious knock on the wall and without even looking extracted a chocolate bar in Turkish wrappings from an invisible shelf that appeared when a tile door on a spring flipped open. Eidel screamed and reached. But her friend's only thought was for the bargaining power she'd just established. There were plenty more like that one, Elkie said, and she knew them all. To prove her point she knocked out another code and a door by the baseboards opened on some sacks of beans. Elkie crossed to the stove and fixed it in one minute. Then she told the Tauber's woman to fetch some water and get it boiling.

Poor Elkie didn't have long to enjoy being in charge. Assigned their own indoor room, the Kotzes would stay to help clean up the place and re-open but inn business was nil. No one stopped at Obodovka after this. The atmosphere of boredom and hopelessness was too much for Eidel who had their couple packed for Moscow by the end of spring, when—to Anton's major heartbreak—their bus would pull away, leaving the other landlady on top again.

For now, the dugout survivors took themselves to wash. On the street men were piling a second or third dead body on a wheelbarrow. Elkie said the town was taking care of the burials, they would even come to Krutonog's this time. The strangers wore their faces behind scarves, sheer philanthropists, maybe. As for other Jews who'd survived, there had to be two or three dozen. Human beings were astonishing. They had a long wait for hot water. People said the line was incredible, there were many complaints. Some, pretty Roza included, had hidden outside the ghetto and only just returned; the gates and most of the barbed wires were all pulled down, Roza said. Now after a week in the icy woods a few asked to be given priority and were answered with jeers. Everyone waited their turn, the forty or fifty who'd survived Transnistria there, including the remnants of a Ghetto Council still in charge. This persistence was bemoaned but no one revolted. People talked quietly of the great number dead. Hardly any children were left. Musya was lucky—blessed, they told her. God's will done. She said yes, she knew it. In truth she felt grateful but more urgently filthy, even after her washed scalp had stopped crawling and she'd stepped into a change of ragged clothes; she felt broken, robbed of everything, destitute, futureless. Her stomach clenched as Sender Kotz walked up with damp-darkened curls and serious eyes.

"Can we go find Russvelt now?"

She warned him, "It could be very bad."

"You promised," he said.

Their route was lined with countless signs of slaughter. Its highest point showed them prospect upon prospect of white thawing fields gashed and trampled, sprayed here and there with gore. Dead livestock and horses, dead people, the blood ripped from them resounded against the eye until the silent Ukrainian land rang like a holiday. The deep ice pooled in the dip of the road before Babiak's was a rust brown-black color. At the top they paused. Steps away in the frozen mud, resembling a playground ball, severed close to the jaw, was a human head, Cezar the rapist's. Pulled out of place, the white boundary stones were circling the site of a campfire the Germans must have made. And again Boris Kotz had been wrong. They were cannibals.

She turned to go but Sender stopped her with a hand, saying, "What about Russvelt?" She squinted across at the big blue farmhouse. Someone was at home, a few roof vents were smoking. Then a cloud end flicked the sun and a beam of light shot up from the snowy blood-splashed yard. It drew her. By the big tree, lying in one of the patches of dead grass and mud showing through, was a hand mirror: Baila's, unluckily cracked but the tortoiseshell undamaged. Musya's face in the glass looked like a chicken's, red and white with the alarm in one dark eye split open. A narrow chain of many footprints led from the front door to the tire-churned road. Slipping the hand mirror into a hidden pocket, she narrowed her eyes at the broken doors of the chicken coop where Sender was about to search—empty, for a relief. "We have to try the house," he said. A crow called and several answered, the first sound in ages.

On the old side porch they found the bedding piles almost untouched, rejected as spoils by every rampager. The house door gave onto more silence. They crept down the hall to his boot stove corner where, among wisps of warmth, the grasspea cripple lay curled on his side, day-napping as usual. Once roused he became joyful at the bit of chocolate Sender had saved for him. Russvelt was on the verge of starvation but otherwise fine. Musya asked after the rest of the household. He licked his lips.

"From the kitchen, she ran. From the vyshyvanky, they went away with the soldiers." Gone forth in single file through the snow, she remembered the uncharacteristic suggestion of orderly obedience there. "Poor Cezar!" the boy laughed suddenly. Sender took Musya's arm.

"Don't hit him," he said.

Russvelt was remembering. "He was trying to protect his sweetheart—they ate him like shashlik!"

"Yes we saw," Musya said. "So you're alone here?"

He nodded. He was lying.

Mrs Yelyuk appeared in the doorway, armed with a long-barreled pistol. "Hah!" she greeted them. The breath from her might have been dangerous, she smelled like something soaked in alcoholic spirits for three million years. Bleary and mean, she waved the pistol and told them to march, go.

Musya stayed where she was. "Does she think we still work here?"

"Maybe you do," Russvelt said. "I do."

"No you don't," she told him. "None of us do."

Sender said, "But she has a pistol."

"That's a different question," she said. So many hours of being cooped up with Eidel might have been showing their effect. Impatient of pedantry, Mrs Yelyuk shouted and brandished her weapon. She pointed them down the hall.

"Oh no," said Russvelt. "Oh God no."

Oksana Babiak's naked corpse lay on the floor of the vyshyvanka room. Her seeping entrails gleamed in the icon candlelight. Her dim eyeballs reflected dull golden flames. Many more candles than usual were lit but most of the icons were gone; incense was smoking. The dead face was all bathed with dried blood. Her jaw had split, brown molars showed through. Some skin was blackening and like her lips had peeled back by now. She'd been dead for days. Her breasts had been cut off, one left hanging; her hairy sex had been sliced and shat on.

Musya felt the hand mirror clank against her knee joints as they wobbled—she couldn't fall down, horror held her fixed in an iron vise. Now she understood why the others had left so cooperatively. Her tongue felt frozen but she managed to ask, she'd learned enough Ukrainian by now, "Who did this?" At her side Sender and Russvelt breathed through their teeth, wetly moaning. "They must have been devils."

Mrs Yelyuk shrugged and said she'd had a lot of enemies, that woman. A few aggressive pistol gestures closed this topic and introduced the next, the old drunkard's plan. This dead body—out—put outside—carried.

"Hire someone!" Musya said. "We are not slaves here anymore—you understand? You have to hire and pay money for workers now." The pistol barrel rose. Sender moaned and threw his arms around her, tight enough to cut off breathing. *This always happens*, she thought. "She's not going to shoot me, don't worry," she told him.

Russvelt disagreed. "She shot Sonya Androvna. She shot her and killed her."

"The hairdresser? For what?"

"Vengeance," he said.

"Well," Musya said, "who carried out Sonya Androvna?"

"No one did. She shot her in the back yard. She made her go outside before she killed her." The Yelyuk was nodding along as she followed, pleased with herself; a psychotic old lying drunkard.

Musya looked down at the task before them. She had no helpful ideas. The houseplants were all toppled, piles of roots like hair. Sender sobbed against her ribs. Out of nowhere a huge regret assailed her, regret that he should see and save this picture of naked womanhood in his mind—Sender Kotz of all people. *He'll never like them now*, she thought.

Indeed, how could any of them seeing a woman used this way recover and go on to thrive or get ahead or simply find a little happiness? They'd remain with their minds in shrouds, hiding, kept from the daylight world because they'd seen how butchers had monopolized Earth and made it unsafe to emerge there. It was too bad, but the dead weren't the only ones who'd stay underground all their lives.

All they could do now was try to behave decently. "Where does she want her?" Musya asked. "In the garden?"

"By the road," Russvelt said. "She says the town is supposed to collect."

Sender Kotz wailed, tears rolled down his face. He'd vomited chocolate all down his front. The overseer had wanted his conversation; now he regretted withholding it. "I was so mean to her!"

Musya said, "You were following your principles." But she couldn't console him. He sobbed brokenheartedly as they hoisted and dragged the overseer's body from the room where they'd labored at her moneymaking schemes for so many thousands of hours combined. Sender's eyes and frame were permanently weakened, his front teeth like Russvelt's deeply grooved by bitten threads. The boys took the legs. There was nothing for it but to handle her, the Yelyuk wouldn't spare even a scrap of cloth from anywhere. First the boys had to help Musya raise the torso from the floor so that she could hook her own arms through the two dead armpits. *My poor arms*, she thought. She had to steady the rotten unwashed head with her own bare chin. There was no question of carrying anything, the three of them combined had nowhere near the strength required. It was lift and step and stagger and lower and drag before lifting again. Jostled loose the hand mirror slipped out from Musya's skirt onto the drenched carpet, lost this time for good.

Here came the hall she'd scrubbed on her hands and knees: "What happened to the husband?" she asked. Mrs Yelyuk who'd located a bottle with a few slugs left raised it to help pantomime a crude response: hanged, clearly. They'd passed three hooded men on a gibbet along the way, Musya wondered if he'd been among them. That two men who'd both raped her might be dead that day on the same stretch of road seemed very strange— but Obodovka was a small town. Strange things happened there and few people knew of them.

Heaped near the front threshold were bags, coats, hats, wraps, prayer books seized and tossed aside by the other women's captors, Musya guessed. Had they been collected for a brothel, the way Eidel said? Could they be laboring in that kind of prison at this moment? Musya wondered briefly until the challenge of the threshold took all her concentration. Then she screamed and now her own chocolate splashed out across Oksana Babiak's dead face—in full sunlight horror incarnate. Mrs Yelyuk gave a dismissive belch and even offered the bottle with a tip before she noticed how little was left. Then seeing the party start down the older footpath she stopped them: no, they should cut across the yard another way to the roadside where the bodies went.

The ground was snowy, slippery, they inched along, Musya backwards. They slid the dead woman on her buttocks across some dead leaves. Now the body started giving gases. One boy stumbled, one dead hip crashed to the ground and they all three ended up on their knees in slush. A shot rang out, terrifying. Smoke trailed from the upturned pistol barrel and a blackbird flock screamed in panicked flight from the branches overhead, *every sparrow reckoned,* Musya thought.

"She did the same thing before Sonya Androvna," Russvelt said warningly.

They regrouped but it felt like the last time they'd be able to manage it. Fiery pains in their backs and legs weakened them. Oksana felt heavier in death at every moment. Her leaking entrails got underfoot more than once. Mrs Yelyuk drove them along with gestures of gun and bottle but now the bottle had gone dry. The gestures slowed to a stop. Her three enslaved laborers paused as she swayed on her feet. She must have been deliberating because a sudden incoherent shout ordered them to keep at their task and she turned back towards the farmhouse. They kept moving until she'd been inside for a second or two. Then they stood with the dead woman bent almost double between them and stared at each other.

Sender said, "We should leave her here, she always loved this tree." When Musya looked up she got a shock: indeed, they were still under the tree. They'd never make it to the road alive.

"Really?" she said.

"Yes. She climbed it when she came here first married, for a bet. To the top. She told me once. Before." More tears of his threatened. Musya said she agreed, the tree was perfect. Sadly, there wasn't time to say a prayer, she told him and whispered a quick, "Eyns-tsvey-dray!"

They dropped the body and scooped up Russvelt between them. Then they ran as fast as they could all the way back to the Jewish quarter.

PART THREE

ODESSA | TRANS-SIBERIAN | BIROBIDZHAN | TEPLOYE OZERO

(1)

Where Musya sat the sun rested full on the top of her head. Mild relief afforded by an intermittent sea breeze didn't change the facts that mattered. Her condition was dire, completely exposed. She had her household on a roadside in Odessa. A journey of weeks seldom supplying any roof overhead here dead-ended with no prospect of shelter.

That dawn, she and the five children had left their overnight camp on the city outskirts and found their way on foot to what wasn't her parents' home anymore. New whitewash, new smells: these days Russians filled the rooms that lined the enduringly narrow, muddy street. And in the front plot outside one small house stood the mother's work table, its surface ruined with red-black cleaver scars and stains left by the blood of chickens whose hard-hearted survivors scuttled around its legs after crickets and such. A woman emerged to menace with enormous forearms from the front doorstep and the Kotz family party moved on, but not before Hodeh had managed to abstract some eggs from the box coops stacked by the old raspberry patch which the boys had picked clean. That had been breakfast. A few more yolk splashes on Samuel Nemo's sailor blouse hardly mattered now, Musya told herself.

Along streets hard to recognize from her dress-fitting days they'd followed broken trolley tracks to where service resumed in unfamiliar cars. During the long wait to board they finally saw Jews, three well-dressed middle-aged couples conversing. One man and wife who'd spent the war evacuated in Almaty had returned to find strange Russians living in their room—a very nice room, by the sound of it, for which the Jewish couple possessed airtight paperwork. With this they waited to see bureaucrats all day long; the other couples too, it seemed, were similarly busy contending for one restoration or other. Musya couldn't even hope for a fate like theirs, stifling in anterooms. She had nothing to claim in Odessa. The couples turned their talk to street crime and with sidelong looks at Musya's berry-stained, road-stained, racketing children, the wives held their handbags closer, respectable women speaking excellent Russian who probably didn't know how many women so like them had been hung from wires around here. She had to agree with them in a way. No question, the whole city had gone badly downhill. Once-charming prospects were pockmarked with rubble and vacancy; everywhere builders added debris; and what was left standing wasn't the same. What had gleamed richly was dim now and had a slapped-together look, raw and rundown at once. Of course the children didn't mind the way she did and rushed from side to side to catch all the streetcar window views in their euphoria.

Nearing the Privoz market, the pavements had become lined with people selling stacks of dishes, samovars, everything, their possessions spread out on the ground for pedestrians to eye and bargain for. Finally the family had climbed down into a Russian crowd that strolled among ice cream kiosks, Hero City banners, and battle victory souvenir stands, its children clutching toy bombers and stiff little flags at face level with five hundred types of blind drunkards and amputees. Meat smoke from open grills was curling up around the market eaves where fixed loudspeakers blared a brass band version of Odessa Mama between patriotic outbursts. Musya's children groaned for meat but the sad fact remained that they couldn't digest it—some chicken pieces from a skewer were all she'd risk.

More Jews were to be seen inside, looking ill at ease. Some she guessed were haunting their own families' lost occupations there among the Privoz market's smoky close-packed aisles. Not much from before the war remained. Like its immediate neighbors in notions and trimmings the old Golbus pompom stall displayed empty shelves through stove-in shutters. But the secondhand goods trade was booming in every corner of the place—a buyer's market entirely, where the last good wristwatch from Hodeh's nest failed to fetch more than a pittance. The hired rooms Musya had promised and longed for were out.

The sun's weight stunned her. She pictured her heat-soaked hair emitting white light edged with molten copper hot enough to blacken foliage at several dozen paces. But she wouldn't put a scarf on. Headscarves dehumanized, she'd decided this sometime along the road south from Obodovka after seeing what came to look like too many collections of headscarves, not women, headscarves kerchiefs and shawls, the patterns busy bright or faded, sometimes clashing but most often forming harmonies to please the human eye; she thought it had to be by design—someone's. Covered women together would blend into something like laundry draped to dry on hedges. The Ukrainian summer had been dotted and striped with them, women displaced, policed, on the move; dodging bands of invalided soldiers, aimless partisans, roving deserters; seeking safety in numbers, distressed women huddling outdoors. Humps of floral print and deep shadow, attention slid from them. From Musya's point of view, to see them was to know they'd be no help at all, not even much of an audience, not often welcoming five hungry children and another young mother who'd be no help to them in her turn. Their foot parties crisscrossed the war-blasted countryside, homebound or fleeing the ruins of homes. Sometimes trucks headed for the Black Sea ports jounced some human cargo along broken highways; and the oxcarts were back, keeping close to the same walking pace Russvelt's leg allowed. But before every checkpoint the Kotz family would set off for the footpaths. Who were they and what were they doing there? And where did they belong? For the most part Musya had no answers.

Every so often in the distance a train engine trailed smoke: first destroyed in the fascists' invasion and again at their retreat, the rails and track beds of Ukraine were under round-the-clock repair now. Beside work gang encampments women on foot collected to trade what they could for what they could get, joining local kitchen gardeners and beggars at the edges of firelight. Sender might pick up a little mending. Welcomed to perform, an orphan act could be rewarded with a meal and some kvass to take away in a red tin pitcher. Musya and her children slept rough in pine woods, in fields of late-sown wheat. The air had seemed full of angels to her sometimes. One morning brought a salt air scent; a day later they'd finally looked down from a rocky hillside, yesterday evening: a great metropolis tumbling between them and the ring of vasty blue beyond. Odessa putting on its lights had looked so welcoming, they'd cheered.

But the view had been deceptive. There was nothing for them in Odessa. She'd led them south to destitution—the least useful of guardians as all the world could see, no cubicle walls or barbed wire intervened this time. The Soviet state would sweep them up like leaves.

"Schnorrer!"

Anton followed through with a derisive toy trumpet blast. She looked up at him from the ground. One hand came up to shield her eyes. Her head ached. "Don't shout at people," she said, as their one-man audience hastened away.

"But he listened for three songs and didn't give anything!"

"Such is life," she told him.

Musya made a reluctant impresario at best. That role was Hodeh's, of course, with Russvelt more surprisingly their top collector of small change in the tank gunner's helmet they'd found, he rattled it so expertly; especially when he and the two-year old star circulated holding hands the crowd would dig deep. A touch of scrofula and the limp of course remained. He'd looked his neediest but up here on the promenade, direct sun had discouraged passersby from lingering to form an audience. The war wounded who monopolized its benches were mainly sunk in alcoholic torpor and all unresponsive. Odessa disappointed profit-wise.

"We should have gone home to Bucharest with the Ernste like she wanted," Anton said, not for the first time. "We could have been in halls by now—famous." Another worn-out complaint: Musya was settling Samuel Nemo in her lap as she answered mechanically:

"You mean I should have sold you to her like she wanted—to a stranger."

"She wasn't a stranger. We knew her," he said.

His brother Sender took sides again. "But we don't know anyone else in Bucharest."

Anton said, "You didn't have to come, you could come here with her to narish Odessa."

"You're narish," Sender said.

"No fighting," Musya said ineffectually. Both boys' tempers, she knew, had been stoked red-hot by the humiliations of their visit to the city seashore from which attendants had chased them off for not being in appropriate swimwear on the sands. Musya might have wept over the incident had she been less full of wonder at herself. When the time came to leave Obodovka she'd fixed her mind with longing on the sea: but why? What had the sea to do with her? She'd never visited the seashore with her parents, they'd lacked the leisure and they couldn't swim. Yet all along she'd been picturing herself lying as she once had with Leon Flohr in the days of their love affair, browning golden, sun-kissed, lulled by surf. Seeking rejuvenation she'd discovered the ugly old truth instead. People like her didn't belong at the seashore. Her best past spit her out.

Of course the children couldn't swim either even if Musya had remembered how; and Russvelt was right, the Black Sea wasn't even a real ocean like the one his uncle Rockefeller's giant white liners plied. Retreating up here to the hillside promenade they'd unpacked the instruments and rolled out the routines. Even Song of Youth had fallen flat, twice.

Hodeh kept her eyes narrowed in the direction of the sparse weekday foot traffic from town. "Give a look," she said. "The man from your photo."

The boys dropped their dispute to clamor, "Where? What photo? Who?"

"From that old wedding." Hodeh pointed.

Like a live carp in a washtub, Musya's heart thudded bloodily for several seconds. Was it Boris after all? She'd thought he might be in Odessa. From the Privoz market she'd led the children to his parents' flat. Fresh signs hung along the quiet back streets indicated a new guest house quarter for workers from various state unions—the writers had one on a shady corner but no writers were about. The hope was faint, but Musya guessed some Kotz or other might have resumed occupation of the old rooms. Maybe his father was right all along and Samuel had lived to return a hero from the resistance caves; or else her husband, a Red Army veteran, comfortably pensioned and fairly intact, would be in there heaping his mother's furniture with extraneous stuff. But they'd found only strangers, not a soul on the premises who'd even recognized the name Kotz. Through a fast-slammed neighboring door Musya might have glimpsed the old sofa but couldn't swear to it before a strange dvornik chased them out onto the street again. Had Boris been there all the time—had he come after them?

It was Falk, however. Musya knew him right away. That Hodeh had too surprised her: most of the big man's beard was missing, the remnant closely shorn, manicured. He wore a fine loosely-fitted bleached linen summer suit as had never been his wont. At the sight of them he staggered and his deep-set eyes snapped wide—gray light poured out. They were recognized.

"My God," he said. "I don't believe it." He approached slowly almost on tiptoe, brought his left hand to Musya's shoulder and squeezed, staring hard at her face. He gave another squeeze. She felt his wedding ring, he'd never used to wear it. "Is anyone— are the others with you?"

"No, we're all that's left—I think," she said. "Unless you've heard anything of my mother? Or maybe some word from my husband, from Boris?"

"Nothing, nothing at all," he said at once, releasing her. He dropped his hand. His voice rumbled sadly, "Such terrible times we've lived though—terrible." He'd changed colognes. His suit was too clean to embrace. He looked around at the silent gawping professionally shoeless children, counting each one with a solemn nod. "I remember some of you," he said. His matchless smile featured new silver bridgework around the incisors. "And this one from before he was born, I think?"

Samuel Nemo pressed his face against Musya's skirt as she introduced them all somewhat vaguely. Falk kept nodding until the sharp trumpet note Anton blew in his direction knocked him back a step and Sender broke out:

"Why did you not come for us? When we were in that place with no shelter for anyone, Mama Kotz sent for you so many times! She said you were coming for us but you never came. And now she's dead—because of you!"

Musya said, "You can't blame him for that, not for everything."

"No, let him talk." Uncle Falk smiled down at Sender. "My friend, believe an old man when he tells you that a long memory is no good without a forgiving heart. I did everything it lay within my power to do for you and your grandparents and more even than that. No one could have done more."

"I don't believe you," Sender said.

Falk continued to Musya now. "It was a terrible time. You can't imagine. I had enough problems explaining how my truck came to be in a restricted military precinct along with my employee lying—found there. Poor Weissbein. I faced accusations."

"Tennible." This was Russvelt. He'd stepped up, seemingly breathless with sympathy. The boy had a knack for winning favor, they'd all come to value it. He'd understood Ukrainian all along; his Russian was wretched, though. "Poor Mister."

"You're got that right, little man," said Falk.

Musya said, "Yes. It was a terrible day." Her look warned Sender to keep mum. Then no one spoke. If Falk had questions about what had befallen them, he wasn't asking any. She gestured at the summer suit. "Are you retired, Uncle Falk?"

"Retired? That's a laugh." He gave a grim one. "I've never been busier. But things, business, it's all different these days. Everything is, in Odessa. You know I converted."

She said, "No I—hadn't heard."

He touched his hairline, barely receded since Liza's wedding day. "It's true. I was baptized two years ago."

"Ah, yes, we wanted to try that, ourselves," Musya said too quickly. A blankness barred her way until she thought to add, without naming names, "Only one of us did it."

"And the rest of you?" Falk, that gentleman, asked with interest.

Musya said, "Oh, still Jewish. Definitely."

"He was drunk," Sender explained.

The wine merchant grimaced. "So was I, believe me. And I wasn't alone. You know it was illegal to be a Jew in Odessa, our Romanian guests made it a crime. We had no choice."

"Tennible!" Russvelt again. Musya had to agree:

"Illegal to be a Jew in Odessa—that is terrible."

Baila Kotz's former lover said, "It was mostly politics. The better ones understood that. There were some real gentlemen in the Romanian officer class, and plenty in the lower ranks. They did good things for the city—rebuilt the opera house, no expense spared. They straightened up a lot for that matter."

She said, "But how—so they—you had opera but no Jews?"

He shrugged. "The Romanians are a musical people, we all knew that going into any occupation. Frankly I never cared for that style of thing but my wife—my new wife—she enjoys it."

As the children murmured Musya said, "I see." Her mind tumbled back to a moment on the front path outside her in-laws' old home where she'd paused, lost for any idea of a next destination. Just then the oblepikha bush had tossed noisily and some pale coral colored berries pattered down unripe to roll among the children's feet. She'd peered in to see familiar bright finch wings flit and flash among the thorny branches where Mama Kotz's babies, or maybe their descendants, battled sparrows for the harvest rights. "Did your new wife convert, too?" she asked.

"No need," he said. "She was never Jewish. Her people are Moldavians, champagne importers, from generations back. She's a lovely woman."

"Of course," she said. Why hadn't he come for them? He looked like he'd never even needed a wash very badly in his entire life—which might not be the case had he come for them, Musya reflected. Hodeh had been tugging at her blouse for a few moments; leaning down she heard a whisper:

"Get money from him."

She straightened up again. "Uncle Falk," she began.

But now he had questions. "Tell me my dear, how did you come by a girl? And what are you doing with your family in the street here—not that it doesn't rejoice my heart to see all of you?"

She explained as well as she could with Anton interrupting constantly that they'd come south from a small town Jewish ghetto after almost three years to look for family; finding none, they'd set out to earn the price of a room with a show of talents. "I don't do much but Hodeh and the boys have a musical act—and Sender, he's an expert-class tailor, he'll mend anything right while you stand there." The irrelevancy of this fact to Falk's case stalled her for a beat or two before she rallied. "I used to see more foot traffic on the way to Arcadia Beach."

He said, "Yes, it's very exclusive out here now." His new flat nearby overlooked the botanical gardens; he and his new wife liked living outside the press of the city proper, he explained. Overhead a single seagull went crying. The sun had dipped and the next sea breeze came with a dismaying little kick to it; the night might turn chilly. Anton wanted wine. Through a screen of plane tree boughs Musya could make out the green-grayest of seas. It green blood pulsed beneath the frothy waves with their silver trim untarnished by time's passage. Falk walked home daily, weather permitting, he said. She fought off a shudder. How could the man live here? How could he stand the memories of his mad Goldie and her end in the ivy bed? With his shrunken beard, what kind of man had he become? That he'd loved his dead wife she didn't doubt; that he'd loved Baila Kotz she knew. One sister lost, then the next: he wouldn't speak of either sister now, she knew he wouldn't. He'd moved on. "And this boy," Falk said suddenly, "is whose?" Russvelt appeared to fascinate him. "He must be one tough malysh to have come so far on that pair of legs."

"He's with us, we take care of him," Sender said.

Now an interruption, as the prosperous figure paused there inspired approach:

weaving, with searchlight eyes, not a young man, one of the war wounded held out one wrist bone stump and a filth-blackened hand and launched into an eloquence which travel from the furthest limits of inebriation left devoured; all that reached them was a drunkard's moan. Falk cursed and hissed through his teeth. "A plague—another deserter—these men are a plague." He hissed again and waved a threatening arm. Instantly Russvelt hissed at the begging man and shooed him off, limping after him as he retreated to his former bench. The boy wore a scowl as he limped back to the wine merchant's side.

"Tennible man!" He turned his eyes from Sender's outraged breathing.

Falk chuckled softly and gave Russvelt's shoulder a pat. "That's right—they helped themselves out of trouble once, they can learn to do it again, yes? This is a jewel you found here," he told Musya.

She caught Hodeh's eye, narrowed by an urgent frown. She said, "We need a dentist, Uncle Falk. The children's teeth—Sender's especially, they're very bad. I don't know where to go."

He said, "A dentist? I know the best, of course."

"Of course you do," she said. "And we could use your help finding a place to stay, a decent room somewhere that doesn't cost too much."

"You're crazy if you hope to find a cheap room in Odessa these days. Half of Moscow is vacationing here—it's all the rage, everyone wants to see liberated Odessa. That Hero City business of His really put us on the map again. I'm not complaining, it's good for trade."

Sender said, "We can sleep outdoors."

"And who's going to protect the females here from men like that?" Falk cocked a thumb at the benches. "You? Really?"

Musya broke in. "Uncle Falk, it's true, we need your help. And, money. Some money. Please, we're related to you—we're your family."

"Well," he stopped her. She might have gone too far and claimed too much, she feared. Sealing bargains wasn't a strong point of Musya's, that was something else Hodeh usually handled. Falk stood with his gray head bent so that a thoughtful gaze encompassed the grasspea cripple whose shoulder touched his jacket hem by now. At last he spoke. "It's true. Family is family. Even when there's no blood tie—I think of young Weissbein, that poor boy was like a son to me." Musya while she considered this an exaggeration held her peace. The wine merchant continued, "You know my wife and I, my new wife, we have no children—again I'm not blessed that way."

"But," she began, picturing Baila's long-ago confession, Papa Kotz's tangled heap of first-place prize ribbons, the box of pornography under an old bed. Didn't Falk ever think of the hero son Samuel as his own to mourn? "I'm sorry," she said.

"Thank you. We've thought of adopting," he added. Then his smile reappeared. "And look at you, with so many more than you had when you first came to us."

She pressed Samuel Nemo closer to her side and said, "It's a lot to handle sometimes, I admit. That's why we need—it's why I beg you for your help, please, Uncle Falk."

He said, "My help? Of course you'll have my help, whatever I can do for you I will. What, did you think I planned to just walk away and leave you to perish here in the street?"

"Yes," said Sender.

Two weeks later they were leaving Odessa by train in a storm of noise. Shell-damaged in the city's liberation, the old Golovnaya station's humming rotunda lay in heaps of pieces on its marble floors; the place would take years to rebuild. Here in the cigarette mists of the temporary depot, loud jangling echoes fell fast from the tin ceiling to multiply against the floor's cement and bounce among the very insufficient chairs. A confusion of loudspeakers pumped strangely rhythmless dance music into the welling uproar. People hurried to shout between bursts of ear-shattering static that heralded amplified voices reciting commands, partial lists of regulations, date time and temperature readings, warnings, news items, greetings, stern reminders and sporadic arrival-departure-delay announcements: not bad, these last. Passenger service to Moscow, restored after non-stop killing labor, would feature no more than a handful of kinks.

"A monumental achievement, a tribute to the people's will," said Falk in a voice that drew nods from a few nearby heads.

The big man had a patriotic platitude habit, possibly acquired from his new wife. She was about thirty-five, genteel and tall, fairly handsome; otherwise fit, she had a horror of Jewish suffering, she couldn't hear it mentioned without feeling the onset of heart problems. "Her heart is too soft," Falk had told the Kotzes to prepare them. "Leave the past away from her, in the past, for my sake." Which hadn't been difficult, since the new wife had done almost all the talking in the time they'd spent with her—four hours, total, they'd counted. She had a passionate interest in tennis and played it daily; in public park restoration and a related small committee seat she held; and in her husband who awed her. Her rosy face and high bosom beamed when he spoke.

"Sometimes," she'd confided, "your Uncle Falk reminds me so much of Him." Her eyes swiveled across her plush spotless living room to where the Father of Nations sat framed in three-quarter profile. "More than genius, it's that they share the same extraordinary modesty of truly great individuals. How much he did for the resistance cause alone, no one here will ever know. And just look what he's doing for your family— look at this little one here. And he'll never take the credit for it—never." Her enchantment with the boy Russvelt, who rattled his new steel leg braces at her side while devouring seed cake, had appeared to be entirely unfeigned.

Indeed Falk had done much for them, and all on the quiet—their lack of papers being nothing to advertise, so he explained. They'd had a room to themselves in a communal apartment on Primorsky where the head was a warehouse manager in his orbit. New items had arrived for them almost daily to replace their ragged wardrobes, all secondhand but good quality, better than the new stuff being made these days, Falk assured them. At odd hours they'd seen a dentist and doctors who'd supplied fillings, vaccinations, bottled vitamins and prescription eyeglasses for Sender and Musya. She didn't like to wear hers. The children's health was good and in some cases close to prodigious. Their digestion improved day by day after a general worm treatment. Tests certified Musya herself as disease-free in every place. She'd added the slip of paper with its stamp to the Kotz family file that she carried in her same old carpet-sided bag.

The bag topped the pile at her feet. Admiring its bakelite handle, the wine merchant said luggage hadn't been so well-made in years. His new wife was skipping the train platform farewells but here was Russvelt, aloof in a three-piece brown corduroy knicker suit that showed off his clanking braces to advantage. His sparse hair was oiled, crisply parted and combed across his bald sore scars. He wore a patriotic red lapel pin and a faint bay rum splash that he kept tugging his collar up to sniff. Russvelt would be staying in Odessa, the new apprentice and heir of sorts to the wine merchant's hopes. Now he told Sender that crying was silly and boys shouldn't. "I always told you I was going to live with rich people," he said.

"I'm not crying over you," Sender cried. His jaws still hurt him from last week's extractions, it was true; but he would miss this strange friend of their joint slavery. All the way to Moscow, whenever Musya paid with cash he'd announce, "That's the money you got for selling Russvelt!" For now he fought tears. A furtive knuckle knocked his new eyeglass frames askew.

Anton gave the bags an angry kick. "Are we almost leaving?"

"Soon," she told him. He didn't like Odessa, he'd been waking up from bad dreams every night and by day complaining about everything there. His new secondhand shoes were too tight. He hated sidewalks and automobiles; he called the harbor smelly; he hated umbrellas for no reason that he cared to explain. The rest of them hadn't cared to argue long and although they'd all disliked their temporary neighbors as much as Anton did, the family had mostly kept to its room after the first few days. Odessa was so full of absences and upsetting changes and bad memories.

Hodeh beside him was chewing her braid again, the old habit was back. New to city life, she hadn't minded at first; but she'd been uneasy ever since Falk's new wife had given Musya some newspaper clippings about war orphans' homes. Hodeh who couldn't read a word of Russian had understood the pictures and their conveyance very well. For as the thin walls of the communal apartment would let them know from first to last, ringing down the old refrain from Krutonog's in tones identical: Musya Kotz had too many children. With only one child or two and Falk's limited help she might have managed to hang on in Odessa, in half a room somewhere. She might have done cleaning or taken in sewing although even this would have been risky; it might have paid to apply for a propiska stamp to work in Odessa but it would have meant scrutiny. Either way, she'd have lost Hodeh—at least. Consensus in the communal kitchen had held that she'd be bound to shed one or two more before she was through. Meanwhile in the war orphans' home Hodeh might be taught skills, Falk had said—real skills, not low street capers. A month from now he'd miss the malachite cufflinks he'd kept boxed up in his closet.

"Soon," Musya told Samuel Nemo, another one who agitated for departure. He liked action and the open road. "Don't be in such a big hurry. It's a long ride."

Uncle Falk had settled an envelope of cash money on them, along with a promise of remittances in future case of need; he'd bought their one-way tickets, too. They'd catch a Trans-Siberian in Moscow. It made nothing but sense, he'd assured her, to leave Odessa. She and the four children she insisted on keeping would be best off and probably more comfortable back where they'd come from in 1941, back in the Far East and Birobidzhan where Musya was entitled to housing and work by her papers. Near as it was to the enemy in Japanese Manchuria the whole place was a closed military zone these days; but they were letting some people in, returning residents, a few intelligentsia. Falk had managed their passage. Hesitant at first, she'd soon come around to his point of view. Just to watch the loudspeaker announcements leave most of her children bobbing among waves of unrecognized words made an argument in favor. At least in Birobidzhan they'd hear some Yiddish which save for a few Russian song lyrics was all her orphan trio knew; for Anton had lost all the Russian his father ever taught him. Poor Boris: going west had done his heirs no good. Shipwrecked on a war not yet won, they were being beaten back to their Jewish homeland.

Falk had to shout. "This is for the best—believe me!" Musya nodded. His breath was sour and he was repeating himself. Things were rising to the surface of the man, she could tell, as their wait for the engine to appear stretched too long. Emotions, memories, remorse: his clean surface was breaking up around the pressure. Pain and blankness flashed in alternating bolts across his face.

"Uncle Falk, I know you did the best you could," she told him at last. But he frowned and shook his shrunken head—he couldn't hear her.

(2)

Panic burst from Musya's throat in a scream. In the midst of reaching, the Number 44 provodnitsa quailed. As Soviet train conductresses went she looked typically immune to being bothered by any variety of human experience, but Musya's reaction and the sound of it got through. She stared, her anger building visibly.

"What do you need with this dirty thing?" she said.

Musya wrenched her quilt away from the taller woman's hands. She was too upset to answer. And too tired: fatigue was making it hard to bounce back from the state into which alarm had plunged her, screaming. As for the alarm, it felt like a terrible mystery, awful. Where had it come from? She held the quilt against her pounding chest with both arms and had to gasp for breath. She heard Sender Kotz say, "It is stained, not dirty."

"*It is stained, not dirty,*" the provodnitsa snapped back in a mocking sing-song. "You people," she resumed in her normal rather toneless tones. "No one can help you." She stalked away, leaving shame and paralysis behind with them.

Musya blamed Moscow, in part. Her third encounter with the great city, this time inconceivably crowded and despite its countless breeze-blown red banners overwhelmingly gray and unwelcoming; every step of it patrolled and sneeringly bullied by armed men wearing otherwise blank slab faces. A capital that could smell victory, overrun with unfinished constructions of over-tall plinths awaiting delivery of monumental feet; meanwhile an incessant clangor of what sounded like forges where the monumental bronze trousers were being creased shook exhaust-soaked intersections down to their curbstones. To their mighty disappointment she'd told the children no, they couldn't stop to sight-see—good thing, as the cross-town congestion posed one unbroken delay. Then the length of the Yaroslavsky station provisioning lines left barely time to board. The family was being installed in haste when she'd felt her hands emptied all at once and her spirit taken unawares. Then the scream—which was still shaking her.

Basic human unkindness, striking repeatedly, had left Musya sore, sorrowing, raw-nerved, primed for alarm. Adding stress, what she'd already suspected, a few hours in Moscow had served to develop into a dead certainty: yes, the war might be won, but not against Jew-hating. Which hadn't gone anywhere.

Of the Soviet Union's Jews, nearly half their millions had survived the fascists' efforts to exterminate them. No one rejoiced at this. The Jews mourned their dead. The rest remained indifferent or worse, some growing adamant about having fought and sacrificed for the fatherland, not for the cause of Hitler's targets. Their preservation and freedom had never been a goal when only the ground beneath the Jews had mattered in the Russian mind, especially. Why couldn't they have just floated off in their tormentors' wake, gone like dandelion down? Why were the Jews still present? Their fellow citizens seemed to ask themselves.

"You shouldn't have screamed," Hodeh said matter-of-factly. She was stashing things on the top storage bunk of their platskartny berth, monkey climbing up and down again. "Just tell us the next time and we'll take care of her, Pretzel and me."

The thought of the sharp scissors which Hodeh kept concealed about her person to this day gave Musya cause for relief that she'd screamed after all. Her limbs unlocked, she lowered herself onto the lowest bunk with a sigh. In the light from the window she noticed some batten escaping through a pea-sized rip in the quilt's sand-colored lining.

Sender hadn't moved. He sniffled. "Everyone is looking at us."

"Good," said Anton, who never forgot about an audience. He also loved heights. "I want the top bunk."

As it was practically on the ceiling, she stayed out of the next argument among the brothers. Her examination of the quilt continued. Another new hole, one of several. She groaned. "All the time I'll have to mend this and nothing to use for patches." They couldn't spare a single garment.

A cheer went up, echoed by muttered prayers. The train was leaving Moscow exactly on schedule.

Musya let her eyelids fall, loosened her grip on the leaky quilt and felt the will that had powered her forward transformed, thrumming—a stretched wire released with a snap.

Her mind spun in place. Words from a hundred arguments she'd had flew out at her like notes from a crazy broken gramophone. Too many children—too many children: she'd brought them all this far, just to go back. She pictured gigantic circles, wheels in time she couldn't escape. She couldn't have pushed ahead on her own another moment—not with so many children. Four, they stood gathered at the window, distracted and safe under a roof for a week. Her seat rocked side to side. Residual tensions slipped through her onto the tracks, only a few returned to pluck at her again.

She looked out and saw the city's gray-black industrial hem give way like grime in a soaking tub to birch groves, picket fences, charming dachas with bright carved fronts. Everyone picked their favorites. Everyone drank hot tea.

Falk had secured the family passage in third-class, platskartny. Sixty or so triple bunks like theirs were set along an off-center aisle in one of the Trans-Siberian's great rolling dormitory carriages. After the private kupé cabin her striving husband had squandered on for their ill-fated trip west, Musya was back where she'd been as an unmarried girl on the way to Birobidzhan. A few modern improvements since 1939 hadn't changed the basic outlines of the experience to come. Strangers were hands-breadths away at all times, coming and going, belching and breaking wind, sleeping, snoring, eating, talking. The hot water ran out less often these days. Towel-blackening incursions of coal smog and cinders weren't quite as frequent. Men, mainly wounded or elderly, were more numerous. Despite including a large-sized contingent of noisy alcoholics they'd prove not at all troublesome—because the railway's provodnitsa class had been upgraded several notches. Gray and almost troll-featured in her recollection, these conductresses were strapping, busty, lacquered-looking in their immaculate two-toned blue uniforms. Especially the male passengers on average admired them without reservation, hastening to assume a nursery calm at the first hint of their displeasure. Their authority rode framed behind glass in pride of place above the giant samovar, immovably fixed as the modest star pinned to his olive-brown tunic. Like him, the Hero of Socialist Labor and Gardener of Human Happiness, they were loved.

Musya dreaded them.

The cathedral domes of Vladimir and the Golden Ring were spotted. "What's that?" and "Where are we?" her children would ask. Knowing little, remembering less, she answered truthfully, "I was only here at night before." Luckily, the carriage could boast several booming-voiced pedants, old men who spieled facts in fierce competition; if the children hushed, she could eavesdrop on a running travelogue.

Here, she translated, was the world's greatest machine gun manufactory. Further on lay a little town with a miracle icon, a place of pilgrimage. Past Gorky came a guard post, a bridge, and a river impossibly silver and wide where the passengers in company rose to salute Mother Volga, Volga Volga, source of song and survival.

"It's real?" Hodeh was amazed.

"It's better in the film, though," Anton said.

The men replaced their caps, blew their noses. Patriotic sentiment ran thick and chin-high down the platskartny carriage aisle like rich white curds, a prosperous wealth of feeling. It seemed no time at all later that the handkerchiefs came out again. A stop at dusk: everyone was peering out past the station lights at the shore of a small round lake. Musya listened. Mothers came here to pray for the safe delivery of their soldier sons from mortal harm, she said, they'd kneel on the lakeshore—this was Lake Svetloyar, its waters were magical, healing, sacred. Its depths hid an invisible city where the pure lived eternally: Kitezh. Up and down the carriage Russian women crossed themselves and their reflections kissed fingertips in the darkening window glass. Sometimes the blessed saw this city when it rose, in glimpses.

"I see it," said Samuel Nemo. "I see Kitezh."

"So do I," said Musya.

The next morning they awoke among the Ural Mountains which Anton complained looked like hills. Presently the train left Europe and crossed into Asia, the precise spot where east met west marked in Russian on a white stone obelisk. Musya remembered Boris watching for the obelisk in vain, hours too late and then vexed almost to tears because he'd already missed it once during an ill-timed lavatory visit on his honeymoon trip with Liza in 1934. She herself had now seen it three times and his older sons twice. *Poor Boris*, she thought.

Between pine-furred Asian hills identically green and brown in every respect to the European hills behind, the Number 44 rolled towards the smokestacks of Sverdlovsk. The historians' duels grew less and less voluble until their broken whispers rasped, worn-down and grim. Trains still changed engines at Sverdlovsk and took on provisions. Droshky drivers still waved their whips from behind a fence on the platform edge and whistled for fares: Musya guessed the halt still left time enough for a round-trip downtown with the traditional highlight, a street view of where the Romanovs had perished. The last tsar of all the Russias and his wife, their daughters and sickly young son, tutors and nurses, lap dogs, executed with bullets and bayonets against a cellar wall. Musya kept thinking of Boris. *"Typical ghoulish garbage!"* She remembered him rejecting her plea that they hire one and go—she'd felt curious. *"How can they expect this country to accomplish socialism with such disgusting tourist attractions on offer at every turn?"* This time through Sverdlovsk she had no wish to leave the platform. Maybe parenthood had changed her. She was treating the family to baked apples when a droshky man with an eye-patch that hid half a mass of wrinkled scar limped right up to her, soliciting:

"Ipatiev house—for the children!" She managed a polite refusal before the platform guard chased the man back to his pen.

Sender stared after him. "Who is Ipatiev?"

In fact she felt herself agreeing with Boris: this history was morbid. "No one," she said. The drivers appeared to be doing poor business. The popular taste for gruesome memories had faded, maybe. "He owned the house where the Bolsheviks killed the last

Tsar Nicolas."

"How does the Tsar live?" Anton shouted abruptly. "The song—How Does the Tsar Live! A classic," he said. He wanted to run back for the tin trumpet and put on a few verses, he saw potential for a paying crowd. The Ernste's teachings told: "True crime sells!" he insisted, fired up by fruit sugar, tugging Musya's clothes in the urgency of his call for an orphan act appearance there on the platform, five minutes, impromptu. She said no to fun and no to profit. "But we're getting out of practice," he complained.

"Not here," she told him.

The Ural mountain twilight was fading when the train pulled itself out of the foothills and onto the Siberian steppe, where it put on speed. Soon, save for the rare silhouette of an outcropping or tree against a faint horizon, the bare brown track margins rushing by in the light their carriage windows cast made all the view its passengers enjoyed. Meanwhile the half-hour mingle on the Sverdlovsk platform had shaken things up in platzkartny class. A new conviviality reached even the Kotzes' bunks, where a fellow female passenger, married, good-looking, Jewish, unwidowed, with misaligned shoulders, had stopped to introduce herself in hesitant Yiddish: her name was Vera, from Leningrad. Caught without her new eyeglasses which she elected to keep off, Musya shook hands and introduced her family. "And my name is Musya. Kotz," she finished.

The woman nodded. "You are the one who screamed."

"Yes," said Musya. "Yes."

"Oh—we all call you that."

"I see." The woman wasn't a bad sort. Her bluntness came from being benumbed—by something. Musya squinted. She asked, to make conversation, "Are you going to Vladivostok?"

"Oh—no—Birobidzhan. Like you. The provodnitsa told us—that is why I want to meet you. To ask what it is like." In fact her ticket was for Khabarovsk, further east, where new settlers first filed their paperwork. She'd always longed to see the Soviet Zion, Vera confided in the Russian where she was far more at home. The place-name Birobidzhan breathed romance for her. A strange digression followed on the sacred human and the symbolism of the fruit tree. Otherwise her tale had familiar outlines. She'd spent the war in Kazakhstan, returning at length to Leningrad where the new house committee head's ex-wife was using her good bed linens, bedroom, bed, everything. Recourseless, she and her son and the man she was with had turned around with their suitcases and left for Moscow as quickly as possible, Birobidzhan-bound. They had no more family. "It seemed like we got a sign," she added. "Many signs—that we are free now to live out our dreams." Being a top-level stenographer Vera had intelligentsia credentials, men of letters needed her. But she hoped to find a place on one of the collective farms doing cheerful song-filled labor; she'd seen In Search of Happiness five times as a young girl and had pored over all the novels. Had the difficulties of kolkhoz life in eastern Siberia been exaggerated for dramatic effect, she wondered? Did the laborers still sing anyhow? Had very much changed?

Musya said she couldn't speak to current conditions in the Jewish Autonomous

Region, although she wished Vera's family luck there. However, she and her own family had spent the last few years in occupied Ukraine. "Under the Romanians. In a Jewish ghetto—prisoners."

The woman frowned, deeply concerned. "But I thought people starved in those places."

"But—we did. We starved."

"You do not look like it."

Musya sat and blinked until her children's hands prodded for a Yiddish explanation. "I'm telling her how we starved, before," she told them.

"Forgive me," their guest continued, "But I just came from Leningrad. I have seen how the starved look. You do not look like them. None of you do." She looked again. "Except maybe the little girl and even she does not look too bad." At this, Hodeh offered a reflexive curse. The woman named Vera gave a nervous laugh and tried sounding out the curse, its syllables. She didn't get it, lacked the Yiddish. Musya was breathing a sigh of relief.

Then: "May leeches drink you," Sender Kotz offered helpfully from the top bunk.

Now the Leningrader blinked, then made a smile. "Such a descriptive language," she said.

Musya tried her best to help a friendship sprout between Vera and herself. It should have been easier. Vera turned out to be a well-read interesting person who'd enjoyed a lot of theater; she'd seen Mikhoels act from good seats many times. Instead the work of cultivation felt very hard, the place all but barren inside her where new friendship would go. With the other Jewish passengers she met, it was the same. What she needed was old friendship first, a therapeutic course of trouble-shedding in the presence of her friend Fanny's warm, wise, capacious heart.

As for Trans-Siberian friendships in general, Jewish passports made a barrier no one crossed—save for the chess players. Jews, Russians, Cossacks, Tatars, they didn't care. Two or three games were always in progress and Hodeh's ranking on the tally board showed a steady climb.

Siberia streamed past the windows, its swamps enlivened by huge flocks of waterfowl and the occasional distant inverted mirage. After long dusks, nightfall was sudden. Finally the moon, full, bright behind its blemishes like a dead face, rode alongside them into the taiga.

In a sawmill, people turned trees into wood for building with. At a coal mine, they climbed down into holes and dug out special rocks to pile outside and later burn for fuel. In a cemetery, people could mark where their dead families lay for remembering later; but it wasn't necessary. Bridges were built over rivers so that trains like this one could cross them. Musya had all the answers, even when she was only pretending to know; the ease of authority kept taking her by surprise.

Her baby's sitting weight made another almost alien sensation. She'd carried Samuel Nemo plenty, but his leisure lap-times he'd mostly spent in Hodeh's care. He still purred quite often. Musya was trying to teach him Russian and improve his baby Yiddish jointly. His mind amazed her with its capacities, its fruitfulness. His beginnings between prison walls weren't apparent at all, unless they might have made his curiosity a little frantic. Demanding names and meanings faster than she could furnish them, he left the window jabbed and dotted with his fingerprints. Anton would lean against her side and interject his own countless questions for hours at a time—it was a real peppering she faced. At quiet moments, the two brothers sprawled at ease among the comforts of her body, on the look-out for bears and wild deer in the undergrowth. They might count past one hundred the freight wagons tearing west on the line alongside. By night they hoped for the tracks to round a bend so they could watch the Number 44 reveal its spooling flanks front and rear in gigantic dotted glow-stripes to their view.

Installed high above their heads, Sender Kotz did almost nothing but read. After lights-out he lay facing the bunk edge and held the pages under the carriage safety lamp's glow. His first new books in over three years—all in Russian, which he was recapturing this way—they were a lot of old model shock-worker romances interspersed with very little better stuff from Falk's new wife's bottom shelf. One afternoon Musya objected: "You're missing everything! Come look out the window with us."

He didn't even glance down. "It is not worth seeing until the lake."

"What lake?" Musya said.

Her confusion was genuine. Now Sender showed an interested face—in fact he was amused and Anton even more so. "You thought Papa was stupid for missing the oblelisk twice." Anton laughed. "And you missed Lake Baikal!"

"It's not funny," she said. Even her baby was laughing at her.

The next day as the shores approached, statistics went flying among the fact-competitors again. Quickly Musya gathered that a major wonder of the planet had two times caught her sleeping. Not today: when her eyes would see the world's deepest fresh-water lake throw itself across the scenery in sapphire and aquamarine, its inland sea-like expanse given up to the ravishment of an unclouded Siberian sky. Her chances of glimpsing unique native species also looked good as there were about a thousand of them living there. And should she take advantage of a scheduled stop, slip off the train and go down behind the station to test its frigid waters, she could count on Lake Baikal to prolong her life. Dabbling her fingertips in it would add a year; full immersion and a swim, a quarter century. Other passengers were already clutching bath towels in readiness.

Of course as soon as they crossed the first trestle bridge she recognized the place right away. This was the Krugo-Baykal, a notorious collection of rock-hewn tunnels, aque-ducts, and cut-into cliffs down which loose boulders rolled with terrifying frequency. A human miracle of engineering, except that the platskartny carriage roof was liable to be smashed through at any time, if the whole train wasn't knocked into the water first—she remembered perfectly well. The rounded green promontories, the faraway violet beauty of mountainous opposing shores that stretched on and on, snowcap to snowcap:

"I thought it was a river," she explained; but she thought the lake view rolling past did everything to justify her mistake. Now she could see, it was simply enormous. The brothers shook their matching heads at her.

"But don't you remember, Papa told us all about it, before."

"But I didn't always listen to him, your Papa," she answered weakly. "I couldn't."

"But he knows everything," Anton said. He often did. She never contradicted him although her disagreement had grown heartier with every day that passed, it felt like.

For Boris Kotz had known nothing. Back and forth across the Soviet Union, end to end, crossing Siberia twice, he'd raced in his naiveté, dragging others along—her family—chasing phantasms. He'd been such an innocent, so unable to pass up a deal and so sure as well that everything worth knowing would be written down somewhere, probably with tables attached. In bed, she hadn't understood what he was trying to accomplish at times until he'd finally admitted: it all came from books, health manuals he and Liza had studied together. He'd produced the manuals; they'd looked out of date to Musya. At the sight of her sister's spiky black notes all over the pages she'd closed them for good, with a shudder. Pretending virginity, she hadn't been able to offer many suggestions of her own.

She'd done what she could. She'd been a young wife and mother of two at eighteen, out of nowhere. Since then she'd given birth and twice miscarried; she'd been terrorized, imprisoned, starved, enslaved and raped in a world war. She'd passed through conditions damaging in every way, she was heavy with what she'd suffered.

So now who would love her?

What man, Musya wondered, would return with her to Lake Baikal on some romantic getaway or honeymoon? Solitary pines leaned across cliffs to look down on secluded inlets that a little boat could reach. White-toothed waves hammered at their sands. Ice water: and a shoreline warmed hot by a Siberian sun that felt unimpeded by atmosphere. She pictured lying there, looking past a bunch of suntanned shoulder muscles into a sky more black than blue at its apex, her eyes tracing cloud wisps in their swirl around the lower depths of infinity. A half hour in Lake Baikal was cold enough to kill a healthy man, she heard someone say; twenty minutes, another argued.

Twenty minutes!

The notion gripped her. What she would give for such a power, to be as fatal as this lake against a man at will—if jumping in would grant it, she'd strip naked and dive, Musya thought. She'd want enough for a lifetime. As it was, she felt plunged into uproar and clammy sweat as her heartbeat started trying to outrace iron pistons. The past sprayed through her mind. Their hands gripping, their putrid mouths marking her, their anger invading, hating, hurting her—the men moving around on top of her memories weren't going anywhere. Neither were the unseen ones who'd left Oksana Babiak in pieces. She was stuck with all of them—and with the pieces. Captive inside and out, Musya Kotz for life, she remained seated, fettered in humiliations, weighed down by babies, with her every nerve and muscle primed for flight. Shadows came out of nowhere. Who would want her, fat and jumpy? The iron wheels' roar doubled and doubled again in her ears.

A moan slipped out between her clamped teeth as she heard the roar rolling towards her. A short tunnel came and went like a whiplash of lightlessness.

"Oh, look!" she heard. And "Oh!" she exclaimed.

They were passing one of the Krugo-Baykal's most spectacular derailment spots, famous since 1941. There in the shallows, a steam engine tipped on its side lay tumbled among a few snapped-off passenger carriages, the submerged parts tinted green and enlarged by the crystal-clear lake water. The provodnitsa's claim that the accident itself had not been fatal was accepted without comment. Then the woman took offense at someone's asking why the wreck wasn't cleared away by now.

"We've had a war to win, in case you didn't notice," she grumbled. "Real Soviet people have been sacrificing everything for the fatherland so that you lot could go on with your useless lives."

No one objected. Platskartny hadn't seen her all day; instead, tantalizing fragments of popular tunes had escaped the locked den where she'd sat by the radio set, smoking against regulations. She'd emerged with many fewer hairs than usual in place, her mood argumenttative, Musya sensed. A general silence prevailed as others sensed it too. No question, the shores of Lake Baikal touched the provodnitsa someplace painful. She had a Red Army boyfriend, whereabouts unknown, was the word.

From Musya's seat the sacrifice of manpower looked well justified. The fatherland was gorgeous. Exhibit A: Lake Baikal, which wore its green hills and brightly-painted wooden hamlets as a vast fancy necklace draping a bosom of natural wonders. Goats danced against jaw-dropping prospects. Far-off fishing boats under sail plied in and out of incandescent mists.

"Excuse me," she heard. It was the lovesick provodnitsa who loomed before her, fists on hips, chin with some unpowdered splotches tilted to point at Musya's knees. "Excuse me—where did you get that?" Gone to stand against the better window view, Samuel Nemo had left the quilt exposed with its repairs in progress.

Musya answered, "I made it."

The rather long neck jerked right, left. "No. That. And that."

"We already told you—it is not dirty, it has permanent stains." The other ignored this and raised her right hand for a final finger-point:

"And that. Those are new, you did not have them in Moscow. Where did you get those patches?"

Musya glanced out to see the lake widen all the way to its furthest, arctic-looking shore. Minute mirror image mountains closed like a blue equator belt around a vast transparent globe of sky in which a few black spheres floated: rock islands. "Go away," she said. "You are spoiling my view."

"Answer me!"

With her eyeglasses in place for a change, Musya could see what she'd neglected to notice before now. Lack of clarity would be no excuse. "They are from a family heir-loom," she said.

"That is my blouse," the conductress countered. She was right. "I have been missing a blouse since Sverdlovsk. I thought someone else stole it, I blamed another girl—but it was you."

"No." From the family luggage, Hodeh had claimed it came, a nice collection of scraps in a durable lightweight wool, light blue, that Musya had forgotten all about packing in Odessa; provodnitsa blue. "You are mistaken." She remembered having felt the usual suspicions but this was a worst case possible. The victim was livid and making threats from a position of authority over a personal loss:

"I could have you locked up," for instance. "That is state property."

"No one stole your blouse—no one in my family. Leave us alone."

"Oh, I will leave you alone, plenty—I will dump you off this train by yourselves and have you sent back to Irkutsk—Irkutsk and beyond."

"Go ahead," Musya told her. "If you think no one ever sent us worse places than beyond Irkutsk, you are out of your mind."

"I do not think so," said the provodnitsa. "Pack your bags for the next stop!"

She surged off in the direction of superiors, an angry squall short one uniform blouse. Halfway to the end of the carriage a knot of passengers stopped her with a burst of special pleading; for the little chess player was in a three-way tie on the leader board, they couldn't lose her yet. Some discreet cash wagers were in play. A few resources were pooled. They cut the provodnitsa in.

According to Hodeh, it was enough for ten new blouses. Safe in their seats as a consequence, the Kotz family faced a blank where Lake Baikal by moonlight had vanished under in-sweeping clouds. Musya regretted the magnificent sunset she'd been too busy to watch properly. And now all their bags were packed. This time she wouldn't unpack anything. She quilted another stitch in a small blue repair and considered the little thief seated there with her Pretzel kicking lightly in his sleep between them. Life with Hodeh went on as it had, Musya reflected. The good she did them cancelled out the bad that followed from her crimes; in truth Hodeh found ways to distinguish herself and be useful in every situation, an admirable person.

"Some people said you break balls," the girl continued.

This took Musya by surprise. "Oh, well," she said modestly.

"Because you stood up to her. They're calling you Worse Than North Irkutsk now."

The One Who Screamed considered this. "I guess it's an improvement."

"Yes," said Hodeh.

Indeed, the next day or two would bring the family several furtive food gifts, bags of cedar nuts mostly—a boon, as four children were proving costly to feed on demand otherwise. Now, too, came requests to add her name into ink-grooved address diaries: just in case their Jewish owners ever needed to know someone in Birobidzhan, they said. She wrote down Magga's street number but whether she'd be living there was uncertain. A relative had sent telegrams on her behalf but he'd had no answer, she explained. People wished her the best. Sometimes she could see almost all the other entries had been scored through.

Overnight the Number 44 climbed east into wet weather. The track clung to mountainsides. Now and then a snowflake struck the window glass. Fog walled off precipitous views, then parted to show valleys lined with smokestacks and furnace blasts that dyed the dripping air in blood and acid shades. Somewhere out of sight, the provodnitsa called.

Moments later Vera the young wife hurried up, red-nosed and wrapped in half a dozen shawls. "Did you hear that? Chita is next! I read everything about Chita when I was a girl—it's where they sent the exiles, all those noblemen who tried to kill the old tsar's father."

"His grandfather," Musya corrected.

"You're both wrong," someone called. But everyone could agree that it had happened after the Decembrist plot.

"The plot—yes!" Vera's shawls jumped as she clapped her hands inside them. Her face was alight. "And their wives—the wives who renounced wealth and titles to follow their husbands into Siberian exile—they kissed their husbands' filthy chains!"

"Yes, the wives, the Dekabristi. It's a famous story," Musya said flatly.

Vera's ecstasy blazed higher. "The Dekabristi! Oh—I wish we had a camera! We could get out and take our photographs on the platform, in the same place they stood. It would be so beautiful." She sighed giddily. "Don't you think we live in the most romantic country?"

"Oh, yes," Sender said. Musya too agreed, of course it was. Vera from Leningrad was a little crazy. She was right about this however.

Downhill from the freezing rain, the tracks found a river to follow through the taiga for a day. Every few hours a small cathedral city rose along their route through a Siberia unchanged for three hundred years, still a nearly limitless labor camp prison. Transported there, hidden from comprehension, convict generations passed and followed one another; criminals and political prisoners, poor poets, poor women, toiling and dying side by side by the million in its spongy vastness, a continent in all but name, mostly frozen and nowadays riddled with unsleeping war-science and secret metallurgies. Shuttered carriage wagons bristling with gun barrels rolled west for unbroken hours at a time. All the track connections were unmarked. No one was supposed to know anything, Musya heard.

The view left her feeling solitary. Her eyes travelled from one face to another at Hodeh's deciding matches, two dozen men and none struck a spark in her—nor did a single one try. She felt low, with a cheated life, stripped of romance while others like Vera with her handsome man kept piling it on.

Hodeh was outplayed at last. The provodnitsa won either way but this result favoring her more, she turned all conviviality. "Her bag of Romanian zhid tricks wore out," she told Musya with a big smile in passing. Unexpectedly teary over this loss, Hodeh cried harder. It hurt her to lose, she said. Years would pass before she played the game again. Musya applied a comforting hug and spoke in a whisper:

"Could you get one of her skirts maybe?" Though fairly well-proportioned, the provodnitsa was built along generous lines. Musya was thinking there'd be enough good wool and lining combined to make a nice little jacket for Hodeh; dark blue would suit her. But the little girl swiped tears from her mouth to declare it impossible—up and down the carriages, the precautions now being taken by the train crew were too robust to risk it, sad to say.

The next morning the taiga was gone. Tall oaks shaggy with brown leaves hid the sky between railway bridges and views of near-completed harvests from sunup to sundown. Around midnight they heard the provodnitsa give her throat some extra clearing for the next stop announcement:

"Kuybyshevkavostochnaya!"

Platskartny class woke itself up with applause. Sleep was already general again by the time they reached some abbreviated signs bracketing a nondescript station; a brief stop, and they moved on again. Anton groaned.

"People live too far away!" He was miserable.

But they were only a few hours from home. Musya told him to get a little more sleep. He said no and clambered down with his tiger-stuffed satchel to crowd her at the window. Within two minutes he was slumped against her ribs, his lips blowing dream bubbles. She returned to watching the furtive, almost silent movement of her own lips in the dimly-lit glass. Determined to avoid any costly repetitions of her first trip east, she'd be practicing Boris Kotz's line all the way to Birobidzhan:

"I'm sorry, no. Tipping is not permitted in the Soviet Union."

A scrim of boiled egg and kvass vendors withdrew and quickly dispersed in the dark as the Number 44 pulled away with a pounding racket. No one waved from the windows because it was half past two. The last of the handful of other passengers to Birobidzhan, strangers, hurried into the station building. Left behind on the platform the Kotz family staggered with sleeplessness among its bags. Musya's mind also reeled.

The provodnitsa hadn't said a word, not even proschai. She'd practiced for nothing.

The night air whinnied. The children looked around them. "Why is it so cold?"

"Because it's Siberia," she said. "In the middle of the night." Overhead haze cast by the station lights failed to obscure the stars, Siberia's sky carpet. Dense in patches as salt grains in sea water they made pools of sea-green glow she'd never noticed. Of course she'd never seen them at this hour before.

"It's worse than Ukraine." Sender pursued the subject. "And it's only September."

"Yes. It's cold, I'm sorry." With the train out of earshot, a metallic clamor coming from some nearby all-night factory began to dominate the scene.

"For what?" Poor Anton: this was him. He burst out sobbing, ugly sobs. Bone-deep griefs tapped at their roots pumped out steadily with a force that wreathed his grimaces in breath clouds. He'd had his heart set on a homecoming show and this empty platform crushed him. "For what? For what?"

"We're all disappointed," she said. "All of us."

"But what are we waiting for?" the others wanted to know.

She cast about for an answer, seeing blanks. Where the man with the half-rotten handcart had stood with his long lips, she recalled him. A crooked cartwheel axle crossed the threshold of her memory with a ghostly squeak. At any moment he'd appear. She wondered where he'd take them—what kind of housing Boris had found this time, far away out here in the autonomous region of the dead. Were the rooms any more spacious? Would Liza be there too, again? Or rooms and houses could be entirely lacking—one step from the platform, Birobidzhan might never have been. Instead maybe a swamp forest through which animals pursued by predators with iron-tipped spears kept crashing would be there to offer a gray-green existence outside history, untouched by Soviet planning, where the family might wander reunited in the form of ground fog.

The station door opened and someone in a uniform called out from the yellow interior:

"Kos? Kotsies?"

In their startlement all five of them went still and glanced towards the Trans-Siberian tracks, the obvious escape route; in fact Samuel Nemo headed that way and had to be caught. Musya temporized:

"May I help you?"

"Why you not coming in?" the guard complained. "Your dvornik expects you. She sent a Nanai."

She felt better. "Oh, good. Will it fit all of us?"

"What are you talking about? Are you crazy? It's—here he is—a Nanai. Don't touch anything!" the guard shouted after the Nanai—not a taxi, but a black-eyed Asiatic-featured person near Musya's small size who, having slipped underneath the guard's elbow, walked up extending a note ten-times folded which read:

I AM MAGGA. HE NANI COUSIN. GO WITH. HOUSE OLD READY.
AFTER BULLET MAKES I GREET YOU.

The Nanai cousin chewed his lips with some scattered teeth. He had skin purple from drink, an unfortunate youth who smelled bad. But there he was, punctual, to fill the place of a dead man. She asked his name.

"I am Yuri!" He shouted when he spoke and stared when he was through. Then he looked down at their bags and began to make conjuring moves with his arms as if to gather them into a mid-air heap; of course nothing happened. The arms kept moving. He was incredibly drunk. Musya didn't know what else to do, except take out some small bill currency and hold it towards his hands, chasing them with cash until he finally plucked and made it disappear into his dirty fur-trimmed tunic folds. She couldn't tell whether he was avoiding her eye or only looking inward. Quite abruptly he grabbed Sender Kotz by the wrist, signaled the rest of them to follow and headed for the station doors, where he turned and signaled again. Sender pulled and struggled unavailingly, bewildered behind his spectacles.

The rest of them looked down at their luggage. The station guard laughed.

"Nanai men don't carry bags, Kotsies—that's women and children's work!"

(3)

Returned to love she felt committed and hopeful. Her eyes perceived brightness again. Once more she took pleasure in her full possession of a working body. She enjoyed the complex counterweights at play between shoulder and hip, left right and left, as she walked across town after posting a reply to Leon Flohr.

It was her usual Monday, these hours free in accordance with her schedule at the Birobidzhan Agricultural Machinery Plant. The old rooming house dvornik who covered replacement shifts there had put her up for a steady job. They worked in different departments: Magga's manufactured bullets, Musya's lathe parts. The plant along with its big machines for making farm vehicles had been retooled for the war effort and ran non-stop. There were a lot of accidents. Musya kept well clear of anything in motion. She worked as a sweeper and also cleaned the shop bathrooms. Her daylight leisure hours today would end in a short night shift. After some hours on a hard cot in the plant dormitory, she'd work days shifts from Tuesday on through. As workplaces went the machinery plant's worst feature was an incessant thudding screech of machine noise. Musya kept her ears plugged with wax-oiled cotton batting, a procedure she thought she had down to a science even if flaws persisted in her push-brooming. Now the street sounds roared and grated against her naked eardrums. When a truck wheel churned a pothole's slush across the windscreen of the next truck behind, the resemblance to gunfire spatter hardly troubled her today.

> My dear Odessa Girl—my Muschka with the beautiful hair, Is there the smallest chance for me to hope you remember a young man—hardly more than a boy—who loved you? It is I, Leon. Or what is left of him. O my dear girl, countless are the hours I've spent remembering our golden times together. I think of the sweet cherry ice we shared at Passazb Arcade. And the night—that unforgettable night!—on Vorentsovsky Lane. I can dare to hope you remember too? Alas, between those happy hours and these of my writing, what a chasm lies.

Musya knew every word. Her heart muscle halted at the chasm and flexed sympathetically—tighter. With her reply posted, every moment brought Leon closer to the ardent comfort in which she longed to bundle him. Like heat escaping from a stove, affection warmed her view of the freezing, filthy, snow-smothered city and the two-story snowdrifts that climbed its crowded building sides all streaked with dreck, like soiled skirts. Human beings were human beings. They behaved terribly, yes, they dumped their night buckets out the windows from sheer laziness. Yet give them an implacable foe and they flamed with capacity to fight and work without rest: and they prevailed. By now they were triumphing. The news of 1945 so far was full of victories, three months' worth and counting. The radio reports playing everywhere came bracketed by march tunes, an unavoidable sound collage of Soviet heroism.

As heroes went, though, these Birobidzhaners couldn't compare to the man whose moustache captured her mouth's recollection at will. If she needed to wait at a street crossing in a mob of pedestrians for their numbers to swell before braving the traffic floods in a herd, Leon's kiss crossed with her; through horn honk choruses and diesel fogs she'd trail with her own lips smiling, parted, tickled. Leon's pen strokes danced behind her eyelids when she blinked. The lettering rounded and even rather childish, a very wholesome hand, Magga had remarked when she delivered it, postmarked Odessa, its contents (a characteristic Yiddish-Russian mix) recently dated Novyi God 1945.

"Manly," said the dvornik. "Not like his."

She'd meant Boris Kotz, who'd sent the dvornik three missives on Red Army post stock full of rambling instructions, some contradictory, regarding his library, papers and specimens. In the third (dated like the rest within a week of his curbside conscription) he'd pledged to take up the problem of the Manchukuo dishware next time. *"Disregard any instructions you might receive from my wife in this matter."* Not one more word had arrived; and of course they'd heard nothing of him in Odessa. *"Allow me to suggest again that you Magga or your daughter might attempt to remove dust from all the shelves and not solely the lower ones."* Packed inside the meticulous printing, here was Boris, his voice. These querulous scraps were all that remained of it. *"Please do not attempt to exercise your own judgment in regard to my books and digests from Germany."* There wasn't a word of German in the place by the time his family returned to the flat. Their sewing machine and tarelka were both gone, too, for the war took everything, as Magga said. As for the daughter, Kitty had enlisted at the declaration of war, right away, and was still with the Air Forces. As for the Manchukuo plates, they'd been called into use by the rooming house pantry years before; people said they gave the place a tone, something civilized. The Kotz family continued to use their own set every day.

And as for the correspondent, the years had delivered no further news of Boris Kotz, only one fateful surprise: all his striving had actually paid off. Complete with triple signatures and seals, thick with officialdom and dated only days before the German invasion, when he'd had his family on a train, the appointment he'd longed for had welcomed them home. The next available spot on the Western Ukraine survey was his— he'd achieved his promotion. Musya Kotz was the wife of a Soil Specialist.

His sons were fiercely proud of him.

> *The silent years between us—dare I hope to bridge them with these words I shape from sorrows? My dear girl, to write you is to live but to think of you again is torment. Again I feel the blade, the blow, the branding iron, the red hot pain that felled me when I heard you'd wed another. Many agonies since*

haven't come close—but dear god believe me, I don't reproach you, not for your marriage, not for anything. I humbly introduce this letter to his home and wish that you will inform Kotz your husband of my hopes for his good health and long years. Only ask him, I beg, that he should allow you to send me word of yourself—a line is all I ask, only to know that you are well. A letter addressed to me here, as you see, at a scene of our old happiness, will reach me without fail.

The Londonskaya Hotel that straddled the top of his notepaper: he'd treated her once to pastries at its café restaurant. She remembered watching the wheeled cart take its time reaching their table. Leon had talked a lot about a money venture, something to do with antiques. Happiness, yes—it had been. At the time expecting a lifetime just like it to follow, she hadn't realized. But she knew better now, she knew enough to take note when it appeared. She smiled at her happiness on this winter's rest day in the Soviet Far East, narrowing her eyes against its brightness even as the brief gray daylight began to expire. And although nearly perpetual nighttime could feel almost unbearable, today (or already tonight, she supposed) it did not. She felt sun bathed.

But what am I saying? Dearest—my heart's love—please tear out those lying lines I wrote just now and destroy them—incinerate them!

Of course she hadn't done this.

I rage—believe me. I burn to have your husband Kotz at the end of my saber, my pistol barrel, I want to feel my bare hands around his throat—I denounce and despise him. Leave him! Love me again.

Re-reading these words she'd still raise her eyes involuntarily sometimes and look around for Leon's rival. The old flat's permanent clutter kept impressions of him close. To Musya's goodbye, what would Boris Kotz have answered? Entirely fogged, his thick lenses looking like rounds of cement, his tight voice crackling with upset, his spittle in play, as an exit line with slammed door likely, something told her: *"Typical romantic garbage!"*

Love me again. And yet again, alas! Alas alas alas alas alas.
I am not the Leon you remember. I am less than he. A man still, a man they call a hero, I call him a pathetic wretch. Yes, a hero. Three years underground with the Odessa resistance—a real underground, we lived under the city cellars in caves. Three years of hell. I saw executions and all sorts of butchery, I saw hand-to-hand combat. I crawled through catacombs in blind darkness—how often then I saw your face, my dear girl, rising to comfort me. I was a leader. Men died, men I sent into harm's way. Remorse drove me. The fascist vermin were always setting explosive traps for us in the tunnels—one of them had

caught my men. My obsession was to track down their sapper teams and kill every last man after subjecting him to torture. And believe me, I knew success. Picture it: a limestone cavern dripping with ice water; the enemy sneaking around, laying wires and dynamite; and your Leon crawling silently up behind with a knife between his teeth. Bloody revenges were mine, dearest. Hero: a word the size of a kopek.

Then every so often came solace. How? From where? Where else but from the thought of you? Oh my dear girl, your broken lover calls to you from the past where he lives day and night among memories of your smiles, your merry laugh, your sweet kisses—dear god, those kisses! How we kissed—how we loved—how we danced, gliding like swans, our two souls in perfect time. Paradise, darling. But now through tears I tell you, your dancing lover will never dance again.

On the last day I was a whole man, the Soviet bombs were falling, the liberation was certain, a matter of hours. I could have waited in a deeper cave with the rest but I wanted another kill, I had bloodlust, I was like a madman. One last team I was hunting, the cleverest, most elusive and most fatal, the very nemesis I blamed for my men's slaughter. That day I found them—only a minute too late. The charge was already laid. The tunnel walls and your Leon inside them were exploded. My survival was miraculous. I awoke to find myself above ground in our Odessa, a clinic patient. To you, dearest of all my heart's resting places, what can I tell but the truth? I saw I'd never walk again. They were gone—my legs are gone.

Magga hadn't wanted her daughter to join up, especially not when she did, not right away. But though Kitty was barely seventeen and her schooling a year short of finished, the girl wouldn't stay home; already desperate to travel and see life, she was ten times more desperate to get to the war. This was a national phenomenon. Young girls besieged conscription offices with demands to be sent west into danger zones, demanding a yes before the time grew too late and the Soviet Union prevailed too swiftly. With all its millions thrown at once into the fray, its fascist enemies couldn't last many weeks. Kitty had been afraid of missing out. Three years later and her only child still absent at the front, the dvornik felt glad to exercise a motherly dominance over the Kotzes' re-installed household. Considering their survival miraculous, the brothers she reverenced with pious looks and murmured incantations, and often spoiled them with treats.

Now it was a question of persuading her to move the family from their upper floor to street level rooms. These were normally reserved for other purposes and Musya faced a struggle, but she planned to be tireless in Leon's interest for his accommodation and his wheelchair's. She was pushing for a solid ramp from street to threshold to replace the perennially loose boards laid out front across the local trash and drainage ditch; she had the ditch on her list to go next. The house would need a bigger bathroom, too. More odd moments passed amid plans for perfecting the loving care to be, once Leon arrived. As the night added cloud cover to its early descent she could feel the frozen atmosphere, compressed, become less yielding to the human form on foot. But a walker warmed herself; whereas the legless hero in his chair would need to go blanketed in fur, maybe bearskins, a future expense to keep in mind. His story didn't surprise her at all, he'd always had tenacity.

> *I'll confess it, I cursed my own vigor for preserving my life. I called down Death to come but my strength barred the door. My will warred against itself. I'd left hell underground for a hell within. My misery was absolute. To end my own life! Resolved, I had to plan carefully, for the clinic is run like a prison. At last the moment came—and found me picturing how you'd react to the news of your lost lover, dead by his own hand, felled by despair, self-murdered, a suicide. It was you, you and the thought of your heart-pang and sorrow that stayed me then. Knowing your sweet true heart, I knew you'd only reproach me for this single fault, that I'd given you no chance to speak and try to save me, no chance to say Stop—Leon—Live!*
>
> *For never doubt, the lion's heart within me would still seize life with all its passion and endure. My potency is unaffected. But without a word from you, I confess, I fear my hours are numbered. How long I'll survive the expiration of my hopes—a few days, a fortnight—it hardly matters. For now my hopes are all I have. You must be—no, you are indeed the earthly goddess of my memories, my dreams, my every thought—a being made for adoration—you, darling, who will never look at me and see a legless man but only and forever his undying love. I beg you—save my life. Send me word of yourself. Call to me, send for me, yes, dearest. You know your Leon, I can live anywhere. A little shelf in your happy home would be enough. Dear God! Pity me and write. Tell me of yourself, your husband, your housing and employment—tell me anything, only pity your old true Odessa lover and don't delay.*

He'd signed it *Yes, Yours, Leon Flohr.* Her hands had been shaking by then, the first time she reached the signature, her coat and boots shedding ice onto a floor mat while life in the rooming house went on as before. Men and women circulated past, some with friendliness for her; she'd felt light touches, heard some murmured pleasantries. From the two-lane traffic in the busy narrow stairway came a cheerful hum. Looking up from the pages, she'd seen herself surrounded by good people doing their best in a good and beautiful world: a glimpse, slow to fade. "There's a pretty smile!" someone said then, he wouldn't be the last. Leon's letter had opened and changed her. Men looked at her more now, ever since, Musya noticed.

Despite the urgency in Leon's closing lines, she'd replied not quite right away. She'd pondered and then she'd made a dozen false starts and as many re-writes for penmanship—she could afford it, with heaps of her husband's leftover stationery still taking up shelf space nearby. What to Boris the inveterate packrat would have seemed terribly little left of all his stuff, to his surviving wife remained overabundant; the children enjoyed the extra playthings however. Of the original flat the family had just the old bedroom and the passageway bunks. Now that the Nanai cousins had gone, they shared sink, samovar, and commode closet with three girl telegraphists who occupied the front room in overlapping shifts. More space to herself would have been nice but her children had round-the-clock company as needed—a godsend with Musya working. When she was at home she had a lot to do and still a lot to dust. Outside a couple of hours on a rest day, time to write letters barely existed.

Of course I remember, she told him.

Outside the Agricultural Machinery Plant School gates stood the usual crowd. Crowds were everywhere in Birobidzhan lately, overflowing its classrooms, filling its wide straight streets with traffic, jamming its bad restaurants. At work round the clock, the capital of the Jewish Autonomous Region was all-in for the war effort. Its zeal had been celebrated by the state, its Jewishness proclaimed as being no barrier to patriotism; its children even sang some Jewish-sounding songs in school. The teachers charged with educating the plant workers' children seemed competent enough; but their Russian-language pedagogy found a pair of stumbling blocks in Hodeh and Anton. *They resist curriculum*, the director reported. In fact Anton still carried a big torch for Eidel (his good teacher, he called her stubbornly) and as a whole the former orphan trio made no secret of hankering greatly after mame loshn and the old career. Although she sympathized, Musya watched until the school doors closed behind them every morning—they'd fooled her in Obodovka but not in Birobidzhan, she wouldn't allow it. Truant children risked too much on these Far Eastern streets full of war-footing traffic and agitated humanity. Terrifying scenarios haunted her.

Meanwhile Samuel Nemo had mastered infant class where he was a dominant personality, made much of by all.

Of course I remember you, Leon. Further down she added, *Of course you should come to me—come quickly—I welcome you with my whole heart.* She told him the truth: that though married she was husbandless, heading a young family of five. Having a husband hadn't done much for her, she admitted. Her own war in Ukraine had been difficult. *I suffered from men*, she wrote. Leon and her children would love each other from the first—she felt this deeply because they shared so much in common. *Real Odessan hearts*, she put a line beneath for emphasis.

Of Sender Kotz she'd boasted to Leon at great length. His academic promise was real and placed him among the plant's leading ten year-old scholars. They could thank the books he'd read over and over again in Obodovka: *It's good we were somewhere that gave him time to read, his teacher told me*, she wrote. Sender wasn't the most popular boy but he had plenty of friends whom he practiced avoiding sometimes. Tonight she watched him cut a lone zigzag through the crowd to the family's rendezvous spot where he greeted her:

"Any letters?"

She told him no, there hadn't been. His face didn't move and its sadness disturbed her into adding, "There will be—only not today."

"You always say that—just stop saying that," he snapped.

So every morning without fail she brought her children to school, when her schedule allowed she walked them home, and there was nothing rarer than a day when no one started a family argument. Other children would pass them in the road, laughing, chattering happily. Musya sighed. "I don't always say that."

His sigh was louder. "You always say that, too."

"I'm sorry." A father figure was what their family needed. Until he arrived as expected, Musya did the best she could—but it felt like she mostly made apologies.

One question preoccupied her and tinged odd moments with unease. Was she really a good enough match for Leon Flohr? After all, he was a major wartime hero whereas she, Musya Kotz—failed poet, overburdened young mother, many times raped—had passed that time at forced labor, mostly sewing. What could she produce to compare to the exploits of a man who'd fought, lived, taken lives, spilled hot blood onto white limestone? Despite its horrors and tragedies hers was a very dull war by comparison. Even Leon's life as a bedridden man close to suicide possessed a vitality that made her own life look feeble to Musya. Adding to the imbalance and the discomfort, it sounded as if Leon had kept himself not just unmarried but unattached, stainless, even pure. Not even officially widowed, she could hardly say the same—far from it.

Unregretted living proof of her faithlessness to Leon's love hurried up, pulling Hodeh by a mitten, his snowsuit knees pumping. His seven year-old brother trailed them by a few steps. In the gate lights' glare Anton's eyes looked huge with exhaustion shadow. He kept flinging himself out of nightmares, chased awake by Fascism, the awful Enemy of Culture. Hulking, incongruously silk stovepipe-hatted, with a hair-covered yellow torso, Nazi armband, gorilla features, a belt full of knives and a large blood-dripping axe carried poised for further use, this monster came from a patriotic wall poster made popular in the years before the war. The artist had planted one of its legs through a framed canvas and surrounded it with wreckage and ruins, tumbled philosophy books, broken antiquities. Angry and watchful only for more to murder and smash, two dots for eyes appeared fixed on the monster's next victims. Many parents had complained, she'd been told. The poster was gone from the school hallway but the damage was done; also city-wide the image remained fairly ubiquitous. Anton kept struggling up out of sleep in the coils of his tiger skin to cry, *"The hat, the hat!"* The rest of the family had learned to sleep through.

Samuel Nemo wore a furious look. He wouldn't tell why. A new behavioral quirk: sometimes he used a human mouthpiece to communicate with his mother. "He won't go back to school again, he says that's final," Hodeh volunteered tonight.

"But for what?" Musya exclaimed. "What now? He loves it there, everyone there loves him."

The baby shook his head violently. "He says they don't respect him," Hodeh said.

Anton spoke up. "They respect him fine, they just won't pay him."

"Pretzel!" She took a firm tone. "Remember what your teacher said—please don't try to make the other babies pay you, it's not nice and it's not good socialism."

"I'm not a baby," he said. He was three years old. "I'm not a baby—I need money!"

People turned to look. "Who doesn't?" someone said. Musya pointed her children towards home. *I have my hands full sometimes,* she'd written Leon honestly. Not in her first reply, granted, but an early one, the fourth one, probably. She couldn't tell for certain as she never kept copies.

When her first reply was in the mail, for a few days she'd been happy waiting for Leon to write back. From the start she'd entertained herself with picturing him in his clinic, her letter open in his hands, his eyes devouring. Happiness, he'd brought her to happiness again. Her mind had moved to the words to come in his reply. What would he say now, what would be the sound of his joy on the page? Or would Leon even precede his letter, his person sped eastward by eager love and kind officialdom? Happy thoughts had filled her mind day and night until one morning, in the middle of the shop floor, revelation struck with force enough to cause paralysis. Her push broom handle hit the concrete with a bang she couldn't hear.

Leon was testing her.

It was the ices. She'd noticed the mistake right away, then brushed it aside—he was entitled to all the mistakes he needed, she'd judged. But she'd been the one in error. This was no mistake, only subtlety, modesty, quivering hope, recognized too late. From her failure to set it right in her first reply, Leon with pain would divine something forgetful and indifferent in her heart towards him; a false conclusion, utterly false and bound to cause a misunderstanding she was desperate to prevent. It took two days almost without sleep to frame words. She opted for a light tone finally: *I'm sure you remember, Leon,* she'd written, *that your favorite stand in the Passazb Arcade was out of sweet cherry ice that day you took me there. I remember how upset you looked when we had to settle for lemon. But here is a secret—I like lemon ice better!*

I'm sure our letters will cross, she'd write.

Favoring different routes for the nightly walk home, the five Kotzes rotated the choice. Tonight was Pretzel's turn. The family set off, Musya keeping the step behind she favored. Once she had all her children in sight, that was when she could relax, plunge into her welcome plans and aim at perfection. Kasha with butter was Leon's favorite dish, although he also loved caviar. Spoons, napkins, sour cream bowl—more for the list. A mind kept busy repelled disquiet.

For how would Leon Flohr adapt to life here in Eastern Siberia's eleventh largest city? Would he be able to forgive its difference from Europe, its distance from everywhere, and most of all the lowliness of its standards relative to the standards Leon himself embraced and indeed epitomized? Would he find a way to overlook its inelegance, not to mention its squalor? For her sake, for her sake of course he would: she could chant love charms all day long but facts remained facts. She was asking a lot of him when she offered this place as a haven. *We live close to nature here,* she'd written mildly. Lifelong Odessans like Leon, she knew from experience, tended to find Birobidzhan a shock. It wasn't just the awful climate's brutality and strangeness, where a single winter week might layer impenetrable fogs over skin-scalding freezes and wrap up with a swamp blizzard of large pale green flakes. No: it was the vacuum in place of advanced civilization that really struck at a person's vitals. More and more these days Musya thought it must have been this shock, delayed but fatal, that killed her sister—consumption had only been its guise. Transplanting Leon from his native Black Sea shore safely would require her to cushion his nerves and spirits as well as his poor body.

She counted on help from the city itself: Birobidzhan—less bad all the time. Almost twenty years had gone by since the original framework to support a human population had been erected from wood, thrown up and left there. In general dilapidated, a lot of it was still in use, as housing stock mainly, smaller places like Magga's with rooms to let and of course the big log-sided dormitory hotels which maintained their grim positions on the major thoroughfares. But every year more fine public buildings and cement pavements crowded them. The street lamps worked better. The weedy street trees Liza Kotz helped see planted had branched overhead, their rows would cast summertime shade dapplings across Leon's chair rides. In booserish hours Musya was happy to note every amenity the city possessed going strong. There was the spot-lit white stucco front of the Universal Store's two handsome levels; also the few dozen shops, the five bad restaurants and cafés, the good Sholem Aleichem library, the State Yiddish Theater reviving, the old cinema with its new marquee at which Sender pointed excitedly:

"The Two Fighters are back!" Released a few years before, this male comradeship tribute was a current household favorite. Luckily, the telegraphists didn't mind bringing children along to the cinema sometimes. One of them had called it a good conversation starter—men missed having families, the girl had said, they missed children.

"Maybe Valia will take you this week," Musya suggested.

"You come," Hodeh urged.

She said no, she wouldn't. *Never*, she meant.

Musya's old love for cinema had deserted her. Since leaving the Obodovka ghetto she'd gone to one film, a matinee of Two Fighters and a terrible experience. She'd lost the knack of being an audience to a screen. Disbelief hampered her understanding. Monstrous, crawling, mud-colored lights resolved into actors squinting on a sun-beaten lot at the Tashkent Film Studio where the opening credits had placed them. Dialogue jabbered out of time with their paint-darkened lips. She disagreed with everyone she knew and thought neither lead was handsome; Mark Bernes did nothing for her. The storyline in her view was equally a zero, there was nothing to see except how some healthy men and women had enjoyed themselves making a film in a nice part of Uzbekistan while Jews in ghettos died of typhus and starved on potato peelings and Leon Flohr, snaking through white mud on his real Odessan belly, never ceased to risk a hero's death in defense of their common homeland. He'd given his legs. Other people had hairdressers. For all her trials, sometimes Musya thought she'd never felt so sadly abused as when she sat watching those disembodied strangers pretend to interest people and burst into song. *When you're here with me, Leon,* she'd written, *we can go if you like—the cinema won't seem so bad with you beside me, I know.* Another underscoring there—she'd also drawn a heart—two. She remembered kisses in a balcony.

"Mine!"

Samuel Nemo, already starting. Musya looked up and felt a little stabbed in a soft place, where her love for a legless man was tender, as her eyes met a pair of two-toned wingtip dress shoes. All the city's shops were strictly numbered by the state but went by unofficial names among its citizenry. The Kotz family's route home tonight would feature the youngest's favorites—window shopping was his passion. The window of Obuvf, people called it, showed off products of the Birobidzhan Shoe Factory in neat leather rows. The pointing mitten moved steadily.

"Those are mine. And those. Not those." Even on the limitless budget of strict fancy shopping with care: "And them, mine also." The rest of the family gazed until he was satisfied. Her baby had flashy tastes for which Musya was at a loss to account.

The dark reddish sky released some snowflakes over the jostling pavements and fed the bright clouds billowing from vents and chimney-pipes, throats and cigarettes and sidewalk braziers. Down at street level, charcoal burned smokily. Aisles of indirect electric light paralleled the shop fronts, to the benefit of street food hawkers who tended steaming samovars and dumpling kettles. The Kotzes dodged string bags and strangers' elbows crooked around slender parcels of dinner meat. The usual school notebooks and writing supplies met them in the display window at Shkolnik, their next stop, where Musya said no, they could not go inside. This pained her as well because the novels on show were definitely new. The family kept to the library of late, they couldn't spend. Musya was saving everything possible for when Leon Flohr arrived.

Economy wasn't the only reason to keep out of Shkolnik, however. Weeks earlier, a shop attendant had caught Anton pocketing a gum eraser. A manager stepped in without delay. There were no second chances in stock: no more Kotzes were allowed across the Shkolnik threshold, who knew for how long. That night on reaching home there'd been a clatter as Hodeh unpacked a major haul. Pencils and pens, a glue bottle, ink pad and rulers, a miniature globe—the gum eraser had been a cheap decoy, this was evident.

"The mean one isn't there," Sender on tiptoe observed with a hopeful tone.

"Mine!" Samuel Nemo shouted over him at an abacus with large brass beads.

"We have five at home," Musya objected. The bargain-hunter Boris had never passed up a single abacus. Was this hereditary? His baby bellowed:

"No! This one! I want this one!"

"Fine, that one we'll have, too." She raised a glove to swipe breath mist from the window glass and tried to read the titles on the unfamiliar spines until a startling volley of knuckle raps announced the mean one, quite present after all, looming over the display, glaring out at them. The familiar index finger wagged, then pointed: onward, elsewhere. While Samuel Nemo made angry noises, an expressionless Hodeh lugged him away with a practiced arm.

Although she knew them to be full of perfections, Musya considered it urgent that her children develop all-around better behaviors by the time Leon Flohr joined their household. Less foot-stamping and sulking, fewer attempts at truancy and infant peer extortion, and no more stealing, zero thefts, none whatsoever—these didn't seem like such unreasonable goals when she listed them to herself. To fall short, to offer less, given such a father figure, a war hero in the home, would feel shameful. Because Leon deserved the best possible family, she found herself lecturing, prodding, nagging at her children—who complained, balked, and behaved even worse as a result. She recognized an impasse and feared she was stuck with it.

Her friend Fanny's voice sounded abruptly in her ear, the rich laughing voice: "*All children steal. This is good—it shows nature's intelligence.*" Musya's step faltered. She couldn't place the occasion but here was a vivid memory of Fanny's warm room full of silk cushions and color. A stuffed toy cat and some battered dolls were under repair on a table beside a spill of talcum powder. Pungent leaves hung in dried gray-blue bunches on the walls. Photographs of the handsome family clustered in frames on every free surface. The Romantic Ballad hummed from the tarelka in this room of the past.

Fanny her sister's friend, her own friend, was long dead, murdered. She was buried in the city cemetery under a small white stone. A year into the war, when the Red Army needed men, the husband she adored had been released from political prison and shipped west towards the battle lines. Freed only to fight, his pen was silent and his whereabouts unclear for months until he made his sudden return to Birobidzhan. A changed man, almost wordless, clearly embittered, his smiles extinct and all his former beauty stripped from him: "Scar, scar, scar," Magga recounted sadly. Where he'd been he wouldn't say. When he spoke he didn't make much sense. He ate like a two-fisted animal and urinated everyplace that had walls, indoors, outdoors, outside his old laboratory building where the civil guards picked him up and brought him home. A few more days passed after that. Fanny sent her children to sleep at the neighbor's place. She must have had a premonition, people said. Her husband attacked in the night and killed her with a roofing hammer. Then he ate some bread and fell asleep. Cross-eyed Sonya hiding in her bed cupboard witnessed it all; she kept house these days for the prosecutor whom she'd impressed and put on airs whenever she returned. Sentenced rightfully this time, the husband would do hard labor for life in one of the northernmost camps.

As for lovely selfish Zara and the rest of Fanny's children, their mother's kin had come and fetched them away to the mountains beyond Baku. According to the dvornik's sources, one ancient man among their company had made chalk marks on the threshold and scattered what looked like bone meal all around the crime scene. Now everyone who occupied Fanny's flat for even a week suffered bad luck.

After all the hope she'd rested in a warm and talkative friendship's renewal—and more, there was a kind of belief Musya had cherished that she'd find the older woman's very presence healing—the news of Fanny's murder had come like an electricity cut; it sent all the lights out in a moment. Talk, laughter, health—out. Weeks later she'd still been groping through murk, unpredictably tearful. Even now, after Leon's letter, the terrible loss hadn't stopped circling her daily existence. Its shadow could dim any view. The the lost brightness felt like it must have been delusion, a sparkle swept away; what was left appeared as reality, brute fact. Fanny was dead, and Musya her younger friend was lonely. In silence, loneliness buried her deep.

Factory workers, delivery boys, school children, kitchen maids, grandmothers, invalids with coughs hurried past in the cold. The scene might as well have been filmed in Tashkent, these people felt like such absolute strangers to her. Even at the machinery plant where she'd been sweeping for months now Musya rarely spoke to anyone. When Leon came, she told herself, she'd bloom again, make friends and smile again, laugh as she'd used to laugh in Fanny's room. *You'll be popular here, Leon,* she'd written. *Smart men are valued here in the East. I'm sure you can even find work to do in an office, if you want that. The people here are good, maybe rough sometimes but honest, good people, even when they have problems.* Musya hoped there hadn't been too much exaggeration in that particular reply.

The last half of the long afternoon queue blocked the way past Khleb 1, the neighborhood bakery. In practiced wedge formation the family squeezed up to the window with its oblique view of the Father of Communism filling the standard central frame on the wall behind the counter. Loaves with golden crusts lined the long shelves beneath him; these objects of Samuel Nemo's fascination were made of painted plaster and kept there on show to signify better times. Two elderly clerks wearing white caps bagged black bread at the counter and frowned. The customers weren't happy either, she could hear their voices shrilling through the glass.

Complaints about food shortages were general but hard to take seriously after a captivity in Obodovka. True, the war bread was very poor, its ingredients suspect. "Forgive this bread," Magga would say. The dvornik collected all the ration slips when issued, standard procedure. Roasted chicken had been off the menu for years but her tenants agreed, they never went hungry. Fish soup and borschts, meatless pirogis, strange berry and root vegetable compotes, preserved mushroom salads sufficed; when the Nanai cousins turned up there might be fresh or smoked pike or game. The children also got sour thick morning milk for their special minors' share. New inhabitants of a world of abundance, they'd relish a piece of awful beet sugar cake like it was a strawberry cream puff from the Londonskaya's café. Sad to relate, sometimes Musya would, too. She'd fallen, her tastes toppled by hardship. At night she'd crawl into bed with groans of relief, pull the earth-stained patchwork quilt up to her chin and sleep instantly. She still thought of it as her wedding quilt. The children claimed she snored.

On the next street they came to Elektrobot, an Ali Baba's cave of modern plug-in wonders where Samuel Nemo was inclined to plant himself until he'd claimed every bright-red appliance. Poor Sender, his feet dragged grooves in the snow as they went along. He loved to browse among books for sale, would never steal, and had nonetheless to suffer the common Shkolnik ban. Musya wanted to do something special for him. She could see sadness tugging him from their midst into a dismal place apart; he was its helpless prey and barely fought. His resignation rebuked her—his predicament was all her doing.

She hadn't said a word to the children about Leon nor his letter, not at first. She hadn't told Magga what it contained, she hadn't told anyone. Bottled up tight, its effervescence buzzing, the delicious secret had quickened her steps, her smiles, her interest in life. She'd started to pay more attention to her clothes and the shine in her hair. She turned down a few sweets. She told jokes at which she laughed first and loudest. One day Sender got her alone and asked whether she was going crazy again.

"Again?" she'd asked, startled.

"Like you were in the dugout, when the Germans were coming." Her rejuvenated personality made him anxious, made his weak eyes start welling salt tears.

"I'm not allowed to be happy?"

"Not if you're the only one," he'd answered her.

Homecoming had stranded Boris Kotz's oldest son amid a new set of privations. Alone among her children, Sender missed Russvelt. He also missed his friend Zara whose mother's death upset him terribly: although Musya had tried to keep the details from them, Fanny's murder was still talked of and the children heard all. As the eldest, his better memory of his mother's old friend made his grief hurt worst. As for the boy Mendel and his sister, they were still in Birobidzhan but attended a different school; the three had met but there was some estrangement. He made new friends, yes, but Sender Kotz was lonely too, and saddened by loss, burdened by harsh memories, and fatherless—he missed his father more than he knew, she thought.

As before, the answer came to her while sweeping. At her very next chance, she'd found a private moment in which to produce Leon's letter and she'd read Sender parts of it, not the whole, just enough to show that something wonderful rode their horizon. Feeling generous and kind, Musya shared the view, as if she were handing him the captain's spyglass for a turn. A hero was coming, an underground Resistance hero and more—she described the man, witty, energetic, restless, debonair. The boy was enthralled, she couldn't tell him enough about Leon Flohr, this Moldavanka charmer turned warrior. His moustache! His white suits! They dissected him in whispers. Then together they'd wept over the dancer's legs he'd lost to fascist treachery. Through flowing tears they'd pledged to build him a new life of love and family in the Soviet Zion. He'd have the home comforts he deserved.

"Tell him so!" Her words, her impulsive idea that Sender Kotz should write his own reply to Leon Flohr, just a few welcoming lines that she'd enclose with a brief explanation: what kindness this would be to the man in the clinic bed! They'd agreed, he'd be the envy of the paraplegics' ward. In deepest secrecy they labored, two now—but separately. Sender claimed the right to be confidential in this, as man-to-man. She hadn't argued. Surely this would spark Leon into writing again. If her own replies had kept him too busy being pleased to make a written demonstration, here was something else entirely, a little boy with his heart on offer. *He's so much more cheerful since I told him you were coming, Leon,* she wrote. *He can't wait to meet you.* Weeks passed. Sender kept writing, sometimes quite long letters for Musya to fold inside her own; she never read them. "Leon's will cross ours in the post," she assured him time and again. Her mind's eye vaulted the polished mahogany lobby desk at the Londonskaya Hotel to seek out a particular mail slot: was it being emptied or was it stuffed full? Run like a prison, Leon had said; Musya supposed that was why he hadn't bothered to give the clinic's address or name but she wished he had, now. She might even have telephoned.

She sent a few postcards. A tinted summer view of the River Bira, indigo currents banked by green rocks: *What was the name of the restaurant on Feldman Boulevard?* she wrote. *It's driving me crazy that I can't remember.* She never mentioned Fanny in her replies to Leon, not wanting to create the wrong impression of Birobidzhan as a violent place.

A stretch of frozen mud beyond the last shop windows became a ragged borderland of sheds and flimsier wooden stalls, where a diesel generator hissed long strings of mismatched bulbs into wavering service overhead—the local night market. Here the dealers in used goods and imports by whom Boris Kotz had been regularly cheated were still ensconced, turning wartime profits alongside more precarious sellers of fish and fresh pelts, wooden ornaments and toys, Chinese slippers, tattoos, illegal tobacco, home-distilled samogon bottled as health tonics, playing card fortunes and paraphernalia for every religious persuasion. Scratchy gramophone tunes contended with an old man playing a bayan. Smells wafted, some irresistibly.

At Musya's call the children gathered to witness a rare production of small bill currency, not very much, which she handed to Sender, "For blinis," she said; his favorite treat. With Anton determined on caviar stuffing and the rest opposed all four hurried off to descend on the blini maker in a mob.

She felt glad to stay where she was and listen to Leonid Utesov singing Temnaya Noch. Famously featured in Two Fighters, the song was everywhere these days; Anton had learned it by heart and liked to sing it to his favorite telegraphist in the front room, cracking his voice with artificial tears on the last verses:

> *I don't fear Death.*
> *We've crossed paths many times on this steppe.*
> *Even now Death is circling my head*
> *In the darkness.*
> *You wait for me,*
> *Wide awake by the crib-side you sit.*
> *All night long your vigil protects me.*
> *This dark night I rest safe.*

Musya inhaled icy air that smelled sweetly of fish. A half-dozen dried river taimen stood on their tails in a barrel frame beside her, thrusting their toothy jaws high into the night above her head. Steps away, two women haggled over pungent dried mushrooms, one speaking Yiddish and the other Chinese: the sale was progressing, however. So it wasn't Odessa, it was lively commerce all the same, exactly the kind of thing Leon enjoyed. The maze of paths among the market stalls wouldn't be too narrow for a wheelchair, she judged. Pushing, she'd bend and sink her lips in the hair on the top of his head, his fine-textured fragrant and warm brown hair. She thought of kisses—those kisses.

In truth she wasn't sure which erotic memories Leon had preserved from

Vorentsovsky Lane of all places. That night hadn't been their best. It hadn't been a night, merely an hour or two around dark. A tall stone address with private flats, one of which he'd said belonged to a friend; a few dim rooms stuffed almost wall-to-wall with upholstered furniture difficult to pick a path through; a strong stink of powered insect poison; a locked window giving on an empty courtyard; at last kisses, followed closely by unusual bother on Leon's part over a messy contraceptive failure—her mental reconstruction of the scene hadn't yielded any clues to his choice of allusion. Quite the contrary: she'd remembered laughing at the red upset that contorted his face; because his contraceptive measures amounted to so little to begin with, his tardiness to care had really struck her as comical. Leon hadn't seen the joke. They'd spatted, parted, and he'd let a week go by before they finally met again. These were all the facts she'd been able to recall.

The evident conclusion had become her occasional torment. Somehow, on a mildewy purple divan three floors above Vorentsovsky Lane, Musya's youth had peaked—she'd attained passion's highest prize, there in the embrace of a soul mate—only for life's devouring corruption to come along and do its filthy business on her heart and mind until today, barely five years later, not a trace was left. The treasured moment survived intact for Leon in his purity; he remembered, not she. They might have made vows for all she knew. Faithful Leon waited. At times she felt near panic. *How can I say this?* she'd written. *Please forgive me, dear Leon, darling man, if I disappoint you in some things. I promise to make you surprisingly happy in others. You can guess which, I think!* Maybe her desires surpassed her dignity in this particular reply but Musya didn't believe she had a choice. She wanted him. Whatever his potency, to some extent they'd need to start fresh, almost like strangers, considering all she might have forgotten, the great blanks between them.

The children dawdled back with smeary mouths, a half-eaten blini for Musya and nothing more. Snacks were dearer just like everything else lately, she didn't need to be told.

"We gave the change to a samovar," Anton finished explaining. She was proud that he was always generous to beggars but still she had to scold him.

"Don't call them that, it's not nice."

Hodeh said, "But it's what the Russians call them."

"I don't care what the Russians call them, calling them samovars is not nice. They are war heroes, they lost their legs, and arms sometimes, fighting for our lives and freedom in the war. And in our home we will not call them samovars."

"They go around on little tables with wheels, though," Anton persisted. "Like regular samovars." Big ones did, the other children agreed.

"I don't care!" Musya cried.

Someone had sucked all the artificial cocoa filling from her portion. The tilt of Samuel Nemo's eyebrows said enough to make the ring around his lips redundant. He was in a greedy mood.

Home was near. With quickened pace the family made no better time, for the vague snowfall had turned decisive. Musya kicked a path through her children's footprints. Best to leave a little early for her night shift, she reflected, not unhappily. Posting a reply to Leon Flohr always left her spirits buoyant for a day or two, sometimes longer. If tonight's boost promised record endurance, this was because a gnawing guilty doubt she'd had was gone, banished by her latest postscript. *I hope*, it read, *you didn't feel offended, Leon, to receive what I sent you last month.* Weeks ago she'd had another revelation, one that told her why the hero hadn't written again or signaled his intentions, why he hadn't come. He was penniless. *Please consider it to be your own. For here is the whole truth— what is mine is yours.* She'd sent him almost all she'd saved by then—far from enough, she knew—for his nurses, his train fare, his debts, his mother's rent of course. *I'm saving again, everything I can. If you need more, dearest, please write to tell me so.*

Someone from the rooming house had tossed sawdust and cinders onto the sagging planks that spanned the ditch out front—a rare concession towards safety. Musya's complaints were having some effect, she decided, picking her way across. The children had already bounded inside and were almost done stamping their boots on the floor mat by the time she closed the front door behind her.

"It's you?" she heard: the dvornik's call.

"Yes, Magga, it's us," she answered, watching Pretzel scramble after Hodeh up the stairs.

Here was a fraught relationship in action. Magga's partiality towards the Kotz boys did not extend to the little black-haired girl. Hodeh she didn't trust. She was watching her hands, Magga said. This had been in the course of reporting a second tenant's stolen wristwatch complaint. "I know what thieves' hands look like." After which Hodeh had pledged to go straight again.

More trouble might be on the way, however, since Hodeh was keeping a cat in their rooms. Other tenants did the same thing, granted, for the place was chronically mouse-infested (and worse: ditch rats got in all the time). Magga even kept a pair of kitchen cats around. But animals in the rooms were against the rules of the rooming house. Anxious to preserve the dvornik's favor on Leon's future behalf, Musya regretted the timing of this small young gray-striped cat whose inexplicable name was Merele. At the same time she could only welcome the decimation of the vast mouse colonies populating her husband's left-behind stuff—to open the large armoire especially had been a test of nerves. Not anymore. And a mouse-free home was a safer home for Leon. Meanwhile the cat named for a carrot slept on all the beds in turn and charmed the three girl telegraphists out of dinner scraps and milk. The girls were on Hodeh's side anyhow, since she'd brought them stockings when no one else could get stockings, not long before she'd gone straight again. As the dvornik's bast soles whisked rapidly closer, Musya felt the usual guilty apprehension.

"Is something wrong?" she asked.

"Do not worry." Magga kept her frown. "It is nothing about your cat."

The war years had thinned the dvornik's red face and baked old and new wrinkles deep into its planes. Responsibilities crowded her days: a shop floor leader among the bullet-makers at the plant, she continued to run everything here in the rooming house; and her daughter's safety at the front was a constant worry. To the Kotz children's intense fascination, she kept Kitty's long black braided plait in a box. The mother bewailed the Air Forces' cruel sacrificial demands but Musya happened to know that Kitty had wanted bobbed hair for ages. She herself had kept her auburn lengths and waves. Leon wouldn't be disappointed. The fact was there'd been no keeping her at home, Kitty's mother said so all the time.

Now she only growled. "If you want to get letters, it is an extra house fee."

"Oh, we won't," Musya lied; but she hated the expense. She watched the dvornik's hands explore apron pockets and other depths within her many layers of clothing. Magga smelled of saltpeter and onions.

"Ah." She extracted a pale blue, postmarked envelope. "This came today. For you— from Odessa."

"It's him!" Sender Kotz rushed to see. "Oh, thank God."

Musya swayed but couldn't move a step. Her mind rang with alarm. Where was the Londonskaya stationery? What had happened? Where was Leon? She had a premonition: bad news. She watched her right hand accept the letter from the dvornik's hand. Without another word she turned and carried it into the parlor, the brothers noisy at her heels. A man sitting reading Izvestiya with his boots unlaced gave a scowl at their entrance and reached deliberately for cigarettes. The front of the envelope swam with words as in a dream, eluding sense; **Одесса** was all that stood out clearly, like an iron ring. She trembled; the page she pulled out fluttered and something heavier dropped to the floor. The writing wasn't Leon's, the hand was even more childish.

"Give a look!" Anton picked up the fallen photograph. "Russvelt has hair now!"

"What?" said Sender. "What?"

How come you don't you write to me again? she read. Her eyes chased through words, front and back. There was nothing of Leon here. In the envelope another sheet: she yanked it out, ripping off a corner in the process. Falk's firm black fine-nibbed lines raked her vision. *The boy thrives, as you can see from the enclosed,* she caught. *He would appreciate a word from your eldest.* Sender was panting, reaching for both letters.

"Is it him? From him? He knows Russvelt? How? Let me see!"

The dvornik nodded, stamping her survey of Falk's penmanship with satisfaction. "Very nice. That's how an important man writes, you can tell."

"Yes, it's from my uncle. My husband's."

"But," said Sender.

"It's a letter for you," she told him. At a loss, she added, "From Odessa. For you." She thought this might kill him. His face, his lips, were bloodless and his eyeglass lenses flashed like searchlight signals as he shook his head in blank dismay. She touched his shoulder and looked around for a water carafe but didn't see one; she thought if he lost consciousness she could carry him outdoors where the snow might revive him. This bitter room was full of smoke and ashes. His laughter crowing, Anton shoved the photograph between them, held high. A profusion of dark curls: it was true.

"And look how fat he's gotten!"

"Quiet!" cried the man with the newspaper.

But it was amazement that silenced them. Russvelt had plumpened so much in six months! Filling out every bit of a round-collared blouse busy with student insignia, he leaned comfortably against the wine merchant's portrait studio chair. Falk himself looked bigger, stuffed with well-being. The new wife looked a little shrunken beside them.

"My God," Sender said.

"Yes," said Musya.

"But—if this came, it means the post is working. Everything can get through now."

"Yes," she agreed.

"Everyone's letters are coming. Thank God." He laughed. His resilience astounded her. "Antosha, you're right, he's so fat now!" He took the pages from her hands and started reading them out loud.

Musya raised her eyes to find the Architects of Socialism, fly-specked and faded, presiding from their time-honored spots on the parlor wall. Had they done this? Had these two men created and spun the stuff that made little Soviet boys something so close to invincible? Was this their real achievement? Not a revolution nor a state, not victorious armies, but a strength in-born among Soviet children, boys and girls who could survive almost anything.

While she was smashed against the ground like a clay tablet.

(4)

After that day's disappointment Musya stopped replying to Leon Flohr.

A few weeks passed and then she sent one more reply, bending to an urge to frame their confusion over the Odessan postmark as something comical, for his amusement. She'd sensed he missed her voice.

Soon her letters to Leon went out on her rest days as before. Gradually they became longer: she wrote more often than before, sometimes for an hour or two every night; the weekly envelopes went out stuffed with pages. Sender wrote too, fitfully. No answer came. *I'm sure our letters will cross,* she'd write until the likelihood was gone. After a point his silence explained itself. As she had long surmised, Leon didn't plan to write, he meant to come in person. But delays beset him; understandably. Imagine the planning required! To manage the crosstown trip between stations in Moscow for a legless man would take a brilliant piece of strategy and that was just one detail among multitudes. Her practical advice overflowed into triple and quadruple postscripts.

Winter's war bulletins ended in a string of major triumphs. Through Poland and beyond the Red Army surged, driving Nazi fascism from stolen lands and freeing its slaves. Warsaw, Budapest, Bratislava, Vienna—liberated. Though exhilarating, to the Soviet people this westward advance felt like it was taking everything they had left. Every particle of sustenance and strength they possessed was being asked of them. All day and all night the Birobidzhan Agricultural Machinery Plant forges blazed. Production was down, though, from frequent lack of raw materials. People stood idle, then threw themselves at the tools and assembly lines for an antic shift or two. Strength drained away. Good food was scarce, the shops very empty, the bread worse than ever. Without what the Nanai cousins supplied, Magga said, they'd have been in trouble at the rooming house.

On the ninth of May, Musya was sweeping. A pair of legs ran past the end of her push broom. A minute later another leapt right over the handle. She looked up. People running in all directions, their arms in the air, weeping, embracing: a fatal accident, a big one, she guessed. Dull with dread, she tugged the cotton from her ears. The world was shouting.

"VICTORY!"

Someone picked her up, whirled her around a few times and left her there swaying. The broom had flown from her grasp to land beneath the assembly line belt where iron pieces were piling up unattended; she watched a few hit the floor. Then with great rattling groans all the machinery in the place started to shut down, as if overpowered by the workers' voices.

"VICTORY! VICTORY!"

A woman hurried past, then more women. Mothers! She followed at a run. It had been so long since she'd run, Musya's body felt like an ungainly weight it hurt a younger version of herself to move. Others struggled likewise. Several corridors away the massive bird flock sound began to reach them. Every classroom in the school next door, erupting in joy, had emptied its shrill celebrations into the schoolyard. The shouting mothers burst into the midst of the screaming children and began a riot of indiscriminate kisses and hugs; some got the teachers, too, in clinches. Everybody loved everyone.

"Let's get out of here," said Sender Kotz.

Her children had found her. She had Samuel Nemo in her arms. The rest encircled and began to guide her towards the school gates. Rockets and big guns were going off all over the city now; booms and whistles and smoke trails filled the air. Hodeh wanted to get home to Merele who couldn't tolerate loud noises. In fact, Musya reflected, pushing her legs to go faster, commotions like this one made the whole family uneasy. Revelers thronged their quickest route and forced them to elbow their way through scenes of rejoicing. Many people danced while firecracker strings exploded at their feet; others stumbled about alone with tears sheeting their faces. Beards dripped. And drunkards getting drunk in vast numbers sang along with a hundred gramophones brought onto windowsills to play the Sacred War march. *Rise up, great nation!* Between the samogon and the unsynchronized recordings, the anthem became a tuneless spirituous roar.

She was panting with haste by the time they reached the rooming house. The place sounded deserted, everyone had gone off to celebrate the victory. Gathering themselves on Musya's big bed, the Kotzes watched Merele bathe forepaws in a sunbeam on a pillowcase, before Anton spoke.

"Papa will be coming home now?"

"Your Papa?" She kept her tone bland. Had Boris survived even two weeks much less four years of warfare? Unlikely as it seemed to Musya, the duty lay with Soviet officialdom to tell his sons for sure, she thought, deciding to require her widowhood in writing. "Yes, he can come home after today," she said; and watched Sender frown. She knew they'd been thinking the same thing almost from the moment of victory.

It was Leon Flohr who'd surely come to them now.

But why not, Musya thought suddenly, both? She could make room for two men. They'd fit. A husband and father to help care and provide for the damaged hero—it would give Boris Kotz a use for his time; finally.

Another cannon salute shook the windowpanes. The cat froze, seemed to knit its gray brow, and resumed licking its stripes.

Anton also persisted. "When? When will Papa come?"

"Soon, I hope." The words on her lips saddened her. This meant Anton would be waiting, too. Another state of suspense she'd created in the home, another barrier to rest and peace: her longings for what she didn't have were contagious.

But Samuel Nemo cried "No! I don't want the papa here."

"But Pretzel, he lives here," Sender pointed out reasonably.

"No!"

Even with Hodeh taking the stranger's side, they weren't going to persuade the man's youngest son, at least not today. Just then the front room filled with excited voices: the girl telegraphists were all home at once to change into dresses before going back outside to continue celebrating. The children and Merele went to watch the uniforms come off. Musya stretched out alone and wrapped herself in her wedding quilt. On the great day of victory over German imperialism, she took a long nap.

A decade earlier, as a youth of promise and model student, Magga's cousin Yuri had won a place at the prestigious Institute of the Peoples of the North in Leningrad, from which he'd been expelled within eighteen months. Drunkenness: Magga blamed Leningrad but more people than not blamed his Nanai nature. There were a lot of national minorities in the Soviet Union that hard liquor left undone; the Nanai were one of them. It was a shame, but Russian culture was dominant, especially in Russia. The Kotzes' first encounter with Yuri in the dead of night at Birobidzhan station had progressed into a family friendship. The young drunkard was a welcome but tragic figure who reappeared at intervals from the upriver forest settlements where his closer family dwelt. He'd come bearing dried and preserved fish, meat, berries, skins and milk products, staples of Magga's unique wartime survival diet and source of the rooming house's single small cash trade, carried on in cheap fur coats from a room above the smoking parlor. A person could always recognize a fur from Magga's by the tobacco whiff it shed. Yuri didn't trap or kill the animals, he just transported the skins. He'd hang around until wired for, at which point he'd be sobered up and sent on his way. He carried a sketchbook around and could draw anything from life.

"But the thing is, Yuri," Musya was telling him today, "we've started living in here. Again. You know this room belonged to us, before." When the previous weekend's departure of the third and final telegraphist left a vacancy too good to waste, she'd shown no hesitation. Who knew when Magga would give up a parlor floor suite? The children were enjoying their new sleeping corner in the front room, a vital step towards the coupled privacy she envisioned for her life with Leon. The furniture was all in use yet here was Yuri tugging the chaise lounge out of place and across the room.

"Are you moving here, Yuri? With us?" Leaping into action to give the other end a push, Anton sounded hopeful. For a short time after their return the Kotzes had shared the flat with Yuri and two or three other transient Nanai goods dealers, a time he recalled fondly for the snatched drinks and sing-a-longs; he'd liked the telegraphists, too, for other reasons. He liked company. Musya was thinking she wouldn't mind having Yuri there every once in a while but the whole noisy mob again wouldn't be tolerable. Meanwhile Yuri's answer Musya couldn't understand. None of them could. Sometimes Yuri spoke too many languages at once—even some Yiddish.

"The balebos?" Anton caught this now. "Yuri, what about the balebos?"

Yes, what about him? Musya wondered. The balebos was the one who'd built the place and been its NEP-era landlord, the man who'd hired Magga as its dvornik and still lived on the samogon she brewed him; neither Jewish nor Siberian but a Moscovite who'd dabbled in esoteric teachings, was the word. Once a man of enterprise, a paralytic recluse now, the balebos hadn't left his room since 1938; despite which he kept up a large acquaintanceship and had many visitors. This circumstance appeared to be a worry for the house committee—it seemed he was inclined to talk with too many people.

"Talk Big Man. Talk Tarabak." Yuri said. Anton sniggered and Musya hushed them both. The Big Cockroach: as common nicknames for their nation's Premier went, some like this were dangerously rude. "Trouble talk," Yuri added though he didn't need to.

"Trouble." An hour later, the dvornik confirmed it. "Listen to this trouble."

They'd heard it by now. The new arrival who lay groaning on the chaise lounge hadn't been shy, he'd made his entrance on a proclamation: bad news, lately gotten from a source he trusted, a thick slice of truth straight from a supper party at the Stalin dacha. Where, over brandy, the host and first Hero of Socialist Labor had remarked himself badly displeased with the Birobidzhan Jews for their failure to build up the Soviet Zion he'd given them.

"I tell you, it means the end of us all!" shouted their new flat mate. Emaciated in some parts, swollen in others, generally bald and pinkish, the old balebos had blue bloodshot eyes, smacking lips, and a dark, fruity smell. He coughed explosively. "*Ack!* We can expect to be shot or else shipped off north to die like starved dogs in the ice. Because no one could get a Jew here to grow a bean!"

Magga shook her head. "He goes and goes like this to everyone these days. It upsets the tenants—you upset the other tenants," she scolded.

"Those fucking Jews, why don't they know anything useful?"

Musya said, "I do not want this man in my home."

"But look at him," Magga said. "He cannot live a year—this is a dead man."

"All of us are dead!" the man insisted. Magga said to ignore him. "Ignore me at your peril!" he said.

"But why here?" Musya asked. "What if we—we might have—if another person—"

He broke in. "And if you think I would spend a single night in the same room where that filthy informant sat brewing his poison, you are out of your mind, Magga!"

The dvornik turned her shoulder to him and told Musya, "You have room. He takes only little." As for the bother, there wouldn't be any: she'd go on seeing to everything. "You will forget he is here."

Doubting that, Musya frowned. "What is his name?" she asked.

"Call me Brother Dead Man!" he cried.

"But he is raving mad," Musya complained. "And he hates Jews."

"He blames them," Kitty agreed. "But so what? Look at him—can he hurt you? Why should you care what he says? He upsets the others, then they talk. That we cannot have here." Her mother nodded.

"No talk. No upsetting. No attention."

The newcomer twisted himself onto one hip to holler up at them. "Don't you understand what I am saying? Look what he did to us less than ten years ago. Look what he did to me! *Ack! Ack!* This is him, your beautiful Stalin, the Tarabak, angry at Birobidzhan—the city is doomed, he will wipe it off the face of the earth. We are all doomed!"

"Tovarisch, please." Kitty aimed her battlefield voice at the paralytic. "Think better thoughts."

Musya told him, "Birobidzhan will be fine, Brother Dead Man."

He shouted back, "I know why I don't run but what is your excuse?"

There was nothing to be done. The front room had slipped from Musya's grasp. The dead man demanded his tarelka, he couldn't live without constant radio news. Which he'd lie there mocking. He made a lot of noise and smells; a pass-out drunkard, he snored. An ideal floor plan collapsed just in time for biting insect season. Children leaked back into the marriage bed to share the misery which Magga's home-cooked salves soothed once more.

Summer this year found the dvornik at a zenith of happiness. Her daughter was home, besholem, safe and sound save for the burn scar stripes branded into her forearms and a troublesome hernia. In the Air Forces she'd served at the front in one of the three all-woman squadrons organized by Marina Kaskina, the great aviatrix. Kitty had stayed on the ground, loading old low-flying Po-2 crop dusters with anti-personnel fragmentation bombs. Plywood and percale, powered by chattering five-cylinder engines, the little biplanes—kukuruzniki, corn-pickers, people called them—turned into flying torches at one hit from a tracer round. They couldn't carry more than four bombs at once; each bomb weighed about sixty kilos. The pilots flew twelve or more missions a night, cutting the engines just over enemy lines to swoop in on their targets like owls. Sortie after sortie, if they survived, they'd taxi back in from the darkness, empty bomb cages white with engine heat, and take off again, loaded at lightning speed. "Do you know how heavy is sixty kilos?" Kitty asked. One bomb after another to haul hoist and load on the run, all night every night—and they'd all been girls on the ground munitions crew, barely more than schoolgirls. Kitty was twenty now. She wore a truss. She'd gotten used to staying up until dawn; she'd also returned with a ferocious smoking habit which her mother deplored, a single flaw to season the dvornik's joy.

Now that she'd seen something of the world, Birobidzhan looked even smaller and duller to Kitty than it had during her restless girlhood. She'd passed through Moscow a few times and what was left of Kharkov, where she'd spent a sick leave, had impressed her greatly. Scorn colored her attitude towards her home city and its inhabitants. Even poor Fanny, whom she'd liked, wasn't spared. The details of the murder didn't even make her flinch. She'd seen a lot of women die—too many good women, she said. And of Fanny:

"She ought to have enlisted. She could have fought, then she might have died for something. Or she might have lived and been a hero and alive now, no?" Kitty pursed painted lips and blew a jet-trail of smoke through them. Her mother swatted it away, objecting:

"No, no, she could not fight, her womb was fallen."

"Yes, a little, it was," Musya remembered.

Kitty said, "So? Whose womb was fine?"

She was the first soldier the children had known and they never tired of hearing her tell them war stories. To Hodeh she became a kind of idol, while Kitty scored points for daughterly rebellion and made a favorite of the little girl. At this time Musya and her family were the closest things she had to fellow combatants on the premises where her injury kept her stuck, more or less unemployable. Her mother had put her in charge of the house committee to help keep the boredom at bay.

One rest morning, she and Musya were sitting alone on the back steps in the sun with cedar cups of cool tea when Kitty asked, "What was it really like? In your ghetto place?"

"I don't know," Musya said. She couldn't think of anything else to say.

Kitty pressed her. She'd been listening to the children's stories, too. "But being locked up like that with everyone dying, and all those dead bodies. They were dead, weren't they?"

"The still people, yes."

Musya watched the purple house swifts pick off a few more small white butterflies that had strayed into the air above Magga's kitchen garden. Then she began to tell—not everything, not all the rapists, but some. The men came to mind first, she didn't ask herself why. The words began to pour from her.

Kitty was a loud listener. Full of sympathetic sighs and whispered oaths, having brought back a large collection of oaths from the front, she finally added to a last loud blasphemy, "Musya, it was because of the children you survived."

"Oh, yes," she agreed readily. "They did everything around the place."

"You lived for them."

She nodded again. "I was lucky to have them."

The dvornik's call came from an upper floor. The daughter groaned and got to her feet. "That was more than luck you had. It was fate," she said, and went off shouting, "I am not your housemaid!"

Left behind with her history invoked but unfinished, Musya sipped tea. She had a letter to Leon upstairs to finish and post. A sound settled in her ears, the rustling jaws of the cabbage worms at work on the big blue-green leaves. Floodwaters opaque with foam gathered outside her scrutiny. There was a pressure. She'd survived, true, she and all her children. Had this been fated? The idea left her vaguely giddy. So frightened she'd been all the time back then, so worried. A fresh cleansing compassion towards her former fearful self surged through her spirit now like fresh water, cutting channels for memories. Kitty's cigarette ends in the dirt reminded her of laundry days back in an old courtyard during Odessa's yellow-skied siege, Baila Kotz's laundry and Roza the smoker who'd left for Marseille. All those escape plans—walking pregnant to Bulgaria! She'd almost forgotten that crazy scheme, it made a really comical story; and there were others, so many more. Even certain scenes from Jewish ghetto life in Obodovka as she might describe them—Boim and Papa's overcoat, for instance, or the Bulbe Fence shows— they were good stories. Leon Flohr's bright face would crinkle with enjoyment at their telling. Another postscript occurred to her.

Dearest, she raced upstairs to write, *I long to hear more, everything, about what happened to you in the resistance—how you lived every day, what you ate, where you slept and what you dreamed at night, how you felt in the mornings. All of it is interesting to me. I have so much to tell you, too. Come quickly, Leon.* Her heart was pounding. She sealed the pages in an envelope, dashed off the Londonskaya's address across the front from memory, and began her next reply without a pause. She began to write about Transnistria.

Until late hours these summer weeks she could write by the lingering window light, sitting up in bed as her children and Merele came and went in a revolving tumble around her legs. Needling gnus and the itch of their stings faded from her consciousness as she struggled for the words to capture Leon's understanding with her own. She told about the forced labor details and the claxon's daily welcome to frostbitten dread: Was this to be the day the ghetto took her children's lives? The starvation breakfasts and the bucket's stink; the daily struggle to wrap squirming little limbs in rags for underwear before they froze; the clumsiness of fingers burning with cold, the clumsiness of inatten- tion, of exhaustion and worry; always awakening to fresh uncertainty: What would happen on the road to Babiak's that day? How bad would it be? Required to survive, condemned to hazard, she'd had to keep going ahead to face what she couldn't risk. *Did you feel something like this in the caves, darling, when you knew the fascists were there?* she wrote. Sometimes what she'd been through looked incredible in writing. She tried to tell how her life in actuality had been dull and full of dragging hours yet it had sped past, accelerated by threat. Her time to live had poured through her fingers like water and when she went to embrace her children their bodies, the holy vessels in her care, were transformed into passing time; she'd embraced rushing water. And the petty crimes to which she'd stooped—she recalled how she'd felt tarnished by her own cunning, lower than drains. The hidden pockets she'd sewn into Sender's clothes and made him stuff with scraps for her wedding quilt, she confessed them through tears. The shame could leave her shaking. The next day she always felt lighter.

Sometimes Musya wished she could re-read her own replies. *But I know,* she wrote, *that you're saving my letters as I plan to save yours, Leon—I know I'll see them again, when you come to me, we'll read them together and laugh.*

At work on the women's bathroom floor one day, while thinking about what to confess next, she felt a tap on her shoulder. Someone with a message from the supervisor's office: she was summoned. *Terminated,* her instant thought. The likelihood was high. This was work she was lucky to have kept. From the first, Magga's influence alone had meant that some mistakes of Musya's, some tardiness and even napping in a toilet stall had been overlooked for comradeship's sake. Now her luck must have run out.

She took the chair indicated outside the office door and made no attempt to imagine what would happen when she got inside. The men and women of the management suite crossed back and forth carrying clipboards or big sheets of paper rolled into tubes; others sat at desks where they talked Russian into telephones. None of this concerned her. As if inside an egg of glass she waited, her mind drifting to kisses—those kisses.

The man who came to the office door to summon her inside was the supervisor. Despite his bushy beard he was a pleasant-looking black-haired man, not too young, probably Jewish, missing some fingers from both hands. He knew her name and called her Tovarisch. Once they'd seated themselves on either side of his desk he told her she was being promoted.

She said, "What are you talking about?"

He smiled. "I am talking about good news. I am giving you felicitations. We are promoting you to a job on the line, a better job."

"But I don't mind sweeping."

"The thing is," he said, "we have a new sweeper coming in. Just out of hospital, a veteran's clinic. He cannot do the line work—he is missing parts."

She gasped. "His legs?"

"No," he said. "No. Some parts, you know, in the middle."

The promotion didn't sound all that good to her. "But," she said.

He flashed the smile that made him a popular figure on the shop floor, Musya knew. "And we expect to keep you in the same spot when the plant returns to manufacturing farm machinery."

She said, "Yes, when will that be?" He shrugged, he didn't have that information. She threw up her hands in a strange burst of energy. "Don't they have enough bullets yet?"

The supervisor looked at her for a long time. "Soon," he said. "Maybe soon. Victory and peace are two different animals, Tovarisch."

She was hardly listening. The second reply, she'd come to believe, had been her downfall.

(5)

The new work wasn't bad. Lift grip twist punch twist rag polish: it was simple and even relaxing at times. Musya never made any bullets in the end, she remained in her old shop. She was an engine lathe parts finisher—not the very ending finish but several steps before. To her line comrades on either side she would always be the Little Sweeper; they'd move her out of the way when the machines were running at top speed. The smiling supervisor made a few appearances. He'd ask her how she was getting on and she'd tell him honestly, the new work wasn't bad but the old work had suited her better. There was no returning, though. The new sweeper, bent and bilious, crept along; despite which he was like an artist with a push broom. The shop floors gleamed. Musya stood off in a small brown pool her own reflection made while peak production frenzies bored through her cotton plugs. With victory the war effort had only paused to refresh itself. Japan would be next, through Manchukuo, people were saying. The Far East was upgraded to an active war zone; everything about this she dreaded. War meant soldiers and camp orderlies and deserters, men in all sorts of pain rampaging; war meant shortages, refugees, prison camps, barbed wire coils to grip the landscape and draw blood from moving flesh. And war meant enemies—it welcomed enemies as to a dance. They entered. What if Japan decided to accept the invitation? Birobidzhan could become a battleground.

"Finally!"

This was Kitty's happiest week since her demobilization. She kicked up her legs—and winced. Samuel Nemo had already caught the exulting spirit. "Finally!" he crowed. They were a group on the kitchen garden steps today. Her big baby had learned to shell beans. Musya was helping him. She said, "Finally what? More massacres?"

Kitty said, "No—finally the East will stop sleeping. The East will finally have to do its part."

Her mother shelled beans in anger. "Don't be stupid. When was it sleeping? We never slept one minute here. The war took everything here."

When a short while later the war in Manchukuo began, the noise of the big guns carried from the front below the Amur River, in Birobidzhan they heard the first shots clearly. That first morning the city was sunless as sky-smothering flocks of terrified birds fled northwards. It didn't take long before only whispers reached them, the sounds of a one-sided conflict. The horizon towards China was striped yellow and black; they had some spectacular sunsets for the few weeks the fighting lasted. Another victory: Japan had surrendered. Kitty sulked around, she hadn't been recalled to active duty and the East hadn't stirred, in her view. The victory celebrations, muted compared to those of May, were soon overshadowed by talk about the monster bombs the Americans had dropped on the Japanese mainland. Who had won what? And other unsettling questions sprouted while discontent grew audible in certain corners, certain front rooms of certain divided flats.

"Why does he accept the surrender, why doesn't he invade Japan? Or France? We're so close!"

"My God, Antosha, should he be such a barbarian?" Sender Kotz along with Musya formed the flat's pacifist faction.

But at eight years old, Anton took after his father. Greedy for the territory, Boris Kotz's second son could look at outdated maps for hours. "He should just keep going. We could beat them so quickly—Japan is weak now and France always was."

"True," Hodeh said. "We could surprise them."

The dead man nodded. "There will never be a better time. We have the momentum, too."

Sender let out an exasperated breath. "Whose side are you on, Tovarisch Dead Man? You were the one who said we had to accept peace and wash our hands of blood."

"Our hands, yes, the people's hands." The old balebos on the chaise lounge rattled dice. He'd been teaching Hodeh to play and gamble at backgammon. Hodeh watched him closely, every movement. They both cheated. He let the dice cup fall still—a feint. "But his hands are a different matter. Let him take everything he wants—seas, mountains, monuments, half the planet—whatever makes him happy. Just so he will be content to keep his hands off Birobidzhan. It is our only chance here."

Musya sighed and put another stitch in the sailor blouse she was mending. "Not this again."

The dead man said, "Do all the deep breathing you want, lady. Unlike the rest of you, I know people. I actually know people." The dice dribbled from the cup, one, two: double sixes and uproar.

Autumn came on with the harvests to be expected after a single season's peace. Most shortages weren't going anywhere. Of course peace was very welcome, everyone said so. Yet grumblers much older than Anton Kotz found common themes in the cessation of hostilities. What, for instance, might have been? Why not keep Manchukuo at least— why give it straight back to China? There'd been a promise to the Allies: so what? How much did a promise like that matter when weighed against the four-year totality of Soviet sacrifice? Many who called him honorable for keeping his word also faulted the pusillanimity of the Wise Helmsman's advisors—he could have done a lot more, they knew, had he been given scope. But so, he was honorable. Pictured frontiers shrank back and turned to constraints. His fellow Soviets could feel that he shared their frustration. Each one shared a heart with him.

Musya Kotz's heart was not for sharing with any head of state. Her affections belonged to a legless man in a clinic bed. At any time her thoughts might drift off to embrace him. Now they cooled his pillow and ran some fingers through his soft brown hair, while Vera from the train kept talking.

This effortful friendship had grown closer, strangely. Musya might have let it lapse but Vera liked a confidante and really needed one. Her life was overfull of drama. In brief, although their young child was his, Vera wasn't married to her handsome man—"Far from it!" she'd say. In Leningrad before the war she'd had a husband, an intellectual who'd somehow managed to emigrate to America with her older child, another boy. Too rancorous for paperwork, even the tiny quantity required by Soviet divorce law, the union's end had never been registered. Her remaining man didn't care and neither did Vera. Two kindred spirits, it was enough that they'd found each other. Yes, maybe if she'd been more circumspect or a least kept quiet, she might have stayed with her husband; if she'd been content with a brief furtive bolthole affair she might have been in America now. But Vera followed her own heart, proudly, always; with the exception of her marriage which had been only a mental decadence.

Today Vera had the usual complaints about the hardships of life among the Jewish Autonomous Region's famous collective farms: the unrewarding toil; the awful land and climate; the uncongenial fellow settlers—hostile, outlandish brutes, all, even the Jews who were vastly outnumbered in the countryside as in the city. "Everyone looks at us like we have three heads apiece," she claimed. They were speaking Russian as Vera's Yiddish had never advanced. Her little family from Leningrad had spent the past year on the move, trying out one kolkhoz after another. It didn't sound like the selection had changed much in the ten years since Boris and Liza Kotz's attempt at the life there. Log huts sinking back into swampland; skin and bones cattle let loose to forage for tree bark in the woods; empty barns, empty fuel tanks; bitter water, bread made with sand; eye disease, coughing, emaciation, failure: every stop was the same, only the next would be worse. At the hellish IKOR farm Vera's handsome man had caught an infection ravaging the collective at that time and passed it to the couple's child—or vice versa, Musya wasn't sure. This was where her mind had begun to wander. Her thoughts brushed Leon's lips with less and less fleeting kisses. She knew that at the end of a long story, the trio was now installed at Birofeld whose working milk barns and apiary made it the least bad of a sorry lot. What's more, because they actually produced things the kolkhoz members at Birofeld had a regular trade with the region's towns and capital. A big honey shipment had brought Vera along today without her family from which she claimed to have needed a break. She said she thought her man was cheating.

This Musya heard. "But I thought you said he was bedridden."

"It wouldn't stop him," Vera said. She ate some more salad with her fingers. Birobidzhan's Jewish restaurant was Vegetarian-Jewish now and widely ridiculed for the beet cutlets it served. Vera's way of charming room bosses had netted them the best front window table for two this lunchtime. A vegetarian "whenever possible," she'd also kept her figure through all her tribulations, Musya noted this a little enviously. Although

Vera's hair could have been thicker. Yes, pulled back across the parting and bound tightly away from the long large-eyed face, her hair could have used a touch less flatness. Not Leon's type, Musya decided.

She said, "I am sure you don't need to worry."

Vera's eyes narrowed. "I wish I had hair like yours, Musya. Nice and full with natural waves. And that color, not boring old brown like mine," she said truthfully. "My man liked your hair very much, you know—he remembers it still from the train."

Disconcerted, she gave a little laugh. "He could only look at you, Vera."

"Men change."

"I am sure he still adores you." Disliking the conversation, she applied herself again to her plate and the cutlet which she found almost inedible. *The critics are right*, she thought.

Vera said, "I know he adores me, this is not in doubt. But he is bored with our life. He stays in bed when he could work—but he's not a beekeeper, he says. We argue. Honestly, I don't know how much longer we'll last here. I am dying to get back to Khabarovsk." This was the administrative center, not far to the east, where they'd spent several weeks filing paperwork; Vera tended to go on about its tsarist-era architecture. "That is a real city," she added as usual.

"Birobidzhan is a real city," Musya said.

"No, it is not. To be a city requires a place to possess history and culture—it should have attractive buildings, public parks, colleges, museums. Things made of brick and stone. Not to mention pavements and river bridges. Concert series. Bookstores."

This smarted: the family's Shkolnik ban was still in place. Musya frowned. "We have all of that here. A river bridge, too. Soon," she added. "They say in a year or two at most. And practically all our main streets are paved now. And look!"

She pointed out the window at a green and yellow autobus, rolling up to its stop out front. Vera claimed she'd seen bigger ones in use by tourist hotels for meeting passengers at stations. Although she'd had the same slighting thought more than once, Musya kept quiet and watched the autobus exhaust clouds draw pale blue cellophane across the view. A half dozen passengers climbed out, helping one another with packages, and dispersed along the wide wooden sidewalk, ordinary men and women, insignificant and small like their city, she supposed. Her eyes returned to the cutlet on her plate; all she'd sliced off and eaten appeared to have grown back but kept its bloody-looking edges. She sighed. The fork felt heavy in her hand. A loud knock-knock rang against the window glass, very near, startling her; at the same moment Vera's voice rose to say, "Musya, look, someone knows you." A gray wave crashed across her mind. Her eyes focused slowly.

It was her supervisor from work, standing there against a green stripe that fluttered like her heart as the autobus behind him pulled away. Then the sunny road was there again but he remained. He must have been one of the passengers; she hadn't recognized him because she hadn't worn her eyeglasses to lunch. In the sunlight his beard was full of reddish strands. He wore a brown leather jacket zipped to the chin and a leather snap-brimmed cap, another reason that she hadn't known him: he wasn't dressed for work.

She hadn't realized they shared a rest day. He was smiling at her as he always did, as if she amused him into momentary fondness. She nodded and returned the smile with her lips closed, mindful that her own teeth might be stained with beet juice. Embarrassment gripped her from all directions. Here she was, displaying herself in a public window while eating a plateful of laughingstock food; there sat Vera smirking in her worst manner; and there he stood with a carrier bag in either hand. Clean laundry wrapped and tagged was packed in one. The gloves he wore made it hard to tell that he was missing some fingers, possibly they were customized, the empty fingers stuffed. Vera wouldn't realize it anyway: *Thank God*, Musya thought. She felt embarrassed for him standing there like a male housewife, so vulnerable to a judging look.

Vera reached and tapped her arm. "Invite him to come in and join us—why not?" Already waving a welcome; Musya's shocked refusal made her frown. To the man outside the communication was clear, of course. His smile became a hard grin. Then he raised one bag to touch his hat brim with a glove, met Musya's eyes for an instant and left. The settler from Leningrad huffed, disappointed, amused. "You have an admirer," she said.

Musya's mind squirmed away. "No, I don't, he is only from my workplace." When would Leon Flohr write again? When would he appear? This felt like a complication, too much for her to handle. She went on. "My supervisor."

"Your supervisor. I see." Vera was smirking again. "And what is your supervisor's name?"

"Dovid," she remembered.

"And is he married?"

She cast around. The ring finger was missing. "I don't think so," she guessed. She'd never wondered.

"Well, the way he was looking at you, he had better not be married," Vera said. She dropped one lettuce leaf and chose another thoughtfully before adding, "Although he probably is. My God, Musya, you eat so slowly."

She nodded and explained, "Ever since the war. When we were starving in the ghetto, we ate as slowly as we could."

Vera clapped her hands. "You see? I told you. Food—you had food."

"Not really."

The Leningrader shrugged and glanced at the empty window. "A good-looking man. Too bad about that awful beard."

She guessed the supervisor hated her after that because his visits to the shop floor almost stopped coinciding with her shifts. No chance arose to apologize, a chance she dreaded more than sought, honestly. All the same he didn't terminate her as she'd feared he might, she'd spent a few days picturing tearful self-defenses. He might simply have run out of time for it. An announcement came: the plant would resume production of agricultural machinery. This meant a great deal of refitting and clamor and rushing around by the supervisor class. From her same spot on the line Musya Kotz advanced new sorts of lathe parts for finishing; otherwise nothing changed. The one who lost her place was Magga. When the bullet making section finally closed she and a lot of other workers were thanked for their war effort and told they were no longer needed on the premises. This was a blow. While she'd come to rely on the income—Kitty still couldn't work—more important was what her shop floor leadership had meant, not only in Magga's daily social life but in her heart, and what it meant to lose this. She had treasured the responsibility and enjoyed the exercise of power. Now she was told to report to the Birobidzhan shoe factory and cut lasts three days a week. That place she hated.

One of their dvornik's final acts as an influential personage accounted for some big changes in the Kotz family story. An academic transfer was involved, a thing Musya could never have managed otherwise. The situation was this: As students at the plant school, Sender and Samuel Nemo Kotz kept thriving. Anton and Hodeh had resolutely failed to do the same. They could get by in Russian now although their marks didn't show it; as for the rest of the curriculum, nothing appeared to have penetrated. Both could beat an abacus at sums but the simplest numerical problem on paper left them floundering. *Dearest, I've got two good students and two very poor ones here,* she'd told Leon Flohr. He'd often boasted of having been a poor student himself, Musya guessed he couldn't mind. The children themselves minded, though. They came to her.

"Hodeh and I want to go to the orphan school," Anton said.

"You're not orphans!" She was tired of it.

"We are," Anton said. "My mama died and no one knows where papa is. And Hodeh doesn't have a mama or a papa or anything."

"She has me. You both have me."

Hodeh said, "But the point is we qualify. For a better school—School Number Two."

"That's a Yiddish school," Musya said. The big local orphanage sent all its children there, Jewish orphans of war who'd been shipped to Birobidzhan from the ruined western shtetlach. Charities in America paid for their food and clothing. "Some of those children only understand Yiddish."

"So?" Anton said. "What's wrong with Yiddish? Mendel and his sister go there, too, and they speak Russian."

"Since when are Mendel and his sister orphans either? Their mother lives with them."

"But she's a mental patient," Hodeh said. "So they qualify."

"Well, I'm not a mental patient," Musya said.

"They sing!" Anton cried. He was really crying, as usual when thwarted. "They have a chorus and they sing Yiddish songs, they get to sing on stage. I want to go there—we want to go! Send us there, send us to School Number Two, please! Please!"

The school visit she promised him to make impressed her. The students all seemed very happy considering their circumstances and the lessons looked advanced, really more impressive than the plant school in that regard. Of course the place was more abundantly resourced, too, thanks to deep-pocketed American charity-givers. Applied to for advice, the dvornik was all in favor of the change and even promised to give "a little push" here and there to make it happen.

"Two in Jewish, Two in Russian. So everything covered."

Kitty agreed. "Yiddish is not so bad now. They are letting it back in again."

Magga's push still had force behind it then. Hodeh and ecstatic Anton were soon enrolled and singing with the orphan chorus in School Number Two. Now they went one way in the mornings while the rest of them headed towards work; which felt like the same old story, as Musya told Leon.

When terrible blizzards kept the city indoors for what would have been Chanukah week at school, Anton's disappointment was tearful. They would have had games and sweets but it was the concert he hated to miss: he loved performing again. Trapped in the housebound flat, he slouched around, blasting occasional notes on his tin trumpet in a despairing way. Yuri who'd happened to be caught there by the snowdrifts as the dead man's guest, snored on undisturbed. The mingled smells of drunkenness and fish lay upon the close air like a deep spreading bruise. Samuel Nemo had rummaged out their old Yiddish picture books which Hodeh, gladder for the time at home than her orphan schoolmate, began reading to him. Favorites quickly emerged and then Hodeh read those, Sender Kotz complained, a thousand times each. Seeing him glum, Musya went up and whispered, "Do you want to write a letter to Leon?" She watched his head jerk away as if from a biting insect: no, he didn't. He was over Leon Flohr, he'd moved on.

Her love endured longer. She wasn't like a fickle child, she told herself.

The electricity which had been fitful went out completely on the second day. Anton's carping turned into a victory taunt: "Now don't you wish we had a menorah? Now?"

But his father had thrown all that sort of stuff away, menorahs were almost all Boris Kotz hadn't kept. Musya promised to replace everything before next year. "Just make a list," she said, wincing at the expense in prospect. Meanwhile she added a querying line: Maybe Leon's mother had kept a few heirlooms to pass along? It was worth a try, she thought, biting her pen.

Brother Dead Man broke out his kerosene lamps, powerful things that made dragons' hisses. She'd never seen the front room brighter nor its condition more grimy, really terrible. The cobwebs with their dead fly spangles looked heavy as an armload of gowns. Indifferent to everything, the two drunkards raised and clinked their calibrated glass beakers and drank to the victory of light in all its forms.

"Now—vecherinka!" Yuri shouted, sending the children into a frenzy. They loved the idea of parties.

"Chanukah vecherinka! Chanukah vecherinka!" Anton jumped up and down.

"Cleaning vecherinka," said Musya, going for the rag supply.

It was a noisy festive singing cleaning sneezing Chanukah party in the end. Kitty limped in early and stayed to sit pointing and giving directions. The Cossack girl lately brought on as a menial hire made appearances connected with food water and commode pails; whatever the substance she tended to spill some. Other tenants flitted in and out, drawn by the light, driven back by the atmosphere, its reeks thickened now by dust and Kitty's cigarette smoke. They all managed to learn a few verses of Yiddish to join in on Oy Chanukah. No one talked of sleep; time had stopped or vanished. At last the walls seemed to sparkle and Musya went to bed. She woke up unknown hours later in the pale blue darkness of her bedroom haven. Samuel Nemo had an arm across her and a cat—not Merele, a second cat who'd wandered into their lives lately—was chewing on her hair. From the front room came voices and new smells, a sharp tangle of charred matter and turpentine. She thought her ears must be playing tricks, maybe from the fumes, because she heard the children calling for more bears.

A few moments later she stood blinking at her clean wall, the long one, now entirely covered in colored splotches and charcoal scrawls, floor to ceiling, black and green around pools of white, here and there some reddish brown: what had they done to her clean wall?

"Put your eyeglasses on," Sender told her.

It was a forest scene in progress, taken from life in wild Siberia, this much Musya could see. Her children stood lined up before it, applying more splotches with rags—her best rags, too. Yuri in his shirt sleeves was busy at the work table which she'd left spotlessly clean and uncluttered. Now it was strewn with what she recognized as her husband's old soil science equipment. There was a lot of glassware and torn paper sacking and a carved stone pestle with a blackened end rolled halfway off the table edge. Substances viscous, one violet-tinged, bubbled in flasks above flaming burners. The old cans of paint she'd forgotten about were all open and running with drips. Yuri was making his own pigments out of soil and rock samples and samogon. "The Tungun peoples are natural chemists," Brother Dead Man explained. Just then Magga entered with a basin and towels, glanced around and shrieked.

"My wall!"

"No, my wall!" cried the old balebos. "They're all my walls, I built them—they're mine! And I'm the one who has to lie here all day long, why shouldn't I have something to look at?" He'd wet himself again. Musya helped clean and change him, she was used to it by now. He grumbled as always and criticized: "You two don't recognize beauty, you know nothing of art."

Stung, Musya retorted. "I know plenty about art. In fact I've published poetry—a poem I wrote."

He sniffed. "Anyone can get published."

"That's not true."

"Stop!" The dvornik waved her hands at them. "Who cares what who published? Look at this dirty wall."

"Come back and see it finished," Sender Kotz told her.

This wouldn't be for days. Yuri's forest was no slapdash affair. The details piled up and the animals multiplied; more bears were the least of it. The bark of every tree was rough or peeling and the needles freighting every pine bough had points. It was mainly the forest floor and trees he had the Kotzes working on. Musya being the tallest had the most needles to do, she used an iron nail; she'd think she'd made thousands but they were never enough for Yuri, he'd step in and add another multitude. According to the dead man, they'd taught him too much in Leningrad about realism in art, now he went overboard. But his animals—Yuri painted all the animals—were another story. With them all was pure simplicity, unerring outline, the merest suggestion of volume. Were they spirits? They could die: a sable hung limp from a snare. They had flesh: in the center a bear and a wolf pack had fought to a standoff; the bear's great chest was gashed open and bleeding. Spotted deer stood at still attention in the picture's depths. Squirrels scampered through its branches past songbirds and owls.

Musya pointed. "Is that the owls' nest, Yuri?" He didn't answer.

"It's not a nest." The dead man, having signaled the family over to the chaise lounge, kept his voice low: "That's his baby brother. The one who didn't make it." They looked around at the lumpen form in the cleft oak branches and saw Yuri add a pale green stripe to its wrappings. "The Nanai practice sky burial." Now Yuri touched stained fingers to his lips and brought them to the stripe. His forest was finished. He stepped back and sat down on the floor.

They'd used up the entire soil sample collection which hadn't been quite enough for a high summer scene; the unpainted patches were snow. The other tenants crowded in to marvel. "A masterpiece," the dead man assured them. All the time Yuri sat on the floor with the children lined up alongside. For hours they gazed straight ahead into the trees. Fascinated, the Cossack girl whispered to Musya:

"You have a very strange family."

I told her, We're only artistic. It's the truth, she wrote. *But how I wish we owned a camera so that I could take a picture of the wall to show you, Leon darling.* It filled almost twenty pages by the time she could get outside to mail her snowed-in reply.

By Novi God the Jewish Autonomous Region was running at full speed again and welcomed its true holiday. The Kotz family came home early from viewing the ice sculptures, happy to miss the fireworks and the crowds. They discovered Brother Dead Man in the midst of thick cigarette smoke and company, he'd taken advantage of the festivities to smuggle a large part of his acquaintance in for a wall unveiling and drinks vecherinka. Some transplanted Ukrainians, some ex-journalists, some widows, old-time Birobidzhaners who remembered Liza Kotz; poor Fanny would have fit right in, Musya thought with a pang. There were several Jews and a few pig-tailed Nanai in the mix, everybody talking all at once. The Ukrainians would always get it in the neck from Moscow, Musya heard one guest say.

Another brought up Hitler's death. No one believed it. He had to be lying low somewhere, the great hoaxster—fire was too easy. As for what he'd visited on the Jews within his reach, the waking nightmare ends he'd brought them to in their millions, tones grew hushed.

"You were lucky," flushed Kitty turned in her seat to whisper. "Believe it or not, Musya, you and your family were lucky."

"Yes." She couldn't bring herself to object; but she'd liked it better when Kitty was giving the credit to fate. Because where was the luck? Death had feasted on her family.

"He was the wave of the future!" the dead man told the partygoers.

Maybe, they agreed. Worse might be to come. And if it did, no one there doubted, it would head straight for the Soviet Far East. Where, if anything, the Great Fatherland War had only delayed an inevitable retooling of the so-called Jewish question. Fact: a region dedicated for settlement would become the race's final killing ground. The skeptics ought to stop fooling themselves—although their belief mattered little since there was nothing to be done, it was already too late.

Musya, listening in fascination, might have learned more that night but her 1945 ended in a panicked search for Anton who'd disappeared. At ten minutes past midnight Samuel Nemo finally found him, passed out drunk in the smaller armoire. Both cats stayed in hiding for another three days.

Slightly troubled herself in the aftermath, she started reading the machinery plant's wall newspaper. Which didn't make her feel much better-informed; still, it gave her mind a pleasant feeling to be busied with facts that rarely stuck around for a day and most not so long—immersive, like warm waves of sand instead of sea. One day she noticed an item about veterans and artificial limb design advances. The Soviet legless were walking all over the place, apparently. She found the newspaper it came from among the piles in Magga's smoking parlor and clipped out all three columns. On the day she sent them off to Leon Flohr, it occurred to Musya that her relations with him had become those of a sister, or even a mother. In his waywardness he'd never answer, she knew, she accepted it; but without her replies something bad might become of him. He needed her backbone.

It felt strange to no longer expect him, because if there'd ever been a time when Leon was most likely to come, it would have been then. Early that spring the Jewish population began a surge which showed no signs of abating as the weeks and months passed. In the vanguard, that's where she'd have looked for him; he'd always liked to be the first in things. Of course Birobidzhan hadn't suddenly come into fashion or even improved as destinations went. Instead the Far East had a labor shortage and Ukraine, especially, was full of Jews whose homes and livelihoods had been lost to them in the war, swept away or purloined or in ashes. Here, they'd been told, were new starts for the taking. Work was plentiful and for the most part conditions could have been worse. The chronically underpopulated kolkhozes did their best to compete for new blood against the region's quarries, lumber mills, gold mines: like the state farms with their oceans of grain to be raised, these hard-work places were always hiring. There were jobs in the city, too, but never enough rooms—and much too little privacy.

"*Paradise, darling!*"

Able to hear Anton's voice all the way from the staircase as she climbed, Musya entered the flat in a bad temper, silently, greeting no one. The time for objections had passed but the point remained sore for her. She hadn't minded the children going through her things because children went through things by nature; as a child she'd taken every opportunity to go through her own mother's things, she'd known every crack in the ancient kidskin gloves, every brushstroke on the painted thimble. As for their finding Leon Flohr's letter, she blamed herself for that. Once she'd stopped carrying it around with her, she might have found a better hiding place. What she did mind was

Anton's reading the letter aloud—or, as now, performing excerpts from memory, like it was a presentation piece—for the amusement of others. The marked and gratifying improvement in his reading skills aside, Anton's glow of happiness aside, the laughter and applause and pleasure shared aside, Musya disliked the whole situation. It rankled. The secondary Nanai cousins who were there on a long visit kept requesting encores. *"My legs are gone—my legs are gone!"* Howls of laughter: this line was practically everyone's favorite, she was sorry to know. Anton used histrionic voices.

At the beginning she'd scolded him for mocking a crippled hero and they'd had a tearful scene until the dead man cut in to say that all melodrama was laughable in times such as these: "The boy is right, he's onto something. Leave him alone."

Anton had needed no further encouragement; while Hodeh asked one question. "If he's real, when do we meet him?"

"Soon." Musya could say no more than, "Soon." He'd be arriving soon and when he did, Leon Flohr would be a father figure to them in the home.

"No," had been Samuel Nemo's answer to that. He opposed any talk of fathers, it was a principle with him.

Musya's entrance today forced an awkward pause. The Nanai watched her from the corners of their eyes. They'd gotten the message: she was sex crazy. Stretched out on his work table stage, Anton was unapologetic. "They're our guests—I'm entertaining them," he said. He'd given himself lampblack moustaches and a head bandage that she considered redundant.

She asked, "Why is Pretzel wearing my clean pillowcase on his head?"

"He's the nurse." Indeed, Samuel Nemo raised Mrs Drobitz's tin pitcher a little in the air: proof. Sender continued—he appeared to be taking the director's part today: "The other nurses are evil but this one is good. She's in love with Leon Flohr and in the end they go off together and get married."

"I see." Musya let her eyes stray to the embattled bear on the wall, besieged by wolves, heart-wounded: yes, this too was realism. She put the sack of fish scraps down on the counter and asked Hodeh, "Will you help me with the cats?" The shrilling pair had caught her shins in desperate serpentine currents, she could hardly take one step.

Hodeh asked for another minute and bent closer to the backgammon board where she saw brilliant livelihood prospects—for the dead man owned her sixty thousand rubles which she expected him to pay. He would never pay. From across the room came a trumpeting cry: *"Stop—Leon—live!"* The cats endured torture until Musya put their dinner on the floor.

"Tamara is getting so fat," she observed.

"Pregnant," said the dead man.

"What?" Musya felt stunned. More cats! Hodeh kept her head down.

"Sure, pregnant, knocked up, you know how it is." He grinned unwholesomely. "The Merele, you know, his potency is unaffected."

"Yes," she said. "I see."

To mark one year since the Great Fatherland War victory, the Birobidzhan Agricultural Machinery Plant shut down early for the day and a party was held for its workers. Attendance was mandatory. Musya didn't care to go and being coerced added not at all to her enthusiasm. When no reply ever came from Leon Flohr to last summer's lovingly crafted Obodovka stories, that great flowering, she'd let disappointment seal her war years. She didn't care to be reminded of them now. On the one hand, her memories were bad; the other hand made a trifling gesture. She felt inadequate. Hardly a person she met didn't seem to have done much more with the time. They'd fought or they'd made things, at the very least they'd listened to speeches and attended parades and informed themselves. And Death had feasted on almost every Soviet family. Sometimes it would happen that Musya knew, she felt it, she and her family had suffered a difference in kind—as Jews, they'd had it worse, no question. But then the old refrain would start to play and its echoes obscure any certainty. Too many children! She'd brought too many children out of the ordeal to convince even herself sometimes of its horrors.

"Better to forget!" she heard a woman's voice ring through the uproar. The party was loud, vodka toasts were being drunk every few minutes. They might all be thinking the same sort of thoughts anyhow, Musya guessed. She sipped kompot and scanned what she could see of the hall for a quieter corner to stand in. Blue-gray, brown, the clouds of cigarette smoke were like a uniform jacket enclosing the scene and within it a cavity where a few couples danced to Russian songs she neither recognized nor liked. Then the amplified gramophone cut off and Musya saw a platform behind the dancers fill with men and light from overhead. The polished wood veneers, the silver and chrome of their instruments flashed—bayan, guitar, balalaika, some woodwinds, a snare drum set, a real ensemble. A huge cheer went up at the first drumroll and introduction, the band members were all plant workers. They played jazz. Musya watched the dance floor swell, the dancers multiply: now there were solo dancers and dancers in circles and lines and clusters of six or more, laughing, shouting, raising vodka bottles as they danced.

The next time she looked at the little stage she recognized her supervisor among the players. Coat sleeves pushed up, tie askew, he was pretending to conduct the number with his ruined hands, waving them around. His smile was enormous. His stocky body kept two or three different times. Now he was going from man to man, crouching a bit to be close to their playing; they didn't seem to mind, in fact they laughed and added notes as if to show off for him. But Musya burned with embarrassment. He always put himself in such ridiculous positions, it really tried her nerves. Just then the crowd shifted and she lost her front row view. All around her head, too close, women from her own line were clapping and calling out, "Dovid! Dovid—that's right, show them how it's done!" A couple of them whistled crudely. Odessa in 1939, 1938, 1937—the further the better from wartime—Musya wished herself back there amidst cream-colored elegance, gleaming parquet and whole, unbroken men. Here instead, far away, roughness and ruination surrounded her; no witty chatter, no sea views, but sawdust underfoot and walls enduringly posted with bids for silence, index fingers held to lips. She wanted to go home; she wanted to go home, kiss her parents goodnight and climb into bed with a heap of film stardom dreams.

She made for the door. A tight squeeze through a shipwreck's worth of shouting time-tossed bodies delivered her into another open space. She hadn't gotten her bearings before a man appeared right in front of her, greeted her, smiling. She looked in the direction of the music and back again: it was him, her supervisor.

Dovid laughed. "Oh, you saw me up there? That's right, that was me. Those are my buddies. Good men. Good memories." Sweat was pouring from him. "I used to play lead trumpet with a few of them—I used to play, you know, myself. I was pretty good."

"Oh," she said. She felt so sad tonight, she could hardly see. The brass cymbals crashed crashed crashed. He was still talking. "What?"

"And balalaika," he repeated. "Among others."

"I am sorry," she said.

He looked down at her kompot cup. "You are not drinking?"

"No. I am going home."

He said, "But how about—would you like to dance?"

"No," she said.

He scratched his jaw through his beard, thoughtfully. "Please," he said.

She shook her head, refused him. "I want to go home. I only want to go home."

Dovid nodded. "You had a hard war I think, Tovarisch."

"Yes, I did." She could make out a clear path to the exit by now. "I am sorry. Goodnight."

"Goodnight, Tovarisch."

After Musya was gone the band kept it up for a few hours longer. There were songs, encores, people had requests. Some climbed up on the platform, they wanted to lead songs or even make starts at speeches. Dancing, they grasped each other's shoulders, arm to arm. A year: no one could quite believe it. They walked out at last into the night a little stunned, big-headed from drink, yes, but also struck with disbelief. It seemed incredible that time could really keep advancing after what they'd been through. The worst thing to ever happen had happened to them; yes, they'd won, but long before that they'd made history. What they'd faced had made them historical figures. Walking around, looking up at the green stars, coughing, using communal lavatories, they were just the same as any general, any head of state—Soviet people, they knew this deeply. They respected themselves for it and yet felt like statistics and not much different from the dead.

(6)

By mid-summer 1946 the city had two topics of conversation: the usual, in the biting insect season, and the novel in the Jewish population boom. They were really coming now, from Vinitsa in large numbers and even more from Ukraine, Jews bent on living as advertised, an honest-to-goodness Yiddish-speaking existence on land made more and more fruitful by every hand's honest toil: the original program had been revived completely, it seemed. Yiddish was displayed everywhere on newly painted signs and printed notices; every wall newspaper had a place for Yiddish pages; there was a local literary journal out, an impressive thing, Yiddish from cover to cover. Musya came home one day to find her half-read copy smeared with blood and insect tissue: the flat's foremost mosquito swat, nothing else rolled up so perfectly, the children told her. All but one of the kittens had been adopted into good homes. Vera had asked for one to be reserved but later changed her mind as there'd been a feline population boom at Birofeld as well. The new people coming in weren't the best, she'd complained on her last visit to town—they were only interested in farming and not at all in culture or history; intelligent discussion was out. Quiet people, "practical as brutes," she'd called them.

A rest day of Musya's found the sunny streets full of traffic. Trucks, motorcars, pedestrians were all more or less converging on Birobidzhan station. A small scattered fleet of wooden handcarts racketed along in their midst. Another train from the west was just arriving—she could see the steam clouds, soot-sculpted. Letters in the post, her next hours free, she decided on a whim to wander along with the flow. She'd left the children busy in the kitchen garden where they had a vegetable plot of their own going these days, and knew she wouldn't be missed for an hour.

She walked, her mind staying on letters. Boris's old envelope supply had begun to show signs of exhaustion. If Shkolnik didn't lift the ban on her family soon, she'd be in trouble. For she couldn't stop writing now—her latest theme was nowhere near exhausted. She'd left the war behind, shelved all motherly advice. Instead Musya was filling her replies to Leon Flohr with memories of Odessa as it had been when they'd loved there. Descriptions of dresses and suit styles in shop windows, names of cafés, restaurant menus, dance floors bands and numbers, movie houses and film plots, every detail she could recall of the films they'd seen together; she wrote too about the burning warmth of beach sand and the sweet tang that a lemon ice left on lips later kissed. Musya put in everything she had. She'd finally understood. Leon would never come because he'd never leave his clinic bed. He couldn't. There'd never even been a chance of it— he'd written his letter to her in a frenzy of hope with his last strength, most likely. He'd never write another. Along with this certainty, she also knew he wasn't dead. Something would have told her, some typhoon of bleakness would have knocked her to the floor the moment he was gone. No, Leon was breathing. Her letters were reaching him, forwarded each week from the Londonskaya straight to where he lay among the legless and otherwise shattered men, those whom war and resistance had taken, ruined, abandoned. He'd received and heard every one read aloud to him. Tears had been wiped from his cheeks. What else was he living for, these days? She'd added this year and more to his life, her devotion alone had sustained him. And all the other invalids, by now they waited for her letters, too. No one else wrote them these days, they'd been quite forgotten. Her words, her memories were all that remained to them of a world irretrievably lost. To the clinic staff she'd become a phenomenon. Up and down the gray ward of the hopeless sufferers there would be no moans, no coughing, only the calm breath of men hearing her latest reply read in a nurse's quiet voice. Leon her darling heard his name but by now Musya was writing to all of them—Leon and the nurse, the invalids and clinic staff, the doctors and the delivery boy from the hotel, the local party staff and press who'd heard by this time about the endlessly loving heart, the real Odessan heart in Siberia that had never forgotten, never lost hope. Her audience: she couldn't disappoint it now.

Lately there'd been sometimes more than one letter to post. Musya Kotz had developed correspondents. All those address books she'd inscribed on her last train journey had yielded a crop of them. Introducing themselves as friends or relations of friends to the big-hearted young Jewish lady who lived in Birobidzhan, they wrote with questions about resettlement in her region. Could she advise them? Could she help? She might have been at a loss except for Brother Dead Man, who practically dictated half the replies. His views on the whole were slightly less doom-laden these days as the old balebos admitted a glimmer of hope—if only the kolkhozes could start producing a generous surplus. "Tell them to bring every seed they can find." He'd insist on a postscript: "Not to forget. Beans, carrots, fruit trees, opium poppies, whatever they can get their hands on."

From across the station road she could hear the faint *oom-pahs* of the Young Pioneers' brass band playing its usual welcome. Already the new arrivals were pouring through the station doors in double file and down the wide steps where porters and room touts stood corralling them. Many wore their pockets torn, carrying their mourning grief on their persons and all that they owned outside their suitcases sewn into ungainly parcels, just like the ones she'd brought along. Seven years later, their destination looked considerably more finished yet somehow little had changed. Mud and drunkards took up half the view. Here came the luggage-heaped handcarts, their wheels groaning like young oxen. She'd seen her fill and was ready to leave when Musya's eye caught on an incongruity. The jacket long, wide-shouldered, with a belt-waisted cinch; the trousers wide and flared; practically an hourglass silhouette—she'd never seen its like on a man, nor such a color. It had to be the latest mode, this ice-blue summer suit. She couldn't look away, she kept staring.

It was Leon Flohr.

Musya's immediate thought was that he must have received the prosthetic limb improvement news article she'd posted to him and put it to good use. Gratification swept through her and she felt radiantly happy for two heartbeats longer. Then she recognized his legs with the kick in the step that she'd forgotten until this moment when she saw Leon hoist a big rucksack onto one shoulder and start walking. On both legs with just a bisel of stiffness, her Odessan lover approached. He didn't recognize Musya but he noticed her breasts. His hungry mouth still had a life of its own. She called out at him: "Leon!" His eyes rose to meet hers. She wasn't mistaken: her first man, her only good one. Now he recognized Musya. She watched his full lips form a curse word. His moustache needed a trim.

He wasn't happy. "You're here?" he said as she walked up to him.

"Yes, Leon, I live here. Don't you—"

"Here?" he interrupted. "In the street? By the station when the Moscow trains come in? What are you getting up to then? Nothing good, by the looks of it."

She heard herself answer in the old Russianized Yiddish he still favored. "No, I work in a factory. This is my rest day." He tossed his head doubtfully and looked around as if for someone more interesting to talk to instead of Musya, who continued: "Have you come here to live—to live in Birobidzhan, Leon?"

He said, "Are you joking? Me? Here? Do I look to you like I have anything in common with the rest of these people?" Musya shook her head. Yet here he was. His scowl deepened. "Maybe I thought about it for ten seconds but now that I actually see the place, no deal. I'll be on the next train—*ah!*" He slapped at his neck and came away with dead gnus and blood on his fingers. His handkerchief was soiled and wrinkled, not like his handkerchiefs had used to be. "I'm not staying here in this hell," he said.

Musya watched the handkerchief back into its ice-blue pocket. "Why didn't you write to me again, Leon, why didn't you answer my letters?"

He gave a short laugh. "Your thousand and one letters? Why should I? My God, you made me a laughingstock at the Londonskaya for a while. Are you happy? You and that boy of yours—there's something very wrong with him, by the way."

"No," she said.

"In fact with both of you, you're both crazy, if you want the truth. You and your crazy stories—who cares about your stories?"

"You read them," she said as it struck her. "But why didn't you answer? And why did you lie, Leon? Your legs aren't gone!"

He stood his tallest to lean down at her. "Why shouldn't I lie? What truth do I owe you? Who are you to me? We had a little thing, then you go off without saying a word and marry your uncle."

"He wasn't my uncle, he was my brother-in-law."

"Ugh." A disgusted noise escaped him. "Who cares? How am I supposed to keep you all straight?"

She stared at him. At close range she could see, his fashionable suit wasn't the freshest; and Leon himself wasn't either. His handsome sandiness looked used up, dusty, even slightly derelict. "Leon, what's happened to you? What's wrong? Your letter—your words were so loving and true. You brought our love back to me. You said—you said yes."

"What are you blathering about?"

She felt dizzy now, edging towards sick. "Our love, Leon. Our—we danced. The ices, the motorcar rides." Now it was his turn to stare. She took a breath. "Vorentzovsky Lane. You remember, Leon."

He said, "You stupid woman. Don't you know I was sleeping with your friends at the same time? All five of you. What a laugh."

Her ears rang. "Leon. That's not true."

"No? Why would I lie now, Musya?" Distantly, she felt gratified that he'd remembered her name. "Think about it. I met you first, where, at the arcade?"

"In the park," she corrected him in a weak voice. "By the fountain in City Park."

"The park, the park, that's right," he nodded, thinking. "So by then, I was already sleeping with your friend Anna for six months and cheating on her with another two."

"Anna!" That was it, the one they'd met outside the cinema that day in the heat—here was the name at last. "My friend Anna." He gave a nod.

"She and I were pretty serious," he admitted. "In a way."

"And." She reached for words, words for objects, for anything solid. "And, Vorentzovsky Lane?"

"What about it?" He shrugged. "My uncle's mekhutn was dealing contraband brothel furniture out of this unregistered flat. I used to take women there—all my buddies did."

She winced. "And Anna? What happened to Anna?"

"Her? It was off and on with us, even after the war came. But she was starving herself for her mother, she gave everything to the mother. Turning herself into a skeleton when she could have lived well—that Anna was a different kind from you, my dear. Long dead," he finished briefly.

Musya felt faint. "And the mother?"

"Thriving." His eyes sparkled. It might be a joke. He still had charm. "Why do you need me to tell you about your friends? You couldn't spare them a letter too?"

She said, "We lost touch."

"Maybe," he said. "Maybe you're not such a good friend."

"I'm a very good friend," she objected. "I have friends. I've lost some, yes—I came back here and my best friend in Birobidzhan was dead—murdered! By her own husband, he did it to her. She loved him, she practically worshipped him and he murdered her."

"Then maybe she's better off," Leon said. "Why weren't the two of them at the front, anyhow? They needed everyone there, even women."

"Shut up," she said. "Shut up, Leon."

"I can tell you," he continued smoothly, "none of your friends had such an easy war as you."

"How can you say that? How can you—I wrote you, I told you what we suffered."

"Please." He smirked. "How bad could it have been when you came out of there with a baby and half a dozen children in tow? It sounds like it was some kind of Komsomol camp."

"What makes you be so hurtful!" she cried at him. "What harm have I done you? I welcomed you, I wanted to give you a home, I offered—everything." He laughed. "Why do you laugh? You wrote me that you were crippled for life, you said you only needed a shelf in my home. And now you laugh at me. Why? What happened to you? Where is your heart, Leon?"

He said, "Don't blame me."

"What?"

"What I said. Don't blame me if you're disappointed that I can do my own walking, Musya. That I'm not some helpless samovar needing you to wheel him to market. I happen to be glad about it, myself." She made a consternated sound at which he said, "Let me finish. Because maybe you expected a better return on your so-called offer—but I'm just one man with nothing but my own wits to live on, one man doing whatever and, yes, telling whatever lies it takes to survive."

Musya felt overwhelmingly defeated. "I don't understand," she said.

"Forget it," he told her, shifting his rucksack. "Listen, you weren't the only one who fell for that letter. A few other women kept writing back, too. None as much as you did, though, my God." As his frown returned she spoke quickly:

"A few—you mean my other friends?"

"How am I supposed to remember?" he said. "I had a long list of names, it was a lot to keep track of—who was here, who was there, who was already dead. I had answers coming in from everyplace. Believe me, it was a real operation. And after all that, no luck. Husbands, babies, sickness, sick babies, old parents lying around, no money, no room— none of you has what I need. Or maybe two or three who would have been fine except they're looking for Mark Behrens in Two Fighters."

"Oh, I hated that film!"

"You're crazy, it's a masterpiece."

"But Leon." Standing there empty-handed she tried to refute him, refute everything. "But Leon, your letter, your beautiful letter to me, it had so much about our love—how could it be written to other—how could you send that letter to anyone else?"

He said, "Easy. One or two variations per woman. I got all the rest from a handbook."

"A handbook!" she exclaimed.

"Of course from a handbook, a manual, why not? A handbook of phrases for writing to women."

She felt shocked. "Where do you get such a thing?"

"Everyone has one," he said. Musya didn't believe him—she didn't trust him anymore, she realized it with a small thud of sadness before she heard him continue. "In your case I can even remember using a lot of repetition, like the handbook advised, because you always used to repeat the same silly stories over and over. See?"

She said, "Did I? Or maybe that was one of my friends."

"I'm pretty sure it was you," he said.

At her next thought, she gasped. "And what about my money, all that money I sent you?"

He stared. Sneered: "What about it?"

The train was long gone and the street traffic had thinned. A few families were left to wait with their belongings on the steps outside the station for transport running late from one of the kolkhozes, no doubt. It came to Musya that so long as she could keep Leon Flohr here on the sidewalk, no matter what, he would be with her—at last. Her year and more of waiting was through. Here he was. "But what are you doing in Birobidzhan, then?" she asked suddenly. "If you didn't come here to be with me?"

"Of course I didn't come here for you."

It hardly hurt at all now, she thought. "Then why?"

"Oh," he said wearily. "I have a promising lead in Vladivostok, that's where I was booked for. But I met a woman on the train, a married woman on her way here to settle. We had a little something nice, to be honest. I thought it might be worth pursuing, but." He gave a look around. "Not in this dump."

She almost smiled. He had a romantic heart after all, an ardent lover's heart. The first man who'd touched her; she spoke to him. "What's wrong with me, Leon? I'm asking you to tell me honestly—what is it about me that you don't want?"

"About you?" His answer feinted. "What do I want with raising another man's children, that's the question. You have, what, three?"

"Four," she answered.

He rolled his eyes. "Right. A low-level worker sharing a room in a godforsaken city made of logs with four fatherless children—no, thank you. Forget it. Also, frankly, you're not as slim as you were."

"I see."

"You've gained a lot of visible weight in the wrong places."

"Yes, Leon, I understand."

Yet he continued, with emphasis: "I can do better. In fact, there's your answer. Why not you? Because I can do better."

She disagreed; at the same time she believed him—although she knew him for a liar. "Were you even in the catacombs, Leon? Did you fight even one day?"

"Yes, Musya, I fought for the resistance in the catacombs, Musya—many days. Two years. And it was terrible. My letter maybe borrowed a thing or two from magazines but I saw my share of terrible. I was laid up with a leg wound, that part was true," he said. "Then I was living with one of my nurses."

"Of course there was a nurse!" she blurted out. He narrowed eyes that were red-rimmed, a little inflamed. His eyes had always had a pale pinkish cast, she remembered now. A pink-eyed devil:

"What are you talking about?" he snarled.

"Nothing."

He looked at her angrily. "Listen, I had nothing to do with what happened—she ratted out plenty of men besides me." It might have been a nonsense language; all Musya understood was that she'd been spared so much. The lives of men such as Leon Flohr, their real lives, touching women, were like rolling massacres. She asked him what had happened next. He said, "About six weeks in prison. And that was a different kind of terrible." One eyelid twitched. Diving towards the nearest relief from recollection's horrors, his gaze fixed on her chest. She watched the contours of a plump bosom exert their customary calmative effect. Leon sighed. "I need to live well again. I need it. Can you understand me?"

She thought she could. "Do you have no children of your own, then, Leon? With so many women." She stopped—he was shaking his head.

"No. Thank God. I am a free man."

Maybe he was infertile. The quick guess sent a jolt of pity through her. One point for Boris Kotz, he could sure multiply. *Poor Leon*, she thought. Although he was a terrible person, really, a true scoundrel. He'd used her heart for a rag. And she? Who'd fallen so entirely for his scheme—what kind of person was she? *"That, that."* Musya heard Mommy's spitting voice. *"That—correspondent!"* Her envelope supply was safe now, she supposed. A regret occurred to her that Leon's train hadn't arrived an hour or two sooner and saved her a fee. Instead, her last reply to him was in a mail bag by now headed west to Odessa, one dead thing confused among living words, a pebble in bread, uncanny and noxious, the handiwork of her delusion. No grateful invalids or local press were waiting at the other end; her audience became a cloud of ash and atoms as she watched. She stood alone now with nothing except what was in front of her: an unpleasant man, Leon Flohr, for the moment. Distantly aware that he'd begun complaining about Birobidzhan, what a dump it was, she murmured, "I knew you wouldn't like it here, Leon."

"I said," he said. "And the only hotel is so expensive."

"Oh yes, especially for what you get," she agreed, having heard this around.

"So," he said. "Maybe I could stay at your place until I get my travel permit in order again."

"Oh, no thank you." Musya drew back as she answered. This was instinct. Mockery, heartsickness, bile—here were her prospects for life in the rooming house should Leon Flohr come and go away on his two legs. She'd be the laughingstock, then. Her children, cheated of the father figure they might have liked in the home after all, would be certain to lose all respect for her. And where would he sleep? His hairy mouth looked hungry again and his eyes had a peculiar light she recognized with a pang as he argued and pleaded. She told him no. "It's impossible, Leon."

He breathed loudly. "You always were a selfish little bitch," he said.

"Oh, Leon." She felt sparks go through her and fail, no anger igniting among the wet folds of intestinal dread at what could happen. Drobitz, Drobitz-Fein, he'd angered her to fury before his character acting career wound up defunct in the dust at her feet. And now would she have Leon Flohr wailing through a bloody mouth as steel-toed sapogis burst his ribs and organs: no. She'd never wish an end like that on him, she would never put an angry wish on him; in her heart, instead, she would bless Leon and wish him safe from the violence of other men, husbands included. She would let him go in peace. She said, "Zay gezunt," and walked away. She never saw him again.

Musya kept walking, fast, away from the station, across the tracks, down a mud-grooved incline. A laundry truck rumbled close behind, passed her, slowed, and pulled up alongside a workers' dormitory with a load of bedsheets, she saw, walking past in her turn. She thought of her own bed, forever to lie Leon Flohr-less, forever empty save for herself lying alone, along with her children, their cats and their kittens, piles of storybooks and mending, schoolwork papers, hairbrushes and combs, biting insects, underwear and sometimes a tiger skin—not really so empty in fact, she supposed. And why not forever chaste? It was her husband's bed, after all, not hers to dispose; his and her dead sister's. In damp weather the mattress still produced occasional whiffs of ancient disinfectant. How impossible for Leon or any man to accept what Musya had offered, a love-life at once too little and too much and at the same time not even hers to offer. She wasn't free. She'd been imagining things.

Further on a few other trucks were threading in and out from the coal dust that sur-rounded a sprawl of warehouses and square-sided sheet metal towers. She passed a clock but didn't bother to read it. The clocks this side of town weren't reliable. She reached a collection of big log-sided huts for machinery storage. While the war was on the place had been full of engine noise and activity. Now quiet, it looked half-abandoned. No sign remained of the Jewish cemetery that had stood here. Across the way, dug up, flattened, piled in parts with empty fuel drums, the former snow hill field lay baking in haze and petroleum fumes. Enlivened by the heat, the drum metal serenaded Musya's arrival with a slow plink-plunk chorus. *Goodbye love*, she heard. *Goodbye, goodbye love.*

If only Fanny could have lived! Musya thought the wisdom of an older confidante might have saved her long before now. Just here they'd met, where her sister lay buried beneath earth and snow—the wondrously florid friend from Baku entering like a fall of fruit tree blossoms. Fanny would have known more about these new storage huts than Musya had been able to learn—namely what lay below them in the ground; or didn't. Her own investigations had yielded only that during the war, time had pressed, and the need for machinery storage had peaked in urgency; and maybe they'd never filed for the right permits, those Jews who'd selected the spot. She'd never come back here since the day after the family's return to Birobidzhan, when they'd made to visit Liza's grave and discovered it obliterated. "For what?" they'd wept. For victory alone? Unspoken answers swirled here like a fiery wind and a midriff blow both at once, marking a place to be avoided even in thought.

No, not a trace was left. What had they done, the wreckers, with the Jewish cemetery lintel and fence and the charity box by its gate? What had become of the gravestones and the tall markers painted with names? Where had all those fading letters gone—into what pit, what fire? And the bones in the graves, the shrouds in threads, the thin hair, the wives and mothers—where were they now? Safe, she decided, safe and serene, far away from feeling even this last humiliating violation; nothing pained them. At most they floated near enough to take occasional amusement from the living and their plights so hopelessly frivolous, their empty lives wasted on trifles and fantasy men. The dead could laugh at crazy women.

The road had been paved but was already shattered, Siberia was merciless that way. Musya went on and began climbing the high bluff towards the river view. She was glad she'd kept the pine cone. The entire pine forest was gone. Contrary to her recollection the drop from this height was not at all precipitous but rather bushy and gradual. The great cliffs were on the other shore. Between ran a vast murmuring glare, the Bira in full summer sunlight. One hand shielding her eyes, she looked across at the spiraling sawdust clouds that marked another new building going up behind the trees there. If all went according to plan, Birobidzhan would have a major growth spurt onto the opposite bank and a genuine bridge would replace the little barge ferry whose ropes were just perceptible above the glittering waves, like hairline fractures. Indeed, it wasn't impossible that her children would grow up in a real city—not Odessa, true, but a place with its own people, its own stories.

With a sigh, Musya thought of all her letters gone for nothing; and Sender's as well. She felt glad, now, that he'd given up sooner. She'd give up too, she'd announce to the flat that she'd posted her last reply to Leon Flohr this day, having reached a conclusion. A chapter in her life had ended, she'd tell them. She'd moved on. Just below her ribs a wiggle or a flutter, something that was happiness declared itself present at being freed from thinking about that man. What she would write to him; what he would think of it; how she could please him; his tastes, his pride, his wheelchair—Musya gasped. She hadn't asked about his mother's health! It was true, he was right, she was selfish, crazy, the worst. She grabbed a piece of broken wood off the ground and tossed it towards the river. It landed well short, in a tree.

Of course, he hadn't asked about her mother. At worst they were even.

She wondered how many of her letters Leon had actually read—quite a few, by the sound of it, before he'd stopped. Would he have gotten them in prison? Then some had arrived since he'd left Odessa for the east, those few he'd never had a chance to read. Which was a pity, because they were good ones. Shedding regrets in the gusty breeze, Musya found one that stood out and remained: she'd miss her audience. The invalids with their nurses, the party men listening in from the shadows, she'd miss night spent inspiring their smiles. Although as she stood there and thought about it, the more and more certain she felt that her letters weren't going unread. They'd reached someone—a young man, she guessed, whose curiosity had been aroused by the heap of identical envelopes inscribed by an attractive female hand—he'd rescued them. A desk clerk, maybe a bellboy—she pictured a frail youth showing wrist bones in a gold-frogged uniform jacket—he collected her letters. High up on the Londonskaya Hotel's dormer floor in an iron bed he spent his nights rereading them as if they were a prayer book.

(7)

Then all her hair fell out.

It was a trying time that produced several possible causes for this happening. Her encounter with Leon Flohr had come as a shock, of course, a real life-changer. For weeks afterwards her every hour had felt halting and incomplete, she couldn't move through time as she'd been accustomed to—her legs, in some sense, were gone. Overall her reactions to everything had slowed. People had to repeat themselves in conversation with her; she read the same parts in storybooks two or three times in a row between unacceptably long pauses; at work she slowed up the line more than ever.

One Thursday they evacuated when the new anti-rust spray finisher malfunctioned and filled the lathe shop with silvery gas. It wasn't her fault but Musya felt guilty, on the chance that the force of her many mistakes had compounded to become a factor in the blowup. The gas affected the exposed workers in various ways, the commonest being headache with a sort of influenza that kept them strengthless and coughing in bed for a week or so. Like her, most recovered and resumed their places; some who'd got it worse kept their headaches and coughs and wound up reassigned; and a few never returned. Dovid the supervisor was much around while all this went on, first at the scene with his arms full of smelly gasmasks and blankets and later to welcome the workers back from their sickbeds. Musya he greeted with a short formal bow and said it was good to see her, he always treated her very formally since the Victory Day dance. He had smiles for the rest of them, with one-two-three kisses, long embraces for the men, private jokes with many women. Laughter rang. He'd marry—she pictured it—a beautiful girl bride with a coin jewelry veil.

Not long after that, but before her hair fell out, the defense ministry letter arrived; finally. Kitty brought it to her on the shop floor. The supervisor showed up and stayed, concerned about whether she might faint, she supposed. She almost did faint. The lack of detail lent the brief message every grim plausibility: Private Boris Kotz, Soil Specialist, his identifiable remains lately recovered, had died in the siege and defense of Odessa, first Hero City of the Soviet Union.

Musya let out a bitter laugh. "Hero City!" Close to home, just as if he'd never left the place: she shook her head. "He must have been furious about that."

Dovid cleared his throat. "Go home, Tovarisch. Take another week."

Kitty led her off through a gentle flurry of well-wishers: *The poor Little Sweeper, the little widow,* she heard them. By the shop door the bent sweeper who'd taken her place which he filled so much more skillfully stood with his cap held to the arch in his breastbone. Tears for her ran down his face and made her start to cry. Kitty spoke with him, taking the threshold at a slow pace; then she paused at every open doorway en route to the street exit. Kukuruzniki-loading Kitty hadn't gone to war with men so naturally remained curious and the Birobidzhan Agricultural Machinery Plant was full of them.

"That boss of yours," she enthused, "he's a handsome one—who cares about a few missing fingers?" Of course girls always loved authority.

Back at the rooming house, among the people who'd known him years before the war, news of Boris Kotz's demise spread fast, like a wildfire of deep satisfaction. "Good," said Brother Dead Man, for example. "If that bedbug had come back here alive, I'd have happily killed him myself." Magga laughed and kept rewrapping his ankle bandages until he shook his feet at her. "Don't laugh at me, I'm serious! Men like Kotz ruined this city— someone from here should have had the pleasure in a just world."

"You had plenty of chances," Magga said.

Kitty exclaimed. "Where is your sympathy? His widow is sitting right here!"

"An informant's widow." The old balebos snorted. "She's better off."

No answer came from Musya. She'd argued this point with him, about Boris, more than once. Her husband had liked to write letters. To express his own opinion in violently-colored prose bolstered by armies of quotations facts and tabulated figures had been his hottest-burning lifelong joy. He was that type—or had been—a man of letters to editors and authorities. It wasn't his fault that he'd been born into a time when letter-writing was dangerous to others. "*When wasn't letter-writing dangerous to others in Russia—which weekend?*" the balebos had challenged with a cry. She hadn't answered.

So, Boris Kotz had been typical. So what?

Musya drank tea. There in the branches on the wall, the sky burial baby made a still point around which her sensations and thoughts revolved painlessly. Far from grieving, she was wondering: What next? So now Boris Kotz was dead. Was he? From his clutter in the corners to his investment saucer in her hand, to the enduring enmity he'd earned: despite the message she'd read, his presence hadn't gone anywhere. But she doubted the defense ministry. In truth she'd never expected Boris to come back alive until today, when all at once it seemed he might enter the room momentarily—a most fitting cap to her recent string of disasters. Boris, unchanged, holding the letter up to his shortsighted eyes and clucking his tongue: *Typical bureaucratic incompetence!*

She cried some more tears. In a way, she'd have liked to see this happen.

The others listened as she wept. "Those poor little ones." Magga's Cossack girl sounded moved.

"Also better off," Brother Dead Man answered relentlessly.

Kitty said, "The youngest will never know his father now. Just like me."

"Like many," her mother said in a firm voice.

A noise from the chaise lounge. "Your man ran off, Magga."

"Any different way you lose a man is the same," the dvornik countered. Musya, who thought she agreed, sipped her tea and rubbed Tamara's belly with a slipper toe, enjoying the mild cat's purr massage. Fatherland War widow benefits had already been discussed. Her family's lot in life might have just seen a dramatic improvement—not enough to entice another Leon Flohr, probably, but enough to retool a few current treats into steady comforts. She was choosing which, when she heard Magga say, "I will be the one to tell them."

"No. I will," Brother Dead Man contradicted. "This is my place," he said.

Musya turned in surprise; but she was in no condition, they told her, with no time to argue. Here came her children and their trampling noises on the staircase. Moments later the flat door burst open to admit all four. Suntanned and fresh from some recreation that had ended in controversy they were all disputing at once until they stopped. Sender Kotz studied the room with care and said, "What's wrong now?"

In reply the dead man drew breath and like a man at a podium said, "Children, we learn today from Moscow that the papa of this family, Soil Specialist Boris Kotz, gave his life in the defense of his country and its autonomous regions, dying a hero's death in the battle against fascism that the Red Army fought outside Odessa Hero City, five years ago. May you inherit all his courage and more, and may you live long to honor his memory. Now let me embrace you." Eight kisses, one for every cheek, and it was done. Her children were formally fatherless. Kitty lit a cigarette and Magga smoked one too, she was dabbling in the habit. The eulogist took several long pulls from his brown glass bottle.

Anton, watching him, said, "That's why he never came for us. Because he was already a hero."

"Sure," said Magga.

Pretzel found his way to his mother's lap. "Don't be sad," he told her.

"It's good to be sad sometimes," Musya said, and kissed him again.

Kneeling among the three cats on the fur-encrusted kilim was a little girl with messy tumbled hair that hid her feelings. Hodeh had been very fond of her own papa, they knew, and might have hoped for another. Kind Sender Kotz joined her on the floor. His spectacle lenses were thoughtful as he surveyed what had changed for himself. Then they flashed Musya's way.

"This means I can go to School Number Two now," he told her.

With his friend, he meant. The other boy's sister playing intermediary, he and odd Mendel had lately reconciled. Though far preferring Sender stay at the machinery plant school where he excelled and could also keep an eye on his unpredictable baby brother, later in a weak moment she agreed to apply for the transfer which went through with surprising ease and rapidity. Now three of her children would be studying with the Jewish orphans of war.

The defense ministry's letter ushered the Kotz family into a time of special closeness. Every night the big bed was full of children who spent their waking hours in one another's pockets—and Musya's. Time off put her in the thick of every crowded and eventful moment, where she found comfort. Exactly this was how her family mourned and came to heal, she remembered. Its unit contracted, grew tighter-knit and entertained itself. Together the five Kotzes gardened and harvested, laundered and mended, swept and window washed. They spent a day at the fancier public baths. Back at home the children set about combing and braiding Musya's hair as they'd used to. She felt a tug and heard alarm cries.

The comb was choked with a large thick hank of auburn hair that had an uncommonly interesting natural wave to it.

"Stop combing," she said. She thought the bath steam must have loosened her scalp somehow. The children tugged on their own locks and nothing happened; of course she was older. Panic-stricken, she held her head out the window to cool it in the twilight. She watched several pale stars appear and catch fire, some more blue and some more golden, until she felt much calmer. The next morning the fabric of her pillowcase could barely be seen through the fallen curls. She felt no pain, only it itched where hair had been. Just smoothing one hand across her hairline made the whole thing come away. The rest didn't linger. One day later all her hair had fallen out.

She saved it in an old embroidered purse with jet bead panels that she stuffed under the mattress. All her life, she'd kept her hair long; through violent worldwide changes in salon fashion as through a typhus epidemic, taking risks, uncompromisingly. Her best feature, her pride since childhood, was gone. She stared into the old fly-specked mirror glass. A complete stranger—a strange atrocity victim: "What next?" she asked. Samuel Nemo's mouth dropped open and he started to bawl.

It was only temporary, Sender claimed. Hodeh disagreed:

"That much hair won't grow back."

"No." Musya didn't think it would either. Scrutiny showed her scalp to be covered in unattractive patches of fuzz and inflammation. Fortunately her brows and lashes grew only somewhat thinner; she'd also end up keeping about half her body hair. The head sustained the all-but total loss. "What will I do?" she asked the four sorrowing pairs of eyes in the mirror glass with her own. Her nose grew red. "I don't want to wear a wig."

Then memory struck.

The scarves were found safe in a box in the back of the big armoire, almost twenty of them, gifts to the dying Liza Kotz from her dear friend Fanny. A few extravagances from the Universal Store and the rest Azerbaijani, direct from home. All pure silk, stripes and paisleys, prints of elephants and phoenixes and fields of heavenly flowers, they had to be the brightest-colored things in Birobidzhan, Kitty agreed when she dropped by. She thought Musya shouldn't be so upset. This was only from stress, in her case delayed.

"Back in the battalion the older women were always losing their hair from the stress. And even mine, look how gray it turned."

"Yes, Musya," said Anton. "At least your hair never turned gray."

"Kitty, you should use hair dye," Sender suggested.

"It's hardly noticeable," Musya said truthfully. Kitty's black hair did show up every gray strand, but her hairstyle was the vital problem. A talent shortage prevailed among the city's hairdressers at this time, no question. "And you're so young, the gray might go away."

"And your hair might grow back," Kitty said. She'd seen it happen. Spoiling Sender's neat scarf pile with a distracted tug, she pitched her voice higher. "And I'm not ashamed, I don't need to use hair dye, I earned my gray hairs while defending my country. Who needs hair dye?"

"Fine, then don't use it," Sender said.

At the end of her week's bereavement leave, Musya chose a green and violet paisley for her head and set forth towards workday number one. She was almost out the door when the old balebos raised himself on his chaise lounge and blew a whistle through some teeth at her.

"Hey! You! What happened to your hair?" He'd spent the entire week in a drunken stupor. She could smell the urine on him.

"It fell out, Brother Dead Man."

"How? Why? Not over your childrens' reptile father, I hope."

She said, "It was stress."

He drew phlegm into his throat and spat it into a dirty bottle. "Make me some tea—strong," he said.

"Make it yourself. I have work to go to."

His morning glower darkened. "What do you know about stress?"

"What do you know about anything?" she shot back. "You spend your life in a drunken stupor."

"Better stupor than baldness."

"You're bald, too," she pointed out, leaving.

"Completely different for women and you know it!" His voice pursued her to the top of the staircase. "*Better pull yourself together, my dear. Stop with all the no-good no-show men!*"

A pause for breath on the next step gave her time to acknowledge: the balebos had a point, but it was long out of date. For who would love her now? Present men, bad men or better, not one, Musya thought. Fat, bald: of course, as her footsteps quickened in the fresher air, looks aren't everything. She could walk as well as ever; dance, probably; and as far as her mind—at least her mind—it was unaffected. Fortunes turned every day. She might yet be loved. Scraps of hope her heartbreak seized and pressed to itself as if to stuff the wound; she knew, honestly, all this was only self-deception. She and men were through.

After the supervisor's brusque welcome back to the line had been tempered by many warmer demonstrations from her comrades, Musya found herself working slower than ever. An hour later she was registering with alarm the unbridgeable width of the gap between her best effort and output—try as she might, not one engine lathe part could she finish as fast as before. Her tools which felt unaccustomedly heavy didn't seem to recognize her hands and wouldn't obey. They must be confused, she thought, and nervous, like a good horse sold to a child or a fool. She refused to stop, she couldn't. She felt like cursing at herself.

Lift grip twist punch twist rag polish.

Slower still. Her distress was almost complete. The mindset that had dragged her half-starved mothering body out of bed to keep its daily appointment with the road to Babiak's—where had it gone? Maybe she needed what was missing, a loud electric device timed to every step to force her limbs to follow. On the wall between the twin portraits of Comrade Lenin and his Best Disciple, Musya's eyes found the shop bell. A few moments' hard concentration broke its silence and plunged her plugged ears into Obodovka, the ghetto at dawn: there it was, the old heart-jolting murderer of rest. She tried a turn at top volume. Lift—*ghrrring!* Grip—*ghrrring!* Keeping at it this way she began to work more quickly. Twist—*ghrrring!* Punch—*ghrrring!* By shift's end she'd made up the lost time. Same method, the following day, she surpassed her best recorded speed. She wasn't fast, not yet, only normal, a bit below average; but Musya thought she could become fast. It was true, the leadership was right to keep pushing. With enough force, nothing was impossible.

Luckily she no longer wrote to Leon Flohr because her new on-the-job routine wouldn't have left her the energy. At home she did the least she could manage. In bed she slept. The letters that came from maybe-settlers began to pile up on a shelf; she planned a night of writing all the replies at once that she kept putting off. The children complained at meals of seeing her take more than her share. They complained of her silence, they wanted more words from her and more attention as well. She'd look away while they were complaining to her face. If all went according to plan and she could only push herself to be a little faster, she was on track to achieve something for the first time: she might meet a weekly quota. There would be satisfaction in that, she thought. A monumental gong's roar to shiver time and leave it level, no more groove left in her brain by her inner claxon's hideous pulsing—it had followed Musya home from the line, of course—this was the prize she chased. It would feel like a new start entirely, she knew it would, when her supervisor came to the shop floor with a handshake and said, "Congratulations, Tovarisch. You did it."

Instead, one morning she watched him lean across his desktop and groan at her:

"What are you trying to do, tell me? Explain yourself." He was clearly upset, red-faced even through his beard. Musya felt terrible. She apologized again for fainting at her post. He cried out, "This is why you should never be a vegetarian!"

"But, I am not. I am really not a vegetarian," she told him.

"Good," he said. He picked up a letter opener and put it down again and crossed his arms again. Musya knew he'd stood by in the plant infirmary until she'd regained consciousness. To everyone's relief she hadn't hit her head against or landed in any machinery. She'd come around quickly and now here she sat, summoned again, while her productivity slipped back down from gain to gutter. She'd also lost a good ear plug. He said, "But how do you explain the way you act recently? Working yourself into what looks like an early grave, as if you have decided, you know, you want to get written up as some martyred Stakhanovite—it makes no sense."

She said, "I only want to meet my weekly quota."

"You do? Why?"

"Because I want to prove to myself that I can."

"But why?" He brought out his hands and leaned across the desk to ask her. "Why now? I have—no one has ever expected you to meet that quota, you know, these are only numbers on a page. You are fine as you are, we accept you exactly as you are."

"But I want to improve."

He breathed frustratedly. "I think, forgive me," he said. "But I think your grief is too extreme."

"My what?"

"Your widow's grief, your wifely grief."

"Oh well, no," she said. "I don't think so."

He said, "But it is clear you take it very far, Tovarisch. As you know, you go into this silence, this killing yourself with work, you go and cut all your hair off in mourning."

"I did not—is that what people think? It that what they are saying?"

"Of course, everybody," he said. "They think the gesture very admirable. A great proof of loyalty."

She sighed. "I did not cut my hair. It fell out."

"What?"

"All my hair fell out."

"Bastards!" The supervisor half rose from his seat, thinking furiously, his brown eyes making like a lighthouse beam on water. "Could it? But no one else's hair fell out, no one—wait." Now he pulled close a notepad and pencil and wrote himself a note, quite dexterously, while he got his breath under control again. "If we assume not from any piece of garbage spray finisher accidents, then." He put down his pencil and studied her scarf-line. "From grief."

"Possibly." Musya looked away from this man she couldn't have, she'd never be near enough to; another hopeless case in the making. Her sad eyes strayed to something new, the very latest issue state portrait framed on the wall beside them. The Leader and Teacher of the Workers of the World posed in a white dress uniform tunic decked with gold braid and enough silk-tagged medals to remind her of Sender's scarf drawer arrangement. She stared harder and frowned. "He looks different, doesn't he? His forehead looks different."

"Higher," Dovid agreed. "More Russian."

Musya nodded. "I wonder how they did that."

He said, "You don't remember me, do you?" She looked around at him again and saw his smile. "I guess not. You never got as good a look at me as I did at you."

Instantly horror-stricken, her mind filled with ox-carts, ice fields, ditches, "Where?" she managed without too much tremor in her voice.

His easy smile persisted. "I was in a truck, before the war—before our part of it that is. You were standing with a lot of children by a field, down from the Bira bluffs. I always remembered you."

"That field is gone now," she said. "We used to play there all the time and watch the animals."

"You stopped us in the road—you remember?"

Musya blinked two tears away. "I stopped—oh! The man I spoke to, the driver."

"No. I was sitting right next to him—but you remember."

She did. "We were frightened. Or I was. For some reason."

"Yes, we could not understand you."

"I know." She frowned at the desktop. Why had she been so frightened?

"Well," he laughed. "I still cannot help you!" She laughed with him. Their eyes met with a sound like motorized tools making sparks.

So, she had an old hold on him.

He said, "Listen, you know, I have contacts, I can easily get you a transfer to the sewing factory."

"No!" she cried, all at once out of breath like she'd been in a footrace. "No, thank you, please, no." His eyebrows looked concerned.

"You do not sew?"

"Of course I sew, I love to sew, my mother—I grew up sewing. But I had, in the war, work, forced labor in a sewing shop. Not a factory, please."

He held up some fingers. "I understand. It won't happen."

"It was the river." She'd remembered. "The ice in the river was breaking up, I had never heard such a noise. The children—I frightened the children. I thought it was the war, or the end of the world, when it was, really—it was only that winter ended." She was thinking this man had beautiful brown eyes as she added, "Siberia is so frightening sometimes."

"Ah." Sadly his eyes fell, and he frowned at his own handwriting. "You heard a lot, Tovarisch." She was wondering how to answer when he asked her to take a walk with him in the fresher air, right away. "You know, to complete your recovery. Please," he smiled, "don't turn me down this time."

Indeed, after all her rude rejections, the chance to oblige him and ease her conscience felt very welcome. She waited outside his office in her old waiting chair while Dovid made a few telephone calls and dictated a memorandum concerning the note uppermost on his desktop. After which he walked her the length of the management suite and then past everyone on the shop floor and outside through the restricted exit. Although Kotz, Musya proved to be the sole exposed living worker left hairless by the anti-rust accident, he would never be easy on this point, always suspecting a connection.

What was hair anyhow but a nuisance? Dovid asked. His beard he hated but he couldn't shave himself—a pencil was one thing but razors were another. "And try finding a good barber in this town." Scissors he could just manage.

The salons were the same way, she told him. A little hesitantly, she suggested that his beard would be too popular to shave. The other women liked it too much—the other workers, that is. "You must know how popular you are," she said.

He laughed. "But Tovarisch, have you not heard? Jewish men have sex appeal these days. And if I still played guitar, forget it—all because of that actor in Two Fighters."

Mark Bernes: yes, it was fact. With the field prepared by his mass popularity in the role of Odessan troubadour-hero, the average Jewish man could reap a lot of Soviet womanhood's attention without any toil. Musya thought of Leon Flohr, eluded for all his fishing. Where had he gone wrong? It helped to be musical, perhaps. As for Dovid who was also far above average, he'd disliked the film in question a good deal less than she. Mainly Dovid thought it had been a nice gesture on the part of the filmmakers to make a film about soldiers—even if they'd only done it to be popular, as she argued, and not for the actual fighting men's sake. He shrugged. "They tried to raise the whole nation's spirits—so they didn't raise yours, it is okay."

"I suppose so," she conceded.

They were on their way to the river by a route Musya would never have taken alone or with children, threading as it did through the intervening work yards beneath a canopy of wires and rope pulleys, crane arms, chains. Blue-brown clouds of dust and exhaust almost obscured the trucks that came and went clattering along empty or groaningly full, with great slammings of gears. On every side shipping crews huddled by loading docks and warehouse workers shouldering boxes trudged past and violent characters of every stripe were evident; and not one was a threat to her, not today.

Dovid had friendly words for a few groups they passed. He told her, "It always cheers me up to see men and women working hard, you know? This is good for the spirit. Look around—things getting done, purposeful effort." He exaggerated, Musya thought, marking the leisurely pace and overall prevalence of lounging with cigarettes. Because they weren't on a walk in America, he said, where they might have witnessed breakneck haste born of fear and exploitation, as Capital forced Labor to perish from overwork's hazards. "Here the worker is valued and treated like a human being. Here you see the pace of dignity." Dovid put a lot of thought into these subjects. In his view, their recent ally in war and victory had plenty to learn from the Soviet Union about proper conduct for modern life—which had to start with the labor question, didn't it? Musya said yes, it probably did. Some mud had splashed her shoe—both shoes, now that she looked. She made plans to clean them as she listened. Dovid's worldview chimed in tune against state-educated bedrock in Musya and left her feeling at ease, as if she were with a friend.

She was having to watch her step now. Mossy log walls cast their path into a shade thickly tufted with clumps of grass and stinging weeds. A few paces past the final logs their way brightened. Dovid beside her stopped and said, "There." He pointed with his bearded chin at something just ahead, across a road. She recognized the fuel drums, she recognized the road. He said, "This is where I first saw you."

"Yes."

She looked down at the weeds, the clay. The road being there meant she was standing—they were standing—where she would never have stood alone or with her children, in the midst of the old cemetery ground. It crossed her mind to think she and Dovid might be cursed for this. Unless here lay some evil spell the two of them were actually breaking. She couldn't take another step. Dovid asked what was wrong. "You're faint again?" She said no. That they might be standing maybe exactly where her sister's grave marker had stood among the rest in an obliterated Jewish cemetery, she explained to him. Murmuring apologies, he said he'd never noticed it. He stepped closer to the road. "But are they still down there?"

"No one knows." So a bleary-eyed clerk wedged in somewhere downstairs from the ZAGS office had told her when she'd rushed in on him, furious, fighting back sobs, the children in no better state crowding behind. Without permits, without a file, he told her, it never existed. Returning days later with more questions she'd found the clerk gone with all his furnishings and his former cubbyhole stuffed with girls at typing tables. "Maybe this kind of thing happens all the time around here."

"That's for sure it does," Dovid said. He mused at the empty ground around Musya's feet. "But good for them, you know? Your sister and her friends. For making the effort in the first place. They stuck with their beliefs and they set themselves apart. They took a stand."

"But they failed."

"Not in their own minds," he answered. "Just because time caught up with them—we all get swept away eventually. You know? Even him with the forehead, the Little Father in whose name someone ordered this. My point is." He paused and turned to nod at a passing eccentric on a bicycle that squeaked. When it was quiet at last he finished. "No one can count on eternity."

He was big on health crusades and for Musya ordered long walks to build up her constitution. Avid about walking, he liked the river routes best. Before the war he'd worked there on the riverside. But not for long—only about fifteen months after he'd come east from Omsk came the German invasion. A Jewish street in Omsk was his home, he was a born Siberian, left motherless young. In life the mother drank and beat him but he'd missed her for years anyhow. He'd never been much of a Yiddish speaker. Despite a long history of Jews in Omsk their numbers in his lifetime there were small and untalkative—just like his father:

"He gave me one advice only. My whole life, one. He tells me, *A healthy bowel is all that matters.*" Musya made some sound. Dovid agreed, it wasn't much.

A few qualifications short to be an engineer, he was a foreman instead. He'd always preferred music to work, making music above all; unluckily that career hadn't happened. In its place he'd always enjoyed working outdoors close to the surface bustle of productivity. Now he had an office job, higher rank and a little lower contentment. Now all the fun was on paper. A defective artillery cartridge had exploded on him during the battle for Moscow. After hospital he'd returned to Birobidzhan partly for the Jews but mostly for the scenery.

"And to climb the Sopka." He meant the tall round hill on the opposite shore which according to him was technically speaking more like a mountain, quite rocky and steep at points, its peak often cloud-bound, its ascent no joke. He felt his fingers all the time and only missed them when they were needed. Still, he thought he could manage the

Sopka. Of course he could, she said.

Dovid came on their mutual rest day to collect her for a sunset walk. Magga's Cossack girl had him waiting in the smoking parlor. On Musya's heels the children all crowded in to get a look at this rare interloper. He smiled pleasantly.

"Only four of you?"

"There used to be five," the oldest said. "Musya sold one."

She couldn't deny it. "Russvelt would have hated Siberia, though."

Anton said so what. "He's orphan, Russvelt, we can use him in our school chorus."

"He has a terrible voice!"

"But he has presence," said Sender, ten now, almost eleven, with excellent Russian. His nine-year old brother's was passable.

"Go away," Samuel Nemo told Dovid. Fluent but terse in two tongues at four, he was antagonized by other men. Their guest asked for more time. "Ney," was the answer.

"Patience," Dovid said. He offered Hodeh a smile. "And you? Another vote for Roosevelt?"

She stared back, possibly twelve, very grim. "What made happen to your hands?"

"I gave my fingers to my country when it needed them."

Samuel Nemo stamped his foot and waved his arms. "Why? Far vos? Why? Siz narish—go away!"

"Why," Dovid said. "Why was because of some big river ice making noise. Why was because of your mother. And you, and the rest of you, sure, you were there."

Then he was clever for he paused and made them ask for the story. Indeed he made them clamor before he gave it to them and told how a beautiful maiden of Birobidzhan had stopped his truck with her manner, her alarm, her mysterious beseeching on the roadside; irresistible. Whatever she'd wanted they couldn't help stopping. Dovid said the scene had stayed with him. Next thing, he went on, he'd found himself in a deep freeze defending his nation's capital against world history's biggest army of fascists, fighting the holy war—except it hadn't felt so clear-cut or holy sometimes. Many times what happened led to asking, *Why fight this battle?*

"I think, maybe Moscow should fall, and the Soviet Union should fall, so that socialism can come back better. Stronger." Their eyes tracked his to the parlor wall and the two Masterminds of World Revolution, hallowed by flyspecks. "You know? I am even thinking I am ready to surrender. But then, here it comes, I picture your mother, that day, this beautiful Jewish girl by the field with all the children. You children." He studied them. "That is what I was fighting for and giving up my hands for. So the fascists would not get you."

Sender Kotz said, "But the fascists did get us."

"Thank you, Dovid." Musya couldn't find more words to say at once. Aglow from his compliment, she felt sorrow for him twist her heart. It made her so sad, the littleness and loneliness of one man in a war. How they suffered, this one and her husband and the rest, the millions. "Thank you so much."

"You are welcome." He pointed at her with his hands. "And here you are. Which means, you know, it worked. I fought for you and you survived."

"Well," she said. "Yes. But."

"But what?"

"We." She shook her head at him. "We were very lucky."

"I do not believe in luck," Dovid said. She registered surprise, having heard him call Dmitri the Small Sweepstakes Winner a lucky dog two days previously. "Well of course I believe in some degree of luck! Dimi has won that thing three times, what else can you call it but luck?"

"He plays too much," said Musya.

Dovid said, "My point is, in this case, ours I mean, our case, I think there is more, I think there is a strong connection. I mean between me fighting for you and you living to be here, you know? Where I am too—when you are the one I was picturing."

"And the children," she admitted, won over as far as she could be.

Dovid nodded. "Exactly. They were there, too."

Hodeh said, "I no, Pretzel no. No connection." Dovid said that wasn't true.

"You ae here now so there is, of course there is a connection."

"He is right." Kitty had slipped into the smoking parlor behind them. "It has got to mean something."

A beat of silence fell before Samuel Nemo threw himself against Dovid's legs and embraced him fiercely.

"Yes, well," Dovid said. "I meant to say this today so here I have said it. Thank you my friend," he told the baby. "Hello again, yes," he told Kitty.

"It is too dark for your sunset walk now," Sender observed.

Musya said no. "Not quite."

Dovid laughed and took them all out to a blintz café, Kitty too. Nearly dominating the night, the two older Kotz brothers showed off a sketchy grasp of facts about the Sopka and extinct volcanoes in the region, all learned from their father—a Soil Specialist, they boasted.

Another walk, a longer sunset.

Another Marshal cast in bronze and erected overnight in the middle of a view. Their leader: "He changed my poem. When it was published," Musya mentioned suddenly. "I have never liked him since."

"You published poetry?"

"One—once. A Yiddish poem."

Dovid kept walking. He said, "I had a girlfriend liked poetry. She used to call me a cloud in trousers, from a poem, she said."

"Ah. Yes." Musya sneaked a look from the corners of her eyes at the bowlegged stride, the broad chest, the jaunty hips and elbows, the up-thrust beard. The girlfriend had been right. "You have a knife in your boot ready for God?"

He shook his head. "A Mauser."

"And where is this girlfriend now?"

"Dust," he answered. "Stalingrad." The bronze uniform at their back resounded silently as they walked away. "A sniper. Decorated. She was something."

When he didn't speak again, Musya asked, "You were engaged to her?"

He hummed under his breath first. "Engaged? I thought so."

"I see." She paused. "But it wasn't an official engagement, then."

He leaned back and looked down his nose at her. "This subject is of great interest to you?"

"Not really," she said, thinking about how they'd both loved war heroes; only his had been real. She kicked a stone almost off the path and Dovid kicked it the rest of the way.

He said, "We men cannot all be like your scientific genius husband and marry every woman we see plus her sister. Like your, you know, Professor Bluebeard."

Musya laughed. "He was not like that."

"Listen, he must have had something—something in the soil maybe." She made some denial and didn't argue the point very strongly, his tone was too heated. Later she'd think very often that this had been a mistake she made. "So," he resumed. "Tell me about this poem of yours." She called it a silly poem that had happened to be chosen—a silly poem whose election from the Soviet Union's vast collective pool of schoolgirl poetry to a place in a hardbound anthology left him impressed. He whistled. "Some silly."

"But the publication part was terrible," she revealed. "Because the last lines were not mine, they were changed. The ending I wrote was completely different. And he put his name right there at the front of the book. So I think he did this. He changed what I wrote. He spoiled my work." She paused and her eyes took in the chiseled fullness of Dovid's mouth. The beard was only a distraction. "And not just mine—maybe every-one's."

Dovid nodded slowly. "He is a fucker."

"I think so, yes." Below their feet the trees that were usually flashing in the windy sunlight stood at rest, already shadowy, breathing coolness and resin scents up at them.

"But what can we do?" he said.

"I do not know," she felt relieved to say.

He stepped towards her, certainly to take her in his arms for a kiss; yet she stepped aside, away. Her supervisor, he was a stranger to her, a strange man. She had nowhere to run. Up here on the Bira bluff the forest cover of her past was gone. Stumps pompom-med with mushrooms stood in a flood of fledgling pines, ankle high, green as lizards.

She kept him behind her. "Was that really true what you said, that you thought of me and the children when you fought outside Moscow?" No answer. She turned to see a dark man streaked with sun like firelight, motionless against a gold leaf ground of molten Siberian sky; an icon figure of a man, he could mean anything. He could rape and kill her now or else he could be too good for her. "It was not something you happened to read in a wall newspaper or a manual maybe?"

"What are you talking about? I told you I always remembered you—what did you think I meant?"

"I do not know," she kept repeating. "You said you came back for the scenery."

"And for the Jews," he reminded her. "Marry me, Tovarisch."

He put his arms around her. They combined. He held her with his hands. She could feel the touch of all ten fingers.

Maybe more.

(8)

Brother Dead Man called Dovid a great improvement on Musya's first husband but he thought she was crazy to marry another Jew. Why on earth put herself at an elevated disadvantage?

"You like him? Have him. Bring him in—move him in, even. Only put nothing in writing." This was a form of fatherly advice she was getting because he'd grown fond of her, he said. Musya wondered how true this was; it didn't feel mutual, not at the moment, for sure.

She said, "I don't need your permission to move him in. Kitty signed the house committee form. And I do not like him—I love him."

He accused her of missing the point. "As usual," he added. The long-winded point involved the familiar terror tale about how husbands and wives would be used against one another in the event of conditions turning politically hostile towards Birobidzhan's Jews. "Which trust me, they will," he said again the next day, when Musya was tired of hearing it.

Dovid who was sweaty from carrying boxes upstairs answered him, "Maybe, sure. I respect your opinions and you could very well be right but this is my bride, you know? I must marry her."

"Self-indulgence," said the dead man.

Dovid laughed. "True! Seriously, your wall forest is a great thing but what you did with that ramp out front, I am truly impressed. I can get the handcart right into the hall."

"That ramp was my idea!" Musya said delightedly.

"Ack! Ack!" Sounding out his disgust triggered the dead man's chronic cough. He griped constantly about the cost of this innovation which he had opposed. "Ack! Too expensive. Not needed."

"But you could use it yourself," Musya argued. "If we got a wheelchair and someone carried you down, you could go outside."

"Outside to do what? Wheel around among the doomed?"

Dovid said, "Why not? First some fresher air, then a little exercise, next thing you could be on a walk with the doomed. Give it a try."

They watched a brown bottle appear from between some cushions on the chaise lounge and a long drink go down the dead man's throat. One belch, then, "No thanks," he said.

There wasn't too much to move in on Dovid's part. Of course no more furniture could fit. One box of books; he liked novels, fortunately. He owned a Moscow-brand suitcase gramophone and a small crystal radio set and kept abreast of technical improvements to be had for both, eagerly reading what he could find and rather haunting the night market stalls for the magazines and vacuum tubes and parts he carried in another box; he also bought and traded musical recordings of which he had a large collection. He was getting out of a semi-private bunkroom in one of the original worker dormitories before the city demolished it. Lately the matter was all over the local wall news, how disgraceful to see Birobidzhan's major thoroughfares so dominated by these wooly mammoth-like relics, hulking hotbeds of social crime, and their great logs' stink of decay, and their yards overflowing with outhouses and mire and small animal pens. New worker flat blocks of concrete should soon replace all the old housing stock. Dovid was only a step ahead of the general eviction notice known to be in the local party organization's pipeline: it was to come, the only question was when?

"People will say I married a widow for her bedroom."

He stood looking around. Transformed by a new coat of bright white paint, the walls were hung with his musical instruments—not as many as he'd owned before, he said, but some he could never part with no matter how impossible for him to play—he loved the sound of them, even in another's hands. (His poor trumpet he'd sold in a bad moment, he said.) Up on a chair as directed with a ball hammer and hanging nails, she'd been too close to see until now. The arrangement showed an artistry that dizzied her; she worshipped him. He'd also moved the bed to the opposite wall, it made a vast improvement. She said people would be a little right.

"Without my bedroom I would never want another husband."

They were on a list for a new mattress. At his insistence she'd thrown away her bag of hair.

As for the children turned from an accustomed bed, they could decide between passageway bunks and featherbeds in proximity to the suitcase gramophone, the crystal set, the backgammon board, the family's modest larder and the balebos, whose enthusiasm for capturing rogue Western short waves was the keenest of all. His tarelka still ran non-stop as similar set-ups did in the average Soviet home. Which suited Dovid, who liked things a little noisy. The children loved it when the newcomer wrapped himself in Anton's tiger skin to chase them through the flat, roaring. Also in bed he liked being loud.

The cats took the passageway.

"You know, Mark Bernes is not Jewish."

Dovid said, "Yes, he is."

"But I know this from someone who knows his family," said Vera. "Except for a little on his father's side, they are not Jews and neither is he."

"Of course he is. You can tell from the film."

"You understand he is an actor?" Vera said. "He is acting."

"Not in this case," Dovid said.

Musya put in, "His accent is not real, I could tell that, Dovid. He might be Jewish but not really from Odessa."

"Yes? You talked to every man in Odessa in your time?"

Vera said, "Fake accent, not even Jewish—and homosexual."

Musya gasped and tried to whisper. "His family friend told you that?"

"No, but it is obvious."

Dovid's derisive shout made the Leningrader roll her eyes: neither could quite believe the other's pig-headed stupidity. It was an impasse and they couldn't stand each other from day one.

Direct from Birofeld on the overnight market truck via ferry, Vera had shown up early for the marriage party—hours too early, not long past dawn, unexpectedly alone. Her frenzied pounding on the flat door more than spooked the kolkhoz deserters who'd appeared without warning the previous day. A Russian-speaking Jewish settler family of five come straight from some swampland to this street address; it was Musya's letter their patriarch had clutched and shook at the flat's occupants:

"Lies! Lies! Lies!"

He was hoarse by then. His family had suffered incredible trials which he'd summarized at length. Now Brother Dead Man finally begged to differ:

"Optimistic views, at worst. But we warned you—the letter did warn you there would be hard work ahead."

"Warned me nothing! What warning—bring seeds, she said. So we bring every seed we can find, like she wrote. What do seeds matter or work matter when the land won't support life? My family is barely alive, sir!" Husband, wife, older children not yet twenty, all good-looking; the entire family looked underfed for sure and full of damaged nerves, darting frightened glances at Yuri's painted wilderness. Their name was Matis. Dovid said they were completely demoralized.

Worse, they were fugitives. An old fact of life in Birobidzhan was how many people fled the region's farming outposts and wound up in the city which never had enough room for them. Unlike those who'd come and gone before, post-Fatherland War settlers like the Matis family had nowhere else to turn. No westbound train ticket would help. Their Jewish homes had been lost to them. So now the law said they had to go back to their assigned kolkhozes and stay there or be subject to arrest. It was a harsh set of circumstances.

"But the thing is, we are getting married tomorrow," Musya had explained. "And we are having a little party here."

"Don't mind us," said the wife who hadn't stopped crying quietly into her handkerchief until this instant. Her mate was even less accommodating:

"We cannot leave until I have complained directly to the authorities."

"So you can stay." Kitty the house committee head had spoken. "Stay here. For the time being it's a perfect cover. No one is about to arrest you for coming to a wedding party."

Musya might have argued but Dovid said, "Yes, agreed. Stay, please. We insist." She'd reeled, thinking about the smoked sturgeon, an all-out expense. He'd said not to worry—everyone had been fed enough at the first party, the big rowdy one at the plant with ribald toasts congratulating the popular supervisor on his new cohabitation with his Little Sweeper. Yet times had changed and they'd had to wait nearly two weeks longer for a ZAGS appointment. To mark the day of the official marriage registration, the couple had planned something more intimate, in the home. Five uninvited half-starved houseguests didn't really fit the program but there they remained and here she was, stuck with them and the bedding they'd brought laid out where possible with Yuri and his uninvited friends already sprawled drunk across half the floor space. Yuri needed better friends, Musya resolved to tell him. At bedtime her children doubled up with the cats and the front room looked like an encampment in a forest scene from Voyna i mir, Dovid said.

Before dawn, everything out there was quiet.

Propped on one elbow, Musya lay and watched the sunrise on the face beside hers in sleep. She was saying her goodbyes to the beard. On this his wedding day Dovid would finally allow her to shave him. He'd coached her through some practice on a large garden beet until she could keep from turning the razor blade entirely purple with the nicks she left. She had a steady hand which he'd called the main thing. His body had another body that surrounded it; she could feel this carapace, warm and very firm, from two handsbreadths away. A little closer and sometimes he almost burned her. All the freezing nights she'd known, not only those but the itching filth, the bites, the searing aches, humiliations, horrors shrank, receded, as he melted the pain from her history. Yet more remained, always more. So often she'd jerk herself out of an embrace she yearned for; or else she'd fall asleep blissful and wake up gasping in panic. How could he stand her?

Dawn was illuminating the mobile creases in his eyelids. A twitch: he was dreaming, maybe of alternatives. He'd said he didn't mind her headscarf staying on, he liked the silk, the feel of it, he said. Musya wondered. All in all, what she could offer Dovid might be less than he deserved. So, he'd had her on trial. Bald, traumatized, far from childless, she wanted the lifetime more he'd proposed, naturally. But she couldn't be unfair to him. Moving closer, she began to kiss him awake so that she could ask him if after two weeks he'd still like to go through with it. Her heart raced: this felt like the biggest risk she'd ever run, disaster's furthest edge.

"Of course I still want to marry you. Didn't you watch me buy a new jacket for the purpose?"

It was second-hand. She gave him another kiss. "You would have bought that jacket anyhow."

"Never." He kissed her seriously. Then Vera's voice in the front room—she couldn't wait, she was saying. Musya heard one of the Matis boys cry out:

"We are innocent! We were lied to!"

"So was I, many times!" Vera was bursting into the bedroom, a red shawl worn loose over her half-buttoned tunic blouse, her color high. "Mushka, for God's sake, I need a place to stay! That man never loved me—he accuses me of cheating but he's the one!"

"So," Musya said, "he won't be coming?" Although what difference it made now to her provisions must be negligible, she reflected.

Vera only stared. "You are right, it is the man from the restaurant window."

Musya said, "Yes, I know, I wrote you in the invitation." She introduced the two.

"You must be the vegetarian," said Dovid.

Already then he didn't like this friend of hers. Mark Bernes came later, at the party. The toasts and speeches were through and everyone was drinking fast before the liquor ran out. Even while arguing, Vera was visibly distracted by another man across the room, a handsome stranger. Matis the kolkhoz deserter had eyes for Vera, too; while his wife and daughter, lost in their own reflections, sat with Yuri staring at his trees. Guests were still crowding in and shoving their way towards the food, what little remained. As for Dovid, he was enjoying his favorite European jazz too much to be troubled by arguments or party crashers. He also loved company, this new husband of hers.

Musya held herself pressed to Dovid's side. She could have stood at the ZAGS counter signing her name for a year. They were married. The music was wonderful. Her children had never looked better, healthier, smarter, more lovable as they monopolized the dance floor, swinging their multicolored curls. Kitty, wedged between the two Matis youths, was pinkly ecstatic to be playing the older woman on one sofa; while her mother on another took cigarette puffs between mouthfuls of sturgeon. The balebos could be spotted on his chaise lounge through a cluster of old Birobidzhaners and their thick tobacco clouds; a strong-smelling pipe glowed in the dark luggage-piled corner where Dovid's fellow Jewish veterans and the uninvited Nanai talked topography and trapping. Voices overlapped loudly. Bottles appeared, samogon flavored with berries, with herbs. The room was hoarse with smoke and song by the time Vera's handsome man arrived and shouted at finding her deep in conversation with a new lover, glad he hadn't brought their child to witness this, he said.

Vera raised her chin and threw back her crooked shoulders. She and Matis had been talking of one thing only: Birofeld. Innocently, two idealists, settler to settler; in truth she'd been persuading him to bring his unfortunate family there, to try one last kolkhoz, that was all, she said. The handsome father of her child looked around at the handsome family in question and exclaimed in bitter surprise:

"You don't have enough already?"

Vera slapped at his face and then rushed out into the hallway sobbing. Displaying a matinee idol's profile, Matis followed. The newcomer accepted a glassful, then another. Magga warned against trouble but the scene stirred the room only briefly since the protagonists weren't known there.

Musya went back to admiring Dovid. Nutty brown, round as the backside of a domra, his face clean-shaven took her by perpetual surprise. He was a touching heartthrob man. While they were dancing, when they weren't dancing, her eyes played across and up and down him without ceasing. Until she heard a curiously familiar noise that emanated from the bedroom and followed it. Sure enough, Sender Kotz had slipped away to try out Dovid's wedding gift to his bride: a fairly new Podolsk sewing machine with a handsome case.

And a motor.

"I'm only letting out a few things," he explained, sharp scissors in one hand. He was right, most of their clothes were outgrown these days. She kissed his head and left him to it.

His brothers and sister with their orphan's trumpet remained inside the party's impromptu song corner where the volume built steadily, Anton's voice at the fore. At some point Musya spotted Vera's two men exchanging bicep clasps as friendship pledges. Then Vera was across the room telling Brother Dead Man and his bosom friends about the Leningrad Writers who'd just been attacked in print by the government. Yes, she knew a lot about them.

"Overrated, completely," Vera said. "Pretentious and overrated." The balebos read to her from the broadsheet in his hand. "What? Yes, rotten and empty, un-ideological, vulgar—it's too bad but this Zhdanov is right." She wouldn't listen to any arguments and instead insisted, "They need taking down, Brother, and it's good to see the government cares enough to act. Let someone else get published for a change in Leningrad." This was how she really felt, said Vera; and no, it didn't make her the worst kind of person, a female censor. "It's not about me—it's the truth. After all that poor city suffered, the Leningrad Writers should have changed!"

"To Soviet Culture!" the balebos toasted. His circle murmured yes, here it was, incarnate in Vera before them. "And Soviet critics, to them. To the beautiful souls of bullies and executioners. Here's to your writers' unmarked graves, too, lady—long live their gravediggers!"

Dovid stepped in. "No one said anything about executing writers, please, Tovarisch Dead Man. Let's all calm down. Hey—we need more drink this side of the room!"

He had an old tattoo. As a young man he'd liked to do things just to try them, for the sake of new experience, he said. In maturity a decade on he was a modern-leaning man who liked to have progress around him. Its visible signs—new parks or streetlights, for example—made him happy. He noticed building sites and storefronts changing hands. Anything in a state of repair drew him like a magnet; he loved to ask friendly questions of work crews. Quite soon his admiring step-children took to spotting and making reports on local conditions to please him, multiplying his eyes on the beloved city Dovid looked ahead and saw taking the regional lead, a more successful modern Jewish-run competitor to Khabarovsk's declining Tsarist-era streetscapes and flab-bound bureaucracy. Here progress happened. Siberia's midsummer harvests were wet; but once the Birobidzhan Agricultural Machinery Plant put its new caterpillar tracks on a sufficient number of new mechanical harvesters, mud would be conquered. Regional productivity would skyrocket. And to Birobidzhan's expanding star on the Far Eastern map would come commerce, manufacturing, culture; hospitals, universities, orchestras: "To the victor," he'd say. He promised many more bookstores. Which sounded good if no longer so urgent since he'd persuaded its meanest manager to lift the family's Shkolnik ban. "No progress without books in the home," was a thing Dovid said everyone knew. Sad to say, the Yiddish stock turned out to be meager. The books weren't being published, the manager explained. Dovid liked to talk books and kept up a lively dinner table conversation in general. Tonight's topic:

Which one of them was toughest?

Across Manchukuo export-ware piled with fish in jelly, the family vied for top rankings. So far, Dovid was best-read; Sender Kotz, smartest; funniest was Antosha the clown; best-looking remained in contention. Missing was the balebos, currently hospitalized with stones in his urine. He'd outlived Magga's promised year and would survive this one too. In his absence, Dovid claimed toughest. He meant to clinch it with one question.

"Who else here ever killed a man?" he asked.

For a few moments nobody moved. Then Hodeh sat up straighter. "I did," she said. "I killed one. Me."

Musya said, "You wounded one. We don't really know if."

"He was dead, Musya." The other children agreed with Sender. If too young to remember the full event, at least familiar with the story, the one Musya didn't like to circulate outside their family, Samuel Nemo was emphatic:

"Hodeh killed a bad man with the sharp scissors. It's a secret." It had been.

When? Where? Dovid quizzed them. High summer in Ukraine, in a field near Podilsk, after the ghetto, after nightfall. Why? Self-defense. Who? A hazardous stranger with designs on their meager travelling possessions but more immediately bent on rape. One-two in an armpit up to the handles plus a sliced ankle tendon was how. They hid the body under vegetation. "But I'm sure he was still moving," Musya always insisted.

"No," Hodeh said. "He was not. He was dead."

"By your hand." Dovid looked at her thoughtfully. "So you win. You are the toughest."

"I agree." Sender spoke for all of them.

"Unless, of course," Dovid began, "unless your mother has any killings of her own to count."

Musya smiled and shook her head. "I tried once but it didn't work."

"Lucky for you," he said.

"No," Musya told him. "The ones who had rifles and bombs to use, you were the lucky ones." He laughed and glanced down at his hands.

"I am not so sure about that."

She had a moment to feel terrible before Samuel Nemo got up and went to crowd Dovid close, crying, "Time!" He pushed at one long sweater sleeve. The others shouted yes. "You promised—show us again!"

No one could decipher the old tattoo and Dovid wouldn't tell them what it was supposed to be or say. The question obsessed his new family. It had to have something to do with a woman but he wouldn't even admit that much. Tonight it looked like the face of a small dark blue animal.

Dovid picked up a menorah made of old brass and some candles for it at the night market. He told Tovarisch Dead Man no: he wanted more Jewish culture in the home, not less. He'd set himself a course of study, a few hours a week at the Sholem Aleichem Library downtown where he was reading his way through the entries on Jewish life and culture in the Large Soviet Encyclopedia. Dovid and his friends the fellow veterans were proudly Jewish, he said. After all, Jews had fought and died Great Patriotic deaths as bravely as anyone else to ensure the great victory.

"Jews were suckered," said the balebos. "They should have stayed home to defend their wives and families. Like that reptile your wife and her sister married—what good was he, putting on the uniform so he could get himself killed in a week. Worthless as ever."

Dovid sat up. "You are talking about a man—a brave Jewish soldier—who gave his life for his family and his country! A hero!" His admiration for his predecessor in the home—for Boris Kotz, Soil Specialist, polymath, intellectual—was sincere to the point of reverence. He'd talked about having big shoes to fill. "Show some respect in front of his widow and sons."

"We heard it already, we don't mind, it doesn't hurt us." This was Sender, his generation's leading pacifist, in an attempt to smother the conflict; but it kept kicking. The dead man ignored him.

"And bravery had nothing to do with it," he said. "Your so-called great victory was nothing but numbers. Hitler lost to our sheer population. The Tarabak had more bodies to spare—period."

"It is a sin to say that," Dovid said.

"You know I am right."

Dovid snorted. "I of all people know how wrong you are, that is what I know."

"Me, too," said Kitty, visiting.

Dovid said he might not be a specialized scientific expert like the previous head of household, but he knew plenty about life's bigger side. According to Dovid, the modern world had just fought itself to a chance at genuine progress. The great nation idea had played itself out, he thought. The next step would require a dynamic multiplicity of individuals organized as peoples, all unique yet undivided, in communion, learning from and helping one another to advance and thrive as human nature intended. Men and women everywhere should learn to respect themselves and their own cultures; and also stop fighting, he agreed with Musya there. But peace was a bonus. Only proud Jews, especially, could thrive.

Despite his own struggles with the language Dovid was all in favor of the Yiddish pedagogy at School Number Two. However the couple was keeping one child enrolled at the plant school for appearances' sake; also to use the benefit. For A Freylekhn Chanukah 1946, Pretzel sat between them and watched his older siblings on the concert stage through jealous tears. More American bounty for the Jewish orphans of war: all the girls in the chorus had on red velvet hair bows and the boys wore red velvet trousers. Anton had a ten-bar solo and another in the encore. It was his favorite costume outfit of all time.

Between numbers Musya glanced around the darkened auditorium packed full of applause-flashing hands and smiling profiles. She recognized a few classmates from the normal school where she'd begun taking courses to qualify for an infant school post. She'd have preferred to teach composition, only as birth rates surged many more openings were foreseen in kindergartens and "extra" students like Musya, all women, were being trained to fill them. Half her fellow students were married, some were too young, some were between marriages and a few played the field. Conversation centered overwhelmingly on two subjects: food and men. Between classes, on breaks, they traded anecdotes and advice. Sometimes Musya would be laughing along, wholly involved, when with a kind of snap the fun would go out like a candle flame, blown out by something like the cold breath of an unsealed tomb: Fanny's. Her friend's murder stood there. Far from laughing now Musya found it hard to contain an anxious concern. These women let men get too close to their bodies. The chances weren't good, her instincts told her, that one of them wouldn't get hurt. The most doting made her painfully uneasy and sad—for poor Fanny had doted. As for doting lovers, this former pen-pal of Leon Flohr's distrusted the lot of them. And when anyone talked of the latest conquest she'd made, in this livid state Musya would see Cesar the rapist at the door; and beyond his shoulder a long line of more drooling rapists with broken minds, talon grips. Didn't her fellow students recognize the danger? Three four five she counted cozied up to sketchy-looking types. Musya wanted to shake them by the shoulders. Didn't they know that conquests weren't for women to decide?

How lucky she was to have Dovid! The benefits were countless. Thanks to Dovid's efforts she had a health exemption that freed her from finishing any more lathe parts—work which really would have been too strenuous now that she'd grown noticeably pregnant. As everyone said, they hadn't wasted one minute. Musya liked being a student again. She enjoyed going to class, getting there, sitting down with her books and notebooks and starting to listen; but she always fell asleep. This pregnancy was ill-timed in that regard alone. Otherwise she felt blissful. She knew Dovid would love his baby. He'd love holding and kissing it. Newborn, squalling, filling his hands—she pictured what his face would look like in those first moments night and day and now, again, as the full chorus hummed its way to the next Yiddish homesickness song in the medley. Dovid had regained his calm after the small argument he'd had with someone a few rows up who'd kept blocking their view. The last storm clouds were gone from his brow which gleamed, winningly frank again. Music perfected him.

For what her body was able to do for this man she loved, her husband, that it could produce what he wanted, a second self for him, his own other, Musya felt almost dizzy with gratitude. After all, despite everything, her body had been preserved. Fatter than ever in pregnancy she was less swollen tonight than shame had been making her feel until she squirmed for years. The numerous degrading violations she'd suffered through the fortunes of war had done damage, yes; not to forget, she'd also come to them from Boris Kotz's disinfected marriage bed. And before that? Despoiled by a predator. Ages past, as a girl from Odessa she'd been ripped from the right way of living. Now her course to happiness had been restored. She was back on the way to her proper destiny, warmed by the stage lights' red-golden glow, fast in a comfortable groove that felt like sunlit open-air freedom.

Hodeh dressed as his Snow Maiden watched from a few steps away as Dovid opened the little present she'd handed him. A surprise to Musya, it was nicely wrapped in Chinese paper, a jewelry box.

Dovid let out a low whistle. "Silver cufflinks. Very nice. Very nice stone, too."

He liked to celebrate Novyi God traditionally so they'd decorated a little fir tree in a bucket with silver paper stars. In the circle of its fragrance they sat welcoming 1947 with a gift exchange. A small part of Musya also admired the thick matching malachite slices but most of her gaped horror-stricken at the scene overwhelming her imagination: Police at the door! She managed, "Where? Here?"

Hodeh rolled her eyes. "How could I get anything here?" This, Musya realized, was true. Grown a little gangly and tall, the girl's best sneak-thieving days were behind her.

"So where?"

"From Odessa." Hodeh swore it was the truth. The other children confirmed it. Anton said he'd seen her find them.

"Where in Odessa?" Even as she asked the question, Musya followed Sender's more honest eyes to the postcard greetings from Uncle Falk and Russvelt. The former grass-pea cripple could write a whole sentence by now. He owned a new bicycle, green. In sadder news, the wine merchant was a widower again. At his new wife's death he'd decided to reverse his conversion and emigrate to Palestine, taking the boy along to the homeland. He must have pulled his last strings, Musya guessed. She felt a twinge of sympathy for the female population of Palestine and parts between—the man was fatal to women.

"They were sitting out in the rain with a lot of other cufflinks," said Sender.

"Sounds legitimate to me." Dovid, clearly very pleased with this extra gift, had done well already. From the children came the newest hard-backed bestseller, a Fatherland War adventure by Polevoy called Tale of a True Man. The hero was a double amputee; everyone, the whole country was crazy about it, Shkolnik's staff said. Then the big gift from Musya, hand-sewn silk pajamas—although Kitty had procured the silk so really these were from the two of them. Staying just long enough to be thanked, Kitty left and missed the cufflinks. Which appeared to be the final gift until Dovid climbed to his feet and with a flash of provodnitsa blue and a flourish of the wedding quilt worn slung across his shoulders in place of an ermine-trimmed robe, announced that Father Frost had saved one for last. They followed him to the bedroom where he gestured at the walls. "Everybody pick one instrument." A gasp went up. "I am giving you music lessons. From me. Forever."

While all four children had itched to get their hands on Dovid's collection, Anton's desire had been almost an agony. But now he turned in desperate circles—"No! No!"—unable to decide or choose. He never could; in time Dovid trained him on everything.

Musya picked a wooden flute but she fell behind on her practice hours and stopped before she learned to play.

The maternity clinic's white and green walls were loaded with health posters and slogans, certificates, anatomical diagrams. Sperm, egg and embryo; the normal and abnormal womb; mother and fetus, bisected with tissues and spines showing: Musya couldn't help it, she thought the illustrations gave the place a heartless and disturbing look. The bare board walls of Krutonog's former fruit canning shed had possessed a simplicity more solemn and more humane. She missed her elegant little fenstster beam, too. Dovid held his palms around her trembling hands and let his scars be gripped through her contractions. There was no doubt in her mind that the experience to come would only look bloodier against the white tiles and be no less agonizing than her experience before. She had no faith in anesthesia.

Her friend Fanny floated in, nude on a gauze-winged swan, one long plump arm extended, its pit unshaved. Fanny was holding out a telephone number for her to copy but the digits kept changing under Musya's pen. It was Leon Flohr's telephone number, he was in desperate trouble and begged her to call.

"Don't worry," Fanny said. "He is impotent, poor man."

Discovering that both her hands held telephone receivers, Musya raised one to an ear. Her dead husband, almost comprehensible, was on the line, talking as Boris Kotz could, non-stop on some abstruse topic he'd be determined to explain. She cast about for a way to break the connection and call Leon but there was no cradle, no button, nothing; which left her the receiver cord to follow. But right away it disappeared into a wall of thorny roses, a wall high as a mountainside. Dead-ended at its foot, her upturned features bathed by the icy perfumed rivulets the roses shed, Musya recognized her conclusion. Her halt here was permanent. From now on there would be impenetrable roses only, and otherwise memories or dreams like memories all made entirely from what lay behind her. In a burst of panic she thrust her arms into the thorns, past her elbow veins; with her flesh tearing she reached towards more life.

Musya woke to find Dovid seated by her bedside, holding their baby against his chest. His son: the two were already good friends. Their wet red faces matched.

While remaining the best possible stepfather Dovid became the best father to a newborn child that anyone they knew had ever heard of, paternity's paragon. In fact he was a highly domesticable man; his being so fond of progress inclined him to share the woman's labor of housekeeping and childcare by his own free and even eager choice; he liked to run things a little, too. He boasted of the modern scientific expertise that went into his diapering, for example. He made jolly remarks about Musya needing only five more children—under the new re-population program, with her tenth she'd be named a Mother Heroine and get a medal from the government. Dovid said he couldn't wait to do his part for the Soviet cause. Like night phantoms or vampires, the anxious lessons of Musya's past melted away in the bright warmth of his happiness and his help and many novel comforts. Clean sheets and towels, warm water, bed service, many pairs of hands: she had it all and more. She had time, a precious legal right of Soviet motherhood, time at home to lavish love on her husband's baby, Dovid's image. She had time to read. She tired of her nightgown and made herself another on the Podolsk out of old gingham; this started her sewing for part of every day. Fairly quickly she made two dresses for Kitty who supplied the cloth and basic patterns. The fittings took hours and the results weren't the greatest, bad enough overall that Musya swore off dressmaking for life.

A warm breeze stirred the new checkered window curtains. Again her eye caught on a jagged dip in one seam; just there Merele had chased his offspring through the gingham. The balebos was right, Musya guessed. Records were being kept of everything. Under cover of his midday nap she'd turned the radio broadcast to its lowest volume; silence would wake him, of course. The baby asleep in the bed crib kept up a droning commentary on a dream. The rest were across the Bira where Dovid had led them by ferry on a round-trip hike to the Sopka's rocky base—a reconnaissance expedition, they were calling it. Musya lay back and thrust her bare legs into the slab of sunlight on the old patchwork. She tasted luxury: quiet solitude. Safe between four walls hung with her husband's musical instruments, she listened to the humming chord coaxed by the planet's rotation from their combined wooden bellies and throats, an orchestral stroke sustained in thrumming waves and circles to accompany her breath.

Occasionally Musya wished for a way to keep kolkhoz deserters from reaching her flat. The regional authorities could be more vigilant, maybe. Matis and his family were far from the last to find her at home in Birobidzhan. They all seemed to get through. Red October remained the final straw for many, the settlement of that name a true hellscape for twenty years and counting. And from Red October had arrived the girl who looked at her too hard, then asked, "Didn't you use to have hair?"

"Yes, of course." She admitted it: long, full, natural waves mostly worn in a thick auburn braid.

"Brown, yes," said the girl. "We saw you—we saw her, remember? Right after we got off the train. You had a big fight in the street with that handsome gonif from Odessa who rode out with us." She was high-strung, almost fleshless and unsurprisingly tubercular if so, with Red October in the picture.

"Oh!" The girl's mother had some nutritional deficiency that ringed her mouth in sores through which she exclaimed, "He was awful. And that awful suit—that blue."

"Who was awful?" asked Dovid. He could follow the Yiddish pretty well by now.

"The one who chased married women—I remember him." The girl's grandfather, who looked healthy, chiming in. He peered at her. "But not this one."

"Yes, you do." The daughter's turn again: maybe the nearness of death had bestowed total recall on her fevered brain. "We watched them from the station steps. Was that the father of one of your children?" she asked Musya next. "That's what we guessed."

She said no, not at all. "He was an old boyfriend. We—we always argued."

"You had a lowlife for a boyfriend, then," the grandfather said unnecessarily, in Musya's view. Then the daughter gave a little cry and provoked the first great crisis of her second marriage:

"Leon Flohr! I've just remembered it. That was his name: Leon Flohr."

A family story Dovid knew well. "The one from the letter," he said. "Your pen pal." *Yes, Yours,* Musya thought.

The drowsing dead man stirred and declaimed, *"Yes, a hero."*

"I am less than he," Anton remembered next. "Wait—did he have legs?"

"Of course he had legs," said the mother. "He was wearing a suit."

The flat fell still. Sender Kotz looked around before he spoke. "Musya, Leon was here? You talked to him?"

She denied it. "No, no, I talked to someone else, a boy I'd almost forgotten. What a coincidence but no, that wasn't me you saw." She sensed a wall of disbelief, darker than the sky-burial forest and closer, not even an arm's length away. "Really, it's not surprising. Leon had so many women with arguments against him. It's funny." She managed a laugh. "He really was awful, you're right."

"And did I hear you call him handsome?" The mother aimed a scolding tone at her daughter. "With that awful moustache?"

Musya felt the crisis slipping past, the drag of its tail yet liable to flick dangerously. She said, "Yes, Leon Flohr, he had a moustache when I knew him, too."

"He lied." Sender was taking this in. "He lied to us in his letter."

Musya said it wouldn't surprise her one bit if he had. Sender look so crushed, she continued, "All the same, though, maybe he didn't. Prosthetic limbs these days permit very lifelike motion, they've made a thousand advances by now."

The grandfather wagged his head. "Lifelike enough to sneak around behind that many husbands' backs on a moving train? Doubtful."

"I should have known," Sender said sadly. "I should have known."

Her husband Dovid kept quiet. What he thought mattered. Musya was glad for his silence as long as they weren't alone, which didn't prevent it from feeling painfully ominous. When at bedtime he still didn't speak, she confessed:

"Of course that was Leon Flohr, that, in the road. But I prefer the children not to know because I never told them."

"Or me," Dovid said. "We have lived together for thirteen months and you never said one word about it."

"It was unimportant."

"Unimportant? You wrote love letters to the man every week."

"I wasted my time."

"I thought you were honest."

"Of course I am honest."

"Then what was tonight about, tell me? *Oh, what a coincidence!*" He was mocking her, sore. "My future wife, brawling in public with a cheap gigolo. Some picture. Some honesty."

She crossed the room and picked up the baby although he'd been fast asleep. His annoyance and surprise turned to relish right away: he was a good-natured baby with a powerful appetite. His father stood there captivated by the view as he tended to be.

But Musya couldn't have a breast out all the time.

Dovid's domestic peace had received a violent blow. Her lie of omission's unmasking had damaged their concord. Of course it had, Musya thought angrily. Yes, she'd hidden the truth. She'd been trying to keep a bad humiliation from turning septic—but she'd been a fool to think she could spare herself anything. Every bad fate flowed right towards her. Sunk in resentments like this on both sides, the couple sniped and grumbled; which turned the baby to crying; which spread discomfort. Momentum was against them. How could they avoid a crash? Dread kept her awake in the dark with wet eyelashes. Once again she needed saving and it might not happen.

It did happen, however, thanks to a most unexpected source of help: the Soviet film industry. Aleksandrov's latest was called Vesna. Musya was resisting up to the last moment. Kitty said, "You love Lyubov Orlova, you have to come along." But a novel in bed and an evening alone appealed far more—as a rule, she still avoided cinema. At last she let the children's pleas persuade her; Dovid hadn't pressed, certainly. Then she felt crowded by him in their seats where he used up all the arm room.

Two hours later they emerged into the chill late-summer night with their love restored, intact, running at full speed. What had happened was Vesna: Spring, spring for the nation, spring for everyone. A solar energy scientist and a musical theater actress hired to play her in a film employ their identical looks to switch life stations for a handful of exquisite hours, some of them involving antique fairytales and harp guitars: here was the plot of it. The sun in test tubes, Pushkin reciting on a film set bridge, Hollywood alive in Moscow; America felt very close, like a brotherly rival. This—cinema like this—was the art of an international power: Dovid wasn't the only one saying so in the crowd that lingered underneath the cinema marquee, reluctant to release itself from Vesna's spell. Glamour, yes; but socialist in content. Both characters Orlova played being serious wholly-committed Soviet professional women lifted by the conscientious use of talent to career success—and love. Their harmless subterfuge didn't lose them the love of the men born to love them. A little mystery, a little moonglow made it easier for love to win. The man moved smoothly into place with only the slightest of comical doubts, he took up his towering position at her side. She put her arm through his. They prepared to surpass themselves.

"Not enough songs!"

Meanwhile a less enthusiastic vocal minority complained. He liked the central number but there should have been more songs, Anton thought. And Kitty said Lyubov Orlova looked old. "All of them did. Couldn't they find anyone young?"

(9)

Elkie stepped from the echelon train and with stride unmistakable advanced through steam clouds along its impressive length. Forty cars, government-chartered, run every few months from Moscow on the Trans-Siberian line, the echelons provided Jews safe transport across the Soviet Union to their national socialist homeland, away from the ruins of their irrecoverable pasts. Thousands had ridden them east since the start of the year. Bewildered hundreds more poured out onto Elkie's path, out into the Jewish Autonomous Region where they'd been told the growing season had another month to run—which couldn't be true. They were shivering: it was September 1947. What would become of these people? Already overcrowded to the point of shortages and price hikes in every direction, the city couldn't take another throng; but all the Jewish kolkhozes protested being sent too many mouths to feed, even Red October was out of room. Limits were being reached and exceeded while the echelons kept pulling into Birobidzhan station with its platform too short for them. New arrivals struggled with bags down a cinder path laid alongside the tracks. From the platform edge where she'd elbowed a place, Musya viewed them uneasily. Where would so many more sleepers sleep? And what would all these Jews eat when they woke in hunger?

Briefly hidden by a luggage pile-up, Elkie cut through. Musya waved. "Elkie!" She didn't feel so easily recognized. But Elkie picked her out in a second and walked up beaming: with her baby like that she looked just the same, Elkie said. Musya introduced Dovid's son in his woolen sling. "The others are here somewhere, they've gone to get a luggage cart." She looked around, blinked at what had been missing from Elkie's postcard and now from the platform: "But what about Eidel? She's not with you?"

"God, no," Elkie said. "We've been through for years. We made it all the way to Moscow and nine weeks later she left me for a Metro driver with huge tits."

A sharp, entirely personal regret over the opportunities she'd missed to visit Moscow's fabled Metro stations and ride on even one underground train gave edge to a genuine sorrow. "I'm sorry, Elkie. What a shame—after all that. Oh, Anton will be so disappointed." He hated disappointment worse than off-key voices. Anticipating how he'd take it, Musya felt dread. She spoke sincerely. "It's sad news."

"I took it hard myself for a long time," Elkie admitted. "But I should have seen it coming. Eidel always complained I lacked ambition. And Metro driver is a flashy job—they get women. It was a long time ago." Her eyes travelled the length of Musya's body in both directions, twice. "You look good, Musya."

"Oh, well." She waved her wedding ring around. "Thanks. You, too." Which was understating it, honestly. Elkie had never seemed to be much affected by Obodovka's privations but of course she had been. Three years free, clean, fed, matured, she and her axe-blade cheekbones shone. Musya hoped the balebos would behave himself.

"You cut your hair," Elkie said.

"No, I lost it. After—after the war. From delayed stress," she added. "And—how was your journey?"

"Long," Elkie said. She laughed. "Very long! But fantastic. Great people, incredible sights. At one stop a bunch of us took horse cabs and went to see where the Bolsheviks shot all those princesses." Her smoky eyes sparkled with surprising tears. "It really affected me."

Frightened girls raising white sleeves before averted faces: "Yes," Musya said. The sad history of the Romanov daughters tore something loose in her, too. Minutes passed. She and Elkie stood on the platform crying together. She thought of all they'd seen—they'd seen a lot together.

"Elkie! Elkie!" The children ran up, joyful but empty-handed; even Hodeh couldn't get a handcart in that crowd. "Where's Eidel?" Anton asked.

"In Moscow with someone else not me to pay for everything and hand wash her dirty underclothes. Please don't kill yourself, Anshel," Elkie added, at his wince-making shriek. "There are other women."

"Be quiet!" He dashed his extravagant bouquet to the concrete and began stamping on it, grinding the petals under his boot heels. "Everyone be quiet!"

Musya explained, "He planned a welcome song." Hodeh had stepped well back with the guitar he'd been practicing the Vesna theme on day and night.

"He can sing to me," Elkie said.

"No! Only her! Only her! I hate this place! I hate this train station!" Anton grabbed Musya around the waist, buried his face against her and wouldn't let go. The baby kicked his red curls with one foot through the wrappings and made a laughing sound. His brother sobbed at him: "Be quiet!" His foot gave Musya's a painful kick, mostly accidental. When she objected, Anton flung himself from her, showed everyone his longest face, and stalked away.

"He hasn't changed at all!" Elkie marveled.

She carried her own bags, none were light enough for the rest of them. The famous oil lamp was long gone. The views from the broad plank sidewalks were full of interest to the newcomer who shared her story as they went along. After Eidel she'd stayed in Moscow, mostly at factory jobs. She didn't like the routines there and had drifted around some, unable to settle on any situation. One day she heard people talking about the new Birobidzhan promotion and like a finger snap she'd remembered the city encircled by beehives and wheat fields and volcanoes that the Kotz boys had often talked about. Farming appealed to her more than a factory. To emigrate required hardly any outlay and minimal paperwork; seizing the advantage of some American charity dollar backing, the authorities were all eagerness to fill those long echelon trains, put a Jew in every seat. Although Elkie's echelon had included one very closed car said to be full of German fascist sympathizers rounded up in Ukraine, on their way to a detention kolkhoz improbably located somewhere in the Jewish Autonomous Region. Unsurprised, Musya drew her wrappings tighter around the sleeping baby. "Yes, it's still Siberia," she said. A fact Elkie called apparent from the temperature. In Moscow it had been a hot summer day not two weeks earlier. "Better the cold than the gnus," Musya told her emphatically.

Steps later Samuel Nemo dragged the party to a halt before the sparkling shop window at Start, their route's transfixing highlight. Here Birobidzhan equipped itself for physical culture. Arrangements of volleyballs and barbells and boxing gloves had been interspersed with hockey equipment and ice skates, snowshoes, skis and tinted goggles to eye-beguiling seasonal effect. It was true: if a person cared to look, the city abounded in winter athletes and sporting clubs and regulation skating rinks where all sorts of teams competed. Elkie made a pleased sound—she loved to watch hockey games. Birobidzhan impressed her more and more.

"You've got everything here," she said.

Musya agreed. "Including two cinemas now. By the way, have you seen Vesna?" She thought it was so good—really maybe a great artwork. Her family had seen it six times together. Shocking to hear, Elkie hadn't, not once. Her broad shoulders shrugged off the Kotz family's collective protest which even Anton rallied far enough to join. Elkie was unmoved:

"I don't care much for cinema, I never did. That was another complaint Eidel had about me. Oh, what a pretty autobus!"

More and more taken with her surroundings, the former housemaid regretted right away that her papers bound her for the land, perhaps far distant from the city; to the end she'd remain mystified by how many people greatly disliked Birobidzhan. With Yevrei inked inaccurately or not on her internal passport, however, some lucky Jewish kolkhoz would be feeling blessed quite soon when her arms were bared for action: so said Dovid when he hefted the bag-weight she'd managed.

Finally Musya's husband met a friend of his wife's he might have chosen as a friend on his own. He and Elkie had much in common, they shared the same kind of decency. As for women "like Elkie" who went with other women, Dovid in his experience had always found them to be admirable when sober. To Musya's relief both men in the flat kept up their best manners and their hands to themselves while the rest talked non-stop, an Obodovka ghetto reunion. By the time they were roaring with laughter over Anton's hoarded skull collection, Brother Dead Man had been shaking his head for an hour. No question, his faculties were on a downward slope. He kept saying, "You people went back to a primitive time there."

In the end, some kolkhoz Jews were out of luck and Elkie didn't need to care for cinema, because her path lay in the direction of the stage. She hadn't left the city yet when she fell for an actress with the State Yiddish Theater downtown who got behind her in a bread queue. Before a week was out they were sharing a room and Elkie was assisting the theater's house manager whose job she'd usurp within the year—she had ambition when she chose. The practice wasn't strictly permitted but Musya's family got many free tickets; after all, she only knew anything about show business because of them, Elkie said.

The problems people had in 1948 felt mostly like the usual at first. Normal joys, normal sorrows: sad things happened, not catastrophes. The war was behind them. In Musya's flat the new year caught the occupants weeping after Yuri turned up underneath a coal wagon in a shipping yard two stops down the Irkutsk line, their family friend and favorite artist, twenty-six years old and dead of exposure. He had some injuries Magga was told were post-mortem. She said his Nanai kin were blaming Moscow's baleful influence, they'd always blamed his ruin on his student days out west at that minorities of promise school—where indeed all his promise had been drawn out and stripped from him. Now he was dead.

The news did not surprise his people but they were taking it hard—everyone was, really. No one harder than Yuri's old patron and drinking companion, the balebos, whose wasted shoulders whipped from side to side with the force of his denial: never, he said, should the blame be put on higher education which had truthfully been Yuri's one chance at escape, a withered hope that had seen him return to Siberia and the early destruction that no man felt more closely than he, the so-called dead man on the chaise lounge. He lay there sobbing overstatements about how Yuri had been like a son to him, the only son he'd never deserted—like a last chance.

"The best of myself I could see in him," he claimed through sentimental tears. A last pure living unbroken bond had been severed by cruel misadventure; on the ground, left to freeze, the closest thing to his own flesh in the world had fed warehouse rats. One big misshapen arthritic fist pounded his sternum: "Our warehouses! Our rats! Our disgusting way of life—we Soviets, we pioneers—men of progress—Ack-a-Ack! What men like me did to Siberia killed him. He should have stayed as far away as he could get."

"There's nothing wrong with progress," Dovid said.

Musya said yes, this was true. She sat comforting children bereft of their friend; whose fault or why, she said, no one could tell them for sure. "You know sad things keep happening. It's just a normal part of life."

The Last Good Almost Year, people would name it, remembering tunes, dresses, pleasures; memorializing its cinema outings and picnics and climbs on the Sopka. The last months of comforting possibilities. In Birobidzhan a synagogue had opened; there was even talk of a Jewish cemetery again. And everywhere talk upon talk about science, in every field of which gigantic leaps were being announced constantly: 1948, so they were told, wouldn't recognize 1968 if this pace kept up; while in atom-powered centuries to come their Earth might have become one great radiant harbor in a blue-black sea of intersecting star routes. Where would governments be, where would world leaders be then? What rankled or overweened today was destined for irrelevance; the worst burdens wore their expiration dates up front. Chances were, people said, the present generation would live to see improvements beyond everyday hopes. They should look for things like miracles to mark the years left them and all their children's futures.

All winter, long after Novyi God, people toasted the future. Colored scarves still draped the lampshades. Couples come to dance crowded into smoky rooms, some swaying in night-long embraces even when their ears were full of swing. Close heat: at times every head ended up sweat-soaked, some bare scalp showing through. Musya got a fugitive satisfaction seeing it happen—they were all the same then.

Wet fringe in stripes, fast-pumped bosom largely exposed as usual, Vera sat working a Chinese sandalwood fan with self-defeating vigor. An unannounced guest, she'd been asked to leave Birofeld but planned to fight it, when she was less exhausted. The complaints she'd left off a few numbers ago when asked onto the dance floor resumed:

"I will tell you what it is—their pathetic success in this ocean of failure out here has turned them reactionary. Socialism is dead in Birofeld."

Even to hear her story was exhausting. Months back, handsome Matis had indeed brought his family to the relatively thriving kolkhoz where Vera lived with hers. No surprise: only shortly, in a twist, their passionate affair drove Vera's man into the arms of his rival's man-eating wife. Thus, suddenly, all four had found themselves much happier: like day and night, they'd agreed. The households had split and recombined, Vera's now-former man contracting amicably for their son to share his bunkhouse corner along with the Matis mother and her trio of young; he'd come from a large family himself and wished his son to benefit from the same experience. Reconciled after soul-ravaging motherhood pain to the sacrifice, Vera handed over the little boy right away and set to work creating a beautiful new household for two better soulmates. Reasonable and perfectly socialist as an arrangement, the swap was also perfectly clean and should have been fine. Instead the whole kolkhoz had met at the so-called House of Culture to cast a secret ballot. The result: she'd been censured and expelled—not Matis, nor the rest, who'd shared the censure; of course her innocent child could stay. Only Vera was out. That is, she might be out but planned on fighting to stay. First she and her crucified nerves required an immediate respite. She'd arrived at the flat with a black evening dress and pumps to match she pulled from a large briefcase that had some silken nightclothes in there, too.

Vera's briefcase sat beside her on the floor at the vecherinka. She hadn't left it at the flat because she might not be returning there tonight—it depended, she'd said. Matis, as it happened, hadn't volunteered to join his lover in exile, not immediately and not after a series of hints. He had a coarse unfeeling streak, Vera confessed.

"Last month when I was lying prostrated, literally fainting from grief at the news about Mikhoels, he called it an overreaction." This was the head of the Moscow State Yiddish Theater, Solomon Mikhoels, a great stage actor as well, in the late years of his prime, cut down in January by an auto crash in icy Minsk, his death a sad jarring shock in Yiddishland—yet also the occasion for a fine memorial show at the Birobidzhan State Yiddish Theater; Musya recalled a good night out and a good homecoming afterwards. Vera hadn't been able to persuade Matis to pay for seats. She'd restrained herself then. Now: "So be it. I will give him an overreaction." Mainly Vera wanted to forget things for a few hours, in a strange man's arms maybe, if fate so decided. She needed to feel like herself again, on the loose in a city again, even one so mean as Birobidzhan: "A free

Soviet woman, passionate about my nation's cultural life. Not the pariah of my peasant serf village." She slapped her fan against the table edge. "I ask you: How many kilometers to where the government has planted an entire town of Ukrainian Nazi sympathizers? But I meet a man and that makes me the problem to cast out—I am the one literally driven away, with all my belongings on my back. Please. Typical Birofeld beekeepers— all they do is fear women."

"You are probably right," Musya said, watching Dovid squeeze into view bearing fresh bottles and glasses. He'd looked unhappy for days. Vera peered around his hips into the jostling crowd; her last dance partner had pledged to return with something special for the two of them. Musya and Kitty unloaded the glassware from Dovid's arms and poured. He sat and frowned.

Vera said, "You have no fear of women, do you, Dovid?"

"Why not?" he answered. "A woman with destruction on her mind is a frightening thing." Another swallow; then he stood up, asked Kitty for another dance and walked away with her on his arm. They disappeared into a wall of cigarette smoke.

"There, you see." Vera flicked her fan after them. "Yours, too."

Musya murmured noncommittally and watched the dance partner emerge from behind Vera's shoulder to surprise her with champagne. Instant romance: the Leningrader had a talent, no question. Which left Musya to enjoy a comfortable pocket of solitude in the midst of an informal dress show to study. By the veiled pinkish light her trained eye noted hemlines and seams, fastenings and bias-cut fabrics, her tastes rejecting the girlishness of half the garments. Although not yet out of training, she kept an eye on her teaching career; in her view, even infant school teachers ought to have smart wardrobes and look like adults. Yet the women's styles these days flattered no one.

A pleasing progress check showed Vera's return to the flat looking unlikely to happen. Even so, Dovid remained a concern. For the moment he used every means to avoid Vera's company; but his sulk went deeper. World events had set him brooding again. This time the Soviet Union was throwing too much of its weight around Czechoslovakia. Matters like this really distressed him—he cared deeply about distant happenings. Why? Because he had plans of his own for those places, in fact for the entire world Dovid had plans. Sometimes Musya could only shake her head and sigh over how, with all her experience of the consequences, she'd wound up with another enthusiast, a full-throated utopian. Her husband dragged poor Czechoslovakia into every conversation. "Let's not be tyrannical," he'd said. The balebos had laughed at him.

"Why not? Why stop at misgoverning your own country when you can misgovern other people's countries at the same time? Why not the world? Why not the solar system?"

"But Dovid," she'd interrupted. "Czechoslovakia is in Europe. No matter what government, they have got better lives than Siberians. It just stands to reason—they have so much more there. History and telephones and paving and bridges." She watched his frown dig itself deeper.

He said, "That is not the point, you know?"

She didn't know. The heat of his concern for Prague mystified her without eroding her affection, indeed it might have added a peculiar luster as his goodness made her fond. Musya felt she was tending him like a family hearth or a fever victim until the coup d'état had passed. To be followed by the next upsetting crisis—and the next. She could see a long lifetime like this unfolding, decades of Dovid disliking the news and then getting sore at his wife and her trying to mollify him or else not bothering—as at present, when she'd let him dance the night away with the dvornik's daughter. Which was perfectly fine: Musya didn't begrudge Kitty the rare occasion to monopolize a man.

Kitty wouldn't have him when the lights were out.

The very back of Dovid's close-shorn head was flat like a dinner plate from birth, he said. She'd bury her fingertips in the dense black nap and let them range across his skull from ridge to plateau, nick to bump, all his shrapnel, like precious jewels to her. His hands, his tongue, his body licked hers like flames. In the forge of her body they'd started becoming another, becoming one. Again. Already, yes. The knowledge a dizzying aphrodisiac: this was the best pleasure, they remembered. Their flesh was crazed.

For Musya and her sister, too, she guessed, the fame of its State Yiddish Theater had always stood in for everything Birobidzhan lacked when compared with Odessa or anyplace civilized. Those who'd founded and built it had been ambitious for the Jewish patriots of Birobidzhan to re-create, even improve on what they'd left behind back home in real cities, and consequently come to be recognized, yes, for making their own vital contribution to Soviet culture. For a time, this had actually happened. The theater with its bright white façade had been an emblem of success as well as hope.

The youth troup auditions were packed as expected. A cold day at the theater, where inside a vaporous tent of human breath and stagelight sparkles milled a deeply competitive talent pool, also as expected, being a good part of School Number Two's well-trained and highly musical student body. Anton paced a tight figure eight in the center orchestra aisleand whispered through his spoken audition piece, an affecting excerpt from Y.L. Peretz. He'd let the moment decide the song, he knew dozens. Every few circuits he paused to tell Elkie in the fourth row that yes, the pit piano was far out of tune, which Elkie kept denying. Musya in the seat beside her thought the piano too quiet and muffled, that was its problem. The black-haired baby wrapped against her chest enjoyed it anyhow. Flexing pleasured limbs against her pregnancy Dovid's first son snuffled and vocalized along in an entertaining fashion: another musical comedy boy, Elkie said. Yes, a maker of happiness like his brothers and his father, Musya thought so.

"This theater was your mother's pride and joy," she reminded Anton.

"Yes, you told me already four thousand times," he said, pacing past. Elkie poured out more hot tea from a thermos as another unwelcome breeze reached them in his wake. Here, Elkie said, was one aspect of theatrical life she didn't care for:

"Too many nerves in it. Unnecessary nerves."

"But I always miss the nerves." Elkie's actress friend was sitting on her other side. "That's why I dread being out of work," she added.

"Anshel Kotz!" A woman's voice came jolting through a megaphone. "Anshel Kotz to the stage, please!"

Anton flew towards the call without a backward look at Musya who'd excitedly splashed tea and as a result spent his entire audition out in the lobby with a handful of snow packed in a handkerchief and pressed to a scalded forehead.

The baby's righteous tears rang deafeningly against the pretty wall tiles and plaster. Musya swayed, bounced, murmured, appreciating the details: Art Deco, she knew. As a young girl fresh from Odessa how she'd glamorized this theater for a time. To find such an elegant piece of incongruity planted here among the desperate mud-choked streets of frontier Siberia, as if the future had visited and left its pledge of loveliness to come; even now her spirits were boosted whenever she caught sight of its white façade gleaming in full sun. A style and place of daydreams. Musya smiled at herself: back then, in the days of her first marriage, she'd given half her time to picturing scenes not so different from today's reality; for here she was. As Elkie's friend she'd been backstage, onstage, at dress rehearsals, here an audition—a real habitué. She'd risen from her starting place to attain what she'd longed for. And for a few steps Musya floated, her mood enormously gratified.

An odd thought struck her then. What she'd just felt, that lift from an ancient goal achieved, must be what her husband sought from the Progress he loved to extoll. Only Dovid would establish this fleeting self-satisfaction on a world-wide and permanent scale. He'd satisfy humanity's finest heart-wishes non-stop. Too bad for the world he loved—also too bad for her husband—it couldn't be done. His destiny's obvious bent towards disappointment cast a melancholy light across Musya's steps as the baby wound down into hiccups. She patted, bounced, asked, "Were you jealous of your big brother?" Not a whisper came from inside the hall. Cold draughts penetrated the padlocked street doors. For a moment Dovid's high hopes saddened her: all high hopes saddened her. Poor Anton today, with a heart set on stardom. Musya knew how that turned out.

A roar of voices, applause, whistles and cheering stopped her cold.

Here was a twist: the audition she hadn't seen would be conveyed by those who had into Yiddish theater lore, they promised. Elkie was still crying her eyes out over Bontshe Shvayg's forgotten grave.

"He's so lucky," the actress kept telling Musya. "You're so lucky—he'll always work!"

Anshel Kotz got the part and a place in the youth troupe, naturally—but this was just for starters. Brilliant careers were launched from such auditions. For now it seemed like fate: the male juveniles being cast would be needed on the summer tour to Khabarovsk. The play, by Peretz Markish, the Yiddish poet, was Ufshtand in geto—Uprising in the Ghetto.

(10)

A child's hand prodded her awake. Musya blinked: almost dawn, not yet spring. Hodeh stood by the bed with her stricken expression resembling burn marks on a blouse in the half light. Her voice shook and fluted oddly:

"He's dead. Brother Dead Man woke up dead."

"How?" Musya fumbled for eyeglasses. "He can't be!"

Yet how ridiculous she sounded! The old balebos had outlived every prediction; still, he wasn't immortal. The last doctor to see him had said exactly this, he'd wake up dead, and soon, if he didn't alter his habits drastically, stop liquefying his brain with samogon. In fact by then his alcohol intake had plummeted, but only because of how fast downhill his mind was slipping—it took less and less to knock him out. Every so often he'd regain enough lucidity to cancel everyone's awareness of his notable decline, which kept surprising them in consequence. His death came as another such surprise.

The night before he woke up dead hadn't offered any hint that the end was nearer than before. A normal evening, the family gathered over dinner plates before music lessons, the tarelka tuned to Tchaikovsky hour, the balebos supine with his face to the forest wall, his stare more or less wild-eyed as he watched the brushstrokes for movement. He spotted some and cried out periodically; this wasn't unusual by then. Partner to his gaze, his thoughts dwelt on wilderness. Strange regrets first voiced at Yuri's death tormented him for the large part he'd played in rendering Birobidzhan inhabitable. He groaned.

"We ruined Siberia."

He'd be dead the next day but none of them knew it then. Dovid called across the room at him good-humoredly: "Who ruined Siberia? You and who else?"

"We filled Siberia with Lenin's lies. Those were the orders. Then the new lies started coming in."

Dovid said, "What lies? What's ruined about it? Siberia seems fine to me."

The dead man's voice wept. "We filled Siberia with our stinking lies and destroyed a holy land. The last pure land."

"There's plenty left," Dovid said.

"Lies and more lies. And then Jews." The dead man's voice droned. "Like the lies weren't enough. What were we thinking? Trainload after trainload—lies and Jews. Like we were trying to exterminate the place."

Dovid's head overheated at this juncture and his final words to the balebos consisted of a barracks-room curse. It wasn't the worst fight they'd had but he blamed himself for the bowel rupture, maybe more than one, that killed the dead man while they slept. It was an unlovely death to say the least. When the bloody and malodorous results were exposed to electric light, what sprawled on the chaise lounge drew shrill heartsick noises from the terrified children. Their four-fold heaving distress besieged Musya's arms where she sat perched among them, awkward with pregnancy, her attempts at comfort muffled by the scarf she had to hold across her nose and mouth. "But after everything you've seen!" Cat fur invisible when she swept lay everywhere on the green and gray kilim. The rise of a fretful cry sent a guilt-stricken Dovid back into their bedroom where his baby son had just stopped sleeping through. She kissed the children's heads. "This isn't so bad, don't be upset. It's not so bad." The cats who'd backed into crouches on the higher shelves to hiss and growl hair-raisingly, they disagreed, she supposed; or maybe they knew better.

The balebos would be missed. Many mourned him. Musya's loving children had made him despite all odds a grandfather figure in the home, difficult to lose. She and Dovid missed something more indefinable, like a piece of equipment they'd used to steer by that had gone and left them prey to uncertainty and drift. Others mourned likewise as around the city the loss of his authority sank in. Who would tell their past and future to them now? Birobidzhan had lost a foundation stone, as some eulogist put it. And with the dead man went his informants far and near, his golden connections. He left his circle in a place of ignorance—the swamps might as well have returned to reclaim the scenes around them.

To the rooming house he'd built came dramatic changes. Magga had run everything for years but only as his agent. His primacy proved unassailable and as long as he lived, she was on top. His death left his dvornik unprotected. Within a week she was summoned for questioning. A man at a desk downtown behind a numbered door, every-thing very anonymous, no names anywhere, not even the place was named. Kitty wasn't allowed inside, she waited for her mother in the street. Magga said the man told her there'd been anonymous reports. They accused her of war-time malfeasance, ration fraud. She denied everything for six hours until he let her go. Downstairs she collapsed into Kitty's arms and begged for cigarettes. She had to smoke a few before she could walk to the autobus stop. By the time they got home, she was enraged. Her face had gone from red to raw meat purple in a permanent way. Nothing about the incriminating report was anonymous to Magga: she knew.

She said, "It was the cheap furriers." From turning small profits in a close room above the smoking parlor on cut-rate fur coats and ushanka, the Ossetians there had organized themselves a faction in the rooming house. At times they'd tried to make some trouble for the balebos but nothing had stuck. Now the restive faction had become a force opposing Magga for control. Who else would have reported it, that she'd fed her tenants Nanai-supplied protein while their meat ration points went straight to the black market trade? Unhelpfully, some truth lay behind the accusation: "But what could I buy?" Magga said. "The war took everything!" That the Ossetians got their raw furs from the same Nanai was a maddening irony. It also meant she couldn't report them in return without implicating herself further. She said, "They have my leg in a trap."

She half intended to disappear up north before the third summons could reach her. The second interrogation had been longer and more grueling than the first. The man wanted names: Magga's partners in the fraud; her suppliers and buyers; her fellow dvorniks doing the same, committing the same crime against socialism. But the names the man wanted he already had, he kept reading them at her, again and again, until confusion took over. Released this second time she'd collapsed on the cold ground one step from the unmarked building. For an hour after she regained consciousness she could only howl at the pain in her ear; for the man had come out from behind his desk and hit her with an oblast bureau directory. After that she'd gone so far as to pack a bag with clothes and inquire about transport. According to her contacts among the market stalls, the ice fishing camps along the northern forest rivers were recruiting, she could have gone within a day. But to leave her daughter felt impossible. The dilemma was that Kitty didn't want to go with her, not now, not when the city had almost become an entertaining place to live. And to sit all day among women cleaning fish: no. She said her mother ought to go north alone.

Hoping to persuade, Magga hesitated too long. Next she was arrested and taken to a different, well-known building downtown to await trial in a holding cell that grew crowded with dvorniks in the days to follow. There'd been some kind of sweep. Eventually the whole group was sentenced as one, in bulk: fifteen years at hard labor, enough for their venal and reactionary urges, the last gasp of the landlord class, to be driven out of them. The verdict report expressed the further hope that this piece of dirty social order's cleansing might finally admit the realization of long-delayed plans to modernize and vastly expand Birobidzhan's housing stock—insufficient to say the least, with conditions ever more abysmal in the giant half-rotten log dormitories that still loomed over too much of its north bank streetscape. With the sludge of wreckers and diversionists rinsed away, the gears of Progress could turn now; so read the brief half-column which otherwise contained no details of either evidence or crime. All the accused had confessed. There could be no appeal. The oblast's newest convicts were off to the Arctic Circle and the most anyone could do was load Magga with every bit of tobacco she could carry after bribing a guard for the chance to exchange stunned farewells. At every attempt to do more, even to learn what was happening, Dovid and Musya and Magga's friends around the city, her daughter above all were told, warned, threatened, depending on the personality in charge, that it was a risky business they'd undertaken. And everyone they approached for advice told them the same thing: help would be hard to come by. For who would care? The Dvorniks' Trial wasn't anything special, it was just the kind of thing that happened, a normal event.

Back at the rooming house, the power struggle turned too unequal to last. Magga's side was weak and steadily demoralized, the Ossetians ascendant. They'd taken charge and removed Kitty from the housing committee before her mother even went to trial. By then, many tenants welcomed the furriers and their replacement dvornik to power. It was nothing personal against Magga and her daughter who'd been there for life; only a time had come and gone. Having no one to enforce the rules of the rooming house brewed disorder. Self-government didn't suit the place. Especially the honor system was a poor substitute for how a neighbor's infraction could become currency in a roiling hallway trade of threats to "tell the dvornik," as like Soviets everywhere the tenants competed for every speck of living space and comfort, any miniscule advantage. This was their normal life the majority wanted again.

It was either the worst cruelty or a saving grace that the charge against Magga left her daughter out of it. There'd have been no surprise in seeing them go as a pair: family groups were common in what people called the gulag, Siberia's prison camp system. The dvornik might have kept her daughter as a comfort; but Kitty was spared. She returned from Khabarovsk where her mother's trial had been held to find a one-day eviction notice on their old quarters and the kitchen locks already changed against her. Homeless, essentially orphaned and now illegally unemployed—where else could she go but into the front room lately shared by the balebos? Where Musya had once more been determined to preserve the vacancy; her family was growing. But they had to move the furniture again and clear out half the front armoire to house the contents of Magga's old icon closet that her daughter had pledged to honor and maintain. They didn't hesitate to welcome Kitty. Except that they now spent half their lives helping re-hang the bed curtain she favored, the one the cats kept pulling to the floor, really, the family joked, she'd always spent so much time in the flat that the difference with her residing there was slight.

Again Dovid offered his contacts at the sewing factory, this time to more avail: an inventory job with tasks and hours allowed by Kitty's hernia was hers. She enjoyed factory work to a degree that surprised everyone, Kitty included. With her contribution, the little household which pooled its resources enjoyed a thriving period: fortunate, since Magga was gone and none of them cooked, so they bought everything downtown at the Gastronom delicatessen.

Under Hodeh's instruction Kitty became a keen backgammon player. She even started to learn a few beginner's pieces on Dovid's mother-of-pearl-inlaid clarinet. A happier outcome for the dvornik's daughter might not have been possible, for her sorrows were so extreme. Her mother had been everything to her, meant everything. The two women had done everything for each other, all Kitty's years before and since the war. Magga's death would have been the gravest loss to her; but it would have been better than this, they all realized it. An anguish kept fresh by fearful surmise, imagining the worst, never knowing: How was her mother? Stiff jointed, small, old, half-deaf, what was her body undergoing right now? What privation, what pain? Was she feverish? Was she begging for mercy?

"Yes," Musya remembered. Where she'd sat and comforted her children after Yuri and all through the dawn the dead man went, she sat again, one arm around Kitty who drank more than was good for her sometimes. It was only natural. Her heaving sobs buffeted Musya, hugely pregnant, and rocked her passenger—he and Kitty bonded early and would always be close. Musya remembered her mother's work table standing bloodstained in the little yard. She remembered heaving guilt-ridden sobs. "I know exactly what you mean. It is terrible," she said.

(11)

A printer's artifice circled Golda Myerson's face in a crowd of fifty thousand Jewish men pressing close to surround her outside Moscow Choral Synagogue. On October 4, 1948, the foreign minister from Israel—the first minister from the new nation of Israel, that is, born in Kiev—had shown up there for Rosh Hashana services. Alone in a sea of men and black overcoats: Musya marveled at the pleasure in the woman's smile. "I am so glad I don't have her job," she said, handing back the newspaper.

Elkie said, "Me, too. Not interested."

"Oh, I would not mind it," Kitty said. Elkie's actress friend said nor would she:

"Travel the world, the best hotels, dress up, get treated like royalty, never pay for anything." The actress was a small slim brunette of unknown age, a Yiddish theater professional and former wartime evacuee who'd played secondary ingénues in several Tashkent Film Studio comedies; no one in Birobidzhan recognized her exactly but the circumstance lent her an undeniable fascination.

"Their own limousines and drivers," Kitty was eager to agree. "And the power."

"Oh, the power, definitely," said the actress. She'd come along with Elkie to see Musya's new baby and to practice holding him. This was a serious actress, always training to improve on stage. A young mother betrayed would cradle so; a conscience-stricken nursemaid elsewise. The baby had yawned and burbled, a willing prop. Now he nursed in Musya's arms. His one year-old brother was fast asleep in the box crib, the other children were at school, and the four young women sat talking pleasantly in comfortable Russian. Indeed it was pleasant to sit at home and entertain guests from the theater, that entrancing world.

"Any news about the orchestra? Will it be coming back?" Kitty asked hopefully. She'd become a frequent user of the family's free seats since two babies kept Musya more housebound than one ever had. Kitty loved seeing musical plays but the house piano on its own gave things a meager, jangly aspect. Sad to say, the public were stuck with it. The theater's budget wouldn't cover pit musicians.

"Siz farbei, gone for good." The actress, who'd lost half her acting colleagues in the same budget cuts, wasn't too enthusiastic about the upcoming schedule. A Russian troupe had recently been organized at the State Yiddish Theater to help it counteract its own nationalist tendencies. In practice this involved a drastic reduction in stage time for the Yiddish troupe, which at half-strength remained overworked. The actress thought there might be one or two choral solos in the upcoming 150 Years of Pushkin program that Anshel could get (he wouldn't, he'd be stuck in the chorus): "But nothing for me, nebekh. Pushkin is so old hat anyhow," she added with a sigh. "I proposed we tour our Mikhoels tribute gala for the region, really as artists in Yiddish theater this is our duty—but no. Refused by management."

"You will have other chances." Kitty consoled; but as Musya well knew, the dvornik's daughter was far from sorry to hear that the Birobidzhan State Yiddish Theater would be performing even more plays in Russian this season—in fact even more than in Yiddish with which she struggled. "It is a shame about your tribute to that actor, though. I liked your number in it," Kitty added with more sincerity. "And that simple way they recited the traffic accident report from Kiev at the end—you could hear people crying."

The actress said ney. "Minsk. Do not believe those lies we're forced to tell. Shloime Mikhoels was murdered."

A shrill horrified gasp escaped the samovar stand where the Cossack girl lingered forgotten, fixated, moth-like before their company's sophistication. The rest made quick signals at the actress to hush and then sat mum. Fortunately the Ossetians had kept Magga's Cossack girl on staff as their new dvornik's helper, a sensible measure that paid hidden dividends to the occupants of Musya's flat, since the girl retained all her former loyalties—unless they were kidding themselves. Who could be sure? She might have gone over to the furriers completely for all they knew; she might have been planted there all along. Except that she appeared utterly simple, open and guileless, certainty was impossible.

Kitty slipped into her former house committee head manner. "You can go now, Katerilena. You shouldn't spend too much time in here."

"Yes, Tovarisch," said the Cossack girl with a hasty bow. She exited.

"That one seems okay," the actress remarked. Elkie chided her in the voice of experience:

"You should never trust any. Not one. All girls tell. They do it to get things extra for themselves. What else? This is human nature."

Kitty nodded sadly. "Even at the front, we always told."

"What a bleak outlook!" laughed the actress.

Musya asked, "But what about the murder? Who murdered Mikhoels?"

"Who do you think?" Elkie said.

Kitty snorted softly. She didn't think and didn't care, she said, adding, "Girl or no girl, this is an unfit subject for conversation."

Musya disagreed. "I don't know," she told Elkie. "Who?" Same reply. Who did she think had done it? Musya found herself blaming backstage osmosis for the stubborn new will to mystify that altered her old friend's verbal physiognomy. She'd never sounded like a bad play before. The actress was no help, she was keeping blank-faced. Her own curiosity getting duller by the second, Musya tried a final time. "Really—who did it?" At which Elkie made her eyes round as eggs and leaned forward to grip Musya's gaze with her own. What was this?

"Mental telepathy," Elkie said. "Thought transfer."

"Oh. Oh."

"I miss seeing musical shows," Kitty complained. "If only the actors on stage could play instruments like in the children's troupe."

"We are not children," said the actress.

The problem with America was inequality, the gulf between rich and poor which was due entirely to one factor: the rich had extra money to put towards land speculation. The amount of wealth that flooded the property markets whenever capitalism was working especially well for the rich was the poor masses' big problem; for under such conditions, under the guise of one land boom or bonanza or other, nothing remained affordable. Each United State was a bleaker nightmare than the last over there for a poor man with a white skin and how much worse for the poor Negroes and native Indians couldn't be calculated. Then religion combined with technologies of culture to keep a largely mythical bourgeoisie hypnotized and render it politically impotent. The whole society was rotten, Dovid said.

Sender Kotz breathed impatiently. "But answer the question! If you could wake up there tomorrow and stay for good, in America, would you do it?"

"With my family."

"Yes, we established that already."

"Forgive me, please," Dovid said. "I apologize if my question served to keep you from more important imaginary business." Obviously stalling; yet it was a tricky hypothetical. Musya sympathized. She was ironing trousers and holding a baby at the same time: also tricky. The laundry didn't press hard enough at a time when Dovid needed flawless creases plus no other cause for reproach, not at a time like this when a search appeared to be on for excuses to fire Jews. To date, probably because he was a Fatherland War veteran, he'd only been demoted, knocked from his desk job down to the tractor shop floor where the line workers out-earned him. He struggled with the change and his popularity slipped when he faced accusations of problem-solving where no problem existed. He'd been required to denounce himself in a semi-public meeting which had stung badly. Dovid expected the trend to blow over, a brief phase of a sort endemic to industry. Simply put, because they'd always been the biggest leaders and organizers, Jews got kicked out the door first. It was always temporary. No one could get along without them. With a baby gurgling against her shoulder in its sleep, Musya wished she felt so confident. A big healthy family took a lot of care.

She volunteered: "I would do it. Wake up in America."

Her family laughed because of course she would, according to their favorite joke of 1949 so far—the one she'd given them, when upon hearing the phrase for the first time she'd exclaimed at how well it fit her, really glove-like. *"Rootless cosmopolitan! That's me!"* Flooded by a sense of belonging that she couldn't recall from her lifetime before, she'd wondered where to meet them, these others of her own kind, other rootless cosmopolitans—the newest vilest enemy among the Soviet People, as Musya was entirely unaware (this being the joke, of course) because she didn't follow political wall news very closely.

"It is a wonder we have kept you here this long," Dovid said. On the quiet, he'd been exploring his options should conditions get worse before they improved. One of his Jewish veteran friends worked as a cement factory foreman upriver at the new Teploye Ozero settlement but had lately decided that enough Soviet civilization was enough: he was heading off to trap furs in the northern forests, a solitary life. The friend had offered to recommend Dovid for his empty place but no one in the family could tolerate the idea of leaving the city, Dovid included. Even so, he said, "I would like to go off alone and live as a fur trapper."

"Well, you can't," Musya said. "You cannot go off alone and live as a fur trapper."

Sender said, "No, she is right. America or nothing. America or the same?"

"Don't rush me," Dovid said.

Days before its annual mid-winter regional tour, the Birobidzhan State Yiddish Theater received a deep repertory cut. With its playwright the poet Markish currently behind bars, Ufshtand in geto was out. Sadly, it was political prison; but people thought he might make it through in one piece because he was so innocent and also famous.

The development struck a blow to Musya and her family's plans by losing their resident juvenile his biggest role by far—six lines plus unison shouting with other Jewish prisoners in revolt against fascist tyranny; no mere walk-on. Should Anton even bother going on the tour now? He might be better off staying at home; between Dovid's music lessons and the excellent choral instruction and touring program at School Number Two, his development might even be hastened that way. But it would also mean everyone else staying home, stuck at winter's dullest point in a two-room flat that four children, two babies, four or five cats and three grown adults were sharing; it would mean feeling cramped. Over the last year, traveling with Elkie's help as parent-chaperones on some of the youth troupe's many tour appearances around the oblast, the married couple and Kitty too had gotten used to perforating time with distance and variety. More air had been getting in than would now. And for Musya there'd be many fewer chances to enjoy adding to the string she'd started keeping in a sort of hidden pocket, another precious instance of solitude.

Meanwhile from Elkie's point of view the decision to cut like this appeared a poor one. Ufshtand in geto was a top crowd-pleaser, never failing to bring them to their feet out on the kolkhozes—no easy achievement in spots where malnutrition reigned. At present the order called for comedy straight down the line on this tour; nothing but comedies, the lighter the better, in Russian if possible.

Dovid barked a sarcastic laugh. "Russian comedies! They're really going to love that out at the Lion of Judah farm."

"They will probably be changing the name," Musya said helplessly. She felt trouble threatening a downpour. Was it to be as the balebos had predicted after all? Tears overcame her. "Those plays were our life stories, Jewish lives—this is a murder of us! A new murder! What is happening? Is this happening again?"

Dovid shook his head and reached to take her in his arms. "This is a couple of ministers doing this." He was angry. "A couple of over-reaching pricks."

Elkie said he was probably right.

Anton never toured again. His parents were sorry. The lost performers in them both had relished the arrivals in far-flung locales; the tractor rides between roadsides and illuminated barns; the making up in old foil-glass mirrors behind curtains sewn from mismatched blankets as the hidden public enters on a tide of talk.

As for kolkhoz life in general, the couple might as well have been visiting different planets. Where Musya saw poverty and isolation producing uncouth young, where she saw adults crushed into silence and premature debility, Dovid saw Jews, a proud unbroken people, heroic, shrugging off privation, Jewish patriots in their own proud homeland—a place truly as predicted by critics the most important guardian of the Jewish national culture. If sometimes they seemed indifferent or half-dead, he argued, the cause was no secret: killer fascists had ravaged their lives, stripped them of loved ones and scattered those who survived to the four winds. Still, they endured. The countryside was looking better and better to him, Dovid said.

Meanwhile the silent endurance he perceived among the Jewish kolkhozes moved him and caused Dovid's religious physiognomy to come more into view just at the worst time. He made a show of the many hours he'd spent downtown at the Sholem Aleichem Library reading the huge mass of material on Jews in the Large Soviet Encyclopedia. He developed an interest in public ritual and only Musya's staunchest refusals kept the family from claiming seats at the new synagogue. Which was fortunate since everyone who attended its next Rosh Hashanah services wound up arrested and charged with trea-sonous Jewish nationalism; if any survived being shot, they were luckier than their rabbi.

Musya and Dovid's friends began to spend a lot of time hushing him, saying to be careful. It wasn't only that his sons were circumcised (plenty had the skill in Birobidzhan although none offered prayers) or that he wanted Sender Kotz at thirteen to prepare for the bar mitzvah which Sender dreaded and would finally manage to avoid. It was that Dovid considered a Jewish people to be something real that existed and should exist, under protection if necessary, in a homeland. This belief was improper now. Like the beloved Yiddish plays none of them would ever see again, Musya's husband put too much national emphasis on the problems of everyday life—so went the verdict at the plant when his work performance was next evaluated at another, bigger meeting. Once again they hadn't fired him; but Jews were nothing special and neither really were war veterans, he was told to remember these points. The rest went unsaid. Even if Dovid could manage to keep his mouth shut, his future in agricultural machinery looked grim.

Her sex life satisfied her, yes. Their sex life, she meant; as Dovid shifted in his chair beside her. He didn't like this medical worker any more than she did. From the mono-tone probing, the pale eyes that never left the questionnaire, the absence of any expression save for the little leaping eyebrow shows of doubt, Musya diagnosed a toxic blend of Jew-hatred and bone-weariness. The noisy corridor outside was mobbed. The last echelon trains had continued to bring far fewer able-bodied workers than invalids and babies and pregnant women to Birobidzhan: "This is what people are talking about," the medical worker had grumbled. What kolkhoz on earth could afford to feed so many mouths surplus to labor? The strains on the medical worker as well were evident. With too many women to quiz and not enough variety among the answers, boredom also resulted. One hand left the clipboard to mask a yawn.

She heard Dovid raise his voice:

"The answer to that question is none of your fucking business."

"What question?" she asked.

"What sexual activities we do in bed together."

"Yes, we are not going to tell you that," she agreed.

The medical worker's flat voice was edged like a saw. "And you have three four five six other children." This was already answered so the couple sat motionless. Here was their dilemma: they had too many children to add another just yet. They'd needed prophylactics but couldn't get them. Now they needed an abortionist. The medical worker glanced up at their silence and then flipped to the end of the survey, not even bothering. "Based on my medical judgment, you people could try to exercise a little self-control sometimes."

"You should watch your language," Dovid said flatly. "And show some respect. My wife is only four children away from being a Mother Heroine, you know?"

"You do realize those awards are intended for Russian women?" Of course they did. The couple sat waiting. At last the medical worker sighed. "I wish I could help you."

Dovid reached into his coat and pulled out savings. "I heard this would be enough."

The medical worker counted, said it would do, then scribbled a note and address on a notepad, tore off the sheet, folded and handed it across to Musya. "This place is clean and fairly modern."

"It had better be clean," Dovid said.

The medical worker grinned and told him to relax. "Time for you to get a hobby, Tovarisch."

She'd walked past the building a thousand times and never known what happened there. What was it like? A terribly long wait on the staircase but otherwise not such a bad experience, she'd have told someone. She had no one to tell, no friends close enough. Dovid didn't want to talk about it. He hadn't been entirely convinced of the need and afterwards the loss of another son or the little daughter he sorely wanted weighed on his paternal heart. The couple kept the whole thing from Kitty and the children, blamed a bad hemorrhoid, and remained uneasy.

Musya felt in a hurry to finish her much maternity-delayed teacher training. She had her two boys by Dovid in a day crèche and was readying herself for exams. Not that she wanted to begin teaching infants—nor did she need to, really. The demand for infant school teachers had never grown so urgent as predicted at the time she'd enrolled. Now, with Dovid's blessing, partly because it would always pay more, she was determined to continue training at the normal school for a composition teacher's post. This idea still drew her, she explained to the registrar. The hard part had been getting the meeting with this busy personage and Musya didn't anticipate trouble over her new plan of studies. She felt a calling to teach composition, she said.

The normal school registrar replied, "We are not accepting any more Jewish nationality students into those classes, Tovarisch."

Musya stared. "You are not?"

"No."

"But." Musya's disappointment was extreme. "But I have been published. A school poem of mine was included in a major anthology."

"Nevertheless."

She floundered for a moment. "Do you have this in writing? Is it an order?"

"Do you want me to write it down for you?" asked the registrar.

"Something else then," Musya said with heat. "What other programs are open?"

"To Jewish nationality students?" The registrar picked up a piece of paper, looked it over, and put it down again. "None."

Musya said, "Since when? I have been a student here for years."

"Yes. In which time you have completed five courses."

"Six," she insisted.

"Five," said the registrar. "Don't worry, you will be credited with six. You will receive your certificate. And then you will go find some infants to teach. There is still a need."

Sitting there, unprepared to change her future, Musya cast frantically through what she remembered of her classwork, lectures, readings, for anything of aid. Her eye fell on the office wall and there she got it. She gestured at the Most Profound Theoretician of Contemporary Times, the Coryphaeus of Science and the white cliff of his sweeping brow. "But don't you think there might be some mistake? He said it himself, that anti-Semitism is the most vicious hangover of cannibalism."

The registrar nodded. "I believe he would know. But my opinion doesn't matter. And there is no mistake, Tovarisch."

"None?" Musya asked. A little hope stirred. "I mean, if it is money you want."

"I am sorry, but no." The fingers of two tired hands met and locked on the registrar's desk. "This is only our world today."

Half-past two in the morning, another arrest, happening across the road where the better flats were. People slept poorly this summer of 1949, they lay awake and listened for the black cars instead. When one came along and god forbid stopped, they peeked outside unless fear held them paralyzed between the covers. The same insomnia had to be striking all over the Soviet Union these months. A new sweep, on a grand scale this time, a massive round-up targeted the rootless cosmopolitans. Thanks to the men at the top, they've been found out in their treasonous campaign to drip poison into the sense organs of Soviet culture, sowing degeneracy, nurturing division, and collecting nefarious rewards from capitalist American hands along the way—this was the story. Unmasked, the villains turned out to be intellectual Jews, for the most part, including editors of

Yiddish-language literary magazines and their contributors in Birobidzhan and elsewhere. Now whole mastheads were under arrest.

In these dark hours, the city also lost lecturers, scientists, institute heads, educators of all sorts, along with their school registrars. State administrators up and down the ranks were targeted as well. The Jewish Autonomous Region's Jewish leadership evaporated into the back seats of black police cars. Doors slammed on protests, on women's tears, the howls of children dulled by engine noise rising, wheels on the road again, leaving— the end of terror felt so sweet and rotten.

From the pillow next to Musya's came a grunt, then speech. "They would have taken your first husband the genius by now, if he was still around."

"What?" She whispered. "What are you talking about, Dovid?"

"You know," he said. "A scientist, a well-educated man, a proud Jew—that's who they come after. The proud Jewish brain workers."

"He was not," she started, stopped. *They wouldn't*, might be closer to the truth, Musya thought, when she considered Boris Kotz, Correspondent. Would he have been suggesting new names to the authorities this time around—again? She said, "Dovid, you're being very silly, please go to sleep."

He said, "I am only saying, good thing for you, Tovarisch, you wound up with a lowly guy like me."

"Yes, I feel grateful all the time." An answer meant more sincerely than it sounded, she realized as his silence lengthened. But shouldn't Dovid know this without her needing to explain? She kept quiet and so did he until sleep found them.

After Elkie's arrest Musya was furious with herself.

She'd been here before. She knew that working at the Birobidzhan State Yiddish Theater carried the risk of a long term in political prison. No chance of forgetting with Sender's friend odd Mendel and his sister always around. Ten years since their father had made the leap from stage design to gulag, never to return; their mother came back mad, she was another who'd worked at the theater.

Yet not one syllable of warning had Musya uttered in Elkie's ear. Instead, swept along, she'd let life alone to suffuse itself with color and interest. Now every choice was a regret for which Musya blamed her own selfishness. Serve tea to actresses and go backstage, go places, tour, meet performers, see new faces, attend the occasional after-show veche-rinka at someone's flat with wild jokes and sing-a-longs: yes, all this was worth something. But it wasn't worth a friend like Elkie, who took the fun in life with her when she was gone; for good this time, leaving the entire flat aghast, they barely spoke about it, only in broken phrases, through tears, wincing. No one saw Elkie again after she left for the September tour run in Khabarovsk. Her co-workers at the theater would be getting arrested up until November when the Council of Ministers finally released the liquidation order and the whole place closed; but Elkie was already tried and convicted by then, pulled off the street in Khabarovsk and sentenced to hard labor for crimes against the state including foreign espionage. A few much-censored postcards were all that would ever come from her, they stopped within a year. Disappeared at the same time, her friend the actress was said to be a suicide but Musya didn't believe anything these days, Dovid said not to.

Gone were eager looks down the road at the white façade in sun. Musya kept her eyes averted, and hurrying from the sight of its boarded-up doors wearing the padlocks and chains of an outlawed joy, she'd notice others practicing the same avoidance. They tried to ward off or simply minimize depression any way they could, now that the State Yiddish Theater wasn't around to help them be happy or optimistic at will; each one had lost a kind of personal talisman. Once an emblem of success and hope, now people couldn't stand the sight of it. A dangerous, dangerous place to work, its vacancy filled the former audience with grief and superstitious dread and nervous anxiety. Here again had been seen, again, what sometimes becomes of the housemaids and the house managers, the bit players and secondary ingénues, sweepers and pit pianists: their insignificance protects them, until it doesn't.

The State Yiddish Theater's liquidation left its most promising male juvenile talent at the end of a string of more and more widely spaced steppingstones, denied a chance at the landmark role his audition had seemed to foretell. Instead Anshel Kotz never left the youth troupe, where he'd long been losing stage time to the Russian juveniles. Now they were all out of work, now it was back to the daily grind of a dull Soviet childhood. Just when he was inconsolable, Anton's bad luck continued. His beloved School Number Two underwent a major management change when its leaders who'd accepted American charity dollars got slapped with treason charges. Pedagogy would now be conducted in Russian, no exceptions. He and Hodeh would struggle academically after this. Even worse, the Jewish holidays were out with the Yiddish language at school. The boys' choral Kol Nidre so polished in practice would never be performed; there'd be no more Chanukah pageants, no more pageant solos, no red velvet trousers anymore. Destined for legend only to remain a might-have-been, Anton's stage career didn't survive.

Still, he could perform at home. Musya loved the way he picked guitar. But on this particular night she found her enjoyment spoiled because his brother Samuel Nemo was late for music lesson. This represented a severe infraction. Ensemble today: Dovid on snare drum and harmonica was leading the rest through one of his own arrangements of an old jazz foxtrot she loved. Hodeh fiddled, Kitty shrilled and Sender coaxed a faltering accompaniment from the handsome but wheezy bayan, a recent night market find. The cacophonous first run-through shook the walls less than usual in the absence of horns: at seven still the littlest in the band, Pretzel had the most lung power.

So Musya had been waiting for him to come through the door when instead she found herself hurrying to answer a stranger's knock. He wore a tall ushanka and a well-maintained overcoat. At his side stood the missing musician with paper ash in his hair, her son who smelled like a gasoline fire. So did the stranger.

"What happened?" said Musya. The stranger had a lot of metal in his smile. Removing his hat, he asked her not to be alarmed, then proffered congratulations: her little boy showed every sign of growing into a fine young Soviet. She ought to be proud. "Did he burn something down?" she asked.

"Who's there?" This was Dovid. The music had stopped. "What's going on?"

"It's Pretzel. He's with a man."

"Just a friendly stranger," the man stood on his toes to explain across her head. "I met your boy at the book burning."

"At the what?"

"I'll take care of this, Dovid," she said. He couldn't afford any trouble. She took a brighter tone with the stranger to ask, "Was that today?" In fact she'd heard something of the kind might be planned but she'd refused to think about it. More terrifying politics—she wasn't interested. She listened now with reluctance to the stranger's eye-witness account. A bonfire had been built from every Yiddish book and piece of Yiddish printed matter that its builders could find, and set alight. Politely, she asked where.

"At the library," the stranger said.

Dovid was on his feet, right behind her. His voice rumbled with threat. "At the Sholem Aleichem Library you burned Yiddish books? At the library actually named for our great Yiddish writer?" Musya asked Dovid to sit down. He inched closer.

"Well, yes, we did." Slight uncertainty entered the stranger's voice. "That's where they were, most of them. It made sense to do it there. I think the name will probably be changing."

"They announced it at school," Samuel Nemo told the floorboards.

"You went to—you ditched music lesson to do that?"

"Dovid, please sit down!" Musya said, and felt him back off a pace or two.

"He went to contribute," said the stranger. "He did his part and then he stuck around, people were impressed. Then it got late and I thought he could use someone to walk home with him—our little hero disagreed, of course." Another flash of bullet chips: the stranger's smile. "The other children had their parents around."

"Yes, of course, thank you." Musya's scalp prickled. Behind her the flat overflowed with sounds of a hurried and desperate search. They'd cleared the shelves weeks ago, hidden everything away when Dovid said to; he'd said it would be temporary, a precaution only. His hours on the machinery floor had been extended again so Samuel Nemo had been getting himself to school and back—such an independent-minded child, she'd congratulated herself more than once. She said, "And so, he gave some Yiddish books to your bonfire?"

"Well, not mine alone," the stranger answered modestly. "It was ordered."

"I see," said Musya. Consternation boiled behind her; now from Sender Kotz a wail: loss. Someone made hushing noises: Kitty. "I see," Musya said again. Who was this person? she wondered, too upset to make out the strange features more than one at a time. A chin pimple, a probing eye, an earlobe broad as his thumbprint: "I am glad it went well."

The stranger said it had, indeed. "Now maybe we can start to have some progress around Birobidzhan. That is all we seek here. Progress."

"Out with rotten bourgeois nationalism," said Samuel Nemo in a rush of consonants. The stranger laughed approvingly.

"He gets it," he said.

Musya nodded. In fact she didn't agree, she believed just the contrary. Samuel Nemo got nothing, he just didn't know any better. Exposed to bad influences at the Agricultural Machinery Plant School, he had merely obeyed orders. Which didn't prevent Musya from feeling furious at him. And the sinister adult friend he'd brought home from the book-burning only added to her aggravation. Pervert or police informer? Either was bad. She kept nodding. "Yes, we're very proud of him. So, thank you. Goodnight."

The stranger said, "He told us his mama is a rootless cosmopolitan."

"That was my sister," Musya said. "My sister was the mother of him, this one, and my older boys. These two are mine, there." She gestured at the box cribs in the room behind and kept her eyes locked on the stranger's face, one dirty fingernail of a nostril at a time. It was difficult not to fall down.

"I see," he said, echoing.

Her legs felt like they were turning to seawater. *I'm being struck dead,* she thought. Her face forced itself into an answering smile for the stranger. She said, "Thank you again for bringing him home. Goodnight," and moved aside to admit Samuel Nemo. Nothing happened. She brought her eyes down to him and said to come inside. "Pretzel Kotz, arayn," she ordered. He didn't budge.

The stranger cleared his throat. "You should be watching your language, Tovarisch."

"Yes, of course, thank you." She'd reached across the threshold for Samuel Nemo's jacket and was tugging hard to no avail. His face was expressionless. She'd turned him to stone. She had to beg him: "I'm sorry, please forgive me, please come inside."

He shoved her against the doorframe and strode into the flat where silence greeted him. They were all on their feet, watching the door until the stranger left politely, never to be heard from again; a pleasant enough man but a book burner. They waited through the clicks as Musya locked the door behind him. The silence lengthened. Dovid couldn't trust his own temper; he picked up his two sons, one in either arm, and took them from the room. That left Samuel Nemo to seize the initiative. Back and forth his eyes raked their faces until he finally burst out crying and screamed: "You hate me! You all hate me!"

Anton responded at once: he did, he agreed, he did hate his brother. Kitty said no, Anton didn't and neither did she. "I don't hate you either," Musya the mother said dutifully. "And neither do your brothers and sisters, any of them." For Sender kept silent. Nor did Hodeh say anything. Pretzel breathed loudly with a face full of tears and waited for Hodeh's silence to end, his agony increasing. Their bond had survived the years intact; he'd remained a beloved pet and a girl's love still helped sustain him. Yet Hodeh liked book-burning no more than the rest. Tears dripped down her face, too. Theirs was a family of readers.

Gone: all the children's Yiddish books, old and new. Poetry collections, hers and Dovid's. Markish. Sutzkever's Siberia. Novels and stories. Y.L. Peretz. Sholem Aleichem. Liza's old Dovid Bergelson's with all her notes inside. Musya said, "And those books we had in the ghetto especially, Pretzel—when I think of how many times we could have burned them ourselves just to keep warm." She gasped. "And my poem— what about my poem?"

"You're not allowed to talk to me!" Samuel Nemo shouted. "You're not my mother anymore—you said!" He went and threw himself face down on his cot. "You don't even know my birthday. And I didn't touch your stupid poem."

"I apologized," she answered weakly. She'd done damage at the threshold, she knew it at the time. Musya had other children with problems however. There sat Sender Kotz, sobbing:

"He got Yankel's Jules Vernes too. That was all we had of—that was all we had!"

She put an arm around him. "We did have it, though. It was there when we needed it."

"But what if we need it again?"

"Then it's there already. It's in our hearts and memories to find again."

He wept. "No, but I didn't put it in my heart and memory—I thought we could keep the books instead. And that way it's always like new. And now it's gone, and Yankel is gone—everything is gone. Oh, my poor little Yiddish!"

After languishing for many months, School Number Two's excellent musical program would enjoy a revival—only for all the best parts to go to the Russian boys who were in the majority by then. Jewish voices were many fewer anyhow, since all who'd been orphans of war wound up dispersed, the older ones shipped out as apprentice labor to hinterlands, their younger siblings divided and dropped off at other care homes around the Jewish Autonomous Region. These were orders: no arguments were possible.

The Jewish orphans of war who remained behind in Birobidzhan were the youngest of all. Nobody wanted them. Stymied over their disposal, the city cleared some ground floor space downtown and opened an infant institute to educate and house them. Not one of Musya's fellow normal school graduates wanted to work at the place, it sounded much too depressing. She agreed but put her name forward anyhow because this was their world today. Almost instantaneously she was hired to teach one of the boys' classes. *More male babies*, she thought.

The saddest classroom in the world contained a heap of diminutive bedrolls by the Lenin corner, a few benches, and a single large writing table that the teacher shared; besides Musya there were a dozen infant souls, motherless, who'd lately lost their older siblings to dispersion. They cried day and night. She instructed them in counting and in the letters of the Russian alphabet, her pedagogy working towards the goal of simple word recognition. At story time she read the requisite boyhood lives of the Soviet leaders to them. They cried all through story time. She remained faithful to her determination as to dress and showed up looking very smart and older than her years each day. As a teacher of infants Musya was strict, fair, and maintained formal distances; the sadness of her workplace, too, she kept at arm's length. Only some days it met her at waking—she pictured an enormous egg, world-sized, and herself pushed to the uttermost margins of existence by its shell—and then she couldn't go well-dressed. To do so felt like a mockery of infants so bereft; what's more, the effort it took was too much. The immense shell of sadness was too big to fight, and too fragile. She'd come into the saddest classroom wearing her comfortable long skirts, her thick soft sweaters and shawls—then how the infants would draw near and start to attach themselves! She'd wind up encircled every time.

(12)

Vera couldn't have picked a worse time to appear. Of course, if she'd come much later she'd have missed them. Musya's family was moving to Teploye Ozero, the new settlement named for the warm lake at its shoulder. With an arduous packing-up far from complete, there was no time to spend on attention to what Vera might say; but in this case Musya couldn't help it:

"There is another man? Another?"

"The primary man—the man of my life!" Vera cried. Even worse than arriving, she'd shown up with enormous quantities of baggage. She couldn't have left a thing behind at Birofeld, where in the end Vera's opponents had been soft and she'd stayed as long it suited her. Now she was on her way to this man, only she needed to do some shopping first. "I cannot wear this awful coat in front of him."

Musya thought it did look bad. "But where is he? Where is the primary man?"

"Here in Siberia, imprisoned. I go to join him at his penal colony, just like the Dekabristi did."

"Oh dear," said Sender Kotz.

His stepfather grunted in accord. Knee-deep in waste paper and wood shavings, the two of them were putting the musical instrument collection into packing crates. Despite their best precautions the snare drum would sustain a ruinous puncture. String music came from the bed-room where Anton shunned work to improvise on mandolin instead; with the suitcase gramophone already packed for safety they let him, it made their work go easier. Musya returned one eye to the babies playing volcanic mountaineer across the floorscape and started folding clothes again while she and Vera talked.

"So he's in political prison? Or is he—was his family some kind of ex-nobility?"

"Them? Noble? Hah!" Vera filled in the portrait: the silvery-blond only child of bureaucrats, Party fixtures inhabiting a gigantic private flat off the Nevsky Prospect, two gray souls whose starry-eyed son had a mouth made from the same stuff as poetry. He'd been a student of her husband's, soon to enter university, he arrived for tutoring. Their love took flame.

Dovid spoke up. "And you complain about my friends."

"It sounds very romantic," Musya said.

Vera said yes. "Love devoured us." Was it real? It was. But could it be? It could not. After placing low on his exams the son fell into argument with his doctrinaire family. Vera was named but she denied everything. What choice did she have? There were scenes. In despair, the primary man enlisted, survived the Winter War in Finland and was stationed in Western Ukraine, a Red Army lieutenant, when Germany struck. He was captured immediately. Two despairing letters with Polish postmarks reached Vera from prison camps before one brought jubilation, for he'd managed to escape. Next she heard, he'd been arrested as he re-crossed the Soviet border. "Such distrust of those poor men, the prisoners of war," Vera wept into a yellow handkerchief. She'd cleared a corner of the chaise lounge to sit and used her swollen briefcase as a footrest. "It was so unfair, so ignorant! People actually thought Hitler could have used mind control to turn them into spies."

"Quite right, there was a lot of that going on then," Dovid observed.

Vera went on. "When I think how he has suffered, my heart feels like a diamond." For years she'd known that this primary man of hers was in the Arctic Far East. Only now she knew exactly where, she'd had word of him. "Why do you think I dragged us here from Leningrad? Why I steeped myself in all that pretense? To seek for happiness—in Birobidzhan, my God." Due north: her course was set. She held the square of yellow linen to her heart-flush and said, "I have reached the end of base emotions."

Before Musya could answer, the flat door opened to admit Samuel Nemo entered in red neckerchief uniform. He'd spent the afternoon downtown at the former State Yiddish Theater, now the City House of Pioneers and Schoolboys; Komsomol property, where they did a lot of shouting. He indicated Vera with a loud cry:

"Hey—what is she doing here?"

"Get changed into something civilized and come help us," Dovid told him.

"No," said Samuel Nemo, who was determined to stay in Birobidzhan, he'd been announcing it almost hourly. Musya sympathized. Naturally in demand, always popular, his power and influence among his fellow schoolboys was even on the rise, now that he went to these meetings downtown in uniform. The Organization Man, Dovid called him. If it were so, then he was marked for the top, he had the aura. Other boys vied for his friendship with tokens and gifts, painted tin airplanes and the like, things they'd seen him point at in shop windows that he refused to return now or part with—they had to be packed yet. He brought home some freshly-inked certificate of achievement every week; those, too, though Dovid favored their destruction. In another time, his loving parents might have promoted this quality Pretzel had of standing out, here as a model schoolboy in the future Soviet leader mode; if they'd thought he might become a leader and thrive as one, they might have encouraged him. At present, when they were practically fleeing town to escape the reach of politics as far as possible, their confidence in that kind of future stood at zero. As the Jew-Hating Campaign kept claiming victims, Musya felt they couldn't separate the boy and his meetings and his popularity fast enough. The time to leave was now. Eight had to be too young an age to charge someone with crimes against the state but she wasn't sure about twelve or thirteen—she wasn't sure about ten. Their budding Young Pioneer continued, "And you can't tell me what to do. You're not my father."

Dovid waved his hand at Musya's voice and said he could hold his own conversations, thank you. So she went quiet. Her husband's nerves were exposed with this move. A transfer had been engineered; in truth he'd lost his place. The men and women at the Birobidzhan Agricultural Machinery Plant didn't want him around anymore. He'd always regret it. He'd pledged himself to the work there, set his heart on the mission to make Siberia boundlessly fruitful. Cement could never enthuse him the same way tractors did—cement wasn't musical, he said. "I'm telling you now," he told Samuel Nemo, who answered:

"Go ahead. You can't make me do anything. You can't make anyone do anything. Anywhere!"

Dovid forced back his temper and sighed—hurt, Musya knew. Also weary of the same argument again and also cautious, no question, careful every day not to antagonize the little boy into reporting him at any organizations downtown: "Then go play with your brother," he said. Pretzel stomped from the room. The first notes came from the zhaleika's cowhorn bell.

Vera said, "My goodness, Musya. Your little boy turned into a Russian."

"So he thinks," said Dovid. His bond with her son had seen better days, definitely, Musya reflected with sadness. He'd used to drape the tiger skin across his back and chase a squealing Pretzel through their rooms—no little boy had ever been more gleeful.

"We're sure it's only temporary," she said.

Dovid said maybe not. "Maybe once a book burner always a book burner." The bonfire story, quickly told, got Vera shaking her head:

"Children destroy so much."

"They are not as bad as cats," Musya confided. "But Vera, what about your son?" For the one thing their guest might have left behind in Birofeld appeared to be him. Always sickly: Musya felt a worry-pang even asking in case she'd missed the news of a tragic end.

But Vera said, "The boy thrives with his bestial father. Ice hockey—he is playing ice hockey in a junior youth league, he hates me for missing some major game today. Can you imagine? What have I to do with ice hockey when the man I love is chained in ice? It feels almost offensive. And the boy will lose his teeth that way, he will wind up needing full dentures at twenty like his father."

"But he—his father." Musya struggled for a moment with chronology. Between the tutoring, the war, the handsome man—whose perfect teeth, now that she pictured him, had accounted for much of his visual appeal: "You must have loved him at the same time you loved the—your lieutenant, no?"

"Yes," said Sender.

Vera said, "I used that love as a narcotic only—a man and child to dull my pain in."

"Really delightful," Dovid said.

"And men don't do the same?" Vera challenged him. "Women cannot do what men do—is that it?"

Musya said, "But what about Matis?"

"Matis is like all other men," Vera said pointedly. Her eyes stayed on Dovid. "He likes to sit around drinking in an undershirt and play the little tyrant in his home."

"You are right, yes, all men," Dovid said. "Other than those in the gulag for high treason."

"Innocent men!" Vera cried.

A high note screeched. *"Be quiet in there, would you?"* The mandolin's tinny song trickled on. Now the flat door opened to admit Kitty and Hodeh with their arms full of wicker boxes: the cat carriers at last. Every cat in sight vanished immediately as the search began for a place to set things down.

"What are all these—oh no, not now, not again," Kitty said. She didn't like Vera because Dovid didn't like her and that was final. Kitty was coming along to Teploye Ozero too. "What ideal timing," she added.

The Leningrader smiled, impervious. "I am only passing through."

Hodeh was counting bags. "Are you going around the world?"

Dovid said, "Yes. An around-the-world manhunt."

"Although I might not be completely welcome here," Vera said, "please know that my feelings towards you all remain as warm and friendly as ever."

"Yes, of course," Musya hurried to say; but as much as their looks threat-ened, no one else said a word. Vera's speech had doused their spite enough to quiet them. So must she have hung on among the beekeepers at Birofeld, employing a thick skin and rhetoric to match. In her own way Vera was admirable, Musya thought with a smile at her. "And you will always be welcome in our home—and our garden, too, they have one where we are going. Once the snow melts, of course. With fruit trees—you love them."

"Dear Musya." Vera smiled back and shook her head. "What have I to do with fruit trees now?" The next day Vera was gone, a little crazy as ever, destination north of Kolyma, true frozen wilderness. Her smile as she waved goodbye was ecstatic.

In truth, Musya could hardly wait to get out of the city herself. Grim, dull, frozen, hideously dark, blighted with disrepair, crammed with a humanity brought low by planning failures and drink, Birobidzhan wore its worst face fixed in place these days. Poisoned rumors channeled among endless shop queues, everywhere a parade of slack faces and eyes inflamed, darting side to side in too many shadow pools of sleeplessness, eyes hilarious with fear and triumph: for someone else had been taken. Denunciation of internal enemies had become a favorite public pastime. Anyone might be next—Musya's family might be next. They felt it. The government's Jew-Hating Campaign remained like a steel beam being driven straight through their every sense of enclosure or safety. Every minute they lived felt broken. 1950 found Dovid and Musya moving house upriver from capital to hill country but behind all appearances they stood stripped naked in a desert, stunned faces turned to find the nearest cover. Ancient instincts put pace into the hammer blows Musya rained on the packing crate lid. Kitty hammered faster still, she always competed for Dovid's praise.

Almost finished, they could hear Anton play around with Temnaya Noch on guitar, slow and unbothered by the hammering out front. Neither did Sender Kotz and Mendel's sister let it interfere with the farewells they said in the corner, where they'd advanced to holding hands. Odd in her own way, the girl continued to share part of a room with her incapable mother but Mendel had gone out with the real orphans as an apprentice. He'd tried to avoid this but he'd failed the foreskin examination. Now he was hours away at a furniture-making concern and a best friend-sister romance had shown signs of developing. "Too bad we have to leave just now," Dovid remarked in an undertone. Looking glum, Hodeh had taken Pretzel to help keep watch on their stuff already piled downstairs for transport, some to go by truck and some the few stops west by slow train to Teploye Ozero. There the household would reunite with its goods in a new home at a convenient distance from the station—they weren't going far enough, Musya whispered, to impede Mendel's sister in her pursuit of Sender's love. The girl acted smitten. Dovid said, "The boy ought to chase first."

The flat door banged open and ended the matter. In walked the new dvornik who didn't like them. At her heels trailed the Cossack girl, struggling with an overweight galvanized bucket and a stubby long-handled push broom. The new dvornik spat at the stack of wicker boxes which hissed and spat back—every cat accounted for since Merele had emerged at last from hiding, dusty and ravenous. They had been spared more tragedy.

"Filthy, filthy people! My new tenants are waiting. Put it there," she rapped out syllables of abuse and command in an angry monotone. Before anyone had time to move she took the broom, dunked it in the bucket which was full of whitewash, and advanced on their forest wall. Two great swipes blanked out the sky burial. Erasure trails dripped down the tree trunks.

"For what?" Musya screamed, Sender screamed, the room was screaming. "Stop! Stop! What are you doing?"

"Look at that!" the new dvornik screamed back at them. "It will need two or three coats—minimum! This family! You should hope I never see you on the street—that is, if they ever let you people back in town. Katerilena, cover it," she ordered and stormed out on them all screaming after her to go to hell.

Their upset was such that they almost missed the babies' swift gravitation towards the whitewash pail. Musya got there just in time, with Katerilena too upset to even offer help; quite unlike herself. Instead she stood there with the push broom in her hands, sobbing words: a flood-release of desperation, this was clear, to be rescued from Birobidzhan, a place about to be left void of what only their family and their flat had shown her, a world so different:

"The way you play your crazy music together. And your beautiful art wall, the most beautiful, all the little animals. And your friends—and, oh, the poor little actress, how sweet she was!" cried Katerilena. "Please let me come with you, take me along, I can work—I will work for you, Kitty!"

As Kitty hesitated, Dovid hurried to say yes, he called it a great idea. "The more the merrier," he added in a comforting voice.

Musya felt exasperated. She said, "Wonderful. That will make four of us who cannot cook."

"I can cook," said Kitty and Katerilena. Both exaggerated.

Dovid looked puzzled. "Who is the fourth—Hodeh?"

"You are!" she told him.

He held up his fingers at her—not enough, being his point. Tempted to debate it, instead she looked away. As if through a tapering blizzard she observed Yuri's infant brother and his spring green stripe grow visible in the branches beneath the whitewash. The dvornik was right about the job ahead.

Katerilena drooped, sob-wearied. She freed one hand from the broom handle to stroke a naked patch of painted pine bark. "I cannot do it. I love this forest so much. It is my favorite thing in the world, I swear."

They knew, they told her. They knew she had no choice. Sender Kotz stood up and took the brush from the Cossack girl's hands. "Let me do it," he said.

"I will help," said Mendel's sister.

In the bedroom Anton strummed unbearably.

They settled in at the new place, where Dovid led the family in a craze for making snowmen. They made snowmen when they should have been unpacking; but it was too much fun to stop. In fact they were luxuriating in the larger home they'd found here in the country. A jumble of tiny rooms and windows (plural) with a Russian stove at one end of a plant worker longhouse, it was a little house within a house, not quite so close to the train station as promised, much nearer the outskirts of the young settlement and a little uphill. They had the open air as compensation and welcomed the bargain.

All around were hills. Somewhat higher up and the longhouse would have had a view between them, across purple wetlands to the distant river's edge—the Bira that curved here. As it was, home overlooked the cement plant, a vast sprawl of smokestacks and industry; colorless, in a way, neither gray nor white nor brown, not unlike the product. The bread of construction, some called it. From the quarry walls that ringed the place, a network of vehicles, handcarts, chutes and conveyors moved limestone and clay from crushing towers to hammer sheds to kilns; another took cooled clinker through its grinding in the mill tower until at last, more like the high-grade flour of construction, really, the finished cement went into the silos, ready for bagging. Musya knew the layout by heart fairly quickly as the children learned and talked about the plant with enthusiasm in these early days. Down its center on a slight tilt ran two immensely long steel pipes that were the housings for the vital structures: the great rotary kilns, with brick-lined interiors that a man could stand up on his toes in. At the kilns' lower end, the hottest of fires was kept burning. The tall furnace building sheltered the firebrick supply bay where Dovid worked.

He was irresistible when it came to making the rest of them stop what they were doing in favor of bundling up again to go out and make another snowman. He'd had himself a pair of hide mittens lined with fur and custom-stuffed. He could shovel when he wore them and shoveled joyfully. There was something of a village meeting taking shape out in the longhouse yard, a snow-bound garden space edged with the tops of shrubbery and low trees, some burlap-wrapped, fruit-bearing as promised. Now their winter sleep made a fence around a swelling population. Family portraits some, the rest stranger snowmen with their mates and young; snow dvorniks, too, and a snow policeman with terrifying branches for arms. One tiny snowman had a gigantic wife whose skirt was a snowdrift where he perched in the shade of her big snowball breasts. Naturally there were cats of snow and even one dog; Dovid said he wanted a dog now that they lived in the country. A few monstrous figures stood out: a cannibal in a crown of bottles; a wraith more snow pillar than man. The gathering glittered brilliantly day and night, for every eye contained a polished steel ball bearing, picked off the ground at the plant on the children's compulsory work afternoons there. Various sizes were used in the cement mills to grind up the clinker—of which plenty made its way home as well, little gray pellets that served for moustaches and such. Everywhere adorned and studded with the excess steel, a host in resplendent finery faced Musya where she stood at her bedroom windowpane. She and Dovid were out there together in the moonlight. The children had given her clinker curls.

Dovid put his arms around her from behind. They liked to quote a poem from a lost and burned collection:

"I'm your snowman," Dovid said. "I'm your snowman in a cloak of skin."

But the snowmen outside gleamed only briefly. A few days' existence found them discolored, their stainless pupils tarnished. Some days the snow the family packed into snowmen left their mittens filmed with oil. The cement plant, Dovid explained, did more to clay and rock than crush, fire, and grind it. Without the proper chemical processes introduced at every step, heated by mountains of coal and furnace coke, fueled by rivers of gasoline, they'd have wound up with nothing but dust, inert powder. Without chemists, without their gas clouds, without jetting gypsum steams and mists of carbon particles, there'd be no cement to bind so magically with water and harden into concrete. And without concrete: truly, the absolute importance of concrete wasn't something to question. After winning a war like that, the Soviet Union must build. So her family's snowmen would turn gray as cemetery stones before their time. As industrial consequences went, better by far were the spectacular skies, not only at dawn or sunset. Shows of colored lights like darting fish and triple suns at high noon were typical effects produced by gases catching in the ever-present dust clouds. In certain strains of moonlight the whole settlement—plant, river marsh, station, Lenin square, outskirts—turned entirely blue.

It was a nerve-wracking job Dovid had. At every crisis the kiln foremen were liable to blame the firebricks. Sad to say, often they were right. With drive gears and rollers engaged, inside their massive housings the great rotary kilns turned on a tilted axis. Crushed rock poured down firebrick lining towards the furnace blaze to cook and then emerge as clinker. Every brick was set by hand. The plant's firebrick source was local and not well managed; lapses in its quality control weren't always caught in Dovid's shop. The brick setters were like a breed apart, sworn to use every brick they were given without exception; no better than wreckers, he sometimes called them. For when enough bad bricks failed it could collapse a kiln lining. That meant a lot of trouble. Shut-downs were an expensive proposition in every way and blame for one was a heavy load to bring uphill at night to a family. A slump in production was no joke in this political environment, Dovid said. His shovel blade bit angrily as he attacked a fresh snowdrift, toiling alone in his snowman garden, digging a plaza. Chopping stove wood might have offered the same relief but an axe was beyond him; Katerilena did the chopping.

The place he'd led them had a drawback that left Dovid's family at a disadvantage. As settlements in the Jewish Autonomous Region went, Teploye Ozero hated Jews more than most. An early sign of this had marked the end of a first visit and fruitless search for Yiddish books at what passed for its library, when Musya got a pamphlet shoved across a desk at her with the remark, "They warned us about people like you." Detailing the traits of the rootless cosmopolitan, the pamphlet claimed to tell How to Spot One. The library clerk had added, "At least you could stay in the cities where you belong." The school-teachers on the whole weren't much better. Every neighborly act at this point was an event.

So it rejoiced Dovid to see some fellow longhouse tenants finally stop being too standoffish to add their own family portraits and monsters to his snow ranks. These were mostly clerks from the cement plant, men, women, their children, and mostly not Jews; although no one discussed it. Musya smiled as her older ones offered to share their ball bearings with the neighbor children in the snow. They won friends so naturally. Good and loving children; but the worst necessity had trained them young and they were also calculating, slow to trust and watchful for allies.

In a sling to match his brother's that Musya was wearing, the two year-old kicked happily against his father's coat. The only father present with a baby strapped to him, Dovid was telling the other men about his work history, hinting at dissatisfaction: "Cement isn't musical," she heard him say. Kitty was chatting with someone new, ano-ther younger man, a boy—just like Vera, they teased her sometimes, Kitty liked them young. She'd ask why not? Young men were better, boys better still; they had ideals and stamina, she'd say, laughing in Dovid's direction. Her meaning was unmistakable; but that Kitty knew anything beyond what hearsay and conjecture had told her, Musya doubted thoroughly. In her war without men, the dvornik's daughter had gone to battle and returned a virgin; enlisting before she'd ever had a boy's caress had left her stuck wanting one. Her injury constrained her and Kitty's looks did the rest, cruel Vera was probably right—but that had been back when they lived in the old flat. Out here in the country, an unattached young woman was a minor phenomenon. What's more, she wasn't Jewish. Her appeal might be higher here. Musya hoped it would be, so that Kitty might find her own primary man and move in with him; and she could take Katerilena along. Still no cook, the Cossack girl had been welcome enough as an extra pair of hands around the place but Musya thought they could spare her come warm weather. She was helping Hodeh roll the midriff of another snow cat, a fat one. The neighbors interspersed their curious examination of Dovid's baby sling with even more curious looks at his household. What did they see? A man with many children and a wife—or maybe a man with unusual social ideas who'd attracted female followers?

Unhelpfully, Musya still spent half her nights back in Birobidzhan, where her school heads declined to release her from service, they were too understaffed. No one else would be assigned there because the place was scheduled to close within another year or so. Issued with her propiska to travel for work was a putevka that guaranteed lodging; but the hotels were terrible, she could never get a private room. Even so, Musya hadn't struggled to escape the situation. She knew her class needed her. Some nights the school clerk had a sofa free; otherwise she slept in their Lenin corner alongside her pupils. A few shared her cot with her, as many as would fit. The former infants were mostly six years old now. By day she taught them Russian reading, writing, sums. Then the slow Friday train back to Teploye Ozero, bearing big sacks from Gastronom onto which her family would fall like wolves; for the settlement was a wasteland when it came to good delicatessen. Her neighbor in the snow agreed:

"But the less to buy, the less to carry. That is an advantage here."

Musya said it was true. "I have a little cart but I need one with better wheels for this hill."

The young longhouse wife wore a sympathetic look. "I could never stand to do that round trip so often, the way the train just crawls."

Her memory offering a torrent of passionate homecoming reunions and tender partings, paired every week, "I like it," Musya answered truthfully.

She had always liked making journeys, being in motion through views. Here, down the river between pickets of trees, the sun ran a trail of red gold or white gold light; sometimes against a deep-dyed blue, a yellow gold. She'd never really changed. A loco-motive window seat would always summon an earliest self, the poet-picturer of love. Who, smitten, would approach her? Someone different from the men who did anyhow, of course, as living men did often approach confront talk at jeer at living women: what would a graceful truly love-struck man say and do—and how would she respond? A brisk rebuff and a flourished wedding band, her normal resort, would feel too unkind. "I love my husband," she'd have to tell him. She pictured green eyes brimming rosily with tears, and a trim black moustache for some reason; a journalist, she thought, this disappointed suitor whose train schedule by cruel coincidence remained identical to hers. She couldn't avoid causing him pain, every ride they shared. He couldn't have her.

That spring Musya turned thirty. She didn't know how her little charges had found out and was very surprised when they marked the day with a song for her and a gift, a pretty worked-leather bookmark. She was touched. By the end of June she'd persuaded two childless couples in the longhouse to adopt a Jewish orphan from her class—in one case, two orphans. It had happened like this: she'd brought the whole class home for an educational excursion, the plan was to visit the chum salmon hatchery on the warm water lake where Kitty worked. Their first hours in Teploye Ozero the boys spent racing up and down the yard between the brown green-sprouting garden rows. Identical cropped heads, state-issue gray woolen trousers and tunic blouses: the neighbors might have mistaken them for tiny prisoners in a riot of freedom, escapees. Not such a big mistake, Musya supposed. The orphans had never gone anywhere since infancy. Their roughness only wrapping, pleasant little boys and literate to boot, they made a good impression not only at the longhouse but also at the hatchery where a senior foreman whose sons were war dead picked another two. Word got around and Jewish orphans of war enjoyed a period of fashion. Demand quickly outpaced supply and soon the older siblings were being called back from their apprenticeships into joyful reunion scenes. The settlement's hardest hearts kept being cracked open by the sight. Tears would pour out, tears Musya very often wept to picture crowned these daydreams. She pictured the Jew-hating librarian with two new Jewish children in the home. All was forgiven. Her heart exulted.

Then the school shut down ahead of time, the property was too valuable. The news caught her unprepared, cocooned as she'd been in stories with far other outcomes. She had to lean against the classroom door to keep from reeling before she could tell it to her students. Crowded around her skirt they stood looking up at their teacher who was everything to them.

Her confusion was complex. She'd spent so much mental time having already rescued each one that to find them all needing it, threw her. This orphan tugging on her skirt with his long fingers: yesterday he'd played his first piano recital in the chum salmon hatchery canteen, encouraged by the adoptive mother she'd given him, an imaginary one who'd herself performed in concert halls. As for who he was in reality, Musya wondered. He seemed unformed to her, not quite right. The impression left a pang. Had she tried less hard to know this little boy because she'd reinvented him elsewhere?

A sense of being squandered struck next and left a bruise. For what had they availed, the hours and hours of picture-making with feats of love in bright detail, what had they availed anyone, especially herself? She thought her colleagues were right to mock her as they just had: really, had she never heard them talking? Of course her cheerfulness had been remarked while everyone else waited crestfallen for the blade to finally drop—*the silly bird*, they'd called her. Musya's students, for their part, had taken her habitual smiles as a pledge of security. Now she had to revoke it and leave their future uncertain, a chaos. If no one in Birobidzhan wanted them, who would?

But she heard herself say to them, "Don't worry." In fact some had found homes through no effort of hers; the class was down to eight worried heads. Her own head she'd bent alongside each to observe how pencil points fashioned Cyrillic consonants more or less crookedly and at times, yes, she'd considered the contrast between present and picture; she'd held both threads in one hand more than once. But not steadily. For the most part she'd maintained parallel scenes that went on without touching—except that success in her daydreams had kept Musya's spirits in a state of artificial elation. Her odd bird-brained cheerfulness had been the result. *Yesterday I rescued you*, she might have said to any one of them a dozen times without lying once—yet it would never have been true. Only each detail she'd pictured had been a brick of empty space, one invisible brick in the wall she'd built between herself and what was happening. She hadn't liked the truth, which only got worse now that she faced it. For if she'd ever been able to do anything real for a single one of her students, it was too late now. She'd let it get too late.

Musya felt her conscience crumpling from overload—as if all her delusional gladness had come freighted with guilt feelings, like a compounding fee that she'd ignored and hadn't paid. Now it was clear, her duty in life lay all along in finding real homes for these orphans. She'd known it; so why had she allowed the knowledge to produce nothing but stories to tell herself? Because why not? Hadn't the war orphaned her too? Wasn't she doing enough by being present? She'd answered yes to herself and kept a smile on while the guilt kept piling up. How to look into the face of a doomed abandoned child she'd rescued in her mind the night before, and not say one word, and not change one thing? It took no special effort; her war had trained her thoroughly. Orphans and exiles, a final end product of Jew-hating in their time, Musya's students were vivid to her but half unreal. Behind her wall she'd loved and loved them; beyond, among their voices, less. She'd pictured them loved by Teploye Ozero; but they never got there. Now they were to be scattered, according to policy, as if any grouping of Jews should be pulverized, and would wind up among various children's institutes across the Soviet Far East with little hope of adoption.

"But you said we'd be adopted!" they cried at her in their intractable Yiddish.

"I said I had a feeling that you'd be—I said I hoped you'd be, that we should all hope."

"No!" Six was a contentious age, she well knew. "You said!"

So they parted on terrible terms, upset on every side, and had no opportunity to reconcile since rough shock and fearful haste accorded best with policy. Musya was out of a job before lunchtime. She spent a lot of severance pay on groceries and then caught the slow train west. The iron wheels clattered. Rail travel sounds: a machine for knitting comforts out of sorrows. After all, her students weren't gone. She'd find them—she'd catch up with them—she'd find homes for them—everything she'd pictured could happen only a little later—human hearts would be regenerated yet, and Jew-hating die out all around her—someday soon.

The hills of Teploye Ozero started immediately, with a steep climb up a set of log stairs from the tracks to the station house—truly a house, painted blue, always missing roof tiles despite being under constant repair. Its street door opened on the most level part of the settlement. Here were police and party offices, schools, the bigger state shops, a public hall, arranged around a Lenin square dotted with bronze busts and struggling young trees, where a warm water decorative fountain steamed in the cold months. The gravel road punished the wheels of her wire-sided cart as Musya turned uphill towards home. Few people were about, adults were at work, children at school. She felt out of place and a little unreal. The sky was enormous, a uniform blue, the clouds no more than specks in it. She climbed towards them.

From the top of the next rise she looked down through towering curtains of bone-colored dust at the cement plant and its quarries, the whole place resembling a catastrophic bleach stain among the folded green and purple hills. Inside the joint-rattling roar of its machinery a certain half-shriek half-groan meant Dovid's job was safe for now—the kilns were rotating. Underfoot the gravel danced minutely. The road around here was always spilling away, the bare treacherous clay showing through. Musya recognized her own cart tracks at the last rise before the longhouse came into sight.

Not many blossoms remained on the fruit trees. Fallen petals whitened the yard where a headless tiger leapt and stalked its prey—two robust, black-headed little boys who ran from it in circles. She stood and watched until they spotted her and raced up with joyful cries to embrace their mother and pillage her skirt pockets of hard candies. Dovid followed with the tiger skin around his neck, his happiness striped with concern. He was flushed, tousled, his kiss a little sweet with alcohol, his chin overdue for a shave. She'd forgotten which shifts he worked, somewhere among these weeks she'd lost track of his schedule.

He said, "This is the day I go hunting boy-goats to feed to my tiger wife when she comes home from her job at the circus. Where they pay her in pickled mushrooms!" he added hopefully. Poor man: he'd been so proud of her teaching job, of her independence, of their modern marriage. It hadn't bothered Dovid what people might think of their household—those who understood must admire it, he'd said, and the rest could always learn how. And those left over could do comical things involving woodwinds and backsides. Musya reached to hand him a bag from the top of the cart but broke down partway there.

"The circus closed," she wept.

He drew the story from her tears, applying an embrace that was warm and typically humorful. She clawed her way towards comfort in its shelter. They'd be fine, he said of her orphan pupils, she'd taught them well and they'd thrive without her. But when his older son asked Dovid, "Why can't they come live here with us?" her sobs redoubled.

Then a voice. "Excuse me. Excuse me!"

A woman, not young, stood there with something in her hand. Musya wiped her face against Dovid's shirt and slipped her eyeglasses back on. Yes, it was the neighbor she'd pictured taking two orphans into her childless home, the one whose hidden loving kindness she'd watched emerge like a seedling, a touching story. "We are busy, please," Dovid answered; but the woman didn't care.

"I don't care if you are busy," she said. "Look at this." It was a ball bearing. "They are everywhere—all over the yard, in the gardens, every plot is infested with these things and it is your fault."

Musya said, "Yes, our fault. Now go away, you have said what you wanted to."

"His fault," the woman said. "Him and his crazy snowmen."

"My apologies," said Dovid. "I—we will pick them up, all of them."

"Too late," said the woman. "They went everywhere. You people, always trouble," she finished. Then she threw the steel bearing on the grass and stalked away.

"Pick that up," Dovid told his sons.

Musya said no. "Don't. Leave it." But the younger one had snatched it up too fast.

Dovid said to let them get a taste for work, why not? He promised a prize to the first who found ten. Clinkers counted separately.

(13)

Balanced on the mattress edge, cradling the sobbing girl who'd collapsed in her arms, Musya felt like she might feel even worse than Hodeh did. Two sets of lungs heaved against her thudding heart. Out of nowhere Death had found them—and now the ruin of a rare shared rest day. The injustice felt crushing. Dovid stood in the doorway of their bedroom, his hands half-extended, helplessly.

He'd run out of apologies. "What do you want me to do?" he asked again. His dog had killed Hodeh's cat Paradise Darling.

Musya rocked and caressed and kept repeating, "I know, I know. It's terrible." How could she help otherwise? She tried, "You have four other cats."

"Five," said Dovid.

Hodeh turned on him. "That one doesn't count, he's not official, I told you!" Screaming it; her fury knocked Musya backwards onto the new bedspread. The girl wanted to kill Dovid, she'd announced, and they all knew her capabilities. The dog's safety was another obvious concern although she'd made no threats in that direction.

Yet. "Okay. Four," said Dovid.

Her wet nose creased the narrow forearm swiped beneath its tip as Hodeh glared at him. "This is your fault."

He said, "How?"

"Dovid, it is, Hodeh's right," Musya put in honestly. "She is your dog and you trained her to be so nervous and angry. But he's sorry, Hodeh—they're both so sorry."

The dog had come to them not too young, well past puppyhood, a compact yellow creature with an outsized wolfish head and a fear of loud noises that might have been innate. But Dovid wouldn't have that. It didn't help when the neighbors' mirth at the animal's screaming flight from a Chinese fireworks party in the garden yard refused to let up, they'd mentioned the incident constantly for days. It was depressing to watch Dovid's sympathy for his new dog lose out to a strange, stubborn pride he'd bolstered with Fatherland War recollections: for there'd been dogs on the battlefield, by his account, who hadn't run, who hadn't gone anywhere. Fearless hero dogs, he wanted one of those. So he'd contributed an outsized sum to the communal longhouse fireworks pot, helping pay for enough to set off almost weekly that summer of 1951, when he'd have his dog out there leashed at his side, marching, executing commands; he'd worked out a method for training. He'd said no dog of his would be afraid of loud noises and that was final. Now the poor thing was out of its mind.

But he'd never admit this. "She was nervous when I got her."

"She was nice when you got her," Hodeh said. "She was a nice dog before she was around you so much!"

"Dogs kill cats," Dovid said. "You know? That is their nature. That they don't do it more often is the result of thousands of years of domestication—that is genetics, scientific fact. And are we humans perfect yet? No, and neither are cats and dogs. Grown-up people understand imperfection. Grown-up people realize how much progress remains to be made." His Russian here was pointed; not unkindly. Hodeh had stayed small and looked as young as fourteen year-old Anton, with whom she shared the bottom of the senior class at the cement plant's secondary school; in fact she was probably eighteen at least. Her Russian still wasn't great. But she seemed content there with the younger students and Musya liked the arrangement well enough. Dovid and Kitty liked it less and less. Was it really wise, they asked, to push Hodeh and Anton both towards three more years of study at the local secondary general? Didn't Hodeh want to grow up in the same way as everyone else? Had she no ambition, no desire to contribute, no drive to mature? These questions troubled them. Dovid went on: "We know things like this happen. So we learn, we accept. If we have to grieve then we grieve and we heal. We move on. You are old enough now to be sensible and do the same."

Hodeh said, "And you are old enough to be stupid, Dovid. Cats are perfect. They do not need more genetics like you do. My cat Paradise Darling was perfect and your dog killed him."

"I would not call him perfect when I caught him twice pissing behind my suitcase gramophone."

"He should have pissed on top of you," Hodeh said, starting to cry again.

"Nice talk," Dovid said. "The point I was trying to make—there was an event today, a tragic one, yes, but not something to tear our family apart over. Damage was done, we lost a good cat, we should remember the good in him and grieve the loss of him together. And move on from it together."

Musya said, "Yes, good. All of us will try to do all those things." She pried the sharp scissors from Hodeh's striking hand and slipped them out of sight.

Now came Katerilena to poke her blonde head around the doorframe. The Cossack girl had witnessed the end of Paradise Darling and recovered the limp torn body from his attacker's jaws, her devotion to Hodeh making her foolhardy—her bitten forearm had needed bandaging even if the wounds thank God weren't serious. "We dug the hole," she said with a stricken face. Hodeh's sobs shook Musya hard again. Now two watched helplessly from the doorway. Katerilena couldn't stand it very long. "I will go pick more flowers," she said and rushed off.

Dovid lasted another minute. Then he said, "I had better make sure they made it deep enough," and left. Hodeh gave another howl. Somewhere the dog howled too.

A real gathering met them at the shady graveside, with many neighbors drawn there for the novelty promised by the family's reputation, Musya guessed, and staying for the picturesque qualities. With the taller shrubberies for backdrop, hair slicked, holding twin armfuls of wildflowers, Dovid's sons stood sentry on either side of the hole in the clay, the sad wicker basket between them. Hodeh wept into Merele's fur; his gray stripes salt-watered to black, the father of the deceased looked content in his mistress's arms but might have been disconsolate. For the funeral rite they had Aleksandrov's anthem to open patriotically, the Kotz brothers on various instruments joined by Kitty on shrill clarinet; followed by a string of family testimonials in the bombastic style—the best and gentlest of cats, "goodnight sweet prince," and so on. Sender Kotz recited a Russian crowd favorite from Pushkin, the farewell ode to life penned by the doomed poet Lensky in the hours before his duel with Onegin, the hero; then Anton accompanied himself on guitar for the Tchaikovsky aria to match that he'd learned from the wings at the old State Yiddish Theater. His voice was out of practice, but the assembly took a loud long pause for sniffling and throat-clearing when he was through.

Next, Samuel Nemo raised a real brass trumpet polished to a molten sheen and blew his loudest note. The assembly heard an agonized cry and turned to see Dovid's dog speeding for the hills. Dovid cursed and took off at a run. Content to forego the earth burial, Musya followed at walking pace.

Her thoughts stayed on poets and the many sad exits they found. How to save them—the poet Peretz Markish, for instance, in his political imprisonment? She pictured leading a citizen's committee from Birobidzhan to Moscow, she and Dovid, to secure his freedom; bringing books and writing materials to him and his fellow poet-prisoners, using hidden pockets to carry secret messages; then meetings with influential men over heavy buffet lunches served from silver; riding to and fro underground and other scenarios capped by success and wild celebration at the capital's hottest jazz nightclub; finally, home, bringing the broken-bodied poet and author of Ufshtand in geto along, by agreement, to serve out his Siberian exile in a corner of their longhouse rooms, a treasured living relic of their married life's best era. By miracle his strength returning, he'd write again; he'd become her teacher; he and she would teach others, enough to give the settlement a reputation for its poets; while certain Jewish orphans adopted there would be drawn to Markish and ease his loneliness. It was a satisfying story.

She discovered man and dog sitting together on a lower slope. The dog was getting its big skull rubbed; the man's thumb dug kindly around long ears whose points quivered, caught between pleasure and doubt over deserving it, Musya guessed. She sat down at the man's other side. A russet cast to the hill grasses all around made her think about skirt patterns, for she had fabric close to that color in storage. The sun was very warm. After snapping its jaws at a few passing flies, the dog brought its chin to Dovid's knee and let out a long moan. Her master put an arm around and gave his dog a hug. He'd been letting his beard come in further and further again.

"Duels are depressing," he observed. "Especially for the winner."

Musya said yes. "They are."

"The dog is not angry," he said. "She just gets overstimulated. It is hard living down there in that house for a dog."

"Of course it is."

Dovid continued: "And she is a good dog—isn't she?" He bent to kiss the dog's head. "She just has a stupid guy for an owner."

"Of course she is a good dog," Musya told them. "And he is a good guy. Smart, too—he knows practically everything. Like that, look." He knew every kind of aircraft liable to be passing and usually had an approving smile for each one. Not today. Only another MiG-15, Dovid said:

"Off to fight Americans over nothing in godforsaken Korea." The whole affair bothered him. That peace had been held so cheaply by the great powers filled him with a sick disgust, he kept shutting off the tarelka during patriotic news hour. And as another wave of funeral music reached the hillside, he shook his head. "This moldy thing again?" It was the national anthem in reprise to conclude, with added strings; his out-of-date sheet music called it the Bolsheviks' Hymn. Much preferring the Internationale, which Dovid said was all the anthem anyone should need, he'd introduced its official replacement to the repertoire while holding his nose but the players had turned out to like it. He'd taught the ensemble well, building versatile and accomplished musicians even where the talent hadn't been the greatest; as in Samuel Nemo's case. Formerly defiant, once severed from his allies in Birobidzhan he'd wound up craving the step-father's approval. And while the one-time future Komsomol officer was the furthest thing from a musical prodigy, he'd amazed everyone with his zeal in practice. Now he played the bayan better than his oldest brother ever would, managing its wheezy bulk with gusto. Sender joined Hodeh on violin these days. "Their tempo is all off," Dovid complained.

"You are a good father," Musya told him. "And a good man, and a good music teacher. As a dog owner you can improve."

He said, "I just keep thinking about ways to make more of a difference around here. Like start a small orchestra, you know? Or a jazz listening night, or a music appreciation club—something. People are hungry for it. Look how they come out for a cat funeral just to hear a little boy band play. If I could start an orchestra and get people to work together and communicate instead of whispering behind each other's backs day and night about internal enemies, rootless parasites—"

"Flabby cosmopolitans," she agreed. That one always stung her.

He said, "Yes, all that garbage. Even just talking about music together—I think it could change things." He frowned downhill.

Musya smiled. It touched her to realize that Dovid had these kinds of daydreams too. Who knew, some of her orphan pupils might join and distinguish themselves in his settlement orchestra's youth branch. Their stories matched so well! A sunlit delight in her marriage flashed and left her radiant as in their wedding photos. Wed fast among their wishes they were deeply wed indeed. She kissed him on the shoulder and said, "You want to have more social life, why not?"

"No, in fact I have a lot of things to say that could be important, a lot of ideas, you know? In my head. I want a chance to talk them through sometimes," he said. "If only to keep my mind keen. I am slipping here. I used to read a newspaper, I read Izvestiya, sometimes one or two others. I barely read the wall news now—when was the last time I read a newspaper?"

"But there is nothing," Musya said. "Dovid, there is nothing true in them." He'd said so himself.

"How can we be sure of that?" he argued now. "How can we be sure of anything if we don't at least try to find out? If we don't actually sit down with other people and talk with them face to face and learn what they know," he finished in midair again.

"I see." She did see. Dovid was lonely. Who wasn't lonely? She said, "You can talk to me about your ideas. You can tell them to your children. You can tell Kitty," she added.

"Yes. Yes," he said, his annoyance growing by the syllable. He'd regret Musya seeing how his imagination flailed around, she supposed. The question became whether he'd let it make him irrational somehow, and when, or not. She recognized a husband under powerful pressures and stress, a man at twenty thousand leagues almost, his actions and movements unfree. Unhappiness in his work at the cement plant, where he was always being put in the wrong, made Dovid's hopes for the home life that much more emphatic, his disappointments there very much keener and sometimes too voluble.

Dog and man alike endured hardships among the family's crowded narrow rooms, no question. The children lashed out frequently and hurt his feelings all the time. They were a passionate race, Musya's children. Knowing his weak point they all knew to aim at his intellect; to call him stupid, gloopy, narish, stabbed deepest. To twist the blade they'd make some unfavorable comparison between his and his predecessor's brain-power. Nothing could ever convince Dovid that his sons were talking nonsense and that Boris Kotz had been almost a simpleton; for some reason he preferred to take the boys' word for their late father's genius. Even the balebos had missed a lot about the man, Dovid said, as his low accusations had shown. Sometimes there'd even be a salute: his wife's first husband, say, was the Soviet hero people ought to be writing best-sellers about, making films about; a real inspirational case. She and Kitty had laughed and laughed at that one.

In truth, the home life was generally idyllic and fun-filled. Dovid did as much as anyone to make it so. He was a good father, a good husband, a good head of household. Except for Musya, he turned the rest into good musicians. He was a perfectionist who led by explosion too often, yes; but he got undeniable results. He said it was for their futures' sake if nothing else that he drove them. In case of hard times, his training meant a gigantic head start on any rival street corner musicians. They should learn from their own history, Dovid said. His two infants were already started on woodblocks, triangle, bells, they shared his gifts rhythm-wise.

Kitty plugged along on clarinet, showing flashes of heart but too little to feature assolo. Maybe she could have moved with her smoking materials to a home of her own by now, Musya thought. Kitty had a good job downhill at the warm lake, Teploye Ozero, where wild species of all sorts besides salmon came to breed and spawn. Its waters never froze, a fact which had singled it out for the late NEP-era chub salmon hatchery plant built on one shore. Now a venerable relic that farmed caviar Kitty helped pack for shipment to mid-level diplomats everywhere, it had no shortage of male employees. Plus Kitty was a restless presence in the settlement, a raw, ungraceful, pink-faced virgin who went out to every commemoration, every brass band event, dragging poor Katerilena along whenever she could: "Bait," Dovid would joke. Being blonde the Cossack girl suffered the excesses of men's attention and disliked going out much. Kitty's suitors came and went. Usually they left a mercenary scent behind: Fatherland War veterans' benefits sparkled in Kitty's eyes for most, no question. They also encountered too much lack of encouragement. The dvornik's daughter found only fault in her suitors. And poor Dovid, when Kitty turned critic on him! She'd go along for days being very kind, more than kind, and then suddenly be mocking his beliefs, his hands, his manhood, harsh stuff.

He always forgave her. Dovid said to blame the gulag that had her mother in its jaws. Magga's welfare never left Kitty's mind, Musya knew it. He asked what Kitty could bring to a man besides a giant worry over something that no one should ever talk about? With Kitty herself Dovid kept up a delicacy, a kind of formal kindliness that Musya liked in him—his goodness again.

As for Kitty, she'd grown cynical. She'd have a lot to drink and then announce, "I am the most interesting person around here and nobody realizes it."

Dovid learned to cook. No other way out but that from their predicament, a constant and sizeable blight on domesticity: their food was awful and it cost too much. Three women shared the household, yes, but without recourse to Gastronom not one had been able to take the problem in hand. Gripped by a strange helplessness they'd always dropped and broken things, mismeasured and burnt things whenever they tried. Sender Kotz had finally stepped in: all the best cooks were men, he assured his stepfather. An afternoon's research confirmed it and the matter was settled. Dovid picked some recipes and begged others from neighbors. Now his wife and the rest shopped, chopped, mixed, applied heat and served under his direct supervision while he reaped praise and credit for every success.

Self-nourished, self-enveloped, the household kept in comfort with its resources pooled. Katerilena's job on the fish farm packing line was messier than Kitty's but paid even better. As for Musya, she'd stepped into a vacancy at the LJIS, as parents called it, after its unofficial designation as the "Local Jewish Infant School." Things got tense for a time in the home when a place teaching the cement plant's infants came open; Dovid would have liked his wife's company at work again. But Musya couldn't stand the change—not another change—and she couldn't stand the noise, the grinding ear-splitting shriek of the rotary kilns all day from close quarters. She had naysaid and resisted and stayed where she was at the LJIS.

The orphan class she'd lost remained with her in daydreams, their braided fortunes filling her mind especially when space emptied out around her, on walks along hillsides for instance. Also on those rest days and precious weekends when Dovid led one of his excursions that she'd declined to join, leaving Musya to luxuriate in some privacy—in her most harmonious and peaceful hours the former infants grew up admirably. Qualifying for a rest vacation that year she'd gone alone to a health resort some fifty kilometers away at Kuldur, a place known as the hot springs-powered beauty gem of the Jewish Autonomous Region, even Vera had raved about it. The clean and pleasant architecture; the wide tree-lined promenades between spas; the bare minutes' distance to nature walks where waterfalls ran like steaming white ribbons through the infinite greenery of resinous forests, the silent owl's dominion—altogether Kuldur had charmed Musya into picturing Dovid and herself along with the much-regenerated poet-playwright Markish as the founding co-directors of a primary school located there, to which the scattered boys would find each his way. In time they'd add the higher grades, an auditorium or two, gleaming laboratories. Her war orphans of yesterday would become the Jewish doctors of tomorrow, achieving lives at the twinned pinnacles of nation and race.

Her husband preferred to vacation at home—although he couldn't get out of Teploye Ozero often enough, at every good weather chance he led the rest of them away on walking excursions. On one, at last, he'd gone back and crested the Sopka. Other plans past and future aimed at notable wilderness spots: a primeval larch grove sheltering mushrooms big as truck tires; a hidden mirror-glass lake cupped in an old volcanic cone. They weren't always in time to see what they sought. Much of the Far East's famous tree cover was already gone, first to the war and then to rebuilding. The sawdust-pale dirt of great sap-smelling truck roads crisscrossed everywhere among the forests that remained; while brooks and streams downhill from working gold mines cleft untrodden valleys with trails the color of unbleached bones in their fern bed carpets. Magnificence remained. Siberia's wildlife no longer teemed but still abounded. With constant look-out for a tiger unrewarded to date, a giant salamander mass migration and a mother bear with two cubs headlined the family's large total of animal sightings.

On a profitless tramp upriver in the direction of some rumored hot spring caves, they ran into bad weather and turned around. Dovid had one of his veteran friends with him on a visit from up north where he lived alone as a fur trapper—despite which the man had a woman with babies somewhere as well now. Musya disapproved more than ever when they brought Dovid's older son home to her rain-soaked and visibly overexerted: infuriating. He wasn't the toughest; she'd only let him go along because there'd be two grown men in the party to carry him when he tired. Dovid wanted his sons to learn the forest's ways early in life, this was important for him. As it turned out, he couldn't take the five year-old's weight as easily as he'd pictured; and the boy didn't like the friend any better than his mother did, he'd ridden him hardly at all. Dovid praised endurance and loved a good adventure. Now his son's face wore a bad-looking flush.

Two days of pain and high fever later, Dovid was frantic. They'd been turned away from the small local clinic bureau. He asked the doctor at the door, "Excuse me, you are Jewish? We are Jewish."

The doctor calmly said yes, she was Jewish if it mattered. A woman of late middle age who'd come to their rooms, the cement plant medical office kept her on retainer for family cases in the settlement. Her examination of the little boy revealed a semi-septic infection of the ear that looked sadly common, she told his parents. Most families in the settlement had a child or two going through this agony—it was, yes. The little boy returned her nod through tears. The day of hiking in the rainstorm might have had zero to do with his illness, "Even if it didn't help," the doctor added, preparing an injection.

"I said he was too young." Musya would always blame the hike anyhow and especially she blamed her husband's friend, a malign influence, in this episode she located definitive proof. "Only five years old—he strained too hard to keep up," she said. Dovid pounded on the doorframe as he left the room and Musya watched a tiny jetting liquid arc escape the needle's tip. The doctor whispered a mild curse at the new calibration but kept her nerve otherwise. Swiftly she delivered the shot and had bent towards her bag when Hodeh's voice came from a shadowed corner:

"Will he live now?" She'd been keeping out of sight. "Is he cured?"

The doctor sat up and told her to approach, take a look. She had an encouraging manner. She told Musya, "I used to spy on the doctors too when I was a girl and my brothers were sick. Let her look. Soon, who knows, young Jewish people will return to the study of medicine as we once did, in huge numbers. They cannot keep us out of the universities forever, can they?" She tousled Hodeh's head. The girl hissed at her and vanished, leaving the doctor startled.

Musya explained. "My daughter had a very unusual war."

"She has the look of a surgeon," said the doctor.

Musya brought these words to mind when she happened on Hodeh later at feeding time. Her cats ate well, Katerilena brought scraps home every day that they mixed with other stuff. Five at least and one loud conjoined purr that reminded his mother of Samuel Nemo's infancy. Their girl-savior: "Would you like to become a doctor?" she asked her.

"No." Hodeh had a startled look now. "What for?"

"I don't know. To help people?"

"I don't like people."

"No," Musya agreed thoughtfully. "But what about a cat doctor—a doctor of animals?"

The girl watched her pets. "No thank you."

Moving side to side for months the painful ear infection came and went. Insufficiently dosed or maybe caught too late, some root of it lingered, uneradicated; maybe it was just a piece of wickedness in life. The little boy lost schooling and fellowship to a lonely sickbed. Siblings and pets went about spiritless, their birthdays and holidays hushed. His parents sat up nights alongside the sufferer, they'd read aloud to him by a little lamp while shrieking blizzards raged to get in, tearing at every seal and windowpane, demanding entry like chapers in subhuman cries. They'd had assurances, their son didn't face mortal danger. No one could say the same of his striking musical gifts. What he could hear grew less and less. They read with voices raised; his brothers heard shouting. Yes there were corrective operations in existence, the doctor said, "But the wait will be years. They are getting far better results in the West anyhow."

"Better than Soviet surgeons?" Dovid was baffled. "Truly? How could that be with what we spend on science and medical research?"

She looked at him. "I hear some of our prosthetics are inferior as well."

This shook him and caused his new hands to rattle. Buckles wires and straps attached some replacement fingers of ungiving synthetic rubber, their sculpted verisimilitude minimal, the beige too pink. A worker's benefit, he was required to wear them on the job but he usually asked someone's help to take the hands off right away in the home, unless he used his teeth, for they chafed in spots. He'd been keeping them on for the doctor, Musya realized. The woman impressed him. He said, "I have no complaints. I also have a less negative viewpoint, Doctor. You know? Perfection takes time."

"Even so," said the doctor.

Biting insect season found his firstborn pain-free at last, and Dovid himself urgently convinced of one thing: Communal living was too unhygienic. From its hallway laundry lines and slops pails to its ashy bread oven floors to its faucets and privies, the longhouse posed nothing but health hazards. His family had suffered enough, he said, and couldn't risk worse. Before the thaw he'd started canvassing the higher slopes where shoddiness mated with disrepair to produce some scattered handfuls of free-standing dwellings. Bad, yet vacancies were rare. Every rumor of an opening absorbed her husband's thoughts and conversation; the latest empty shack held him obsessed. Musya told him so often, she didn't want to live up here but her husband was set on it. Since the plan was for Kitty to move along with them she detected no advantage, only inconvenience, further from work and from everything else, further from help in an emergency. She was panting by the time she caught up with him. Another scene had sent him storming off uphill. The dog looked winded too. The gnus seemed no less thick.

Dovid greeted her with a neutral glance and said, "Don't you just feel so much better up here?" She watched him fill his chest with air a couple of times. Below the ridge they stood on sloped the roof of a shambling cabin covered in a lot of moss punctuated by tin chimney vents, a lot of lichen and rust. But the place got too much shade from the surrounding hills, she complained.

"It is empty for a reason, Dovid."

He said, "This will not be our last home, I promise you. Think of it as a step, you know? Just one step, Tovarisch."

Sighing, Musya turned and gazed in the direction of the Bira. They were still too low to spot it. Only the river's purple wrap was visible, a swelling expanse of marsh channels choked with drowned waterfowl, a new record number this spring of 1952; another upsetting report. As for the bluffy view downhill, the monumental cement plant sat in skirts of perpetual dust storms at the usual dead center. From its smokestacks eruptions like crumpled sheets waved their stains at the sky's apex. She thought the rotary kiln noise was worse at this height. Dovid said yes, because they were further away.

"It only sounds worse because you can hear better," he said.

"I don't see the point, Dovid," she said. "Won't we feel even more trapped with each other, more likely to fight?"

"Absolutely the opposite," he said. She'd heard this claim before.

"The rumble feels worse here, too," she added. Dovid said to blame the imagination in her feet; this was the hard part of the landscape. Musya disagreed. Cement-making shook everything around them without ceasing. The plant's furnace blasts, crushers, grinders, immense straining gears; the drills and detonations at its belt of quarry walls; the rattling weight of the trucks and wagons busied between them—the gnawed-on quarries retreated and those engines' trips grew longer all the time. Musya pictured a general planetary leveling in the service of Soviet construction, every jagged place scraped smooth. Here was the plan: to flatten one-sixth of the globe and build straight roads across it between precast concrete housing blocks. She said, "In fact everything feels worse up here—this whole slope is depressing. You cannot make us move up here."

"Make you." Dovid scowled. "So you are with them down there. I am a bully, you think."

"Oh, of course not." Weariness advanced on her almost in leaps. Here came discussion of the scene that had launched his angry exit uphill to this his dream property, almost hidden as it was from human view. The children called him a bully, the old complaint. He forced music lessons on them individually and even worse was the ensemble playing, he'd keep them sitting in a room at practice for hours, an occasionally abusive perfectionist. They claimed his treatment of them was a form of slavery. "They only wish you would change, Dovid."

"Do you wish I would change?"

She did. Dovid couldn't shake his disposition towards being dissatisfied. What's more, he couldn't seem to step in and out of it as he'd used to. She said, "Sometimes you are very predictable."

He reared around at little at that. "When have I ever been predictable one day in my life?"

An example was almost too easy to find. "About the nation's gratitude you are." That was different, he said; but it wasn't. Another Victory Day had lately come and gone. No longer a national holiday—a fact which Dovid hated separately—this one had been marked by another non-recognition of the Jewish Fatherland War veterans. Every year on the same date a special order of thanks had been extended on the Soviet people's behalf to another nationality; but never yet the Jews. By annual tradition Dovid had grumbled about the omission. A folded treasure of his wallet remained a years-old newspaper column clipped from the Birobidzhan Star: every Jewish recipient of their nation's highest military honor, Heroes of the Soviet Union, their names set down in black lines ever worse for wear. But the victory had still been fresh when he'd started asking what their Generalissimo was waiting for—what was taking his gratitude to the Jews so long to be spoken? Musya remembered May-time in the old flat, when Brother Dead Man would be sprawled out on his chaise lounge, calling poor Dovid crazy. *"You want that basilisk to look at you harder?"* Every year the same: predictable. She said, "By now I completely agree with you, the Jews' turn should have come sooner. Even so, Dovid."

He shook his head. "No. No. Your son is right." The last time he'd asked what was taking so long, Sender Kotz who was going through a dour sixteenth year had said it would only be someone making a bad joke if it ever happened. Dovid had stormed out. The children's numbness to his hurt had the power to enrage him. Now he was conceding defeat only to continue as before. "So why not just tell the joke and get it over with?" He agonized himself, Musya thought. Here was Dovid's problem, a belief that he was being injured when he was only being impatient. And then making the rest of them share his mistaken pain; which became his family's problem. To which he replied with heat. "Don't tell me what my problem is. And how many times do I have to tell you? I am not a bully."

"I know," she agreed. "But you know Anton wants to try leading his own arrangements with more Yiddish songs and you are standing in his way, Dovid."

"He doesn't understand the concept of apprenticeship."

"Fine." She disliked being in crossfire as much as ever. "Fine. But as for the nation's gratitude—wouldn't you rather be thanked sincerely? Wouldn't that be worth waiting for?" Musya tipped her chin at the skepticism in the slanting look he threw her. "You don't believe it could happen? Someday?"

Lately she'd been picturing a surprise visit of state to her model primary school in Kuldur, near the spa. While she'd been running its pedagogy more or less solo these days, word of her innovations had spread and sparked interest in high places—maybe the highest. Meanwhile back in Teploye Ozero and reality, more and more Jewish parents were making Musya's class the choice for sons and daughters whose very infancy brimmed with confidence and promise. It was a real pleasure to teach them. On the whole, hope and pleasure touched her every day and left her feeling more satisfied than her husband; which made a small division, one they used their still-ardent bodies to bridge.

He said, "And you all say I'm the dreamer in the family."

"Do we?" she asked his mouth.

Out-of-the-way empty shacks had their uses, she and Dovid weren't the only couple to know. They tied a handkerchief around the front door handle to signal temporary occupation. The place was cold like to store meat, even Dovid admitted, life wouldn't work there. They stayed in the longhouse.

The year would bring them news of friends by post. From Elkie word never came but Vera wrote often. Her moods rode a pendulum between exaltation and despair: the usual, only facing the tundra. By coincidence the population of the gulag had recently peaked. She'd found work right away in Kolyma's gateway city, Magadan, as a skilled stenographer must wherever record-keeping is a place's raison d'être. Far to the north lay her goal, a platinum mining camp where the primary man was at forced labor. Bribed perimeter lapses there kept the lovers exchanging messages with fair regularity but so far Vera hadn't been to see him. In and around her department worked men positioned to approve her travel papers, all sorts of men who could further her efforts in various ways, some who had genuine influence. One bureau head in particular had claimed willingness only to hesitate—when the string to pull was there to pinch, he'd refrained. Why should he help another man to have her, he'd demanded in a stairwell? His heart was involved now, Vera wrote. "Poor Magadan!" was Dovid's comment. But Musya liked to think of the gulag city benefitting from the romantic Leningrader and the bracing, probably welcome love tonics she brought to a cold dark troubled place; her craziness a sparkling flame there, kindling distraction, perhaps saving lives in mis-filed forms and documents left unstamped.

The most welcome word came from another part of the gulag where prisoners were resourceful. A message passed through a network of tundra peoples, including Nanai who'd expedited delivery to Kitty: her mother was alive, conscious, mobile. *Here work is hard*, read one line in her note, penned in her own effortful hand. The daughter rushed to throw open the doors of the icon armoire and fell to her knees, babbling thanks for note and knowledge alike—for the packages she sent were being received at least on occasion. Socks and gloves, chocolate, herring, tea, tobacco of course: Magga said to send more.

Mendel's persistent sister did more than write—indeed she'd been a regular guest. She turned out to have a passion for geology and relished the opportunity for field work. Sender Kotz would be alongside in a well-mannered way to haul her spare picks and specimen bags. Her presence was more agreeable the older she got, Musya found. The same held for her brother, who reappeared that spring. His unwelcome apprenticeship behind him, he'd taken a job at the Birobidzhan sewing factory—where all Dovid's old contacts were gone, at least Mendel didn't recognize their names. A tall dark-haired young man with a high nervous forehead, he had his mother and his sister in a bigger room already. Right away he'd begun encouraging his old friend to give up school and come join him at the factory, with his tailoring skills Sender could write his own ticket there, Mendel said—but the answer was no, the parents were opposed. Some university programs would still accept Jews, it was just a question of finding them—that, and patience. They wouldn't give up, the mother said.

In August the Soviet government massacred a dozen of its own citizens, Yiddish poets and writers who'd been charged with Jewish nationalism, treason, the standard list by now; in the hours following a secret trial that got talked of, taken from their prison cells and shot, men who had visited Birobidzhan and written of it, men who'd written for its journals and its Yiddish stage. Mendel and his sister had brought the news from a literary club they'd joined in Birobidzhan—their family couldn't learn a lesson, people joked. Maybe it was so. The club even risked having contacts with people tracking the case, from the arrests to the so-called confessions. Sad to say, the final report could be verified.

His Ghetto Uprising had counted badly against the poet Markish, dead among the rest. Championing Jews and Yiddish culture in the Soviet Far East proved fatal. Her teacher, colleague, co-founder, fellow poet-in-residence, bosom friend—so: Musya would never meet him. She felt this fact carve out a good-sized space of perpetual darkness that some part of her would dwell in for the rest of her life. A further deep and painful sadness spread shadow-like around the loss of Dovid Bergelson, her sister's former heartthrob novelist—he'd written the book on Birobidzhan, more than one. They were all out of print. Her own son had helped burn the last copies. *Our poor little Yiddish*, she thought.

At the same time, Musya couldn't shake her surprise at how much older than their years the two young visitors looked. Caressed and consoled in the seat between them Sender Kotz might have been a child weeping. "But Bergelson was always such a patriot," he sobbed.

"It does him no good now," said Musya. She watched the siblings' eyes meet across her boy's red-brown curls. They disapproved of her; thought her odd, no doubt; odd, coarse, unfeeling. Only her mind was full of still people stacks and library flames. If their poems were lost, what did it matter when poets died? Because it had already happened.

Once, her determinedly carefree youth had insulated Musya from a time of purges, a government attack on enemies within, conducted through mass arrests and show trials, torture, countless executions, millions sent to Siberian labor. First, all this had been a background to ignore; then it was history. She'd merely lived through these terrors which had sunk her sister's life, Liza's time of trial just as Transnistria was hers. The past divided so was mostly bearable. Now this: history reprised itself too fast and all her sister's side crash-added onto her own could not be borne, an hour like this was too unfair. She stood there trying to catch her breath. Her mind was in dust clouds through which she gradually recognized one of those periodic obliterations that happen in this, the Ernste's old World of Delusion. She knew, too well, how unsurprising the injustice of these murders. For justice was not a human quality. The claims of Lenin's inheritors were all bobe-mayses. Time improved nothing, it lacked that purpose. All earthly help could be absent now and for ages to come. And the habit of picturing otherwise was an enduring childhood greed for story, self-indulged at more or less lifelong expense. Musya, with all her orphan plans, had been taking pastime pleasure in the midst of catastrophe, surviving on images. They couldn't sustain a mouse. She was without protection from the super-weapons turned on her. An infant school teacher, a Jewish woman, Odessa-born, a wife and mother, one Soviet woman was not so small that she could elude every single attempt to exterminate her entire culture.

As for which, she ought to have been there taking bullets with the Yiddish writers, Musya considered. It wasn't only in her mind that she'd lost a colleague—he really had been. But she'd had her chance denied her. She might have had a career as a poet if the General Secretary had only kept his editorial hand to himself; many great poets published first in youth. Injustice piled on injustice. She remembered hearing how Liza had asked for a prison term with her comrades, how she'd felt cheated. Here was a similarity in them. A deep wrenching twist in her chest like something's attempt to escape and join its fellow cheated heroines and poets in a common grave, smothered by the same heavy shovel loads of dirt, prolonged itself.

Her breath was affected, Musya never breathed easily after this. So far as hill climbs went she declared the longhouse her topmost limit. All noises outside frightened her after this, too, which made another argument against isolation. She insisted they stay where they were but Dovid was stubborn and only moved his search to the lower slopes. Leads were few, little affordable. Then local housing rates went up like a firework on the strength of the fast-spreading rumor that Birobidzhan would be wiped off the map as some kind of continuation of the Yiddish poets' massacre, a general punishment. In Musya's family they assumed that Brother Dead Man's warning had gotten loose again in the whispery underground. The settlement prepared for an influx of Jewish refugees from the capital whom fear would make deep-pocketed. Some arrived, fewer than hoped; meanwhile another cement plant foreman paid to occupy the very last empty cottage. Dovid's family remained in the longhouse; for him, another injury.

Near the close of the year they heard also from Falk, prosperous in Haifa with a Beirut sideline, his temples quite gray and finally receding. If there was another woman on the scene by now, she hadn't made it to the family portrait. A father-son pair, the wine merchant sat embraced by the former grasspea cripple who stood otherwise at attention, limbs and midriff straining the confines of an Israeli Youth Corps uniform with a big set of muscles: Russvelt had really filled out. "You see," Musya observed to nobody in particular. "I'm not the only one." They put the photo on the little shelf above the Russian stove with the rest of the Novyi God 1953 greetings. Then on the holiday Dovid took his well-practiced ensemble out into the main hall to play modern swing for the longhouse to dance to if it liked. A qualified success given the number of noise complaints—yet not everyone had such conservative tastes and there'd been plenty of dancing with enough appreciation. Gratified, Dovid declared himself more than a match for his portly counterpart in the patriarchal armchair. He too was prospering, yes, in his own socialist Zion, and more enviably fruitful in children than most; a man—maybe not a business mogul or a scientific genius—but a man respected by his neighbors and even admired for his gifts.

A dark afternoon gathered them around the Russian stove and a half-prostrate Katerilena who'd hurried home with Kitty from the hatchery break room. Another terrible story: word leaked from ministerial kitchens on the caviar route. Since the war, beyond any doubt, the Soviet head of party and state on personal terms as a man had come to hate Jews full time, he'd gone completely over to it—this wasn't rumor but fact, Kitty said. He'd been hit by Hitler's aftershock maybe too hard and directly, he'd taken the worst lessons full on.

"The balebos was wrong. He always told everybody Birobidzhan would get wiped off the map."

"Annihilated," Sender remembered. Hodeh nodded.

"Not anymore," Kitty said. Instead, military police would round up all the Jews left in the rest of the Soviet Union for shipment by train to the Far East, all five million or so; for their own good, they'd be told. The trains carrying them would stop periodically so that guards could unload a lot of able-bodied men to dig a trench and then shoot the men so they fell down dead in it. The survivors would be disembarked at Birobidzhan station, sent down its front steps and marched through a gate. Downtown would lie surrounded by a barbed wire wall. No more than rumor? Kitty drove it in: "That's why the big expansion to the other bank—the regional authorities plan to move everyone else and keep the Jews on the old side. The zhid side now."

"Another ghetto," Sender's lips were gray. "My God."

Musya swallowed panic. "I'm so glad we moved out of the city," she said with all her heart.

Katerilena pulled herself upright to say no. "You don't understand—you will have to go back there too. The people around here will kill you otherwise."

"Our neighbors? Of course they won't."

"Yes," the Cossack girl insisted, devastated. "They will. He will make them do it."

Before she could argue, a commotion in the window glass caught her eye. Anton was dancing naked with one of Dovid's vodka bottles in the garden yard, in the snow. The yellow dog leapt as it circled him, panting clouds and kicking up ice crystal veils about his hips. They grabbed coats and hurried him inside before too many neighbors saw.

"Cement is very musical—cement is so musical!" Anton sang to no tune.

Then in March the great man died, their leader. What did Stalin die of—how? He died from death. Death killed him. Only death could, it took the force of death, like electricity but greater, like whatever beats the atoms into molecules but harder.

Late on the holiday given the Soviet Union to mourn, Dovid miscalculated and brought out the ensemble again. Musya didn't try hard enough to prevent him. Refusing his players' advice that they open with Aleksandrov's old Hymn, instead he led off with the sprightly theme song from Vesna. Within two minutes the peaceful hallway had become an angry mob scene rebuking his family for its show of disrespect. *Zhid* and *zhidy* foamed from many lips.

"Well," he said afterwards. "At least it wasn't mass-murder, that's progress already." Even so, his pride was crushed.

Their doctor escaped with her life, she was happy to tell them the story, by hiding in a forest; black cars were sent for her too late. It had been the dead of winter, as they recalled, when a bad flare-up of old falsehoods saw the Soviet Union's Jewish doctors marked for round-up and extermination. "Your husband is right," she said. "All Jews should know how to live in a forest." Safety returned with the funeral in leadership. But the experience had been enough for her, the last sufficient drop to make an ample patience overflow its cup. Her limits breached, she had divorced herself from the society around her. She said part of her had never left that forest.

"No of course," Musya said, "It won't."

"I might try to emigrate if I were younger. Moscow is bound to start raising the quotas now." Israel for her, the doctor thought. Her relatives who lived in New York City she couldn't stand.

Meanwhile there was good news for the patient and his family. The Soviet Union still had some top specialists of the ear nose and throat after all—and one would be in

Birobidzhan quite soon, coming to consult with its hospital staffs. The specialist wouldn't visit Teploye Ozero of course, but had offered to see a few cases from the settlement at a city clinic; the doctor had referred Dovid's son and he'd been granted a date and an hour in May. There wouldn't be a better chance to find out what could be done.

(14)

A heavyset woman sank down beside her and gave Musya's arm a convivial pinch. "I couldn't keep my figure either," she said.

At this interruption to her steam-gazing, Musya smiled and said yes, it was a losing battle. She tried to time her bathhouse visits to the emptiest hours but perfect success had eluded her again. Now as usual she felt crowded. All her life, maybe lonely but not once alone: tossed from her cramped family into a swelling non-stop procession of men, babies, children, other women, rapists, owners, even from ghosts she'd had no privacy. Nothing changed.

Boris Kotz was back. He'd returned the previous night, after so many years. She'd been trying to rescue further details of his visit from her foggy mind. She'd been in and out of sleep, just like the first haunting. A familiar pinkish glow bathed the slope-shouldered figure whose movements were hesitant, as if will in the afterworld were flickering, its wires time-corroded. He must have come along with the furniture from the old flat, she guessed. Thin as in life the hair needed trimming. The ghost had finally stepped away from the wallpaper, made straight for its favorite old desk, and busied itself with locked compartments: Boris was searching again. "What is it this time, Boris?" she tried to ask but nothing happened, she couldn't speak to him this time. And it took no time at all to find what he was looking for; she could see it in his fist when he turned although it was imaginary: a key. Crossing the bedroom that she shared in Teploye Ozero with her beloved second husband—Boris didn't give their bed a single glance—he unlocked a closet that didn't exist and threw open its two-paneled doors.

Musya had needed to squint as a blast of artificial light illuminated mirror-glass shelves packed top to bottom with souvenirs on a single theme. The silver-black blades of facial hair, the brow like a looming iceberg, the stars and the epaulettes, repeated and repeated; glittering as if by torchlight, the Father of Nations' far-seeing gaze met the bedroom from embossed tins and inkwells, nesting dolls, chess sets, etched mirrors and shot glasses, carved wood and malachite keepsakes, musical jewelry box lids; everything Stalin. Her dead husband's translucent hands moved between items, beating like a trapped bird against her eye in his indecision. No; that wasn't what he wanted, nor that one either. Why had he collected all this stuff? She willed the question to materialize inside his dead brain since her lips were frozen. Unsurprisingly, no answer came before the carnival-colored light dimmed and failed. Boris had already faded.

"Dovid!" she whispered and woke him with a shake. "Dovid, my dead husband was just here."

He rubbed an arm across his face. "Who—the genius of science?"

"He came to visit his collection, he's keeping it here in our wall."

"Hmm. I have no room for it, whatever it is—I hope you made that clear, Tovarisch."

"It's souvenirs of him, you know? Your Generalissimo. At his highest forehead. Tea glass holders, matryoshki, lacquered everything. Thousands. Boris must believe they're a good investment."

"Go to sleep." Dovid had turned back onto his shoulder, away from her. After a few quiet breaths, his voice came again. "He's probably right."

Musya doubted it then and now, as she wondered at the visitation's true significance. She couldn't forget how quickly, back in Obodovka, a coincidental meeting with the old pompom man and his tidings of her father's death had followed the last one. Had Boris in the afterlife become her bad news harbinger? She hoped not. Their appointment with the top middle ear repair specialist was two days away. The entire household wished that the little boy they'd known would be restored to them—for while present even in their rhythm section, he was missed in quiet.

"Women are supposed to be fat." The puckered figure steaming next to her spoke contentedly. "It is our nature."

Musya said, "It was Ukraine, for me. When I almost starved to death there—it made my body store everything."

"All women's bodies store everything. How else are we supposed to live?"

"Well, they say we should exercise more."

The fat woman laughed. "They have been saying that for a long time."

Of course the clinic visit was planned as the main event but a few hours cinema shows around Birobidzhan would be included, Musya hoped. Its bath house wasn't too bad but for cinema Teploye Ozero had only a single small barn-like place with hard narrow benches and lights that stayed on while the film ran. Really better were those summer nights when crews arrived by truck with a projector and portable screen and something decades old in canisters to play down on the lake park or Lenin square. Tsirk beneath the stars had been entirely delightful except for the ferocious insect bites it left.

Was Boris scolding her frivolity again? Or was she being warned against the soft beginnings of forgetfulness? Her dead husband and his dead mother who'd died in her hands, united so fiercely in their stubborn feud, locked in mutual contempt for one another's character—after this long, they'd grown more alike than not to their survivor, so much so that Musya remembered them both, whenever she remembered one these days, almost in the same thought. She asked the fat woman, "Did you ever see a ghost?"

"Not too many," was the answer. "You put out a pan of water, that keeps them off."

"Ah," Musya said. "I will try it."

"And buy new furniture."

She nodded gratefully. "I think so too. That is good advice."

Dovid had them booked at a trade union hotel in Birobidzhan with not the best reputation. It would be a small room so they hadn't brought everyone. Anton, Kitty and the Cossack girl were staying behind; Sender was along but he'd bunk with Mendel's family. Even now they could just fit on their facing passenger benches. Musya had claimed a window seat with the river view and put Dovid on her left where she liked him. He could watch the scenery above her head. The children large and small milled excitedly around the seats and aisle until all massed by her lap as they chugged above the warm lake shore. Waves and wild shouts poured out at the chub salmon hatchery where, on schedule, tiny with distance, a party of two waited by the last shed to see the travelers off for luck. Katerilena was the one jumping up and down with both arms in the air. Kitty's wave was slow and she stood and blew a cloud of cigarette smoke.

Then the settlement was behind them.

They'd picked up the latest Birobidzhan Star and gone straight to the cinema listings. Two fantasy films appealed, either Sadko or May Nights; either way, wall-to-wall Rimsky-Korsakov. Which Musya said she wouldn't mind, not all conservatism was terrible; but Dovid grumbled. The train hadn't gone much further when he announced his own ulterior reason for wanting this trip to Birobidzhan: a surprise plan to instigate the paperwork required for emigrating their household to Israel. Musya groaned softly. He'd talked of this before. His four year-old at her knees said no:

"Never!" He loved his present life. The brother beside him watched the view, oblivious to the topic. Both their black curly heads nodded in time with the iron wheels. The older children kept quiet except for Samuel Nemo who called it a great idea.

The mother disagreed. In her view, as scene changes went, Israel was too much more of the same. She'd never lived anywhere yet that hadn't pitted her life against Jew-hatred. What might as well have been God-sized global powers in violent collision had brought it down like lightning on all her days and her parents' and their parents' days before them. What had she learned except to take cover? What Dovid proposed, Israel, was a place she pictured as utterly open, a windswept salt desert baked by the non-stop blinding hellfire of the entire world's Jew-hatred. Why anyone would seek a situation not just so exposed but so closely surrounded by enemies, was a little beyond Musya's com-prehension. As for her husband, she considered that he'd caught this crazy idea from their doctor and now had too many Mediterranean prospects on the brain to consider the drawbacks, he was a man sun-blinded. "Our life is here, Dovid," she insisted reasonably.

He said, "This one is, yes. But we are still young enough to start another life there. Bring this one, start a new one—what could be better?"

"You mean." She looked at him. "Will Kitty come too?"

"Of course Kitty will come. Why that face?" he asked.

She said, "But why would Kitty come to Israel? She's not Jewish."

He said, "She can be. She will be. And then she can bring her little mother over God willing when Magga gets out."

Musya took a little breath. "You mean for them to convert?"

He said yes. "Sure. What does Magga care? As long as she can keep her icons, she wil be fine."

"I think you take it very lightly, Dovid," she objected, "now, when you cared so much to be an expert on being Jewish before."

"I don't take it lightly," he said with emphasis. "But I also don't see why Kitty and her mother should not have the same chance at a better life as the rest of us. Katerilena is not Jewish either, for that matter."

Musya gaped at him. "She is coming too?"

He said, "She is young, she will thrive there."

"My God."

She returned her eyes to rolling basketwork of blue and green the window framed as a trapped feeling descended. If Boris Kotz collected Stalin flasks, this one collected women. Now she understood.

"How would we even go there, Dovid?" asked Hodeh.

Dovid said, "How do you think? Your mother has her uncle in Haifa, we'll ask him to sponsor us."

"But he is not really," Musya objected. "I don't want to ask him for anything, Dovid. We cannot do that."

"Why not?" He frowned. She could only shake her head. Sender Kotz wouldn't like it, that was the reason. Indeed:

"We are not asking that son of a bitch for anything." This was Sender.

"This is not your decision to make," Dovid told him. "It is mine."

"And mine," Musya said. "And this is not decided yet, not at all."

Samuel Nemo spoke up again. "I think it is a great idea. You were really smart to decide it, Dovid." At eleven, he remained more set than the rest on trying to please the man he'd once defied and ease his dislike.

Dovid shrugged at him. "The idea is not original with me, it is a serious movement. As you would know if you would bother to learn anything about your religion—like I did, yes, your mother is right. I read a mountain of words." The figures rose, Musya thought, every time her husband related the number and length of the entries his eyes had digested on Jews and Jewish contributions to the nation. "And Jewish culture," he said. "In fact, here is what you should do, Pretzel. When we get to the city, why don't you take some time to visit your favorite library and ask for the Large Soviet Encyclopedia, find the primary entry on Jews, and instead of throwing it on a fire you should copy out the whole thing in writing, every column, every word—then maybe you can come to me and praise my decision to move this household to Israel."

"The primary entry," the boy repeated to get it right, his face burning.

Musya shook her head. "But you are not a bully, Dovid—no, of course not."

He said, "That's right, I'm not. If anything," he added, "I am an educator."

"The Coryphaeus of Education," Sender Kotz put in.

Dovid snarled. "Very nice."

"And what about the cats?" said Hodeh suddenly. "My cats."

"There are cats in Israel," Dovid told her.

"So you will leave your dog here?"

He said, "Taking a dog is different, Hodeh. Dogs can do work, an individual dog can be useful." Now he had an argument on his hands only the girl didn't say anything. Her black eyes were frozen wide in a worried stare.

Sender took a bored tone. "You sre always like this, Dovid. Every time when the nation fails to thank the Jewish veterans again, you are like clockwork."

"And what is this sneer?" Dovid asked him. "You think you sre better than Israel, too?"

"They barely exist except as a Western imperialist welfare state—they have no culture there at all."

Dovid gave a laugh. "Yes? You prefer a culture where all the Jewish poets are assassinated every fifteen years?"

Musya told him to lower his voice on the train. She said, "It is true, Dovid, you always start bossing everyone after Victory Day."

"Don't tell me what I always do," he said. "I am not ashamed of my consistency."

Even on a slow train the eastward journey wasn't long. They walked through Birobidzhan station and onto the broad front steps where Mendel's sister met them. The look she threw Musya had a chill in it. Then she and Sender Kotz were gone. It was nice to see Yiddish writing on the street signs again but no one spoke any. The hotel was as bad as feared, the dinner abysmal. Then cinema tickets were found not to come any-more through the old normal grilles one by one across marble countertops; instead some bureau in an office had got its claws on them all. Its representative, in turn, demanded an array of non-resident surcharges and, when met with protest, declared all performances Sold Out. There was no recourse with this sort of individual in seats of authority and they were everywhere.

The family wouldn't see May Nights, then, Dovid said, leading the way down the sidewalk. They'd enjoy a real one, instead, touring their hometown and capital city—briskly, to drive off the chill in the air. As the rest of them followed, Musya fought a sinking feeling; for it meant there'd be no let-up. She'd been counting on the musical to make a pause.

Now her husband would keep talking. In this way he attacked their resistance. They all knew the game. He had an advantage here, too, for the other side was short its two star antagonists; meanwhile their younger brother was dying to appease him. At dinner he'd gained an unexpected second ally in his youngest son, he of "Never!" It was Dovid's explanation of land ownership that did the trick. Musya sat and watched the emigration spark take flame: Israel was now another boy's unwavering goal. Always of uncertain help in an argument of words, Hodeh had gone quiet as clay. But then Musya thought this idea wasn't bad, to let talk wash over them. Would they crumble? She thought not.

Dovid felt too disillusioned to stay in the Soviet Union. Its forests pillaged, the bodies of water and land ruined for industry, for construction; but where was the progress? Not in Siberia, not in the famine-nipped Far East, where nothing changed. Work remained brutal and the culture low where it hadn't been exterminated. Crops failed constantly for lack of basic sense. The ravaged land could not in any case sustain life safely, not when it was running with poisons from weapons materials mining—his friends the trappers had seen mutations. Dovid's voice went on and on. He was signaling his presence, hoping someone friendly might recognize and stop to greet him. He was even leading them along a familiar route in the direction of their old gas un shtibele. But he and his family were like strangers here in Birobidzhan, their faces mirrored in Start's window full of Dinamo pennants and footballs unknown.

They kept on and crossed a few alleys where the usual sunflower patches were in leaf and still no sign of human tending. A final corner turned and there the old rooming house stood, changed almost past recognition, certainly improved, all its surfaces upgraded, facing the road across a concrete culvert where the ditch had been. A wide cement slab with railings led to a front door joined now to a business entrance. Where dead flies had once ringed the baseboards of the smoking parlor stood a fur coat shop behind a thick pane of plate glass; registered and everything, it had a city number sign. The shop was closed for the night but a pair of rose gold electric bulbs had been left burning in the window to display a few sumptuously-draped mannequins of mixed headless height.

"This all started with that ramp of yours, Tovarisch, believe it," Dovid said. And to achieve this result at such a speed, the scale of the bribery that must have been required verged on staggering. Dovid marveled at the enterprise of the ever-conniving Ossetians. "The fur looks better too, you know?"

His youngest son drew close. "Is it mutated?"

"I would not put it past them," Dovid said. He circled Musya's waist with an arm to ask, "Do you wish I would get you a fur coat made from genetic monstrosities?"

"I get more from you than a fur coat, Dovid," she laughed. The man could be exasperating but he charmed her.

That night at the hotel Hodeh waylaid her by the women's toilet door. In the feeble hallway lights her distress made a flicker; indeed the girl trembled. This was rare. Musya murmured something.

"Don't give in." Hodeh spoke through strained lips. She couldn't leave her cats behind, she didn't need to say it. "Don't give in." Musya reached to offer an embrace that she hoped would be comforting but Hodeh stepped back, away—she wanted more from her. "Promise. Promise we won't leave."

Again she reached and this time Hodeh let herself be embraced—another wounded child of disaster with the usual demand, that Musya bind herself in place, here in Birobidzhan, to staunch the heartbreak. This could be her role in life, she supposed. "Don't worry," she said. "Don't worry."

The next morning Hodeh smiled. She'd been waiting with Musya and the rest in front of a bureau downtown when Dovid exited stormily without even a piece of paperwork. Everything necessary would have to be done first in Khabarovsk, the clerks had told him, every interview and filing.

"But what are our chances?" Samuel Nemo asked. "Did they say?"

Dovid answered sourly, "Not good. As if they would know. What are you so happy about?"

"Nothing," said Hodeh.

He didn't get much better news at their clinic appointment, though it could have been worse. There were some drops which would wipe out the last of the old infection; they did help. The boy wasn't stone deaf now by any means. There were hand alphabets easy to learn and devices to be had from the Social Defense ministry, personal electric hearing amplifiers whose miniaturization and manufacture alike were on the cusp of booming; there was hope in that direction. But for now, the ear repair specialist gestured at Dovid's hands. "You see, we can fix some things but not everything."

Dovid said, "You call these fixed?"

The specialist looked dismayed and said, "They look quite serviceable."

"They are not," Dovid said. "My son here—could he get better treatment in Israel?"

The specialist said no. Dovid didn't believe it. They argued back and forth until the specialist said, "Then go to Israel. Why not? Maybe you will experience a modern miracle. But good luck because you are never getting to Israel first—Moscow is taking fewer applications than ever, believe me."

Back in the street Dovid gave way to fury. He raised his arms to bite at the straps. "Help me why doesn't someone?" he growled and struggled as too many hands tried to pull off his prosthetics. "Throw them out—throw them on the ground!" he ordered but Musya said no. She put them in her shoulder bag which Pretzel was happy to carry in her place.

Outside the older cinema Sender Kotz waited as planned to join them for Sadko; unexpectedly, he'd brought Mendel and his sister along. He greeted the young sufferer, his brother, asked him the news. The little boy shrugged and smiled. He must have noticed how deaf he'd become yet displayed few signs of minding—he heard through his skin, through his fingertips, they'd all watched him. Sender's news was bad: no tickets, again. Today's was a special benefit matinee for sewing factory pensioners, who'd made a line along the sidewalk out front an hour before-time, a frieze of crocheted shawls and humps.

Dovid gave a shout of laughter. "Enough of this fucking city today—enough!"

What would they do now? Disappointment wiped Musya's mind clean of suggestions. It was hours before their train back to Teploye Ozero. As the rest began debating, she occupied herself with the youngest boys and a naming game they played sometimes where she'd point at things and give the Yiddish words to match the Russian. Bruder was braht; schvester, sistra. The odd pair she was sure didn't like her: according to Sender Kotz, they thought she had a strong personality. Strong meaning what? Too abrupt, too pushy, she guessed. So let them see, here she was leaving others to deliberate and decide, keeping her mouth shut and her soul gentle like Bontshe Shvayg's, barely listening to an excursion get planned. Two pretty dresses she'd brought along and barely had her coat come off since they'd arrived. Now a trip across the river: she agreed, yes, it would be interesting to see where the rest of its citizens would have lived once they'd penned all the Jews on this side of Birobidzhan.

As he helped her off the gangplank Dovid said something Musya didn't catch. A bitterness in his expression kept her from asking to hear it again—she didn't want to hear it—and she turned away as if refusing him an answer. There was the river, they were on it, the Bira, its further shore a little lost in haze. The sky too was misted with cloud stuff, only here and there feathered. The children and Sender's tall friends had gone ahead and collected along the far rail to look out at the water which appeared breeze-blown, almost placid; but debris caught in its waves shot past. There was a torn fringe of shore ice where the shallows froze at night long into springtime. The deck of the barge ferry rose and fell underfoot.

"Maybe we don't really have time for this, Dovid," she said.

He came up beside her, his breath warm and strong kvass-laden. The fried fish and potatoes at the outdoor place above the ferry landing had also been excellent, he should have been happier. "That's what I mean," he said. "If you had ever come climbing the Sopka with me, you would remember how short this ride is." It was true, a single visit to the south bank, years before—mud, construction, gnus in swarms—had been enough for Musya. "How can I forget the way you refused to come along and watch me wave from the summit?"

"You know I wanted to spend that whole weekend home in bed reading. It is because I am a terrible wife to you, Dovid." She hugged his arm. The wood-draped Sopka reared its deceptive cliffs on the opposite shore. "It was a great achievement, you should be proud."

"I was," he said. "But compared to what I expected to get out of climbing that rock, how could it last? It was too much. Like thought I'd finally reach the top and—what? I'd become whole and young and optimistic again, be some whole new man standing there, at one with his land at his feet. *Siberia!* And then nothing like that happened. Nothing happened."

"But why would anything happen?" Musya asked.

He decided not to understand and said, "Exactly. What was I dreaming?" He threw a look back towards the landing, the loitering officials, the underfed animals, the filth. "Look at this place. It will never be as good as Israel."

She considered a more panoramic view. Blue and green, striped with brown bluffs and sandbars, its horizon trimmed with ancient volcanic swellings: "This is not so bad, Dovid."

He disagreed. "To come within a year of being the final graveyard of the Soviet Jewish people is bad enough, Tovarisch. But the restaurants also stink and the climate is awful."

"But we have been so happy here. And the children."

"What about the children?"

She sighed and looked around. "Everything about them." Children in her home, in her infant class, in her spa-forest dream world where she housed hundreds by now: as usual, she had too many. As a circumstance it made her feel bound in place and influenced her arguments. She resisted uprooting. Something much the same had happened once before. When it became time to leave Obodovka she'd found excuse after excuse to postpone their departure; long after they'd had anything to stay for, when they were almost alone in the liberated ghetto with no more sustenance, her children had finally prevailed and she'd started walking.

Dovid urged her now. "Imagine living someplace that's still at the center of history after thousands of years and not forgotten in thirty by everyone including God. Imagine raising children there."

"Well." Musya sighed. "Maybe."

He told her to picture warm nights and sea breezes, flaky Jerusalem pastries and conversations and wine; café tables crowded with new friends, strangers, Yiddish speakers, Americans. "And the music. Real Western music, no limits." He had a poignant look then. "I miss being a pioneer," he said. At times he missed the war years, he missed comradeship and struggle. "There is satisfaction in fighting a good fight—I know you don't agree. It is true though. Even getting out of town the way we did, even being a persecution target felt like something. And now, nothing. Now I am just a guy who lives in the country," he said. "You know?"

"What is nothing, Dovid?" she asked him. "What is nothing?"

He didn't answer, he turned and walked across the deck towards a small cluster of ferry workers and passengers. Musya followed. A barge rope had gotten caught on a big tossed-up rotten branch not far from shore. It might have been a blackened antler.

"Dovid," she called. "Why are you getting involved? You know you have no way to help."

He turned and said, "Yes I know I am not a genius like your first husband."

Then he shouldered his way in among the other men. They'd tugged all they could. A few were reaching for where the rope was tangled. Dovid did the sensible thing and ducked under the railing to kick down at the rotting wood. The rope came loose but the rest of the log rolled to the surface at the same time. Another dripping branch, it was a dead pine, reared up and caught Dovid and swept him into the water, pulled him underneath as it sank again and took him downriver in the fast current.

"Dovid!" She was frozen at first and could only call. "Dovid!"

He surfaced once, quickly. A barge worker threw him a rope but it went through his hands.

"No! Dovid!"

Haste and panic drove her against the railing with such force that her eyeglasses flew off her face into the water. She could see nothing but a white-hot globular shape-shifting glare. It was like she'd lost him in the noonday sky.

"Dovid! Dovid!"

Her mouth and throat had become like an instrument combined from all musical instruments, ivory and cowhide and cedar and catgut and brass; she heard her voice producing sounds from every cell in her body, her toenails shrieking. Musya shielded her eyes with both hands. Now the river looked rock-like. Dovid was under there. She threw herself at his rescue but iron chains bound her fast to the deck. Later she'd realize these must have been her children's arms around her.

She'd used all her screams. In her mouth instead a piece of Sender's old heart prayer was stuck repeating: "I, Musya Kotz a sinner—I, Musya Kotz a sinner—I, Musya Kotz a sinner." Her breath didn't stop. As she kept breathing, the immensity of heaven, pale blue, wordless, trackless, entered and left her erased.

When she woke up, her children were older. It was the same day, the same hour, what had occurred was coming back to her too quickly in pieces; and there were her children, no longer as she'd thought they were. Here was fact, actuality: taller, more worn-looking but somehow more handsome than before, the eldest were proving competent to manage every detail of the catastrophe while she lay there in and out of comas. As for Dovid's two, bawling their grief non-stop directly at her side, even tears could not restore the childishness to which her mind had pinned them before. New boys sat there.

Now all her children were fatherless.

In another moment of lucidity Musya realized she felt awful. She licked her lips and tried to speak. She asked, "Am I going to die?"

"No!" came an angry voice. Then a face, pink, weeping: Kitty's. This was a shock. "You will be fine."

Musya didn't think so. The past was too forceful. "But isn't this my deathbed? Aren't you going to chant? Aren't you here to wash me? Isn't this my deathbed?" The little boys increased their wailing. She felt more and more uncomfortable; a moment later she let out a cry. Then her heart joined her sons' heartbreak, noisily, until the next blackout.

In truth, most of managing was being done by Mendel and his sister. Natives from birth of its systems, the pair knew the city's service bureaucracy inside and out. Their contacts reported it doubtful that any charges would be pressed for the multiple criminal acts Dovid had committed, as determined at the scene. The law would say his interference had endangered the other ferry passengers along with its crew—a kind of sabotage that continued in the risks imposed by his drowned body in its elusiveness, in the chance it had of fouling some piece of river commerce or pulling the poor individual tasked with its immediate recovery overboard, maybe to drown; another life risked. Even avoiding the worst, like any manhunt on the river this one consumed time and resources. Spared prosecution, Dovid's family would be made to feel resented.

Every authority figure without exception demanded to hear the same thing: why he hadn't been wearing his artificial hands. And Kitty wanted to know this especially when she arrived. Sender had telephoned with the message: Dovid, killed on an excursion. She'd brought Anton to town while Katerilena stayed behind to look after the animals. "Why wasn't he wearing his hands?" She'd been asking almost every time Musya regained consciousness.

"He wanted music without limits," she told Kitty, she told them all. "He thought Siberia was ruined." As answers went, she didn't satisfy a single person. The hands got confiscated and were never returned to her.

They'd come to town just as room shortage season had peaked and they couldn't squeeze another night from their squalid hotel. Musya had an idea that she and the children would go down across the railroad tracks to the sheds where the old Jewish cemetery had stood; she pictured close-set corrugated walls divided by wildflower alleys. There they'd camp among memories and shades. Before she could form the suggestion, she'd wound up instead on a small shawl-draped sofa in Mendel and his sister's room.

Where too lived the mother, a permanent psychiatric invalid with a strong bottled medicine habit and a rail-backed chair in which she spent most of her time filling sheets of scrap paper with minute chessboard square patterns. Musya sat and stared at one, she'd been holding it in her hand for a long time, her mind drifting. The bereaved could please themselves—she decided this was a valuable lesson these moments were teaching her. The room was quiet save for the burr of the other wife's pencil. Maybe making a minor escape, their children had left them alone. Pinned all over the walls were others like the paper scrap Musya held, grids missing pieces, fractured, twisted, blown apart. Without her eyeglasses she had to stand up, get close, walk around. Soon she remarked: "I think these are good—this is very good, what you draw."

The mother hadn't spoken a word yet since their arrival so Musya was surprised to hear her say, "I was an architect."

She turned, impressed. "Don't you need a lot of training for that?"

"Years." She also had remnants of beauty. "Then I followed my husband into the Yiddish theater and became a set designer."

"Ah. I see." The husband had been a dramaturg but Musya wasn't sure exactly what this entailed. "A romantic story, then."

"I made a mistake."

"But," she answered, "I always heard, the productions were excellent back then, he must have been very talented." Tried and sentenced to ideologically regenerative labor in the gulag, leaving two small children, a boy and a girl, he hadn't been heard from since 1938. This woman his wife had been arrested, questioned, sent away and returned robbed of sanity. Now she didn't reply. Musya looked again at the work in her hand. "Then this is a building?"

"It is what's left of a building."

"I see."

What struck Musya as strangest of all about Dovid's death was that everything she'd ever done and felt and lived and suffered hadn't been enough to save him.

Samuel Nemo appeared in front of her. "My baby," she said. "You're my first baby."

"Mamenyu, pay attention. Please," he said. It was something of importance. A paper, he handed it to her. Handwriting, Pretzel's own. "I went there like he said, Dovid, I went to the library to find the primary entry on the Jews, to write it all down. I was going to—I thought when we—we could put it with him. But look."

Musya stood up and asked for her coat. Never in one hundred thousand years would she have thought to visit the Sholem Aleichem Library on this particular day but now she went there directly. Bad news was a favorite topic in downtown Birobidzhan and made her easily recognized.

"Your family stole library books," said the central clerk.

Musya said, "Your library burned library books." But they wouldn't let her past the desk. Samuel Nemo had to fetch the volume in question from the Large Soviet Encyclopedia. She brought her face close. It was true, as he said: the primary entry was barely one hundred words. From Dovid's mountain all the rest were missing. Even so the volume's weight tired her arm.

> "Jews" is the name of various nationalities which originated in the ancient Jews. They are not a nation since they do not have any common language, territory, economic life or culture. Yiddish is spoken by Polish, German and, in part, English and American Jews. In the past it was spoken by Russian Jews. In Russia hard-working Jews have the possibility of engaging in all occupations and professions and take an active part in building communism. Thus in the U.S.S.R. there is no Jewish problem. Jews are being assimilated in the general population.

"It's the new edition." 1950, the clerk told her. "We got it last year."

Musya nodded. "You should burn this too," she said.

"Grieve at home," the clerk requested. "Please, not in the library. Go home to where you live now and grieve. And send our books back."

"Why not here?" Musya cried. "Because you are afraid? You think something terrible followed me in here—the same thing that wiped all the Jews out of your books, maybe you think it might get you next? Well—you are right!" From all over the library voices came shouting for quiet, so many men reading newspapers. She shouted over them. "You are not safe—none of you!" Hands led her out the door to the sidewalk. Once again she faced no immediate charges but the limits of civic indulgence were probably being stretched. Mendel suggested staying inside.

"Until," he said.

They all knew what he meant. Another night ticked by. The odd family's friends and neighbors were being generous with bunks so Musya's whole household was near—her surviving household. She wept her pillow wet straight through. It had some exotic grain stuffing, Mendel's sister wasn't pleased that she'd probably spoiled it.

The Kotz brothers came to her formally, after lunch. Sender couldn't talk for crying so Anton was spokesman.

"If Hodeh has to go out to earn parnosseh then we will go with her."

"Why would she?" Musya asked. "Who would want this?"

He said, "But with Dovid gone—she'll need to earn her way."

The older brother collected himself a little. "I can, a job, the sewing factory."

Musya said no. "Hodeh should stay in school. You should all stay in school as long as they'll keep you. Take your time." After everything they'd been through, children like hers should not be required to enter the Soviet workforce; she believed they deserved an exemption.

The blue river Bira held Dovid to herself, she'd made him her consort and king of all her waters. Spotting him on the gangplank she'd stumbled, tumbled, smitten: their family's loss, of course; but a river's love was stronger. His hair had turned blue, and his blue beard would soon grow long enough to reach all the way back to Teploye Ozero, Musya told his youngest son who watched her mouth with a worry line between his brows. She said, "You don't believe me?"

Hodeh spoke for him. "He doesn't know all that Yiddish."

"He doesn't?"

"You only taught him a few words before."

"Yes. I forgot," she said. This one, now she remembered, had slept in his father's arms through an entire broadcast of Pique Dame back on the old flat's tarelka, the whole opera with narrative interludes, he never woke once. Dovid loved to make a human cradle for his sons. That night Tchaikovsky put his poor arms into cramps, he'd made a clown show of his pain to start her laughing. Why, why had she laughed when she ought to have stroked his arms and planted kisses on him everywhere, this man she idolized? His arms into which she'd escaped with her life, his body that had been her sanctuary— lost, cold and waterlogged and lost to her. Holy fire had gone from her existence. She was a dead pripetshik.

Hodeh spoke again. Musya didn't understand right away. "Curse? What curse?" she said.

"Mine," Hodeh said. "On Dovid. Because I didn't want to leave. Are the others right? That I cursed him—so it's my fault?"

"They don't think that," Musya said.

"Yes they do."

She looked at Hodeh uncomprehendingly, this girl with the strangest beliefs. "But how could it be your fault when it was my fault? Who needed you to curse him when he had me?"

After the telephone call arrived on the third day came the trip to the police morgue. Musya's feet propelled her forward, she had no sensation of willing this, past the dead in rows. The surroundings reminded her of the obstetrical clinic and how she'd felt there, knowing the conditions to be light years beyond the Obodovka ghetto's, infinitely better—and yet they felt worse, somehow more inhumane. Row upon row of freezer lockers passed on either side: Who did these men who'd built this place think, she wondered, they were fooling?

The police kept Dovid's head in a covering, she never saw his face again. Oily, strangely so, he threw off a scent of chemical flowers; the boat crew that picked him up had packed him with cleaning fluids. His ridiculous tattoo that he'd never deciphered for them—too late. His ruined troubadour's hands. His cloak of skin.

They buried Dovid in Birobidzhan where the city cemetery had a Red Star veterans' corner. Fanny wasn't far away. The setting was damp and the earth would stick to the fingers. A slight commotion at the graveside marked the alcohol-delayed arrival of Anton and Kitty, who maybe shouldn't spend the kind of time together that they did, Musya considered, as she watched their weaving approach. Anton was sixteen. He had the ancient satchel in his arms. They'd bury Dovid in the Siberian tiger skin, this was his sons' tribute to him. A murmur approved: friends, men and women from the old lathe parts shop floor, fellow veterans, fur trapper families, over two dozen mourners had found their way to the place in addition to the old bandmates who'd shown up at the place with instruments; there were several trumpets present, for as a trumpet player he'd been the best of them all, they said. Everybody was standing there, tears pouring down. Dovid lay in an open box, sewn into his shroud. To Musya, she and the rest of them were nothing but a garland of seaweed wrapped around him there, floating with him on a marshy shore.

Anton unfurled the tiger skin and draped it, still burnished, glowing, unquenchable, on top of the terrible linen. With a great cry Samuel Nemo threw himself across the body. He beat at the stripes and sobbed, inconsolable; for he and Dovid had never been reconciled. Sender Kotz held his youngest brothers close. At last Hodeh went to the weeping boy's side and drew him back with her thin arms.

Musya watched helplessly. She wept for her children and yet her own grief held her fast, a wasteland spectacle beyond compare. The amount her body missed him already was enough to leave her staggering. Dovid's children, his friends, not a soul standing there hadn't suffered, she knew. Most had endured some hell on earth more or less lengthily. But no one else could know what it meant for Musya to lose Dovid, no one could count that far, she thought. Her Paradise Darling, yes. She held her own sobs in a hunch, against a ruined dress. She tore off her paisley headscarf to loud gasps and threw it at his hidden face, let them close the coffin lid upon it. Only for Dovid's sake, only in his arms had she been something more than bald and fat, scabby and unlovable, Musya wept.

Onto her bare head Mendel's sister slipped her brother's hat, a sort of fedora that he told her to keep. Finally a sputtered shriek of trumpet notes led the way into the single hymn appointed by Dovid's survivors:

> *Arise, you cursed and branded masses!*
> *Arise, you famine-stricken slaves!*
> *Arm your consciences for battle—we have our human race to save!*

Our minds revolt in outraged struggle;
of our former bonds let there remain no trace;
the earth to rise on new foundations:
> *Unified, from nothing,*
> *shall we be all and one!*
Comrades, rise and forward march, let us fight the final battle:
The Internationale shall be the human race!

(15)

The yellow dog rocketed across the grass and leapt ecstatically among the legs of the returning party; from her little dog past she feared abandonment. With her children flowing in around her, safely delivered, Musya walked a little way into the longhouse rooms. A cat-ravaged burlap sack had released potatoes across the clay-tiled floor, they made the narrow-waisted constellation. Orion, was it? Whom could she ask? No one believable, no authority. Rising in her way she perceived old uncertainties she'd gotten used to sailing past; as if an inland sea were being drained, all the old reefs and wrecks of her formerly manless state, even the outlines of defenseless girlhood, stretched before her. Musya's ears rang—she couldn't face the home quite yet. She found an old pair of eyeglasses and went back to the garden yard.

Overhead some kind of aircraft roared in anonymous flight with no one to tell its name. Musya looked towards the river. One missing view past her sand-colored view splotched with purple and green—there it was. The bereaved, she could see what she wanted. Her mind supplied the indigo, the stripe, the water witch's ribbon that had snared her love. She commanded the Bira to stay, the stronger witch from here. Then it was gone in the weak lenses. Grief conferred no powers.

The dog sat staring calmly towards the cement plant and the path uphill that Dovid always took. His dog was happy; patience and devotion made her so. She was under a spell that Musya recognized and missed to the point of pain. As she added to the dozen apologies she'd told the dog already, her sore heart felt suddenly more swollen on the animal's behalf and a sob broke from her chest. The dog heard a difference, turned her great wolfish head, and gave a questioning whimper.

Behind them a door banged and Kitty stumbled out into the garden yard. She hadn't stopped crying. Her face with the drink or two she'd just taken had turned the new flamingo color they'd been pushing for the summer season back at the Universal Store in Birobidzhan. From what she appeared to say now, noisily through obstructing tears, Kitty ought to have been present on the fatal trip, she claimed the medical putevka could have been stretched to a third adult.

"But the room was too small," Musya objected, a little fog-bound. Kitty's point looked absurd to her. "Why should you have been there?"

"Because I can swim!" Kitty screamed. "I can swim! I could have saved him, don't you understand?"

Musya mind filled with icy currents, speed, submerged tree trunks like torpedoes, everything hurtling, even the needles on a drowned pine branch—pictures of a ruined forest rushed downstream, made antithetical to life; its own roaring vengeance. "No," she said. "No."

But Kitty wouldn't be persuaded. Frantic with angry regrets she kept talking. Always, she said, there'd had to be these ludicrous occasions with the wife alone, a regular sacrifice he couldn't neglect or else there'd be trouble in poor Dovid's life. Musya was never satisfied, Kitty said.

Musya looked at her. "What are you talking about? You know? Forget it. I don't care. I don't want to know. Don't tell me."

Kitty shouted, "Typical!" Then she started talking. A lengthy history: hers, Dovid's, Musya's; their schedules, their opportunities. "That day you lost your job," Kitty said. Only an hour earlier home and she'd have caught them, this was one claim. Musya heard all sorts of first times and next times and a usually or two; mostly she heard Kitty's frequent refrain and variations: "What about me? What was I supposed to do? What about my happiness in life?"

Without any doubt, everything the dvornik's daughter knew about the monologue form she'd learned at the State Yiddish Theater, the influence was extremely apparent, Musya thought, listening with somewhat uncertain attention; for marvelment distracted. The pink-faced unsophisticated girl she'd first seen bent across the bloodstains on her sister's dying body; the wounded air war veteran frozen in a virginity with nowhere to go; the profane and argumentative after-hours drunkard whose painful life bought her infinite forgiveness, who clung to this family she came close to abusing—beneath this long-familiar floor lay a Kitty she'd never suspected: a grown woman whose tastes weren't limited to boys. A woman who had tried to steal her husband; and might have succeeded to some degree, as seemed indicated by Kitty's account. Musya felt herself starting to shake at these revelations.

"But what about your hernia?" she asked weakly.

Kitty stared. "It's a hernia."

"Fine," said Musya. "Fine." How could it matter now? But she couldn't give up, either. She fought herself aside. "But I think if what you say was anything, it was not like you say, not that much, probably closer to nothing."

"Closer to nothing? Let me ask, did you two discuss how I would come to Israel too?" She nodded. "So what does that tell you, Musya?"

She paused to think, and answered. "He said Katerilena was also coming."

"That was not the plan," Kitty said.

Musya stared. "You were in love with him."

"So what if I was? I liked him first," Kitty said stubbornly. "From the first day I saw him at the plant. You never even looked at Dovid before I liked him."

This was craziness, Musya thought. A terrible notion burst upon her. "And that's why you refused to go north to the ice fishing camps and help your mother escape—that's why you wanted to stay?"

"He wanted me to stay," said Kitty. "Not to leave."

"Who?" Musya said. "Dovid? Yes he did want you to leave."

"No he did not."

"He said it was Magga's only chance."

"Only in front of you," Kitty said.

What was the truth here? Dovid could have said anything, that wasn't the question. But what had been going on—what had happened? Yes, between her orphans at first and her health cures at Kuldur more recently, she and Dovid must have spent a hundred nights apart, even more. It might have been too many. On the other hand, it had never felt bad. She'd had a happy marriage.

As for the marriage's entirety, Musya would never know the truth, she could only accept this. What was past was beyond her human reach to recover. So, did it matter? What she'd believed—that Dovid had always been no more than kind to Kitty out of pity and decency—might have been ludicrous. Musya lost nothing in that case. Marriage, happiness, children, didn't go anywhere. Of her body's pleasure in her husband's not one single swooping flight was altered by a stitch-length. Was the atmosphere of time a little stained like a blue polluted sky? Yes; but probably not forever, Musya thought. Whereas poor Kitty might have been seduced; she might have had a secret love affair with Dovid; she might have pursued him for more than he regretted giving once or twice; or she might be lovelorn to the point of lunacy because he'd never touched her. Whatever the facts in her case, she'd let her own mother get arrested and sent to the gulag for them. Poor Kitty had bad outcomes either way. "Your conscience must hurt," Musya said.

"Shut up," said Kitty. "Who are you to talk about a conscience? You set your sights on him and stole him from me."

"Hah!" said Musya.

"Then he was never good enough for you. Like coming from Odessa made you so great—I know from your sons, you know, they told me your father was a dvornik too."

"Only briefly!" Musya said.

Kitty kept on. "Then Dovid was stupid, you called him stupid every time he made you angry."

"I did not." Musya feigned certainty. Had she done that?

"You did," Kitty said. "Then you start having one abortion after another."

"Two abortions!" Musya shouted. In fact she'd had three.

"Liar!" Kitty shouted back.

Musya raised her chin bravely and almost lost her hat—one hand was quick enough and caught it. She'd just remembered how she'd laughed at Dovid and the show he'd made over his Pique Dame cramps, yes, at first. But then she'd stroked and kissed his arms, the recollection was clear, she hadn't been remiss, not that time.

Of course everything she'd done to tend and soothe him hadn't been enough.

"Then you refused to go to synagogue with him when he begged you." Kitty was still talking.

Musya said, "What business is that of yours?"

"Don't attack me for the truth," Kitty said.

"The truth? But I don't like organized religion, I don't want my children to be religious."

"But they are. You cannot stop them," Kitty said. "He hated it that you tried."

"That whole synagogue was arrested," Musya reminded her. "And the poor rabbi—Dovid could thank me for saving us."

Kitty said, "He didn't. He said you had no conception of offering strength in numbers."

"Oh!" Musya let out an aggravated cry at this conversation in general. "Fine. Then why did he choose me instead of you? Because he did choose, he did like me, believe me, you know? Dovid married me. So why?"

Kitty said, "Because you went bald and you had a hard war."

"That's true," Musya said. "Both those things are true—but they are not why"

"They kept him with you, though," said Kitty. "They kept him loyal." He'd been more than loyal, Musya had nothing but certainty on this point among all others. Before she could say so, Kitty added, "And you were Jewish."

"He loved me from the past, you know," Musya said. "He came back to the Far East after the war for me."

The other woman nodded. "His great roadside ideal, yes. A nice story."

"It was more than a story—it was true. That was truth!"

"So what?" Kitty said. "His needs went beyond ideals, they went beyond stories."

"I understood," she answered, "Dovid's needs, my husband's needs, very well, thank you." Kitty let out a dramatic laugh and asked why in that case the man could keep neither his hands eyes nor mouth to himself. Musya didn't like how Kitty's pink features were set. "So what are you telling me? My husband was some monster, he needed a woman every minute, more and more? More than me, maybe more than you. Katerilena—was she part of this? Or maybe he did something to Hodeh, is that what you are saying?"

"To Hodeh? My God, of course not, what kind of man do you think he was? Yes maybe Katerilena he might have tried something on a time or two but Hodeh, he considered his own daughter."

"I thought I knew!" Musya wept with suddenness. "I thought I knew what kind of man he was."

"You thought he adored you."

She raised her face. "He did adore me! He did! And I am the mother of his children—not you, Kitty. Only me. Froy un muter," she quoted through sheets of tears. They veiled her from the other woman who flickered there with her soldier's persistence. "He must have pitied you because you were a virgin—you're the one he pitied!"

"No," said Kitty. "You were. Dovid always felt guilty after that accident on his old shop floor, when all your hair fall out. He blamed himself even though there was probably no connection." Kitty blamed stress, Musya knew she would have told him so. "He blamed himself for your illness."

"I am not ill," Musya said.

"Suit yourself," said Kitty. Before she could answer, the yellow dog rose with a growl as a dark rumbling streak, some kind of aircraft's dog-sized shadow passed across the garden yard. A MiG-17, Kitty exclaimed. "We're sending in the new ones," she added with vigor, watching from her tiptoes until the jet fighter vanished. Musya studied her.

"You are sure it's not the other—the fifteen?"

Kitty was quite sure. The wing angle, the fuselage, everything looked faster. To her own relief, Musya believed her—about aviation, that is, she believed Kitty. As for the rest, it already wearied her faculties so much that she felt half-ready to concede the rest. She thought their conversation must have done the dvornik's daughter good, in any case. For a change Kitty looked unburdened, forthright, returned almost to youth. Only fresh canvas showed her sorrow in relief. She'd lost her love, no matter what was true. Poor Kitty, too bad she hadn't made a better choice; or maybe she'd had what she wanted.

Musya sighed. Even her heart would be crowded while breaking in this life, she supposed; even her widowhood she'd need to draw a blanket wall around for privacy. "I'm going back inside," she said. But on the doorstep she found herself caught in a squeeze. Katerilena blocked her way while at her heels came Dovid's dog. The Cossack girl wore the heartsick look of someone directly involved who'd just overheard the previous conversation. If there was a trace of guilt, Musya didn't perceive it.

"Don't worry," she said. The dog slipped past them into the hallway and waited there with an unreadable expression for Musya to follow. She started, then she paused to turn and call:

"Wait—did he ever tell you what his old tattoo meant?"

Kitty blew a cloud of smoke and nodded yes, he had. "It was a little bulldog. Because he'd always wanted one"

"Ah. Good."

Other scenes would follow, other duels to the same draw. The last of the Manchukuo dessert plates would crash against a wall one night. But there was no question of the household coming apart when no one had anywhere to go. In fact they faced the dismal prospect of a stranger or two being moved in on them forcefully. Only just then someone had an afterthought—no one confused it with mercy—and put a stamp on it. The dvorniks were pardoned.

And Kitty's mother came home to her daughter alive. She lived with them now. Since long before the ground thaw she'd been toiling in their garden patch day and night. Magga loved the soil, she loved everything living; she had other things going in pots and window boxes. Sad to say, the family table got the meagrest share and stayed mostly stocked from shops, for the old woman ate up almost every bite she grew. But who could blame her? As Kitty said, she'd lost a lot of vitamins. Fortunately, Magga left Musya's flowers alone. Marigolds, zinnias, margaritkas: she guessed prisoners in the Arctic Circle got no chance to learn how deliciously certain blooms could assuage a well-developed famine hunger. Of course the children wouldn't agree, back in Obodovka they'd always protested Musya's plain floral dinners. Born to criticize, these were her children. Some stalks of chamomile; she grew masses to make bowel-treatment tisanes to treat the periodic complaints common to people who've survived being murdered by starvation, painful episodes which didn't serve to make any of them less anti-social.

Musya lowered herself onto the wooden bench and fanned her face with a battered fedora brim. Carrying water from the outdoor tap across the yard to the garden table had left her winded. Mrs Drobitz's tin pitcher, the old battered red thing that she only used for flowers now, she'd only filled it halfway. Once she'd used to manage it brimming across ten times the distance. The progress of her decline hadn't set aside its power to shock for the occasion, plainly. Even on her birthday came this jolt. She closed her eyes to announce in a voice that cracked, "This is a depressing world, gentlemen!"

The old former dvornik hadn't raised her head from the leafy border. Only Dovid's dog interrupted a rest day sun-bath to send a look across the grass at this familiar remark. Her constant companion, the yellow dog bedded on the old wedding quilt at Musya's feet and made a figure of authority and daily order in her classroom at the LJIS. Widow and dog both came closer to thriving this way. Their life involved no very great exertion, a good thing since the dog especially had struggles. They took the hills slowly. They practiced pausing. And neither one remained too proud to be pulled in a cart sometimes, despite the experience being, yes, a depressing one. They were popular but soon they'd face forced retirement.

Musya looked at the dog. They missed Dovid still. "What, you don't agree with Russia's greatest comic writer?" Fresh recognition sparked a drowsy doggy smile. The velvet-plush eyelids had already drooped shut; next the great head lolled and followed, lowered and returned to a well-earned doze.

She went back to trimming stems with the old sharp scissors, long-retired to floral duty. When it came to their couple, Dovid had been a bigger reader overall than she and the one to read Russian, quote Gogol, quote poetry. Month by month since his death she'd slipped into her husband's place among words, assuming his share of attention to written language. She read and read where before she'd sat dreaming by the tarelka. As Musya read she'd tap and tap her leather bookmark on the cover in a way that tortured Kitty's nerves. Surprising everyone, she'd also insisted on maintaining a well-informed home; to this end she scanned all the wall news she passed for discussion points. And each week Musya could barely wait to get her hands on the latest Birobidzhan Star. Her eyes had a thirst for the Yiddish pages.

Dovid's first son flickered up to her side, smiling, fish-like, half-naked in the style of Tarzan the Ape Man from Hollywood. Ever since its little House of Youth Culture had screened that trophy film quartet, shirtlessness had taken hold settlement-wide, a craze among males of all ages. Musya worried too much over the boy's health to stop objecting. While his bowels were fit as any in the jungle, he looked frail to her, his old infection ever-incompletely cured, his ribs violet-shaded, his clavicles a narrow wishing ledge over twin shadowed pools. The deaf boy declined a lecture, only wanting to give her a kiss and deliver the big bunch of wild pinks and purples he'd scoured from the hillsides. He took up Musya's little notebook from the seat, for she was writing now and then, and flipped through its pages in his usual way without understanding a word; but even his Russian studies had lagged. Another quick embrace and he was through the longhouse door.

Seconds later she heard him at drum practice, the band's demon rhythm section, its heart, soul, and occasional star. Although it was in this sense an all-star ensemble—even the shy violinists, even the shrieks of Kitty's clarinet inspired a following. "Too modern for my ears," Musya would say of certain of the other woman's solos, trying as usual to be agreeable. Her success rate not being the greatest, she acknowledged. The way she took a stand against any change in furniture, anything new, her refusal to hear arguments for it, even—this wasn't pretty.

In fact argument would be a weak point with her ears so unreliable these days. Her pride in the wax plugs she'd used to fashion for the shop floor looked misplaced in retrospect, when she had the sensation of wearing a set that wouldn't come out; worse, they'd trapped a shrill incessant jingling like a fly inside her skull. Magga, adding her own broken ear to their number, had taught the entire household a deaf prison language that was very much at odds with the one they'd attempted to learn from the state-issue course booklet. Once more Musya's family found its tongues mixed and difficult to sort.

A household incompletely restored, still bereaved, half-deaf, deviled by bowel complaints, and better understood among themselves than by their neighbors, they turned isolate—with exceptions. At rare times they went into public and performed. All but Musya and the old dvornik did, that is; for Katerilena had shown herself to possess a distinctive singing voice, she could really croon. The chub salmon hatchery kept asking the ensemble, which went by Dovid's patronymic, back to play swing at its twice-yearly dances. They'd shone at two of the settlement's May First arts festival programs and appeared likely to become a permanent feature at the cement plant's Revolution Day banquet, a big occasion with a grand piano, where Dovid's youngest son stood pounding out boogie-woogie figures for Ale Brider straight from his father's American short waves.

So much that would have pleased Dovid to have in life, possibly even enough to have solaced his insulted heart, came to them after he was gone. Their own pleasure in the applause they earned was bittersweet and mildly skeptical. Would their contribution be so welcome if the father figure were still around running things? For they never had been welcome then. Maybe if he hadn't been too fearsome a hero among men of lesser intellect and worth, his loved ones decided, Dovid might have pushed further ahead.

And Musya also thought a little stage career might have satisfied the man's mental hungers far enough that he wouldn't have needed distractions like Kitty. Because as for the rest, if Kitty's claims were true then Dovid's despair had been deeper than she'd known—Musya hadn't grasped the measure of it that she'd thought she had. Kitty was right, his needs had yawned engulfing anyone's ability to meet them. A cold lightless pit had reigned inside him all along.

"Either that or he liked easy thrills and couldn't resist," had been Vera's reply to this confession.

"Maybe he was right," Musya insisted then. "He should have gone like his friends to live alone as a fur trapper."

Vera said, "Maybe. Only he needed three women to cook for him."

It was true: Vera had an answer for everything except her own heart, she'd said, while making the briefest of visits on her way back to Leningrad. She travelled alone. Thanks to a miracle pardon the primary man had been released, the blissful lovers reunited, a cosmic circle completed with a snap around the wrist of divine eternity. This was as expected but then fate had astonished her. Despite being possessed of every legal right and title to his family's large private flat off the Nevsky Prospect, the love of her life had announced a wish—nay, an intention—to remain in Kolyma as a foreman at the platinum mine. There as a prisoner he'd impressed the management in his favor, they'd asked him to stay on. He wanted to stay. He found the work enjoyably interesting and his mind was full of ideas for improving conditions under which the men still forced into the mines there labored, unpardoned. Vera said no.

"I said no," she said. "Do you have any idea how horrible it is there? No, you don't," Vera had asked and supplied in the same breath.

"Well," said Musya.

Vera said, "Maybe you think so but believe this, wherever they kept you for the war was some dollhouse compared to what goes on in Kolyma."

"It was not," said Musya definitively. "But what about love, Vera, what about the Dekabristi?"

"What about them? I'm telling you, those women were on the Côte d'Azur compared to Kolyma." She'd also overstayed her propiska and had been forced as a result into a tricky grapple with the smitten bureau head while claiming his assistance. She could not wait to put Siberia behind her, in the past: a footnote, she'd call the entire adventure. "To live someplace so inhospitable to life, honestly, I think it shows a lack of self-respect," Vera said.

"But some people will always have to be here. Some to make the cement, someone else to teach their children."

"Necessity! Compulsion!" The Leningrader couldn't live that way. "The only oxygen is in major cities," she said. Even so, Sender Kotz suggested that she wouldn't pass up the Côte d'Azur if it were offered. The idea made Vera smile her sad smile. "No, never. My heart is Russian. I could never leave my country."

Sharing goodbyes down at the station, Musya hadn't felt convinced of their finality, for Vera had always been popping up again. "Don't let your figure go too much more, Musya," she'd cautioned from the steps of the two-berth cabin carriage; her bureau head had done well by her, Vera had to admit. The farewell party caught another glimpse of her, silvery through a rolling windowpane she stood framed in her cabin door, her face alive with recognition, passion, maybe outrage, maybe fear, before a well-dressed male's imposing figure rose to block their view with pinstripes. Worrisome at the time; but the mystery liaison must have ended safely. For here a card from Vera brought birthday wishes and news. She was working in Warsaw, attached to something in cultural development. Vera loved Poland. The men were like fire gods.

Musya sighed and replaced the card in its envelope. She felt a little jealous but then she didn't have Vera's energy. Now, back when she'd been nimble, she might have made a dent in Polish manhood, too. These days she had a tremor in her hands. Their Jewish doctor had put her through several tests and said the results probably wouldn't be good. What did she expect? She'd been starved, exposed to many diseases, an industrial accident victim; heart-scarred, systemically acid splashed and seared by the screams of her children and other people's children, she carried a lot of damage around in one small frame. On the other hand, said the doctor, "Plenty of sick women fat like you hang on for ages." Musya thought she'd try to secure one last rest vacation to Kuldur where she could sit on a balcony looking at trees.

Sender Kotz and his oldest friends surprised her coming up behind with their arms full of water iris for the birthday arrangement. Mendel and his sister had been regulars for years at family celebrations. They remained very odd, believing for instance that the Soviet space program was sham, nothing but a studio production organized by Jews enslaved under Stalin's orders and never liberated. Somewhere up above the Arctic Circle or maybe in Kazakhstan, was their claim, Jews labored in gargantuan underground shops over tinfoil models and snippets of film, while Yiddish theater greats coached goyim playing scientists through triumphal photo-sessions. Ideas like these would have been too extreme for either of her husbands, Musya thought; and then she wondered. In any case there was no talking brother or sister out of them.

"Ah!" said Mendel. "My old hat. You still wear it?"

She did, all the time. And the sister praised her headscarf. It was one Dovid hadn't liked so she'd never worn it; she'd found it lately at the bottom of a pile. She kept getting compliments on having a new one although the entire collection was more like antique, gifts of twenty years ago that might have been heirlooms when her sister's friend Fanny presented them. Some were so fine that in these times they'd have taken the most dramatic black market extravagance to acquire—and to quell any rumors on that count, Musya would always explain. Every scarf she wore had been a gift between dead women, one of them her sister, she'd say, who wouldn't even have been forty years old had they lived. She got the impression that people walked away thinking she'd had a sad life. Of course Sender's friends already knew her silks' history.

Musya was thirty-six that day.

"You don't look it," said Mendel. "You look ten years younger."

"Well, five," said Sender. That made Mendel's sister laugh. Though long convinced that there was true warmth in the odd siblings' affection for her, Musya's certainty had never waned that the offer—which remained open—of a home with them in the city was still being pitched to Sender with one big positive: she, Musya Kotz, wouldn't be there. But he was too loyal to ever go and leave her.

Not that his paying customers around the settlement were about to let him escape. Graduated with awards, he'd now begun studying for entrance examinations to university, a process that could take years in the Soviet Union; Boris Kotz was one she'd known who'd gotten caught there. Meanwhile Sender would slip into his grandfather's thimble; for he'd developed a secret sideline as their peerless young king of alterations and tailoring for both sexes, by appointment. Musya helped him when she could, since it had been her idea in the first place. No, Sender was stuck there.

His younger brother was another story. Anton would be the first to leave. From Tepoloye Ozero's point of view, while his musical gifts would be missed there'd be a measure of relief in this one's departure. His brooding presence on guitar at the festival last May Day had inspired emulation, and now much of the settlement's youth had slacked off at its studies, grown its hair too long, taken to drink and composing. He was in addition a personally charismatic figure in a small pool of options. Mothers and fathers grown weary of having to keep their daughters behind deadbolts would be very glad to see him go.

It was a farewell concert the players planned to give themselves on her birthday. Anton was going away to work, a job on the road with a truck outfit that took a movie screen around to isolated places; all above board, official, only small. With the other generator technicians he'd double in the band that accompanied the silent reels. He'd recommended himself to the crew at a show they'd put on downhill in the Lenin square; they'd hired him on the spot but his papers had taken some ordering. Tomorrow he'd be catching a lift to overtake them on the Irkustk road.

Musya had also met this crew. Anton, she feared, was going on the road to dissipation. But he'd travel all over Siberia, he'd see the Chinese border, the far north's green glowing sky shows, the peaks of Kamchatka. He'd live. He'd sing with the light of camp-fires on his face.

And what would become of her baby, Samuel Nemo? Would he ever be elected, win power, lead? His persistence wasn't in doubt. He'd stayed fiercely determined to emigrate to Israel as Dovid had wanted. In this project his staunch ally remained his youngest brother, the piano player. Musya they would bring along, they told her so all the time, wearing her down the same way their father had started to. She'd waver. Maybe she ought to emigrate to get her other boy the best ear surgery in Israel. Maybe she ought to try and make the application, go to Khabarovsk, file the paperwork. In that case, she'd concluded, Musya welcomed the rest of them to decide. If they wanted her cooperation, they should make it feel like floating. Her next flight she required to be effortless.

Here they were, on their way to practice, her emigrants, the pair of them, with a few stalks of chocolate lily and some buttercups. "We have stinky flowers for you, Mame-nyu," Pretzel said, kissing her. But the brown flowers made up for their smell with dramatic flair; she was happy to add them. She put her arms around the boys and pulled them close and held them to herself tightly for a long time, kissing the tops of their foreheads over and over until at last they squirmed and struggled free, ran off to practice. They wanted to own farmland and houses, they craved democracy; but they could do nothing to shake her belief that all the trappings of citizenship only hid tyrants' schemes.

She noticed Magga coming up the yard with some radishes in her fist. These were not for eating, Musya knew, but rather an ingredient in a premium Kolyma samogon recipe the old former dvornik was intent on recreating and using to seize market share from her fellow bootleggers around the locality. One or two experimental versions could cut the moon in half like a melon, really powerful stuff. They'd lost floor space to the still equipment which meant some inconvenient doubling up. Musya's room felt very crowded with Kitty sleeping there. But the eventual proceeds, combined with what Sender Kotz's tailoring brought in, would keep the best fresh vegetables and fruit to be had on their table; fresh meat, good bread; the mother and daughter's tobacco.

It might all end badly—but then, what didn't?

Even in Musya's old floral summer shift Magga looked old, decrepit. Her pace was good, though, better than Musya's. She wasn't far from the longhouse door when it flew open and Hodeh emerged. This was awkward. The two faced each other. Magga appeared to be growling. She'd missed a sharpened teaspoon dear to herself from the gulag and she blamed Hodeh for taking it. Now she swung a fist around Hodeh's face, not making contact. While Hodeh stood evading blows the ground around their feet had filled with cats and old Tamara leapt up the next time Magga swung; claws caught her arm. She gave a cry and kicked her feet around as Hodeh slipped away.

Poor Hodeh, she'd lost another papa. It was enough to cut her off. Something of her wildness had returned along with some thievery, a small outbreak or two. She didn't talk much and wasn't sociable. Her hair she didn't brush enough made a black unruly cloud around a face half-pinched, half-unapproachable. When she wasn't impossible to find she kept close to home where she stalked around, trailed by her many cats. The devoted Katerilena usually followed; yes, there she stood in the doorway, watching Hodeh go. Some people would always trail sadly after certain other people for private reasons of their own, motives how hidden even from themselves no one could measure, Musya noted.

Katerilena believed that with her character and accomplishments, Hodeh ought to be more popular. Not content to half-drag her on stage at every performance, she pushed her towards society. Cracking at one suggestion, in a startling impulse that left her too nervous to speak, Hodeh had joined a student backgammon and chess club. At last she went to one meeting, Sender Kotz persuaded her. He and the Cossack girl waited outside while she played a few games. After that her club attendance was perfect. Backgammon possessed her for now, she carried Brother Dead Man's old board with its blots and dice rattling inside with her everywhere. She'd begun coming home from the Lenin square with winnings that she counted in secret and hid—a heartening development, Musya considered. And now today, most unexpectedly, a gift from Hodeh's own hand, an envelope full of that cash, maybe all she'd won; for Hodeh cared nothing about money. As for flowers, the rose bouquet she'd proffered stood safe beside Musya's bed, too openly ill-gotten to display. Whatever happened to her, Hodeh remained admirable.

The bunch of violets slipped into her hand by the widower next door had been another surprise that morning, Musya kept thinking about it. Of course there'd always been more love going on around her than she'd realized at the time. Always came revelations. She sat down and fanned herself again with the warmth of late summer. She thought the oak trees looked thoughtfully at one another's wine-streaked branches.

A hand caught her eye, a wave. Musya smiled and replaced her eyeglasses; with the previous pair lost in the river, she wore them on a pin-chain these days. A neighbor from the longhouse who'd paused there cheerfully now reached into a pocket and produced for her another ball bearing, recovered, after all this time, in a garden plot. People knew she collected them. She was sincerely delighted to have it and said so.

Who would love her? Everyone loved her.

She bent to her notebook again to write: *The birch leaves rustle in a rain-bearing breeze*

אין אָ רעגן-שייַכעס ווינטל שושקעןַ די בערעזע בלעטער

and stared at the page until a shadow crossed it. The Cossack girl was coming with a bowl of fruit for the table. And for Musya she carried a cup of tea; another kind person.

Katerilena's hands asked what she was writing about.

"Oh." Musya filled her eyes again with the blaze of golden green, the sunlight, and laughed. One shoulder gave a little shrug. "Men."

TO READERS

Thank you for reading a Nostalgistudio book. This is the second edition of a novel originally published in Summer 2018. Its kind readers overlooked many quirks, errors, and deficiencies and offered all sorts of praise. Yet a consensus was emerging that LAMENT was too long. All a writer can do at that point is another series of edits to make the work feel shorter, and hope for success. The publisher can go further. The second print edition is nearly 150 pages shorter than the first because the font (Parkinson Electra, from Adobe) has been reduced from 11 to 10. This also makes it a cheaper book to produce, buy and ship, all positive benefits. Confidence is high.

The Glossary is new to this edition; it is not exhaustive but aims to be helpful. A comprehensive book list follows for readers interested in the subject matter and the research behind LAMENT. Google Translate led a long list of digital resources consulted at almost every point. Links to many on-line sources and inspirations, including Soviet films and songs, can be found at the publisher's website, **nostalgistudio.com**. People, events and places in the novel are based on life, although a Jewish cemetery in Birobidzhan is not known to have existed.

Questions, corrections as to fact, and other comments are all equally welcome and encouraged. Thanks especially, all who've recommended LAMENT to other readers. More comprehensive acknowledgments are to be found in the Author's Afterwords. Please visit the publisher's website to join in conversation with her and the reading public, or e-mail **contact@nostalgistudio.com**.

With LAMENT, author Liz Mackie launched Nostalgistudio, an independent publishing company for high-quality American writing. Three volumes deep into FAMEPUNK, her picaresque historical-fantasy novel set in the world of women's tennis, she's also published a poetry collection (DUG FOR VICTORY: POEMS FROM RIP-TV) and a travel novella called THE HAPPY VALLEY. Her website www.liz-mackie.com collects her on-line writings. A long-ago graduate of Swarthmore College, she lives and works in New York City.

GLOSSARY

alteh kaker: Yiddish; insult; dirty old fart

balabatische: Yiddish; prosperous, proper, self-regarding

balebos: Yiddish; boss, head of house, landlord

bayan: Russian; a button accordion

bissel / brekhl: Yiddish; a little bit, a morsel, a little bite

bobe-mayse: Yiddish; old wives' tale, tall tale

Bontshe Shvayg: Yiddish; the saintly title character of a renowned story by Y.L. Peretz

chervontsy: Soviet; plural of chervonets, basic unit of Soviet currency; usually called a ruble

Dekabristi: Russian; the Decembrists, army officers noblemen sentenced to Siberian labor for their role in 1825's December rebellion against the new tsar Nicolas I; some of their wives followed them into exile, including the famous Princess Trubetskaya

domra: Russian; traditional stringed instrument, a long-necked lute

dvornik: Russian; building superintendant or concierge, responsible for sweeping hallways and stairs

gas un shtibele: Yiddish; colloquial for home, the street and house

Izvestiya: Russian; "news," the major newspaper in the Soviet Union

kolkhoz: Soviet; a state-owned farm worked cooperatively by the worker-residents of a collective

koorvah: Yiddish; prostitute

landsman: Yiddish; a fellow Jew from the same town

lapti: Russian; traditional footwear woven from tree bark fibers

mame loshn: Yiddish; the Yiddish language, mother tongue

Mamenyu: Yiddish; "Mommy" with extra endearment

mekhutonin (pl.) mekhtoyniste (fem. sing), mekhutn (masc. sing): Yiddish; in-laws by marriage

Moldavanka: Russian; an historic neighborhood in Odessa, Ukraine; known, through the work of Isaac Babel and others, for its literary associations with Jewish gangsters and con men

mumeh: Yiddish; aunt

nafka: Yiddish; whore, whorish

NEP: Soviet; New Economic Program (1921-1928), Lenin's economic policy for the Soviet Union which included elements of capitalism, entrepreneurship, and free markets

NKVD: Soviet; People's Commissariat of Internal Affairs; police arm of the Soviet state, precursor to the KGB

parnosseh: Yiddish; earned living, daily bread

Pashli: Russian; Let's get going!

pressure papka: Russian; the pressure folder on a Singer-designed sewing machine

pripetshik: Yiddish; hearth, fireplace

propiska: Russian; a residence permit, used to determine work eligibility, and stamped on the Soviet internal passport

proshchai: Russian; farewell

putevka: Soviet; a voucher for travel lodging

Sah: Romanian; chess term, "Check"

samogon: Russian; home-distilled alcohol, moonshine

samovar: Russian; traditional urn for boiling water; colloquially, a legless veteran

schnorrer: Yiddish; insult; sponger, freeloader

schnur: Yiddish; daughter-in-law

Stakhanovite: Soviet; a model worker producing far above quota, named for minder Alexey Stakhanov; similar to Shock Worker

tak: Ukrainian; yes

tarelka: Russian; a wired radio receiver shaped like a plate

tsitskeh: Yiddish; breast

valenki: Russian; traditional boots made from felt

Velykden: Ukrainian; Easter

vyshyvanky: Ukrainian; traditional blouses with embroidered decoration

zakuski: Russian; a spread of appetizers and hors d'oeuvres

zay gezunt: Yiddish; goodbye, go in good health

zhaleika: Russian; traditional wind instrument, a hornpipe

PRINT SOURCES

Akhmatova, Anna; trans. D.M. Thomas. *Akhmatova Poems*. New York, London, Paris: Alfred A. Knopf, 2006

Alexievitch, Svetlana. *La guerre n'a pas un visage de femme*. Paris: Éditions J'ai Lu, 2005.

Applebaum, Anne. *Gulag: A History*. New York: Anchor Books, 2003.

Babel, Isaac; ed. Nathalie Babel. *The Complete Works of Isaac Babel*. New York and London: W.W. Norton, 2002.

Beinfeld, Solon and Bochner, Harry, eds. *Comprehensive Yiddish-English Dictionary*. Bloomington and Indianapolis: Indiana University Press, 2013.

Benanav, Michael. *Joshua & Isadora: A True Tale of Loss and Love in the Holocaust*. Guilford, Connecticut: The Lyons Press, 2008.

Bergelson, D. (.pdf, Internet Archive) *The Jewish Autonomous Region*. Moscow: Foreign Languages Publishing House, 1939.

Conlon, Joseph. (.pdf) *The Historical Impact of Epidemic Typhus*. Web Article. Montana: montana.edu, 2007.

Conquest, Robert. *The Great Terror: A Reassessment. 40th Anniversary Edition*. Oxford: Oxford University Press, 2008.

Deletant, Denis. (.pdf) *Ghettos in Transnistria*. Washington, D.C. : Center for Advanced Holocaust Studies, United States Holocaust Memorial Museum, 2005.

Emiot, Israel. *The Birobidzhan Affair: A Yiddish Writer in Siberia*. Philadelphia: Jewish Publication Society of America, 1981.

Gessen, Masha. *Where the Jews Aren't: The Sad and Absurd Story of Birobidzhan, Russia's Jewish Autonomous Region*. New York: Nextbook, 2016.

Gessen, Masha. "The Dying Russians," *NYR Daily*: Sept 2, 2014.

Groys, Boris. *The Total Art of Stalinism: Avant-Garde, Aesthetic Dictatorship, and Beyond*. London and New York: Verso Books, 2011.

Halle, Fannina. *Women in Soviet Russia*. New York: The Viking Press, 1933.

Halle, Fannina. *Women in the Soviet East*. New York: E.P. Dutton, 1938.

Havryl'iuk, Natalia. (.pdf) "The Structure and Function of Funeral Rituals and Customs in Ukraine," *Folklorica*: Volume 8, Number 2; 2003.

Ilf, Ilya and Petrov, Evgeny. *The Golden Calf*. Rochester, NY: Open Letter, 2009.

King, Charles. *Odessa: Genius and Death in a City of Dreams*. New York and London: W.W. Norton, 2011.

Kochan, Lionel, ed. *The Jews in Soviet Russia Since 1917*. 3rd Edition. Oxford: Oxford University Press, 1978.

Kotlerman, Ber Boris. *In Search of Milk and Honey: The Theater of "Soviet Jewish Statehood."* (1934-49). Bloomington: Slavica, 2009.

Kucherenko, Olga. (.pdf) "Reluctant traitors: the politics of survival in Romanian-occupied Odessa," *European Review of History: Revue Européenne d'Histoire*, 15:2, 143-155.

Kunitz, Joshua, ed. *Azure Cities: Stories of the New Russia*. New York: International Publishers, 1929.

Leder, Mary M.; ed. Laurie Bernstein. *My Life in Stalinist Russia: An American Woman Looks Back*. Bloomington and Indianapolis: Indiana University Press, 2001.

Levin, Nora. *The Jews in the Soviet Union Since 1917: Paradox of Survival*. Volumes 1 & 2. New York and London: New York University Press, 1990.

Lovell, Stephen. *Russia in the Microphone Age: A History of Soviet Radio, 1919-1970*. Oxford: Oxford University Press, 2015.

Malaparte, Curzio. *Kaputt*. New York: New York Review Books, 2005.

Medvedev, Roy. *Let History Judge: The Origins & Consequences of Stalinism*. New York: Vintage Books, 1973.

Morris, Jan. "In Potemkin's Steps," *Literary Review*: August, 2011.

Müller, Herta. *Cristina and Her Double: Selected Essays*. London: Portobello Books, 2013.

Newby, Eric. *The Big Red Train Ride*. Pleasantville, NY: The Akadine Press, 1999.

Newell, J. (.pdf) *The Russian Far East: A Reference Guide for Conservation and Development*. McKinleyville, CA: Daniel & Daniel, 2004.

Peretz, I.L.; ed. Ruth R. Wisse. *The I.L. Peretz Reader*. New Haven and London: Yale University Press, 2002.

Phillips, Sarah D. (.html) "'There Are No Invalids in the USSR!': A Missing Soviet Chapter in the New Disability History," *Disability Studies Quarterly*, Vol 29, No 3, 2009.

Sakevich, Victoria I. and Denisov, Boris P. (.pdf) Working Paper. *Birth Control in Russia: Overcoming the State System*. Moscow: National Research University Higher School of Economics (HSE), 2014.

Schaechter-Viswanath, Gitl and Glasser, Paul, eds. *Comprehensive English-Yiddish Dictionary (based on the lexical research of Mordkhe Schaechter)*. Bloomington and Indianapolis: Indiana University Press, 2016.

Shternshis, Anna. *Soviet and Kosher: Jewish Popular Culture in the Soviet Union, 1923-1939*. Bloomington and Indianapolis: Indiana University Press, 2006.

Singer Manufacturing Co. (.pdf) *Instructions for Using Singer Sewing Machines Nos. 127 and 128* (With Attachments 12064). USA: The Singer Manufacturing Co., 1930.

Sutzkever, A.; trans. Barbara and Benjamin Harshav. (.pdf) *A. Sutzkever: Selected Poetry and Prose*. Berkeley: University of California Press, 1991. http://ark.cdlib.org/ark:/13030/ft5qnb3zy/

Thomas, Bryn. *Trans-Siberian Handbook*. 7th Edition. Surrey: Trailblazer Publications, 2007.

Weinberg, Robert. *Stalin's Forgotten Zion: Birobidzhan and the Making of a Soviet Jewish Homeland; An Illustrated History, 1928-1996*. Berkeley: University of California Press, 1998.

Weinstein, Miriam. *Yiddish: A Nation of Words*. New York: Ballantine Books, 2001.

Wiener, Leo. (.pdf) *The History of Yiddish Literature in the Nineteenth Century*. New York: Charles Scribner's Sons, 1899.

Zucker, Sheva. *Yiddish: An Introduction to the Language, Literature & Culture: A Textbook for Beginners, Vol. 1*. New York: The Workmen's Circle, 2013.

AUTHOR'S AFTERWORD

Almost five years ago, my Russian friend and neighbor Lara Mikhaylova invited me to a family dinner and said she wanted to tell me a story she'd heard from one of her clients. Lara works with seniors in a Russian-speaking medical office, and the story concerned two Jewish sisters who grew up in Odessa before the outbreak of the Second World War. Knowing that I'm a writer, she wanted to tell me the story so that I, in turn, might be inspired to write about these sisters, their family, and the ordeals they faced in the Soviet Union. And in fact the whole thing captured my imagination right away.

Living in Brighton Beach, Brooklyn, its sometime namesake, had made me familiar with images of Odessa as a picturesque and literary Jewish city on the Black Sea. But I'd never known about how the Soviets had set aside territory for Jewish settlement in the Siberian Far East, never heard of the place called Birobidzhan. I was equally unfamiliar with Transnistria, the area of Romanian-occupied Ukraine where one of the sisters was trapped by the Nazi invasion of 1941 and locked up for a time in the Jewish ghetto of Obodovka. As Lara's daughter Marianna and I listened, we were searching for these unfamiliar places and their histories on our smartphones and soon realized how rare this story had to be—and how important it was to save and tell it, not only for those Jews who survived and are descended from the times of tragedy, but for the many who never had a chance to survive.

With a little page of notes I'd brought home from dinner, one night I sat down and started at the beginning of this story about two sisters, their family that's not so unlike many families, and their different characters—spinning fiction from the real events. The writing felt like it would go quickly. My idea was to work the plot into a fast-paced "female-centric" mid-length novel and be done in about eight months. As one of its eventual characters adapts the Yiddish saying to go, "Woman plans, God laughs." It took four and a half years of steady work, constant reading and research, some Beginner's Yiddish classes, and some times requiring simple perseverance before I made the final draft edits on the very long novel you hold.

LAMENT follows Musya Kotz and her sister Liza to many grim places, all based on life. Yet as I've kept the particular story Lara's client Betya told in constant view, handling the images and words to do justice to the true facts inside the fiction I was building through a difficult stretch of years for me personally and for the rest of the planet in general, what emerged is a survival story, yes, an astounding one—also miraculous and nonetheless tragic—a story that resonates loudly with contemporary events, strong-man states, refugee crises, wars and women's and children's suffering—the story of an imaginative well-meaning romantic young woman who loves movies and poetry and sun-bathing but whose happiness and freedom are stripped from her always—

who longs for perfect love even while she's marked for racial extermination—who winds up penned, enslaved, her body violated—left without refuge, unprotected in motherhood, to see her children made homeless, penniless—haunted in exile, burdened with trauma, shunned and targeted—at last to lose the dearest people, pets, and places, and still preserve her sense of humor and a welcome-giving heart—this woman's presence has been a strengthening tonic to me every day. I hope LAMENT's readers find they derive something of the same benefit from the finished book in turn.

Finally, to Betya, and to Lara and and her daughters, Marianna and Katharine, and her mother Bronya—and to the women of Ukraine and the women of Russia and their descendants in Brooklyn, Israel, and everywhere else—I offer back this story not my own, written with gratitude.

Liz Mackie
New York, Summer 2018

AUTHOR'S AFTERWORD *(Second Edition)*

Picking up where I left off in 2018, some more explicit expression of gratitude are owed to a wonderful teacher, Dr Eve Jochnowitz, and my fellow Beginner's Yiddish students for two terms at YIVO in Manhattan. Long live Yiddish! . . .Dr Kaori Kitao, my former art history professor and forever friend, shared so many of the hours that contributed a most important form of inspiration to LAMENT. Thank you, Kaori, my tireless companion and guide through the endlessly rich cultural life of Jewish New York City. I'm grateful to YIVO; to the Museum of Jewish Heritage - A Living Memorial of the Holocaust, and to its resident company, the National Yiddish Theatre Folksbiene; to Paula Vogel and the cast and creative team of Indecent on Broadway; to the New Yiddish Rep; and to the Chamber Music Society of Lincoln Center. . .I was working for OppenheimerFunds while the novel was in progress—thank you to a good company that was. I remain grateful for all my colleagues and friends there at the office, and now at work from home with Invesco. . .A million thanks and more for my sister Claudia, my strongest and fiercest supporter. . .And the intrepid early readers whose generosity of time and attention meant everything to this writer—Maire, Anna, John, Jeni, Vikki, Noelle, Margaret, Chris, Linda, James, Lynne, Alex, Athena, Rhea, Charlotte, and Myrna, my mother—my loving thanks to all.

Liz Mackie
New York, Summer 2020

www.ingramcontent.com/pod-product-compliance
Lightning Source LLC
Chambersburg PA
CBHW070924100726
47908CB00001B/96